STORMING INTREPID

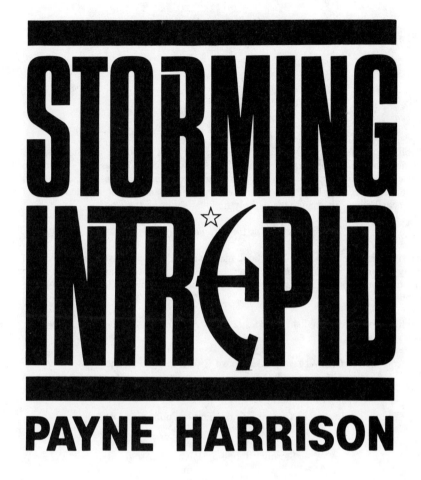

STORMING INTREPID

PAYNE HARRISON

CROWN PUBLISHERS, INC.
NEW YORK

Published by Crown Publishers, Inc., 225 Park Avenue South, New York, New York 10003

CROWN is a trademark of Crown Publishers, Inc.

Manufactured in the United States of America

Library of Congress Cataloging-in-Publication Data

Harrison, Payne.
Storming Intrepid / Payne Harrison.
p.   cm.
I. Title.
PS3558.A6718S7 1989
813'.54—dc19   88-22905

ISBN 0-517-57133-1

Design by Jake Victor Thomas

10 9 8 7 6 5 4 3 2 1

First Edition

ABH-5451

For Paula,
who took my hand and walked beside me on
the
Long March(es)

Acknowledgments

There were a great many press officers within the armed forces, NASA, and the educational community who were most kind in providing me with data for this book. The existence of these professionals is a reflection that the free flow of information concerning American military and space affairs is a strength, rather than a weakness, of our society.

I would like to extend my appreciation to Neil and Judy Robinson, and to Don Davison and Lee Dean for their help when this manuscript was in its formative stages, and to Mike Reed and Margie Cruse for their efforts in bringing this project to fruition.

Craig Covault and Bruce Nordwall of *Aviation Week* were very generous with their time in fielding my questions, and I am grateful to them.

To my agent Jan Miller and my editor Jim Wade, I would like to say I was uncommonly fortunate to be in the hands of such superb professionals.

Tom Clancy and Stephen Coonts were very kind to extend their assistance, and it was most welcome.

A special note of thanks goes to Tom McElmurry, former deputy commander of the Air Force test pilot school and NASA veteran who helped manage the Skylab and space shuttle projects. Professor McElmurry was most gracious to provide a review of the manuscript. Any technical errors that remain are mine and mine alone.

Finally, for Mom, Dad, Sis, and Fannie Mae, thanks for your help, all along the way.

The Prelude

In the predawn twilight, the *Marshal Nedelin* was a ghostly, almost surreal image—as if it were a latter-day *Flying Dutchman* gliding across the sea.

Although it resembled a warship in many respects, the vessel carried no missiles or guns on its deck. Instead, it bristled with electronic gear of every size and description—dominated in particular by a large radome just forward of amidships. If required, computerized controls could keep the radome's dish antenna stable, even in heavy seas; but that was unimportant at the moment, for the Pacific Ocean was dead calm this November morning.

In spite of its vassal states and all its power and bluster, the Soviet Union possessed few genuine friends in the world—particularly in the region south of the Tropic of Capricorn. And without sympathetic governments, the Kremlin had few safe harbors where it could establish sensitive electronic outposts.

Because of this dearth of friendly real estate, the *Nedelin*, and a half-dozen ships like her, had been forged in the Black Sea shipyards of Nikolayev and dispatched across the high seas on electronic tracking missions vital to the Motherland. They were eminently capable of monitoring the outreaches of space, while remaining safe from intrusion and totally under control of their Soviet masters.

Below decks on this November morning, the *Nedelin*'s computers rapidly plotted a trajectory. Then, at the proper moment, the radome's dish antenna pivoted and fired its monopulse radar skyward, probing for an ethereal object hurtling somewhere through the ionosphere. Back and forth the beam traveled, until a sailor was rewarded with a luminescent blip on his cathode-ray screen. The young man punched a button, and the ship's UHF radio immediately transmitted a facsimile of the image to a Molniya communications satellite, where a transponder bounced the signal to another antenna half a world away.

1

KALININGRAD FLITE CONTROL CENTRE,
SOYUZ SOVETSKIKH SOTSIALISTICHESKIKH REPUBLIK (CCCP)

"Sixty seconds to reentry fire, Comrade General!" barked the mission commander.

"Very well," came General Shenko's soft reply.

Col. Oleg Malyshev, the mission commander, spun his chair back to the monitor, forcing himself to concentrate on this last, critical leg of the journey. He'd scarcely left his post for the past fifty-two hours, as the small army of paper tea containers surrounding his feet would attest. Yet in spite of his mounting fatigue, the tall, thin officer with blond hair and Slavic features was unwilling to delegate even minor tasks during this crucial phase of the enterprise.

Row upon row of monitors and their attending technicians radiated out from the huge Mercator world map projection on the forewall. Each person stared intently at his individual screen in the spacious Flite Control Centre, and in spite of the air conditioning that labored to keep the equipment cool, all were sweating like pigs—their rivulets of perspiration triggered by stress rather than heat.

Malyshev, who was unusually young to be a full colonel in the Soviet Aerospace Forces, couldn't worry about General Shenko's nonchalant manner now. Nor could he worry about the other general—this one in a green serge uniform—watching attentively from the glassed-in observation deck. His only thoughts could be of his duty. "Thirty seconds," he said into his headset microphone, and added, "Commence final arming sequence on engines one and two."

THE *MIKHAIL SUSLOV*
ALTITUDE: 163 MILES ABOVE THE SOUTH PACIFIC

Lt. Col. Dmitri Bulgarin popped up the arming circuit's safety cover and flipped the toggle switch from SAFE to ARM, causing the nearby annunciator light to change from red to green.

"Fifteen seconds," crackled in his headset.

Although the entire reentry firing procedure could be done automatically, Bulgarin's stick-and-rudder nature refused to entrust this one vital function to the spacecraft's on-board computers. He was, after all, a pilot.

Bulgarin's copilot gazed through the windshield at the earth's horizon, which appeared above them and inverted. This was because

2

the *Suslov* (named for the long-dead Politburo ideologue) was traveling upside down and backward—a seemingly unorthodox position for a winged object, but necessary for the retrofire braking action to take effect.

The word *Fire!* reverberated in his eardrums and Bulgarin mashed the trigger button, causing the Tumansky liquid-fuel engines to thunder to life—but in the vacuum of space the thunder was silent. It was only from the vibration and mounting g-forces that the two cosmonauts knew the ship's engines had responded.

SOUTH PACIFIC
14° 16' SOUTH, 119° 27' West
ALTITUDE: 61,000 FEET

"Spyglass, this is Rabbit's Nest. Target is coming up on your position now. Begin traverse at zero-one-seven degrees on my mark."

"Roger that, Rabbit," replied the chief master sergeant, as his pudgy hand gently rotated the focusing knob on his console.

The specially modified high-altitude Boeing 767 was cruising over the South Pacific preparing to do what it did best—take a very expensive picture. Its call sign, "Spyglass," was appropriate, for the 767 was a flying observatory designed to take pictures of man-made satellites in low earth orbit. Aboard the aircraft was an exotic reflecting telescope that could scan the heavens through a hole in the plane's humpback roof. The scope consisted of a network of ultrathin flexible mirrors arrayed in a honeycomb fashion. These "rubber mirrors" could be bent and focused by computer to compensate for atmospheric distortion and produce images of astonishing clarity—so clear that one could read a license plate from a hundred miles away.

The position of Spyglass over the South Pacific had been determined by four NavStar global positioning satellites. From 22,300 miles above the earth, three of the satellites continually transmitted time and positioning data to the 767, where an onboard computer triangulated the information, then spat out the aircraft's exact coordinates and altitude. A fourth satellite acted as a double check to ensure the 767's internal clock was accurate. It was. So accurate, in fact, that the aircraft was directly beneath the *Suslov*'s orbital path, which had long been tracked, computed, and plotted by the North American Aerospace Defense Command's Spacetrack radar/computer network. Spyglass was now in position to take its picture.

"Mark," said Rabbit's Nest.

"Roger," replied Spyglass, and the chief flipped a switch to start the aircraft's digital video recorders.

"C'mon, sweetheart," coaxed the chief. "C'mon, be sweet, lift your skirt for me."

The neighboring technician looked askance. He had always thought the chief's near-sexual relationship with the equipment was a little bizarre, but thought it better not to say anything.

Despite the chief's urging, the TV monitor remained blank except for the twilight sky. The *Suslov* spacecraft was traveling at 17,000 miles per hour, while the Spyglass airliner limped along at a meager 500 mph. That meant the 767 had only a tiny window of time to find the Russian orbiter. The seconds ticked by and the screen remained blank until, finally, the chief sighed and decided the *Suslov* wasn't coming to him. He was about to start a search pattern with the telescope when a delta-shaped object popped onto the screen.

"Awright!" he howled. "We nailed the little bastard." Giddy with his success, the chief quickly adjusted the dials for greater magnification. Then he leaned forward to inspect the Russian spacecraft pictured on the monitor. His concentration was so intense that, when the image erupted before his eyes, he involuntarily recoiled from the screen, and it took a few seconds for his mind to comprehend what his eyes had witnessed. Then it dawned on him. "Sweet Jesus!" he cried while keying his microphone. "Rabbit, this is Spyglass! We got the target on screen and he's firing his retro rockets! I say again, target has initiated retrofire. Christ Almighty, what a picture!"

"We copy that, Spyglass," replied a dispassionate voice. "Put it through on RealTime."

"Roger, Rabbit," he said, while nodding to the neighboring technician, who threw the appropriate switches. Almost immediately the same image appeared on another screen at NORAD headquarters, deep inside Cheyenne Mountain in Colorado.

THE *MIKHAIL SUSLOV*
ALTITUDE: 107 MILES
COURSE: NORTH
POSITION: CROSSING THE ANTARCTIC CIRCLE

Twenty-three years of iron discipline in the Soviet armed forces had prepared Dmitri Bulgarin for the next twenty minutes of his life. He had to control the distilled fear and not let the image of his wife and daughter intrude on his thoughts. Their lives had been richer in many ways because he was a cosmonaut. But the state exacted a toll for the privileges it granted, and now the toll was due.

When the retrofire ceased, Bulgarin immediately pivoted the spacecraft into the correct reentry attitude of 32 degrees inclination. The *Suslov* was on a descent gradient toward the earth and would soon begin striking the first errant molecules of the lower ionosphere. Much like an airborne swan landing in the water, the *Suslov* would decelerate from a speed of almost 17,000 miles per hour to 1,500 mph in the space of twenty minutes. The resistance of the atmosphere, which provided the braking action for the winged spacecraft, also generated frightful surface friction, heating the leading edges of the vehicle to temperatures of 2,800 degrees Fahrenheit. Small wonder that most meteorites were vaporized before they hit the earth's surface.

To keep it from being incinerated, the Soviet space shuttle, like its American counterpart, had been surfaced with heat-resistant silica tiles. Unlike the American shuttle, however, something had gone horrendously wrong during the reentry phase of the *Suslov*'s predecessor, the *Buran*. While descending from its third voyage into outer space, the *Buran* had burned into a cinder.

Bulgarin was painfully aware of the previous shuttle's fate as he watched the surface-temperature gauge start to climb and felt the buffeting grow more intense. "Altitude eighty-three kilometers . . . eighty . . . seventy-eight . . ." The strain in Bulgarin's voice became more pronounced and his radio transmission grew weaker as the *Suslov* plummeted into the "black hole" of reentry. The fireball enveloping the orbiter was so intense that it stripped the electrons from the surrounding air molecules. As a result, for twelve minutes the spacecraft was covered in a sheath of ions that was impenetrable to radio waves.

As a reddish glow filled the windshield, Bulgarin tightened his grip around the control stick.

On its *third* voyage, the *Buran* shuttle had been incinerated during its descent through the "black hole."

The *Suslov* was now reentering the atmosphere from its *fourth* journey into outer space.

KALININGRAD FLITE CONTROL CENTRE

As the spacecraft hurtled above the Indian Ocean, it was tracked by the massive phased-array radar complex on the banks of the

Caspian Sea. The Flite Centre's computers digested the radar data and plotted the orbiter's path on the large Mercator map projection, which now held everyone's attention. There was nothing the technicians could do but wait until the *Suslov* emerged from the radio blackout.

"Eight minutes of communications blackout remaining," announced Mission Commander Malyshev, to no one in particular.

The ground track of the *Suslov* advanced on the screen, and the tension in the spacious room became palpable.

"Seven minutes." Malyshev's voice was little more than a whimper now, and his throat felt like a dusty road. He started to reach for a nearby cup, but reconsidered. His system simply couldn't absorb another ounce of tea.

The hulking General Shenko took a very long drag on his Chesterfield cigarette and exhaled slowly. He loved the American tobacco more than he dared ever say.

Malyshev's sweat-drenched blond hair was now pasted to his temples. He murmured, "Five minutes."

There was a collective sigh from the technicians. The *Buran*—which means "snowstorm"— had disappeared with six minutes of blackout remaining. The *Suslov* had now passed beyond that threshold. Maybe the *Buran* tragedy had been a fluke after all. Maybe the Russian shuttle was truly a sound spacecraft. Maybe there was reason to hope.

"Four minutes."

Yes, maybe there *was* reason to hope. Even General Shenko's basset-hound face was showing a flicker of life.

On the plot board, the *Suslov*'s ground track advanced again.

"Three minutes." Malyshev's voice had returned. It looked good now. Very good indeed.

"Commander!" It was the radar liaison officer over the intercom. "I have the Caspian radar station. They say the image is fading from their screen!"

There was stunned silence.

"Confirm that report!" barked Malyshev.

The radar officer held the headset tight against his ears, then slowly relaxed in his chair. "Caspian station confirms, and says the image fragmented before disappearing from their scope."

"Communications officer, try to contact them!" ordered Malyshev.

The young communications officer began murmuring into his microphone, trying unsuccessfully to mask his sobs. Colonel Bulgarin had been his friend. At Star City he was like everyone's favorite uncle—a person who always made you feel special. He followed his orders and signaled the *Suslov*, but he knew it was useless.

As the young officer's murmurs went on, a communal shock spread throughout the room. Every person felt his mission and sense of purpose had vanished along with the *Suslov*—every person, that is, save for one.

"General Shenko, as a representative of the Committee for State Security I must ask you to accompany me." The voice was gentle. Almost benevolent.

General Shenko turned and confronted his counterpart in the green serge uniform of the *Komitet Gosudarstvennoy Bezopasnosti*. Shenko was grateful this one wasn't as arrogant as the garden variety Chekist.

"Very well," replied Shenko. He took his pack of Chesterfields off the console and stuffed them into the breast pocket of his rumpled uniform, then turned to leave the Flite Centre. Over his shoulder he gave one last instruction. "Tell Baikonur not to waste a second," he said flatly.

Malyshev nodded as he watched the door close behind his general.

A final puff of Chesterfield smoke seemed to hang in the air.

BAIKONUR COSMODROME, TYURATAM, KAZAKHSTAN REPUBLIK, CCCP

The gargantuan doors of the shuttle hangar slowly rumbled open to reveal a duplicate of the *Mikhail Suslov*. The size, shape, and markings of the winged spacecraft appeared to be the same as the original shuttle, except for black, sootlike impressions along its side. Had the genuine *Suslov* survived, the reentry friction would have burned similar markings onto the white fuselage.

Ground technicians hurriedly hooked the nosewheel onto the tow tractor, and as soon as the doors cleared the wingspan, the duplicate began moving out onto the 5,000-meter runway built especially for shuttle landings.

The special tow tractor used only a fraction of its pulling horsepower, since the replica *Suslov* was fabricated from sheets of phenolic plastic laminated to a plywood frame. Its core was hollow except for some steel ingots loaded aboard to provide it some stability in heavy wind.

When the decoy reached the end of the tarmac, a ground crew detached the hitch and attached a deployed braking parachute to the tail section. A generator cart was wheeled underneath the craft and started, then a technician plugged the electric cable into a connector on the decoy's belly. The connector was hooked up to a network of heating coils imbedded in the plastic skin.

A covey of rescue and ground-service vehicles then drew up around the decoy as if the genuine *Suslov* had landed.

The ground crew chief surveyed the scene and was satisfied with himself that the exercise had gone a lot smoother—this time.

UNITED STATES SPACE COMMAND HEADQUARTERS, SPACE DEFENSE OPERATIONS CENTER, CHEYENNE MOUNTAIN, COLORADO

Gen. Rodger Whittenberg, Commander in Chief, United States Space Command, stared intently at the television monitor while the *Suslov*'s reentry burn was replayed for the third time.

"Okay, that's enough," he told the airman, then turned to the colonel. "I want to see the digital pix from this tape as soon as they come out of the laser printer, and I want a Keyhole pass over Baikonur ASAP. We need to see how well that shuttle held up on reentry."

"Yessir," replied his intelligence chief. "We had a KH-12 slated for a pass over Krasnoyarsk to check on some new ABM construction, but that can wait. The Keyhole's flight path has already been altered, and she'll be coming over Baikonur in about forty minutes. We'll catch it in daylight on the first pass."

"Good . . . good." At least we don't have to worry about getting Keyhole pix these days, Whittenberg thought.

After the American shuttle *Challenger* exploded in a fireball over the Atlantic back in the 1980s, and NASA had been unable to get so much as a kite aloft for the longest time, the United States, the richest and most technically advanced nation on earth, had limped along with a single KH-11 Keyhole reconnaissance satellite in orbit. The dearth of photointelligence during that period was grave, and it lasted over two years—largely because the defense establishment had painted itself into a technological corner. The new generation of reconnaissance satellites, the KH-12s, had been designed specifically for shuttle transport and couldn't be launched by any other means. No shuttle, no satellite. It was that simple.

But times had changed, and for this Whittenberg was grateful. When the current administration came into office, the new President had embraced both the space program and Star Wars with an almost rabid vengeance. Calling it his Final Frontier agenda, he galvanized the

American people behind a renewed effort in space. So effective was he that one newspaper columnist wrote, "The halcyon days of the Apollo program have returned to planet earth." This rekindled emphasis on space was not lost on Whittenberg, who was in essence the American military space "Czar." Now, instead of a single, aging spy satellite, he commanded four new-generation KH-12 satellites that crisscrossed the globe in various orbits.

Whittenberg left the Space Defense Operations Center, usually called "SPADOC," and started the long walk through the underground passageway toward his office. As always, the subterranean journey irritated him. Whittenberg had been a pilot in the Strategic Air Command for years, and he was the kind of man who liked wide vistas. Working inside a high-tech salt mine was not to his liking, but since he'd been hand picked for the SPACECOM post by the President, there wasn't much he could do about it. He suppressed his discomfort one more time and hustled down the tunnel toward his destination.

Chosen because of its location and geologic complexion, Cheyenne Mountain had been developed into a unique engineering marvel —almost on a par with the Golden Gate Bridge or Hoover Dam. It had taken three years of blasting to hollow out the granite innards of the mountain, and another two years to build its four-and-a-half-acre latticework of fifteen underground buildings and assorted passageways. This hard rock inner sanctum housed what could best be described as the central nervous system of America's defense capability.

In a heavily guarded compound on the exterior of Cheyenne Mountain, a forest of antennas pulled in a kaleidoscope of signals from remote sensors all around the globe. On the Arctic tundra the Ballistic Missile Early Warning System (BMEWS) aimed its over-the-horizon radar toward the Soviet Union and beamed its data back to Cheyenne Mountain. Twenty-three thousand miles above the earth, an infrared launch detection satellite called Teal Sapphire kept watch over Soviet missile pads, ready to send a warning should a rocket lift off. Under the sea, American hunter-killer submarines tracked their Russian counterparts, providing location data on enemy missile boats via ultralow-frequency radios that could transmit underwater. All of these signals were relayed to the exterior antennas compound by satellite, landline, or microwave link, then they were carried by fiber-optic cables into the basement of the mountain.

SPACECOM, which included the North American Aerospace Defense Command (NORAD) under its flag, possessed within Cheyenne Mountain the most massive array of computing power in the free world. Although its equipment was not as fresh from the factory as the National Security Agency's computers, or as state-of-the-art as those on the Star Wars platform, in terms of sheer size and bulk Cheyenne Mountain was the world's largest computing center. It had to be. For in the event of a nuclear attack, it was from the mountain that the President would receive those precious minutes of warning to initiate his country's response. The electronic sensor information collected by NORAD was fed into the computer complex, where it was sorted, analyzed, and collated, then routed to the proper screen within SPADOC. All of the information on the technicians' monitors, and on the large projection screens that dominated SPADOC, was on call to the NORAD commander in his "Cockpit" or "Crow's Nest," which overlooked the cavernous room. In the event of an ICBM or bomber attack, the NORAD commander could quickly piece together a picture of the situation and pass on warning and assessment data to the President and major military commands.

Since it was obviously an inviting piece of real estate for Russian target selectors, Cheyenne Mountain was the most attack-hardened facility in the U.S. inventory. To ride out an attack, the mountain possessed sufficient food, water, and power to last for thirty days—and in a nuclear war, thirty days is a long time. Two massive 25-ton steel doors sealed off the mountain from the outside world, and the entire complex of buildings "floated" on a bed of thirteen hundred heavy steel springs designed to cushion the impact of a nuclear explosion. But although it was hardened, a direct hit by a multimegaton warhead could knock out the fortress and render it useless.

However, in contemporary times, NORAD's role had become redefined by the expansion of warfare into space. It now kept track of some fifteen thousand pieces of man-made hardware orbiting the globe, and alerted the proper authority whenever a satellite changed course or attempted some strange maneuver. Yet its basic mission of hostile missile surveillance had remained unchanged for decades.

Cheyenne Mountain was one of three military space installations outside Colorado Springs—the other two being Peterson Air Force Base and Falcon Air Force Station. The latter two were aboveground, causing Whittenberg to envy those who worked there.

*   *   *

"Coffee please, Barb," Whittenberg told his secretary while striding into his windowless office. Windowless because fifteen hundred feet of solid granite stood between him and the wilderness exterior of the mountain fortress.

Whittenberg leaned back in his chair, rubbed his eyes, and contemplated what he had just seen on the SPADOC monitor. The thought of a viable Russian shuttle program profoundly disturbed him. SPACE-COM intelligence estimates showed the United States had long held a substantial lead in shuttle delivery systems and a technical superiority in Star Wars deployment. The combination of the two made for a comfortable edge. But now one of those gaps was narrowing, and he didn't like it. Not one bit. A year had elapsed since the last Soviet shuttle launch, leading Whittenberg and others to speculate that something was amiss with their spacecraft. But now the Russians had renewed their activity, putting them well on their way to a viable shuttle program. It was following a scenario similar to their fighter plane development, where for years Soviet aircraft had been inferior to their Western counterparts. But slowly, with determination, the Soviets came close to catching up with the West, developing the Su-27 Flanker and MiG-29 Fulcrum fighters in the late 1980s. The latest models of those two aircraft were good. Too damned good, as far as Whittenberg was concerned. The American technical edge had eroded with fighters, and he was afraid it could happen with the shuttle, too.

He picked up a green phone that was a direct line to the Chief of the General Staff, United States Armed Forces—his immediate superior. "Admiral," he said into the receiver. "This is Whittenberg at SPACECOM. Here's the situation."

ALTITUDE: 512 MILES
ORBITAL INCLINATION: 73 DEGREES

Five hundred and twelve miles above the earth a tiny vent opened on the side of the KH-12 satellite, allowing a small jet of hydrazine fuel to escape. With this last, gentle nudge its optical cameras would be in correct position to survey the entire Baikonur Cosmodrome complex in southern Kazakhstan.

The KH-12 possessed two lenses of a fixed focal length and one with a zoom capability which projected the target's image onto a focal plane of electro-optic sensors rather than film. The satellite's on-board computer converted the image to digital information, then transmitted

11

the signal via a relay satellite to the National Photographic Interpretation Center (NPIC), located in a warehouse-style building at the corner of M and 1st streets in Washington, D.C.

On command from the ground, the satellite's lens covers slid back, allowing the cameras a full view of their target. There was no cloud cover, and conditions were superb. As the Keyhole traveled from north-northeast to south-southwest in a near-polar orbit, its cameras began clicking and didn't stop for twelve minutes.

NATIONAL PHOTOGRAPHIC INTERPRETATION CENTER, WASHINGTON, D.C.

A half hour after the data arrived at NPIC, the pictures were electronically analyzed and "massaged" by a Cray-Y/MP supercomputer. This computer enhancement of the *Suslov*'s image was so sophisticated that it allowed the photo-interpretation analyst to view the shuttle in a three-dimensional form on a color television monitor.

After studying the 3-D image, the analyst turned off the monitor and picked up one of the laser-printed color photographs from the pile on his desk. With old-fashioned stereoscopic magnifying glasses he scrutinized the shuttle carefully.

Neither the old technology, nor the new, allowed him to discern that the *Suslov*'s skin was made of plastic.

CHEYENNE MOUNTAIN

Col. Peter Lamborghini stood at the lectern in the giant conference room and reviewed his notes. By nature, the SPACECOM intelligence chief liked to be precise and accurate, and he knew General Whittenberg demanded no less. His predecessor had been fired by Whittenberg less than a month before for failing to measure up.

Lamborghini was a former fighter pilot who had been in the intelligence field less than a year, but had grown in the role. So much so that General Whittenberg—known to his staff as the CinC (an acronym for Commander in Chief)—had tapped the colonel to fill the intelligence slot usually occupied by a brigadier general.

Running down his notes one last time, Lamborghini unconsciously felt his tie to make sure it was straight. He was a second-generation American; his father's family had come from Italy and his mother's from Norway. The mixture of Mediterranean and Nordic genes had produced an offspring of compact, medium build with raven-black hair, angular features, and blue, blue eyes.

Those blue eyes now looked up and down the conference table and saw an assortment of generals and colonels who were extensions of Whittenberg's mind and authority. The responsibility for American security above the earth's atmosphere ultimately rested on Whittenberg's four-star shoulders—Star Wars, the military shuttle, NORAD, and space reconnaissance had all been consolidated under Space Command, and it was the CinC's charter to make it work. Whittenberg had told Lamborghini more than once that SPACECOM was too big for one man to grapple with by himself, so he relied heavily on the staff to be his eyes, ears, and brains, and to always come up with the answers—the right answers.

Yet in exercising his power, Whittenberg—who was very big, very black, and very, very smart—was sometimes surprisingly gentle. Given his six-foot-five frame and the twinkle of his four stars, the former B-52 pilot rarely had to be gruff to get his point across. But when required, as Lamborghini knew, the CinC could turn into an absolute hard-ass in the blink of an eye. It seemed Whittenberg was either the gentle giant or General Ogre, with no middle ground between the two. The SPACECOM staff labored assiduously to keep him in his "gentle" mode.

Lamborghini had just finished his note review when the aide entered and announced, "Gentlemen, the commanding general." Everyone around the huge conference table rose as Whittenberg strode into the room, and as always, the tension seemed to increase with his presence. He was closely followed by his chief of staff, Maj. Gen. Michael Dowd, also known as the "Bull."

"Please be seated," said Whittenberg, while lowering himself into the big leather chair. As always, the CinC looked restless. His close-cropped, Afro-style haircut was liberally flecked with gray, as was the pencil-thin mustache under his pug nose. His blue uniform had nary a wrinkle in it, and the six rows of ribbons above his left breast pocket seemed to say, "Don't even think about messing with me." He nodded to his chief of staff and crisply ordered, "Okay, Bull, I have to leave for Washington in a couple of hours to give the Vice President a personal briefing, and I want to be up to speed." The Vice President was the administration's point man for the Strategic Defense Initiative. "Let's wrap this up as soon as we can."

"Yessir," replied the burly chief of staff. He turned and nodded to Lamborghini. "Go ahead, Colonel."

"Sir," began Lamborghini from the lectern, "three days ago on 4 November, at twelve thirty-two hours Zulu time, the seventh Soviet shuttle mission was launched from the Baikonur Cosmodrome in a polar orbit with eighty-three degrees inclination. The mission continued for seventeen orbits with an apogee of one hundred sixty-nine miles and a perigee of one hundred forty-two miles."

On the screen above the colonel, a Mercator world map appeared with a wavy line indicating the *Suslov*'s initial orbital path.

"Shortly after we obtained the launch detection, verification, and plot of the spacecraft we scrambled Spyglass to grab some pix, but there was a delay due to the fact she was on temporary assignment in Australia."

The squat but massive chief of staff leaned over and muttered to the CinC, "She was taking some downrange imagery on a Midgetman test shot out of Vandenberg."

Lamborghini waited until the chief of staff had finished his comment, then continued, "When Spyglass finally made it out of the Royal Australian Air Force base at Woomera and got into position, she caught the orbiter at the precise moment of retrofire on orbit seventeen at an altitude of one hundred fifty-seven nautical miles."

The map was replaced by a photograph of the *Suslov* with a fiery tail.

"Pure-dee luck," said the Bull.

"Certainly was," agreed Whittenberg, as he took a gulp of coffee from a mug emblazoned with the SPACECOM insignia.

Lamborghini continued, "An hour and fifty-three minutes after the Spyglass flyby we had a KH-12 pass over Baikonur which caught the shuttle on the ground at the end of the recovery runway."

A new slide came on the screen depicting what appeared to be the *Suslov* with various vehicles parked around it.

"We had an IR pass ninety-seven minutes later, after sunset; but as you can see"—another slide popped up, this one showing a grainy infrared image with a reddish hue—"the orbiter had not been moved. Only some of the vehicles had been withdrawn."

The heat-sensitive elements of the KH-12's infrared system clearly showed the outline of the replica *Suslov*. Had the genuine *Suslov* survived, its surface would have remained quite hot from the reentry friction. The heating coils that ran under the replica's skin had the same effect on the satellite's sensors, so no one in the room had any reason to suspect the shuttle was a phony.

"SIGINT?" queried Whittenberg, using the acronym for "signals intelligence."

14

"Only traffic analysis, sir," replied Lamborghini. "The Soviets had two tracking ships deployed—the *Marshal Nedelin* and *Vladimir Komarov* in the Pacific and Indian oceans respectively—and NSA monitored most of their transmissions through the Eardrum system. But as is the case with many of their sensitive missions, the radio transmissions were scrambled."

"All right," said Whittenberg, "the Vice President is going to ask me what it all means, so let's crystallize our position."

"I think it's quite apparent, General," said the deputy chief of staff for operations, a tall, thin brigadier who was never without his meerschaum pipe. Because his mathematical skills were legendary, Brig. Gen. John Fairchild had long since been stuck with the call sign of Sir Isaac, in honor of Sir Isaac Newton. He lit up his pipe and continued: "Our initial SDI testing"—you couldn't call Star Wars "Star Wars" at Cheyenne Mountain—"demonstrated that the shuttle was vital, even crucial, in retrieving essential parts for repair. We were all surprised to find its uniquely critical role evolved into providing the transport *downlink* from the prototype platform, rather than carrying equipment up to it. We simply did not foresee how fundamental that element was. In any case, as our testing progressed, the Russians saw they would have to have a viable shuttle program if they were to build a Star Wa——er, SDI system."

Everyone chuckled, and Sir Isaac's ears turned a slight shade of pink over his gaffe.

"Well, what I'm trying to say," added Sir Isaac defensively, "is that we've learned you can't build and *maintain* an SDI platform without a shuttle system. As long as the Russians didn't have a shuttle they would've had a bitch of a time maintaining a platform. Now they have one."

"And that is definitely bad news," grumbled the Bull.

"I'm afraid it is," agreed Whittenberg.

"At least they haven't matched our technical breakthrough," said the adjutant.

"So far," countered the CinC as he turned to Lamborghini. "Colonel, time's running short. Would you be good enough to sum things up for us?"

"Yes, sir," said Lamborghini as he quickly shuffled his notes. "There was a time gap of one year, one month, and four days between the previous Soviet shuttle mission and the one that occurred on 4 November. Because of the time expended between launches, we speculated something was wrong with their program. With this successful mission it appears they fixed whatever the problem was and are back in business. This is historically characteristic of their space program—that is, to continue to press forward even after major setbacks. An operational shuttle provides them with the missing transport link to assemble and maintain an SDI platform in space. Their heavy-lift capability already surpasses our own."

"Thank you, Colonel." Whittenberg looked up and down the table. "Anyone have any parting remarks? Anything we haven't covered? The floor is open for speculation. I won't hold anybody to their comments." And they knew he meant it.

"Sir?" It was Maj. Lydia Strand, Lamborghini's intel deputy—a striking brunette whose looks were surpassed only by her intelligence.

"Yes, Major?" prompted the CinC.

"Well, sir," she offered, "after the Russians' previous shuttle launch there was an absolute crackdown on access by the Western press to officials in the Soviet space program. I mean, zip has come out of there over the last year, and the Russians always play their space heroes up to the nth degree."

"As we have," Whittenberg pointed out.

"Yes, sir," agreed Strand, but added, "I would be curious to see what happens to press access after this mission."

The SPACECOM CinC pondered the thought for a moment, then said, "Your point is well taken, Major. I'll mention it to the Vice President if you have no objection."

Strand smiled. "No, sir. No objection."

THE KREMLIN, MOSCOW, CCCP

The General Secretary stood by the bay window of his baronial office, watching the season's first snowfall drift down onto Cathedral Square. It was a great irony that the Kremlin was populated by a regime which passionately embraced atheism, yet within its stone walls was a network of old structures that recalled the passionate faith of the Russian soul. Walking across the Kremlin grounds, one could see separate churches honoring the Archangel Michael, the Twelve Apostles, the Dormition of the Virgin, and the Annunciation. Additionally, there was the Church of the Deposition of the Virgin's Robe, as well as Wall Towers dedicated to Saint Peter, Saint Nicholas, and the Saviour.

To be sure, for the Party faithful there was also a statue of Lenin to complement the mausoleum that held his waxy embalmed remains. But by and large, the Kremlin grounds were dominated by beautiful old churches capped with onionlike domes, and the falling snow gave the scene a fairyland appearance. The snowfall, although late in coming for the year, was the time-honored sign that the city would soon be in the full grip of another leaden winter. But the General Secretary's mind did not absorb the spectacular view from his window or the turning of the seasons. Instead, he pondered the future—in particular *his* future—and the Politburo meeting that would convene in two hours. His energetic mind tried to anticipate the various courses the conclave could take, and he found none of the alternatives appealing.

Alexei Fyodorovich Vorontsky had struggled all of his adult life for the attainment of power, and upon reaching its pinnacle he found himself shackled by the very forces that had propelled him there. His ascension to the post of General Secretary of the Communist Party—in essence, the contemporary Russian throne—had been achieved by crushing those who had failed to make the leviathan Soviet bureaucracy perform to the state's expectations. By following such a career strategy he had no shortfall of victims, for so ponderous was the Russian bureaucratic engine that no measure—no matter how harsh or sweet—could force it to achieve the state's fanciful expectations. Year after year GOSPLAN, the central planning bureaucracy of the Soviet Union, generated reams of projections and production targets for Russian factories and collective farms. The production of everything—from toothpaste to light bulbs to cigarettes to automobiles to nuclear reactors—was controlled by the omnipotent tentacles of GOSPLAN. Yet so restrictive were GOSPLAN's controls that production targets were hardly ever met, and factory managers were routinely purged and replaced with fresh talent. The ridiculous production-targets-to-fired-managers cycle had become almost boring in its predictability. But such was the proletariat's paradise.

The General Secretary knew the game and played it masterfully. As Minister of GOSPLAN he had parlayed his powerful position to a seat on the Politburo, and it was from there he'd pulled off one of the most stunning political coups in decades by deposing Mikhail Sergeyevich Gorbachev as General Secretary of the Communist Party.

Upon attaining the post of General Secretary, Gorbachev had purged the "old guard," or the last remaining elements of the Stalinist and Brezhnev eras, but only after a long and bitter power feud with the old-line conservatives. "New blood"—as he called it—was injected into the Politburo, and a flurry of "progressive" programs were implemented—*perestroika* and *glasnost*, he called them. Yet despite all of the publicity-laden "reforms" and a missile treaty with the Americans, Russia was still a police state. *Perestroika* was challenged every step of the way by Gorbachev's political enemies, who rankled at the very thought of dismantling their bureaucracies and cutting deals with the Americans. Only by the slimmest of margins did Gorbachev remain in power. His saving grace was that there was some progress, albeit glacial, with the economy—and the troops had come home from Afghanistan.

But then the worst possible thing had happened. KGB intelligence revealed that the Americans had achieved the feared "technological breakthrough" with their Star Wars space defense system. A breakthrough so far-reaching and transcending that the specter of an impotent Soviet nuclear force was, in fact, a very real possibility—and it could happen much sooner than anyone could have anticipated. Such a fearsome possibility had unleashed violent and destabilizing forces within the Politburo, causing its militaristic and conservative members to demand a crash program to catch up with the Americans in space weapons. Gorbachev resisted, arguing it was too expensive.

The militaristic forces—who had opposed the pullout from Afghanistan—rallied around the GOSPLAN minister, and another power struggle ensued, causing divisiveness . . . and bloodshed. During the midst of the conflict, when it seemed he might tip the balance and retain his post, Gorbachev flew to Leningrad to consolidate his support among the Party leaders there. He was successful in his mission, but on the return flight to Moscow his Ilyushin jetliner mysteriously exploded in midair.

No investigation was ever made into the "tragic incident" of Gorbachev's demise, and from that point forward, opposition to the GOSPLAN minister quickly melted away and he had a cakewalk to the post of General Secretary.

Upon achieving his lifelong goal, the new General Secretary had acted swiftly to satisfy his military and conservative constituency. The missile treaty with the United States was scrapped, Afghanistan was reinvaded, and—most critical—an incredibly expensive crash program was launched to catch up with the Americans' "technological breakthrough" in space defenses. The General Secretary was a masterful politician, but in satisfying his conservative constituency he now found that he could run, but couldn't hide, from the compelling truth. And the truth was: if the Soviet Union's five million men under arms and

25,000 nuclear weapons were stripped away, Russia would be a Third World country—and a poor one at that.

The General Secretary's rush to catch up with the Americans had bloated the Soviet military budget to such a degree that the typical Russian was being bled white, and the state's ability to bottle up dissent became more fragile with each passing day. Rioting over food supplies—once isolated in the more remote Soviet *republiks*—was occurring with greater prevalence, in provinces closer to Moscow. Times were bad. . . . Worse than bad. And now his position as General Secretary was in jeopardy. After embracing the space defense system and placing its development in his personal portfolio, he soon learned from the Americans' experience that a viable space shuttle fleet was an essential tool in building and maintaining a Star Wars platform. The Politburo would not look kindly at the loss of a *second* space shuttle. Not kindly at all.

The agenda of the upcoming Politburo meeting would have one topic—the second failed shuttle mission, which by implication would mean a failed General Secretary. And the image of failure was frightening to him. Without a space shuttle or a technical breakthrough like the Americans', the Rodina—the Motherland—was stuck with an expensive, inoperable Star Wars project and millions of hungry, and angry, citizens. These facts would not be lost on the Politburo.

The General Secretary rubbed his eyes. In the dim light Vorontsky looked like the quintessential Russian that he was. Some said that with his swarthy features and heavy eyebrows he resembled Leonid Brezhnev. His large frame had once been heavy muscled, and as a young man he'd been a hammer thrower for the Soviet Union in the Olympics. But the hard muscles had long since surrendered to fat. He was growing old, tired, and soft.

A light tap on the door roused him from his stupor.

"*Da?*" he said absently.

The door opened to reveal a wiry, diminutive man dressed in a well-tailored English double-breasted suit.

"Ah, come in, Vitali," the General Secretary beckoned. Vitali Kostiashak, Chairman of the KGB, walked up to the larger man and spoke in measured tones—the voice of a civilized man speaking of a grossly uncivilized act. "General Secretary, I have come to personally inform you that General Shenko was executed by military firing squad forty-five minutes ago. His failure to develop an airworthy space shuttle had placed the state in very grave jeopardy." Then he added deferentially, "I thought it might help you," and he nodded toward the adjoining Politburo conference room.

The General Secretary contemplated Vitali Kostiashak with feelings he rarely experienced in this room—feelings of trust, confidence, and even warmth. Always surprising was this little Chairman, whom Vorontsky had sponsored and promoted to the Politburo. This diminutive man who possessed a penchant for English-tailored clothes and a complexion so dark he might have come from New Delhi rather than the Ukraine. A scholar with a Princeton Ph.D. and blade-sharp mind who, at times such as this, could be ruthless beyond belief. It was Vitali Kostiashak who had arranged for a kilogram of plastique explosive to be concealed in the wheel well of Gorbachev's Ilyushin jet while it was on the tarmac at Leningrad.

"General Shenko gave many years' service to his country. . . . I knew his family. It is regrettable he should come to such an end as this."

"General Secretary," replied the KGB chieftain, "after the American breakthrough it became critical for us to develop our own reusable shuttle system. It was General Shenko's responsibility to bring such a system to fruition. He failed. One must deal with such failure with ultimate firmness."

Vorontsky sighed and massaged the bridge of his nose. "As always, Comrade Kostiashak, your analysis is most precise—particularly as it concerns the subject of failure." His heavily lidded eyes returned their gaze to the window, and he paused some moments before saying, ever so softly, "I fear I will not be General Secretary much longer, Vitali. . . . So many years I have struggled. To have come so far and to reach such an end as this because of some damned airplane in *outer space* is more than I can fathom." A moment passed, then he turned and brought his two hammerlike fists crashing down on the desktop. "Two billion rubles!" he cried. "Up in smoke! In an instant! For the *second* time!" The outburst seemed to vent the remaining energy from his lumbering body, and he collapsed into his huge leather chair.

Kostiashak did not interrupt, but took note that his patron was beginning to show the telltale signs of age.

The General Secretary covered his face with a pair of huge hands. "What good is a damned shuttle if it burns up after three or four flites? It is useless! Utterly useless!" He sighed, and then pointed at the conference room. "They will soon be asking for my head," he murmured apologetically, "and yours along with mine, I'm afraid. . . . My dear friend, I hope I have not shortened so promising a career. You are a grandmaster, are you not? What does one do when one's king is exposed and defenseless?''

Vorontsky raised his watermelon-sized head to face his young protégé, who had taken the liberty of lighting up a Pall Mall. But instead of a look of dejection, the diminutive Chairman's Indian-like features seemed vibrant, and the corners of his thin mouth betrayed the flicker of a smile. These signs were not lost on the General Secretary—a consummate politician who had read through many a stone face in his career. "Vitali. What is it? Is there something you have not told me?''

Kostiashak tapped the ash of his cigarette into a porcelain ashtray sitting on the rosewood desk. "Yes, General Secretary. I must confess. There is something I have not . . . disclosed.''

The former hammer thrower felt his pulse quicken. "Then do not keep it from me, Vitali. Tell me what it is.''

The KGB chieftain did not answer at once, but took a long pull on his Pall Mall and exhaled slowly, causing the smoke to rise in tiny curls around his dark eyes. In a soft voice that was charged with an undercurrent of excitement, the grandmaster whispered, "You were mistaken, General Secretary. Our king is not defenseless . . . but to win the game we must risk everything.''

THE FIRST DAY

Four months later

Day 1, 1238 Hours Zulu, 4:38 A.M. Local
VANDENBERG AIR FORCE BASE, CALIFORNIA

She was beautiful.

Poised above the Pacific surf at Point Arguello, and illuminated by the gantry klieg lights, the American space shuttle *Intrepid* looked both lovely and powerful as she waited for a spark to ignite her fiery tail. The sleek-winged orbiter was pointed skyward, married to the bright orange external fuel tank and flanked by the pair of giant solid booster rockets. Together the four elements made up the "launch vehicle" of the *Intrepid*, and her beauty was surpassed only by her complexity. Sitting there, the spacecraft stood eleven stories high, weighed 4.5 million pounds, contained hundreds of moving parts, and carried so much volatile liquid fuel that the gigantic external tank contained internal baffles to prevent the fluids from whirlpooling as they were drained during launch. The orbiter-tank-booster vehicle possessed six major systems—from avionics to propulsion to life support—and hundreds of subsystems, all of which had to work in harmony if the spacecraft was to heave itself aloft.

On this moonlit night, the landscape surrounding Space Launch Complex Six at Vandenberg seemed deserted and eerily still, except for the occasional jackrabbit and a wispy, cloudlike contrail swirling around the top of the bright orange tank. Earlier that morning, 143,000 gallons of liquid oxygen, chilled to minus 147 degrees centigrade, had been loaded into the giant external tank. Once inside, the top layer of the "O-two" oxidizer became warm enough to "boil off" and change into gaseous oxygen. When the expanding super-cold vapor was vented from the tank, it hit the warmer atmosphere and left a telltale contrail whipping in the wind.

A fuzzy voice came through the headphones. "*Intrepid*, this is Launch Control. Seal your O-two locks."

The shuttle commander's thumb flipped a switch that read o2 valve—et (for "external tank") from the open to the close position. Inside the external tank an aluminum valve rotated and the white contrail immediately disappeared. Pressure was now building up in the liquid oxygen tank like steam in a capped tea kettle. The *Intrepid* had eight minutes to launch or reopen the valve; otherwise, the tank would rupture and the ensuing explosion would turn the launch complex into a small Mount St. Helens.

"Roger, Control. O-two locks are sealed." It was a cold, hard, and self-confident voice that responded.

"We copy that, *Intrepid*. We have a visual on the O-two seal."

"Roger," came the icy reply.

Maj. Frank Mulcahey chuckled to himself that the pilot in the adjoining chair enjoyed talking about liquid oxygen because, as a well-worn joke around the complex suggested, the shuttle commander's blood probably ran at about the same temperature.

"*Intrepid*, seal your H-two locks," ordered Launch Control.

"Roger, Control." And the liquid hydrogen tank, which held the second component of the shuttle's volatile fuel mixture, was closed off.

Mulcahey, the *Intrepid*'s copilot, was the true picture of his Irish ancestry with his red hair and red mustache, and the tough boxer's build that reflected his feistiness. A native of Boston, he'd spent most of his adult life in fighter aircraft before joining the SPACECOM astronaut corps. He now ran his brown eyes over the multitude of gauges, dials, and liquid crystal displays on the control panel, looking for any aberrant behavior in the launch vehicle's subsystems.

Human eyes and reflexes were woefully inadequate to handle the 34 million pieces of information processed during a shuttle launch; so to fill the void, five on-board computers gobbled through the data, monitoring thousands of functions and even checking on one another. If a dispute arose between the computers concerning a flight procedure, they would vote among themselves to settle the argument. The shuttle was so computer-dependent that firing the engines, liftoff, guidance, and reentry could all be done without the human element. Mulcahey mused to himself that the absence of the human element had extended to the flight commander's chair. Perhaps that's how the commander pictured himself—just another silicon chip or circuit performing a function.

"Move APUs to 'inhibit.' " It was a quiet but firm order.

Mulcahey responded with a terse "Yessir" and flipped a switch to shut down the orbiter's auxiliary power units during the launch phase.

"Control," radioed the commander, "this is *Intrepid*. APUs have been switched to 'inhibit.' Over."

"Roger, we copy, *Intrepid*. Out."

Mulcahey eyed the launch clock, which showed less than two minutes to ignition of the main engines. He half turned in his chair and said through the intercom, "How're you doing, Jerry? Ready to go?"

Dr. Jerry Rodriquez, mission specialist, smiled and said, "You bet. Everything's A-OK."

The two men laughed at Rodriquez's use of the expression coined during Alan Shepard's first Mercury spaceflight. It was now considered dated and more than a bit hokey, which was precisely why they laughed. The *Intrepid*'s commander, however, did not join in the levity. His face remained impassive, his expression remote and closed.

"Iceberg." That was the shuttle commander's call sign, and Mulcahey figured it suited the man well; for Col. Julian Kapuscinski always seemed to have more of an affinity for computer chips and flight controls than people. He rarely displayed anger, or warmth, or humor, or any of the other emotions associated with the human condition—in particular, fear. Whatever the commander's faults, Mulcahey thought with admiration, Kapuscinski was utterly fearless. And Christ—what a flyer! On Iceberg's second shuttle mission, this one out of the Cape, the solid rocket boosters (SRBs) had just separated when a light blinked on the control panel indicating a rupture in the liquid hydrogen component of the giant external tank. Iceberg immediately separated the orbiter from the tank and then, using the maneuvering thrusters, pulled the spacecraft into a tight loop. Nothing by the book, but if he'd waited a few seconds longer, the ensuing explosion of the external tank would have obliterated the orbiter. His subsequent landing on the Cape runway was called nothing less than Promethean by columnist George Will.

Needless to say, NASA, the Air Force, several insurance companies, and the government of Indonesia—whose $85 million communications satellite he had saved—heaped praise upon Iceberg by the truckload. There was even a White House ceremony at which the President anointed him as "a latter-day Chuck Yeager." Yet in spite of the publicity, all Kapuscinski would say about his salvation of the orbiter was: "It's just another flight." Which, of course, only served to enhance his reputation.

After the hoopla died down, historical X-rays taken of the external tank before liftoff revealed a flaw in its liquid hydrogen component. NASA engineers heaved a sigh of relief that it was the faulty component—and not the tank system—that had broken down.

27

*　　*　　*

"Hmmm. That's strange."

The launch director turned his head. "What is it, Doc? Anything the matter?" Launch directors typically were a little skittish at T minus one minute and thirty-seven seconds.

The flight surgeon hesitated because it was a minor aberration, but he decided to tell the director anyway.

"It's Kapuscinski. His heart rate is at one oh six and we still have over a minute to ignition. His pulse has never exceeded eighty-five, even after ignition."

"Iceberg?" The launch director was incredulous. "You're kidding? Must be something he ate. Either that or he's a little tense about the special cargo on board."

The doctor sighed. "You're probably right. It's not something to abort the mission, but it does concern me a little."

"Right, Doc. Let's not abort. Just keep an eye on it, okay?"

A launch director's career was not enhanced by aborts.

"*Intrepid*, this is Launch Control. SRB APU start is go. On-board computers engaging now. You are cleared for launch at T minus twenty-three seconds."

"Roger, Control," replied Iceberg. "*Intrepid* out."

Mulcahey felt the perspiration start to line his palms. There were no switches to be thrown now, no buttons to be pushed. Everything from this point was controlled by electronic impulses racing through silicon wafers.

The capsule communicator, or "Cap Com" in the Launch Control bunker, who handled radio traffic with the crew, ticked off the countdown: "Eight . . . seven . . . six . . ."

Around the pad, six giant nozzles popped up, spewing out horizontal geysers of water at the base of the spacecraft. The engines of the shuttle vehicle generated such tremendous acoustic energy that the pad had to be cushioned with a blanket of water during launch to prevent the sound waves from literally bouncing back from the concrete apron and damaging the orbiter. To provide the sound-absorbing blanket, a gravity-fed system of deluge nozzles released 760,000 gallons of water onto the pad and into the exhaust ducts in a thirty-second period during liftoff.

". . . five . . . four . . ."

The three main engines on the orbiter fired in sequence within three tenths of a second. The shuttle lurched forward about a meter, and a

Twang! reverberated in the cockpit as the "slack" in the brackets holding the orbiter to the external tank was taken up.

". . . three . . . two . . . one . . . SRB ignition!"

The computers triggered the two solid-fuel rocket boosters, and their fiery plumes joined those of the orbiter in the exhaust pit. The roar was deafening as an eruption of smoke, mixed with steam, shot high above the launch gantry.

Mulcahey checked the main and SRB engine lights and shouted, "All green!"

For three seconds 6.5 million pounds of thrust—roughly equivalent to one fourth the energy blast that leveled Hiroshima—heaved against the combined weight of orbiter, tank, and boosters, until finally the explosive bolts that held the solid-fuel boosters to the pad blew and the spacecraft began its ascent.

For those in the control room the sight of a live launch, particularly at night, never failed to fire the emotions.

"*Intrepid*, we have lift-off! You look good. The tower's been cleared and you are go for roll."

"Roger, Control," said the icy voice. "Starting roll maneuver now."

The dialogue was superfluous, for it was the orbiter's computers that commanded the booster engine nozzles to swivel, or "gimbal," rolling the vehicle 120 degrees on its axis into a "heads down" position.

Mulcahey said nothing as he watched the machometer and time-lapse clock. It never ceased to amaze him that something this big could go from zero to Mach 1 in fifty seconds.

Day 1, 1248 Hours Zulu, 2:48 p.m. Local
KALININGRAD FLITE CONTROL CENTRE

"Launch detection, Comrade General!"

"Where?" It was a plaintive demand.

"Vandenberg. Initial course one-eight-seven degrees. Launch signature analysis coming up now." Mission Commander Malyshev paused, allowing the full report to trickle into his headphones from the Soviet Aerospace Defense Warning Centre. "Confirmed. Infrared signature indicates shuttle vehicle launch profile."

"I want constant updates!" wheezed the general.

"Of course, sir. The plot is coming up on the board now." A short

29

luminescent line, aiming south out of California, appeared on the Mercator map projection.

Lt. Gen. Likady Popov slammed down the receiver and turned to the two civilians in the glassed-in observation deck. "The American shuttle has lifted off at the same time and direction as we anticipated."

"Excellent!" exulted the hulking General Secretary, while his diminutive companion—a chess player who often concealed his emotions across the chessboard—was more circumspect. Nevertheless, it was difficult even for him to contain his elation.

"Yes, yes. This is quite good. Very good indeed," purred the little KGB Chairman. "There are many things to come, but this is the most critical step, is it not?"

Popov did not respond. The harried, stocky, and overweight general in the rumpled uniform was wary in dealing with these two.

"Come, come, General," coaxed Kostiashak. "You must learn to relax. Have you any idea what this can mean for us? . . . Cigarette?"

Popov eyed the KGB chieftain. The diminutive man's black hair was always combed straight back and never out of place, and his Indian-like features seemed to be perpetually hidden behind a veil of cigarette smoke. Cautiously, Popov extended a hand and took a Pall Mall from the solid gold cigarette case while the little man's other hand proffered a flame from a Dunhill lighter. Popov accepted the light and inhaled deeply. The last month of his life had been sheer terror. In the dead of night, the fifty-nine-year-old Director of Spaceflite Operations had been roused from a peaceful sleep by a pair of goons in the green uniforms and flown by helicopter to the KGB Chairman's dacha on the Moskva River. Ever since then he'd been in the company of Kostiashak himself or one of his henchmen, making preparations for something he still could not believe. An engineer by nature and training, Popov feared the political side of Soviet life; and he was acutely aware of the fate of his predecessor. The late General Shenko had been a capable man.

To embark upon an exercise such as this was inconceivable to Popov. And to do it with such oppressive secrecy—even for a Russian—made it almost impossible. He had not seen his wife and son since he left them in the middle of the night a month ago. No doubt they thought he'd been arrested.

"When can we expect communication?" asked Vorontsky.

"That," replied Popov while scratching the ragged fringe of gray hair around his bald head, "is totally out of our hands, General Secretary."

The phone buzzed. Popov ripped the receiver off the cradle and yelled, "What?"

"Solid boosters have separated."

Day 1, 1250 Hours Zulu
THE *INTREPID*

The flash from the explosive bolts caused Mulcahey to blink, then breathe a sigh of relief. On this, his fifth shuttle mission, it was still hard to forget the *Challenger*. The image of its solid rocket booster corkscrewing into the external tank was an indelible memory for him, and he was grateful the *Intrepid*'s spent projectiles were now tumbling toward the Pacific Ocean.

"*Intrepid*, this is Mission Control at CSOC." The acronym, standing for Combined Space Operations Center, was pronounced "See-Sock." "We copy SRB separation."

"Roger, CSOC," replied Iceberg. "We have clean separation on SRBs."

After the *Intrepid* had cleared the gantry tower at Vandenberg Air Force Base, control of the mission immediately passed to the Combined Space Operations Center at Falcon Air Force Station outside Colorado Springs. The CSOC facility was almost identical to NASA's Mission Control room in Houston.

"*Intrepid*, this is CSOC, please advise on your status, over."

Iceberg ran his eyes over the gauges. "Going through Mach five, altitude twenty-eight miles. Main engines at ninety-eight percent of rated power."

The combination of orbiter and external tank hurtling through space made for an odd picture now—something akin to an airliner copulating with a barn silo. But even without its outrigger boosters, the *Intrepid* continued to accelerate, pushing Mulcahey back into his seat with a force of three g's—or three times his own weight. This would be the maximum g-force he would experience during the mission, and ordinarily three g's would be a piece of cake for the former test pilot. But on a shuttle launch the g-force was constant, unlike the short duration experienced in fighter-plane turns. The copilot's stubborn nature didn't want to admit it, but he was uncomfortable, and he'd be glad when they reached orbit. His brown eyes kept darting over the instruments. He felt that his fifth shuttle mission must be charmed, because everything was operating

31

beautifully. The Iceberg said nothing. He never did unless speech was required.

At an altitude of eighty miles the orbiter's engines "gimballed" again slightly, putting the spacecraft into an ever-so-shallow dive. The liquid fuel was almost expended now, and the big orange external tank had to be aimed on a trajectory back to the open sea; otherwise, pieces of it could fall back to earth, Lord only knew where. The tank was almost half the length of a football field, was twenty-seven feet wide, and weighed thirty-nine tons empty. It was simply too big to burn up completely on reentry, and so it had to be aimed at a remote corner of the Pacific where its charred remains would splash down harmlessly.

The computers gave the command for the main engines to shut down, and the orbiter and tank "coasted" together for another twenty seconds. Explosive bolts fired again, and the maneuvering thrusters were automatically triggered to steer the orbiter away from the separated spent tank. Once it was clear, Mulcahey watched Iceberg take manual control of the shuttle and put them into position for the orbital maneuvering system (OMS) rocket engines to fire. These were the smaller engines which allowed the spacecraft to change orbits and also provided the critical retrofire for their return to earth. The three astronauts experienced a slight jolt as the OMS rockets burned for forty seconds.

"Okay, Jerry. You can relax now. We coast for another forty-five minutes," Mulcahey said.

Rodriquez was well aware of the flight plan and knew the orbiter's systems better than Mulcahey. He even had one more shuttle flight under his belt than the copilot. His Ph.D. in mechanical engineering from Cal Tech and seven years in training as a mission specialist made him eminently qualified for this particular mission.

The *Intrepid* was en route to the prototype platform of the Strategic Defense Initiative, which was circling the earth in a polar orbit of 430 miles at 83 degrees inclination. In forty-five minutes the *Intrepid* would fire its OMS rockets again to execute an orbit "insertion burn," which would place it in a roughly circular orbit 126 miles high. After all the flight systems were checked, another series of lift, insertion, and correction burns would be executed to place the *Intrepid* in rendezvous position with the platform, where its payload would be transferred—a very sensitive payload. So sensitive that nothing could go wrong with this particular mission. That was why Rodriquez, Mulcahey, and Iceberg had been selected. They were that good.

Actually, Iceberg hadn't been on the original manifest as flight commander. He was the backup. The primary slot had belonged to Jarrod McKenna, who was everybody's first choice. The squire of the astronaut corps, McKenna looked like a test pilot sent over from Central Casting. An all-American quarterback from Yale (of all places) and a Rhodes scholar, he passed up the chance to play pro football and instead joined the Air Force, where his career took off like an F-16. Promoted early to full colonel, he was truly the chosen of the chosen—an extraordinarily gifted pilot, a brilliant leader, physically attractive, and politically acceptable to everyone. He was a natural choice for this crucial journey. But four days prior to launch he had come down with a severe case of intestinal flu. He'd been in the cafeteria and doubled over right after breakfast. Rodriquez remembered it. Scared hell out of everyone. Paramedics called and everything. The doctors said he'd pull out of it in a week or so, but he was scrubbed for the mission. Rodriquez was disappointed. He'd rather have McKenna as the jockey instead of the Iceberg, but what did it matter—it would only be for a short time.

As soon as they reached the platform, Rodriquez would deploy the payload from the cargo bay with the remote manipulator arm and then transfer to the platform himself to oversee installation of the two Star Wars components. Two members of the platform crew would ride back down with the *Intrepid*, and that would be that.

Rodriquez was thirty-six years old, but looked much older. His dark Latin features were heavily lined and his hair streaked with more gray than most men his age. His nose was flat and his ears betrayed a hint of cauliflower. His climb out of the Los Angeles barrio had taken a toll, but it was a toll he had been willing to pay. Spaceflight was the payoff. He was in orbit, and anxious to return to the SDI platform. He hadn't seen it for nine months and was fiercely excited at the prospect of, in a sense, laying the final brick. By now the orbiting station should have taken on its full hexagonal shape. Powered by a nuclear reactor, the platform was surprisingly small and manned by a crew of thirty-two who were in the final phase of teching out and debugging the systems. When it was finally operational, so the scuttlebutt went, the platform could truly negate much of the nuclear arsenal of the Soviet Union. Much earlier than anyone could have dreamed just a few years ago.

Funny, he thought, that something so staggeringly powerful would have to rely on two relatively small parts to make it all work.

Day 1, 1310 Hours Zulu, 6:10 A.M. Local
CHEYENNE MOUNTAIN

"Lookin' good, General," opined the bespectacled duty officer. "She's through lift-off and initial OMS burn in good shape. Not much that could go wrong now. She'll be back on the runway at Vandenberg in forty-eight hours—if the weather holds."

"How long till their next OMS burn?" asked Whittenberg.

The duty officer peered at his time-lapse clock. "Thirty-eight minutes, twenty-three seconds to the next burn, sir."

CSOC at Falcon Air Force Station outside Colorado Springs was several miles away from Cheyenne Mountain, but its activities were also Whittenberg's responsibility. However, even with his lofty rank, the CinC couldn't be in two places at the same time, so he monitored shuttle missions through the Space Defense Operations Center inside the granite fortress.

"Okay, I'm going to get some coffee and go back to my office," said Whittenberg. "If anything, and I mean anything, turns into a hitch, I want to know about it yesterday. Got that?"

"Yes, General," replied the duty officer.

"Pete, would you mind hanging around and keeping an eye on things until they dock with the platform?" It was Whittenberg's polite way of giving an order.

"Be glad to, sir," said Lamborghini.

The general said, "Thanks," and walked out of SPADOC.

"What's with him this morning?" asked the duty officer. "He's been pacing up and down like his wife was having triplets."

Lamborghini patted the young captain on the shoulder. "Don't worry about it, son. When you get your fourth star, you'll understand."

Day 1, 1349 Hours Zulu
THE *INTREPID*

"Ignition!" ordered Iceberg.

Mulcahey pressed the red button and the OMS rockets fired in another timed burn, inserting the *Intrepid* into low earth orbit.

"Okay, Jerry," said Mulcahey. "We're gettin' in the groove now. A coupla more burns and we're up to the platform." Executing a rendezvous with an orbiting object that was 430 miles high and traveling at 17,000 miles an hour had to be taken in stages, with deftness and skill.

"Rodriquez," intoned the Iceberg, "see to the doors."

"Roger . . . sir." Rodriquez had decided he didn't like Kapuscinski. Didn't like him at all. He truly was a real cold bastard. But never mind about that now. There was work to do. Rodriquez unplugged his intercom cord and shoved it into the pocket of his flight suit. The crew areas of the shuttle were environmentally controlled, and the astronauts did not wear the pressurized space suits during lift-off—only the light blue coverall flight suit and a crash helmet.

Rodriquez unbuckled his harness and giggled as he floated out of his chair, weightless. Mulcahey knew what the feeling was like and laughed, too. Whatever the rigors of astronaut training, they all became worth it when you floated totally free from gravity for the first time.

Rodriquez gently propelled himself to the aft crew station, where he slipped his flight boots into special shoe clips. The simple anchoring device would prevent him from drifting away while he operated the workstation controls. The aft crew station was U-shaped, with a battery of instruments, switches, and buttons. Rodriquez powered up the electronics, then peered out the window into the cargo bay. It was pitch-black. He flipped a safety switch and moved a lever marked CRG BY DRS from CLS to OPN. There was a hum, then a slight vibration as the latches slipped back and hydraulic pistons engaged, pushing the 33-foot doors open. What greeted Rodriquez was a spectacular sight—the earth's azure horizon against a jet-black background. Had he not been weightless his knees would have buckled, for the scene always left him awestruck—and reminded him what a long hard climb it had been from his impoverished youth to this window on the earth.

The skin of the shuttle became extremely hot from air friction during launch, so the inside panels of the cargo bay doors were lined with radiators which, when the doors opened, dissipated the heat buildup. Without a timely venting of the heat, the life-support system would be unable to keep the cabin cool.

"CSOC, this is *Intrepid*. Cargo bay doors are open and secure," radioed Iceberg.

"Roger, *Intrepid*. Your next OMS burn is in ninety-three minutes. Enjoy the ride. Out."

Iceberg stared out the window at the Indian Ocean. A small bead of perspiration from his upper lip broke free and floated in front of his eyes. He deftly caught it between his thumb and forefinger and mashed it. His heart was racing, so he took a long, slow breath to quiet the thumping in his chest. In a sense, the Iceberg was melting. . . .

It had been such a long journey for him. So very, very long to reach his elusive grail. Many times he had questioned himself. Questioned his purpose. Questioned his own resolve. Questioned why he had to lead such a sterile existence. But for each question she had had an answer. When he wavered, she was firm. When he cried, she had consoled him. Wait . . . be patient . . . the time will come, one day. You are not to question, she admonished him. You are to obey. It is your duty. And he was never able to disobey her.

He unzipped the breast pocket of his flight suit and took out the picture. The face that stared back at him possessed hard, stern Slavic features. But there was a trace of softness in her brown eyes, penetrating eyes that had evoked the only deep emotions Kapuscinski—the "Iceberg"—had ever known. And as incredible as it might seem, the events that propelled him into the left seat of this spacecraft had started with her, almost fifty years ago.

Mulcahey craned his neck to peek at the photograph in Kapuscinski's hand. "Say, Berg? Uh, mind if I ask, who is that?"

Iceberg did not look at his copilot but instead continued to stare at the worn picture. "It is my mother," he replied softly.

Mulcahey *almost* said, "I didn't know you had a mother," but caught himself before it slipped. Instead, he commented, "Oh—I don't recall you ever mentioning her."

A pause.

"She died. When I was nineteen. . . . I was in my second year at the academy."

"I see," said Mulcahey, but he didn't, really. He was just trying to be polite. But the sight of Iceberg gazing at the little photograph caused Mulcahey to eyeball the pilot more carefully. Although his flight skills were second to none, Iceberg had always been a weird guy. He was thin—even gaunt; there wasn't a trace of body fat on the man's physique. He worked out on a rowing machine by the hour. His close-cropped hair was gunmetal gray, the eyes black, and the hollow cheeks gave him an almost cadaverous appearance. Mulcahey shrugged and looked away.

Iceberg replaced the photograph and took another long breath. It was now, he thought. The long journey's end was now. Slowly, now that Mulcahey wasn't looking, he unzipped the thigh pocket on his flight suit and extracted a small, cylindrical object about the size of a 12-gauge shotgun shell. On the side of the cylinder was a pressure-sensitive button that released a stainless steel projectile, propelled by highly compressed carbon dioxide gas. It could be used only once. And that time was now. Iceberg put a sharp edge on his voice and barked, "What was that!?"

Mulcahey and Rodriquez both spun their heads.

"What was what?" Mulcahey asked nervously. He didn't like the pilot's tone.

With a stone face Iceberg said, "I saw the smoke-detector light flash."

Mulcahey's blood went cold. There was nothing more terrifying on a spacecraft than fire. Ever since Gus Grissom, Ed White, and Roger Chaffee had died in an Apollo capsule fire while on the pad at the Cape, the very thought of fire while in space evoked a standard reaction of raw panic.

"The annunciator didn't come on!" protested Mulcahey, trying to wish the danger away. "Which one was it?"

"Avionics bay number two," replied Iceberg grimly.

"Oh, shit!" cried the copilot.

The avionics bay was the worst possible place for a fire. Smoke detectors would trigger the automatic halogen fire extinguisher within the bay; but if that didn't work, the only way to gain access to the bay and fight the fire was to remove bulkhead panels in the lower-deck crew compartment. And that took time. Time that could allow the fire to spread.

"Rodriquez!" Iceberg's command was flint. "Get down there and see what you can make of it."

"Right! Let me get my oxygen on and—"

"Forget the oxygen! There may not be time, you fool!"

Standard safety procedures called for the flight crew to put on their portable oxygen packs in the event of a fire, but Rodriquez decided not to argue about procedures just now, or take offense at Kapuscinski's remark. He'd do that later. For now, he followed orders and pushed himself to the hatchway leading down to the crew compartment deck. He struggled to unscrew the hatch wheel, finding it difficult to get a foothold in the weightlessness.

The crew areas of the shuttle were divided into two sections. The flight deck—which included the cockpit and cargo bay workstation —was topside, while the crew compartment—which contained storage, sleeping areas, kitchen, bathroom, and airlock access—was below. After the *Challenger* disaster, NASA had decreed future orbiters would have a safety ejection mechanism. A slide pole escape

37

system was installed on the older shuttles, but the newer models—like the *Intrepid*—possessed an upgraded system whereby the flight deck was a self-contained capsule that could be ejected with all hands during launch, up to about 120,000 feet. The hatch sealed off the flight deck from the crew compartment until final orbit was achieved, then it was opened to allow passage between the two chambers.

When the hatch wheel finally yielded, Rodriquez yanked the lid back and shot through the passageway hole headfirst.

"CSOC, this is *Intrepid*," said Iceberg. "We have a problem."

"We read you, *Intrepid*. State your problem."

Iceberg had rehearsed well. "We received a momentary flashing light of number two smoke detector in the avionics bay. The annunciator did not, I say again did not, go off. Rodriquez is investigating now."

"Roger, *Intrepid* . . ." There was a pause. "*Intrepid*, we do not, I say again we do not, copy a smoke detector alarm on the telemetry monitor. We've alerted flight engineering. They'll be on standby in case you need them. We recommend you proceed with a circuit check."

"Roger, Control," replied Iceberg. "We will comply with a circuit test of the smoke detector system. Stand by. . . ."

"Well, I don't see any other lights," said Mulcahey, starting to relax a bit—but pulling out his auxiliary oxygen mask just the same. "I think another detector would've gone off by now if there was a real problem, don't you?"

They were Maj. Frank Mulcahey's last words.

In one swift movement Iceberg shoved the cylinder under his copilot's chin and pressed the button. There was a popping sound as the projectile shot into Mulcahey's brain, causing him to convulse and give a little cry. Almost immediately blood started oozing out of the small hole in his chin and into the weightless chamber.

Rodriquez sailed through the hole, not stopping to secure the hatch lid. He immediately faced a bank of storage lockers—much like the kind one would find in a bus station. They were secured to the bulkhead panel, which provided access to the avionics bay. He reached behind the top locker and popped a safety catch. This allowed one row of the lockers to come free. He ripped it away and pushed it toward the back of the compartment.

The front bulkhead panel was secured by six recessed butterfly screws. The screwheads could be pried out of the recesses with a screwdriver, or a strong fingernail, and unscrewed by hand. Rodriquez pulled a screwdriver out of the on-board tool kit and was starting to engage the first screw when he heard a popping sound from above, followed by a little yelp. He hesitated, and was torn between continuing his task and going back to investigate.

Then he heard the hatch clang shut.

Iceberg slammed down the lid and spun the wheel as tight as he possibly could. Then he unzipped the other thigh pocket on his flight suit and pulled out a simple bicycle-cable lock—the kind with a combination mechanism. He ran it through the hatch wheel and around the restraining post, then locked it. There would be some play in the wheel, but the steel cable would prevent it from being opened.

He then pushed himself back to his cockpit seat, where Mulcahey's blood was beginning to be a problem. Iceberg fished in his copilot's breast pocket and came up with a handkerchief. Most astronauts carried them, not wanting the mucus from their sinuses to escape into the weightlessness. He capped Mulcahey's chin with the handkerchief, then shoved the corners up between the flight helmet and the dead copilot's temple. He looked at his handiwork for a few moments until satisfied it was a good temporary plug.

Sliding back into his seat, Iceberg started flipping control switches on the orbiter's oxygen/nitrogen life-support system, just as he heard a metallic pounding on the hatch lid.

Rodriquez was no fool. But none of his academic or astronaut experience had prepared him for a situation such as this. Rather than rush for the hatch, his first instinct was to establish communication. He fished out the plug to his intercom headset and shoved it into a nearby port.

"Frank? . . . Berg? What's happening? Did you shut the hatch because of the fire? . . . Hey, guys. What gives?"

Nothing.

He unplugged the headset and floated up to the hatch. The wheel would turn a little, but not much. That told him something was very wrong, for there was no locking mechanism on the hatch wheel. He pounded on the lid with his screwdriver and had started to yell when he heard a hissing sound.

When the Grissom-White-Chaffee Apollo capsule went up in flames, it was largely due to its one hundred percent oxygen atmosphere; and in the wake of that disaster some bureaucratic chowder-head got the revelation that pure pressurized oxygen around electrical wiring could be dangerous. So, for safety considerations, the shuttle's life-support system was designed to simulate the earth's atmosphere with a mixture of twenty-one percent oxygen and seventy-nine percent nitrogen. The oxygen was carried aboard the orbiter in cryogenic—that is, liquid—form. A controlled boiling chamber converted the super-cold liquid into vapor, then it was warmed by a heat exchanger before being introduced into the cabin. The nitrogen was carried aboard in pressurized tanks. The two gases were mixed through a regula-tor/sensor that purged the cabin atmosphere as required, and intro-duced one gas or the other to keep their prescribed level constant. There was, of course, a manual override switch on the shuttle commander's console that controlled the regulator.

Rodriquez knew the *Intrepid*'s systems as well as anyone. The hissing sound told him the purging fan had been turned on to siphon off the existing atmosphere in the crew compartment. The hissing, in itself, was not unusual, and a scientific instinct tried to tell him this had something to do with the fire; but another instinct, this one from his youth in the barrio, told him he could be in another kind of danger.

Once again he pounded on the hatch.

"Frank! . . . Berg! . . . Somebody answer!"

Nothing.

Rodriquez began to notice his breathing was more rapid. He floated to the oxygen indicator, and his eyes widened when he saw the needle resting on 12% OXY . . . Then it started falling to 11% OXY. There was no question in his mind now. Somebody was trying to kill him.

He thrust himself to the locker that held the portable oxygen system. He yanked out the mask, pressed it to his face, and flipped the switch—but no oxygen flowed to his nostrils. Because the tube wasn't transparent, he couldn't see that it was blocked with epoxy glue which had been injected by hypodermic needle. He discarded the mask and went to the second oxygen system, only to come to another dead end. His chest was heaving now. There was one more emergency oxygen system on this deck, but something told him it would be just like the others. He flew to the airlock and hit the pressurization switch to try to get some oxygen that way, but the red MNL OVR RDE light was blinking and the air wouldn't flow. Rodriquez knew the override switches for the airlock and the cabin environmental system were all in the cockpit, and there wasn't anything he could do—except, maybe . . .

He grabbed the floating screwdriver and pushed himself to the bulkhead panel which sealed off the avionics bay. His chest was heaving like a quarter-miler's now. Frantically he pried loose each of the butterfly screws and unscrewed them from the panel. He was becoming a little giddy now, and light-headed. The last screw popped free. All the color was fading from his vision. Everything was black-and-white.

The panel came off. The room was spinning. His hand floated inside the bay and pulled on a drawer filled with circuit boards. It didn't budge. He yanked again. Images were dimming. The drawer pulled free. With his last conscious effort, Rodriquez grasped the butt of his screwdriver and brought it down as hard as he could on one of the brittle plastic circuit boards. It shattered, causing fragments to float out of the bay and into the cabin.

To his credit, Rodriquez had taken the only action which might have saved his life, and that was to break the circuit which controlled the purging fan and the manual override switch on the oxygen/nitrogen regulator. But his strategy didn't quite work as planned. The lack of oxygen in the cabin had blurred his vision, and instead of hitting the circuit board labeled OXY/NIT, Rodriquez brought the butt of his screwdriver down on the board marked OMS.

Day 1, 1445 Hours Zulu, 7:45 A.M. Local
CHEYENNE MOUNTAIN

"What happened?" demanded Whittenberg.

Lamborghini nodded to the duty officer and said, "Play it back." The young captain punched a button on the digital recorder and they all relived the *Intrepid*'s last transmission.

"We notified you immediately, sir," said Lamborghini. "This came in just seven minutes ago. CSOC has tried raising them on all four transponders and has gotten zip. Telemetry also ceased shortly after the transmission. Spyglass is at Andrews. If we scramble them now they can be in position for a flyby in about six hours."

With his jaw muscles flexing, Whittenberg nodded. Lamborghini grabbed the yellow phone and immediately started barking orders. That was one thing about his intel chief, Whittenberg thought. He answered your question before you asked it, then pointed the way.

When the colonel hung up, Whittenberg looked at his watch. It was not quite 8:00 A.M. "Assemble any of the staff who've already arrived.

41

Then have McCormack from CSOC piped into the conference room on a secure line.'' The CinC didn't wait for an answer, but spun on his heel and left.

Eleven minutes later the conference room was filled.

"Okay, Colonel," ordered Whittenberg. "Bring everyone up to speed."

Lamborghini ran through a quick brief on the situation and took his seat.

"Did we miss anything, Chet?" Whittenberg queried the speaker-phone box.

"No, sir," replied Maj. Gen. Chester McCormack from CSOC. "That about covers it. We even tried to raise them from the SDI platform with no success."

"All right, gentlemen . . . and lady," said the CinC, to include Lydia Strand, Lamborghini's deputy. "That's where we are. Where do we go from here?"

No one spoke at once, and Whittenberg didn't rush. He knew it would take some time for them to absorb the problem. It was the deputy chief of staff for operations—the professorial General Fairchild—who spoke first. He was a brigadier who cut a strange-looking figure, for his bald head was in the shape of a light bulb, and it seemed a bit large for his thin body. His peculiar appearance was further amplified by the meerschaum pipe that always seemed to be hanging from his mouth. But when "Sir Isaac" talked, everyone listened. "Let's consider the options," he began, through a haze of pipe smoke. "First case, there was a fire on board that reached the liquid hydrogen or oxygen fuel cells and blew the orbiter apart. While this is possible, I feel the fire-suppression systems and the design of the craft make this unlikely."

No one challenged the Ph.D. in electrical engineering from MIT.

"Besides," he continued, "Spyglass will soon tell us if this is so or not. . . . Second case, the spacecraft is intact, but the crew are dead. In such case the orbiter and payload can be salvaged. . . . Third case, the crew are alive but life-support systems are damaged and they are operating on emergency systems. If they cannot effect repairs—and being without ground communication, this will be difficult—they will be dead before any rescue effort could be mounted."

No one was comfortable with the detached way Sir Isaac sized things up.

"Fourth and final case," he concluded, "they are alive, life support is functioning, and they have only lost their communication, and possibly some other functions."

There was another lull.

"Chet," asked Whittenberg, "they were on auto controls for their final OMS burn, weren't they?"

The Commander of SPACECOM Flight Operations said, "Roger, General," through the speaker box. "They had fired their initial orbit insertion burn and were supposed to go through a systems check before their next lift burn. They were on auto."

"So if they're alive and the computer and OMS systems weren't damaged, they could still be programmed to fire the next burn?" asked the CinC.

"Mmmmm," McCormack hedged. "I suppose that's possible."

"How long till the next burn was scheduled?" queried Sir Isaac.

There was a pause, then the box spoke: "Eighteen minutes."

"Okay," said Whittenberg. "We wait eighteen minutes. If nothing happens, we start considering the more unattractive alternatives."

Day 1, 1515 Hours Zulu
THE *INTREPID*

Iceberg watched carefully as the oxygen meter needle inched back up to twenty percent. He'd kept it at one hundred percent nitrogen in the crew compartment for twenty-five minutes, which was long enough to asphyxiate anyone several times over. Also, he knew Rodriquez wouldn't have procured any relief from the portable oxygen packs. He'd taken care of those before launch, right after the ground crew had certified them as being in great shape. The recollection caused him to smile at his own cleverness.

Iceberg was sure Rodriquez had died, but he couldn't shake a desire to be certain. He floated to the hatch, took off his helmet, and held his ear to the lid for some minutes, listening for a sound. There was none. Slowly he dialed in the correct combination to the bicycle lock, then removed the cable from the hatch wheel. He carefully turned the wheel, raised the lid slightly, and peeked through a slit. He needn't have worried. Rodriquez was floating spread-eagled in the far corner, with the unsecured bank of lockers lightly bumping his leg.

Iceberg lifted the hatch and secured it, then pushed himself through. He turned Rodriquez over to see his glaring eyes and blue face. The death mask of the mission specialist showed that his end had been a painful one, but the grisly picture unnerved the shuttle commander not at all. Having released the manual override switch from his cockpit console, Iceberg started repressurizing the airlock. When the light turned green he opened the door and shoved the mission specialist's body inside. The airlock allowed passage from the crew compartment to the cargo bay of the orbiter. It was ordinarily used to provide access for extravehicular activity (EVA), but Iceberg was now using it for storage. After stuffing the remains of Rodriquez inside, he quickly traveled back up to the flight deck and unhooked Mulcahey's seat restraints. He pulled the dead copilot below, shoved the body into the airlock chamber alongside Rodriquez, and sealed the door. It was then Iceberg noticed the floating plastic fragments. He whirled around to look at the avionics bay. More fragments. He shot across the deck to inspect the damage. Shards of the shattered circuit board stuck out of the slot marked oms; and for perhaps the first time in his life, Iceberg took in a little gasp.

Kapuscinski's understanding of electronic flight control systems was better than that of most pilot astronauts, but still, he was not an electrical engineer. Engineers, in fact, were often looked upon disparagingly by pilots—and he was a superb flyer. So the shattered circuit board gave him an intuitive feel for what had happened, but he wasn't certain—and he was a man who liked absolute certainties. He dashed up to the cockpit and flipped the orbital maneuvering system switch from SAFE to ARM. The light stayed red, refusing to turn green. He screamed, "*No!*" and pounded the armrest of his chair. He tried the backup system and the result was the same.

"*No! No! No!*" he wailed. Never in his life had Iceberg unleashed such emotion. "No, Mother, *please*. Tell me this *cannot be!*"

With the butt of a screwdriver, Rodriquez had crippled the circuits of *Intrepid*'s OMS retro rockets. The spacecraft was, quite simply, unable to return to earth.

Day 1, 1545 Hours Zulu, 8:45 A.M. Local
CHEYENNE MOUNTAIN

Out of control.

That's what Whittenberg thought. The whole damn technology thing had tailspun out of control. For somewhere out there, circling around in space, was $4 billion worth of exotic hardware—possibly blown to pieces by a short circuit in a five-dollar breaker switch.

Prices had definitely gone up. As a young stableboy growing up in Kentucky during World War II, Whittenberg had been exercising one of the stud farm's three-year-olds when a P-51 Mustang screamed over them at treetop level. The horse was so spooked that the animal parted company with the young rider. It was at that point, Whittenberg told friends, that he'd decided to forego a career as a jockey and become a pilot instead. Everyone always laughed at the story, because at six feet five inches and 230 pounds, he was an unlikely candidate to ride at Churchill Downs. But while humorous, the story was true. Being buzzed by a P-51 was a transcending experience for the youthful Whittenberg. Much later, when he was an instructor at the Air Force Academy, he looked up the original 1944 cost of a P-51 aircraft. It turned out to be $47,000. About the price of a good sports car these days.

Whittenberg also remembered his first B-52. The eight-engined behemoth was awesome, and so damn complex! He figured that weapons systems couldn't possibly get more complicated than the cockpit of his first B-52. But they did. First the Hound Dog missile, then laser-guided bombsights, then electronic countermeasures, and electronic counter-countermeasures, then cruise missiles. He'd consumed countless technical manuals during his Strategic Air Command career, and it had reached the point where he simply couldn't keep up. He could only manage people whose job it was to keep up on their respective tiny pieces of the Big Picture. He had inner doubts about his, or anyone's, ability to tie all of the little pieces together. Sometimes, like now, it got to him, and he almost wished that Mustang had taken a different vector on that day so long ago . . . almost.

Whittenberg had yearned all of his life to be a fighter pilot, and the one perk of his four-star rank that he truly relished was his "stick time" in a Talon T-38 trainer, which allowed him to retain his flight status. But in the early days of his career, because of his black skin and enormous size ("Sorry, Lieutenant, we don't have a shoehorn big enough to slip you into one of these itty bitty Sabre Jets—why don't you step into one of those big ole bombers over yonder . . . ha, ha"), he was relegated to flying the larger aircraft.

So it was in bombers he'd made his reputation, particularly flying missions out of Guam over North and South Vietnam—as the ribbon on his chest denoting the Distinguished Flying Cross would attest. It had happened on the first mission of the Christmas bombing in 1972. The bombing raids over North Vietnam had been halted during the fall of that year while Kissinger was in Paris putting a "peace agreement" together with Hanoi's Le Duc Tho. But the negotiations broke down after Nixon's election, causing the President to embark upon a strategy of bombing the Vietnamese back to the negotiating table. Unfortunately, the bombing halt had given the North Vietnamese plenty of time to repair and replenish their air defense batteries.

On the first mission after the hiatus, Whittenberg's squadron was assigned to strike the port facilities at Haiphong, which possessed one of the heaviest concentrations of antiaircraft weapons in the history of air combat. B-52s were a particularly sweet target for the surface-to-air missile (SAM) batteries because of their size and lumbering speed, so on this mission a flock of "Wild Weasels" flew in ahead of the bombers to neutralize as many SAM launchers as possible. The Weasels were specially equipped F-105 Thunderchiefs that would "clothesline," or intentionally let a SAM radar lock on to them, then unleash their own tracking missiles to home in on and destroy the SAM radar antenna. This would blind the SAM battery until the antenna could be rebuilt. Unfortunately, a Weasel often had to contend with an incoming SAM missile while lining up its own shot. In essence, the process often became a high-speed game of chicken, and sometimes the Weasel's missile came in second.

On that mission over Haiphong, however, no amount of Weasels could contain the flock of missiles that screamed toward Whittenberg's squadron. The entire rim of the harbor seemed to come alive with SAM launch signatures. Sizing up what seemed like a hopeless situation, Whittenberg released his bomb load prematurely and commanded his squadron to release airbursts of radar-confusing chaff. He then put his own lead B-52 into a steep diving turn, turning *off* his black box of electronic countermeasures and turning *on* his navigational transponder. The resulting multitude of radar images apparently confused the Soviet-built fire-control computers, causing them to lock on to the one clear signal which emerged from the electronic clutter—i.e., Whittenberg's transponder. The remainder of his squadron made it through unscathed that morning, but not Whittenberg. The first incoming SAM clipped his B-52 on the wingtip, causing it to cartwheel at 23,000 feet. Whittenberg and his copilot and tail gunner were the only ones able to eject.

Whittenberg never saw the rest of his crew again, except for his tail gunner. They landed not far from the coast, the young enlisted man suffering a fractured leg on impact. For eleven days they evaded capture, the big black officer carrying the young Louisiana airman on his back. The North Vietnamese, who had become very astute at tracking down American pilots, combed the area thoroughly while Whittenberg communicated via his survival radio with Navy search-and-rescue helicopters. The Navy choppers were able to drop some supplies, but couldn't risk exposure long enough to make a pickup. Finally, Whittenberg radioed for a raft, which was dropped to them on their final night. He carried his gunner to the coast and into the surf, then inflated the raft and started rowing. Just before dawn he popped a flare, and a Sikorsky Sea King plucked them out.

His entire crew received the Distinguished Flying Cross. Except for himself and his tail gunner, the award was made posthumously. How many airmen and B-52s had been saved that day by his actions was impossible to tell. All Whittenberg knew was that writing letters to his crew members' families afterward was the toughest thing he'd ever done in his life. He almost left the Air Force after that.

But he stayed. And his reputation grew. As squadron commander, then as wing commander. Then the stars started rolling his way. Every unit he'd touched was goosed to its top proficiency. During a duty tour in Washington he took time out to get a master's degree in international relations from Georgetown University, and after that he was named Superintendent of the Air Force Academy—a posting that made four stars almost a sure thing. It became everybody's foregone conclusion that he would eventually be CinCSAC—Commander in Chief, Strategic Air Command. It had been his dream. But just when the apple seemed his for the taking, the new President came into office, along with a latter-day gunslinger for a Vice President, and the two of them turned the Pentagon topsy-turvy to find just the right "Space Czar" for "their" space program. The computers kept spitting out Whittenberg's name. And so he landed in Cheyenne Mountain. He now wished he'd wound up anyplace else.

"All right," Whittenberg said. "I make it five minutes past OMS burn. Anything happen on your end, Chet?"

"Negative, sir," lamented McCormack through the speaker box. As Commander of Flight Operations, he considered the men on board *Intrepid* "his" astronauts.

Whittenberg turned to Michael Dowd and asked, "How about it, Bull? Any deviation of their orbital path?"

The chief of staff's nickname, Bull, came partly from his linebacker build and pugnacious appearance. And his rough features reminded people of the bull on a package of Bull Durham chewing tobacco. All that was missing was a ring in his nose. He made one last query into the phone to the Spacetrack duty officer in SPADOC, then hung up and said, "No change in orbit, General."

"Very well," said Whittenberg, while rubbing his temples. "Of all the options Sir Isaac has outlined for us, I have decided that we will proceed on the premise that the *Intrepid* is dead in the water and cannot maneuver, but the crew is alive. We are to mount and execute a rescue operation with the priority of first saving the crew, then salvaging the payload. Since time is of the essence, we will not wait for the Spyglass pictures, but start immediately." He paused just a moment to let everyone absorb his comments, but no more than a moment, then turned to his deputy chief of staff for operations. "Okay, Sir Isaac, what's our status?"

Like any four-star command structure, the SPACECOM staff was huge, but out of its giant organization chart an inner circle of advisers had emerged upon whom Whittenberg relied heavily. Lamborghini was the former fighter pilot who had an intelligence officer's instinct for finding the right answer; Bull—the two-star chief of staff—was Whittenberg's surrogate, who raised hell, jumped up and down, pounded the table, and made sure the staff's work was cranked out on time; and Sir Isaac, the operations man, was a one-man "brain trust" who spoke with a quiet, detached air. He'd never been a pilot, but he knew more about launch systems and the shuttle than anyone else inside or outside SPACECOM.

There were a few moments of silence as Sir Isaac fired up his meerschaum pipe again and contemplated the ceiling. Then, without consulting any notes, he said, "Of the shuttle fleet, *Atlantis* and *Christa* returned from the SDI platform just nine and twenty-one days ago, respectively, and are in the turnaround pipeline. Neither one could launch for another three weeks at the very least." He paused to release a puff into the air. "*Discovery* is slated to enter the Rockwell hangar at Palmdale in two days for scheduled maintenance, just as the *Antares* comes out. The *Constellation* is on the pad at the Cape, scheduled to launch in eight days for deployment of an Anik communications satellite and a COSMAX astronomical telescope."

Sir Isaac didn't say what everyone already knew—that the *Columbia* had long since been retired, and the new administration had ordered up four new shuttles to get their "Final Frontier" program on track. When the President announced to an open-mouthed press corps that his fiscally conservative administration was going to buy four new orbiters at a price tag of $2 billion apiece, the former auto executive couldn't help joking that he'd gotten a fleet discount. Yet in the same speech he'd also announced the newest shuttle would be named *Christa*, in honor of the teacher who'd died aboard the *Challenger*, and for whom he'd wept on that fateful day.

"So all we have in the gate is the *Constellation*?" asked the Bull.

"That's correct," replied Sir Isaac. "The soonest we could get the *Constellation* off the pad would be seventy-two hours, give or take, depending on *Intrepid*'s flight path at the time. I haven't run a rendezvous flight plan through the computer yet. But if we do use the *Constellation* that presents us with two problems."

Whittenberg already knew what they were, but wanted them verbalized anyway. "Continue," he ordered.

"Yes, sir. Since the *Intrepid* is in a polar orbit, we'll have to extricate the *Constellation*'s payload. It's way too heavy for a polar launch. That means we'll have to send up the Anik and COSMAX later, and that screws up the scheduling pipeline for at least a year."

Sir Isaac was referring to one of the basic limitations of orbital mechanics. The earth rotates from west to east at about 900 mph. This provides equatorial launches, traveling east out of the Kennedy Space Center, with extra lifting power—sort of like jumping from a running start. Unfortunately, this "rotational boost" is lost when a shuttle is fired into a polar orbit—which is sort of like jumping from a standing position. As a result, equatorial launches from Florida could handle payloads almost twice as heavy as polar launches from Vandenberg Air Force Base in California.

"Also," continued Sir Isaac, "there's another problem with going out of Florida. We've only launched a few satellites into a polar orbit from the Cape, and that was back in the sixties. As I recall, those rockets were launched due east over the Atlantic, then were put through a dogleg maneuver that sent them south. There's no way we could execute a dogleg maneuver with the *Constellation*. It would require too much propellant. If we launch the *Constellation* from the Cape it will have to go directly south and pass over populated areas during its ascent. I suppose such an action would require Presidential approval of some sort."

"I think you suppose right," said Whittenberg. "You find any flaw in his thinking, Chet?"

"Negative, General," replied McCormack.

"I agree with everything Sir Isaac has said," continued Whittenberg, "but the *Constellation* is the only vehicle we have at this time that can pull something like this off. It's got to be *Constellation* and it's got to be now. Chet, you and Bull and Sir Isaac start mapping out the flight plan. If Spyglass comes back with pix showing *Intrepid* is blown to pieces, you can take this matter up with my replacement. Until then, I'll talk with the White House and NASA, and get control over the launch switched to Chet at CSOC. Everyone else get his ass in gear. I want that bird off the pad in seventy-two hours, max.''

Day 1, 1545 Hours Zulu
THE *INTREPID*

Control.

That had been the guiding force of his life. Control and purpose. Now, once again, he had to become a creature of absolute discipline and retake control of himself and his situation. No more childish outbursts. No more wailing. Once again, he told himself, be the superb test pilot. Assess the problem and correct it. Be scientific and detached.

First, take stock. Put things in order. There were still droplets of blood floating in the cockpit. Iceberg drifted out of his chair and retrieved a hand-held vacuum cleaner from the crew compartment. He methodically swept the flight deck's air of the red droplets, and then went below to clear the crew compartment of floating circuit-board fragments. After securing the vacuum cleaner and floating oxygen packs, he carefully inspected the damage to the spacecraft's electronics. Iceberg cursed. That *damned* Rodriquez. He'd always despised the man's flippant manner.

It appeared the only circuit board damaged was the one marked oms, which carried the primary and backup systems for the maneuvering retro rockets. Carefully, Kapuscinski plucked out the remaining shards and fragments from the circuit casing and put them in a waste container, then gently pushed the circuit drawer back into place. He replaced the bulkhead panel and tightened the butterfly screws, then reattached the storage locker to the panel. Lastly, he put the floating screwdriver back in the tool kit. Satisfied everything was in its proper place, he returned to the left seat of the cockpit.

Methodically, he ran through the instrument checklist and found all major systems were functional, including the reaction control system (RCS), which allowed the orbiter to change position up, down, and

50

sideways, with small pitch and yaw thrusters in the nose and tail. That is to say, with the RCS thrusters the *Intrepid* could change its attitude *in* orbit, but it couldn't *change* orbits or execute retrofire. Also, the circuits which allowed the hydrazine and nitrogen tetroxide fuel to be transferred from the larger OMS fuel tanks to the smaller RCS fuel tanks that had been taken out by Rodriquez. That meant Iceberg could maneuver the orbiter, but would have to do so sparingly with the existing RCS fuel in the smaller tanks. Life-support systems were in order, and there was enough oxygen and supplies for three men for eleven days—thirty-three days for him alone.

He punched up the orbital path data on the flight computer, which showed the *Intrepid* was in a circular polar orbit with an altitude of 126 miles. If he was left in this pattern long enough, the orbit would eventually decay and the shuttle would fall into the atmosphere to break apart in an uncontrolled reentry. However, such an orbit decay from this altitude would probably take a couple of months.

For the time being he was alone, with no other vehicle, from either the SDI platform or the ground, that could be of immediate danger to him. That would change, though. It was his guess that efforts were under way at this very moment to get some kind of vehicle aloft—and fast. He had to find some way of reactivating the OMS retro rockets. He'd crossed the Rubicon, and his only way to survive was to get down from orbit before the Americans found a way up. It had to be done, and he knew he couldn't do it alone. He needed help, and that meant communicating with his new masters.

On the communications panel of the pilot's console, there was a device which had a liquid crystal display with a numeric keypad underneath. It looked very much like a simple ten-key electronic calculator, but in fact it was a radio transmission scrambling device called "Oracle." This device could be wired into virtually any military aircraft or tactical radio and was immensely popular with all three services because of its effectiveness, simplicity, and durability. However, widespread popularity did have its drawbacks.

The spy ring which had so devastated the Navy and compromised its most jealously guarded cryptographic secrets had not ended with the arrest of John Walker, a sleazy submarine warrant officer who sold out his country for some spare pocket change. Operating independent of Walker and unbeknownst to the FBI was another communications warrant officer—this one on a frigate—who had copied an Oracle technical manual and passed it to his Soviet case officer between cruises. About the same time, a file clerk at Pacstar Communications in Los Angeles—the manufacturer of the Oracle system—had photographed circuit diagrams of the system while the design engineers were at lunch and passed it on to her case officer on the West Coast. The KGB's Technical Directorate had pulled the elements together to fashion a working model of the system.

While these intelligence losses were devastating, having an Oracle terminal did not, in and of itself, give the owner access to all scrambled radio traffic. Fortunately, eleven identical digits had to be punched into the microprocessor of the Oracle transceiver for the communications to pass back and forth unscrambled. Without the exact same digits, the Oracle was useless; and with 99,999,999,999 permutations and combinations, the likelihood of anyone tapping into the same eleven random digits during a brief transmission was—to say the least—remote.

Iceberg punched in the eleven digits he had committed to memory. He'd obtained the numbers from the proprietor of a ramshackle rare book store in Lompoc, California—the same person who'd given him the little cylinder with which he'd killed Mulcahey. Next, he checked the Global Positioning System on the *Intrepid*'s NavComputer, which gave him the spacecraft's position, altitude, course, and speed (or vector).

Normally, the orbiter communicated with Mission Control at CSOC through the tracking and data relay satellites (TDRS), which were two geosynchronous satellites that relayed radio transmissions from the shuttle to the ground. The Russians had their own Kosmos 1700 communications satellites that worked on much the same principle, but it had been decided from the beginning that the *Intrepid* would not use the Kosmos system, except as a last resort. That was because satellite relay transmissions were much easier to intercept than point-to-point radio signals. Therefore, the *Intrepid* would aim its directional radio antenna at a ground-based receiving station and communicate only while it was overhead. This cut down the "time window" for communications, but it improved security—at least long enough to get *Intrepid* on the ground.

The NavComputer told Iceberg the *Intrepid* was over the Arctic ice cap, and after one more orbit the spacecraft would be crossing Soviet airspace in far eastern Siberia. Iceberg had memorized the positions of the Russian ground-based Orbita tracking stations, and he could see from the navigational plot that he would have a communications time window of about four minutes as he sailed over the small naval station of Valkumey—a dismal outpost on Chaunskaya Bay that emptied into the East Siberian Sea. There was precious little there, except ice, tundra, a pier—and an earth-station dish pointed expectantly at the sky.

Day 1, 1800 Hours Zulu, 8:00 P.M. Local
KALININGRAD FLITE CONTROL CENTRE

The communications officer sat bolt upright as if he'd been goosed with an electric cattle prod. "Commander! I have a transmission on the preset S-band frequency coming through the encryption device." A table had been set up next to the commo officer's console, with a large metallic box resting on top of it. Several coaxial cables ran from the box and into an open panel on the console. The commo officer held his earphones tighter. "The transmission is coming through clearly . . . in English."

Col. Oleg Malyshev, the mission commander who had presided over the burn-up of the *Suslov*, nodded to the commo officer and said, "Switch to my microphone." The young man did as instructed, and Malyshev listened . . . not believing what he was hearing.

"Flite Centre, this is *Intrepid*. Do you read? Over. . . . Flite Centre, this is *Intrepid*. Do you read? Over."

Malyshev tried to ignore the three men standing over him and concentrated on the transmission. As a former military attaché stationed in London, Malyshev knew the English language fluently. He keyed his microphone switch. "*Intrepid*, this is Flite Centre. We read you five by five. Repeat, we read you five by five. What is your status? Over."

Of the troika standing behind Malyshev, Popov was also fluent in English, and Kostiashak spoke the language better than most Englishmen. General Secretary Vorontsky had a tiny foreign vocabulary. All three men wore headsets.

"Flite Centre, this is *Intrepid*. Listen and listen good. We have trouble. The other two crewmen are dead, but one of them managed to damage a circuit panel before he died. The damaged panel controls the rockets of the orbital maneuvering system. All other systems are functional, but I cannot, repeat cannot, fire the retro rockets."

Malyshev was stunned, but kept his mind working. The spacecraft had only a small window of time to communicate, and he couldn't waste a millisecond. "*Intrepid*, this is Flite Centre. Can you repair the damage?"

53

"Negative, Centre. I do not have the on-board capability to make any repairs. I can still maneuver the pitch and yaw thrusters and my fuel cells are functioning properly, but the OMS engines are dead. Got that? Dead. Whatever solution there is, it has to come from you, Flite Centre, and it's got to be fast. The Americans will not leave me up here."

"What is your life-support situation, *Intrepid*? Over."

"Approximately thirty days of life support," said Iceberg testily. "But we won't have near that long. Do you understand?"

The time window was about closed.

"Yes, *Intrepid*, we understand you. We will study the problem and advise you two orbits from now when you pass over the Irkutsk station."

"Roger. Will comply. *Intrepid*, out."

Malyshev ran a hand through his sweaty blond hair. He was amazed at how flat and detached the American's voice had been. Particularly since he'd just reported an unmitigated disaster.

"I did not understand the transmission," complained the General Secretary. "What did he say? When will he be landing?"

Popov, Kostiashak, and Malyshev all sought to avoid his inquiring glance, and no one volunteered to translate. Their reluctance was not lost on Vorontsky, who said, "Vitali—tell me at once. What did the pilot say?"

The KGB Chairman paused, but did not mince words. "The pilot—*our* pilot—had to kill the two other crewmen aboard. Apparently there was a struggle of some kind, and some of the electronic equipment aboard was damaged. His life-support systems are functioning, but he cannot fire his retro rockets. That is to say, he does not have the capability to fire his rockets and return to earth."

The General Secretary crashed his headset down on the console. "*Cannot return to earth?* You mean he has killed two American astronauts and now he is *stuck* up there?" Entire rows of technicians slunk down into their chairs, trying to disappear under their consoles. "Why was this not planned for? What do you think the Americans will do? They are not going to sit on their hands and let this spaceship and its cargo drift along! No! They will find some way to retrieve it! Then where will we be?" Vorontsky paused, collecting his breath and his thoughts for another salvo. "Vitali, you are responsible for this! It was you who persuaded me to pursue this insane conspiracy!"

Mission Commander Malyshev had been boar hunting once. He'd

seen one of the animals go berserk after being wounded by a poorly aimed shot. It was much like this.

The KGB Chairman was surprisingly unemotional. "General Secretary, let us not jump to premature conclusions. There is a problem, yes. But we do not yet know the full dimensions of the problem."

"We know the goddam ship is stuck up there and not coming down!" screamed the General Secretary. "In St. Peter's name, man! We are talking about our heads!"

"Quiet, both of you!" Heads spun around to look at Popov, holding up a hand to indicate he wanted silence. This commanding posture was 180 degrees from his usual flustered demeanor. A few moments passed before he muttered, "Yes . . . yes. It could very well work." The stocky general turned to Malyshev. "Find Vostov. Wherever he is. And get him to the flite conference room. Then go pull whatever engineering charts we have on the American shuttle. Now!"

Malyshev fled from the room, joyful to be out of the danger zone.

"What are you doing, General Popov?" queried Kostiashak.

Popov looked at the KGB chieftain and the General Secretary with contempt. Two space pioneers had died—Americans, true—but kin in many ways to their Russian counterparts who ventured into the ether, and all these two vermin could think about was their own skins. Perhaps the contempt helped stiffen his spine. With a look of disdain, Popov responded to the Chairman's question with, "Do you not understand? I am an engineer."

Day 1, 1800 Hours Zulu
ALTITUDE: 22,300 NAUTICAL MILES
ORBITAL INCLINATION: 006 DEGREES

Drifting quietly in the vacuum of deep space, moving in sync with the rotation of the earth, was a remarkable piece of engineering that most technicians could only dream about and never touch, for nothing quite like it existed on the ground. Shaped like a huge ice cream cone with a beanie propeller on top, this object was Eardrum, the present-day successor to a string of satellites known by exotic code names like Rhyolite, Jumpseat, Magnum, and Vortex. Of this technical pedigree, Eardrum was probably the most aptly named, for it was America's biggest electronic eavesdropper in space.

Russian radio transmissions, telephone microwaves, TV shows, radar signals, car phones, missile telemetry—they were all scooped up by Eardrum as if it were a giant vacuum cleaner, then transmitted to the National Security Agency's compound at Fort Meade, Maryland, where they were sifted and analyzed.

It was by far the largest artificial satellite circling the earth—even eclipsing the Star Wars prototype platform in size. It was so big, in fact, that it had had to be assembled piece by piece in low earth orbit before being boosted to its higher, geosynchronous position.

Its huge parabolic reflector had to be of enormous dimensions—a diameter of 720 feet—because a high-gain antenna was needed to capture faint radio signals. So sensitive was the apparatus that, when combined with its ultrahigh-speed frequency scanner, even directional microwave transmissions could be picked up by the Pacific Eardrum, or its sister satellite drifting over the Atlantic. And directional microwaves carried a treasure trove of telephone conversations.

But there was also a dark side to possessing exotic equipment like Eardrum. Years ago, in a case similar to that of the Walker spy ring that ravaged the Navy, the deep dark secrets of the old Rhyolite satellite had been compromised by two young ne'er-do-well traitors —Christopher Boyce and Andrew Daulton Lee (also known as the Falcon and the Snowman).

After his first briefing on the Eardrum project, Whittenberg decided that, while he was in charge, nothing about this satellite would have so much as a chance of being compromised. Under his personal supervision, draconian security measures were implemented. Every component of the project was kept tightly compartmentalized, and only a tiny handful of engineers knew the full scope of the satellite's capabilities, which were vastly superior to those of its predecessors. Not even the chairman of the board of TRW or the mission specialists who assembled the components in space knew Eardrum's true powers —nor did Iceberg when he keyed his microphone switch over the East Siberian Sea.

Day 1, 1838 Hours Zulu, 1:38 P.M. Local
KENNEDY SPACE CENTER, CAPE CANAVERAL, FLORIDA

Lt. Col. Phillip Heitmann banked the Gulfstream III to his left, while watching the instruments on his head-up display. The holographic image allowed him to look through the windshield of the aircraft and scan his flight data at the same time. The readout from the TACAN microwave landing system told him he was 8.6 miles from the runway, while the altimeter indicated the aircraft was 13,428 feet above the ocean. At 7.5 miles from the runway Heitmann pushed the hand controller forward so the GS-III headed down in a 22-degree glide slope—seven times steeper than that of a commercial airliner.

The Gulfstream aircraft had been specially modified to react and behave exactly like the shuttle orbiter, and Heitmann was taking his usual practice landing approaches prior to launch of the *Constellation*. Every shuttle landing was a "dead stick" landing with no propulsion whatsoever. You got only one shot at the runway, so it had to be good. This was the second of what would be fifteen practice approaches for himself and Maj. Jack Townsend, his copilot. It had been six months since his last shuttle mission, and the barrel-chested former Marine test pilot was looking forward to his upcoming trip on the *Constellation*.

The Gulfstream's engines throttled back automatically at pre-arranged settings to give it the same "feel" as the orbiter on approach. Heitmann watched carefully as the elevation and distance clicked off. At two thousand feet altitude and 350 mph, Townsend said, "Initiate preflare," and Heitmann pulled back on the hand controller. The glide slope was reduced from 22 degrees to 1.5 degrees in a maneuver that consumed about fifteen seconds. "Arming landing gear. . . . Landing gear deployed," relayed Townsend. Heitmann saw he was ninety feet above the ground, with the black tarmac rushing up toward him. Airspeed and altitude continued to decrease, until at 216 mph the Gulfstream was gliding a few feet above the runway.

The aircraft's wheels did not touch down. Because the orbiter was a much bigger flying machine than the Gulfstream, Heitmann kept his aircraft a few feet above the runway to simulate the same perspective he would have from the shuttle's cockpit on landing.

As they neared the end of the runway Townsend turned a switch from AUTO to MANUAL and said, "Green." The aircraft was now back on manual control and Heitmann shoved the throttles forward. The Rolls-Royce Spey engines responded with twenty thousand pounds of thrust, and the Gulfstream picked up speed. Townsend pushed the appropriate lever to the UP position. There was a whirr and a few clunking sounds as the landing gear retracted into the wings and nose.

"Three greens," Townsend said, adding, "Not bad for an old fart."

Heitmann grinned. "I suppose an air crapper like you could do better?"

"You bet your ass, old man." Townsend enjoyed ribbing Heitmann about the gray strands in his rapidly thinning hair.

"Okay, pussy," countered the Marine pilot, "the weather's not too bad today, so we'll let you try the next one."

This time it was Townsend who grinned. The two men were close, and their mutual insults were a reflection of their friendship. The *Constellation* would be their third mission together, and they were both anxious for lift off.

Heitmann was watching the altimeter go past five thousand feet when his headset crackled. "GS-Three, this is Control. You are to return to base at once."

The two pilots looked at each other—their curiosity aroused. "Control, this is GS-Three," replied Heitmann. "What's the deal? We just started our approaches."

"Eagle One is flying in from CSOC in Colorado. His ETA is forty-five minutes from now, and he wants to see you both in his office when he gets here."

"Roger, Control. You talked us into it." Heitmann banked the Gulfstream around for a conventional landing. "Eagle One" was the call sign for Maj. Gen. Chester McCormack, Commander, SPACE-COM Flight Operations. A Nordic-looking dynamo who had elevated the practice of ass-kicking to a fine art. Nobody liked getting on his bad side.

"Got any clue why Eagle wants to see us?" Townsend sounded a little apprehensive.

"Beats me." Heitmann shrugged. Then he turned and leveled his gaze at his partner. "You ain't screwin' the old man's wife, are you?" The slim, unbalding Townsend had a reputation with the ladies.

"Certainly not," said the copilot in mock indignation.

"How about his daughter?" asked Heitmann.

Townsend paused for the full effect. "Not for at least a week."

Both of them burst out laughing.

Jacob Classen chomped on a tuna fish sandwich and poured the first of what would be many cups of coffee. Although a voracious eater, Classen was always skinny as a rail. That was because he ran marathons to relax. And though he was only forty-nine years old, his hair was white. Not gray. White. He was manager of Pad 39A at the Kennedy Space Center, and the tension on his job fluctuated somewhere between oppressive and unbearable. It was now rapidly approaching the unbearable phase. His pad crew was embarking on a "fire drill" maneuver to yank out the *Constellation*'s delicate payload and make the spacecraft ready for a "dry" launch, and he had no idea why. He'd been told not to ask questions and just do it—quickly.

Not one to question his orders, even though he was a civilian working for NASA, Classen had given instructions for the rotating service structure of the gantry to be rolled into place. As he watched from the small service trailer, the enormous superstructure began its long, slow swing that would envelop the orbiter like a closing door. Once in place, environmental seals would be inflated along the side of the orbiter and the closed payload room of the superstructure would be purged with clean air. In this pristine environment, the cargo bay doors of the orbiter would be opened and the payload transferred to the superstructure.

Classen figured unloading the *Constellation*'s payload was going to be a first-class pain in the ass. The Anik communications satellite was pretty standard stuff, but the COSMAX was an X-ray telescope and had to be handled carefully to keep its calibrations in line. Delicate instruments had problems enough with the rigors of a rocket launch, but dropping them during an earthbound transfer could be a career-limiting experience for a pad manager. Although the launch director was screaming at him to hurry, Classen wasn't about to bobble that $300 million COSMAX.

Day 1, 1903 Hours Zulu, 2:03 P.M. Local
NATIONAL SECURITY AGENCY, FORT MEADE, MARYLAND

In the basement of the main building at the National Security Agency compound resided a machine unlike any other computer in the world, for it was custom-designed and manufactured by the NSA's own staff, in conjunction with outside contractors. This hypersecret device—nicknamed "Pandora's Box" by her architects—was not very big, and to the untrained eye it looked like nothing more than a black polyhedron, four feet by four feet by eight feet, laid lengthwise. There were no gauges or displays on the exterior aluminum panels of the polyhedron, but inside was an intricate series of gallium arsenide computer chips that enabled it to process data many times faster than even a Cray-Y/MP supercomputer. So powerful was Pandora that it generated tremendous heat and had to be cooled by a custom-designed air-conditioning system. The chilled vapors were funneled up through the floor, causing a constant hum.

When the Eardrum satellite downloaded its stewpot full of electronic signals to the NSA's earth-station dish, they were first converted into digital information, then fed into Pandora. The mystical computer digested the data, then worked them like a wrangler at a cattle chute—rapidly sorting the electronic signals by carrier band and type of transmission. After the sorting was complete, Pandora plucked out the gemstones in the stewpot—such as a Defense Ministry telephone call from Moscow to Murmansk, or a conversation on a Zil limousine radio car phone—and routed them to an analyst for examination.

If the electronic signal was telemetry—which was the transmission of data from a satellite to the ground, like a spy satellite photograph—Pandora had a slick trick up her sleeve. She could take the date, time, and bearing of the telemetry signal, then triangulate the position between the Pacific and Atlantic Eardrums and compute an orbital path for the satellite. This path information was matched against the orbits of known Soviet satellites so the source of the telemetry could be identified. If there wasn't an existing Russian orbital plot in Pandora's memory banks that matched up with the signal, then the signal was flagged on an analyst's computer screen.

As it was now.

"Coffee, Evan?"

Evan Littleton checked the dregs of his cup. "Yeah, gimme a warmer."

"Gotcha," said his colleague, Ernie Marks, who grabbed the cup and trotted down the hall to the coffee machine.

Littleton stretched, then tapped his keyboard to call up another bunch of signals from the Eardrum satellite for analysis, and found there were two flags blinking on his screen. He found it difficult to concentrate on this, his first day back from vacation. The bespectacled Littleton had gone cross-country skiing in Vermont with his girlfriend of six months, who worked in the cryptanalytic division. They had come back engaged.

But now he put the thought of his betrothal out of his mind and tried to focus on the two blinking flags. The first one, Littleton guessed, was probably a Progress "drone" space capsule ferrying supplies up to the Russian Mir space station. The Progress drone had no crew and was navigated totally by an onboard computer and ground controllers. After it docked automatically with the space station, its cargo of food and supplies was unloaded, then it was jettisoned and sent back into the atmosphere to burn up. Littleton was 98 percent sure it was a Progress drone because the amount of telemetry was tiny, and it bore the characteristics of other Progress signals. A "no brainer," Littleton thought.

The second flagged signal was harder to figure. Its orbital path showed a polar inclination with an altitude of 122 miles. It matched nothing in the current inventory of orbiting Russian vehicles, which included more than ten thousand pieces of space hardware. He typed in the word ANALYZE and hit ENTER. There was a slight delay as his request queued up for Pandora behind several others. Then, in a blink, the words were erased and replaced with the cryptic message:

```
ANALYSIS: VOICE COMSEC
SIGNAL ORIGIN:
      TERRESTRIAL: 67 DEGREES, 21 MINUTES NORTH;
                   171 DEGREES, 14 MINUTES EAST.
      CELESTIAL:   71 DEGREES, 38 MINUTES NORTH;
                   173 DEGREES, 51 MINUTES EAST.
                   63 DEGREES, 12 MINUTES NORTH;
                   169 DEGREES, 23 MINUTES EAST.
ALTITUDE: 122.7 MILES
INCLINATION: 83 DEGREES
```

"VOICE COMSEC" meant it was a voice radio transmission and the communication was secure, or scrambled—which was typical of communications on a manned Russian Soyuz mission. This, however, puzzled Littleton, because he hadn't seen any alert memos about an upcoming Soyuz launch. (The Soyuz was the Russian manned-vehicle workhorse.) Also, the tracking data showed part of the transmission was moving and the other part was stationary, which indicated the space vehicle was communicating directly with a ground station. This was unusual, too, because the Soyuz ordinarily communicated with ground stations via the Kosmos 1700 satellite system—just as American spacecraft did with the TDRS satellites. But Littleton shrugged. Things like this had happened before. Those Russkies racked up over a hundred launches a year, and it was easy to lose track of one before lift-off—even a Soyuz.

He typed in the codes to transmit his data on the two flagged telemetry items to NORAD, where the orbital path information would be matched with the exact vehicle.

Ernie Marks returned with the coffee. "Here you go, Slugger. Or should I say skier? Or should I say married skier?"

Littleton grinned.

"Anything of interest?" Marks asked.

"Naw, not really. I just sent a couple of unknowns to NORAD for identification. Looks like a recently launched Progress drone and a Soyuz. Maybe the Soyuz is heading up to the Mir to change crews. It's about time, I suspect."

"Hmmmm," murmured Marks as he pushed his glasses up on a crop of sandy hair—a sure sign that he was puzzled. "I don't remember seeing anything in the alert memos about a Soyuz on the pad."

"Yeah, well, it's happened before. Anyway, it's NORAD's problem now." Littleton didn't even mention the ground communication link. "Besides, I got a shitload of stuff to wade through this afternoon. Can't futz around with this."

"Yeah," agreed Marks. "Leave it to our esteemed colleagues in Colorado."

It never occurred to either of them that a voice transmission above the Soviet Union could be anything but a Russian spacecraft.

Day 1, 2111 Hours Zulu, 11:11 p.m. Local
MOSCOW

Grigory Vostov had retired early and was sound asleep when he awoke to a pounding on his apartment door in the Mulzeny Prospekt. Groggily he gained consciousness and flipped on the bedside light.

"Who could that be?" mumbled his wife.

"Mmmphf," was the only response the middle-aged, overweight scientist could muster as he pulled on his robe and slippers and absently scratched his scalp of dark, thinning hair.

Unlike the typical Russian, Vostov did not have a fearful knee-jerk reaction to a knock on the door in the middle of the night. That was because his technical genius insulated and protected him from the vagaries of Russian political life, and bequeathed upon him and his family the benefits of the *nomenklatura*, or the elite of Soviet society. Quite simply, he knew himself to be an indispensable man in the Soviet Union. The country and the Party would protect him because they needed him. Therefore he had no fear of them, or of the knocking on the door. In fact, he was severely incensed at having his slumber disturbed. His ample girth waddled through the richly appointed seven-room apartment—a regal privilege by Moscow's standards— and stopped at the door. "Who is there?" he demanded.

"State Security," came an equally demanding voice through the door.

Although Vostov had friends on the Politburo, this response unsettled him, and caused his sleepiness and aloofness from politics to evaporate. He was indispensable—wasn't he? He had nothing to fear—did he? Carefully he opened the door, and was stupefied to find a KGB colonel, captain, and sergeant facing him.

"Grigory Vostov?" demanded the colonel.

"*Da*," said the scientist tentatively. "What is the meaning of this?"

"You will get dressed and come with us immediately."

"But why? What is happening?"

The colonel had been told he had carte blanche to expedite Vostov's collection. "Now, Comrade! Or you will not live to see the dawn."

Vostov blinked with his mouth open and took a couple of reflexive steps backward. He was often arrogant with his own staff—it was his right, after all—but he sensed this was not the time for a confrontation, nor were these the people with whom to have one. Retreating back to his bedroom, he quickly threw on some clothes and an overcoat and told his wife to keep quiet.

Downstairs the KGB colonel shoved him into a waiting Zhiguli sedan. The car tore through the frozen slush and headed toward Kaliningrad, just north of the city.

By God, this was an outrage! Vostov thought, and his old arrogance began to resurface. His friend Gudenov on the Politburo would hear about this! . . . Maybe even the General Secretary himself would be told. Vostov was the Chief Designer of the Soviet Union. One of the most prestigious positions in the Rodina and the Academy of Sciences. He certainly would not let a Chekist colonel get the better of him. Didn't this fool know that he—Vostov—was a national treasure?

On October 4, 1957, an SL-1 booster lifted off the Baikonur launch pad and heaved a twenty-seven-pound spherical object into orbit. An object which the world came to know as *Sputnik*. The guiding force behind this pioneering scientific achievement was, for many years, a mysterious figure to the West. The Soviets took special pains to keep everything about this man cloaked in secrecy, and for over a decade they would refer to him only by his title of Chief Designer. In fact, his name was Sergei P. Korolev, and in many respects he was the Russian counterpart to the Americans' Werner von Braun. His skills were legendary in scope, and almost single-handedly he brought the Russian space program to world prominence. Had it not been for Korolev's extraordinary talents, the Soviet space effort might still be on a par with Albania's.

On that glorious day in 1957, Vostov had been a junior engineer on Korolev's staff, and his star had risen steadily ever since. Vostov was now *the* Russian authority on rocketry and propulsion systems, and possessed a resume that was the envy of the Soviet Academy of Sciences—he'd been Venus Lander chief engineer, project director for the Salyut and Mir space stations, and designer of the Energia heavy-lift booster vehicle.

That last one—the Energia booster—had been the only bright spot of the Soviet shuttle program. The Energia had successfully heaved the *Buran* and *Suslov* aloft. It was the orbiters' reentry design that had failed somehow; and, luckily for Vostov, he'd had nothing to do with that.

Because of his track record and his noninvolvement with the orbiter design, a month earlier Vostov had been anointed with the coveted title of his former mentor. He became the new Chief Designer of the Soviet Union.

Along with the title, he was given full authority to find out what was wrong with the Soviet shuttle and *fix it*. Well, he'd soon put things right there . . . he hoped. Even Vostov had to admit the previous team of shuttle engineers were very competent . . . and they had disappeared, along with General Shenko. Vostov's technical expertise was in rocketry and propulsion, not aeronautics. Surely they didn't hold him responsible for the shuttle's failure. They'd just made him Chief Designer, hadn't they? Hmmpff. Well, Gudenov of the Politburo would hear about this.

The Zhiguli wheeled to a stop outside the Flite Control Centre. Vostov was hustled inside and literally shoved through a conference-room door by the burly KGB sergeant. He was confronted by three men across a long table, which was covered with unrolled engineering diagrams. The scene astonished him. In the center was the insufferable

Popov, looking unshaven and fatigued in a wrinkled uniform. On his right was a small, dark-complected man in a double-breasted suit; Vostov knew the man only by reputation but recognized him. Then the Chief Designer's heart skipped a beat. On Popov's left was . . . was . . .

The General Secretary barked, "Get over here, Vostov!" The Chief Designer did as he was told. Lord in heaven. Not even Gudenov could help him now.

"Listen to me, Chief Designer," implored Popov. "Listen and do not interrupt. We cannot waste a single second." Little love was lost between the two men. "An American shuttle—the *Intrepid*—was launched seven hours ago from Vandenberg. A loyal Soviet was inserted on board as a member of the crew. He has killed the other crew members, and the shuttle is now controlled by our man. Do you understand what I am saying, Vostov?"

The Chief Designer was stunned, but gave a quick nod. However, his acknowledgment did not mean he believed what he heard. How could something like this happen and he not know of it? This couldn't be real. It had to be a dream.

"Our man controls the spacecraft, but something happened," continued Popov. "Perhaps there was a struggle. The circuit board controlling the retro rockets was damaged, and he cannot fire them. He is stuck up there, Vostov. Do you understand? Stuck up there. And we—you—have to get him down before the Americans respond. Is that clear?"

Another curt nod. This was no dream. It was a nightmare.

Popov grabbed the diagrams in front of him. "As we both know, these are the mechanical drawings of the American shuttle, based on information the Comrade Chairman's Technical Directorate has provided us over the years." Popov's finger pointed to the posterior view of the orbiter. "The American shuttle has three large main engine rocket nozzles and two smaller retro-rocket nozzles. They are all useless. Is it possible to fabricate some kind of engine and attach it to the tail to bring it down? Tell me, Chief Designer. Tell me."

For Vostov it was almost too much. The sudden awakening, the drive in the night, the KGB, the General Secretary, and the American shuttle they were trying to . . . to . . . hijack! Vostov could only gape.

"We are waiting for your answer, Chief Designer." The Chairman's words sailed across the table like a viper's hiss. "You would not want to meet the same end as General Shenko."

Vostov gulped and tried to get a grip on himself. His engineering talents had brought him this far. They would extricate him from this predicament. He pulled the diagram toward him and studied it for a few moments. Start with information, he told himself. Obtain accurate data. "What is the shuttle's altitude?"

Popov was quick with his response. "Circular orbit. Altitude two zero three kilometers."

Well, thought the Chief Designer, that made things infinitely easier. If the shuttle had been in a higher orbit it would have been an impossible task for a—what was the American expression?—"jerry-rigged" device to bring the orbiter down. "Are his pitch and yaw thrusters still working?"

"*Da*," replied Popov.

Vostov stared at the diagram. God in heaven! To capture an American shuttle! If he could bring this off, *he* could well be appointed to the Politburo. They could take the American spacecraft apart and find out what was wrong with their own orbiter. Vostov began to grasp the import of the opportunity. "Leave me alone for a few minutes," he commanded.

Popov jerked his head, indicating the three men should leave the room. They walked into the hallway, leaving the Chief Designer transfixed before the engineering drawings.

Outside in the hall, the former hammer thrower was apprehensive. "Do you honestly think this can be done, Popov?" asked Vorontsky.

Popov felt like a weary teacher tutoring a not-so-bright pupil. "There are some things in our favor, General Secretary. First, the *Intrepid* is in low earth orbit. Low enough that its orbital path would eventually decay in two months or so, and it would tumble in an uncontrolled reentry. The thrust required to propel an object out of low earth orbit, even an object the size of the shuttle, is relatively small. If the Chief Designer can come up with a way to fabricate a thruster and attach it to the tail, then we may be able to retrieve the vessel."

"But can he do it?" The General Secretary wanted assurances.

"He is the Chief Designer of the Soviet Union, and his specialty is rocketry," Popov explained patiently. "He was Korolev's star pupil, and every project he has undertaken for the Rodina has surpassed everyone's expectations. If any of the Motherland's sons can do it, it is he. If he cannot, then we have failed."

The General Secretary was about to issue an unveiled threat when Vostov's voice rumbled out of the conference room.

"Popov! Get in here!"

Day 1, 2250 Hours Zulu, 3:50 P.M. Local
CHEYENNE MOUNTAIN

With her nose buried in a clipboard, Maj. Lydia Strand walked through the NORAD Space Defense Operations Center, scanning her satellite run sheets. NORAD's worldwide Spacetrack radar system monitored the orbital paths of all Russian satellites, and through telemetry analysis NORAD had a pretty good idea which ones were photoreconnaissance birds. NORAD routinely kept major commands informed about Russkie recon cameras passing overhead, so sensitive American hardware could be concealed from the high-resolution lenses. The F-117 Nighthawk Stealth Fighter Squadron at Nellis Air Force Base in Nevada was constantly ducking in and out of hangars to avoid detection, as were the Northrop stealth bomber prototypes based there.

One irritating characteristic of recon birds—to Russians and Americans alike—was their ability to change orbits. This happened rarely, because it consumed precious fuel, but it did happen. When a deviation was detected by the Spacetrack system, the NORAD computers immediately started beeping and blinking to notify the Spacetrack monitors in SPADOC. The new orbital path was then plotted and the major commands, like the Strategic Air Command, were notified.

Lydia Strand, Lamborghini's deputy, was gathering the latest run sheets on the recon birds for a routine afternoon staff conference, which was being held despite the turmoil over the *Intrepid*.

She had joined Lamborghini's staff four months ago, when her star-studded ascent up the Air Force career ladder had taken an unexpected turn. After graduating summa cum laude in physics from the University of North Carolina, Strand had joined the Air Force ("It seemed like fun") and entered the pilot training program. Much to her surprise, she found herself to be a highly skilled pilot, and she embraced her newfound love with an overwhelming passion. She graduated number one in her flight school class at Sheppard Air Force Base, and as a reward, received an atypical assignment for a woman pilot—flying F-16s back and forth to Hill Air Force Base in Utah. Hill was the worldwide center for large-scale repair and maintenance of the F-16, and it was her job to fly the Falcons into and out of the garage and give them "test drives," so to speak. When repairs were completed on an F-16, she'd take the Falcon upstairs and put it through the wringer over the Wendover Bombing Range. These shakedown flights usually went smoothly, but one time there had been a glitch, and she'd had to punch out. While drifting down in her parachute, she was transfixed by the sight of a $20 million aircraft spiraling into the desert. It was a painful spectacle, and the accident rattled her confidence—so much so that she quit sparring with her male counterparts in practice dogfights over the Wendover Range—contests she had regularly won, much to the chagrin of her macho comrades.

To restore her confidence, Strand's boss persuaded her to apply to the NASA astronaut program as a pilot. While a number of women had been selected for the astronaut corps as mission specialists, nary a one had been assigned as a shuttle pilot because of a Catch-22—you couldn't be a shuttle pilot unless you had experience flying high performance aircraft. "High performance aircraft" was a euphemism for "combat aircraft," and women were barred from flying in combat. They were usually relegated to flying transports (exciting), except in exceptional circumstances, such as Strand's.

She'd applied to NASA shortly after the *Challenger* disaster, when the space agency's fortunes were at a particularly low ebb. Maybe some reverse discrimination was working for her during the selection process, or maybe one of the committee's judges was overcome by her intellect and stark beauty; but whatever the reason, she got her acceptance letter and moved to Houston. The two-year pilot training curriculum restored her confidence, and she was assigned as copilot on the *Antares*, where she performed well on a payload mission to the Star Wars platform. Four months later she copiloted the *Discovery* on a satellite recovery mission, and again her performance was straight out of the manual. There was chatter in high places at Houston and Colorado Springs concerning her possible appointment as the first woman commander of a space shuttle mission. But then an imponderable happened. She became pregnant, and had to make a choice—either be an astronaut, or be a mother. She opted for the latter, and petitioned the Air Force for reassignment. The Air Force complied and moved her to Colorado Springs, where she landed on Lamborghini's staff. Her husband, whom she'd met and married in Houston, was a software engineer at NASA. He followed her to Colorado and obtained a similar job as a civilian with CSOC.

As disappointing as it was to leave the astronaut program, she enjoyed her intelligence billet, finding it fascinating. Almost as fascinating as Noah, her eight-month-old son.

"Anything I should know before the staff conference?" she asked.

T/Sgt. Bill Matthews played with his keyboard. "Ummm, nothing new since the run sheet you have, except for a couple of items that just came in from our spook friends at NSA. Hang on a minute and I'll get them matched.'' He hit a few keystrokes and waited for the computer's response. "Yeah, this was a Progress capsule that went up to the Mir space station yesterday. Hasn't been jettisoned yet as far as we can tell. Telemetry analysis and Spacetrack plot both confirm.''

"Okay,'' said the major. "Anything else?''

Matthews typed in a few more keystrokes while Strand reviewed her run sheets. She glanced at her watch. Only ten minutes till the conference.

The keystrokes that Matthews punched in called for a comparison of the NSA telemetry data from Eardrum against the existing orbital paths of known satellites. However, unlike the NSA's Pandora, the NORAD computer compared the telemetry against *all* known orbital paths, regardless of their country of origin. His green CRT screen displayed the matchup:

ANALYSIS: VOICE COMSEC

SIGNAL ORIGIN:

      TERRESTRIAL: 67 DEGREES, 21 MINUTES NORTH;

                         171 DEGREES, 14 MINUTES EAST.

      CELESTIAL: 71 DEGREES, 38 MINUTES NORTH;

                       173 DEGREES, 51 MINUTES EAST.

                       63 DEGREES, 12 MINUTES NORTH;

                       169 DEGREES, 23 MINUTES EAST.

ALTITUDE: 122.7 MILES

INCLINATION: 83 DEGREES

PATH SOLUTION: STS-202L

"Uh, Major,'' stammered Matthews, "I, uh, think you better look at this.''

Strand looked up from her clipboard and read the screen. She already knew that STS-202L was the latest Space Transportation System—that is, shuttle—mission, and "COMSEC'' meant it was a secure radio transmission. She didn't pay attention to the coordinates, and simply assumed they pinpointed the location of the *Intrepid*'s last transmission before it went off the air. "Two zero two Lima. That's the *Intrepid*, isn't it?'' she asked.

"Uh, yes, ma'am.''

"So, what about it?"

Matthews punched a few buttons, then said, "Look at the plot of the signal source, ma'am." A Mercator world map appeared on Matthews's screen with a wavy line indicating the *Intrepid*'s orbit. Three white dots were astride the orbit line, blinking over far northeastern Siberia.

Strand shook her head, as if trying to clear a garbled circuit. By nature she was a person driven by logic, and her logical mind couldn't accept what her eyes perceived. It was like looking in a mirror and seeing the reflection of a stranger's face—it wasn't supposed to be there. But the blinking white lights, like Lady Macbeth's spot, wouldn't disappear. They kept blinking and blinking until finally evidence overcame logic, and the realization imploded on her like a freight train.

She gasped. "But that's . . . that's . . ."

"Yes, ma'am."

"Dear God . . ."

When her F-16 had flamed out over the Utah desert she'd had the same cold, sickening, sinking feeling as she reached for the eject handles. Something was wrong. Terribly, terribly wrong. Those dots on the screen. They simply could not be. Strand looked around the room, almost in a daze. She needed help. There was Lamborghini across the room. "Colonel!"

Whittenberg lowered himself into the big leather chair, the strain of the afternoon having taken its toll. He'd been on the phone for hours talking to the Chief of the General Staff, the Secretary of Defense, NASA, and the Vice President, explaining in patient detail what had happened and what they were doing to rescue the *Intrepid*. Whittenberg's orders were straightforward: "Try to rescue the crew and save the payload." At least the Spyglass pictures had come back showing the *Intrepid* was still in one piece, so maybe there was someone up there to rescue after all.

The CinC poured some coffee from the thermos pot. He wouldn't be getting much sleep the next few days, and SPACECOM had its regular business to attend to. He nodded to his chief of staff. "Okay, Bull, let's begin and wrap it up as soon as we can. I want to check with Chet and see how things are coming at the Cape."

"Yes, sir," replied Michael Dowd as he scanned the room. "Uh, sir, I was going to lead off with intel, but Colonel Lamborghini doesn't seem to be here."

Whittenberg looked at the colonel's empty chair. "Hmmm. That's odd. You can usually set your watch by him. Well, send someone to fetch him. We'll start off with Sir Isaac instead." Whittenberg tried not to show his irritation, but the edge on his voice wasn't lost on anyone.

The Bull was muttering to an aide to find out where the hell Lamborghini was when the double doors to the conference room burst open and the SPACECOM intelligence officer lunged through, with Major Strand on his heels. "General!" he shouted. "We've got trouble!"

Everyone was taken aback by the force of his delivery. Lamborghini was always a cool one. He never got rattled. What was happening? Had SAC gone to DEFCON One?

"Okay, Colonel," Whittenberg said cautiously. "What seems to be the problem?"

Lamborghini went to a wall phone and punched in an extension. "Okay, Matthews, patch it through to the conference-room screen." Not waiting for an answer, he went to the control switch at the lectern. He took a few deep breaths. These men needed accurate information, he told himself. Not hysterics. He caught a few more breaths, then ran through a quick brief as calmly as he could. Then he spun a dial on the lectern and a Mercator map appeared on the big overhead screen, showing the wavy line and blinking lights over the Siberian coast. "And that," he concluded, "is the flight path of the *Intrepid*. The white dots are the radio transmission points."

No one spoke, and there was a prolonged silence—until a *clunk* was heard from the middle of the table. Sir Isaac's meerschaum pipe had fallen out of his mouth and onto the hardwood surface.

To say the room was shocked by Lamborghini's demonstration would not capture the true essence of the moment. It was more like a collective stroke.

"Jesus H. Christ," was all the Bull could say, while the rest of the table looked like a mass dental examination, for every single mouth was wide open.

As stunned as he was, Whittenberg had to summon up thirty years of military discipline and get a grip on himself. "Colonel . . . does this mean what I think it means? That the *Intrepid* is communicating with a *Russian* ground station?"

"Yes, sir. That is what the data indicate."

There was a pause. "Are you certain the information is accurate?" asked Dowd.

Lamborghini spoke precisely. "I just got off the phone with the analyst at NSA. A civilian named Littleton. He's double-checking, but the signals came through the Eardrum satellite and went through normal analysis."

The chief of staff felt a little relieved. "Those spooks at NSA have been wrong before." But no one echoed his opinion—or was it wishful thinking? "Has CSOC been able to reestablish contact with the *Intrepid*?" Dowd asked.

"I checked with Mission Control before I came, sir," replied Lamborghini. "Nothing from the *Intrepid* since it went off the air."

Whittenberg's mind was spinning. The *Intrepid* talking to the Russians? It was not to be believed. But if it was actually happening, some member of the crew had to be doing the talking. His gaze fell on Strand. "Major. You were in the program with the *Intrepid*'s crew. You probably know them better than anyone here. Did any of them ever seem, well, unstable to you?"

Strand sorted through her memory banks carefully before answering. "Rodriquez always seemed like a bit of an airhead to me, but maybe that's because the guy was so smart. You know, he was like the flaky kid who slept in class and never studied, but always got A's on his tests. He never broke the rules. He was just flaky." She conjured up the copilot. "I got to know Frank Mulcahey fairly well. He was the practical joker. Real solid pilot and conscientious father. Loved a good time. Air Force Academy. Typical red-white-and-blue American boy who was proud of his Irish ancestry." She paused.

Whittenberg prompted, "And Kapuscinski?"

She tugged at her chin. "Kind of a weird bird, sir, but of the three he was probably the least likely to do something like this. Whatever *this* is."

"Why is that?" asked Sir Isaac.

"I'm a little hazy on this, but I seem to recall his parents were Polish refugees after the war. They'd endured some incredible hardships at the hands of the Soviets. His mother was, uh, well, raped by some Russian soldiers, or so went the rumor. He didn't talk much, but if the subject of Russians ever came up during a conversation it was like waving a red flag in front of a bull. He hated them. Deeply. If he's diverted the *Intrepid* it would probably be to try to bomb Moscow. Also, sir, he's an incredible pilot. We went one-on-one in a couple of T-38s out of the Cape one afternoon, and he nailed me before I knew where he was coming from."

"So, as far as you can tell," asked Whittenberg, "there's nothing to indicate any of these men had gone . . . round the bend, so to speak?"

"No, sir," she replied.

Whittenberg digested this for some seconds, then shook the tree. "All right, people. Talk to me. What do we do?"

Lamborghini responded. "Well, sir, I think we should first verify that the information is accurate."

Sir Isaac had retrieved his pipe and was rekindling the light to calm himself. "I agree," he muttered between puffs. "If we bump this up the line, the first thing the Pentagon will want is confirmation. Eardrum is a powerful tool, but triangulating from that distance leaves room for distortion and error. It's happened before." Once more, no one challenged the electrical engineer from MIT.

"But if Eardrum has problems, how do we confirm?" asked Dowd.

Sir Isaac thought for a moment. "Pete, did you say the communication was directly between an earth station and the spacecraft? It did not pass to a communications satellite—ours or theirs?"

"That is correct, sir," replied Lamborghini.

"Hmmm." Sir Isaac tapped his teeth with his pipestem. "Then to be absolutely certain, it would be best to insert a listening post between the ground station and the spacecraft, so it would be directly in the path of the transmission from either side."

There was a long pause as everyone mulled over the problem, until finally Strand said, "SR-71."

Whittenberg raised an eyebrow. "Exactly what do you mean, Major?"

"Simple, sir," she replied. "Just take a plot of the Russian earth station locations that can communicate with a spacecraft, and overlay it with the *Intrepid*'s orbital path. Pick out a point where the two intersect, and sandwich in an SR-71 during the time window the *Intrepid* is overhead."

Strand made it sound simpler than it was. Ever since Francis Gary Powers's U-2 had been knocked out of the sky by a Russian SAM in 1960, overflights of Soviet territory had been a sticky subject. They still happened, but usually they were just probing flights on the periphery of the country. Spy satellites had eliminated much of the need for overflights, and improved sensors on reconnaissance aircraft allowed them to fly along the border in "stand-off" missions to pick up intelligence without crossing the border. So overflights were very rare these days. Any penetration of more than two hundred kilometers inside Soviet airspace required the approval of the Secretary of Defense.

Lamborghini went to the phone again. "Matthews, punch up the *Intrepid*'s flight path for the next twelve hours." A few seconds later a series of wavy lines appeared on the Mercator map, each one slicing the earth a few degrees west of the previous one. The intel chief looked up at the big screen. "We should be able to plot the Russian earth stations in no time at all, and match them with the orbits."

Whittenberg ran through everything in his mind, but it was impossible to absorb. Lord in heaven. The *Intrepid* talking to the *Russians*. It was too bitter to contemplate. *If that payload fell into the wrong hands . . .* that was all the impetus the CinC needed. "I'll call SAC and get a Blackbird for us. Pete, you and the major get cracking on coordinates where *Intrepid* might communicate with the ground. I'll want you to feed it to SAC's intel people as soon as you've got it. Keep in contact with the NSA people, too. Bull, I want you and Sir Isaac to start putting together contingency plans on what we should do, or could do, if the *Intrepid* has, in fact, become a . . . a . . . what the hell do you call something like this, anyway?"

There was no answer, until Lamborghini offered in a strained voice, "I believe the intelligence term, sir, is 'rogue elephant.' "

Back in his office, Whittenberg picked up the red phone that was a direct line to the Commander in Chief Strategic Air Command, in Omaha, Nebraska. He knew that within fifteen seconds the CinCSAC, his deputy, or his chief of staff would pick up the other end.

Having attained four-star rank, Whittenberg had precious few peers, and among his peers there were even a smaller number of people he could genuinely call his friends. But Bernard Dooley, CinCSAC, was one of those. They'd been pilots in the same B-52 wing and tossed down more than a few beers together. Dooley was godfather to Whittenberg's eldest daughter. It had been a dead heat between the two of them for the CinCSAC job, but when Whittenberg went to SPACECOM he was happy his old friend had gotten the post in Omaha. He was also relieved when the voice on the other end said, "Dooley."

"Bernie, it's Rodg."

"Hey, how's my favorite jockey?" It was Dooley's standard greeting, a lampoon on his friend's size and Kentucky heritage.

"Not so good," said Whittenberg. "I got a problem and I need one of your Blackbirds."

"Aw, shucks, anything for the father of my favorite daughter." Dooley had four boys and always prided himself on his female godchild. "I just talked with my recon guy this morning. His Blackbirds are pretty backed up for five or six days. 'Course, for a bud like you maybe I can move your slot up a day or two. What's the problem?"

Whittenberg told him the problem.

Twelve minutes later a flash message was fired off from Omaha under the CinCSAC's personal signature to the 9th Strategic Reconnaissance Wing Detachment at Mildenhall Royal Air Force Base, England.

Day 1, 2250 Hours Zulu, 12:50 A.M. Local
KALININGRAD FLITE CONTROL CENTRE

"But are you certain this will work?" whimpered the General Secretary.

Vostov thought the man sounded like a little boy. "I will have to verify the exact specifications," said the Chief Designer, "but quite frankly I see no alternative. We take a small Progress solid-fuel engine and fashion a collar around the anterior end. We then insert the anterior portion into the shuttle's center main engine rocket nozzle—much like stacking one drinking glass on top of another—and clamp it to the lip of the nozzle. The collar will act as a brace to hold the engine firmly in place during the retro firing of the Progress engine. After the fuel is spent, an explosive bolt on each clamp will fire, releasing it and triggering a small spring to push the engine out of the nozzle."

Popov was impressed. No matter how big the Chief Designer's ego might be, this demonstrated he was entitled to it. The man had been roused out of his sleep in the middle of the night, told an unbelievable story, ordered to pull these politicians' asses out of the fire—and he'd done it. Of course, Popov did not belittle his own contribution. The concept, after all, was his idea.

"Extraordinary," said the General Secretary.

Vostov beamed. Perhaps the Politburo was not an impossibility after all.

The KGB chieftain exhaled a puff of smoke from his Pall Mall. "What do we have to do to bring this brilliant design to fruition?"

75

Vostov could see this little man was going to be nettlesome. "We must first design the collar to exact specifications so it will fit the outside of the Progress engine and the inside of the shuttle nozzle. The design must then be molded and cast." Vostov took a few moments to think about transport. "We will have to launch two vehicles—a cargo vessel to carry the components and a Soyuz to carry two cosmonauts to install the collar and engine."

"How long will all this take?" asked the General Secretary.

The two engineers looked at each other, both thinking through what had to be done. Vostov said, "To design and fabricate the collar, working around the clock, will take no less than forty-eight hours. Probably more when you consider the problems associated with the explosive bolts. Comrade Popov?"

Mentally, Popov went through his inventory of launch vehicles at the Baikonur Cosmodrome. "I can have an SL-4 booster for the Soyuz, and an SL-14 for the Progress engine ready in two to three days. However, that does not include the time you will need to load the engine and collar in a launch shroud and install them on the SL-14. We cannot do that until your fabrication is complete."

"So we would need three to four days," Vostov reflected.

"Then I would suggest you not waste any further time discussing it," said Kostiashak.

The two engineers took the Chairman's remark as more than a "suggestion."

"Chief Designer, you begin immediately on the collar design and line up the fabrication facilities," ordered Popov. "I'm sure the General Secretary will see to it you receive every assistance. I will start preparations for the launch vehicles and select the Soyuz crew. You will also have to coordinate with my people at Baikonur to fit the engine and collar into the cargo shroud."

"Agreed," said Vostov. The Chief Designer scratched the stubble on his flabby chin and paused, then asked rhetorically, "What if the Americans try to launch a vehicle to rescue their shuttle before our preparations are complete?"

There was another pause before the General Secretary asked in a sheepish voice, "We can do something to stop an American rescue, can we not, Popov?"

Popov took a deep breath. He didn't like being party to cheating—whether at cards or an international treaty. The United States and the Soviet Union had signed a treaty outlawing anti-

76

satellite (ASAT) weapons two years previously. But at Vorontsky's direction, Popov had hidden something away. "Yes, General Secretary," he said gravely, "at Plesetsk." Popov referred to the second-largest Russian launch facility at the Plesetsk Cosmodrome, which handled military payloads, and where *no* treaty inspection teams from the U.N. were allowed to set foot—ever.

"Then I suggest you make contingency preparations at Plesetsk as well—without delay. Is that clear, Comrade General?" queried the KGB chieftain.

Popov sighed. "Quite clear, Comrade Chairman."

Day 1, 2331 Hours Zulu, 6:31 P.M. Local
LAUNCH CONTROL BUNKER, KENNEDY SPACE CENTER

The supervisor held the glass doors open, allowing the janitorial crew to enter Firing Room Two of the Kennedy Space Center Launch Control Complex. In the old days of the Apollo program it took some 450 technical personnel in a bunker like this to get a Saturn 5 rocket off the ground. But lift-off preparations were so computer-driven now that only ninety launch technicians were required in Firing Room Two—one of four such rooms at the Cape.

The cleaning crew shuffled slowly into the big room, which was filled with consoles and computer terminals. They had little, if any, inclination to hustle, for theirs was a lousy job that paid the minimum wage.

The janitors ordinarily cleaned up the Space Center office buildings at night, but when there was launch activity a cleaning "detachment" would be farmed out to the firing room bunker to tidy things up. Usually it was only the night before a launch that the bunker was fully manned. But somehow, this evening, things seemed different.

Rosita Coronado, a small Hispanic woman wearing a blue uniform, moved slowly down the aisle of consoles, wiping the countertops and being careful not to disturb any papers lying about. Then she emptied trash cans into her gurney that held open a big plastic trash bag. No one paid much attention to her as she methodically worked her way down the aisle. Nor had anyone noticed she carefully avoided being assigned vacuum cleaner duty. The reason was that she couldn't hear anything with the machine running.

"Okay, start O-two valve seal test on fuel cell number two, now."

77

The skinny power systems technician killed his microphone, then pulled off the headset and draped it around his neck. He turned toward his neighbor and grumbled, "This is the most screwed-up deal I ever heard of. The whole weekend's shot to hell, we've got to crunch eight days of launch prep into less than three, the payload's being yanked out . . . and they won't even tell us what this is all about, either. It's shit like this that makes people cut corners, and you know what happens then."

"I know, I know," said his compatriot. "I was here, in this very chair, when *Challenger* went down. Mark my words, with this kind of launch pressure, one of these days something like that . . ."

Rosita had to keep moving, causing the voices to drift out of earshot. She progressed slowly down the aisle, until . . .

"Say, lady?"

She didn't turn, but kept moving.

"*Señora?*"

Rosita stopped and turned to look at the technician with the set of earphones slung around his neck.

"*Sí, señor?*"

"You forgot my ashtray."

She gave him the dumbest look she could muster. "*Señor?*"

He held it up, full of empty butts. "The ashtray. You forgot it. *Comprende?*"

She gave him a look of mock horror. "Oh, *sí, señor*. So sorry." She took the ashtray from his hand and emptied it into the plastic bag, then meticulously wiped it clean and replaced it by his elbow.

"*Gracias,*" he said.

She nodded and turned back down the aisle, pretending not to hear him mutter "Dumb Mexican" when her back was turned.

The cleaning crew finished up quicker than usual, responding to the supervisor's entreaty of "*Undele! Undele!*"

Upon completing her night's labors, Rosita took the bus home to a ramshackle frame house outside of Orlando. She didn't bother to doff her blue uniform, but immediately went to the bedroom closet and extracted a battered Smith-Corona typewriter with a microcassette memory recorder.

Actually, the technician at Firing Room Two had been wrong on both counts. Rosita wasn't dumb, and she wasn't Mexican. Cuba was her homeland. Where many years ago, when she was a little girl, her father and brother had died a slow and horrible death in the cellars of Juan Battista's prisons. She and her mother had fled to the Sierra

Maestra mountains, where they took refuge with a ragtag band of rebels under the command of a young renegade physician named Fidel Castro. When Battista fell, it went without saying that she became a Communist to her marrow. To spy for the cause was an honor. Bending over her typewriter, she pecked out her message, in Spanish:

EXTENSIVE ACTIVITY KSC LAUNCH BUNKER. CONVERSATIONS INDICATE PREVIOUS LAUNCH SCHEDULE ACCELERATED. PROB-ABLE LAUNCH WITHIN 72 HOURS. ONLY ROCKET ON PAD IS SPACE SHUTTLE CONSTELLATION.

—WATER LILY

She'd chosen the code name Water Lily herself, an ironic tribute to her successful masquerade as a refugee crossing the water from Cuba to the Florida Keys.

She looked at her watch. Time was short. Quickly she changed out of the blue uniform, rewound the cassette, plucked it out of the typewriter, and placed it into the false bottom of a makeup compact.

She left her house and caught another bus into downtown Orlando, where she transferred to the airport express shuttle. At the Orlando Airport, Rosita went directly to a bench situated near a gift shop and sat down. She took out the compact and checked her face—and her watch. At precisely the right instant, she closed the compact and placed it beside her, just as an aristocratic Mexican woman—looking stylish in her Adolfo outfit—sat down. Rosita left, and the recent arrival picked up the compact to study her own high cheekbones and carefully applied Lancome makeup. After indulging in a moment of self-approval, the Latin beauty dropped the compact into her Hermes purse and rose to catch the airport subway for the Mexicana Airline gate.

Later that same day, Rosita's message would be encrypted and transmitted from the Russian embassy in Mexico City to a waiting satellite dish at 2 Dzerzhinsky Square in Moscow.

THE SECOND DAY

Days are based on 24-hour Zulu military (Greenwich Mean) time

Day 2, 0550 Hours Zulu, 8:50 A.M. Local
MIDAIR REFUELING OVER THE BARENTS SEA

Maj. Felix "Catman" Griggs watched the fuel indicator needle creep to the top of the gauge. When it passed the FULL mark at 61,000 pounds, he said, "That's it, shut 'er down."

"Roger," replied the KC-10 boom operator as he extracted the aluminum pipe from the Blackbird's fuel inlet vent, just aft of the rear cockpit.

A few gallons of the JP-7 fuel dribbled out of the boom and washed over the backside of the SR-71 in sheets, causing the aircraft's black titanium skin to glisten in the morning sun. There was no danger of a fire, for the subzero temperature at 35,000 feet inhibited that. Besides, the JP-7 had a higher combustion point than regular JP-4 jet fuel. That was because the Blackbird's turbo-ramjet engines required a very special diet.

The boom operator in the underside pod of the KC-10 raised his hand in a wave. "Tallyho, Catman. Good hunting. See you in a little while."

"Roger, Fillup-One. Thanks. Catman out." Griggs watched the big KC-10, a tanker version of the civilian DC-10, lumber off on a bearing of 000, true north, where it would fly in a long rectangle until their scheduled rendezvous later that morning. Griggs then banked his SR-71 to a heading of 169 degrees, while the reconnaissance systems officer (RSO) scanned the astro-tracker and NavChronometer on his control panel in the backseat. The timing and navigation on this mission were going to be very dicey indeed, and they would have to work in tandem to bring it off.

The two men had been shaken out of bed in the middle of the night, by the detachment commander no less, and hustled to the recon briefing room at Mildenhall Royal Air Force Base. They'd crammed five hours of mission planning into one, then hauled ass to link up with the KC-10 over the Barents Sea.

They hadn't been told what the mission was about, but that wasn't unusual. They were only told where and when to fly and what to do. The what and when didn't bother Griggs. It was the *where* that had shocked him out of his sleepiness in the briefing room.

Their Blackbird was headed deep inside Soviet airspace.

Currently they were 473 miles off the Russian coast, west of Novaya Zemlya, which was the long, desolate island that extended a Soviet finger into the Barents Sea. Griggs and his RSO had often flown up to the edge, and even a little over, the Russian border from Finland, or flown over the coastal submarine base at Polyarny—taking pictures with side-oblique cameras, or collecting imagery in foul weather with the Blackbird's SLAR (side-looking airborne radar). But probing the frontier was one thing. A deep penetration was something else again. Particularly since they had to cross some of the world's heaviest air defenses to complete their mission. Terrific, Griggs thought. "Talk to me, Pretty Boy," he ordered.

The backseat RSO, Capt. Thomas "Pretty Boy" Floyd, scrutinized the astro-tracker navigation system and the NavChronometer while punching data into the flight computer. "Come to one-seven-one and bring it up to six hundred knots. We'll go to initial altitude in about forty seconds."

"Rog," replied Griggs.

Floyd ran through his flight data one more time. He didn't have to be a Rhodes scholar to figure out they were on some kind of ELINT (electronic intelligence) mission to listen in on a Russian spacecraft. Probably some satellite telemetry. What he found puzzling was why they had to listen in over Perm, seven hundred miles inside Soviet territory. Usually the Russians downloaded their telemetry to earth stations via a relay network of communications satellites at unpredictable intervals, just like the Americans. But on this mission the detachment commander had emphasized timing, timing, timing. It simply didn't make any sense. Oh, well, just try to concentrate on the mission, Floyd thought. Forget about the Russkies and their nine thousand surface-to-air missiles, their twenty-two hundred interceptors, and their ten thousand air defense radars. They wouldn't mind a little seven-hundred-mile penetration by the Blackbird, would they? Naw.

"Go to initial altitude on my mark," ordered Floyd.

"Roger," replied Griggs.

"Three . . . two . . . one . . . mark!"

Despite its power, getting an aircraft as large as the SR-71 through the sound barrier was not an easy thing to do, so pilots of the Blackbird used a maneuver to propel the aircraft past supersonic speed while conserving fuel. Griggs pushed the dual throttles all the way in and put the spy plane into a shallow dive. This combination of dive/thrust rapidly pushed the machometer indicator past the speed of sound. Griggs then pulled back on the stick and pointed the nose of the Blackbird almost straight up. This "dipsy-doodle" maneuver produced a slingshot effect that catapulted the spy plane skyward at an incredible rate of climb.

The two men felt the pressure build up in their orange space suits while watching their altimeter needles spin round and round.

Day 2, 0610 Hours Zulu, 9:10 A.M. Local
SOVIET AEROSPACE DEFENSE WARNING CENTRE, MAGNITOGORSK, CCCP

"Unidentified aircraft, Sector seventeen-D, approaching the coast on a south-southeast heading. . . . Altitude fifteen thousand meters and climbing . . . fast. . . . What do you think, Comrade Colonel?" asked the radar controller.

Looking at the map projection from his post in the Crow's Nest, Col. Valery Leonov of the Soviet Air Defense Force said through his telephone, "I do not have to think about it. At that speed and rate of climb it has to be one of their SR-71s. No matter. It will probably turn west and head toward Kola before too long." Leonov guessed the surface-to-air-missile batteries at Archangel and Pechora already had it locked in and a target solution computed, but neither battery was about to unload an expensive SA-5 missile at a target that was always out of reach. The paperwork demands of the elephantine Soviet bureaucracy explaining wasted missiles was beyond a Westerner's comprehension.

After a West German teenager landed his Cessna in Red Square several years ago, the Soviet Aerospace Defense Command had gone through a bloodletting unlike anything since Stalin's time. Everyone from generals to lowly captains had been busted and purged from the Air Defense Force. During this turmoil, SAM battery commanders feverishly sought some target, *any* target, at which they could unleash their missiles. The officers in the Aerospace Warning Centre were told to "damn the paperwork" and shoot something—*anything*—down. It was during that frenetic period that some zealous SAM crews successfully defended the Motherland from two weather balloons that had drifted over the Kola Peninsula from Norway and wasted dozens of SA-5 missiles shooting at SR-71s probing the northern coastline.

But slowly, things got back to normal. Paperwork demands resurfaced, and commanders became reluctant to face the embarrassment of weather balloon inquiries. Pressure from superiors about wasted missiles grew to the point where no one was going to cut loose with an SA-5 unless it was a sure shot.

Even so, it was absolutely maddening for Colonel Leonov how those Blackbird aircraft could play tag along the Rodina's coast and the Air Defense Force couldn't do a damn thing about it. The best surface-to-air missiles in the Soviet inventory could only reach an altitude of thirty kilometers—roughly 95,000 feet. The damn Blackbird could fly five kilometers above that. The SA-5, with a conventional warhead, would explode harmlessly below it.

The only way they might catch one, assuming they could probe through the SR-71's devious electronic countermeasures, was to put a high-altitude interceptor astride its flight path and fire an air-to-air missile at it. Even then, odds were against a hit. If the missile approached the Blackbird head-on, the mutual closing velocity of over five thousand miles per hour was too fast for the missile's guidance system to react and hit the target. If a tail shot was fired, it would have to be damn close, because the SR-71 could almost outrun a missile in a dead heat. About the only way to nail one was to get lucky with some kind of an underneath/side profile shot from an interceptor. But that wasn't possible unless you knew exactly where the Blackbird was going and could lie in wait for him. Leonov had no idea where this one was going, so his final option was closed.

Absolutely maddening.

But still, Leonov had to at least make a gesture to show the capitalist swine the Rodina knew he was there.

"Scramble the 11th Interceptor Regiment at Archangel," ordered Leonov. "If he turns west toward Kola we may at least have a shot at him."

"At once, Comrade Colonel."

Day 2, 0615 Hours Zulu, 9:15 A.M. Local
THE BLACKBIRD

At 75,000 feet, Griggs eased back on the throttles and gently pushed the stick forward to level off the Blackbird prior to their final climb and high-speed run. "How're we doing, Pretty Boy?"

"On track, Catman. Ready to go max?"

"Ready," said Griggs firmly.

Maj. Felix "Catman" Griggs physically resembled his radio call sign, for he was wiry and catlike and sported an upper lip of bristly whiskers. Capt. Thomas "Pretty Boy" Floyd, however, was the antithesis of his call sign, in that his face was uglier than a mud fence. Yet for some unfathomable reason, women were profoundly attracted to him.

"Okay . . . okay . . ." muttered Floyd nervously as he monitored the readouts from the astro-tracker and NavChronometer.

"Okay . . . okay . . . okay . . . now! Put the spurs to it, Catman!"

"Roger." Griggs shoved the dual throttles all the way forward, causing the air-intake cones on the General Electric J-58 engines to start pulsating in and out. The pulsing action regulated the airflow pattern into the engines, transforming them from turbofans to ramjets. The compressed air and JP-7 fuel exploding in the combustion chambers produced a combined thrust of 65,000 pounds, propelling the Blackbird at a speed nearly twice as fast as that of the supersonic Concorde.

A product of Lockheed's famous "Skunk Works," the SR-71 looked like a black hooded cobra with wings, and had always enjoyed a mystical reputation. No air-breathing aircraft, before or since, had been able to match its speed and altitude capabilities. Only thirty-two of the aircraft were built in the early sixties, causing them to be collector's items in every sense of the term—not only because of their singular abilities, but because the special tooling used in their construction no longer existed. Secretary of Defense Robert McNamara had ordered Lockheed to destroy the special tooling so the SR-71 would not compete for funding with his pet project—the FB-111 bomber. (In fairness to McNamara, the FB-111 was a fine plane for the Air Force—if the U.S. ever went to war with Canada.)

Griggs and Floyd concentrated on their instruments with intense silence as the Russian coastline approached them. With any luck at all they would complete the round trip of fifteen hundred miles and be out of Soviet airspace in less than fifty-five minutes.

On the edge of the stratosphere Griggs watched the sky turn to twilight as he leveled off for the last time. Then he let his aircraft come up to its fastest gait, like a thoroughbred on the backstretch.

The SR-71 was now exceeding the velocity of a .30-06 rifle bullet.

Day 2, 0630 Hours Zulu
THE *INTREPID*

They had been the most exasperating hours of his life. There was absolutely nothing, nothing, he could do but sit and wait. To have come to the very threshold of success, then have his triumph shattered by a broken plastic circuit board—well, it was enough to make even an Iceberg crack.

He'd eaten a little, rehydrating some of the freeze-dried food in the pantry. But his appetite was barely active. He'd avoided checking on the bodies of Mulcahey and Rodriquez floating in the airlock, for he knew they were dead. Mostly he kept himself strapped into the command seat, watching the inverted horizon and trying not to think of the *Constellation* on the pad at Kennedy. Would they launch into a polar orbit from Kennedy? Probably not. He hoped the *Intrepid*'s last message about a fire had convinced them everyone on board was dead. They wouldn't risk sending a shuttle near Miami. It would be a political decision to do that, and no politician would be insane enough to risk another *Challenger* disaster over a major city. They'd send up a recovery ship from Vandenberg, he kept telling himself. And that would take time.

Iceberg willed himself not to look at the clock. When he'd passed over Irkutsk earlier he hadn't even activated his transmitter. The message from the ground had been brief: Stay off the air. We're working on the problem. We'll contact you over Perm.

The *Intrepid* was just passing over the Arctic ice cap. He'd be able to talk to them in about twelve minutes.

Day 2, 0630 Hours Zulu, 9:30 A.M. Local
SOVIET AEROSPACE DEFENSE WARNING CENTRE

If a Russian and an American airman could trade places between the Soviet Aerospace Defense Warning Centre in Magnitogorsk and NORAD headquarters in Cheyenne Mountain, they would be struck by the similarity of the two facilities. At both locations large projection screens dominated the giant room, and there were rows and rows of consoles. Both the American and Russian centers had a Crow's Nest overlooking the entire facility, where a colonel was on duty at all times to respond to any "bogie," or unidentified aircraft or missile. Still another similar aspect was that just as CSOC Mission Control outside Colorado Springs was separate and apart from Cheyenne Mountain, so was the Aerospace Defense Warning Centre separate and apart from the Kaliningrad Flite Control Centre. With General Secretary Vorontsky and KGB Chairman Kostiashak keeping their operation tightly under wraps, not even Colonel Leonov in the Crow's Nest was aware the orbiting spacecraft and the Blackbird were approaching a rendezvous. To him, they were separate and distinct.

Leonov—who was middle-aged and somewhat overweight with a thick crop of wavy gray hair—looked at the northern hemisphere map projection on the wall, which showed North America and Russia in a circle around the Arctic ice cap. He spun a dial on his control panel and the projection zoomed in on the Soviet Union west of the Urals. A white dot moving south was the SR-71.

Leonov scratched his chin. Blackbird overflights were rare, and it was his guess this SR-71 was out to get something the American spy satellites were unable to capture. What, he couldn't imagine, but that wasn't his concern. Of the few overflights he'd been briefed on, he knew the Blackbirds always exited Soviet airspace at a different point from where they entered. This one had not turned west toward the Kola Peninsula as he'd expected, but instead had crossed the coastline south of Novaya Zemlya on a bearing almost due south. If it continued in that direction, it most certainly would not turn due west, because it might come within range of the Moscow antiballistic missile defenses, and those Galosh missiles *could* reach the Blackbird. Also, if it continued on its present southerly course it would reach Afghanistan, and, in view of the Soviet reinvasion, that seemed an unlikely destination, to say the least. Neighboring Iran had long been hostile to the United States, so it certainly wouldn't land there. China, Pakistan, and some Persian Gulf Arab states were possibilities, but there was no historical precedence of Blackbirds operating out of those countries. Therefore, the SR-71 would most likely turn slightly southwest and land in Turkey—a NATO country. Either that, or it would turn back north and link up with another tanker for refueling.

Leonov carefully inspected the Barents Sea airspace, and the only bogie he could find was making its way slowly toward Spitzbergen Island. The other blips on the screen were Russian military or civilian aircraft. He lifted the phone on his console and punched in the radar operator who had first alerted him. "That bogie headed toward Spitzbergen. Have you identified it?"

"Yes, Comrade Colonel. It apparently is a tanker. We tracked two bogies that joined into one radar signature, then divided. The American Blackbird separated from that signature."

"Hmmm . . . Are there any other tankers east of Spitzbergen?"

"No, Comrade Colonel," replied the radar operator. "Only what you see on the plot."

So, no other bogies off the coast except for the single tanker. That,

Leonov felt, would indicate the Blackbird was surely headed for Turkey, because whenever an SR-71 exited over the northern coastline on previous overflights there would always be two tankers—one over the Barents Sea and one hovering over the Laptev Sea. The wide spacing of the tankers gave the Blackbird an exit point almost anywhere along the north coast of Russia. And given the SR-71's speed, it was an impossible task to cover the entire coast, even for the Rodina's awesome air defense capabilities. But since there was only one American tanker off the northern coast, that would indicate the spy plane was headed for Turkey.

Leonov pulled out a three-ring binder from under his console and flipped it open to the section outlining the 77th Interceptor Regiment at Tbilisi on the Turkish border. He found what he was looking for and quietly swore under his breath. The 77th Regiment had the sophisticated MiG-29 Fulcrum fighters, but they were armed with the medium-range AA-10 radar-guided missiles and close-range Aphid heat-seeking missiles. It would be useless to send those against the Blackbird. The damned spy plane would be too high, too fast, and out of range. A waste of time. He flipped to another section in the binder, and here it looked more promising. The 11th Interceptor Regiment out of Archangel, which he had just scrambled, had MiG-31 Foxhounds, and they carried the long-range AA-9 radar-guided missiles.

The colonel pondered this, then looked at the plot. The SR-71 was still racing south over Russia, but the tanker over the Barents Sea was altering its course and turning back to a southerly heading. Hmmm. Why was the tanker doing that if the Blackbird was headed for Turkey? If, by the off chance, the spy plane returned from whence it came, then maybe, just maybe, he could spring a very clever surprise on the mystical American aircraft. He pushed the button to buzz the communications officer.

"Yes, Colonel Leonov?"

"Patch me through to the squadron commander of the 11th Interceptors who is leading the scramble."

Day 2, 0634 Hours Zulu, 9:34 A.M. Local
THE BLACKBIRD

Griggs looked down and saw the curvature of the earth, then he turned his gaze skyward and witnessed a host of stars twinkling in the dark sky above him. Traveling on the edge of the stratosphere always provided a spectacular view, but Griggs knew his backseater was ignoring the panorama. The RSO had his eyes glued to the instruments. "How's it lookin', Pretty Boy?" he asked.

"So far, so good," replied Floyd. "We've been scanned by search and SAM radars since we crossed the coastline, but nobody's popped a missile yet. Three hundred miles to target. I've already got the ELINT sensor going."

"Roger."

Traveling at forty miles per minute made three hundred miles a short distance. Although it was the fastest air-breathing plane in the world with the unclassified world speed record of 2,193.6 miles per hour (and a classified record of 2,623.4 mph), even the SR-71 would have a very small time window with which to eavesdrop on the *Intrepid*. With a speed of 17,000 mph, the spacecraft would quickly overtake the spy plane as it flew above Perm.

Day 2, 0642 Hours Zulu
THE *INTREPID*

Iceberg checked the Global Positioning System and figured he was within range. He keyed his mike switch. "Flite Control Centre, this is *Intrepid*, do you read? Over. . . . Flite Control Centre, this is *Intrepid*, do you read? Over."

"This is Centre, *Intrepid*, we read you. Listen carefully. Our engineering people have examined the problem, and we think we have devised a way to get you down. But we must know, do all of your control functions except the retro rockets work properly?"

"Yes. I've checked them a dozen times. I can do everything except transfer fuel from the OMS tanks to the reaction control tanks. I have plenty of fuel in the RCS tanks now, though. What do you have in mind?"

"*Intrepid*, we are going to fabricate a device that will allow us to attach one of our solid-fuel rockets to the rear of your ship. We will be sending up a Soyuz spacecraft and a cargo vessel with the materials and assistance to help you accomplish this. It is taking some time to fabricate the attachment device, so we will not be able to bring you down for four to five days. Can you hold out that long?"

Iceberg almost laughed. "I don't like it, but what choice do I have? Five days is a long time. The Americans might try something."

"We are watching the American situation very carefully, *Intrepid*.

We are prepared for any contingency. Stay off the air but keep this channel open. We will keep you informed of any developments. You are a brave man, *Intrepid*. You will be greatly honored when you land."

Iceberg sighed. "Yeah. When I land. *Intrepid* out."

Day 2, 0642 Hours Zulu, 9:42 A.M. Local
SOVIET AEROSPACE DEFENSE WARNING CENTRE

The other phone buzzed, and Colonel Leonov picked it up. Now he was holding a receiver in each hand—one to the squadron commander of the MiG-31 Foxhounds, and one to the radar operator who'd just rung him.

"Colonel, the tanker has turned again," said the radar operator. "It is now heading east on a bearing toward its previous refueling point."

Brusquely, Leonov replied, "Very well." Then he switched receivers and said, "Fox Leader, it appears this Blackbird aircraft may go out the way he came in. Do you understand what I've instructed you to do?"

"Roger, Colonel. But if we do what you suggest we will not have much fuel to get home."

"I know that. I am a pilot myself. Do not go to afterburner until I tell you. . . . And that is not a 'suggestion.' Is that understood?"

"Understood, Colonel," replied the leader of the Foxhounds. "But it is on *your* order we are firing our missiles." Which meant the Aerospace Warning Centre would be responsible for the paperwork.

"We have standing orders to shoot down any aircraft that violates Soviet airspace, Fox Leader. Is *that* understood?"

"Roger, Colonel. My squadron is deploying now."

Leonov's trap was really quite ingenious. The SR-71 had speed, but at 2,500 miles per hour it was much like a supertanker in that it couldn't alter course very easily. The plan had two premises—one, that the Blackbird would exit on the same axis that it had entered Soviet airspace; and two, that it would be traveling with its throttle wide open. The eight interceptors were strung out on a line one hundred miles long. If it looked as if the Blackbird would follow the same path, they'd all go to afterburner and scoot to their maximum altitude of eighty thousand feet, where they would all fire their AA-9 missiles underneath and astride the enemy aircraft. Each of the Foxhounds carried four missiles, but it was unlikely they'd have time enough to fire more than two apiece. The AA-9s had the range to go the final thirty thousand feet and possibly hit the SR-71 from an angle perpendicular to its axis of advance. Even a magical airplane like the Blackbird would have trouble flying through sixteen missiles . . . or so Leonov hoped.

"Colonel!" cried the young radar operator.

"Yes?"

"The spy plane is turning!"

Day 2, 0646 Hours Zulu, 9:46 A.M. Local
THE BLACKBIRD

Griggs brought his throttles back ever so carefully before starting a long banking turn to a northern heading of 349 degrees.

The mission had been laid on so fast there simply hadn't been enough time to make arrangements with the Turkish government for the Blackbird to land at Encirlik Air Base in central Turkey. Nor had there been time to deploy a second refueling tanker from Alaska with JP-7 fuel to cover the Blackbird's possible exit points over the northeast Siberian coast. The SR-71 was forced to violate normal procedure and go out the way it had come in.

"Get anything?" asked Griggs.

"Yeah," replied Floyd. "There was some traffic on that S-band freq we were told to watch out for. Hope it makes somebody happy. Let's get outta here."

"You got it. Just keep an eye on the threat board," implored Griggs.

"You got that straight."

Griggs finished out his turn and pushed the throttles up to their stops.

Day 2, 0647 Hours Zulu, 9:47 A.M. Local
SOVIET AEROSPACE DEFENSE WARNING CENTRE

The radar operator watched the blip intensely. It *was* going back the same way. Almost the exact reciprocal of its original bearing. Maybe they *would* bag an American Blackbird. "Colonel?"

"Yes, yes. I'm watching it on the plot board." Leonov picked up his other receiver while watching the large white blip approach the string of smaller red blips. Red blips denoted the friendly fighters. "Fox Leader, I see your aircraft are deployed."

"That is correct, Comrade Colonel," replied the pilot in a mocking voice.

I'll deal with this insolent bastard later, thought Leonov while dabbing some perspiration from his forehead with a white handkerchief. "The American spy plane is approaching your position from the south on a bearing of one-five-nine. He will be in range of your southernmost aircraft in approximately twelve minutes. If he stays on this course he will, I believe the nautical term is, 'cross the T' of all your aircraft. Go to afterburner on my command."

"Acknowledged, Comrade Colonel. We will do more than 'cross his T.' "

Day 2, 0657 Hours Zulu, 9:57 A.M. Local
THE FOXHOUNDS

"Go to afterburners, now! Now!"

Fox Leader winced from the loud transmission in his headphones. Then he keyed his mike and said, "You heard the colonel, Comrades. Go to afterburners but do not, I repeat do not, activate your radars until we pass twenty thousand meters. If we are to catch this Blackbird we must surprise him." He cut in his fighter's afterburners, injecting raw fuel directly into the Foxhound's tailpipes. The twin-engine aircraft leapt in response, and Fox Leader pointed it straight up in a textbook interceptor climb.

Classic fighter doctrine calls for gaining altitude on your opponent, then pouncing on him out of the sun before he knows you're there. A modern-day, high-tech nuance to that doctrine calls for the use of look-down, shoot-down radar in conjunction with a fighter's missiles. In this case, however, the Foxhounds would be looking up and shooting up. And when they topped out at 25,000 meters, Fox Leader wasn't going to waste a single second loitering around looking for a nebulous target. His fuel was rapidly disappearing with the afterburner climb, and a dead-stick landing in the Foxhound was out of the question. Its stubby wings gave it a glide pattern like a lead shot sinker.

They passed through 20,000 meters, and a red light blinked on the Leader's control panel, indicating the target acquisition radar had been activated. "Anything, Koldunov?" he asked.

The backseat weapons system officer scanned his screen. "Nothing yet, Leader."

The altimeter dial spun past 23,000 meters. "We have him!" cried an excited voice over the radio. "Fox Leader, this is Fox Four! We have missile lock!"

"Then shoot! Shoot!" yelled Leader.

"Leader, this is Fox Three! We have him, too! Engaging now!"

Fox Leader's pulse was racing. He'd never fired a missile at a real enemy before.

Day 2, 0659 Hours Zulu, 9:59 A.M. Local
THE BLACKBIRD

"Uh-oh."

Griggs didn't like the sound of that. "What is it, Pretty Boy?"

"Threat board shows we've been illuminated in the X-ray band. Looks like a bandit with Doppler radar. . . . Yeah, they've got lock-on, and . . . hey? . . . What's this? Another illumination. It's got lock-on, too. . . . I count three . . . four missiles approaching. Christ, they're close! Where'd they come from? Turning missile sucker on now . . . Shit! *Another* illumination! What is goin' on? Catman, I don't like this."

The missile sucker was an electronic countermeasure device that could "bend" the radar signature of the Blackbird, causing the hostile missile to receive a false impression of the aircraft's actual location. Like an electronic ventriloquist, the sucker mechanism could "throw" the Blackbird's radar image up to a mile away.

Most of the Foxhounds' missiles, however, were unable to catch up to the SR-71, or even its false image. The spy plane's speed was simply too great. Only a few of the projectiles reached the periphery of the "sucker ghost," triggering their detonation; and Griggs and Floyd were going too fast to see the distant firebursts.

It was the last aircraft in Fox Leader's string that did it. In his youthful zeal the weapons system officer, on only his third mission since flite school, loosed his missiles prematurely—letting them fly off before his fire control radar had acquired the target. His attempts to regain control of the AA-9s only served to confound them and they became, quite literally, unguided missiles. One missile strayed and was caught between the genuine Blackbird, the "sucker ghost," and the Foxhound's own radar sweeps trying to regain control of it. This multitude of electronic signals peppering the AA-9 so confused the missile that its proximity fuse went loco and exploded.

The blast was far enough away from the SR-71 that the aircraft was not hit directly by debris, but the spy plane had to fly through the explosion's shock wave, which kicked it into left yaw. This was sort of like skidding sideways in a car when the left front tire blows out.

As the Blackbird yawed to the left, its fuselage blocked airflow into the port engine, causing it to flame out. Basic physics kept Griggs and Floyd going in a straight line, and like a pair of sunglasses on the dashboard of that skidding car, they were smashed into the right bulkhead of the SR-71's cockpit. Floyd was knocked unconscious and Griggs was dazed, but the pilot had the presence of mind to reach out and pull the starboard throttle back slightly. Simultaneously he pressed hard on the right rudder pedal and dropped the right wing a little. Griggs figured they were probably dead anyway, but to have any chance at survival he had to get the spy plane back into proper trim.

The reason the Blackbird could operate in rarefied atmospheres, at altitudes in excess of 110,000 feet, was that its incredible speed forced enough thin air into the ramjet intakes for combustion. Without the high-speed ram effect, airflow would be too weak and a flameout would result. Griggs was painfully aware of this as he tried to restart the port engine. He hit the ignition switch but the dead ramjet refused to come alive. The spy plane's speed had dropped too far for a restart, and Griggs knew the Blackbird's remaining power plant would soon become oxygen-starved and die. So instead of letting the starboard engine choke itself off, he carefully eased back on the throttle even farther. Then, using all of his pilot's instincts, he got the aircraft into proper trim, just as the starboard ramjet started going *chug . . . chug . . . chug*. He then cut the throttle completely as Floyd began to regain consciousness.

"Ca-Catman . . . what happened? . . . Damn . . . my head."

"Never mind that now!" yelled Griggs. "Just hang on!"

The Blackbird was coasting down in an arc at Mach 1.9.

Griggs knew he had no choice but to take the spy plane down to a lower altitude where he could try and restart the SR-71's turbofans in a thicker atmosphere. But as his aircraft descended, he felt his gut tighten up like a board.

An unpowered supersonic dive into enemy territory was more frightening than anything he'd ever experienced.

Day 2, 0701 Hours Zulu, 10:01 A.M. Local
SOVIET AEROSPACE DEFENSE WARNING CENTRE

The Blackbird's radar signature was lost in the flurry of images caused by the Foxhounds' exploding missiles. But finally, the spy plane's white blip was reacquired on the radar scope, and the operator noticed its altitude and speed were falling. Slowly at first, then faster. "Colonel, I think we hit it! . . . It is falling!"

A collective cheer went up through the cavernous room, and the loudest voice among the chorus was the colonel's. He had shot down an American Blackbird. How glorious! Could a general's epaulets be far behind? "Where will it impact?" Leonov asked.

The operator studied his screen. "He is continuing to fall. It looks like he will come down somewhere north of Pechora on the Bolshezemelskaya Tundra."

"Obtain the closest fix that you can. The wreckage may yield us some secrets, as that American U-2 did many years ago . . . probably before you were born, my friend."

The young lieutenant turned around and smiled at his colonel in the Crow's Nest. It was such a triumph—one to be savored.

Day 2, 0702 Hours Zulu, 10:02 A.M. Local
THE BLACKBIRD

A staunch Roman Catholic, Griggs whispered a prayer, while Floyd kept up a low chant of "Ohshitohshitohshitohshit."

Their aircraft was arcing over into a steep dive and descending through 90,000 feet.

Griggs's plan was to keep the Blackbird in proper trim as they descended into thicker air below 50,000 feet. Then he would open the engine cones and let the airflow hit the spinning turbofan blades. If the turbofans maintained enough RPM, he could restart the engines. A nice strategy, but plenty could go wrong. If sufficient airspeed wasn't maintained when he opened the air intake cones, the turbine RPMs could drop below the minimum level required to execute an airstart. Or maybe the port engine had been damaged in the attack, so even if they got one engine started the spy plane would have to limp along at an altitude well within range of SAM missiles and fighters. Lovely.

"Okay, Pretty Boy, here we go," whispered Griggs in a tight voice. At 45,000 feet he slammed open the air intake cones and hit the two ignition switches simultaneously. A wave of relief swept over both men as the two turbofans came to life. Griggs pushed the throttles halfway in to give the Blackbird enough power to slowly pull out of its dive.

They had just plummeted through 39,000 feet.

Day 2, 0705 Hours Zulu, 10:05 A.M. Local
SOVIET AEROSPACE DEFENSE WARNING CENTRE

The white blip halted its descent. It was moving again.

"Colonel! The American spy plane has stopped falling. . . . He is moving again . . . slightly in excess of Mach One."

Leonov felt a pang in his chest. "What sector?" he cried.

"Fourteen-G."

The Foxhounds had already turned for home on their thirsty fuel tanks. To scramble another flight might take too long, so the colonel pressed a button that connected him with the 128th Air Defense Battery at Pechora.

"Captain Vydinsky," came the immediate reply.

"Captain, this is Aerospace Warning Centre! Do you have a bogie on your screen in sector fourteen-G?"

"Of course," replied Vydinsky. "We have been tracking this activity carefully. It appears some Foxhounds have been taking shots at it."

"Is it in range?"

"*Da.*"

"Engage it now!"

Seven seconds later four long-range SA-5 Gammon missiles roared out of their bunker pads, which ringed the phased-array radar complex at Pechora.

Day 2, 0706 Hours Zulu, 10:06 A.M. Local
THE BLACKBIRD

Griggs leveled off the Blackbird at 37,000 feet to check out the systems before returning to a higher altitude.

"Aw, shit."

"What is it, Pretty Boy?"

"We got another lock-on . . . and, yep, missile fired. This one's coming from the ground, though."

"Hit the missile sucker," ordered Griggs.

Floyd toggled some switches, but his indicator needles didn't move. "Looks like the sucker's gone dead. Can we outrun this one?"

"We're certainly going to try," replied Griggs in a squeaky voice.

Luckily, they were already at supersonic speed and could forgo the "dipsy-doodle" maneuver. Griggs shoved his throttles all the way in and pulled back on the stick. He was at 37,000 feet, which gave the SR-71 about a six-mile lead on the ascending SA-5 Gammons. All he had to do was make it to the Gammons' 90,000-foot service ceiling before the missiles did.

Day 2, 0707 Hours Zulu, 10:07 A.M. Local
SOVIET AEROSPACE DEFENSE WARNING CENTRE

The radar operator stared at his screen intently as the blip of the Blackbird raced upward, trying to shake the pursuing Gammons.

"He's climbing, Colonel, but the missiles are gaining!"

Leonov's heart was pounding. "Good, good."

The young lieutenant continued watching his scope closely, mesmerized by the scene. He'd never seen a race such as this. The missiles were closing . . . closing . . .

Day 2, 0708 Hours Zulu, 10:08 A.M. Local
THE BLACKBIRD

The SR-71 climbed through 80,000 feet.

"They're closing fast, Catman," said Floyd in a tight voice.

"I hear you." The aircraft was now at an altitude where the turbo-to-ramjet conversion could take place, and Griggs held the throttles hard against their stops.

"Still closing," said Floyd.

Griggs watched his altimeter spin past 84,000 feet. "Come on, baby, come on!"

Day 2, 0709 Hours Zulu, 10:09 A.M. Local
SOVIET AEROSPACE DEFENSE WARNING CENTRE

The two blips almost converged.

Almost.

At 31,000 meters the Blackbird's blip continued climbing, while those of the Gammon missiles seemed to hang in place for a few moments before starting on a downward arc.

"Colonel . . . the American spy plane has . . . pulled away."

Leonov did not reply. He sat there dumbfounded, contemplating the stacks of paperwork he would be filling out, for weeks on end.

He could kiss his general's epaulets goodbye.

Day 2, 0745 Hours Zulu, 10:45 A.M. Local
MIDAIR REFUELING OVER THE BARENTS SEA

The boom operator deftly inserted the aluminum pipe into the Blackbird's fueling vent.

"Contact, Catman. Starting flow now." The operator opened a valve and the JP-7 liquid began gushing from the KC-10 into the spy plane's near-empty fuel tanks. "So how'd it go?"

Griggs was too tired to respond intelligently. "Just a regular milk run," he mumbled.

Day 2, 1200 Hours Zulu, 2:00 P.M. Local
STAR CITY, CCCP

Lt. Col. Vasili Lubinin attempted to guide the aluminum strut into the nearby receptacle hub, but his initial momentum from the backpack thruster had diminished. He was sorely tempted to close the remaining distance with a little swimmer's kick, but he knew such an attempt would bring an admonition from the tank controller—because swimming kicks didn't work very well in outer space. Luckily, his teammate, Maj. Sergei Yemitov, reached out and pulled the strut a final meter into the hub's waiting receptacle. Yemitov then closed a clamp over the strut with a definitive *click*.

"Many thanks, Sergeivich," said Lubinin.

"We are a team, Vasilivich," responded Yemitov, as indeed they were. So much so that the major addressed the colonel by his first name without reservation.

"All right, you two," instructed the controller, "back up and let us see the handiwork of this marvelous team."

The two cosmonauts readily complied, propelling themselves away from the structure with squirts from their maneuvering backpacks.

They were traveling through a water tank roughly half the size of Madison Square Garden, where for the last hour they'd been constructing a large geodesic dome with prefabricated aluminum struts and hubs. When the Soviet Star Wars platform was eventually constructed it would have to be assembled in orbit piece by piece, and the dome assembly was good exercise.

Lubinin and Yemitov continued thrusting backward and upward until they obtained a better perspective on their construction efforts. Their maneuvering backpacks were a modified version of the genuine spacepack. The underwater model produced thrusting squirts of water with small internal propellers, while the spacepack propelled itself with tiny jets of pressurized nitrogen. The movements of the cosmonauts were slower and more cumbersome in the water than they would be in the vacuum of space, but it was the best simulation that could be manufactured on earth.

The two men hovered above the dome and smiled at each other through their clear plastic helmets. They had assembled the dome swiftly and precisely, making the most of their time, which was limited by the oxygen in their life-support tanks. Pilot cosmonauts like Lubinin and Yemitov typically received more cross training—like the dome-assembly exercise—than their American counterparts, and there were two reasons for this. For one, the primary American space vehicle was the shuttle, which was much more complex to pilot than the Soviet Soyuz, and therefore the flight training demands on the American shuttle pilots consumed the bulk of their time. The other reason was that some Soyuz models could carry only two people; there simply wasn't room for a third mission specialist. So Lubinin and Yemitov spent a good deal of time in the huge training tank, carrying out exercises to prepare them for extravehicular activity outside the spacecraft. Someday the Rodina would build her own Star Wars platform, and when that day came, they'd be ready.

"Excellent work, Comrades," commented the controller. "You may exit the tank and take some refreshment."

The two men smiled again and began propelling themselves toward the rim of the tank, looking otherworldly in their bulky spacesuits. Just below the rim, they lowered themselves onto an elevator platform and shut down their backpack thrusters. Then they helped each other disengage the maneuvering sections of their backpacks from the life-support sections and placed the equipment by their feet. "We are in position," said Lubinin. "Hoist away." The controller threw a switch on his console and the platform heaved the cosmonauts out of the water. The two men groaned as the weight of the suits settled on them for the first time in over an hour.

Technicians helped the two men off the platform and onto the staging area, where their helmets were removed. The cosmonauts experienced a little light-headedness as they went from a pure-oxygen environment to a normal nitrogen/oxygen mix. The white-coated technicians had begun the unclasping and unzipping process on the suits when the tank controller poked his head through the door. "Lubinin and Yemitov. I just received a call. General Popov wants to see the two of you in his office immediately."

The cosmonauts looked at each other, and as well as he could, Yemitov shrugged in his spacesuit to indicate he had no idea what the summons was about.

"Very well," said Lubinin. "Tell the Comrade General's office we will be there as soon as we get out of these things and change." The controller nodded and disappeared.

Doffing the suits took another five minutes. The cosmonauts then adjourned to the locker room before peeling off the final layer of Spandex body garments. Chilled water passed through plastic tubes woven into the Spandex suit to keep the cosmonauts cool; yet in spite of the coolant, they sweated while they worked. Yemitov muttered to himself that the foul smell sometimes encountered inside a spacesuit certainly took some of the glamour out of being a star voyager. After a quick shower the two men put on their workaday flite suits and fur-lined coats, then walked out of the simulator complex toward the headquarters building. A recent snowfall had covered the campuslike grounds with a white blanket.

The simulator complex building housed not only the enormous water tank but also the shuttle simulator and mockups of the Soyuz spacecraft. And it was just one piece of the sprawling campus known as Star City, located outside Moscow. If given a choice, Russians tend to gravitate toward single, huge enterprises rather than smaller, multiple endeavors—and Star City was a prime example. It was the focal point for cosmonaut and spaceflight training and contained the simulator complex, administrative office buildings, an education center, athletic facilities, laboratories, a movie theater, and living quarters for the cosmonauts and their families. The creature comforts enjoyed here were among the best the Soviet Union had to offer, including special shops that carried scarce Western goods. An indication of the cosmonauts' fine life-style was the fact that virtually no black market existed at Star City, and it was not unusual to find a VCR in some of the apartments. In short, cosmonauts had a pretty good deal by Soviet standards, and an emergency summons from Popov could mean something was amiss.

As they hustled across the grounds, Lubinin looked like a burly football guard running interference for the nimble Yemitov. The older cosmonaut was big-boned, with dark, swarthy features, while Yemitov was compact, trim, and blond, and his blue eyes gave him a look of vulnerability.

Lubinin read his comrade's thoughts. "Do not worry, Sergeivich," he comforted. "I am certain it is nothing serious."

Yemitov looked at his friend skeptically, but didn't contradict him. "I hope you are right. I would not want anything to go wrong just now. Sasha . . . she, she is pregnant."

Lubinin stopped in midstride. "Sergei! Why did you not tell me? This is joyous!" He embraced his friend. "Now do not worry. I am sure everything is all right. If not, I shall make it right." It was a boast, but one that Lubinin could probably back up. With the Russians' two top shuttle crews dead, he and Yemitov were now considered the "hot" team in the cosmonaut corps. Yemitov had nothing to fear about his position. In fact, it was because of his proficiency that he was being summoned to Popov's office.

The two cosmonauts walked into the glass office building and took the elevator to the eighth floor, where Popov's male secretary pointed toward the general's office and said, "Quickly." The cosmonauts walked in and saw the stocky Popov sitting behind his desk, just hanging up the phone. They were shocked by his appearance. The general looked like hell.

The aide closed the door behind them.

"Vasili . . . Sergei . . . Sit down," began Popov. "I have a mission for you. Something you cannot imagine. From this moment forward you are totally incommunicado. No contact with anyone other than mission personnel. Is that clear? What you are about to undertake is surely dangerous, but the two of you are the best qualified for this task and I do not have the luxury to ask you to volunteer. You are needed now. Are you prepared to do your duty?"

The two cosmonauts looked at each other, then back at Popov, and nodded.

Popov nodded as well, and said, "Good." Then he proceeded to brief them on how they were going to lasso an American space shuttle and bring it down to the Baikonur Cosmodrome.

Two jaws dropped. It was Yemitov who recovered first. "You mean we may actually capture an American shuttle?" he asked incredulously.

"Not just the shuttle," said Popov, "but the payload as well, which contains some critical components for their space defense platform. It will be a windfall beyond our imagination."

"Incredible," whispered Lubinin, before regaining enough composure to ask, "You said the pilot killed the two other American crewmen on board?"

"*Da*," replied Popov. He did not amplify the statement, for there was nothing else to say.

Lubinin looked down and shook his head. He had always felt space travelers formed a special fraternity that somehow transcended national borders. A double murder in space quickly shot down that heroic assumption, and he found the truth painful.

"How do we proceed from here?" queried Yemitov.

Popov scratched the fringe of sweat-stained gray hair on his bald head. "Chief Designer Vostov is over at Flite Centre. Get over there right away and have him explain the design of the collar mechanism. Make sure you understand everything you need to know. There is no purpose in going into orbit and not knowing how the damned thing works. Is that clear? If Vostov causes any problems, let me know immediately. I am sure you have many questions, but they will have to wait. Learn all you can about the docking collar first. Then we will talk again. I am handling launch preparations personally. That is all. You have a car and driver at your disposal. Go."

Still dumbfounded, the two men rose and left.

Popov was spent. He couldn't remember when he'd slept last. He heaved himself up and waddled to the door to speak to his aide. "Wake me in two hours, and do not disturb me unless the General Secretary or the Comrade Chairman calls . . . no, if they call, tell them I am out on the grounds. Only wake me if they appear in person . . . and then take your time about it." Popov didn't wait for an answer. He was beyond caring. Slamming the door, he collapsed on the divan and was instantly asleep.

Day 2, 1303 Hours Zulu, 3:03 p.m. Local
SHEREMETYEVO AIRPORT, MOSCOW, CCCP

There was a whirring sound as the Aeroflot jetliner's flaps extended to 100 percent. Yuri Shevetchenko peered out the window, watching the snow-covered farm plots grow larger and larger in his field of view. Finally they disappeared altogether, replaced by the black runway tarmac rushing past. The middle-aged man, wearing an ill-fitting suit, turned to his companion and excitedly said, "Hold on, Andrei! We are going to land!" The tires of the aircraft squealed, and all the passengers pitched forward as the pilot engaged the thrust reversers. The jetliner's speed decreased quickly, and the captain turned off onto a taxiway cleared of snow.

"Ahhhh, Moscow. Much too long, yes, Andrei?" His younger companion smiled and nodded. Shevetchenko said, "Now perhaps we can buy some decent vodka, get a real meal." Then he whispered like a conspirator, "And maybe find a real woman."

The nineteen-year-old Andrei blushed, but smiled again. "*Da*. It will be good to see Anna again. I only hope she has not forgotten me. We have been away six months, after all."

"Forget a man like you? Impossible. You are *unforgettable*," joked Shevetchenko. "Besides, we have three weeks in Moscow. You will probably be married by the time our leave is finished." The young man turned red and smiled again. Shevetchenko was his superior, mentor, and friend. The husky, dark-featured, fifty-two-year-old bachelor was an electrician at the Baikonur Cosmodrome, and the slender, baby-faced Andrei was his assistant. The older man treated him like the son he'd never had.

The airliner braked at the gate and the flight attendants opened the door. "We have arrived. Let us be off," commanded Shevetchenko, and the two men joined the surge for the door. Exiting the airliner, they walked a couple of hundred meters down the long concourse and entered domestic passport control, where their internal CCCP passports were stamped by a scowling clerk (all Russian passport officials scowl). After passing through passport control they collected their luggage at a carousel and went through yet another check at domestic customs control, where their luggage was inspected by an incredibly bored uniformed official. Finally they walked out of the airport and clambered onto a bus for the hour's ride into central Moscow. There was little conversation between them during the journey, for each man had his own agenda to think about. Andrei contemplated his Anna and the new pair of Levi's jeans he'd picked up for her on the black market. Yuri thought of something else.

Upon arrival at the Metro station near the Rossiya Theater, the two men exited the vehicle and prepared to part company.

"You will be sure to come to my parents' flat next Thursday?" asked Andrei. He didn't ask his friend to call him, because only one in six Muscovites had a phone in their residence.

"You can be sure of it, my friend," replied Yuri. And with that, the two men embraced. Young Andrei started walking toward his parents' apartment building, while Shevetchenko disappeared into the Metro subway station. He paid his five kopeks at the kiosk and boarded the first eastbound train. The ride took only a few minutes, and at Dzerzhinskaya Station he transferred to a different line, traveling up to Komsomolskaya Station, where he quickly exited.

The Moscow Metro system in general, and Komsomolskaya Station in particular, best demonstrated how aberrations could appear in Russia where one least expected them. While New York City's subways are best known for their grime, graffiti, and vigilantes, Komsomolskaya Station looked like a grand opera house transplanted underground. It was clean as a hound's tooth. A string of elaborate chandeliers hung from marbled archways, illuminating frescoes and intricate mosaics that depicted scenes from Russian history. It was a spellbinding scene for those who experienced it for the first time. Shevetchenko, however, was not a newcomer; and he paid little attention to the artwork as he took the escalator up to ground level.

Pulling his coat close around him to keep out the cold, he made his way north through Sokolniki Park, which was deserted except for some skaters on the park's main pond. Walking slowly through the grounds, he paused now and again to carefully check his rear. Anyone following him would be revealed in the open, snowpacked spaces. Satisfied he was alone, he exited the park and walked over a small bridge that spanned the frozen Jauza River. The term *river* was perhaps a bit grandiose. In reality, the Jauza was a minor tributary stream that fed into the larger Moskva River. He walked a couple of blocks farther, then turned around to retrace his steps and recross the bridge. He stopped by the wooden sign that declared REKA JAUZA, and took some time to scan the area once again. Nothing. From his pocket he extracted a simple white thumbtack and pushed it into the bottom right-hand corner of the wooden sign. Hastily he left the area in search of a café and warm tea.

Nightfall was quickly approaching.

Day 2, 1338 Hours Zulu, 6:38 A.M. Local
CHEYENNE MOUNTAIN

Lamborghini gently tapped the big man's shoulder.
"General?"

Whittenberg awoke, and blinked a few times to get his bearings. He looked around the conference room, then up at the colonel. "Thanks, Pete. How long was I out?"

"A little over an hour, sir."

"What time is it?"

"Zero-six-thirty-eight, sir."

Whittenberg rubbed his eyes. "You wouldn't wake me without a reason. What's the word?"

"Bad news, sir. The results of the Blackbird flyby just came in from NSA. They definitely confirm a transmission between the *Intrepid* and a Russian earth station."

Whittenberg brought his giant fist down on the table and spat, "*Dammit!*"

"Yes, sir," agreed Lamborghini in a weary voice. "The Blackbird almost got its ass shot off in the process, too, but made it out okay."

That cooled off the CinC as he murmured, "Hmmm. Remind me to send a personal note to General Dooley. I owe him one for that. . . . Is everyone here?" Bleary-eyed officers were filing back into the conference room. Uniforms were rumpled by now, and faces unshaven. "Everybody get some coffee and sit down. We've got to sort this thing out in a hurry."

Cups were filled and seats taken.

"All right, we have an unbelievable, unprecedented situation here," lamented Whittenberg. "I don't know how it happened and neither do you; but it's real, it's deadly serious, and we have to keep our wits and deal with it. Let's take it one step at a time. Intel, give us a recap of where we are."

Lamborghini didn't go to the lectern, but remained seated at the table. "Sir, we have definite confirmation of a secure voice transmission between the *Intrepid* and a Russian Orbita earth station receiver at Perm. Yet the spacecraft has refused to respond to any of our own transmissions—on any frequency. We have reviewed the service records of Kapuscinski, Mulcahey, and Rodriquez, and have found nothing anomalous to indicate they would singly, or collectively, do something like this. In fact, their records are unusual in that they're virtually devoid of any black marks. The orbit pattern of the *Intrepid* has not changed, and the spacecraft has gone past its first reentry window for a touchdown at the Baikonur Cosmodrome shuttle runway—and this brings up a tough question. If the *Intrepid* is indeed trying to defect, then why hasn't it attempted reentry for a landing at Baikonur?"

"I grant you that the spacecraft has gone past the reentry window," concurred Whittenberg, "but even so, if it's not a defection, what else could explain the *Intrepid*'s scrambled radio transmissions over Perm?"

No one had an answer.

"Very well, then," said the CinC. "Regardless of its passby of Baikonur, we have to assume the worst—that the *Intrepid* is indeed a defector. In just a little while I'm going to have to place a conference call to Admiral Bergstrom and the Secretary of Defense and brief them on the situation. They're going to ask me for a proposal on how we respond to this. What do we do?"

There was a prolonged silence.

Lydia Strand, Lamborghini's deputy, absently felt the clasp on the back of her head to make sure her long, dark hair was up in place before saying, "Sir?"

"Yes, Major," said Whittenberg.

"I agree that the *Intrepid* must definitely have gone over. I mean, there simply is no other explanation for its behavior. Now if we take that premise as a given, it means there has to be a *reason* why it passed up Baikonur on its first go-around."

"And the reason?" asked Sir Isaac as he stoked up his pipe.

Strand cocked her head to one side. "I think it can only mean that the *Intrepid* is either damaged or the controlling party is not a pilot—which would mean it was Rodriquez."

"And?" prompted Sir Isaac again. He was following her train of thought.

"If the shuttle is damaged, or if the controlling party is unable to fly the spacecraft through reentry, then the Russians would have to send someone up to repair it or fly it down, or maybe send up one of their own shuttles and transfer the payload to it. Whatever the case—"

"They would have a launch vehicle on the pad ready to go, or would be hastily assembling one. Maybe as we speak." Sir Isaac finished the thought for her, then looked at Lamborghini. "Colonel?"

The intel chief picked up the baton. "We get every Keyhole satellite we have to start eyeballing their launch facilities, pronto—right, sir?"

"Right," said Whittenberg. "Tell SPADOC we want passes over Baikonur, Plesetsk, and Kapustin Yar, ASAP. Tell them to change orbits if need be and not to spare the fuel. Go make sure they get it right. Now."

Lamborghini nodded and left the room.

"Any other thoughts, Major?" asked Whittenberg.

Strand furrowed her brow. "It's imperative we get to the *Intrepid* before the Russians do. And whoever we send up should have the means to prevent the *Intrepid* from falling into Soviet hands."

"You mean, if we send the *Constellation* up after *Intrepid*, the *Constellation* should be able to shoot down or disable her?" asked Michael Dowd, the chief of staff.

"Yes, sir," replied Strand.

"Well, that's just charming. Real charming." The veins on Dowd's neck started to stick out. "The last time I checked I didn't see any air-to-air missiles mounted under the *Constellation*'s wing. What are we going to do? Send the *Constellation* on a ramming mission? If we do, that leaves three astronauts marooned in orbit with no way of getting them down. Plus we blow up a cool seven or eight billion dollars' worth of equipment in the process. And you can forget about an antisatellite missile. Our farsighted President saw fit to send those to the shredder a year ago!"

Whittenberg reached over and gently patted his chief of staff's ham-hock shoulder. "Take it easy, Bull. All of us are wound up pretty tight over this thing. Rest easy. I need you."

Dowd sighed. "Yes, sir. You're right. I'm sorry. And I apologize to you, Major. I hope you know I wasn't sniping at you personally."

"Yes, sir," replied Strand sympathetically.

"It's just, well, the *Constellation* has no armament, we can't ask the pilots to go on a kamikaze mission, we have no ASATs, the SDI platform isn't armed yet. We're just flat on our ass. And I feel like we're being played for some kind of suckers—that part especially I just *don't like.*"

Whittenberg leaned back, closed his eyes, and thought carefully before he spoke. "I assume everyone here has an Omega clearance?"

All heads nodded. An Omega clearance was far over and above a Top Secret classification. It was used for only the blackest of the "black," or supersecret, technical programs—such as the Eardrum satellite. The selection of the term *Omega* was not an accident. Since it was the final letter of the Greek alphabet, it signified that whoever leaked Omega material was at the end of his career.

"What about the Kestrel?" asked Whittenberg.

Dowd raised an eyebrow, then instinctively looked around the room. Before answering he focused on Fairchild. "Sir Isaac, has this room been swept?" Which meant electronically inspected for listening devices.

"Yes, Chief," responded Sir Isaac. "Just before the afternoon conference started, as per standard procedures."

Everyone was sensitive about the Kestrel, because not only was the technology hypersecret, its very existence could be construed as a violation of the antisatellite treaty. If some errant Congressman or staffer leaked that to the *New York Times* there would be hell to pay—several times over. So far, there had been no leaks. But now, given the *Intrepid*'s current situation, the ASAT treaty appeared to be a moot issue.

Still, Dowd looked around once more before speaking. "The Kestrel? Sir, that just isn't feasible. Lockheed just delivered the prototype a month ago. It's still going through avionics testing. The weapons systems have never been fired in a space environment. We haven't even conducted full-scale wind-tunnel tests yet."

"Sir Isaac, have all the avionics and weapons systems been installed?" Whittenberg reflected that ninety-eight percent of being a commander was prodding people in a direction they didn't want to go.

Sir Isaac pinched the bridge of his aquiline nose before saying, "Yes, General, they've been physically installed. But as the chief of staff said, there's still a lot of debugging to do. We figured on four more months of avionics/electronics testing at Edwards, then wind-tunnel tests back at Lockheed, then static firing of the weapons from the SDI platform, and probably a dry-run flight before we load on the missiles for a mission test. In all, sir, I think we're a minimum of nine months away from a full all-systems-check ride."

Whittenberg sipped from his cup. "LTV delivered the Phoenix-VII and the new prototype Sidewinders a few weeks ago, didn't they?" He was referring to an updated version of the radar-guided Phoenix missile system used by Navy interceptors and a specially modified model of the infrared-guided Sidewinder air-to-air missile which had been a mainstay of American fighter aircraft since the Vietnam War. Both missiles were manufactured by LTV and had been redesigned to operate in a space environment.

Sir Isaac replied with a very slow "Yes . . . sir."

"Both missiles, in many respects, rely on much of the same technology that has been around for years, right?" queried Whittenberg.

"To a degree, yes, sir."

"Well, I don't like it any more than you do, but we'd better see what we can do in a makeshift way to get the Kestrel up and running. Even so, we have to go ahead and send up the *Constellation*. If nothing else, she could prevent the *Intrepid* from being . . . well, boarded."

Whittenberg's big shoulders drooped and he shook his head. "Lord . . . 'boarded.' I thought piracy was a thing of the past."

His staff said nothing, but they felt a wave of sympathy for their CinC.

Whittenberg mentally shook and refocused himself. "Okay, I'll call Admiral Bergstrom and the Secretary and tell them it is our opinion the *Intrepid* has definitely defected, and we're sending up the *Constellation* to try to prevent the spacecraft from falling into Russian hands. In the meantime, we'll see what we can do with the Kestrel prototype to use it as a backup if need be. Bull, you get the honors of calling Chet at the Cape and informing him that the *Intrepid* has defected. I know he was busy getting the *Constellation* ready for launch, and I didn't want to spring this on him until we were sure, but he's got to know right away. Tell him to stay on top of the *Constellation* preparations and crank up the Kestrel's flight crew."

"Yes, sir," replied Dowd.

Whittenberg turned to Fairchild, his one-man brain trust. "Sir Isaac, I want you to get cracking on the Kestrel prototype. Crank up the LTV engineers and see if we can put something together for a possible launch. Anything you need, say the word."

The hawk-nosed brigadier ran a cleaner into his meerschaum pipe. "Roger, sir. And I have an idea that may allow us to put some armament on the *Constellation*. But I have to check a couple of things first."

"Do it," ordered the CinC. "Major Strand, I want you to tear the service records of Kapuscinski, Mulcahey, and Rodriquez to pieces. Go back to square one. Take nothing for granted. Talk to anyone you need to, but keep the purpose under wraps. Use your own staff people, or call in CID or FBI to help you. I want to know who the hell this defector is."

"Yes, sir," replied the brunette major tentatively. "But I'm really not any kind of trained investigator."

"Granted. But you know these three men better than anyone here. Bringing someone in from the outside to head up an investigation and getting him briefed would take too much time. And time is something we have very little of at the moment."

"But what about Colonel Lamborghini?" she asked.

"I have a feeling," Whittenberg sighed, "I'm going to Washington. And he's coming with me."

Back in his office, Whittenberg once again picked up the green phone that was a direct secure line to the Chief of the General Staff of the United States Armed Forces. It rang once. "Bergstrom," came the reply.

"Yes, Admiral, it's Whittenberg at SPACECOM. Would you patch the Secretary in on this line? I have something to tell both of you."

"Hold on." There were a few buzzes and peeps before another voice came on the line. Whittenberg methodically went through the results of the SR-71 flyby and what SPACECOM planned to do to recapture the *Intrepid*. There was a prolonged silence before the Secretary spoke in his aristocratic Southern drawl.

"Well, General, this is definitely going to require the President's attention. I think you'd better come to Washington and bring the pertinent data with you. I'll call the White House and get a meeting of the National Security Council convened. This thing is incredible. Who the hell knows where it might lead? Maybe this is only a part of some kind of subversive plot. Maybe it's the prelude to an attack of some sort."

"I've got NORAD at full alert status," said Whittenberg. "SAC is at DEFCON Four. I wouldn't recommend going to DEFCON Three with them until we have a better handle on things. It might tip our hand."

"Agreed," said the Secretary.

"Do as the Secretary said, Rodg," ordered the Admiral. "Get your information together and hightail it to Washington by the fastest conveyance possible."

"Yes, sir. I'll be leaving Cheyenne Mountain in a few hours, as soon as I get some updated satellite pix in."

"Hmmm." Bergstrom's voice took on a guarded tone. "Since the payload was so critical on this mission, maybe we'd better get Havelichek and Sharp out here, too. I'm sure there's going to be some questions about the severity of any potential loss, and they can field the questions better than anyone I've got in the Pentagon."

Whittenberg winced at the words *potential loss*, but he agreed. "Yes, sir. Will you arrange for their transport?"

"They'll probably beat you here."

Day 2, 1500 Hours Zulu, 10:00 A.M. Local
KENNEDY SPACE CENTER

Maj. Gen. Chester McCormack leaned back in his office chair. Although he was fifty-two, his blond hair showed not so much as a hint of gray. He was still trim as a board and, as the phrase goes, "rakishly handsome.'' So handsome, in fact, that early in his career he'd taken a lot of guff for being the model in an Air Force recruiting poster. But the pretty face concealed a hard-nosed general who prized discipline and always liked to be in control.

McCormack was in his office, talking with astronauts Phillip Heitmann and Jack Townsend about the procedures they would use on their rescue mission to the *Intrepid*. Also present was Maj. Sandford Watkins, who would be the extravehicular specialist on the mission. Although he was an Army major, the sandy-haired "Sandy" Watkins was able to serve in SPACECOM because it was a "unified command," meaning it drew on all three branches of the armed forces for its people. Watkins had a Ph.D. in mechanical engineering from Texas A&M and had designed some modifications to the manned maneuvering unit backpack. His technical credentials and gymnast's body made him eminently qualified to handle the EVA.

"Okay," said McCormack, "loop around it at six hundred meters for an initial visual, then come in to about three hundred meters and see if you can signal with a beacon from the *Constellation*. If you get no response, suit up Sandy and send him over for a look-see. Remember, though, I want a minimum of three hundred meters separation at all times. Maybe their fuel cells conked out and they have an O-two leak. Who knows? But I don't want to take a chance of damaging the *Constellation* if *Intrepid* blows up for whatever reason. So keep the distance."

"Roger, General," responded Heitmann, the mission commander. "No problem. We'll be careful. What I'm concerned about is this polar launch over Florida. There's gonna be a lot of flak about that."

"No doubt. But that's a decision a little ole two-star like myself won't be making. You guys just worry about bringing whoever's left back alive."

Heitmann nodded. "Yes, sir. All I can say is that the *Intrepid* must've had a technical glitch of some kind. With Iceberg up there you can rule out pilot error altogether."

"No argument there," concurred the general.

The phone rang and McCormack answered. It was Dowd, the SPACECOM chief of staff, on the other end. "Yes, Bull, I'm just going over things with the crew now. . . . Okay, hang on a second." McCormack punched some buttons on a keypad recessed into the side of his phone. "All right, can you hear me okay? . . .This scrambler has always given me problems. . . . Yes . . . yes . . . go on. . . .''

There was a prolonged silence. The shuttle crewmen were reviewing their flight plan notes when Watkins looked up and noticed McCormack's tanned complexion had assumed a deathly pallor.

The general said nothing, but continued to listen to the chief of staff. Finally, after some minutes, he silently hung up the phone. By this time all three men had taken notice that McCormack's face had turned ashen.

"Uh, General?" queried Townsend. "Anything wrong?"

Some seconds elapsed before McCormack could find his voice. With a croak, he said, "There's been a change in plans."

Jacob Classen's slender frame heaved a sigh of relief as the payload canister holding the Anik satellite and COSMAX telescope was finally secured to its transporter. It had been a long and tiresome exercise to transfer the delicate instruments from the *Constellation* to the gantry, to the payload canister, and finally onto the transporter; but the unloading was finally over with, and now maybe he could grab a little nap.

The driver of the payload transporter fired up the engine and started backing away from the rotating gantry superstructure with the vehicle's "creep" mode. The bizarre flatbed transporter with forty-eight wheels could travel forward, backward, sideways, or pirouette on its own axis if need be. But right now it was simply inching away from the superstructure at 0.014 mph. Once clear of the gantry tower, it would rev up its engine and drive off toward the payload processing building at a thunderous 2 mph.

Classen took off his hard hat and ran a hand through his white hair. He handed his preflight clipboard to his deputy, then headed for the service trailer and his cot. He had always promised himself not to be a victim of the proverb "Tired men make mistakes."

Day 2, 1500 Hours Zulu, 5:00 P.M. Local
KALININGRAD FLITE CONTROL CENTRE

"The beauty of the design is its simplicity," crowed Vostov. "The Progress solid-fuel engine will be secured inside of the mating collar prior to launch. All you have to do is insert the 'male' end of the collar into the 'female' center engine nozzle, then install the explosive bolt clamps," he said while pointing at the diagram. "Brilliant, is it not?"

Cosmonauts Lubinin and Yemitov nodded their assent. Popov needn't have worried that Vostov might be uncooperative. The Chief Designer was so effusive about his design creation that the main problem was getting the man to shut up.

114

"You know, of course, I completed this design in a matter of hours, to exacting specifications."

"Yes, Comrade Chief Designer," replied the swarthy Lubinin. "Which brings up an important point. The tolerances on this mating collar must be precise. If the circumference of the collar is too large, it will not fit into the nozzle. If it is too small, the clamps may not reach over the lip of the nozzle. Are you sure about the specifications?"

In a condescending voice, Vostov said, "My dear Lubinin. The Americans are fools. They publish all of their sensitive scientific data widely." Vostov instinctively looked around the conference room, which had been converted into a makeshift drafting room, before speaking. "Our Comrade Chairman of State Security would have you believe his spies are working feverishly to steal away our enemy's precious secrets. Hah! It is often a matter of going into an American bookstore or library for the data. The problem is not too little technical information. It is too much. Look at this," he said, gesturing to a pile of books and documents on the conference table. He extracted one and opened it to a page which showed a cutaway schematic diagram of the American shuttle.

Lubinin and Yemitov looked on and were surprised. Their access to such material was limited, and they were somewhat in awe of the pile of documents on the table. Yemitov's blue eyes blinked as he murmured, "Amazing."

"Yes, amazing," echoed Lubinin. "But if the Americans are such fools, Comrade Chief Designer, why do they have a successful shuttle program, while two of the Rodina's orbiters have burned into cinders during reentry?"

Vostov's ebullience vanished. He looked at Lubinin carefully, detecting a steely character behind the friendly round face and brown eyes. Apparently this cosmonaut was not one to be trifled with. "I was allowed to examine your service record," the Chief Designer said cautiously. "You flew combat missions in Afghanistan, is that not so?"

"*Da*," replied Lubinin.

"It also reported you shot down two Pakistani F-16s, I believe."

Lubinin shrugged his muscular shoulders. "*Da*. They said we violated their airspace. We charged them with violating Afghan airspace. To tell the truth, I cannot say who violated what. I was too busy dodging their Sidewinder missiles to pay attention to navigational matters. In any case, it taught me to respect American equipment."

The overweight Vostov nodded his understanding. "You know, I had nothing to do with our shuttle's airframe design, and I have not a clue as to what caused their destruction. I was only recently given authority over the entire program."

"Yes, Comrade Chief Designer," said Lubinin in an understanding voice, "I know this. But the engineers who designed our shuttle obviously had access to this mountain of data, and still it failed. In view of this, you can understand my concern about precise specifications?"

In an uncharacteristic human gesture, the Chief Designer put his arm around the cosmonaut. "I understand, Comrade. And Vostov shall not fail you."

"That is comforting, Comrade Chief Designer. Now then. Two questions. First, how do we trigger the engine?"

It was back to business. Vostov said, "You will be given a remote-control triggering device to ignite the solid-fuel motor. You will have to be in EVA and outside the Soyuz capsule to make sure it works, because the remote transmitter is small and emits a weak line-of-sight signal. You will have to trigger it. The American astronaut cannot. You also must communicate with the American about the precise timing and inclination of the firing angle. I assume that is why the two of you were selected. You both speak English, do you not?"

Lubinin nodded, then asked, "Where do we go from here?"

"I will take the drawings to Leningrad and have the collar cast," replied Vostov in a businesslike voice. "Popov is having the launch vehicles prepared at Baikonur, and the collar will be shipped there as soon as it is completed. When it arrives I will personally supervise the welding of the collar to the Progress engine. We will meet again at the cosmodrome."

Day 2, 1630 Hours Zulu, 8:30 A.M. Local
LAWRENCE LIVERMORE LABORATORY, CALIFORNIA

"Boosters breaking through cloud cover. . . . Initial launch detection profile indicates twenty-three vehicles and increasing. Time to impact of lead missile elements is twenty-eight minutes, twenty-three seconds. . . . Infrared and velocity analysis define elements as SS-11, SS-18, and SS-19 booster vehicles . . . missile count now eighty-seven and increasing rapidly. . . . Time to impact of lead elements is twenty-seven forty-two."

Thomas Havelichek scratched his dark red beard while watching a bird's-eye view of the northern hemisphere on the custom-designed thirty-inch color monitor. Out of the Soviet Union a forest of white pencil lights, representing intercontinental ballistic missiles (ICBMs), were arcing northward toward the Arctic Circle. Beyond the polar ice cap lay their targets in North America.

Havelichek could have superimposed the numeric attack data onto his screen, but he felt it distracted his attention from the graphic display. Instead, his assistant read out the flight profile data on the attacking missiles, while he operated the SDI platform's fire-control systems. "Okay, Gilda," he said, while tapping his keyboard, "reactor power to ninety-three percent. . . . Target acquisition and prioritization initialized. Isotope is charging . . ."

Gilda's voice was acerbic, like the quintessential Jewish mother she was. "Time to impact now twenty-five minutes, fifty-seven seconds, vehicle count two-one-four and still increasing . . . initial booster separation of lead missiles should begin within thirty seconds . . ."

The pencil shafts of light continued northward, approaching the Siberian coast.

"Target prioritization complete . . . isotope is charging . . . will initiate pulse on lead elements. . ."

"Vehicle count at three-two-seven . . . still increasing . . . lead elements have booster separation . . . second-stage failure on three vehicles . . . lead missile elements have entered exoatmosphere. . . . Time to impact twenty-three minutes, sixteen seconds." Gilda, with her pear-shaped body and ink-black curly hair, peered over her half-moon glasses and said, "You'd better move your ass, Thomas."

Havelichek's narrow face was transfixed on the screen as he kept tapping the keyboard. "Relax, Gilda. We've got another four minutes of postboost left. Besides, no sense firing unless we have a bunch of them in the exoatmosphere phase . . . reconfirming acquisition and tracking . . . isotope is energized."

"Time to impact twenty-two minutes, thirty-two seconds," said the Jewish mother.

"Auto systems engaged. . . . Graser pulse at full power. Commence firing!"

On the screen another light beam—this one bigger and bright red—originated above Severnaya Zemlya island on the northern Siberian coast and began intersecting the leading edge of the white pencil lights, taking out ten to fifteen ICBMs with each pulse. After disposing of the lead elements, the red beam began working its way down the pencil-light forest.

Gilda watched her screen. "Eighty-three kills and climbing." With each "kill" the deceased white pencil light disappeared from the screen. "Uh-oh. Launch detection! FBB! Looks like SS-30s."

FBB was the acronym for "fast-burn booster," a rocket that burned super-efficient propellants and could halve the time of a typical ICBM's boost and postboost phase. The distinctive infrared signature —caused by a bigger and brighter exhaust plume—and greater velocity made FBBs easy to identify. But because of their speed, the SDI platform's battle management computer had to reprioritize the sequence of targets. Otherwise, one of the FBBs could slip by while the Graser beam was engaging slower targets.

"Target priority is adjusting," said Havelichek. The Graser beam stopped momentarily. "Isotope recharging."

"Lead missile wave is destroyed. Time to impact of new lead elements has been rolled back to twenty-four minutes, twenty-two seconds, but FBBs are moving up. Vehicle count now four-one-four." Gilda peered over her half-moon glasses again. "Isn't he clever? Slipping in the FBBs during an isotope recharge."

"Oh, yeah. Clever as hell," responded Havelichek, while rubbing his high forehead. "His timing is a little off, though. He should've launched them a bit sooner. . . . Recharge complete. Graser at full pulse power. Commence firing."

Again the red beam began zapping the white pencils; but after being zapped, one pencil beam continued toward the Arctic ice cap. Havelichek turned to his assistant. "Hey, what's the deal? I thought I nailed that one."

Gilda checked her screen. "No, Thomas. You nailed the first stage of an FBB just *after* it separated." She turned to him. "So sorry. You're doing well, though. Kill count is up to one-seven-four."

He pursed his lips. "Recharging."

"Except for the one you missed, time to impact of new lead missile elements is now twenty-three minutes, fifty-two seconds. . . . Oops! Submarine missile launch detection." She studied the readout. "South of Bermuda in the Atlantic . . . four ballistic missiles. Bearing appears to be headed for . . . Washington. Impact time just over seven minutes. Looks like they're out of range for our platform."

Havelichek leaned back and smiled. "Look again." From above Newfoundland another red beam appeared and zapped the four ballistic pencil beams climbing out of the Atlantic.

Gilda scanned her clipboard with a puzzled expression. "I don't see a second platform on the defensive elements list."

Havelichek grinned. "You don't see a submarine launch on the offensive elements, either."

Gilda stared at him for a few moments, then understood—and giggled. "You are sooooo sneaky. When did you insert it?"

"Last night," replied Havelichek. "That's why I wanted to run the exercise early this morning, before Buford had a chance to recheck the program."

The red beam over the Siberian coast continued zapping the Russian ICBMs with astonishing speed until all were erased from the screen.

"Exercise concluded," announced Gilda. "Five hundred forty-three kills and one miss that impacted." She inspected her screen. "It appears Detroit has been totally wiped out."

Havelichek shrugged. "Doesn't bother me. I drive a Mazda."

Just then the door burst open, revealing an ogre with cauliflower ears, who looked as if he'd once played defensive tackle for the Rams. He was puffing and pawing like a fighting bull. "And just where the hell did that second platform come from?"

Havelichek greeted the ogre with a friendly smile. "Welllll, good morning, Buford."

The man's temple artery was pulsating against his scarlet face. He appeared on the edge of blind rage. "Don't 'good morning' me! I want to know where the hell that damn platform came from!"

The exchange was taking place in the Conflict Simulation Center of Lawrence Livermore Laboratory, a facility which enabled scientists to simulate combat conditions in a computer environment. An offensive tactician would sit in one room while a defensive tactician would sit in another, and they would play out a battle scenario in a simulation powered by Livermore's Computing Center. The exercises often resembled a highly sophisticated chess match. Havelichek—and his nemesis Buford—had just finished a simulated nuclear ICBM attack on the United States. Buford was in charge of the offensive Russian missile strategy, while Havelichek played defender with the Graser weaponry aboard the SDI platform.

"Well, Buford," recalled Havelichek casually, "yesterday morning I read the battle scenario memo you sent me and I didn't see anything programmed in on a submarine launch." Buford seemed to deflate a little. "So, seeing how things were a little slow yesterday afternoon, I thought I'd check out the battle program, and lo and behold, would you believe somebody—I have no idea who—dropped in a Russkie

Typhoon-class sub off the Bermuda coast. Well, figuring fair was fair, I programmed in an extra space platform late last night.''

Buford tried to regain his lost momentum. "You can't expect an attack to go by strict parameters. There's always going to be an element of surprise.''

Havelichek's narrow face broke into a wide grin. "I guess that's fine, just as long as you're not the one being surprised. Right, Bu?''

Buford blew a gasket. "Listen, Buster! I had an Assistant Secretary of Defense observing in the other simulator. You made me look like a fool!''

Havelichek sighed. "You don't need *me* to make you look like a fool, Buford.''

With that, Buford emitted a little choking sound, spun on his heel, and slammed the door.

Gilda adjusted her glasses. "You were a little hard on him, weren't you?''

He shrugged. "I dunno. Maybe so. He's ridden my ass ever since I came to this place. Basically, he's just a bully. And it's gotten worse over the last six months.'' Havelichek was thirty-two. Buford was fifty-two. Everyone at Livermore knew that within another year or so Havelichek would be Buford's boss, and Buford wasn't coping very well. He took cheap shots at the younger man every chance he got, but Havelichek always seemed to stay one step ahead.

Havelichek was Assistant Director for Computing Sciences, Lawrence Livermore Laboratory, attached to the Strategic Defense Initiative Group. A child prodigy mathematics whiz and a computer science Ph.D. from Stanford at age twenty-three, he'd spent his entire career at Livermore and was the chief technical guru for the SDI's battle management system. It was his revolutionary design in computer technology and artificial intelligence that made operating the platform feasible. To stop a ballistic missile attack, the amount of information that had to be handled was so vast and the time required to process the data was so compressed that conventional computers—even Cray supercomputers—were woefully inadequate for the task. Havelichek had designed the revolutionary PRISM battle management computer, and it was his team who brought it to fruition. It was a foregone conclusion around Livermore that he'd be named Director of Computing Sciences for the entire laboratory before too long.

The door opened again. This time it was a petite blonde.

"Dr. Havelichek?''

"Yes, Ginny.''

"Dr. Waverly wants to see you in his office at once. He emphasized the 'at once.' " Waverly was Livermore's executive director.

Havelichek looked at Gilda, and both shrugged. He said, "Okay. Tell him I'm on my way."

He told Gilda they'd get together after lunch, then walked out of the simulation building toward the headquarters complex. Havelichek possessed a slender, somewhat frail-looking torso, but his trousers concealed a pair of legs that were strong as pistons. That was because his passion was cycling, and he routinely racked up 150 miles on his Peugeot ten-speed every week. Those legs now carried him swiftly across the campus.

The Livermore Laboratory was a sprawling hodgepodge of office and warehouse-type buildings that probably held the largest concentration of hard-science Ph.D.s in the world. Established in 1952 and operated jointly by the University of California and the Department of Energy, Livermore was established with one express purpose—research in and development of nuclear weapons.

Since its founding, however, the laboratory had grown and expanded to embrace a mind-numbing range of scientific and defense projects, from laser fusion to biomedical research to artificial intelligence. The computer center alone linked up four thousand personal computers and nine Cray supercomputers throughout the complex in a network called LABNET. If you went to lunch in any of the laboratory's cafeterias you'd hear conversations about plasma physics, laser isotope separation, tandem mirror fusion, kilospud spectroscopy, aerojel, and multimegajoules rather than talk about the Rams and the Giants.

The centerpiece of Livermore, however, had become Star Wars. And Havelichek was one of its two key players. The other key player was waiting in Waverly's office when he arrived.

"Oh, hi, Garrett," said Havelichek as he entered the executive director's office. Sitting there was Garrett ("Don't call me Gary") Sharp—the inventor of the Graser. At thirty-two, Havelichek was the old man of the pair. Sharp was twenty-nine years old. The younger scientist also had a beard and was of medium build, but unlike the eagle-eyed Havelichek, Sharp wore an incredibly thick pair of trifocal glasses.

"You wanted to see me, sir?" Havelichek asked Waverly.

"Yes, both of you," said the portly Waverly from behind his desk. "I know this is unexpected, but you boys are going to Washington today."

The two scientists looked a little surprised. "What for?" asked Sharp.

"Beats me," said Waverly while tossing down a candy from the bowl on his desk. "All I know is that I just got off the phone with the DOE Secretary, and he said to get the two of you to D.C. fast. Very fast."

Havelichek's curiosity was aroused. "Okay. I've got a grip packed in my office. I'll have Gilda call TWA—"

He was interrupted by the *whop-whop-whop-whop* of rotor blades cutting through the air. Out the window they could see a giant Sikorsky Sea King helicopter descending on the helipad near the headquarters building. On the side of the aircraft was painted U.S. NAVY.

"You can forget the grip!" shouted Waverly over the noise. "I was just told to put you two on that helicopter—now!"

Day 2, 1630 Hours Zulu, 8:30 A.M. Local
EDWARDS AIR FORCE BASE, CALIFORNIA

The ringing pierced his unconscious like a cold ice pick, triggering waves of stupefying pain that were vicious in their intensity. He pulled the pillow tight around his head, but the ringing was like a persistent jackhammer, refusing to stop its pounding salvos. From the depths of an Olympian alcoholic haze, his hand reached out and pushed the phone off the bedside table, causing a crash and jingle that were too loud to bear. Enraged by the noise, he groped for the receiver, and with all the consciousness he could muster, a demand poured from his lips: "Who the fuck is this?"

The response was not long in coming.

"This is fucking Major General Chester McCormack! Is that you, Monaghan?"

Throughout his naval career, Cmdr. Leroy Monaghan had employed a vast array of instant hangover cures—black coffee, hot and cold showers, a shot glass of clam juice, and the like. One Filipino madam told him a drop of lighter fluid on the back of the tongue worked wonders. He tried them all with varying degrees of success, but he never remembered anything quite so efficacious as a pissed-off major general on the line. He sat up at attention and stammered, "Uh, yes, sir . . . sorry, sir. Didn't know it was you, sir. It's just that, well, I was off today, sir, and wasn't expecting—"

"Save it, Monaghan. You're back *on* duty. Get your butt cranked up and get over to the hangar, then call me back on a secure line. I'm at my office at the Cape. Get hold of Barnes and have him meet you there."

"Uh, yes, sir. But, uh, what is this all about?"

"Didn't they teach you anything about COMSEC in the Navy? Just move it, Monaghan. My secure phone had better ring within thirty minutes."

The connection was terminated.

Into the dead line Monaghan said, "Yes, fucking General, sir," and saluted. Then he collapsed back on the bed as the hangover rolled over him like a leaden ocean wave. "Uhhhhhhhh, Jeeeesuuuusss." The elixir of the instant cure had abruptly failed him.

The previous night a retirement party had been held for an outgoing warrant officer at the Edwards officers club—which, of course, degenerated into an interservice drinking bout between the Air Force retiree and Monaghan. After consuming beer, martinis, Singapore Slings, Boilermakers, Southern Comfort, Black Russians, Cutty Sark, White Russians, Amaretto, Irish whiskey, Courvoisier, Moët & Chandon champagne, and Wild Turkey, Monaghan had no recollection of who won the contest. Or when or how he got back to his room in the bachelor officers quarters. The alcohol consumption the previous night had been staggering. Even for him.

But the yoke of duty called. He slipped down to the floor and pulled his address book off the bedside table. When his bloodshot brown eyes were finally able to focus, he found the number he was looking for and groggily punched it in. After two rings there was an answer.

"Hello?"

A pause.

"Davey . . . this is . . . Mad Dog."

"Oh, hi, Dog. What's happening? I thought we were off today."

To Monaghan the voice on the other end sounded youthful and full of pep. Disgusting. The hungover pilot struggled to form the words. "We were off. Just got a call. We're supposed to go to the hangar right away. . . . Meet you there."

"Darn," said Barnes. "I was gonna work on my cycle today. But okay. I'm on my way. I'll see you there. . . . Say, you don't sound too good. Are you okay?"

"No," mumbled Mad Dog, "I'm not," and he hung up the phone. The trip to the bathroom was painful beyond anything he could recall in recent memory. He filled the washbasin with cold water and submerged his head for some minutes before coming up for air to greet his own image in the mirror. Strands of red hair were plastered against his rough features. He might have been a hockey goalie who'd stopped too many pucks with his face. "Leroy Monaghan, Commander, United States Navy," he muttered to himself. "Just how the fuck did you wind up in the middle of the fucking California desert with a bunch of fucking air craps?" Not waiting for an answer, he resubmerged himself before stepping into the shower.

Monaghan's route to Edwards had been circuitous indeed. When the Kestrel project developed steam, Whittenberg decided to cast out for a Navy or Marine pilot to groom as chief test jockey for the prototype. In a quirk of timing, Whittenberg's request for pilot candidates hit the desk of Vice Admiral "Dixie" Creighton, Commandant, U.S. Naval Air Test Center at Patuxent River, Maryland, just as the commandant hung up the phone after talking with his wife. Admiral Creighton's spouse had informed her husband that their eldest daughter had been seen sneaking out of the BOQ room of a certain Commander Monaghan in the wee small hours that very same morning.

Within the week, Creighton had Monaghan's orders cut for SPACE-COM, and he was sent across the continent to Edwards and the Kestrel project—much to the delight of the commandant and his wife, and to the chagrin of their daughter. It took her an entire week to find another pilot to bed down with.

Stumbling out of the shower, Monaghan didn't bother to shave. He pulled on his flight suit and wobbled out the door to his Porsche 944.

Air Force Capt. Davey Barnes buckled the chin strap on his crash helmet and fired up his brand-new Honda 500cc Interceptor motorcycle. Next to an F-16, he thought the cycle was the most fun you could have with your clothes on. He dropped it into gear and took off.

Barnes lived off base in an apartment in the town of Lancaster. His route to work involved weaving through some side streets before getting on the main highway that led to Edwards. He approached an intersection without slowing down because, having traveled through it almost every day, he knew the cross street had a stop sign and he had the right of way. What he didn't know was that the driver of an approaching station wagon had dropped a lighted cigarette between his legs and was searching frantically for it when he barreled past the stop sign and into the intersection. There was a skidding-crashing-scraping sound as the station wagon clipped the front wheel of the cycle. Barnes was pitched up in the air and did a lazy somersault over

the hood of the car before coming down on his left leg with a
sickening *crack*.

Day 2, 1800 Hours Zulu, 11:00 A.M. Local
CHEYENNE MOUNTAIN

Maj. Lydia Strand set down her coffee cup and once again stared at
the three personnel files in front of her. Each one was crammed with
evaluations, biographical data, old addresses, transfer orders, and the
mélange of paperwork that military people accumulate during their
careers. She'd gone through each file three separate times looking for
some clue that would tell her which crewman on the *Intrepid* was a
traitor. Sitting alone in the conference room, she felt more perplexed
than ever. Her lack of experience as an investigator left her with
nothing but her own common sense and intellect to guide an inquiry
into the lives of Kapuscinski, Mulcahey, and Rodriquez. But the
general had said, "Do it," and that was that.

CM/Sgt. Tim Kelly walked in with a fresh pack of cigarettes. He'd
been briefed early that morning on the *Intrepid* affair, and had been
chosen by Strand to help her sort things out. He wasn't an investigator
by trade, either, but had been in the intelligence field for seventeen
years of his thirty-year hitch. He was built like a fireplug, and the crew
cut on his bullet-shaped head was always trimmed close. Strand had
instinctively liked him from their first encounter in the intel section.

"Any leads?" he asked.

Strand tapped the files and sighed. She was already red-eyed and
tired. "Nothing. A big zip. Each one picture-perfect. . . . I feel a little
over my head here, but I guess we've got to do the best we can. I talked
with the chief of staff and he agreed it might be good to have some
expert assistance on this. We're supposed to have an FBI agent
assigned to us shortly." She leaned back. "What's your guess?"

The sergeant lit up. "I would say that something like this would
have to be motivated by one of two things. Extortion or ideology."
Kelly gave credence to the truism that senior NCOs ran the armed
services. He didn't have a college degree, but the man was a
self-taught scholar. His quarters were crammed with books on psy-
chology, Russian history and language, Star Wars technology, and
defense strategy. During the Vietnam War he had interrogated North
Vietnamese prisoners and had been on the intelligence crew that
worked on the heartbreaking Son Tay POW rescue mission. After

125

Vietnam he was assigned to the debriefing team which handled Soviet defector Viktor Belenko when he flew his MiG-25 Foxbat fighter to Japan. The CIA had dangled a job in front of Kelly more than once, but he elected to stay with the Air Force.

"Extortion or ideology? How do you mean?" asked Strand.

Kelly played with his lighter and said, "I mean, he's either defecting on his own volition or being forced to do it."

For the next hour they went back and forth over Kelly's thesis, looking for some glimmer of an opening that would lead them to the *Intrepid*'s defector. They enjoyed no success.

Finally, Kelly said, "Okay, what about Kapuscinski? That's Eastern European extraction, isn't it? Maybe he longs to be back with the kinfolk in the old country?"

Strand opened his folder. "Two hundred and twenty-three combat missions in Vietnam, the Distinguished Flying Cross, a Silver Star, and two Purple Hearts. Flew F-105 Thunderchiefs and F-4 Phantoms. He's an ace. Shot down six MiGs. Doesn't sound like a Commie sympathizer to me."

"Me either," Kelly agreed.

"Besides," said Strand, "if you knew Iceberg, you knew his feelings on Vietnam. He was always sorry we hadn't finished the job with nuclear weapons."

Kelly raised an eyebrow.

"Seriously. Also, his parents came from Poland. A rumor circulated among some people at NASA, which I happened to overhear, that his mother had been raped by a gang of Russian soldiers during World War II."

Kelly shook his head. "Christ. We take our safety and security for granted, don't we? Can we talk to the mother? Is she still living?"

Strand looked grim and replied, "No. She was killed during a robbery in Chicago years ago."

Kelly continued toying with his lighter. "What about Rodriquez? He climbed out of the slums in East L.A. Scholarships all the way. Maybe his early poverty instilled some kind of sympathy for a socialist order of some kind?"

Strand thought about that one. Although incredibly bright, Jerry *was* a flaky guy. Didn't care much for a U.S. presence in Central America, she remembered. Flaunted authority sometimes. "Maybe," she said.

The phone rang, and Strand answered. After listening for a few seconds she said, "All right. Bring him to the conference room." She hung up and turned to Kelly. "Our G-man is here."

Shortly thereafter, an Air Police security man escorted the FBI agent into the room. Strand and Kelly looked up . . . and up . . . and up some more. Kelly thought the chief of staff had mistakenly sent them someone from the Chicago Bears.

A huge hand extended and a rough voice said, "Hi. Walt Tedesco. Special agent. FBI Denver office."

Strand and Kelly shook hands carefully—not wanting any fractures —and introduced themselves.

The agent checked out his surroundings. "So, quite a setup you guys have here. I went through half a dozen security checks to get in. I had no idea all this was underground."

Kelly nodded while checking out Tedesco. The Chicago Bears connection had occurred to him because the agent looked like the Bears' head coach, Mike Ditka—widow's peak, mustache, and all. "Yes, sir," said the sergeant. "We don't get many visitors under the mountain."

"Well, I don't mind telling you I was a little flustered to get a call from the Director himself this morning," said Tedesco, "telling me to hightail it down here and report to you people. I've been told to give you whatever assistance you need."

Strand was relieved. "Good. Now then, Agent Tedesco, sit back and relax. I have something to tell you which you simply are not going to believe; but it's important that you do believe it. And quickly."

For the next twenty minutes Strand crisply related the *Intrepid* affair, while Kelly poured coffee and watched the G-man's eyes get bigger and bigger. Finally, when they looked as if they would pop from their sockets, Tedesco bolted out of his chair and began pacing back and forth.

"This is *incredible*! Absolutely *incredible*! It's a thousand times worse than the Walker spy ring. I know. I worked on that case when I was stationed in California." He continued pacing back and forth, like Ditka on the sidelines, working himself up. He stuck out his sledgehammer fist. "Don't you worry, little lady. I'll take it from here. I'll have twenty agents on this case inside of an hour and we'll start ripping apart everything you've got on these people . . ."

Oh, terrific, thought Strand. They had to send me a Mr. Macho.

". . . I promise you by this evening we'll have—"

"No," stated Strand.

Tedesco was knocked off balance. "Pardon?"

"I said no," she repeated.

The agent was stunned. "What the hell do you mean, no? We've got to find out what happened. Did it occur to you there may be more than one person involved? He may have an accomplice right on this base. Under your very nose. We've got to—''

"Agent Tedesco," said Strand firmly, "please listen to me carefully. First of all, I am in charge of this investigation, by order of General Whittenberg. Until you hear otherwise, you are working for me. Secondly, if you unleash your SWAT team and start turning everything topsy-turvy, people are going to start asking questions about why *we're* asking questions. That means the press probably gets involved. If there is an accomplice, I don't want him flushed out before we're ready, and a newspaper story will do that in a second. Additionally, everything we're doing is highly classified. So from this point it's just the three of us. We use our brains and proceed with discretion. We talk only to those people we need to talk to. If there's a screw-up, it's my head, not yours. Now if you have a problem with any of this, just say so. I'll have my boss call your Director and we'll secure a replacement for you without delay.''

The G-man was chastened. He gulped and murmured, "Uh, no . . . I, uh, don't think that will be necessary."

Kelly covered a smile with his hand. The FBI agent wasn't the first man he'd seen the major cut down to size. So much for the young lady's fear about not being up to the task at hand.

Suddenly there was a glimmer of recognition in Tedesco's eyes. "Say, weren't you that woman pilot on the space shuttle a couple of years back? I remember a write-up in *Newsweek*."

"Yes," she acknowledged. "That was me."

As if Strand had passed some litmus test, Tedesco said, "Oh, okay."

"Fine," she replied. "Now then, here are the three personnel files. I want your recommendation on how we should proceed—given the restrictions we face."

With twenty-two years in the bureau, a good chunk of it in counterespionage, Tedesco knew where to start. "After I review the files, we start going backward—in time, that is. We go through their living quarters and look for any physical evidence. Talk to relatives, friends—discreetly, of course. We'll have to develop some type of cover story. Look at bank accounts, credit card accounts—anything that might leave a paper trail to something out of the ordinary. And that means we start wearing out shoe leather."

"All right," agreed the major. "Each of us will take one of the crew. Agent Tedesco, I want—''

"Call me Walt."

"Okay, Walt. You take Rodriquez—that's spelled with a *Q*, not a *G*. I'll get you an office so you can review his file in detail. I guess you could say he looks the shakiest to Tim and me—sorry to say. His quarters are in Houston, though. He was a civilian with NASA. We can arrange for your transportation. Come to think of it, we may need some extra support from your bureau to check out immediate and extended family to make sure they're safe. That could be another facet to our extortion scenario."

The agent nodded. "No problem there. We'll take care of that right away—and be quiet about it, too. I presume family addresses, et cetera, are in these files."

"Correct," she said. "Tim, you take your fellow Irishman, Mulcahey. He lived on base at Peterson. He was the only one with a wife and kids. Maybe you'd better get over there and make sure they're okay. If they are all right, see what you can find out about Frank—in an oblique way. Go easy when you talk to his wife, Katy. On second thought, I know Katy. Maybe I . . ."

"No, Major." This time it was Kelly who was firm. "I know Frank and Katy myself. Not well, but I do know them. I'll be careful."

Strand heaved a sigh of relief. "Thanks, Tim. You'll have to play it by ear on how much to tell her. As Walt said, we'll dream up a detailed cover story later."

"Understood."

Finishing up, Strand said, "I'll take Iceberg. He lived in the BOQ at Peterson."

"Who?" asked the G-man.

"Iceberg—radio call sign for Kapuscinski. Sort of a nickname."

"I see," said Tedesco. "We'll need some warrants, too. I'll take care of those on an *in camera* basis."

"A what basis?" asked the major.

"*In camera.* Lawyer talk for 'secret in the judge's chambers.' " A few moments passed before Tedesco started laughing. "I'd love to see the judge's face when the U.S. Attorney tells him the probable cause on this one."

Day 2, 1930 Hours Zulu, 1:30 P.M. Local
AN F-14 TOMCAT OVER KANSAS

The long black hose began winding into the backside of the KC-135 tanker aircraft, yanking the fuel cone off the Tomcat's intake nozzle.

Navy Lt. Mike "Blackjack" Pershing hit a toggle switch and watched his fighter's small fuel intake arm retract into place at the base of the cockpit canopy. When an F-14 ran on afterburners it consumed fuel at a prodigious rate. It was the Tomcats' second midair refueling on this trip, and they had one more to go before reaching Andrews Air Force Base outside Washington, D.C. It was an unusual way to travel, but it allowed them to finish the transcontinental journey in a little over three hours.

Pershing watched the tanker bank to starboard, then radioed to his wingman in a jocular voice, "We be all full up, Sweet Thang." He raised his left hand to flash a thumbs-up sign.

The wingman raised a thumb in reply. "Roger that, Blackjack. Ready whenever you are."

Pershing hit his intercom switch. "How 'bout you back there? You ready?"

Havelichek was definitely *not* ready. He wished he was back at Livermore shooting down Russkie ICBMs on the computer. After leaving Waverly's office, he and Garrett Sharp had been whisked away by the helicopter to Alameda Naval Air Station in San Francisco Bay, where they'd donned flight pressure suits and been plunked into the backseats of two high-performance interceptors. Next thing they knew, they were streaking across the Great American Desert at Mach 2.

"Say," asked Pershing, starting to become concerned. "You okay back there?"

"Uh . . . yeah, I think so," replied Havelichek in a quavering voice. "It's just . . . I, well, I think we left my stomach back in Oakland."

Pershing laughed. "Hey, don't sweat it, Rice Chek." Havelichek had already been anointed with an aviator call sign. "I'll get you there with all your internal organs intact. The old man said it would be my wings if I screwed up playing taxi on this mission. I don't know who you guys are, but you must be some kinda heavy-duty dudes. I'll bet we're setting a record for prolonged afterburner flight."

"I'm honored to be aboard," replied Rice Chek nervously as he watched the F-14's swing wing rotate into its swept-back position.

Pershing punched his mike button again. "Kansas City Center, this is Tango-Oscar-Mike one-one-four. You have a military flight plan and special clearance for our mission. Request permission to climb to four-seven thousand for supersonic vector on bearing zero-eight-seven, over."

There was a brief pause. "Roger, one-one-four. We have your flight plan. You are cleared and have no traffic in your immediate area except for your KC one-three-five. Over.''

"Thank you, Center. One-one-four, out." Pershing switched to his flight communications frequency. "Okay, Sweet Thang, see you at four-seven thousand on my countdown . . . three . . . two . . . one . . . hit it!''

The afterburners on the fighters kicked in, and the two Tomcats streaked skyward in an 80-degree climb. Havelichek was heard to remark, *"Shhheeeiiit!''*

Day 2, 2003 Hours Zulu, 10:03 P.M. Local
FLITE DATA COMPUTING CENTRE, PLESETSK COSMODROME, CCCP

"An interesting problem," commented Ivan Pirdilenko, the Data Centre director.

"Problem?" There was apprehension in the General Secretary's voice. "Why is there a problem? Our missile can shoot down the American rescue shuttle if it is launched from their Florida cosmodrome. Is that not so?''

Pirdilenko pulled on his Vandyke beard. "Oh, yes, of course. We can certainly do that. But it is my understanding you do not wish to damage the American shuttle—the *Intrepid*, I believe you called it—which is already in orbit. Is that not correct?''

"*Da*," replied the General Secretary.

"Aha," said Pirdilenko. "Therein lies the problem.''

General Secretary Vorontsky was becoming agitated, and his heavy features turned into a scowl. "I do not understand," he confessed.

Having sensed Popov's reluctance to employ the antisatellite weaponry if need be, KGB Chairman Kostiashak had decided it was best not to entrust those preparations to anyone but himself. He prevailed upon the General Secretary to fly with him to the Plesetsk Cosmodrome, where the Russian antisatellite resources had been hidden away from U.N. inspection teams—in violation of the ASAT treaty signed with the Americans. At Plesetsk they tracked down the Data Centre director, a gaunt, spidery man of fifty named Ivan Pirdilenko, who was unimpressed by the lofty status of his two visitors. However, he seemed fascinated by the technical puzzle they'd brought him. It was Pirdilenko and his staff who formulated and programmed the orbital paths of the seventy or so satellites that lifted off from Plesetsk every year. He was also one of the leading authorities on Soviet ASAT technology, having designed the weapon's guidance system.

"It is really quite simple," Pirdilenko observed. "You said the American rescue shuttle would undoubtedly try to rendezvous with the *Intrepid* spacecraft as soon after launch as possible."

The General Secretary nodded.

Pirdilenko rose from his desk, which was surrounded by Kosmos computers and disk drives. "I will explain," he said patiently, then motioned to the KGB chieftain. "What is your name?"

The small man exhaled a puff of Pall Mall smoke. "Kostiashak," he replied.

The Data Centre director sounded like a strict headmaster. "Come over here . . . and put out that cigarette. There is no smoking in the Centre."

Kostiashak obediently crushed out his cigarette and stepped over to Pirdilenko.

"Now then, General Secretary," began Pirdilenko, "this is the problem. Let us say that Kostiashak here is the rescue shuttle launching from Florida." Pirdilenko took several steps back, putting some space between himself and Kostiashak. "Let us further assume that *I* am the *Intrepid*, traveling in orbit at seven kilometers per second. Since the initial lift-off and ascent of the rescue shuttle is relatively slow, Kostiashak must launch *ahead* of me if we are to rendezvous. Otherwise, I will pass him. . . . Once he has launched and we have achieved our rendezvous"—Pirdilenko walked up until he was abreast of the little man—"it will be impossible to destroy the rescue vessel without damaging the *Intrepid* as well. The two spacecraft will be traveling close together, and our antisatellite weapon is not, ah, 'surgical' as the Americans say. It scatters pellets in a wide pattern, and both spacecraft would undoubtedly be hit." The director pulled at his Vandyke beard again. "In order to destroy the rescue vessel without damaging the *Intrepid* spacecraft, we must strike the rescue shuttle *after* it has launched from Florida and is in the ascent phase, but *before* it makes rendezvous with the *Intrepid*—like my example with Kostiashak here. That is a terribly small time window in which to identify, track, launch, and intercept the target . . . and we have never attempted any test that simulates such an occurrence. Now do you understand the problem, General Secretary?"

Vorontsky was not pleased. "I am afraid I do, Comrade."

Pirdilenko continued, "Adding to this problem is the fact that the Americans will undoubtedly launch from their Florida cosmodrome when the *Intrepid*'s orbit intersects their location." The Data Centre director went to a globe on his desk that had a maneuverable ring around it, giving it the appearance of a gyroscope. He placed the ring over Florida in an approximate polar orbit. "That orbit is somewhat out of range of Plesetsk—we would have to wait two, perhaps three, hours until we passed under their orbital path to launch our ASAT missile. By then the two shuttles would have had ample time to achieve their rendezvous."

General Secretary Vorontsky looked shaken, and Kostiashak was wary when he asked, "Are you saying there is no way of stopping the rescue shuttle without destroying the *Intrepid* as well?"

Pirdilenko took off his glasses and cleaned them with the tail of his white laboratory coat. "Ordinarily, yes. But in this case we have an extraordinary advantage. This is not like a game of chess, for we *know* what our opponent's next move will be, and we can anticipate that move to . . . checkmate him, if you will." He replaced his glasses.

The KGB chieftain spoke but one word: "How?"

Pirdilenko seemed unconcerned that lives were at stake. He saw it simply as a technical challenge—like a chess match. He motioned the two men to return to the globe on his desk. "Come closer," he beckoned, and for the next ten minutes he explained in patient detail how his plan would work—how he would spring his checkmate and blow the *Constellation* out of the sky without harming the *Intrepid*. When he finished, the General Secretary was beaming once again.

"Brilliant," proclaimed the former hammer thrower.

Kostiashak nodded agreement.

"Tell us, is there anything you require?" asked the General Secretary. "Anything at all?"

Pirdilenko knew what he needed. "I shall require the orbital data from the Aerospace Defense Warning Centre so I can compute the intercept vectors and program the flite data into the weapon's on-board computer."

Vorontsky was absolutely floating at this point. He'd always been intoxicated with technology. "Amazing. You mean you can actually program a computer that will fly into space and guide this antisatellite weapon?"

Pirdilenko pulled open his desk drawer. "Of course, General Secretary. Actually, we program the flite instructions onto a silicon chip such as this"—he pulled out a sample from the drawer and held it in his hand—"and insert the chip into the on-board circuitry."

Vorontsky smiled, then picked up the computer chip—which was smaller than a kopek—and inspected it reverently. "Incredible," he whispered. "Which one of the Motherland's factories produced this miracle? The Soviet Electronics Institute at Kharkov?''

Pirdilenko shook his head.

Having once been the GOSPLAN Minister, the General Secretary prided himself on his knowledge of Soviet production facilities. "Hmmm. Then it must have come from the Defense Manufacturing Centre at Volgograd.''

Again, Pirdilenko shook his head.

Stumped, the General Secretary asked, ''Then who made this device?''

"Texas Instruments,'' replied Pirdilenko.

"*What?*'' cried Vorontsky.

"*Da,*'' said Pirdilenko clinically. ''We obtain them through a shell company in France. I prefer the semiconductors of Texas Instruments, but when they are not available we use Fujitsu. Those come through another shell company in Singapore.''

As incredible as it might sound, American, European, and Japanese semiconductors could be found in Russian sonobuoys, missiles, ships, and aircraft for the simple reasons that the Soviet product often didn't measure up and many models of Western semiconductors were widely traded on secondary world markets. Even with export restrictions and the cooperation of reputable companies who manufactured the goods, Western governments were powerless to stem the flow of sensitive technology into the Soviet Union via shell companies, subterfuge, and espionage.

But while this technology transfer was frustrating for Western governments, it was a great embarrassment to the General Secretary. Upon learning the point of origin of the semiconductor in his hand, his jowls fell. Throwing the silicon chip down, he said through his teeth, "See that Comrade Pirdilenko gets everything he requires, Vitali.'' Then he stormed from the room.

Kostiashak decided to flout the Data Centre's "no smoking" rule and lit up another Pall Mall. He watched the door close behind the General Secretary before speaking. The KGB chieftain admired confidence and detested arrogance. Pirdilenko had confidence—therefore Kostiashak felt at ease with him. ''I will see that you receive the data from the Aerospace Warning Centre, but do not contact them directly.'' Kostiashak pulled out a card. ''If you require anything, call this number—anytime, day or night—and speak to me personally. Talk to no one about this matter except those who are subordinate to yourself, and be sure that you can rely on their discretion. Is that understood?''

"Ummmm." Pirdilenko's mind seemed to be elsewhere as he continued stroking his Vandyke beard. "Did you say your name was Kostiashak?" he asked absently.

The KGB chieftain nodded.

A few seconds elapsed before Pirdilenko's face brightened. "Of course! I remember now. It was years ago . . . you were a lad of, what? Thirteen? Fourteen? You defeated Berkofsky in the Moscow District semifinals with a brilliant Sicilian Defense."

"And was beaten in the finals by Leskov," added Kostiashak.

"Bah," harrumphed Pirdilenko in dismissal. "Leskov was an old man. He was relying on experience. I remember. I was there. You were the sensation of the tournament. The youngest grandmaster in years. You could have gone on to be Soviet National Champion. Perhaps even world champion. You had the gift. Why did you give it up?"

Kostiashak allowed himself a moment of reflection. "My father was a diplomat. We moved abroad, and I developed . . . other interests."

Pirdilenko sighed. "A pity. We must have a game sometime."

The little man exhaled his smoke slowly. "You do not understand, Comrade Pirdilenko. We are in the grandest game of all."

Day 2, 2130 Hours Zulu, 4:30 P.M. Local
ANDREWS AIR FORCE BASE, MARYLAND

Peter Lamborghini felt a hum and bump as the landing gear on the T-38 Talon trainer deployed and locked. Whittenberg had the aircraft on approach to runway zero two left at Andrews, while Lamborghini watched the Maryland woodlands from the backseat. The SPACE-COM intelligence officer was unaccustomed to riding in the backseat of a T-38 and didn't like it. But the CinC seemed to take some comfort in being at the controls on this trip, and God knew the man could use a little comfort right now.

Lamborghini looked at the huge lumberjack shoulders framing the canopy in front of him. He'd served under Whittenberg for two years, and it had been the best assignment of his career—even if it didn't involve flying. The giant black man was simply a dream commander. Smart, tough, decisive, fair, and above all he listened to you and acted on the facts you brought him. Lamborghini had known some generals who would've simply rejected the notion of the *Intrepid* communicating with the Russians and coasted along in a fool's paradise. Not Whittenberg. He acted on hard data.

And Lamborghini wasn't beguiled by Whittenberg's sometimes

paternal manner. The man could change into Lord of the Jungle in a split second. Lamborghini remembered his first tour as duty officer in the Space Defense Operations Center. He was sitting in the SPADOC Crow's Nest that overlooked the spacious room when Whittenberg strolled in for a casual visit. There was a rule at SPADOC that when the duty officer picked up the phone, he expected to talk to someone on the other end of the line—at once. Whittenberg picked up the phone and punched a button for a test check with one of the BMEWS radar monitors. The operator was two stations away, conferring with a colleague. After the third buzz, Whittenberg leaned over the Crow's Nest rail and barked, *"Somebody'd better get on that phone!"* The entire mountain reverberated from the intonation, and every spine in SPADOC snapped ramrod straight. He handed the receiver to Lamborghini and said simply, "Never again, Colonel."

In spite of that reprimand, Lamborghini was always grateful he had landed at SPACECOM—although his career path to Cheyenne Mountain wasn't exactly planned.

Peter and his wife, Juliet—a blond, blue-eyed beauty of Norwegian extraction—got married the day after their graduation from the University of Wisconsin. Juliet had stuck by her husband through two tours in Vietnam, reared his daughters, gone through move after move, and endured more banal cocktail parties than she could count. She was also a damn smart lady who had goals of her own. When their daughters were old enough and the family was stationed at Hill Air Force Base in Utah, Juliet Lamborghini enrolled at the University of Utah School of Law. She'd kept her ambitions on the back burner long enough to get her children reared, and now she didn't intend to put her career aside any longer for anyone or anything.

At the same time Juliet obtained her law degree, Peter had been promoted to full colonel and was up for vice commander of an F-16 tactical air wing—the final stepping-stone to his own command of a fighter wing.

The four-star Commander in Chief of the Tactical Air Command (CinCTAC) interviewed Lamborghini at length for the job. Everything was going beautifully, until Peter proudly told CinCTAC that Juliet would soon begin practicing law.

The gorillalike CinCTAC said, "No."

Lamborghini asked, "How come?"

CinCTAC said, "A vice commander's wife has too many responsibilities. Tea parties. Unit picnics. Mother Superior to the junior officers' wives. Things like that. You know. Has to be done.''

Lamborghini protested. "But *I'm* the one who'll be vice commander. Not her. Besides, she's sacrificed enough for my career as it is.''

CinCTAC said, "Sorry. It's nonnegotiable. Take it or leave it.''

For the only time in his life, Peter Lamborghini went into a blind rage. So much adrenaline emptied into his bloodstream that he truly couldn't recall much of his last conversation with the CinCTAC. All he could remember were fragments like "Pigheaded . . . Neanderthal . . . brainless . . . throwback.''

Peter didn't get the vice commander's job.

And the very next day he and Juliet decided to submit his paperwork to retire from the Air Force. She'd practice law and he'd open a flying school, or do something equally benign. It was a bitter end to a gilded Air Force career.

Then he got a phone call from Rodger Whittenberg—inquiring whether Peter and Juliet would be good enough to come down to Colorado Springs for a weekend visit? "I'll send my Sabreliner for you,'' he said.

The Lamborghinis traveled to Colorado, and the weekend was simply a dream. The two couples got along great. After a cookout dinner, Whittenberg drew Peter aside for a private chat. He told Peter SPACECOM had obtained approval for development of a prototype spaceplane fighter. Code name "the Kestrel.'' A Lockheed executive would be project manager, but Whittenberg needed a deputy project manager who would report directly to him at SPACECOM.

"Of course, it would also mean an orientation ride on the shuttle. Are you interested?'' asked the SPACECOM four-star. "I'd heard you weren't happy at TAC.''

"You heard right,'' replied Peter. "But what about my wife?''

"Lovely lady,'' observed Whittenberg. "What about her?''

"She wants to start practicing law,'' said Peter cautiously.

"Fine. My wife's been a teacher for over thirty years. I think it's important for a wife to have her own career.''

A month later Peter and Juliet moved to Colorado Springs. Their eldest daughter transferred to the University of Colorado in Boulder, and their youngest enrolled as a junior in the neighborhood high school. Peter got his orientation ride on the shuttle *Antares*, while Juliet got a job in the litigation division of a Denver law firm. Although her commute back and forth to Denver was a bitch, especially in the winter, Juliet and her husband were as happy as a couple of pigs in slop. It got even better when Whittenberg pulled Peter onto his staff as the assistant intelligence officer, and later promoted him to chief of SPACECOM's intelligence billet. Everything seemed to be clicking on the right cylinders.

Until the *Intrepid* went rogue.

The Talon touched down, and when their speed dropped enough, Whittenberg applied the brakes.

"Nice touchdown, sir," observed Lamborghini.

"Coming from you, Pete, that means something," replied Whittenberg. He radioed the tower for instructions and was told to taxi to the temporary duty hangar by the pilot's lounge.

"What do you make of that?" queried the CinC as he pointed. "A couple of Navy F-14s are parked by the TDY hangar. Wonder what they're doing on Air Force turf."

Lamborghini had spent his time at the Pentagon, too. "In Washington it could be anything. Maybe the Navy's giving a joyride to a couple of Senators."

"Yeah. Maybe so. I've done that a few times myself. . . . Of course, that never compared with the time I got to take up Angie Dickinson for an 'orientation ride.' "

"Are you serious?" asked a disbelieving Lamborghini. "When was that?"

"Back when I was superintendent at the academy. Bob Hope came through with one of his shows and she was in the group. I thought it would be a nice gesture to give her a spin."

"Uh-huh."

"She looked pretty good, even in a pressure suit."

It was one of those intimate moments between superior and subordinate when the lines of authority disappeared and two men communicated on equal terms.

Whittenberg sighed. "I hope you don't mind me laying this briefing assignment on you, Pete. I'll field any questions that come up, but I thought it better to have somebody else grapple with the details."

"No problem, sir."

"You ever met the President?"

"No, sir," recalled Lamborghini. "I met the Vice President a couple of times on his visits to SPACECOM, but never the President."

"Yeah, well, I don't want to sugar-coat it for you," muttered the CinC. "I've briefed the President and Vice President a number of times. If the two of them get their feathers up it's like being caught between a couple of buzz saws. But like I said, I'll handle the questions. Just lay out the situation for them.''

"Yes, sir. I think I'll be able to handle it. I've briefed Admiral Bergstrom before. If I can get by him, the President should be a piece of cake.''

Whittenberg chuckled. "Yeah, he is an old salt, isn't he?''

"Yes, sir.''

"Did you bring the slides?'' It was the third time Whittenberg had asked.

"In my flight grip, sir.''

Whittenberg taxied toward the ground crewman and cut his engines when given the sign. He popped the canopy just as an Air Force captain walked up, saluted smartly, and asked, "General Whittenberg?''

"That's me, son.''

"Please come with me, sir. I've already closed out your flight plan.''

The two men climbed out of the plane, carrying their flight grips. They entered the pilot's lounge and quickly showered off the caked-on perspiration. Besides the cleansing, the shower helped recharge the exhausted men. Also, Whittenberg didn't want to face his Commander in Chief while wearing a flight suit. He felt there was a very good chance this afternoon could be the twilight of his military career, and if he got shot down he was at least going to be in proper uniform.

Following the captain out to the tarmac, they boarded an Army Blackhawk helicopter that was warming up. Upon climbing aboard Whittenberg recognized the other two passengers. "Hello, Dr. Havelichek, Dr. Sharp,'' he said in greeting. "Always nice to see the two of you. I'm sorry it had to be under these circumstances.''

"Good to see you, too, General,'' Havelichek shouted over the growing noise of the rotor blades. "Can you tell us why we're here . . . and where we're going?''

He shouted back, "You'll find out in a few minutes.''

The Blackhawk lifted off, and after it gained altitude, Whittenberg could see the Washington Mall in the distance.

Day 2, 2200 Hours Zulu, 5:00 p.m. Local
THE WHITE HOUSE

The Blackhawk helicopter touched down on the south lawn of the executive mansion, and the foursome of Whittenberg, Lamborghini, Havelichek, and Sharp was escorted off the aircraft by the Air Force captain. They were led to the west entry, where the captain guided them past several uniformed guards and into an entryway which looked like a phone booth with a rubber-cupped camera lens protruding from the wall. Each person was required to put his left eye against the rubber cup while a strobe flash was triggered and an electronic photograph of his retina was taken. The pattern of retinal blood vessels on the back side of the eyeball is as distinctive as a fingerprint, and each man's photograph was matched with a historical computer file of previous White House visitors. Lamborghini's in-processing took the longest because he'd never visited the executive mansion before, and a new file had to be created. Upon completing their verification, they were quickly led through a doorway and into the reception foyer of the West Wing.

Standing in the middle of the black-and-white checkered floor was Admiral Jason Hawthorne Bergstrom, Chief of the General Staff of the United States Armed Forces. To call the old salt "crusty" would be an understatement. He looked as if seawater had been hitting him in the face for thirty years—which was, in fact, the case. His enormous bald head possessed only a fringe of white hair around the perimeter, and between his teeth he chewed on the biggest, most foul-smelling cigar Lamborghini had ever seen—or whiffed. There was hardly a square inch on the Admiral's blue Navy uniform that wasn't covered with battle ribbons or gold braid.

Long before the new administration had taken office, one of its priorities had been to make the Defense Department "work." Through decades of interservice rivalry, and the propagation of layer upon layer of bureaucrats, the Department of Defense had succeeded in developing a structure that couldn't even manage itself—let alone the nation's security. The "command and control" that was supposed to be exercised by the Joint Chiefs had become a joke. There were so many lines of authority between services and major commands that a Pentagon organization chart looked like the tangled strings of a marionette. And weapons procurement? That was a quagmire of pork barrels and corruption.

The Goldwater-Nichols reform law had gone a long way in correcting those problems, but the new administration went even farther. The old Joint Chiefs structure was scrapped, and in its place a General Staff system was imposed. Under the Secretary of Defense was a Chief of the General Staff who was now the uniformed military "czar." Under him were ten major unified commands whose commanders, or mini-czars, reported directly to him—such as the European Theater, Pacific Theater, Strategic Air Command, and Whittenberg's SPACECOM. The separate Navy, Air Force, and Army departments still existed, but they were pretty much for training and administrative purposes. The Chief of the General Staff now had total control over all promotions and budgeting for all branches of the service, and weapons procurement was managed directly out of the White House by a staff of professional purchasing executives.

The political hue and cry against this restructuring was unlike anything the Defense Department had ever seen. The President and Vice President, however, had wisely put the issue on their election platform, and upon winning by a landslide they enjoyed a clear mandate to carry it off. Several assistant secretaries of defense and a dozen four-star generals had to be fired before the Pentagon finally got the message a new era had dawned. And the man chosen as the inaugural Chief of the General Staff was Admiral Bergstrom.

Whittenberg extended a hand, "Hello, Admiral."

Bergstrom took it. "Hello, General." Whittenberg noticed the old salt didn't call him Rodg as he often did.

Acknowledgments were made all around.

The admiral looked at his watch. "The Executive Committee of the National Security Council will be convening in the Cabinet Room in about fifteen minutes. You got everything you need?"

Whittenberg nodded. "I would like Colonel Lamborghini to set up his slides prior to the meeting, and I would like to check back with my chief of staff on a secure line to see if anything has changed at SPACECOM since I left."

"All right. Captain, show the colonel and the good doctors into the Cabinet Room. We'll join you shortly." He turned to Whittenberg. "We'll use the White House Chief of Staff's office to make your call." The two men walked past the appointments secretary and down the hall to the corner office, which housed the third most powerful man in the United States. "He's in with the President right now, so go ahead." Whittenberg walked into the office that had belonged to Alexander Meigs Haig and James A. Baker III, as well as unfortunates like H. R. Haldeman and Sherman Adams. He picked up the phone and punched in the numbers. His conversation with the Bull was brief. Nothing had changed. Whittenberg hung up.

"My chief of staff says the situation is still the same."

The admiral grunted.

"May I ask, sir," queried Whittenberg, "what has the President been told?"

The old salt grunted again. "This happened at a god-awful time, you know. We're in the middle of a state visit by the new French President. He's talking seriously about bringing France back into NATO and even participating in a Euro-American SDI program. This *Intrepid* thing could blow the whole deal to shit. Anyway, the President has been hard to pigeonhole today. We told the Vice President everything and he said hold off telling the main man until you got here. The President knows something is wrong with *Intrepid*, but he doesn't know what."

Whittenberg nodded. "So he gets all his bad news at once."

"That's about the size of it." The admiral jerked his head. "Come on." They walked back down the hall and into the Cabinet Room. Lamborghini was just finishing his preparations.

Whittenberg turned to Havelichek and Sharp. "Has Pete told you what this is all about?" The two men nodded like zombies.

The Cabinet Room was a brilliant white with a dark ebony table. At one end of the room there was a fireplace with a model of *Old Ironsides* resting on the mantel, and above it was a Gilbert Stuart portrait of George Washington. Whittenberg, the scientists, and the admiral took their places at one end of the table, while two Presidential aides fretted up and down the room restraightening pads, pencils, and ashtrays for the umpteenth time. The President had a penchant for cigars—Cuban cigars, before he was elected—and therefore smoking was allowed during Cabinet meetings.

The door opened and in filed the secretaries of Defense, State, and Treasury; the National Security Adviser; the directors of the Central Intelligence Agency, the National Security Agency, and the FBI; the White House Chief of Staff; and the Undersecretary of Defense for the Strategic Defense Initiative. Lamborghini looked at the group and swallowed discreetly. This, he thought, is definitely the heavy artillery. A rivulet of sweat trickled down his armpit.

For the most part, the individuals who comprised the NSC Executive Committee (EXECCOM) possessed Ivy League pedigrees, with a couple of Rhodes scholars thrown in. There were several attorneys who, as a matter of course, shuttled back and forth between government service on the Potomac and their law practices on the Hudson. Between tours of duty in Washington, the lawyers would return to Manhattan to serve on the Council of Foreign Relations, read the *New York Times*, lunch at the Century Club, bill outrageous legal fees to their blue-chip clients, and embrace the illusion that the conduct of American foreign policy fell within their personal domain. Lamborghini looked down at his boss, who was the son of a hired hand on a Kentucky stud farm. He was the only black face in the group, and unlike the other men present, he hadn't been born with a trust fund. Whittenberg's net worth wasn't in seven figures—or even six. But Lamborghini knew his CinC to be a fine man, so the SPACECOM intelligence chief resolved that despite the heavy artillery aura and the economic disparities, he was not going to let his general down in any way, shape, or form, no matter how intense it got.

There was no idle conversation as there usually was before an NSC EXECCOM meeting. Everyone knew the score except the President, and no one felt comfortable making chitchat about the *Intrepid* debacle. The door opened and the President entered, followed by the Vice President. Everyone rose in somber formality.

The men who have held the office of the President of the United States came to the office through a career in politics or, in a few cases, the military. The two men who had just walked into the Cabinet Room had shattered that historical axiom by scoring the most startling upset in American political history.

The President was the son of Italian immigrants and had skyrocketed to fame by taking over a bankrupt car manufacturer and turning it into a financial juggernaut, earning him the nickname "Patton in Pinstripes." His face resembled a cross between a boxer's and a Marine drill sergeant's, and he was known for kicking ass harder than any CEO in American industry—except, maybe, the Vice President.

The son of a Kansas farmer, the Vice President had attended West Point and founded an electronics company with $3,000 in borrowed capital. Twenty years later he sold his company to Boeing for $1 billion. He had served several Presidents as a private envoy. Once he mounted a private rescue mission and sprang two American POWs from North Vietnam, years after the war ended. He won their freedom when the United States government was powerless to do so; and as a result, his name became a household word. Ordinarily, being the Vice President is much like being a professional speechmaker and partygoer—all style and no substance. A former VP, John Nance Garner, once remarked, "The Vice Presidency isn't worth a pitcher of warm spit." This administration, however, had a different idea about that, too. This Veep became the *Executive* Vice President of the United States; or, in another way of speaking, he became the country's chief operating officer. The White House Chief of Staff reported to him, not directly to the President. He controlled access to the chief executive, and he gave certain projects his personal supervision, one of which was SPACECOM.

Since taking office with 63 percent of the popular vote, their administration had been characterized by hard-nosed policies, draconian budget cuts, a tax increase, a paucity of diplomatic niceties, the first budget surplus anybody could remember, and a trimming down of the international trade deficit. On the day after inauguration, the two men slapped stiff tariffs on auto imports for a two-year period. They told the American car makers, "You've got two years to put your house in order, then it's open season." The United Auto Workers and industry executives howled, "That's not enough time!" The President snapped back, "It's more than I got. We won World War II in four years. Two years is plenty of time to get off your ass and make a better car." The UAW and executives gulped, then decided to quit fighting each other and fight the Japanese instead, and when the tariffs came off the Americans seemed to hold their own.

Both men, however, saw space as America's future, and here they opened the checkbook—and to spearhead their military effort in space they selected Whittenberg, who now sat before them.

The President took his place in the middle of the table, with the Vice President sitting directly across from him. "All right," said the former auto executive, "what's this all about?"

The Vice President nodded to Bergstrom, who began. "Mr. President, we have a serious situation with the space shuttle *Intrepid*. An unprecedented situation. I've asked General Whittenberg to come out from SPACECOM and outline what's happened."

The President nodded a greeting. "Hello, General."

"Good afternoon, Mr. President. As Admiral Bergstrom has said, we have an unprecedented problem here, and I would like my intelligence officer to give you a detailed overview of the situation as it now stands. Then I'll field any questions."

"Fine," said the President, apparently impatient to get on with it.

"Yes, sir," said Whittenberg. "Colonel Lamborghini, if you please."

The President cocked an eyebrow. "Lamborghini?"

"Yes, Mr. President," replied the colonel.

A genuine smile came over the former auto executive's face. "You any relation to Ferruccio?" he asked, referring to Ferruccio Lamborghini, founder of the legendary Italian sports car company.

Lamborghini shook his head. "Only in the sense that all Italians are brothers, Mr. President."

The chief executive, who prized his Italian heritage, laughed. "Right on, Colonel. Go ahead."

Peter began to understand why he'd been selected for this particular briefing. He spun a dial on the lectern, causing the lights to dim and a slide projector to come to life. "Sir, on Wednesday, at twelve forty-seven hours Zulu time, zero four forty-seven hours Pacific Standard Time, the space shuttle *Intrepid* was launched from Vandenberg Air Force Base on a mission to ferry certain components up to the prototype SDI platform." A slide popped up showing a globe of the earth with the initial ground track of the *Intrepid*'s orbit aiming out of California.

For the next twenty minutes Peter Lamborghini explained in detail how communication had been lost with the spacecraft after a suspected onboard fire, how a rescue effort had been started, and how the Eardrum satellite had picked up a radio transmission between the *Intrepid* and "a Russian Orbita earth station in Chaunskaya Bay, on the far northeastern coast of Siberia."

The President blinked. He wasn't sure he'd heard what he'd heard. "Siberia?" he repeated.

"Yes, sir."

He blinked again. "But that's in Russia."

"Correct, sir," noted Lamborghini. Finally it hit home, and the chief executive came out of his chair. "Our shuttle is talking to the *Russians?*"

Lamborghini took a deep breath. "Yes, sir. That is what the data indicated. That there was communication between the spacecraft and the Soviet earth station."

"Why wasn't I told this earlier?" He eyeballed his Secretary of Defense in the low light.

"Sir," said Lamborghini, gently but firmly, "if I may, the Eardrum' information indicated there was communication, but as you can see on this slide, we had only three signal sources, and the Eardrum satellite operates from such a distance that there was significant possibility for error."

The National Security Agency Director chimed in, "That's correct, Mr. President."

The President plopped back down in his chair and adjusted his rimless glasses. "So? What does that mean?"

"It means we felt it prudent to confirm the information before notifying the White House," Peter explained. "We contacted the Strategic Air Command and arranged for an electronic listening flyby with the SR-71 reconnaissance aircraft." Another slide flashed up showing the ground tracks of the SR-71 and the *Intrepid*, and the

Russian earth station at Perm. "After we received the approval of the Secretary of Defense, the SR-71 penetrated Soviet airspace and inserted itself between the spacecraft and the earth station at Perm. The Blackbird aircraft was fired upon during the mission but made it out safely, and it was successful in picking up a secure voice transmission between the *Intrepid* and the ground. In short, we have definite confirmation that our spacecraft is talking to the Russians, and not to us."

The ordinarily loquacious President was at a loss for words. "I . . . I don't understand . . . I mean, how could this happen?"

Whittenberg started to interrupt, but Lamborghini kept on. "Sir, the crew consists of Shuttle Commander Colonel Julian Kapuscinski, Air Force Major Frank Mulcahey as copilot, and Mission Specialist Geraldo Rodriquez, a civilian on loan from NASA. We have reviewed the service records of these three men in meticulous detail and have found nothing to indicate they would do anything disloyal."

"Kapuscinski?" The President's eyebrows twitched in recognition. "Isn't he the one I decorated a year or so ago? Saved that shuttle from blowing up?"

"Yes, sir," said Peter tiredly. "As I mentioned, the records of all three showed they were the finest crew we had. But the fact remains that one of the crew is in control of the spacecraft and is talking to the Soviets. I have one of my best people working with the FBI to review the service records again to see if we can ascertain who on board has . . . defected."

The President was still in shock. This was a little different from choosing tailfin designs. "Well, still, I, uh, what does this mean?"

Now Whittenberg was on. "Can we have the lights, Pete?"

The lights came on and the projector powered down.

"What it means, Mr. President," said the general, "is that we are in jeopardy of losing the shuttle *Intrepid* and its payload to the Soviet Union. There can be no other explanation of the spacecraft's behavior as far as we can see, and there is no sense in mincing words, sir. The loss of the shuttle would be severe, but the loss of the payload would be devastating. With regard to the orbiter itself, its loss would be mitigated by the fact the Russians have already developed their own shuttle system. Their most recent mission occurred last November, as you will probably recall. Make no mistake—losing the *Intrepid* would be damaging and expensive, but it would be sustainable. However, the loss of the payload would be something else again. Admiral Bergstrom has brought Drs. Havelichek and Sharp out from Livermore to explain exactly what is on board and what the loss could mean. Dr. Havelichek, would you outline the situation on the PRISM system?''

Havelichek's narrow face had turned a ghostly pale—the only color on his countenance was now provided by his dark red beard. He felt as if he'd just come off a merry-go-round traveling at 78 RPM. In one day he'd gone from fighting with Buford to supersonic flight in an F-14 to the White House—and now the spotlight was on him. He wanted to scream, ''Leave me alone!'' and hide under the table; but he knew that wasn't feasible, so he took a sip of water and cleared his throat. ''Ahem, Mr. President, I, uh, hope you realize this is as big a shock for me as it is for you—I was only informed a few minutes ago myself. But I'll try to recap the situation concerning the PRISM Battle Management System and describe what is aboard the shuttle.''

''Please do.'' The President's voice had become stone cold.

Another sip of water. ''Yes, sir. As you're aware, one of the primary problems of operating an SDI system is handling the enormous amount of information during a ballistic missile attack—tracking missiles, prioritizing targets, dealing with thousands, perhaps tens of thousands, of ICBMs, decoys, chaff, electronic countermeasures, and the like. Conventional computer technology simply was not up to the task—even supercomputers. Conventional silicon-chip technology faced a fundamental limitation—a 'speed limit,' if you will—that had to be overcome. That is to say, electrons pass through conventional semiconductors at a relatively.slow speed. Slow in the scientific sense, that is. Switching time for a supercomputer semiconductor is about fifty picoseconds—or a trillion switches a second.

''At Livermore,'' he continued, ''we looked for ways around this fundamental 'speed limit.' We did so by building upon the research started at Bell Labs and developing a functional *optical* switch that utilizes pulse laser light waves. This is quantumly faster than electrons traveling through a solid like silicon, or even gallium arsenide. The switching time of this optical device is about twenty-five femtoseconds, or quadrillionths of a second. . . . Now, in addition to that, we incorporated this optical switch into a parallel-processing computer architecture which, in effect, multiplies the number of computations that can be done simultaneously.''

The Secretary of the Treasury broke in. He was a white-haired financier who had been appointed to his post just six weeks prior and was a Star Wars neophyte. ''Forgive me, Doctor, but exactly what are you trying to say? In simple English?''

"Well, sir," explained Havelichek, "what it means is that we can achieve computing speeds with the optical PRISM computer that are about twenty-four hundred times faster than the Cray-Y/MP supercomputer."

The Secretary blinked. "Did you say two thousand four hundred times faster?"

"Yes, sir, but that's not all there is to the PRISM system."

The Secretary, who had left one of Wall Street's premier investment banking firms to join the Cabinet, was mentally trying to gauge how much money he could make underwriting the initial public stock offering on the PRISM computer company after he left office. He'd have to corner this Havelichek fellow after the meeting. "There's more?" he asked.

"Yes, Mr. Secretary," replied Havelichek. "The PRISM system uses an artificial-intelligence 'expert system' to acquire the targets, prioritize them, and operate the Graser. The complexity of this AI expert system is state-of-the-art, because the PRISM computer itself was used in its formulation. It is so advanced, in fact, that if necessary the PRISM system can reprogram certain elements of its own software *while an attack is in progress* to achieve the most effective response to the incoming threat."

The Secretary was taken aback. He stroked his walruslike mustache and muttered, "Extraordinary."

The President cut in. "Dr. Havelichek, we know all this. The key question is, what's on board the *Intrepid*?"

Another sip. "Well, sir, I was working closely with Dr. Rodriquez, since he was going to install and power up the PRISM system on the platform. The element that is on board the *Intrepid* is the, uh, central processing unit of the system."

The President's jaw dropped. "You . . . you mean the guts and brains of the system, don't you?"

"Well, yes, sir. That's about the size of it. I, ahem, guess I should add that the artificial-intelligence software—the 'expert system' stuff I was talking about—was loaded into the core memory of the CPU before it was delivered to SPACECOM at Vandenberg."

The President fell back in his chair and closed his eyes. "You mean our leading-edge computer technology . . . the hardware, the software. Everything is on that shuttle?"

Havelichek gulped. "Yes, Mr. President."

"Jesus God Almighty," wheezed the chief executive.

There was a prolonged silence.

"Mr. President," lamented Whittenberg, "I'm afraid there's more. Dr. Sharp, would you explain?"

Garrett Sharp held two Ph.D.s from Cal Tech, one in physics and one in nuclear chemistry. To the group of heavyweights in the Cabinet Room he looked like something of a nebbish with his thick glasses and scraggly brown hair and beard; but he understood the atom, and the unfathomable energy locked inside, perhaps as well as any living scientist. He spoke in a soft monotone without inflection, so that a statement from him such as, "Your hair is on fire" would carry the same urgency as "Pass the salt." Although rarely intimidated or excited, he was now deeply disturbed, because he knew what the loss of the Graser could mean. "Mr. President, Mr. Vice President, in order for everyone to understand what is involved here, I think it best if I review a few of the technical issues first."

No one objected.

"Very well. The Graser, as most of you know, is a weapon of staggering power. It draws on much of the laser technology that has been around for decades, but in many ways it is quantumly different. To explain, in conventional lasers the atoms of a given substance—like a ruby crystal—are stimulated, causing the electrons to oscillate between an energized and dormant state. The energy of this oscillation is released in focused infrared light waves. During the initial development of SDI, it was proposed that conventional lasers could be used to shoot down hostile ICBMs. Although this made for an intriguing theory, there were some inherent flaws in that line of thinking. First of all, to generate a laser beam powerful enough to 'kill' a missile, the beam would have to be of a relatively short wavelength—that is to say, the shorter the wavelength, the stronger the beam. But unfortunately, as the wavelength shortens, the power required to generate the beam goes up dramatically; and it simply wasn't feasible to lift tons upon tons of power generation equipment into space. Now to get around that problem, some people in the scientific community voiced the opinion that the laser could be based on the ground near a large power source, and the beam could be bounced off orbiting mirrors to hit their targets. This idea also proved to be unfeasible, because the optical and reflective surface tolerances on those mirrors would have to be so incredibly precise that, as a practical matter, it simply became an impossibility." Sharp paused and collected his thoughts before going on. "In addition to these limitations was the fact that lasers, even of short wavelengths, have relatively narrow beams. Hitting a missile traveling at eighteen thousand miles an hour with a narrow beam was an incredibly difficult task—even with the rapid-fire capabilities of a laser combined with the PRISM Battle Management System. It's sort of like shooting a .22-caliber rifle at a clay pigeon over three thousand miles away.

"Finally, X-ray lasers were examined, but eventually dismissed as potential ABM weapons because they required the detonation of nuclear weapons as their power source. This was deemed too 'messy' an alternative. So, in a nutshell, all of these factors made the laser unattractive as an antiballistic missile weapon.

"On the other hand," Sharp continued, "the gamma-ray laser, or Graser, presented a very attractive alternative of unbelievable potential. That's because the Graser device causes the *nucleus*, not the *electrons*, of the atom to oscillate and generate the energy pulse. If you gentlemen recall your basic college physics course, you know that a proton or neutron in the nucleus of an atom has over eighteen hundred times the mass of an electron. Suppose, for example, an electron had the mass of a baseball. If your son threw that baseball at your neighbor's home, it would break a window. If he threw the equivalent weight of one proton, it would be like throwing the family car, and it would probably level the house. That gives you an idea of the difference in scale between the raw material of a laser and that of a Graser. It does not, however, give you an indication of the scale of the energy released."

Sharp paused and took a sip of water. "With the Graser, the nuclei of a rubidium isotope are stimulated by X-rays. These nuclei then oscillate into a 'lase' pulse, and the funneled energy is released in the form of gamma rays. The wavelength of these gamma rays is incredibly short—less than an angstrom—and they are released in an energy beam approximately four kilometers wide. This beam width is amply wide enough for targeting purposes. Indeed, it can strike down several missiles or warheads in a single pulse. And the power requirements to operate the device are minor, relative to the laser."

Sharp paused again to collect his thoughts, then continued, "The final issue I wish to point out is that the energy released in the Graser pulse is approximately twenty trillion watts. Quite enough to obliterate any missile."

Again, the Treasury Secretary broke in. "Did you say twenty *trillion* watts?"

"Yes, sir," replied Sharp.

The Secretary's walruslike mustache twitched as he puffed on his cigar and mentally tried to get a handle on the number. "That sounds like a lot," he said finally.

"Yes, sir. To give you some idea, the power output of all electric power plants worldwide, nuclear and conventional, is about two point three trillion watts."

It took a few seconds for the numbers to sink in on the Secretary. When they ultimately registered he exclaimed, "Good God!"

The President bored in on his new money man. "You keep your mouth shut about what you hear in here, Milton. Understand?"

The Secretary gulped. "Yes, yes, of course, Mr. President. But, my God, the power. I had no *idea*. How on earth does this contraption work?"

Sharp didn't flicker. He might have been describing how an electric train worked. "Conceptually the process is surprisingly simple. As I said, the nuclei of a rubidium isotope are stimulated by X-rays, then 'lase' into a pulse at the isotope's own wavelength and are released in the form of focused gamma rays, which are out of the visible light spectrum. I know, Mr. Secretary, that the amount of energy we're talking about is beyond comprehension, but that is the kind of power locked inside the atom. Nuclear fission, even fusion, is relatively inefficient compared to the Graser. In fact, when we make comparisons to fusion energy in our lab work we have to use a logarithmic scale. However, you have to keep in mind we're talking about a nanosecond pulse, not a constant. Even so, the scale is overwhelming. For example, if I had a glass"—Sharp held up his drinking glass—"full of the rubidium isotope, the power output generated by a gamma-ray laser pulse could be equal to a hundredth of one percent of the energy of the sun."

The Secretary's hands were shaking. "A *glassful?*"

"Yes, Mr. Secretary."

"That means if you had a . . . a swimming pool full of this, this iso-whatever-you-call-it, you could *generate the power of the sun?*"

Sharp looked at the ceiling, running through some equations in his head. "No. I don't think you would need an entire swimming pool."

The Secretary's mustache was quivering now as he nervously fingered his gold watch chain. "How much of this ruby stuff does it take to make this Graser space gizmo work?"

"Approximately half a thimbleful," Sharp replied flatly.

"*Half a thimbleful?*" The money man felt weak. He longed for the frenetic stock-trading floor at his old firm. It seemed a much safer place to be right now.

"Yes, Mr. Secretary," explained Sharp. "And that was the major problem in developing the Graser. You see, fourteen common chemical elements make up ninety-nine percent of the earth's mass, and the bulk of the one thousand, eight hundred and eighty-seven isotopes that exist come from the remaining one percent of the earth's matter. The biggest hurdle in developing the Graser was finding the right isotope with a natural wavelength that could be used for funneling the stimulated nuclei. I mean, laboratories all over the world searched for *years* trying to find the right isomer substance for the Graser. It was a difficult process, but we found that an extremely rare isotope of rubidium worked best.''

"What the hell is that? I never heard of it before,'' complained the old financier.

"Rubidium. I guess I should point out that it is not to be confused with ruby crystals, which are commonly used in lasers,'' explained Sharp. "It just has a similar name. Rubidium is the sixteenth most common element found on earth. It's a soft, silvery-white metal, and for many years it was thought to possess only seventeen isomer forms. . . . An isotope, by the way, has the same chemical properties as a given element, but possesses a different atomic structure.

"Anyway, a few years ago the National Laboratory at Oak Ridge, Tennessee, discovered that there was an eighteenth isotope to rubidium, and much to our surprise at Livermore, we found it had excellent qualities for the Graser. This isotope was rubidium-98, or Rb-98, for short. Unfortunately, however, rubidium-98 is an extremely rare isotope. It is radioactive and has a half-life of approximately fourteen months. We obtained it through a long and arduous laser diffusion process at Oak Ridge, and it took us eleven months just to produce that half thimbleful. With a half-life of fourteen months, you can understand the production problem.''

The Secretary was still aghast. "I just can't believe it. You produce twenty *trillion* watts with a half thimbleful of this ruby stuff?''

"Yes, Mr. Secretary,'' responded Sharp without emotion.

In a gesture he had not made since he was an altar boy, the Secretary made the Sign of the Cross, and he didn't care who saw it. "With something like this, you could wipe out an entire city with a single blast, couldn't you?''

Sharp shook his head. "No, sir. The Graser only works in a vacuum. The gamma rays rapidly disperse when they hit the atmosphere. It can only be used against missiles when they are in the exoatmospheric phase—or, in simpler terms, when they are in the vacuum of space.''

The Secretary sagged with relief. "Thank God for that.'' Compared to the Graser, a little thermonuclear warhead seemed like a toy.

The President was rubbing his temples. "I have to ask you, Dr. Sharp. What part of the Graser system was aboard the *Intrepid*?"

Sharp took off his glasses. "As you know, Mr. President, we designed the Graser in components so it could be easily installed and deployed on the platform. The structure of the device is like a hub and spokes. The Rb-98 isotope is housed in the hub, and the X-ray channel rods of the SDI platform are arranged around the hub like the spokes of a bicycle wheel. The six channel rods feed their X-rays into the isotope, then the gamma rays are pulsed out from the hub."

"You haven't answered my question, Doctor." The chief executive sounded like an undertaker.

"Well, sir, the hub component of the Graser was on this flight. It really isn't very big; and as I said, it was designed for easy deployment and installation."

The President was slow to whisper his final question. "That hub unit. Did it contain the rubidium isotope?"

The room was deathly still.

"Yes, sir," replied Sharp.

Everyone in the room exhaled as if he'd been hammered in the solar plexus.

The Treasury Secretary had to ask. "If the Russians got hold of this, could they figure out what it is?"

Sharp replaced his glasses. "The Soviets have some brilliant scientists, particularly in the field of theoretical physics. I have no doubt that they could figure it out in a very short period of time. Additionally, the hub unit is, as I have said, pretty much self-contained."

The Secretary crumpled the remains of his cigar. "You mean, all they have to do to make this thing work is shoot it with some X-rays?"

Sharp shrugged. "Essentially, yes. As I have said, conceptually the device is surprisingly simple."

Another mass exhalation.

The President asked, somewhat rhetorically, "Let me make sure I understand what we're dealing with here. We are in danger of losing a space shuttle, a state-of-the-art, highly classified computer system, and an antimissile weapon that has a capability beyond anything the Soviets ever dreamed of. . . . Admiral, what would it mean if the Soviets captured the *Intrepid* intact?"

The answer was easy. "Sir, it would be nothing less than catastrophic. A hundred times worse than the sale of that top secret software and milling equipment to the Russians by Toshiba and

Kongsberg. That technology transfer allowed the Soviets to fabricate submarine propellers that are only a tenth as noisy as their old ones. Any single element on the *Intrepid* would be a serious loss, but all three, particularly the Graser . . ." His voice trailed off. "Additionally, to our knowledge, no other country in the world knows about rubidium-98, nor has anyone duplicated our laser diffusion process. We'd be handing over our most precious defense secrets on a platter."

Now the President bored in on Whittenberg. "General, the *Intrepid* must not—I repeat, must *not*—fall into Soviet hands, whatever the cost. Can't we shoot the damned thing down?"

Whittenberg knew that question would be asked. "No, sir. We no longer have any antisatellite missiles. They were destroyed in compliance with the ASAT treaty signed two years ago."

The President was slack-jawed. "Well, surely we, well, I mean, surely we squirreled away one or two missiles just in case, didn't we?"

Whittenberg was firm. "No, sir. We complied with the treaty. All of our ASATs were destroyed in the presence of a United Nations inspection team."

Now the President was angry. "Well, you'd better come up with *something*, General. And fast."

The tension in the Cabinet Room was now palpable. "If I may, sir, I would like Colonel Lamborghini to outline our response. Colonel?"

Again, Peter lowered the lights and fired up the projector. This time a wide vertical pattern was painted over a map of central Russia. The colonel spoke carefully. "Sir, while we must assume the *Intrepid* is trying to defect, there is something that has been puzzling about the spacecraft's behavior."

"What do you mean by 'puzzling'?"

Lamborghini remained cool and explained, "If the *Intrepid* was going to defect, it would most certainly retrofire and land on the Soviets' own shuttle recovery runway at the Baikonur Cosmodrome in south-central Kazakhstan near the Aral Sea, as shown on this slide. However, the *Intrepid* has already gone past the first reentry window— as outlined by this pattern—without returning to earth. Its orbit has remained the same."

"So what does that mean?" asked the President.

Whittenberg responded. "We can only guess, sir, but it would seem that a defector would want to get the *Intrepid* down as fast as possible. If that course of action was not taken, it could only mean that the spacecraft had experienced some type of malfunction, or the person in control of the vessel was unable to pilot it down for reentry. In either case, the Soviets would have to send someone *up* to retrieve the payload, and that would mean their spacecraft were being prepared for a launch, or were already on the pad. Pete, the slides.''

Lamborghini ran through the Keyhole satellite pictures of the Baikonur, Plesetsk, and Kapustin Yar launch facilities.

''As these slides show, Mr. President, the Soviets currently have nothing on the pad at any of their three cosmodromes, and these pictures came in just before we left Cheyenne Mountain. The fact that no rockets were on the pad, ready to go, would indicate that *Intrepid*'s pass by the reentry window was *unplanned*. That means there's probably some type of problem on board the spacecraft, and that means we've got some time.''

The President perked up. ''Go on. I'm listening.''

''The space shuttle *Constellation* is on the pad at Kennedy. It was going to be launched in a week to deploy a communications satellite and a telescope under a civilian contract with NASA. The mission has been transferred to SPACECOM and we are accelerating the launch preparations to get her off the pad in about forty-eight hours. Our instructions to the *Constellation*'s crew are to try to board the *Intrepid*, but if that proves to be impossible, they are to disable her so she cannot execute reentry. Should any Soviet spacecraft appear, they are to inject themselves between it and the *Intrepid*.''

The President gave a quick nod. ''All right.''

The Secretary of State shook his head and sighed. ''Warfare in space. I suppose it had to happen.''

Whittenberg continued, ''Additionally, I have ordered that launch preparations be made for the Kestrel spaceplane prototype to act as backup, if need be. It is very much in the experimental stage, but other than the *Constellation*, it is the only vehicle we have that can be made launch-ready in a matter of days. The weapons systems of the Kestrel are something of an unknown—the missile prototypes were delivered from LTV only a few weeks ago. But the Kestrel is better than nothing.''

The President nodded again. It was some seconds before he spoke again, and when he did his voice was dripping with venom. ''This is a potential disaster, General. It should never have happened.''

Whittenberg didn't even try to duck. Responding evenly, he said, ''Sir, I have no idea how the defection of the *Intrepid* occurred. I am totally at a loss to explain it. All I can say is that SPACECOM is my command, I personally approved the crew assignments, and I assume full responsibility for whatever happens to this spacecraft. You may have my resignation at any time, but I would prefer to have this matter resolved before it is accepted.'' Whittenberg remembered an old bureaucratic axiom: If you walk in with your head under your arm, it's hard for anyone to decapitate you. Besides, it was how he really felt.

"No, General.'' For the first time the Vice President spoke up, causing heads to turn. The Veep appeared to be a perpetual coiled spring, with his restless energy, darting eyes, and crew cut that looked like a crop of steel bristles sticking out of his head. "Nobody is resigning,'' he said emphatically, ''unless it's me. I've been through the service files of the crew, and I agree they all had exceptional records. Nobody could have foreseen this. Nobody. Hell, the President and I decorated this Kapuscinski fellow ourselves not too long ago. I doubt if he's the problem, but what if he was? We'd look like fools. And we were certainly fools to have signed that antisatellite treaty.'' It was rare to hear a Vice President talk in such a manner in front of his boss. But this one had his own power base, and never shied away from using it. Also, everyone in the room knew he was leading in the primaries and would probably be the next President, and no one wanted to buck the crown prince. "So, no,'' he continued. "This isn't an equipment failure, or a system failure, or anyone's *fault*. The Russians got to one of the crew. It's as simple as that. How, I can't say. Drugs, money, sex—who the hell knows? But there's no way any person in the system could have stopped this. I'm totally convinced of that, and trying to play Monday-morning quarterback won't solve a damn thing. This situation is just a damn fluke.'' He looked at Whittenberg. The two men had grown close over the years, and that bond surfaced now. "But having said that, just fix it, Rodg.''

Whittenberg nodded. "Yes, sir.''

Although somewhat chastened, the President reasserted control and turned to his Director of Central Intelligence. "Bobby, do you know anything about this?''

The DCI, a man who employed thousands upon thousands of analysts, agents, computer specialists, and scientists, a man who had access to some of the world's most exotic technology, a man who presided over an operating budget greater than the gross national product of several countries in the world, said, "No, Mr. President.''

"Well, you'd better shake the tree, and be damn quick about it. Call in all the chits you have to, but find out whatever you can about what the Russians are up to.'' The President turned to the Secretary of Defense. "Sam, look into any, and I mean *any*, contingency response

156

we would have if the *Intrepid* retrofires before our people get up there. I'm open to anything.''

The former Senator responded in his Southern drawl, ''Yes, Mr. President.''

The Secretary of State was next in line. ''Winston, get Ambassador Yakolev over here right away. I want the Russians to know we know something's up. Maybe it'll scare 'em off.''

Admiral Bergstrom injected himself. ''Mr. President, do you think it appropriate to go to a higher level of military alert? You know, as President Nixon did back in the '73 Arab-Israeli War. Shall we rattle a saber to let them know we mean business?''

The President scratched his head. ''Winston, what do you think?''

The Secretary of State was quick with his response. ''I would say yes, Mr. President, except for the presence of the French President. If we went to a higher level of military alert while he is a guest in our country it could give him the feeling of being caught in a crossfire, and that might not be a good thing to do in view of how well the visit has gone thus far.''

''Hmmm. Good point. Very well. Stand down for the moment, Admiral. Everyone else get cracking. I've got to get dressed for dinner. Winston, let me know the minute Yakolev arrives. Mr. Vice President, please keep tabs on things while I'm tied up.''

''Certainly, Mr. President.''

''Colonel Lamborghini?''

The intel chief was caught off guard. ''Uh, yes, Mr. President?''

The President allowed himself the trace of a smile. ''It's always nice to meet a brother. Don't let your extended family down.''

Lamborghini nodded in acknowledgment. ''No, sir. I won't.''

The chief executive left the room to prepare for a state dinner.

Day 2, 2300 Hours Zulu, 1:00 A.M. Local
MOSCOW

The night was achingly cold. Yuri Shevetchenko pulled his worn workman's coat closer as he walked past the faceless warehouse buildings in the Zuzino Prospekt. His feet had been crunching the frozen snow for almost an hour while he meandered on a labyrinthine path through the Prospekt, stopping every few blocks to check for an unwanted companion. Finally, he came to a doorway on Odesskaya Street and looked around one last time. The snow-covered boulevard was deserted. The door opened from the inside, and he quickly stepped over the threshold. Warm air rushed over him as he stamped his feet. Then he sagged against the doorway.

"Good evening, Lamplight." His host spoke Russian, but with an unusual accent. "Drink?"

Shevetchenko sighed. "A very, very large vodka, if you please."

His host, a man with sandy hair and unremarkable looks, was also dressed as a workman. He motioned Lamplight toward the potbellied stove in the middle of the room. Next to it stood a table and two chairs. "Get warm," he offered, "I'll pour." He produced a liter of Stolichnaya vodka and filled two glasses.

Shevetchenko drained his glass quickly and said, "Another." His wish was granted. Lamplight lovingly studied his glass before saying, "They control alcohol very carefully at Baikonur. It is rationed, but appetites cannot be controlled as easily. Some of the technicians tried straining anti-icing fluid through bread and drinking it. They went blind, I believe." He gulped down half the glass.

"We thought you had been discovered," said the host. "It's been over six months. I was happily surprised to have seen the thumbtack on my way home this evening."

Lamplight nodded. "They are shorthanded at Baikonur. My normal duty tour was extended."

Yuri Shevetchenko was a spy. Pure and simple. What's more, he was a spy with a purpose. During Stalin's reign of terror, when he was a small boy, some uniformed men came to his family's apartment and took his mother and father away. He never saw them again. No explanation. No grave. No epitaph. Just gone. Forever. He never forgave the state for that, and took a blood oath the state would pay. A lot of victims from that era felt the same way, but Shevetchenko was somewhat different in that he went about his revenge in a very methodical way, and he was in no hurry. He took his time. The "reforms" and the denunciation of the Stalinist era by Khrushchev and Gorbachev impressed him not at all. The state was the state, and he was going to even the score, however long it took. His strategy was simple. Being a Russian, he knew the most precious thing any Russian possessed was a secret. Find a way to compromise the state's secrets, and the state would feel the pain.

Having no family influence, Shevetchenko attended trade school and became a simple electrician. He was patient, and waited for the right opportunity. When he secured a job as a staff electrician in the Council of Ministers Building—which was a stone's throw from the Lenin Mausoleum—he felt his time had arrived. Surely there were all sorts of secrets in the ministers' building, weren't there? While waiting for a secret to surface, however, Shevetchenko stumbled onto something that was infinitely more precious. Something that profoundly affected his life. That discovery was White TASS.

Except for a brief period during Gorbachev's *glasnost*, information within the Soviet Union has always been tightly controlled. The government-sponsored newspapers, *Pravda* and *Isvestia*, publish little hard news and are devoid of debate on public issues. The TASS news agency—a Soviet version of the Associated Press—is also tightly throttled. However, there is an additional function that the TASS news agency performs which only the privileged few in Russia know about. This is White TASS.

In essence, White TASS is the mirror the Soviet elite hold up to look at themselves and their country, and it works this way: Foreign TASS correspondents stationed abroad regularly read what the *Times* of London, the *Washington Post,* and *Le Monde* have to say about the Soviet Union—such as stories on arms control, Afghanistan, or "Kremlinology." The correspondents condense this information and send it to Moscow on a special White TASS circuit. Summaries of these sensitive dispatches are prepared in the Minister of Information's office and distributed among senior Kremlin officials. Circulation of the summaries is severely limited, and the raw teletype White TASS dispatches are discarded in the minister's trash cans, which are routinely emptied into bins that are carried to the incinerator in the building's basement.

Shevetchenko was working on a basement fuse box one day when he happened to spy a roll of White TASS teletype paper in the trash bin. He read. And was thunderstruck. He had had no idea what was really happening out in the world, and the White TASS dispatches were like a revelation—a window on the world and his own country, unlike anything he'd ever seen. He returned night after night and pored through the dispatches. It was in the darkened Council of Ministers basement that he learned about the invasion of Czechoslovakia, about Afghanistan, about Solidarity, about Chernobyl, about how abysmally poor his country was compared to the West. For years he read, and his resolve to strike back at the state became more firm.

Finally, he decided it was time to establish contact with someone in the West. But who? And how?

As to the who, White TASS may have saved his life. Shevetchenko was appalled to read historical pieces on the British intelligence community, and how it was rife with spies like Kim Philby, Guy Burgess, Donald Maclean, and Anthony Blunt. And as for the Americans, he was particularly shocked to read how an unstable CIA recruit—one Edward Lee Howard—was given precious information on America's top "human intelligence" network in the Soviet Union and then turned traitor.

Because of these stories, Shevetchenko decided to avoid the Americans and British directly. France and Italy were also out of the question. Their governments were crawling with Soviet sympathizers. So where to go? And how?

His answer came with his assignment to a work detail at the Australian embassy. Foreign embassies in Moscow have minimal custodial staffs and are forced to call on host-country support for things like plumbing and electrical repairs. While fixing a light switch in the office of the Australian trade chargé, Shevetchenko simply dropped a note in the man's in-basket outlining his intentions. Shortly thereafter, he was christened with the code name Lamplight and he had been spying ever since.

As fruitful as Lamplight's job in the Council of Ministers Building should have been, it wasn't. His access to sensitive documents was quite limited. Ministers and their staffs were usually arrogant members of the Party who refused to associate with a common workman. So when an opportunity came for a transfer to the Baikonur Cosmodrome, Lamplight leapt at it—ostensibly because the pay was better to compensate for the cosmodrome's remote location. For the last five years he'd been on a rotation routine of three months at Baikonur, one week in Moscow. On each return he was debriefed by his Australian case officer, and the information he provided proved invaluable. Nothing was better than a pair of eyes and ears inside Russia's largest launch facility.

"So what do you bring me this time, my friend?" asked the Australian.

The two men had known each other for some time. A tape recorder was on the table in plain view. It did, however, have a thermite self-destruct mechanism that would trigger itself automatically unless periodically reset.

"Something that may be extraordinary. I simply do not know." Lamplight consumed another gulp of the vodka. "Four months ago the shuttle, it was called the *Suslov*, was in preparation for launch. As you know, I do not work on the rockets. I only repair the electrical equipment in the buildings. Even so, I could see it on the launching pad. A colossal thing. Anyway, a few days before the launch I was ordered to make a repair on a circuit panel in one of the warehouse hangar buildings, where security was unusually tight. I took notice of the increased security because it was just a warehouse hangar that was rarely guarded. A soldier took me to the utility room through an outside door. He told me to stay in the room and make the repairs, and not go inside the hangar under any circumstances. He probably would have stayed with me, but it was time for a shift rotation and he wanted to leave.''

"So you were left alone?" asked the case officer.

"*Da*. More vodka, please." The bottle of Stolichnaya was half gone, and Shevetchenko continued his story. ''I thought another guard would appear, but apparently I was misplaced in the shift change. I went ahead and completed the repairs, and then remained in the utility room until after midnight. I listened through the sheet-metal door, but I could not hear anything in the hangar. The door that opened into the hangar was padlocked on my side. I forced it open with my tools, trying not to make too much noise. I waited, but no one came, so I went inside. The hangar was dimly lit and deserted . . . and there it was.''

The case officer cocked an eyebrow. ''There was what?''

"The *Suslov* shuttle, or what appeared to be the *Suslov*. Even the name was painted on the nose.''

"What do you mean, 'appeared to be'?" queried the Australian.

Another drink. ''It didn't look right to me somehow, so I took my stepladder—I usually carry one with me—and used it to climb up and inspect the rear engines and tail.''

"And?" prompted the Australian.

"They were made of plastic.''

"Plastic?''

"*Da*," said the Russian. ''In fact, I could make the whole thing wobble slightly just by rocking back and forth on the engine. I did not rock it too hard because I was afraid I might detach the engine—or what looked like an engine—from the body.''

"You mean, you were looking at some sort of fake?''

"*Da*. It appeared so to me.''

The case officer was incredulous. ''I don't understand. Why would they make a plastic replica of this *Suslov* shuttle?''

Lamplight shrugged. ''I have no idea. All I know is that shortly

thereafter all support personnel—cooks, janitors, repairmen like me—
were bussed into Tyuratam for a week. It is not unusual for us to be
transported off the base, but ordinarily it is just for a launch. Our
remaining away for a week is unusual. When we returned, the shuttle
and booster were gone from the pad.''

"Hmmm.'' The case officer's mind raced. "This sounds extraordinary. Did you see anything else?''

The Stolichnaya was almost all gone now. "Nothing. I replaced the
padlock with a spare from my tool kit and was able to leave unnoticed.
I never returned.''

The case officer was a pro. "What if somebody tries to unlock that
padlock and can't? Can it be traced to you?''

"No,'' said Lamplight with self-assurance. "Everyone mixes up
keys. They will simply open it the way I did and replace it.''

The case officer seemed satisfied. "Good. This may be hot. I'd
better get it out fast. I'll contact you the usual way if we need to meet
again before you return to Baikonur.''

Lamplight nodded and tossed down the last of the vodka. He
replaced his gloves and hat, and exited by a back door. The case officer
watched him walk down the sidewalk with a wavy gait, then shook his
head. If he himself had put away that much vodka inside of an hour it
would've meant a trip to the hospital. These Russians must have
pickled innards, he thought. As Lamplight disappeared around a corner
he whispered, "Take care, mate.''

The case officer's title in the Australian embassy was that of
assistant cultural attaché. But in fact he was Moscow station chief
for the Australian Secret Intelligence Service, a small but highly
competent organization that was better known for its efforts in the
Pacific Basin. It was also highly regarded for its ability to keep a
secret.

He waited fifteen minutes before leaving after Lamplight. It was
well after 2:00 A.M., and the freezing Russian wind cut through his coat
like a well-honed blade. The Metro subway had already shut down for
evening, so he had a long, frigid walk back to the embassy.
Additionally, he had to follow a mazelike route to make sure no one
was behind him—with a source like Lamplight, you had to exercise
extreme care. Finally, with frostbite approaching, he made it to the
embassy gates and the welcoming shelter from the cold.

Upon entering the building he went directly to his office, started
some coffee, and began writing out a report in longhand. Typewriters—even manual typewriters—could be picked up by electronic

bugs, and he had no doubt the embassy was wired eighteen ways from Sunday. Upon finishing his report he put the original in an envelope and sealed it with his personal wax emblem. He addressed it "Eyes Only—Director—ASIS," then put his feet up to wait for the dawn. The envelope would go into the diplomatic pouch, then off on the 8:40 A.M. Aeroflot flight to Tokyo. Upon arrival at Narita Airport, the diplomatic courier would switch to a Qantas 747-SP airliner for the long haul to Australia. It would be in the ASIS Director's hands in Canberra in twenty hours. Slow, but this kind of intel you didn't even think about entrusting to the encryption room.

He poured more coffee and thought about the warm sandy beaches at Perth.

Day 2, 2400 Hours Zulu, 2:00 A.M. Local
FLITE DATA COMPUTING CENTRE, PLESETSK COSMODROME

Ivan Pirdilenko's spidery frame was hunched over the computer keyboard as he scrolled through the navigational program on his monitor one last time, searching for any hidden bugs. The flite plan for the antisatellite projectile would have to be most precise, and because of this he was unwilling to entrust his programming efforts to the Soviet-built Kosmos computers in the Data Centre. Instead, he cranked out the flite plan program on his Digital Equipment MicroVAX 3600 minicomputer. The American VAX machine had also been purchased through a shell company in France, and was so popular among Pirdilenko's staff that he had to personally control access to it.

When he was at last satisfied the program was purged of all bugs, he made the appropriate keystrokes and the electronic instructions were loaded into the Texas Instruments computer chip housed inside the navigational cartridge. After the data transfer was complete, he rang for his assistant and detached the coaxial cables from the cartridge.

Pirdilenko allowed himself a moment of reflection. If he pulled this off for the General Secretary and the KGB chieftain, he would likely be promoted to director of the entire cosmodrome. As Data Centre Director he virtually ran the cosmodrome now, because his superior was a Party hack who was drunk half the time. It would be a tremendous advancement for his own career.

"You summoned me, Comrade Director?" asked the young assistant dutifully.

Pirdilenko scratched his thinning hair with his long, skinny fingers.

"*Da*. Take this cartridge to Major Somolya in Flite Operations. Have him install it in the warhead immediately." Pirdilenko looked at his Seiko watch. It was 2:00 A.M., but he was accustomed to working bizarre hours. "We have over four hours until launch. That should be ample time to complete preparations."

"At once, Comrade Director."

After his assistant left, Pirdilenko pulled on his Vandyke beard and smiled. Perhaps this Kostiashak fellow was correct, after all. This *was* chess on a grand scale.

THE THIRD DAY

The long black Cadillac Fleetwood limousine pulled through the White House gate and up to the visitors' entrance. A Secret Service guard opened the rear door and out stepped Ambassador Yevgeny Yakolev, wearing tuxedo and overcoat. The well-tailored tux fit his rotund body snugly, and a homburg hat covered the few wisps of white hair that still remained on his head. He'd been attending a Gershwin concert at Kennedy Center when an aide had finally tracked him down. The old diplomat refused to wear one of those infernal beeping devices and was known to go off by himself without telling anyone. This wasn't the first time one of his assistants had had to play hide and seek.

Yakolev was known for two things—he was a survivor, and he was an honest man. In Russia, those two attributes were not always compatible. As a lad of fifteen he'd carried a machine gun from Stalingrad to Berlin in the Great Patriotic War, then later he'd built an academic career at Moscow State University. His field was Western European history, and he was called upon from time to time to perform special studies for the Foreign Ministry, where he gained a sterling reputation for his succinct analyses.

After Gorbachev was murdered and the GOSPLAN Minister had clawed his way into the General Secretary's slot, the Politburo members were apprehensive and wanted a reliable man in Washington. A man they could trust, and one whom the Americans would trust as well. With all the upheaval going on within the Kremlin, the Politburo didn't want the Americans skittish, too. As a result, the new General Secretary found himself compelled to select Yakolev—a man who had no vested interests or career ambitions in the Foreign Ministry, but who was well respected in diplomatic circles. He'd also been a professor to several Politburo members when they were younger men attending the University, and was universally liked.

Yakolev took the post reluctantly, because he was an old widower and didn't want to leave his children and grandchildren. Also, Western Europe was his field, not North America. But he was a lifelong member of the Party, and he felt the posting was his duty to the state, so he accepted.

As expected, the Americans came to respect Yakolev. He never promised what he couldn't deliver. He wasn't intoxicated by press conferences, but returned the phone calls of reporters. He spoke in clear language instead of *Pravda* gibberish. He was the antithesis of the legendary Anatoly Dobrynin, who had been the Kremlin's envoy to Washington for over two decades. Dobrynin was master of the "back channel" communiqué and could change his spots faster than a chameleon. By comparison, Yakolev was rather plodding, but he was trustworthy. What you saw was what you got with Yakolev, and the President was aware of this as the aging ambassador was ushered into the Oval Office of the West Wing.

Yakolev felt something was amiss. The fact that he'd been tracked down and taken away from his beloved Gershwin music was one indication. The second hint was that the President was receiving him in the Oval Office. Usually the President liked to work out of a less formal office in the old Executive Office Building, and Yakolev had been there on many occasions. The Oval Office was used for occasions of stiff formality, and this appeared to be such an occasion, for seated behind the desk was the President, and standing on his right was the Secretary of State, while on his left was the Secretary of Defense. All were wearing white tie and tails. They'd been pulled out of a state dinner honoring the French President when the Soviet ambassador was located. The Vice President had remained in the State Dining Room to cover for the three men. All hoped they could return before their absence became too obvious.

Sensing the somber tone of the occasion, Yakolev walked forthrightly to the President's desk. "You wished to see me, Mr. President?" he asked.

The chief executive nodded. "I did, Mr. Ambassador, and I'll come right to the point. I have received some disturbing information from my people in the Defense Department that an agency of the Soviet government is communicating with an American spacecraft which was launched yesterday morning from California."

Yakolev offered a blank stare. "I beg your pardon?"

The President turned to his left. "Mr. Secretary, if you please."

The Secretary of Defense handed the ambassador a typed sheet outlining the specifics of the *Intrepid*'s behavior, and in his gentle Southern accent he read through the details.

After the Secretary's explanation, Yakolev looked even more

befuddled. "You are saying that you have lost communication with one of your space shuttles . . . and it is now talking with someone inside the Soviet Union?"

"That is exactly what I am saying, Mr. Ambassador," replied the President.

"Preposterous," said Yakolev, and in dismissal he tossed the paper onto the President's desk.

The chief executive's voice became hard. "I assure you, Mr. Ambassador, it is not preposterous. This spacecraft is carrying some critical components for our Strategic Defense platform. It went off the air without explanation. We sent one of our reconnaissance aircraft deep into Soviet airspace to verify the radio transmissions between this shuttle and a Russian earth station. It was confirmed beyond question. Your people even tried to shoot down our intelligence plane. Check it out."

Yakolev shook his head slowly. "Mr. President, I am not one who puts much faith in this technical gadgetry you Americans embrace so passionately. You treat it like some sort of religion. Like your American football. I have no idea what you are talking about, but I would wager it is some type of malfunction with your equipment. As I recall, there was some speculation that our Committee for State Security was responsible for blowing up your shuttle—the *Challenger*, I believe it was called. Are we to be blamed for everything that goes wrong with your space adventures? I have heard the rumors concerning your so-called scientific breakthrough with your space platform, but I am highly skeptical. You have constructed this platform under the tightest security and now you claim we are trying to seduce your spacecraft. It is absurd."

The President eyeballed Yakolev for a moment, then decided to try another tack. "Mr. Ambassador, we've spent some time together, have we not?" The old man nodded. "We've had dinner several times. You've been up to Camp David. You've played with my grandchildren. Have you ever known me to tell you less than the truth?"

Yakolev returned the stare. "No, Mr. President."

The chief executive softened his tone. "Then, Yevgeny, believe me. Our shuttle went off the air, and we know that someone in your country is communicating with it. There is no question about it. The payload on this shuttle is critical to our nation's defense, and if I let it fall into Russian hands, I will be impeached on Monday and lynched on Tuesday. I cannot, *I will not*, let anything happen to that shuttle. Now, I implore you. Communicate the seriousness of this matter to

169

your people and let them know that any attempt to tamper with that spacecraft will be regarded by the United States as an act of war.''

Yakolev pondered the words *act of war,* then slowly reached out and picked up the paper he had tossed away. In a more deferential tone, he asked, ''All of the particulars are on this sheet?''

The Secretary of Defense responded, ''Yes, Mr. Ambassador. The launch and orbit data, and information on our reconnaissance mission.''

The ambassador sighed. ''Very well. I will communicate your concerns to the Foreign Minister. But I maintain this must be a technical malfunction.'' He looked at his watch. ''It is well past midnight in Moscow. I hope you realize I will not be able to give you a response until the morning.''

The President nodded. ''I understand, Yevgeny. But please. Do not take this lightly.''

The butterball Russian chuckled. ''Did you know, Mr. President, that I was wounded four times by the Germans in the Great Patriotic War?''

The President shook his head.

''And did you know that I am missing two toes on my right foot from frostbite I suffered during the advance on Berlin?''

''No, I didn't.'' The President was telling the truth, and he was miffed that the CIA's dossier on Yakolev didn't have that information.

''And did you know,'' continued the ambassador, ''that I spent much of my young manhood dodging the NKVD while trying to build a teaching career?''

''No.''

The old man smiled a paternal smile. ''Now that you know these things, perhaps you will understand why I do not get excited so easily.''

Now it was the American's turn to chuckle. ''Very well, Mr. Ambassador. But please. Communicate quickly.''

Yakolev nodded. ''My cable will be waiting for the Foreign Minister when he arrives in the morning.''

After Yakolev had left, the President turned to his Secretary of State. ''What do you think, Winston?''

The man from Foggy Bottom—who might have stepped off the cover of *Gentlemen's Quarterly*—helped himself to one of the Don Diego cigars from the humidor on the Oval Office desk. ''Obviously,

Mr. President, Yakolev is telling the truth when he says he doesn't know anything. We've all known the man for some time, and he has an inability to lie effectively. There's really nothing we can do on the diplomatic end until the Foreign Minister responds.''

The President grunted. "Sam, are we *sure* the *Intrepid* is communicating with the Russians? I mean, we'll look pretty foolish if Yakolev is right.''

The Secretary of Defense, a Southern aristocrat with bony features and horn-rimmed glasses, fingered his white tie and said, "Mr. President, I personally went over the telemetry data with the National Security Agency people a dozen times. The evidence looks solid. The *Intrepid* is talking to somebody in the Soviet Union. When the Foreign Minister gets the ambassador's cable, that will put the Russian leadership on notice that we've been alerted. Let's hope it will scare them off.''

"And if it doesn't?'' asked the chief executive.

"We proceed with General Whittenberg's plan as he outlined it in the NSC meeting,'' replied the Southerner. "Additionally, Admiral Bergstrom's staff is putting together a contingency operation in case there's a glitch with SPACECOM's efforts. We'll present it to you and the Vice President after the dinner this evening.''

The President nodded. "Whittenberg knows to alert us immediately if anything changes with the *Intrepid*'s situation?''

"Of course, sir.''

The President took off his rimless glasses and rubbed his eyes. "This is the craziest damn deal I ever heard of in my life. It's a helluva thing to happen to Rodger, too. I know you had your eye on him to take over Bergstrom's job when the admiral retires next year, Sam, but that may turn out to be impossible.''

The Secretary of Defense became defensive, and he took off his glasses, too—a sure sign he was getting his feathers up. "Mr. President, I think the Vice President was correct when he said this affair wasn't any one individual's fault. It would be unfair to single out General Whittenberg.''

"Oh, I agree completely. It's just that if the Russians do capture or mangle the *Intrepid* in some way, the Vice President and I will be impeached, you and Winston will be out on the street, and whoever is the new President will bust everyone in SPACECOM down to buck private—and there's not a damn thing any of us could do about it.'' The chief executive checked his watch. "Okay. Let's get back to the party.''

Day 3, 0130 Hours Zulu, 6:30 P.M. Local
BIGGS ARMY AIRFIELD, FORT BLISS, TEXAS

Warrant Officer Greg Hogan stepped off the loading ramp of the C-141 Starlifter to make way for a forklift rolling into the cargo bay. He made a notation on his clipboard, then turned to his cigar-chomping colonel, who was wearing the crossed-cannon-and-missile insignia of the Army's Air Defense Artillery branch on his collar.

"Now let me make sure I've got this straight," queried Hogan as he replaced the fatigue cap on his bald head. "I'm taking five cases of Stingers, a dozen RPV target drones, and an RPV team to *Cape Canaveral*?"

The colonel flicked his cigar ash. "You got it straight, Mr. Hogan." Due to some obscure military protocol, Army warrant officers were addressed by the title of "Mister."

Hogan absently pulled on the bill of his fatigue cap. "I would sure appreciate it if you could tell me what this is all about, sir."

The colonel chomped down on his stogie. "All I know is that I was told to grab my top Stinger instructor, put him on this here Starlifter with the RPV team, tie a pretty ribbon around it all, and kiss 'em *adiós*—and to keep my mouth shut. I suggest you do the same."

The Stinger was a hand-held, heat-seeking surface-to-air missile; the RPVs, or remotely piloted vehicles, were training targets; and Hogan was an instructor at the Air Defense Artillery School at Fort Bliss.

The crew chief of the C-141 yelled down from the cargo bay, "We're all secure up here. Let's move."

Hogan popped to attention, saluted smartly, and yelled over the growing engine noise, "Yes, sir. I'm just hoping this aircraft doesn't divert to Nicaragua. Or Cuba."

The colonel returned the salute. "That's what we're paid for, Mr. Hogan."

The warrant officer sighed. "Yes, sir," he said, and walked up into the cargo bay.

Even before the ramp had closed, the Starlifter was taxiing toward the runway.

Day 3, 0130 Hours Zulu, 6:30 P.M. Local
PETERSON AIR FORCE BASE, COLORADO

Lydia Strand was exhausted. She'd spent the last three hours probing around Kapuscinski's BOQ room and didn't care much for the exercise. She found it as distasteful as it was frustrating. Distasteful because she didn't like to violate someone's privacy, and frustrating because she hadn't found so much as a glimmer of a clue.

Strand was a handicapped person. But it was an invisible handicap. She possessed a brilliant mind (the University of North Carolina does not pass out *summa* degrees in physics without good reason), but her intellect was wrapped in a package of stunning beauty—long dark hair, cool gray eyes, and a figure that was 9.8 on the Richter scale (although her flying career had caused her breasts to sag a little from pulling g's in F-16s). As she tried to do her job, too many people—men and women—failed to look past the pretty exterior. The women would often be envious, while the men would either fixate on her looks or try to prove they were God's gift to the female order. Not everyone was fair-minded like Whittenberg, Lamborghini, or Kelly. There were plenty of people in SPACECOM who simply refused to take her seriously. She had to prove herself every day, and that caused her to remember why she loved flying. In a dogfight there was a winner and a loser. Period. She had deflated many a macho fighter jock in her time, and that was what kept her going. Proving she wasn't just another pretty face.

But times like now got to her. She'd been given a heavy responsibility and wanted to produce. But she was tired and at a dead end. She slammed the metal desk drawer.

Strand had found Iceberg lived an austere existence. In the two-room BOQ suite there was some government-issue furniture, a closet full of uniforms and a single civilian suit, a bookshelf of flight manuals, and an issue of *Flying* magazine on the coffee table. The small desk revealed nothing except a file of paid bills, some NASA and Air Force records, bank statements, and a box containing medals and citations. The odd thing about it all was what she didn't find. There were no pictures on the wall of fighter planes or spacecraft or family. No beer in the small refrigerator. No Holy Bible on the bookshelf. No issues of *Playboy* lying around. No love letters in the desk drawer from girlfriends—or boyfriends. No fishing rods or skis in the closet. It was as if all the humanity had been purged from the rooms, and the remaining artifacts were government issue. After going through his effects, all that Strand could piece together about Iceberg was that he was a colonel in the Air Force, had won a lot of medals, had $33,428.22 in a Mountainview Savings & Loan account, used Crest toothpaste, and paid his bills on time. The bills were ordinary, too. Exxon and American Express were about it. Nothing flashy. The only thing left was a series of paid invoices to a self-storage warehouse in Chicago.

Since the BOQ was a big washout, all Strand could think to do was go to Chicago and track down his old home addresses. Maybe somebody who knew him—or his parents—would still be around and could shed some light on the guy. . . . She shivered. "Iceberg" was the right call sign for the man. Picking up the phone, she dialed Chief Master Sergeant Kelly back at her office.

"So how was Katy?" she asked.

"Worried," Kelly responded. "I only told her there appeared to be a problem on the *Intrepid*, but couldn't talk about it because it was classified. I asked her if Frank seemed okay before he left. She said he was thrilled to be copilot on the *Intrepid* and was happy as a clam. She pressed me for more information, and I decided to back off. Told her to call me if she had any problems."

"Good. Heard anything from Walt?"

"Just that he'd left for Houston."

"Okay, I need you to do something for me. When Walt calls in, tell him I'll need one of those search warrants for"—she flipped through the paid bills—"the U-Stow-It warehouse at 1731 Grindell Street in Chicago. I've drawn a big zero here, and I'm going to Chicago to see if I can rustle up something from the old homestead. . . . I'm starting to feel like a fool on this."

Kelly comforted her. "You're tired, Major. Go get some sack time. There's nothing you can do in Chicago until the morning, anyway. I'll keep the chief of staff informed."

"Thanks, Tim," she said wearily. "Have you heard from the Colonel?"

"Yeah," replied Kelly. "He and the CinC were getting some sleep before they flew back in their T-38. They're probably sawing the logs right now."

"Think I will, too. If you would, please make some arrangements for my transport to Chicago tomorrow. I'd like to depart here at zero-six-thirty. That'll put me in there early enough to get some work done."

"You've got it, Major."

"Thanks, Tim," she mumbled, and hung up.

She dropped the invoices into her briefcase, walked out, and locked the door behind her. She'd give Noah his bath, kiss her husband, and crash.

Day 3, 0130 Hours Zulu
THE *INTREPID*

The hickory stick came down on young Julian's shin with a terrible *whack*, eliciting a terrified scream from the eleven-year-old boy.

The adolescent thug who wielded the stick put his face close to his victim and snarled, "You fucking little Polack. We don't want your kind around here. Do you understand that?"

Julian struggled against the other two bullies who were pinning his arms to the ground, but the thirteen-year-olds were bigger and stronger than he.

Whack! Another scream.

The stick wielder shoved his weapon in Julian's face. "You get your scum shit Polack ass out of our neighborhood. My old man says your kind of filth doesn't belong in America. Go back where you came from. You understand, Polack?"

Julian cried.

Whack!

Another scream. "Ye . . . Yes! I understand!" he wailed.

One of the bullies looked down the road and sounded an alarm. "Davey! Somebody's coming." The three young hoodlums quickly released their victim and fled from the vacant lot, which was behind a construction site. The tall grass had provided them with ample concealment.

Once free, little Julian rubbed his shins, then ran home crying.

His mother was there, as always, and he fell sobbing into her arms. She kissed away his tears and rocked him back and forth in a soothing motion.

"They . . . they said we weren't . . . real Americans," he cried. "They . . . told me to leave. . . . Oh, Momma, I want to go away from here. I hate them. . . . They hurt me."

Victoria Kapuscinski held her son tightly, then dried his tears and led him to the sofa. The time was now, she felt. Yes. The time was now. She rose and dramatically closed the drapes to darken their modest living room, then she returned to the sofa and held him close. "Do you trust your mother, Julian?" she asked softly.

He sobbed. "Yes, Momma."

She stroked his hair. "In all things, do you trust your mother, Julian?"

"Oh, yes, Momma, I trust you."

175

She continued stroking his fine blond hair. "I have something to tell you, Julian. A secret. Something so secret I could not tell you before now. A secret you must never tell anyone. Since your father died last year, there are only you and I now. Do you understand, my son? Only you and I. If you ever tell anyone this secret, the Americans will come and take us away, and we would be separated forever. Do you want that to happen, Julian?"

Frightened, Julian hugged her tightly. "Oh, no, Momma, *no*."

"Can I tell you the secret, my son? The very special secret? The secret you must not share with anyone? Ever?"

Slowly, Julian nodded.

"Good," his mother whispered, then repeated, "Good. Now tell me, Julian, do you hate the American boys that hurt you?"

He hugged her. "Oh, yes, Momma. I *hate* them. They called me a Polack."

She took his face in her hands. "You must hate them, Julian. You must hate them, and all of their kind, for all of your life. They are Americans, Julian. They are evil people. All of them. They are poison on this world. And all of your life you must hate them and never become one of them. Do you understand me?"

Julian nodded. "I *hate* them, Mother. I will always hate them. They hurt me. I will never be one of *them*. I am Polish."

She stared into his eyes with an incredible intensity now. "No, Julian. No, my son. You are not Polish."

Puzzled, the boy stared back. "If . . . if I am not Polish . . . then what . . . what am I, Momma?"

Her eyes were like burnt embers as they held his gaze. "This is the secret, Julian. You are about to learn your true identity. Your true destiny. You were born in this country, my son, but you are not an American. And you are not Polish. You are something special. Something so very, very special."

Totally bewildered now, the boy stared back and asked, "What am I, Mother?"

She kissed him on the forehead, and ever so softly she whispered, "You are a Russian."

Iceberg came awake with a start to see beads of perspiration floating around his face in a weightless dance. It took him a few seconds to realize that he was in the cockpit of the *Intrepid*, for the dream had been so incredibly real. He closed his eyes and sighed before murmuring, "Yes, Mother . . . I am a Russian."

*　　*　　*

Little Julian's indoctrination began the very same day he learned of his true heritage. And every day following, for an hour, sometimes two, sometimes three, Victoria Kapuscinski would drum into her son, over and over, the evils of America. How the rich exploited the poor. How the Americans let the Nazis overrun Mother Russia before lifting a finger to help. How the ruling American elite kept the masses hypnotized with a gagging river of patriotic propaganda. How the capitalist system fostered violent criminals. How the American "democracy" was an illusion the wealthy used to stay in power. And, finally, Victoria told Julian the story of her own life, and how her mission from the Generalissimo was now his mission.

With the father dead, the bond between mother and son fused until it was rock-hard—they were each other's lifeboat in a hostile land. She tightly controlled his access to the "outside world." There was no television or radio in the house. With her hidden source of money, Victoria placed Julian in a small, all-male private school that emphasized academics. She dropped him off when classes began every morning and picked him up immediately afterward. Girls were to be avoided.

It was these three elements—his isolation, the sense of purpose that was drummed into him, and his life-raft relationship with his mother—that crystallized Julian Kapuscinski's acceptance that he was truly a Russian.

And turned him into a borderline psychotic.

Day 3, 0146 Hours Zulu, 3:46 A.M. Local
PLESETSK COSMODROME

The technician checked the readout on his oscilloscope for the fifth and final time. It was correct, and he turned to his superior. "All warhead systems are verified, Comrade Major."

"Disconnect it," came the reply.

The technician unscrewed the coaxial cables from the bottom of the cone-shaped object and clambered down the platform ladder with his equipment. Two airmen unblocked the wheels of the carriage platform and began rolling the antisatellite warhead toward the SS-N-9 liquid-fuel booster vehicle. Major Somolya, looking like a munchkin in his winter uniform, closely supervised the transport. Using an electric-powered motor carriage—which was about the size of a Mack truck—the two technicians guided the base of the warhead inch by inch onto the "headless" booster. Finally it was in place.

"In position, Major!" yelled one of the technicians.

The major motioned to another airman at the booster's midsection, where an open panel exposed some switches and dials. "Seal it!" commanded Somolya. The airman threw a switch which triggered a pneumatic ring seal around the base of the warhead. A *chunnnggg!* sound was heard as the ring seal popped into place. Now the ASAT warhead was permanently attached to its maneuvering rocket, which was also the final stage of the SS-N-9 booster.

"Close it up, Valery."

"At once, Major." The airman shut and secured the panel door.

"Commence transport," ordered Somolya.

American launch centers typically use large "crawler" track vehicles to transport missiles to their launch pads, but Russians utilize a system of rails and locomotives to carry their rockets from assembly hangars to pad. A diesel engine fired up and began pushing the SS-N-9 rocket through the hangar doors and into the bitterly cold night.

Plesetsk was situated in the far northern latitudes—not too far from the Arctic Circle. At this time of year the sun rose late and disappeared early. The cold was a nuisance for the missile crews, but they were used to it. The Soviet Union was far and away the technological leader in winter launches. The *Challenger* disaster had occurred when it was launched in the middle of an unusual Florida cold snap. The frigid weather prevented the O-ring of its solid rocket booster from sealing properly, and the *Challenger* went down. It was a painful lesson in cold-weather launches.

Although smaller than Baikonur, Plesetsk possessed dozens of launch pads and was the world's busiest spaceport. If the Kennedy Space Center was the Neiman-Marcus of space travel, then Plesetsk was K-Mart, designed for high-volume traffic. It handled the bulk of Soviet military payloads, such as optical reconnaissance and electronic listening satellites, and fired off a rocket approximately every six days. Therefore the SS-N-9 booster rolling out of the hangar did not arouse undue suspicion.

Upon reaching the pad, it took about six minutes for the missile to be raised into place by a telescoping hydraulic jack. Once it was in position against the tall gantry tower, a starfish network of smaller gantries closed around the base of the booster to hold it in place until launch. The major watched the scene under the glaring klieg lights while technicians in the gantry attached the dimethylhydrazine, nitrous oxide, and nitric acid fuel lines. An electronic umbilical was also plugged into the side of the rocket. It was through this umbilical that the missile's vital signs would be monitored by the launch bunker.

Day 3, 0412 Hours Zulu, 11:12 P.M. Local
THE WHITE HOUSE

The President frowned. "Are you sure there isn't a better way, Admiral?"

The chief executive, along with his secretaries of State and Defense, the Vice President, and Admiral Bergstrom, was leaning over a table in the Treaty Room of the White House, eyeballing a map of Southwest Asia. The white ties were all undone now, and the tailed jackets thrown on a chair. The group was reviewing the President's options should SPACECOM's efforts with the *Constellation* and Kestrel fail.

"Sir," said the admiral crisply, "there is no sense in pussyfooting. This is the only nonnuclear option we have. If we send in B-1s, they would be precluded from using their nuclear-tipped cruise missiles to blast a path to Baikonur, and that would make them sitting ducks over the flat terrain of the Kazakhstan steppes. I could round up plenty of B-1 crews that would volunteer to take a shot at it, but that's not the point. The problem is having a reasonable certainty of success. Without the cruise missiles, the B-1s just don't have a piss of a chance —period."

The admiral was referring to strategic bombing doctrine that calls for using nuclear-tipped cruise missiles to take out SAM radar/missile bases and fighter airfields ahead of the B-1s' flight path—that is, to "blast a path" to the primary target, where the B-1s would drop their main bomb load. The B-1 was a capable airplane, but it couldn't be expected to fight the Soviet Union's antiaircraft defenses without using all of its resources. Particularly over flat terrain where it couldn't use its ground-hugging flight navigation system to bob and weave through valleys and mountain passes.

"But what if the stealth bombers had to make some kind of forced landing?" asked the Vice President. "Then the Russians would have the shuttle *and* the stealth aircraft to analyze."

The admiral released a cloud of foul-smelling cigar smoke. He was still wearing his dress whites from the state dinner. "If we don't use

179

the stealth bomber prototypes, then we're back to using a 'surgical'—I never cared for that term—nuclear weapon to hit the *Intrepid* when it lands at Baikonur. And if we're going to do that, there's no sense in using the B-1s. We might as well turn the *Tennessee* loose."

The thought of firing a submarine-launched nuclear missile into Soviet territory didn't sit well with the group.

"Well," sighed the Secretary of State, "let's hope the *Constellation* gets up there before we have to make that kind of decision."

"Beg pardon, sir," said the admiral, "but if we're going to have so much as an option of using the stealth prototypes, I have to have approval to get the ball rolling now. The bombers, their crews, ground-support aircraft, weapons, and all the horseshit that goes along with it will have to fly ten thousand miles just to get to the staging area. And speaking of a staging area, I need your help."

The diplomat raised an eyebrow. "How so?"

"Diego Garcia is just too damn far away from the Iranian coast to use as a staging platform—over two thousand miles. As I explained, if it looks like the shuttle is going to come down, the bombers have to stay on station near Baikonur for almost ninety minutes to make sure both orbits of the *Intrepid*'s reentry window are covered. That means a nine-thousand-mile round-trip between Diego Garcia and Baikonur *plus* ninety minutes on station near their target in a deadly situation. A crew has only so much endurance. Those macho SAC pilots will tell you it's no sweat, but we've got studies up the kazoo that prove different. Prolonged flight stress cuts down on reaction time and proficiency. And to make this confounded thing work we'd better have sharp, well-rested crews on station. So I want a staging area two thousand miles closer to the departure point than Diego Garcia—either Pakistan, Turkey, or Oman."

The Secretary rolled his eyes.

"What about it, Winston?" asked the President.

The Cabinet officer's male-model features were beginning to look a bit haggard. He took a deep breath. "Make it Oman. The Sultan's a good man. He'll play ball in a pinch. He knows how to keep a secret, too."

"Good," pronounced the admiral. "I'll get with you on the particulars later, Mr. Secretary, but if you gentlemen will excuse me for a moment I'll call General Dooley at SAC and get the planes in the air. I want them over the Atlantic before the sun comes up."

"Absolute security on this, Admiral," said the President in his finest ass-chewing voice. "Nobody knows about the bombers unless they have a compelling need to know. That even includes Whittenberg. Got it?"

Bergstrom said, "Yessir," and exited the room.

After the naval officer left, it was the Vice President who spoke first. "He doesn't mince words, does he?"

"Nah," agreed the President. "Besides, that's what we pay him for." While crushing out his Don Diego cigar, he turned to the Defense Secretary. "Sam, I hope none of this stealth business has to go through. When is the *Constellation* getting off the ground?"

The Southerner adjusted his horn-rimmed glasses and looked at his watch. "It's eleven-thirty now. She'll be launching around four-thirty A.M. day after tomorrow—by that I mean Saturday morning. About twenty-nine hours from now. Any early risers in south Florida are in for a big surprise. Uh, by the way, Mr. President, in view of the seriousness of the situation I feel we should notify the appropriate members of the Congressional leadership about the *Intrepid.*"

The President took off his glasses and pinched the bridge of his nose on his drill-sergeant face. "And read about it in the *Washington Post* in the morning? No thank you. Our honorable Speaker can't go to the men's room without holding a press conference. No. This will be our little secret until the *Constellation* gets up there. After that I really don't give a damn who knows." He paused and looked at the ceiling before continuing. "We really put all our eggs in one basket, didn't we? The *Intrepid*, I mean. If the Russians get their hands on that thing I'll be lucky—make that damn lucky—if the American people only lynch me."

"Us," added the Vice President.

The President gave his Veep a wry smile, then turned back to his Cabinet officer. "Sam, just so I'll know, where's that *Tennessee* submarine now?"

"It's cruising in the Indian Ocean about four hundred miles north of Madagascar, Mr. President."

"You mean the Malagasy Republic," corrected the Secretary of State.

"No," said the Pentagon chief with a thin smile. "I mean the Democratic Republic of Madagascar—formerly known as the Malagasy Republic."

The diplomat's ears turned crimson over his slip up.

The two men had sparred verbally with each other since their Moot Court competition at Columbia Law School.

"Move the *Tennessee* in closer. If you think that would help," offered the President.

"Yes, Mr. President," replied the Pentagon chief. "It's heading for the Iranian coast now."

The chief executive sighed. "Well, between the *Constellation*, the Kestrel, and the stealth bombers we should be able to nail the *Intrepid* before the Soviets grab her—I hope. Using the *Tennessee* is something I'd prefer not to think about."

The Secretary nodded. "I quite understand, Mr. President."

The door opened.

"They're in the air," announced the admiral.

Day 3, 0430 Hours Zulu, 9:30 P.M. Local
NELLIS AIR FORCE BASE, NEVADA

In addition to the regular military air traffic control radars on the base, an Airborne Warning and Control System aircraft, better known as an AWACS E3-A Sentry, circled the perimeter of Nellis, looking for any errant low-level aircraft that might be in the vicinity. The rotating "Frisbee" radome perched on the airplane's back allowed it to sweep the mountainous nooks and crannies around Nellis where conventional radars could not see.

"Nellis Tower," radioed the AWACS, "this is Sentry Alpha. Looks all clear from here."

"Roger, Sentry Alpha. Thanks." The twenty-one-year-old tower controller brushed his brown hair back from his forehead, then keyed his mike again. "Ghostflight Three, you are cleared for takeoff on runway zero-two right. Wind is south-southeast at seven knots."

"Roger, tower," came the reply, and a C-141 Starlifter cargo transport rumbled down the runway.

The tower controller watched it lift off in the moonlight, then muttered into his microphone, "Ghostflight Four, you are cleared for takeoff."

"Roger, tower," and a KC-10 tanker aircraft quickly followed the Starlifter. It would act as a flying filling station for the entire 10,000-mile journey, because touchdowns were forbidden until the staging area was reached.

182

Finally, the controller punched his mike switch for the last time and said, "Ghostflight Leader and Ghostflight Two, you are cleared for takeoff at your discretion."

"Roger, tower, and thanks," came the firm reply.

Two objects, looking like unearthly batwings in the landing lights, roared down the tarmac and took off into the night sky. The controller squinted and tried to follow them with his eyes, but with their jet-black skin, he quickly lost them in the darkness.

The radar operator aboard the E3-A Sentry never saw them.

Day 3, 0430 Hours Zulu, 6:30 A.M. Local
LENINGRAD METALLURGICAL INSTITUTE, CCCP

Chief Designer Grigory Vostov strapped on a pair of protective goggles and watched closely as the technician powered up the Black & Decker circular handsaw. The final product was about to be unveiled.

A loud grating sound was heard as the saw sliced through the plaster skin covering the hardened aluminum casting. After the cutting was finished, the technician carefully pulled the plaster away to reveal half of the mating collar that would be used to attach the Progress engine to the tail of the *Intrepid*. He then repeated the process with the second half of the collar.

Vostov went over the castings with hand calipers, and upon finishing he smiled to himself. The final product was superb. The two collar halves would be welded together around the Progress engine after they were transported to Baikonur.

Vostov had used the classic lost-wax process to cast his collar for the Progress engine. It was a process ordinarily used for smaller castings, but it provided a precise finished product. And precision was what Vostov needed.

The Chief Designer had chosen the Leningrad facility because of its up-to-date equipment and superb staff. He slapped the chief technician on the back. "You have done well, my friend. I will see to it that your efforts are rewarded."

"Working with you is reward enough, Comrade Chief Designer."

Vostov nodded in agreement.

"Are we finished here?" came a question from behind.

Vostov turned. It was the same KGB colonel who had originally roused him from his slumber in his apartment. He'd been there all along, but Vostov had forgotten him.

183

With great flourish the Chief Designer announced, "We are ready."

Day 3, 0430 Hours Zulu, 6:30 A.M. Local
PLESETSK COSMODROME

The dimethylhydrazine, nitrous oxide, and nitric acid fuel spewed into the combustion chambers of the dual SS-N-9 engines and ignited, creating a thrust of 280,000 kilograms. Smoke belched out the vectored exhaust pit, and the booster strained against its restraining gantry for three and a half seconds.

In the launch bunker the technician shouted, "All green!"

"Release!" howled Major Somolya in reply. The technician hit the red button on his console, and the starfish gantry fell away, unleashing the missile into the morning darkness. As it rose, the tail of flame quickly turned a circle of snow on the pad into water, and then steam.

The airmen in the assembly hangar scampered to the door to watch the surrounding white countryside grow light as day from the exhaust plume's illumination. It was a breathtaking scene—one they felt privileged to witness. But all too soon the rocket veered northward and disappeared into the black morning sky, leaving the frigid cosmodrome covered in darkness.

Day 3, 0432 Hours Zulu, 9:32 P.M. Local
CHEYENNE MOUNTAIN

The young, baby-faced lieutenant was at his console when the red light started blinking. He quickly grabbed the phone to the duty officer in the SPADOC Crow's Nest. "Launch detection!" he shouted. "It just broke through the clouds, sir!"

Sir Isaac held the phone away from his ear. "It's all right, Lieutenant. Just settle down and give me a zoom of the location on the center screen."

"Yes, sir!" Another shout. There weren't many secrets inside Cheyenne Mountain, and everyone's nerves in SPADOC had become frayed. Whether it be by the water fountain, in the cafeteria, or in the washroom, the one topic of discussion in the entire complex was the *Intrepid*. Everyone knew something was afoot.

"Looks like it's coming out of the Plesetsk Cosmodrome, sir!" hollered the lieutenant.

With the CinC en route back from Washington and the chief of staff finally getting some sleep, John Fairchild—Sir Isaac—was minding the store inside the mountain. Everything that could be done was being done at the Cape, at Edwards, and at Vandenberg. Until the *Constellation* was ready to go, Sir Isaac felt the best place to watch over things was in the SPADOC Crow's Nest, where he could monitor the *Intrepid* minute by minute and examine the satellite pix of the Russian launch facilities the moment they arrived. If this launch detection was indeed coming out of Plesetsk, the Russkies had certainly wheeled out the rocket and fired it off in a hurry. A KH-12 pass only six hours before had showed nothing on any of Plesetsk's launch pads.

A large map of northwestern Russia was projected on the giant center screen.

"I should have a bearing from the BMEWS radar in just a second, sir."

"Very good, Lieutenant," said Sir Isaac patiently.

The young officer tapped his keyboard, and a luminescent line popped up on the screen aiming north-northeast out of Plesetsk.

"Bearing zero-zero-seven, sir."

Sir Isaac tapped his hawklike nose with his pipestem. "Punch up the *Intrepid*'s current ground track, will you, Lieutenant?"

A few seconds later a second luminescent line appeared, parallel to the first and about two hundred miles to the west. The Russian launch was directly in line with the *Intrepid*'s orbit, but it was traveling in the *opposite* direction and a little bit to the east. Sir Isaac found this to be quite puzzling. Why would the Russians send up something that was the direct reciprocal of the *Intrepid*'s flight path? It didn't make any sense. But whatever it was, anything that close to the American shuttle was too much of a coincidence for Sir Isaac. The brigadier picked up a phone that was a direct line to the National Military Command Center in the Pentagon. They would pass the word to Admiral Bergstrom in about ninety seconds.

Day 3, 0436 Hours Zulu, 6:36 A.M. Local
KALININGRAD FLITE CONTROL CENTRE

Mission Commander Oleg Malyshev let the reports trickle into his headset, then picked up the phone and buzzed the glassed-in observation booth. "The main booster has separated and all systems are functioning properly, Comrade General. We will have second-stage shutdown in approximately three minutes."

"Very well, Commander," replied Popov as he hung up the phone and turned to his two companions. "The antisatellite missile is proceeding according to plan. When it reaches the top of its elliptical orbit we will fire the engines again to propel it into a circular flite path."

Both men nodded.

Bemoaning his exhaustion, General Secretary Vorontsky said, "Vitali, I am going to get some sleep. Awaken me should anything happen." Then he turned his swarthy face on Popov. "When will the Soyuz launch from Baikonur?"

"In approximately forty hours," wheezed the general. "We must wait until our launch preparations are complete and the *Intrepid*'s orbit passes over the cosmodrome." Popov looked as if he had one foot in the grave. His face was gray as his cigarette ash, and his eyes completely bloodshot.

Vorontsky nodded and left.

"Do you have all of the data you require from Pirdilenko in Plesetsk?" asked Kostiashak.

Popov looked at the KGB Chairman. Did this man never sleep? He seemed to possess some hidden reservoir of energy. His slicked-back hair was always in place. Even the creases in his pants remained razor sharp. "Yes, Comrade," sighed the general. "Additionally, we routinely receive launch-detection reports from the Aerospace Warning Centre, and we will be able to respond immediately should the Americans launch a rescue shuttle from their Florida cosmodrome."

Kostiashak flicked an ash. "Very well. I shall remain here to . . . observe."

Popov found it difficult to conceal his irritation. "Well then, Comrade Chairman, if you will excuse me, I must attend to the launch preparations."

Kostiashak smiled politely. "By all means, General."

After Popov left, Kostiashak pulled long and hard on his Pall Mall. He disdained Russian cigarettes, for they were like smoking a rope wrapped in cardboard. American tobacco was only one of the luxuries for which he'd developed a taste while at Princeton. Another was Scotch whisky. He exhaled the lungful of smoke and allowed himself a few poignant moments with his memories. Ah, yes, America—the land of plenty. So powerful and so rich, yet with millions in poverty.

So technologically brilliant—and metaphysically shallow. Ruled not by a king or a parliament, but by a cabal of uncontrolled press lords. It was not to be believed, really. Americans had no . . . discipline. And the Chairman greatly admired discipline. But in his beloved Russia, even Kostiashak had to admit that discipline had run amok. The Soviet Union had turned itself into one large armaments factory that could not feed itself. His country was descending into an oblivion from which there would be no return. It had to change . . . *had* to. And the young KGB Chairman had reached back through time—into the inner bowels of Moscow Centre at 2 Dzerzhinsky Square—for the instrument to make it change.

Vitali Kostiashak had been born the son of a diplomat. Although Ukrainian by blood, he'd been raised in foreign embassies for most of his life—where he often found himself an unwelcome visitor in a strange land. To combat the usual isolation of Russian diplomatic life—typically accentuated by the suffocating controls imposed by the KGB *rezidentura* within the embassy—the young Vitali threw himself into his studies, where he demonstrated a singular aptitude for mathematics and chess.

When Kostiashak reached his eighteenth birthday, his father was anointed with a prestigious posting to the Soviet embassy in Washington, where he served on Dobrynin's staff. It was with Ambassador Dobrynin's influence that the elder Kostiashak obtained a special dispensation for his son to attend Princeton, where the young Vitali did exceptionally well. He emerged eight years later with a Ph.D. in international studies from the university's Woodrow Wilson School of Public and International Affairs.

While at Princeton, Kostiashak developed a fascination with American history, in particular the American Presidents. He found the Presidency possessed a more convoluted, more bloodstained, more treacherous legacy than the Russian czars could have ever hoped to achieve—from the Civil War, to Japanese-American concentration camps during World War II, to the Tonkin Gulf Resolution, to John Wilkes Booth, to Teapot Dome, to Lee Harvey Oswald, to Watergate.

Yet it was during his study of the Presidency that Kostiashak struck upon an intellectual candle that would guide his professional life. He was in the Firestone Library, studying late one night as he often did, learning about a particularly magnetic President named Franklin Delano Roosevelt. Kostiashak read that when Roosevelt was Assistant Secretary of the Navy in 1914, he'd run for the nomination to the

United States Senate from the state of New York. He was creamed by the Tammany Hall political "machine," and was despondent over his loss. Sensing the young man's depression, an old pol took Franklin aside and told him in a consoling voice, "Son . . . remember. First, you have to get elected." For Kostiashak, that one phrase—"You have to get elected"—was like a revelation, for it told him that to accomplish anything with his life—whatever it might be—he had to be in a position of power.

With his Ph.D. from Princeton and his father's sponsorship, he obtained a position in the Foreign Ministry, but the younger Kostiashak soon found that power sprang from the Party, not from the ministry's bureaucracy. In a highly unusual move, he left the Foreign Ministry to join the *Komitet Gosudarstvennoy Bezopasnosti*—the Committee for State Security. It was a move that greatly chagrined and disappointed his father, but delighted his new masters. Inside Russia, the KGB was looked upon with contempt—and even though it employed a number of capable people, it was best known as a bunch of hoodlums who did not possess what they coveted most: class. Kostiashak was one of the exceptions who brought the KGB some class, and his superiors recognized this. As a result, his rise was meteoric, and he became widely respected for his brilliance and charm—as well as his ruthlessness.

It was during a counterintelligence operation that Kostiashak hitched his wagon to the rising star of the GOSPLAN Minister, who, upon Gorbachev's fateful demise, rewarded him with the post of KGB Chairman. Kostiashak was thirty-seven years old.

It is difficult for those in the West to comprehend the scope or nature of the power a KGB Chairman commands. It's as if the reins of the FBI, CIA, Military Police, National Security Agency, and Border Patrol were all concentrated in the hands of a single man, who had the license to wield the power like a Mafia enforcer—with no restraint imposed by the courts or the press. Like many things Russian, the KGB wasn't terribly cosmopolitan or elegant, it was simply massive. Some 400,000 of their number—which included agents, spies, troops, guards, data analysts, clerks, executioners, economists, wiretappers, cryptanalysts, cooks, forgers, microwave engineers, waiters, henchmen, and assassins—all fell under the power of the Chairman. And Kostiashak, who was singularly cosmopolitan and *très élégant*, never shied from the use of power.

It was shortly after he assumed his duties behind the gray stone walls of Dzerzhinsky Square that Kostiashak became privy to a basement file which held the "secret of secrets" of Moscow Centre. A file which had been passed down from Chairman to Chairman in a macabre legacy that reached back to the time of Lavrenti Beria—the dreaded chief of Stalin's secret police, the NKVD. It was from this ancient file that the young Chairman chose his instrument.

Kostiashak, the former grandmaster, had played multiple-board chess with a variety of worthy opponents before. He found it a stimulating exercise for his warp-speed mind. But it was only that—an exercise. The *Intrepid* was real. And to win this very real, very deadly game he had to have the American spacecraft on Russian soil. *Had* to. Everything depended on that. He had no doubts the Americans would launch a rescue mission from their Florida cosmodrome. He intuitively felt it from the beginning, and Water Lily had confirmed it. He also sensed Popov's reluctance to employ the antisatellite device. One could never tell when a man like Popov would rise up in some moralistic outrage. It was a nuisance, but one that had to be anticipated. The American shuttle *Constellation* could not be allowed to reach the *Intrepid*, and therefore it would be best to have some insurance should Popov prove to be unreliable.

The Chairman picked up a pad and scrawled out a message. He then rang for his KGB colonel.

"You summoned me, Comrade Chairman?" asked the colonel.

"*Da*," replied Kostiashak as he handed over the folded paper. "Take this to the Communications Centre and have it encrypted and sent without delay. Watch over it yourself to ensure it is handled quickly."

"Certainly, Comrade Chairman," replied the colonel. He turned and departed.

Kostiashak called after him, "And bring some cigarettes from my office when you return."

Day 3, 0537 Hours Zulu, 7:37 A.M. Local
MIKOYAN AIRFIELD, OUTSIDE LENINGRAD

The loading ramp of the Antonov-72 Coaler transport closed up, sealing the docking collar, the Chief Designer, and his KGB escort into the cargo hold.

The Coaler looked like any generic military transport, except for its two engines. They rested on top of the wings, thrusting forward in an extreme overhang. The aircraft appeared somewhat comical—as if it were holding up a gigantic pair of binoculars to see where it was going. And this one knew where it was going. It roared down the runway and lifted off on a vector toward the Baikonur Cosmodrome.

Day 3, 0600 Hours Zulu, 8:00 A.M. Local
THE KREMLIN

The Foreign Minister prided himself on being an early riser. Although he was eighty years old, he looked fifteen years younger, and was always at his desk no later than 8:00 A.M. His brushlike black hair showed only a few flecks of gray, and the skin around his face did not hang down in jowls, but remained firm and tight. Only the liver spots on the back of his hands betrayed his true age. A brisk swim every morning in the private indoor pool at the Kutuzovsky Prospekt 26 building kept him fit as a fiddle, and he enjoyed casting a scornful eye on his soft subordinates who straggled in later than he. Often with hangovers.

He hung up his coat and Borsolino hat, then sat down at his desk—which had once belonged to Czarina Catherine the Great, and had been appropriated from the Hermitage Museum in Leningrad. Following his standard morning ritual, the Foreign Minister sipped his tea and began plowing through the overnight cable traffic before reading his copy of the *International Herald Tribune*, which was flown in for him each morning from Paris.

The cable traffic from Washington came first, of course, although he was watching the communiqués from London these days with great care. The British elections were near, and it looked as if that Thatcher woman was finally on her way out. She'd always been a royal—ha, ha—nuisance; but at long last, Britain's recurring unemployment problems were finally undermining her adminstration. Her opponent was a firebrand liberal who'd promised to evict the Americans from their airbases if elected, and it looked as if that was a real possibility. So much the better, thought the Foreign Minister. Someday all Europe will be ours, and we will not have fired a single shot. All it took was patience. And for one who'd survived Stalin, Beria, Malenkov, Kaganovich, Khrushchev, Brezhnev, Andropov, Chernenko, Gorbachev, and now General Secretary Vorontsky, the Foreign Minister knew something about patience.

190

He picked up the leather folder containing the Washington cables and read.

Then he reread.

Then he reread, again, and scratched his head. In his fifty plus years of foreign service he'd never read anything quite like this. He picked up the phone and buzzed the Soviet Minister of Defense on a private direct line.

"*Da?*" came the reply.

"Ah, Konstantin," purred the diplomat, "I am pleased you are in."

"Of course, my dear Foreign Minister. What is on your mind?" The military chieftain was always direct.

"I have received a rather disturbing cable from Yakolev in Washington. The message concerns something that does not make any logical sense whatsoever, but the ambassador insists the American President is genuinely concerned."

"Yakolev is a good man," observed the Defense Minister. "What does the cable concern?"

The Foreign Minister cleared his throat. "It appears the Americans believe that we are communicating with one of their manned spacecraft, which was launched approximately two days ago."

There was a pause.

"What?" asked a perplexed voice.

The Foreign Minister explained again.

"I do not understand," said the military chieftain.

"Nor do I," said the diplomat, "but I will send a copy of the cable over to you at once. Please investigate and get back to me without delay. I do not think it appropriate to disturb the General Secretary with this unless it turns out to be something of substance. He has already left for a long weekend at his dacha in Usovo."

"As you wish," promised the Defense Minister, "without delay."

Day 3, 0630 Hours Zulu, 9:30 A.M. Local
SOVIET AEROSPACE DEFENSE WARNING CENTRE

The duty officer colonel looked rather odd. He was standing at attention, saluting with his right hand while holding the phone receiver in his left. "No, Comrade Minister," he said nervously, "I know of no such occurrence. It is inconceivable."

The Defense Minister's thick voice came through the line. "I quite agree, Colonel, but our ambassador would not trouble us unless he had reason. You did almost shoot down an American spy plane, is that not correct?''

"Yes, Comrade. I was not on duty at the time, but I read the reports. There was nothing about communication with an American space-craft.''

"Hmmm," murmured the thick voice. "Review the reports again and talk to the colonel who was on duty at the time. Find out if he knows anything concerning this matter. Then call me back with verification within fifteen minutes.''

"Of course, Comrade Minister.''

When the line went dead the duty officer finally lowered his salute and collapsed in his chair. Both of his hands were trembling. He'd never spoken with a Politburo member before.

He found it terrifying.

Day 3, 0645 Hours Zulu, 8:45 A.M. Local
KALININGRAD FLITE CONTROL CENTRE

"I have no idea what you are talking about," said Popov into the phone.

"I felt as much, dear Likady," purred the Defense Minister, "but with this cable from Washington I had to investigate.''

"I quite understand, Comrade Minister," replied Popov. "I can only speculate that the Americans have had some technical malfunc-tion with their spacecraft, and they are attempting to blame it on the Rodina for propaganda purposes. I seem to remember the Americans tried to generate some false accusations about Soviet agents being responsible for their space shuttle disaster several years ago. This could be a similar situation.''

The minister pondered this for a few moments. "Good point, Likady," he agreed. "You are most probably correct." Then he changed the subject. "Someday we must go hunting in the taiga. As we did in the old days.''

"Those were grand times, Comrade Minister," said Popov with feigned enthusiasm. "I will never forget the Siberian bear you bagged with a single shot—from that ancient musket of yours.''

The military chieftain chuckled. "I still have the hide on the wall in my dacha. Very well, old friend. I am sorry to have bothered you. Should anything unusual occur along this line, leave word with my office.''

"Certainly, Comrade."

After the line went dead, Popov slowly hung up the phone, then turned to look down the gun barrel which had been aimed at his temple. "You can put that away now," he said in a strained voice. "I am in too deep to turn back."

Kostiashak pocketed the small Beretta automatic and lit up another Pall Mall. "Quite correct, General. I hope you will forgive the firearm, but I truly could not chance your disclosing anything at this point. You and the Defense Minister have known each other for many years, is that not so?"

"Since we were cadets at Frunze," replied the stocky general.

Kostiashak nodded. "Old ties die hard. Should your resolve in our enterprise waiver, do not forget your wife and children are vulnerable."

Popov turned scarlet with rage. "You . . . you . . . ."

The Chairman swiftly held up a hand. "Restrain yourself, General. We are embarked upon a course, and I will not allow anything to disrupt it. Too often dreams of greatness are stopped short because the dreamers lack the will. Continue with your duties and do not impair our efforts. The rewards could be great if we succeed."

"I want nothing from you," spat Popov through his teeth.

The Chairman shrugged. "As you wish."

The general glared at his tormentor. "The Americans know," he said finally.

Kostiashak exhaled another lungful of smoke. "I have never been one to underestimate the Americans. I have lived among them. Now, continue with the launch preparations."

Day 3, 0655 Hours Zulu, 8:55 A.M. Local
THE KREMLIN

The Foreign Minister's private phone jingled. "*Da?*" he answered.

"Yes, my dear Minister," replied the military chieftain, "I have the information you requested."

The old diplomat picked up his tea cup and leaned back in his leather chair. "Ah, yes, Konstantin. Thank you for responding so swiftly. What have you learned?"

"I spoke with the duty officer at the Aerospace Warning Centre," recounted the Defense Minister, "and he confirmed that we fired upon an American Blackbird spy plane—almost downing it, I might add."

The memory of a Cessna landing in Red Square was not yet erased. "However, they know nothing concerning communication with an American spacecraft."

"Very good," said the Foreign Minister.

"I then spoke with General Popov in Spaceflite Operations. He, too, knew nothing about communication with a foreign spacecraft. He did, however, suggest what was motivating the Americans."

The old diplomat put down his tea. "And that was?"

"He speculated the Americans may be experiencing difficulty with one of their spacecraft—perhaps another disaster is in the making like the one of a few years ago—and they intend to claim we are responsible for any problems that occur, for propaganda purposes. Therefore they have fabricated this story of our communicating with their spacecraft—to 'set us up,' as their saying goes."

The Foreign Minister rubbed his temples for a moment. "Of course. That must be the reason. I recall that space disaster of theirs—the *Challenger* it was called. An agent in their 'free' press suggested our state security people were responsible for its explosion. We quickly defused that rumor with our vigorous diplomacy. Yes, Popov may well be correct. I will communicate your findings and General Popov's thesis to Ambassador Yakolev. That should put the Americans in their place, and put this matter to rest. As I said, I did not wish to disturb the General Secretary unless it was a matter of urgency. . . . Also, I am leaving for a holiday at my dacha in Vilkovo. I did not want this to interrupt it."

Vilkovo was an exclusive resort enclave on the Black Sea for Politburo members.

"Vilkovo, you say?" The Defense Minister's interest picked up. "Perhaps I shall see you there, my friend. I am leaving myself in a few hours. It is time for a respite from this harsh Moscow winter."

The Foreign Minister smiled. "Quite true, Konstantin. I hope to see you there. And thank you for investigating this matter so promptly."

"Not at all," purred the thick voice.

After he hung up, the Foreign Minister dashed off a cable in longhand, then rang for Kulikov, his aide-de-camp.

"Yes, Comrade Minister?" asked the supplicant aide.

The old man held out the cable text. "Read this, then have it sent to Yakolev without delay. I am leaving for Vilkovo this afternoon. You are to remain here over the weekend and notify me immediately should any further cables arrive from the ambassador. You have my private number in Vilkovo?"

"Of course, Comrade Minister," replied Kulikov, trying to conceal his anger at having his own weekend plans demolished.

"Very well. See to the message." And with that, Kulikov was dismissed.

The Foreign Minister looked out his window and saw that snow was falling once again. He drummed his fingers on Catherine the Great's leather-topped desk. Perhaps he would leave early for Vilkovo.

Day 3, 0645 Hours Zulu, 10:45 P.M. Local
EDWARDS AIR FORCE BASE

"Oh, great! That's just great. I really needed this just now. Shit!"

Monaghan held the phone away from his ear to allow General McCormack to vent his fury. The general had just been informed that Capt. Davey Barnes had finally been located—in traction at Lancaster General Hospital, where he would remain for at least six weeks. That meant the Kestrel was without a weapons system officer.

When the roar from the phone began to subside, Monaghan decided to hazard a question. "So, uh, where do we go from here . . . sir?"

"You let me worry about that, Monaghan," replied McCormack testily. "You just make sure that bird gets armed and on the transport in one piece. Think you can handle that?"

"I believe so . . . sir."

"What's the status on the arming?" asked the general.

"The LTV people are here now. I think they've got the Sidewinders installed and have started to work on the Phoenix."

"You think? Jesus, man, don't you know?" yelled McCormack. "Didn't I make myself clear about what's at stake here? This isn't some kind of piss-off test spin, Monaghan, do you understand that?"

"I understand somebody got his teat in a wringer and wants me to ride a rocket upstairs to pull his ass out of the fire . . . sir."

Monaghan's biting response caused McCormack to snap, and in military parlance, the general "went ballistic." Monaghan heard a gurgling sound through the phone. "All right, *Commander*, I wasn't going to tell you this, but no sense in pulling punches now. You were fixing to be drummed out of SPACECOM next week. I was already cutting the paperwork. The only reason you got on the Kestrel project in the first place was that oversexed recommendation letter Admiral Creighton gave you out of Patuxent. I don't know how much you paid him to write that epistle, Monaghan, but it must have been a nice piece of change. You're a helluva a pilot, I'll give you that. But you're the sorriest excuse for an officer I have ever seen—in any branch of the service.''

"I never knew there was a problem in that regard . . . sir," said Monaghan innocently.

The gurgling sound returned. "Not a problem? Listen, bozo, officers in the United States Armed Forces do not, I repeat do not, drive a Hertz rental car into the main pool at Caesars Palace at three o'clock in the morning! With a Senator's daughter in the front seat!''

"The accelerator jammed, sir."

"That's not the way I heard it. You took her up on a dare. The only reason you weren't busted then was the Senator wanted the whole damn thing hushed up. But forget that. Obviously, I'm not getting through to you, Monaghan, so let me put this to you in terms even you can understand. If you play this one by the book and act like a good little soldier—excuse me, good little sailor—then when this *Intrepid* mess is over, whether or not you go upstairs, you get mustered out of the service nice and easy. Take your twenty-six years, retire to Pensacola, and get drunk on the beach. No sweat. You're happy. We're happy. Okay? But if you fuck this up, then so help me I'll see to it your retirement benefits are frozen for so long you'll be a dried-up geriatric prune before you see your first pension dollar. Am I getting through now, Monaghan?''

"Uh, yessir . . . I understand, sir."

"Now you get the Kestrel armed and on the road to Vandenberg. I'll get you another backseater. That is all, Commander."

And with that, the line went dead.

Monaghan looked at the receiver for a few moments, then dropped it on the hook. That air-crap general gave a new meaning to the word *prick,* he thought. But who the hell cared—maybe this had been overdue for a long time. He scratched the red stubble on his craggy features and leaned back in the swivel chair. It groaned under the load of his husky body.

Leroy "Mad Dog" Monaghan had been the bane of the United States Navy for twenty-six years. But despite their ongoing efforts to bust, court-martial, or muster him out, he always managed to beat the odds one last time. Indeed, at times it seemed he led a charmed life. Such as:

While executing a routine landing on the carrier *America,* Monaghan's A-4 Skyhawk snagged a defective arresting wire, causing

196

it to snap at the anchor joint. The unleashed cable sailed across the deck and wrapped around the Skyhawk's landing gear like a bullwhip, just as Monaghan tried to "bolt" from the ship and take off again. The deck crew watched in horror as the lassoed Skyhawk plunged over the edge, only to see Monaghan's rocket-propelled ejector seat pop up from below like a high infield fly. His chute deployed, and Mad Dog came floating gently down on the carrier deck—standing up. After a few stupefied moments, the deck crew burst into spontaneous applause.

Then there was the time he flew cross-country as a passenger on a TWA jetliner, en route to a naval aviation convention in Washington. After knocking down a long series of in-flight cocktails, he fell asleep with a lighted cigarette in his hand—unintentionally igniting the madras sport jacket of the gentleman in the adjoining chair. Roused from his inebriated sleep by the screams of his fellow passenger, Monaghan instinctively tossed his drink on the smoldering jacket to douse the flames—remembering too late it was the remnants of his 100-proof vodka stinger. The madras jacket went up like a torch, and pandemonium broke out on the plane until a flight attendant was able to spray the sport coat with a fire extinguisher. Women screamed. Children cried. Men swore. Smoke everywhere. Emergency landing. Ambulance to the hospital. Police called. When the clothes of the olive-skinned victim were finally cut away in the hospital's emergency room, the doctors discovered a tiny .22-caliber revolver hidden in his jockey shorts. Fingerprints were taken, and it turned out the victim was a wanted member of Iran's Islamic Jihad Shiite terrorist group. He'd been part of an Air France hijacking three months earlier, which had ended with four innocent deaths at the Beirut airport. Monaghan went from facing a personal injury lawsuit to instant hero.

And the list went on and on. His entire naval career had been a balancing act between disaster and glory—fueled by his unending quest for the perfect party and his unmatched skill as a pilot. More than once he'd been asked if Mad Dog was his call sign or true Christian name.

Leaving the hangar office, he walked toward the Kestrel just as the LTV engineer approached him.

"How're we doin'?" asked Monaghan.

The gangly, middle-aged engineer shoved a small screwdriver into the sleeve pocket of his coveralls and grumbled, "Sidewinders are loaded and we're going through systems check now. My crew has started to attach a Phoenix to the right pylon."

Monaghan nodded.

"Say, if you don't mind my asking," asked the engineer, "this whole deal seems a little screwy. Why were seven engineers yanked out of the factory this morning and flown up here from Dallas with no explanation? I thought we were months away from a live fire test."

Monaghan looked up at the technicians working on the Phoenix installation. "Schedules change. But never mind about that. Just make sure these honeys work when I pull the trigger."

The engineer bristled. "They'll work, Commander. I've slept with these babies for three years, and I know what they can do. They've got redundant systems, independent/dependent guidance and lock-on, vectored thrust, and anything else you want to name. They're state-of-the-art. You just get 'em in the ballpark and turn 'em loose."

Monaghan nodded. "Okay, okay. Don't get your feathers up. All I'm trying to say is that it's real important they work the very first time. You might even say somebody's life depends on it. Catch my drift?"

The engineer's eyes bulged in their sockets. "Are you saying this . . . is not a test?"

"I didn't say anything, including what I just told you. Got that? Just make 'em work the first time. Okay?"

The engineer gulped. "I promise you, Commander. They'll work the first time. I, uh, better check on the Phoenix."

"Right," concurred Monaghan.

The man from LTV climbed up the scaffolding over the Kestrel's right wing and huddled with his technicians. Every few seconds one of the techs would stick his head up and look over at Monaghan, then go back to the huddle. When they broke up the men from Texas went back to work with a grim intensity.

So who cares if they know? thought Monaghan. It's my ass going upstairs. Besides, if this turns into an honest-to-God shootin' match, nobody's gonna keep that under wraps for very long.

He began walking around the spacecraft, making another visual inspection for the umpteenth time, and wondering if he would actually have to ride this thing out of Vandenberg atop a Titan 34-D rocket.

The Kestrel was a small experimental fighter plane designed to operate in a space environment. It had been named after the smallest member of the falcon family—a feisty little bird also known as the sparrowhawk.

The Kestrel's airframe design resembled that of the shuttle in many respects, but there were some major differences. It was much smaller than the shuttle, even a little smaller than an F-15 Eagle fighter; but like the shuttle it had a low-wing configuration, meaning that the fuselage rested on top of the delta wing. The cockpit had tandem seating—one behind the other—for the pilot and weapons system officer (WSO). The weapons systems were too complex for a pilot to cope with while maneuvering the spacecraft, therefore all the weaponry was controlled by the backseat WSO. Located behind the two-seat cockpit were compartments for the hydrazine and nitrogen tetroxide fuel that was used by the spacecraft's single main engine and the network of pitch and yaw thrusters. The main engine could be used for changing altitude while in orbit, maneuvering, reentry, and, in some situations, pursuit of enemy spacecraft, while the pitch and yaw thrusters allowed it to whirl and spin in any direction.

Because it would operate in the vacuum of space, the aerodynamic configuration of the spacecraft was designed for reentry—not for atmospheric maneuvering like a conventional fighter plane. In space, sleek aerodynamic designs were unnecessary, but even so, the designers couldn't help themselves and gave the spacecraft a rapier look.

Like the shuttle, the Kestrel used elevators on the trailing edge of the delta wing; but instead of the single vertical tail stabilizer, it had dual rudders on the upturned "winglets" at the tip of each wing. The control surfaces of ailerons, rudders, and elevators were, of course, useless in space and would only come into play during the Kestrel's atmospheric reentry, approach, and landing.

The Kestrel's heat shielding was a little different, too. The shuttle used a network of thirty thousand fragile silica tiles to protect its aluminum skin from the friction heat of reentry, whereas the Kestrel used a process developed by Lockheed that bonded a solid layer of reinforced-carbon-carbon shielding directly to a thin film of asbestos felt, which in turn was bonded to the spacecraft's titanium skin. This bonding gave the spacecraft a more "seamless" heat shield than the shuttle, which was always in danger of shaking loose some of the delicate tiles during launch or reentry.

For weaponry, the Kestrel was outfitted with special versions of the Sidewinder and Phoenix air-to-air missiles that were also designed to operate in a space environment.

The conventional Sidewinder was an infrared, heat-seeking missile designed for close "knife range" air-to-air combat. Its liquid-nitrogen-cooled nose cone locked onto the hot tailpipe of an enemy fighter, and like a bull terrier it wouldn't let go until its victim was dead.

(Subsequent models of the missile were sensitive enough not to require the hot-tailpipe signature, and could acquire a head-on target profile.)

The space version of the Sidewinder followed this same basic concept, but with some alterations. Because it flew in a weightless environment, its special solid propellant burned slower than conventional fuel, giving the missile a range of 150 miles. Also, because it operated in a vacuum, it had no aerodynamic fins. Instead, steering was provided by the tail nozzle's vectored thrust, meaning it could swivel and point the exhaust plume in any rearward direction—sort of like steering a boat with an outboard motor. However, when the Sidewinder was in the terminal phase of closing on its target, the vectored thrust couldn't provide sufficient maneuvering for extremely tight turns. Therefore, a double ring of small solid-fuel thrusters around the nose cone gave it the ability to execute incredibly precise movements in the final targeting phase as well as providing spin stabilization.

Its guidance system allowed the missile to have target lock-on through an infrared telescope sensor in the Kestrel's nose before it was fired, or it could be released in a given direction and told to "search and destroy" until it found a target with its onboard sensor, or ran out of propellant. When the Sidewinder finally pounced on its prey in the terminal phase, its annular blast fragmentation warhead would slice the victim spacecraft into chopped liver.

The Kestrel carried the Sidewinder in a recessed nacelle, sandwiched between the upper and lower plates of the wing. When fired, it was ejected from the nacelle by a cartridge of compressed nitrogen gas before the solid propellant ignited.

During the Vietnam War, the Sidewinder developed a devoted following among American pilots. When the missile locked on to a North Vietnamese MiG, it would signal the pilot with a *grrrrrrr* in his headphones—like an angry dog straining against his leash; and when released, it would often scurry into the MiG's tailpipe.

The Kestrel's Phoenix missile possessed many of the attributes of the Sidewinder, in that it also had vectored thrust, slow-burn propellant, nose cone ring thrusters for terminal phase maneuvering and spin stabilization, and an annular fragmentation warhead. However, the guidance system was different. The Kestrel possessed a state-of-the-art long-range, Doppler-pulse radar that was operated by the backseat WSO. The spacecraft's radar could guide the Phoenix to the target, or the WSO could switch the missile to its own organic radar system after launch, which also had a ''seek and destroy'' mode. The advantage of the Phoenix over the Sidewinder was range—with the powerful Doppler radar it could engage a target up to 500 miles away. This far outstripped the conventional Phoenix range of 127 miles, but operating in a space environment, distances can be deceiving. To engage a head-to-head orbiting target at a mutual closing velocity of 34,000 mph, or roughly nine miles per second, the Kestrel would have to acquire, lock on, and fire the Phoenix within a maximum of forty seconds. Therefore, it was virtually impossible to engage a head-on target without assistance from the ground. However, if the Kestrel was traveling in the same orbital path and direction as the target, it could take the Phoenix—traveling at a relative catch-up closing speed of 2,500 miles an hour—up to twenty minutes to execute a rendezvous and reach a target that was 500 miles distant.

Because the Phoenix held much more electronics and propellant, it was about three times thicker in the body than the Sidewinder and could not fit into the narrow wing nacelles. Nor could it be mounted on a pylon underneath the wing, because the Kestrel's belly surface had to remain smooth for the aerodynamic rigors of reentry. Therefore the missiles were mounted on pylons on top of the wings. Prior to lift-off they were covered with protective aerodynamic shrouds which were jettisoned after the Kestrel reached orbit. And prior to reentry, the pylons would be jettisoned so that the control surface of the Kestrel's wing would not be impaired.

In addition to the weaponry, the Kestrel was crammed with just about every electronic goody the Lockheed engineers could think of to cram onboard—from NavComputer to Global Positioning System to ring laser gyros to Autoland and threat warning systems.

Finishing his walkaround, Monaghan reflected that the Kestrel looked a great deal like the old Dyna-Soar project that had been under development during the early 1960s. Unfortunately, that prototype had been competing for funding in the shadow of the Mercury-Gemini-Apollo effort. As a result, it had never built up a constituency of its own and was scrapped by NASA in 1963. Too bad, thought Monaghan. If we'd kept Dyna-Soar going we wouldn't have had to play catch-up ball with the Kestrel.

There were two motivating factors for developing the Kestrel. One, the Graser was an extremely effective weapon, but its gamma-ray beam was several kilometers wide, and that could be a problem when friendly targets were mixed in with enemy targets—like satellites traveling shoulder to shoulder in the same orbital path. The Kestrel was a more "surgical" weapon and could pick out its target from a group of bogies. The second reason was that the Soviets already possessed a prototype spaceplane fighter and had successfully orbited and retrieved a scale model several times. The President wasn't about to let that one go by. Period. But what the American President didn't know was that the Russians were unable to translate their success with the spaceplane model to the full-sized shuttle.

Monaghan went into the hangar chief's office. "You got the transport lined up?" he queried.

The chief pushed his baseball-style cap back up on his head of thinning blond hair. "Yes, sir. A C-5N will be here in about an hour and a half."

Monaghan nodded and looked at the hangar door. "Can that C-5 back into here? I wouldn't want to move the Kestrel outside during a Russkie flyby," he said, referring to Russian reconnaissance satellites.

"No problem, Commander." He tapped the bulletin board with his pencil. "We get daily printouts from NORAD on the Russians' observation window. Besides, we'll have a tarp over it when we roll it out to the Galaxy."

Monaghan seemed satisfied, and wrote down a phone number. "Okay, the LTV people won't be finished for another six hours. I'm going back to my BOQ and get a little sack time before we roll. If our beloved General McCormack should call, tell him I'm in the head, then call me at home."

The chief shrugged. "Suit yourself."

Back in his quarters, Monaghan opened a closet that contained various and sundry memorabilia he'd accumulated over the years—a nice way of saying "junk." For several minutes he rummaged around in the closet like a bear in a beehive, until he found what he was looking for under a case of empty Bacardi bottles. It was a videotape.

He powered up his TV and VCR, then dropped in the tape and started the rewind.

Kapuscinski, Mulcahey, and Rodriquez, the general had said. One of them had gone over—defected—and it might be up to the Mad Dog to put the skids on whoever it was. Rodriquez he'd never met. Mulcahey had been the copilot on one of his two shuttle orientation flights. Kapuscinski he knew.

The tape stopped its rewind and Monaghan hit the play button. There was a whirring, then a title appeared on the screen:

RED FLAG

AIR FORCE vs. NAVY

Red Flag was a training exercise that pitted the best fighter pilots in the Air Force against one another in mock aerial combat. Sometimes Navy and Marine pilots were invited by the Air Force to participate in a simulated shoot-'em-up competition—just as Monaghan had been invited seven years ago. The videotape had been taken by Monaghan's gun camera during his last engagement of the competition.

When Air Force and Navy fighter jocks square off, old interservice rivalries heat up to a white-hot pitch, and some zealous ground crew chiefs would load live ammunition into their pilot's aircraft if given half the chance. During this Red Flag match at Nellis Air Force Base in Nevada, Monaghan had been flying an FA-18 Hornet. Going into the last day of the competition, Mad Dog was enjoying himself immensely, having waxed four of four air-crap pilots in mock dogfights over the Nevada desert. Two of his victims belonged to the elite Aggressor training squadron at Nellis—American pilots who played the part of the bad guys in the air. The Aggressors flew with Russian tactics, wore Russian flite suits, and thought they were really hot shit. Monaghan couldn't help but crow about his shoving it to the Aggressors. That was really sweet. But then things changed.

On the last day of competition, Monaghan was matched with his only remaining contender for the Red Flag trophy—some air-crapper named Iceberg. What happened then, Monaghan still had a hard time believing.

The tape played, and Mad Dog went back in time.

Mad Dog's Hornet and Iceberg's F-15 Eagle executed a lateral cross at seven thousand feet. Monaghan yanked back on his stick to try to gain altitude on his opponent, but Iceberg put his Eagle into the same maneuver. Going past Mach 1 with his afterburners screaming, Mad Dog craned his neck back to look out the top of his canopy, only to see Iceberg doing the exact same thing in the Eagle. They were heading straight up in a dead-heat, back-to-back interceptor climb. Monaghan saw that neither aircraft was gaining on the other, so he changed tactics. He threw his Hornet into a series of scissor switchbacks, causing the Eagle to sail past him. This gave Mad Dog tail position on the F-15, but he couldn't lock on to the Eagle's exhaust pipes because it was headed directly into the sun. He had to wait for Iceberg to make a move.

At 52,000 feet, Mad Dog saw the Eagle pull out of the climb, go over in a loop, and plunge straight down in a power dive. Monaghan followed and groaned under the strain of the eight-g turn—he couldn't allow the air-crap to get behind him. Mad Dog anticipated that Iceberg would start pulling up and go into a climbing turn, but he didn't. The Eagle kept going down—straight down. Monaghan followed, and began lining up his Hornet's head-up display targeting circle on the F-15's blazing dual tailpipes; but before he could hold it steady long enough for a kill, Iceberg started jinking the Eagle back and forth, then he put the fighter into a spiral—still headed down. The Eagle's spirals were too wide for the targeting scanner's sweep, so Mad Dog cursed and rolled his Hornet in behind Iceberg, following him down toward a canyon. The spirals became tighter and tighter—and the rugged Nevada mountains drew closer and closer. Water vapor enveloped the wings of both aircraft as the extreme lift created by the tight turns sucked the moisture right out of the ambient air. Monaghan pulled the Hornet almost to nine g's, the point at which blood is literally pushed out of the brain and blackout occurs. But Mad Dog fought back into consciousness and began inching his aiming circle toward the Eagle. Closer . . . closer . . . mountains . . . almost there . . . altimeter . . . almost got him . . . into the canyon . . . put him in the ring . . . altimeter . . . canyon floor . . . closer . . . I've got—*Ridgeline! Pull up! Pull up! Pull up!* Mad Dog yanked the stick all the way back and went through nine g's, blacking himself out for a few moments before yelling, "Jesus! The damn fool plowed into the mountain!" Shaken to his core, Monaghan steadied his climb, then leveled off to regain his equilibrium. God in heaven! he thought. The crazy sunovabitch flew right under the overhang beneath the ridgeline! I didn't clear that ridge by a fingernail! I'd better call this in—

Beeeeeeeeeepppp!!!

The warble of Monaghan's threat-warning receiver told him he'd been locked on. He whirled around to look behind him. *No!* It *couldn't* be!

"Mad Dog, this is Red Flag Base. You are a kill. I say again, you are a kill. Chalk one Hornet and a trophy up to Iceberg. Game's over, gentlemen. Return to base."

What the fuck is going on? Monaghan asked himself. That Eagle *could not* be Iceberg. He'd just seen him crash. He kept his Hornet steady while the Eagle pulled up alongside him. Monaghan's eyes caught the six tiny North Vietnamese flags painted on the Eagle's fuselage, just below the canopy. Yeah. It was Iceberg . . . but *how?*

Iceberg returned Monaghan's stare. No wave. No thumbs-up. No friendly salute. Just a clinical once-over by the champion. After the cold-blooded appraisal was completed, Monaghan watched Iceberg lower his sun visor, then bank and pull away.

Monaghan kept his Hornet level for a few seconds, then shook his head. "I saw what I saw," he told himself, and pulled the FA-18 back around toward the ridgeline.

The terrain around Nellis is full of rugged, bone-dry, sawtoothed mountains, similar to a moonscape. Monaghan flew over the jagged ridge twice, trying to recreate what had happened, but it only made him more puzzled than before. He'd seen Iceberg fly under that ridge overhang. He'd seen it. Mad Dog shook his head one last time and made a visual fix on the location, then headed back for the runway.

After landing and securing the Hornet, he commandeered some-body's Bronco and drove it overland to the small canyon where the Eagle should have crashed. When the vehicle couldn't negotiate the rugged terrain any farther, he got out and walked up the canyon floor. The scene that greeted him was unbelievable.

Monaghan climbed up to the base of the jagged ridge—where Iceberg should have impacted—and inspected it more closely. Beneath the top of the ridgeline there was the rocky overhang—which he'd seen from the air—but underneath the overhang was a large natural arch that had been formed through eons of erosion by windblown sand. Monaghan climbed into the arch, which he estimated had a diameter of about fifty feet. The arch couldn't be detected from above because the overhang concealed it. You had to hug the canyon floor to see that it was almost a perfect hole in the base of the craggy ridge. That son of a bitch Iceberg had flown his goddam F-15 Eagle through the goddam arch at 500 goddam miles an hour. In the pursuit, Monaghan hadn't been quite low enough to see that the hole was there. That's why he'd had to pull the Hornet up to clear the jagged ridge. After the Eagle popped out the other side of the arch, Iceberg had found Mad Dog in nice level flight—the perfect target.

Monaghan shook his head and walked through the arch. He estimated the Eagle had maybe six feet of clearance for each wingtip, and that rattled him even more. Mad Dog figured his own Hornet had cleared the top of the ridgeline by three centimeters at best.

In a dogfight the concentration of the pursuer on the target is so intense that the pilot becomes oblivious to anything else. Just like formation flying. Monaghan remembered when an entire four-plane formation of the Thunderbirds, the Air Force aerobatic team, crashed during a practice session. Three of the pilots were concentrating so hard on their tight formation with the leader that they followed him right into the ground.

Monaghan surveyed the arch and knew that Iceberg's move must have been a well-thought-out and planned trap. He'd intentionally lured Monaghan into a lose-lose situation. If the Hornet wasn't plastered against the ridge while trying to follow the Eagle, Iceberg would nail Mad Dog after he pulled up the FA-18 to avoid it. Either way, it spelled T-R-O-P-H-Y for the Iceberg. It was a wicked strategy that was as clever as it was crazy. It had meant almost certain death for the Hornet—as well as a certain trophy for Iceberg. Not being familiar with the terrain, Monaghan had escaped with his life by the narrowest of margins. A stunt like that wasn't just crazy, it was . . . well, any flyer who would endanger a fellow fighter pilot for a goddam tin trophy was . . . psychotic.

Monaghan had thought about reporting the incident, but didn't for three reasons: Nobody would believe Iceberg would be crazy enough to fly an F-15 through a hole in a mountain; any complaint by Mad Dog would be dismissed as the crybaby sniffles of a miffed Navy loser; and the gun camera video recording had run out of tape three seconds before Iceberg's disappearance under the overhang. So Mad Dog had had to let that one slide, but he never forgot . . . or forgave.

Monaghan turned off the tape and went to the refrigerator to grab a beer—a regular habit, as demonstrated by his generous paunch. He popped the top and walked outside to watch the moon over the distant Sierras. It was a crystal-clear desert night, and the stars were dancing above Edwards Dry Lake.

Slowly and methodically, Monaghan's mind recapped the Red Flag competition one last time. He was totally convinced there was no question. Iceberg had deliberately tried to splatter his Hornet on a mountainside just so he could capture some two-bit championship. Any sicko who would pull something like that was capable of anything.

After he drained the last of his beer, Mad Dog's hefty forearm muscle flexed, causing the can to crumple in his hand. He'd made up his mind.

Kapuscinski, Mulcahey, and Rodriquez. McCormack had said they didn't know which one had gone over.

Monaghan's money was on Kapuscinski, and as far as he was concerned, if the Kestrel went up, that motherfucking snake Iceberg was dead meat.

Day 3, 0900 Hours Zulu, 2:00 A.M. Local
CHEYENNE MOUNTAIN

Whittenberg and Lamborghini straggled into the conference room, still wearing their green flight suits. They looked drawn, haggard, and grimy with stubble on their chins. They'd grabbed a few hours' sleep before heading back from Washington, but it hadn't been near enough to recharge them fully. The long hours and stress were taking their toll.

Whittenberg called a conference of the staff members who were not sleeping, and one by one they waddled in and plopped down in their chairs. The chief of staff had just awakened, and he was probably the most refreshed of the group. Everybody else looked like yesterday's poached eggs.

Whittenberg nodded wearily to Dowd. "Give me a status check, Bull."

"Roger, sir. Let's start off with intel. Chief Kelly, what have you got?" The chief master sergeant had been minding the intelligence shop while Lamborghini and Strand were away. He quickly explained how they were investigating the *Intrepid*'s crew members with the help of an FBI agent.

After Kelly was finished, the Bull said, "Okay, Sir Isaac, what do you have?"

Fairchild turned to face the CinC. "I spoke with General McCormack a few minutes ago. Preparations are proceeding at the Cape and the *Constellation* should be ready for launch by zero-four-thirty Eastern time tomorrow morning. The Kestrel is in the process of being armed, and will be transported to Vandenberg in about five hours. Also, General McCormack asked that you call him as soon as possible, sir."

Sir Isaac then rose and went to the lectern, his huge nose and skinny frame making him look like a buzzard poised on a fence post. He punched a few buttons, and a Mercator world map appeared on the screen showing the ground track of the *Intrepid*. "Something occurred during your flight back from Washington that is disturbing," he began, while pointing at the screen. "This is the ground track of the *Intrepid* as of four hours ago. At zero-four-thirty-two Zulu we received a launch detection in SPADOC of a missile coming out of the Plesetsk Cosmodrome."

"At zero-four-thirty-two?" asked Whittenberg. "That was fast."

"Yes, sir. As you'll recall, our last KH-12 pass had occurred only six hours prior and there were no vehicles on any Plesetsk pads at that time. The Soviets wheeled this one out and launched it in very short order.'' Sir Isaac punched another button and a second wavy line appeared, parallel to the first. "This is the ground track of the Plesetsk vehicle. It is virtually on a direct reciprocal orbit to the *Intrepid*, but with one major difference. It is traveling in a circular orbit at a higher altitude of two hundred twenty-one miles.''

"I don't think I like this,'' muttered the CinC.

"Neither do I, sir,'' replied Sir Isaac.

"Has Admiral Bergstrom been informed?''

"NMCC was notified immediately, sir.''

"Your assessment?'' asked Whittenberg.

Sir Isaac stoked up his pipe. "Take your pick, sir. It could be an ELINT bird, SIGINT, PHOTINT, IR, you name it. Whatever it is, it seems to be passive. NSA hasn't picked up so much as a bleep of telemetry from it.''

"What about an ASAT?'' queried Lamborghini.

Sir Isaac rapped his teeth with the pipestem. "It's not impossible, but there are several arguments against that line of thinking.''

"Such as,'' prompted the CinC.

Sir Isaac stared at the ceiling for a few moments before speaking. "I would anticipate an ASAT would mirror the *Intrepid*'s altitude or travel below it, but as I said, this vehicle's altitude is significantly higher. In conducting ASAT tests, the Russians have historically kept the warhead in the same orbital altitude as the target, or else placed the warhead in a lower altitude and put it through a pop-up maneuver in the terminal targeting phase. Also, Russian ASATs have always traveled in a co-orbital flight path. They've never traveled in the opposite direction. So this violates any historical precedent.''

"What about that test they ran just before the ASAT treaty was signed?'' Lamborghini was referring to a dual launch detection that had been picked up out of the Baikonur Cosmodrome. One SS-N-9 missile went due south, another went due north. What happened exactly, NORAD couldn't say for sure, except that on the very first orbit the two payloads were destroyed somewhere over the South Pole—where the Spacetrack radars had a blind spot. Their flight paths had been kept at such a low altitude that their debris quickly fell to earth before NORAD got a good handle on whether it was an ASAT test or something else. Right after that shot, the antisatellite weaponry treaty was signed.

Sir Isaac shrugged. "Your guess is as good as mine. But if that was an ASAT, they've only had one test.''

"Yeah," said Lamborghini. "One successful test."

Again, Sir Isaac shrugged. "We simply can't say for certain. But consider this: If the Russians are indeed trying to capture the *Intrepid*, why would they shoot it down with an ASAT?"

Lamborghini mulled that one over. "Maybe they can't retrieve the *Intrepid* and want to shoot it down to prevent us from arming the platform?"

"If that's the case," countered Sir Isaac, "then why haven't they gone ahead and destroyed it?"

There was a period of silence. No one had an answer.

"So you're still saying it could be anything?" asked Whittenberg.

"That's about the size of it, sir," Sir Isaac sighed.

"That may be," said Lamborghini as he ran a hand through his sweat-stained raven hair, "but this is another uncomfortable coincidence. It must have something to do with the *Intrepid*. What, I don't know, but there has to be a link."

Kelly thought his boss looked bad and offered a suggestion. "Maybe we should put Spyglass on it?"

Lamborghini was about to respond when Whittenberg said, "Yeah. Let's do that." Then he scratched his stubbly chin. "But for this, we'd better pull out all the stops. Let's put the Hubble on it, too."

Dowd smiled wryly. "Leeds will have kittens. That's his personal wet dream."

"Screw him," said the CinC.

Back in his office, Whittenberg put in a secure call to McCormack at the Kennedy Space Center.

In an apologetic voice, McCormack said, "Sorry to dump this on you, sir, but we have a major problem with the Kestrel."

"What is it?" asked Whittenberg.

"The weapons systems officer . . . you know him, Air Force Captain Davey Barnes."

"Sure, I know him."

"He was en route to the Kestrel hangar when he got racked up on his motorcycle," recounted McCormack. "He's in the hospital for at least six weeks."

Whittenberg winced. "Damn!"

The two generals knew what Barnes's accident meant. Since the Kestrel was in the prototype stage and had been developed under such a blanket of secrecy, only a primary test crew had been selected and trained on its systems. There was no backup pilot or WSO.

"I guess that scrubs it," lamented the CinC.

"I'm afraid it does, sir, unless you want to give up one of your staff people."

Whittenberg's eyes narrowed. "You mean Pete?"

"Yes, sir. He was deputy director for the Kestrel project before he went to your SPACECOM intelligence slot. He's the only one I know of who is flight-qualified and knows the systems."

Whittenberg frowned. "Yeah, but he hasn't done any hands-on work with the Kestrel for over a year."

"I know that, sir," observed McCormack. "But the only other people who know enough about the systems are civilians with LTV— and we certainly can't ask any of them. I don't like it either, General, but I say it's either Pete or we stand down at Vandenberg."

Whittenberg closed his eyes. "I guess you're right. I'll talk to him and get back to you."

"Thanks, General. I hope the *Constellation* can take care of everything and the Kestrel won't matter."

"Yeah, me too."

The conversation seemed to be over, but McCormack didn't get off the line.

"Anything else?" asked Whittenberg.

"Yes, sir," said McCormack, somewhat sheepishly. "I just wanted you to know, I told Monaghan that however this *Intrepid* deal turns out, either way, when it's over he's outta here."

Whittenberg didn't second-guess his commanders. "You're Commander of Flight Operations, Chet. It's your decision. When we brought Monaghan on he only sounded good to me because Admiral Creighton gave him such high marks."

"Yes, sir, I know."

"Seems a shame. I hear he's an incredible pilot."

"Oh, yes, sir," agreed McCormack. "When you can find him sober."

Lamborghini leaned back in the chair, absorbing what his boss had just told him. He thought Whittenberg looked awfully bad. The four olive-drab stars on the shoulders of the CinC's green flight suit seemed to bear down heavily on him. Lamborghini felt a sense of loyalty to this man who'd rescued his Air Force career, and he didn't want to let him down. He said, "I have no problem giving it a try, sir. It's just that I feel awfully rusty on the systems."

"That's what I told Chet," recalled Whittenberg. "If you think it's not feasible, just say so. No sense sending you up if we don't have a reasonable chance of making it work.''

Lamborghini thought back to his briefing at the White House. About what it would mean if the Russians got hold of the *Intrepid*, the PRISM computer, and the Graser. "I know it's a long shot, sir, but considering what's at stake, I think we'd better give it a whirl."

The CinC nodded. "Okay. I'll call Chet and tell him you'll be on your way to Vandenberg after you've got some sleep. I don't want you leaving here tired. Get at least six hours under your belt before you take off.''

Lamborghini didn't argue. "Ask General McCormack to have all the tech manuals ready for me at Edwards. I think it best I do some simulator time before launch, and it would be helpful to have the manuals on hand. I just wish I wasn't going to be in the backseat.''

"I understand," said the CinC sympathetically. "Also, just so you'll know, Monaghan and Chet had words with each other. Don't get caught in a pissin' contest between those two."

Lamborghini chuckled. "I'm not surprised. I only knew Mad Dog briefly. He was coming into the project just as I was leaving. I liked him, but he didn't strike me as General McCormack's type."

Day 3, 0948 Hours Zulu, 4:48 A.M. Local
GEORGETOWN, WASHINGTON, D.C.

When Dr. Percival Leeds was selected by the President and Vice President to head up the National Aeronautics and Space Administration, they thought he would do for NASA what Whittenberg had done for SPACECOM—and to a degree they were right. He'd helped galvanize the country behind a renewed space effort. But if the truth were known, his galactic ego had worn out his welcome at the White House and he was on very, very thin ice. On a highly confidential basis, the Vice President had already retained the executive search firm of SpencerStuart to look for a possible replacement.

Leeds was a peculiar character who could best be described as a slothful dynamo. He was born the son of famed astronomer Herbert Leeds, one of the pioneers in the field of radio astronomy and director of the Lick Observatory. Percy adored his father, and always assumed he would follow in his old man's astronomical footsteps. Unfortunately, Percy also adored lying on the beach alongside a bikini-clad companion. So much so that he remained on the sand throughout the bulk of his ten-year student career at a major California university.

In deference to his father's stature (and a desire to get Percy out of their hair) this major California university (which shall remain nameless) awarded the younger Leeds a Ph.D. in astronomy, with the understanding he seek employment out of state.

Percy agreed, but with his slipshod academic record, he soon found it impossible to obtain work in his arcane field of astronomy. Potential employers would take one look at his dissertation and shudder. "Ahem, *Dr.* Leeds, didn't anyone ever tell you there is no *e* in 'quasar'?"

So there he was. Dead in the water, pushing thirty, with no marketable job skill. It was scary. But then, a twist of fate. Through a friend of a friend, he got a job selling X-ray medical equipment, and his career took off like a comet. He found that he had a gift for putting complex technical terms into simple, clear language. That skill, coupled with the fact that he always presented himself as *Dr.* Leeds to physician customers, made him the company's top salesman. His superiors took notice, and he rose quickly, eventually becoming chairman of the high-tech conglomerate that had hired him as a salesman. And that position served as a springboard for him to become a major fund raiser for the Presidential campaign of a former auto maker.

After the election, Leeds was tapped for NASA because the President saw him as the perfect "Mr. Outside" for the space program—and he was. Indeed, he became a media darling for the agency, constantly on the road proselytizing for bigger and more expensive space ventures. With his blond hair, boyish good looks, and trademark horn-rimmed glasses, he became a regular guest for Johnny Carson, Phil Donahue, Oprah Winfrey, and any other talk show NASA's publicity people could book. And he was incredibly effective on Capitol Hill. He could coax money out of parsimonious Senators like nobody's business—especially for a project that became his obsession, the Hubble space telescope. He saw the Hubble as his vindication of sorts, for in exercising control over the space telescope he demonstrated that he truly was, at long last, a full member of his father's scientific community—and it gave him the credibility to return to that university in California with his head held high.

Unfortunately, though, Leeds's success brought on an acute case of Washingtonitis, a severe affliction that often topples Cabinet officers and Congressmen. Leeds became intoxicated with the media attention and started believing his own press releases. His ego expanded like a supernova, and the White House came to regard him as a royal pain in the arse.

But at the moment, Leeds wasn't paying much attention to the White House. He was riding the crest of his own wave. In addition to the Hubble telescope—and his newfound credibility in the scientific community—Leeds had his own NASA jet, his own publicity staff, his own Georgetown pad, and—as he liked to boast—his own pack of groupies.

It took three rings before the young lady was awakened. Irritated, she shook the figure beside her. "Hey, honey . . . your phone is ringin'."

"Mmmpppffff." He fumbled over his buxom companion for the receiver, and in the process his knuckles accidentally bopped her on the nose.

"Ow!"

"Uhhhh . . . terribly sorry, Julie. My apologies."

"The name's Rhonda."

"Uh, yes, I was going to say Rhonda. You will excuse me." He snagged the receiver with an irritable "Yes?"

"Dr. Leeds?" came the voice through the phone.

"Whom were you expecting?" asked Leeds sarcastically.

"I'm sorry to awaken you, Doctor. This is Rodger Whittenberg at SPACECOM headquarters in Colorado."

Leeds exhaled, not bothering to mask his annoyance. "General, do you have any idea what time it is?"

"I make it about four forty-eight A.M. your time, Doctor."

Leeds growled, "What on earth do you want now, General?"

"As I said, Doctor, I'm sorry to bother you, but something has come up and we require your assistance immediately. We need the Hubble telescope to pass from NASA's control to SPACECOM's. There are some, uh, vital observations we have to make without delay."

Leeds felt his fury building. "Right this minute?"

Whittenberg didn't mask the edge on his voice, either. "Right this minute, Doctor."

Leeds's cork popped. "You listen to me, General! I don't know what kind of toy-soldier games you're playing out there in Colorado —maybe the altitude's gotten to you—but if you expect me to jump out of bed at five in the morning and pop to attention for SPACECOM, you're insane! I run NASA, and it's a civilian agency and don't you forget it—ever! You've already commandeered my COSMAX shuttle, and now you want the Hubble, too? What the hell for?''

"I'm sorry, Doctor. I can't say. But I need it now.''

The NASA Director growled again. "That's what you said about the *Constellation*, too, if I recall. Well, General, you're not getting any more of my toys to play with. I keep the Hubble under my personal supervision—I happen to be a *scientist*, you see—and I don't care to have any of your bloody militaristic paws on *my* telescope. Go play with your goddam Star Wars platform!'' And with that, the receiver came crashing down. "Guess I told that black bastard where to go.''

"You sure did, honey.'' She inched toward him. "Gee, you're cute when you're mad. . . . Listen, since you're up . . .''

He emitted a low, hungry laugh.

She giggled, "I mean, since you're awake . . .''

He reached for her. "I know what you meant.''

Ten minutes later the bedside phone rang again, interrupting Leeds at a very crucial juncture. Outraged, he ripped the receiver off the cradle. "All right, General! That's enough! I told you to take your—''

"Stow it, Leeds. This isn't General Whittenberg.''

The NASA Director recognized the voice. "Uh, Mr. Vice President?''

"That's right, Leeds. Now you listen, and listen to me but good. You get your butt out of bed and hightail it down to Goddard, and make goddam sure General Whittenberg gets control of the Hubble telescope and has any other assistance he may require. Do you hear me?''

The astronomer stammered, "Uh, well, yes, Mr. Vice President, of course, but I feel I'm entitled to some kind of an explanation. What's this all about?''

"Certainly, Doctor. The explanation is that until you hear different from me or the President, your agency and all of NASA's resources are working for General Whittenberg. And don't give me any back talk. If you don't bust ass down to Goddard right now I'll see to it your next posting will be studying penguin shit at the South Pole. And we'll have a new NASA Director by the time the sun comes up. Is that clear?''

"Uh, uh, yes, Mr. Vice President.''

"Now get moving and call the General the minute you get to Goddard—on a secure line. Now *do it*.''

The line went dead, and Leeds rolled out of bed.

"Say . . . where you goin'?" whined his companion.

While pulling on his pants, Leeds muttered, "Can't talk. Gotta go."

With a pouting mouth she whimpered, "Don't forget my cab fare."

Day 3, 1100 Hours Zulu, 3:00 P.M. Local
BAIKONUR COSMODROME

Flashes from the electric arc welder illuminated the entire hangar like a giant strobe light. Vostov watched through protective goggles as the welder guided his electric torch down the side of the docking collar, generating a waterfall of sparks along the way. Understandably, the technician was a little antsy about passing hundreds of volts through an aluminum collar wrapped around a solid-fuel rocket, but the Chief Designer assured him there was no danger.

When the second seam was completed, the two men pulled off their goggles. Vostov walked around and carefully inspected the welds, and how the collar fitted against the exterior of the Progress engine.

The early models of the Progress cargo drone had used liquid-fuel engines. There are many positive things to be said for that type of propulsion system. Liquid-fuel engines are easy to start and stop by turning the fuel flow on and off, and the energy-to-weight ratio of liquids is better than that of solid fuel. But unfortunately, liquids can also be volatile as hell. Two years prior, a Progress drone had been on final approach to the Mir space station when it simply blew up for no apparent reason. Luckily, it was far enough away from the Mir that the space station was not damaged, and the five cosmonauts on board were not injured. The explosion was considered a fluke until the same thing happened again a month later. After that, Vostov immediately went to work on a solid-fuel version.

Most solid-fuel rocket engines are essentially a metal cylinder casing wrapped around a rubbery fuel. The fuel is ignited at the bottom of the exit nozzle and simply keeps burning until it's expended. Designing a solid-fuel engine that can be turned on and off at will is tricky. Vostov came up with a method that fed granules of the aluminum powder fuel and the aluminum perchlorate oxidizer—about the size of BBs—into a combustion chamber. The fuel flow into the chamber could be turned on and off as required by an innovative pressurized nitrogen system. It was another Vostov marvel.

"You are an excellent welder," announced the Chief Designer.

"Thank you, Comrade," the tradesman replied.

"That will be all," Vostov said in dismissal, and the welder gathered up his gear. Vostov beckoned to a lieutenant colonel, who hustled up with several technicians. "Give this a few more minutes to cool, then begin loading it in the launch shroud. When it is prepared, come awaken me. I will be in the temporary quarters building."

The lieutenant colonel saluted. "Of course, Comrade Chief Designer."

Vostov turned to the cosmonauts, Lubinin and Yemitov, and gestured to the welded collar on the Progress engine. "You approve?" he asked, as if it were a dare.

The two men took a walkaround of the finished product. Lubinin allowed himself a smile. "Everything appears to be in order, Comrade. I trust the measurements are precise."

"Precise," responded Vostov, "and well ahead of schedule, as you might imagine."

Lubinin's head, situated on top of his oxlike neck, nodded approvingly. "Very well, Comrade. Just get us up there, and we will bring down that American shuttle for you."

Day 3, 1109 Hours Zulu, 1:09 P.M. Local
MOSCOW

If a Harvard Business School professor ever had the inclination to investigate the management styles of Politburo members, it would make a fascinating study, to be sure; for in exercising their power, this small cabal of fifteen men used arcane techniques that were something to behold. Many Politburo members used the fear-and-intimidation management style. A couple led by example. One tried to be benevolent, while another passed out cartons of American cigarettes as a reward for excellent performance by subordinates.

But the distinctive management style utilized and embraced by the Foreign Minister was that of *humiliation*. At every opportunity he would berate, ridicule, belittle, insult, or impugn his subordinates, and impress upon them how utterly unfit they were to serve in the glorious Foreign Ministry. No position paper, no report, no drafted cablegram was ever worth more than the paper upon which it was written, as far as the Foreign Minister was concerned. And he seized every opportunity to point out these failings to his underlings. "If you presented the Foreign Minister with Michelangelo's *David*," lamented one staffer, "he would ream you out for wasting a perfectly good piece of marble."

216

Now understand, whenever the Foreign Minister dealt with his own superiors he would turn into supplication itself. But with subordinates, the octogenarian minister would remind them over and over and over again that their station in life was just slightly below the level of whale shit on the bottom of the ocean.

The reason subordinates put up with such humiliation was because the Foreign Minister held the key to that juiciest of plums—a posting outside the Soviet Union. Assignments abroad—particularly in Western Europe or North America—were the most coveted jewels in all of Soviet society; and if you had to wallow in the whale shit to grab one of those foreign jewels, well, that's what you did—as long as you eventually landed in Rome, Madrid, or Ottawa.

Aleksandr Kulikov, aide-de-camp to the Foreign Minister, had been wallowing in the whale shit for a very long time indeed. The willowy, almost delicate Kulikov possessed features that were somewhat androgynous, which seemed to accentuate his forlornness. Early in his career he had been blessed with a delightful three-year posting in Paris, where he fell in love with cognac, French food, French architecture, French women (all of them); took weekend trips to Loire Valley; and earned high marks for his performance from the Russian ambassador. It appeared his star was rising in the ministry, for upon his return to Moscow he was awarded with what seemed to be a prestigious position, one that would greatly enhance his career. He was selected as aide-de-camp to the Foreign Minister himself. Kulikov figured he would have the position for a year or two, then be rotated back to Paris or some other choice Western capital.

He was wrong.

Because he was a very efficient aide, the Foreign Minister had kept Kulikov enslaved in the same position for the last *ten* years, subjecting him to a daily regimen of insults, contempt, degradation, abuse, and humiliation. Despite Kulikov's constant entreaties for reassignment, the Foreign Minister refused to let him go, and kept him on such a short leash that the poor wretch was scarcely allowed to go to the water closet by himself.

After enduring seven hellish years of insults, contempt, degradation, abuse, and humiliation from his superior, Kulikov snapped. Utterly snapped. Like a dry twig. At the end of work one day he picked up and *ran* to the apartment of an old friend stationed at the French embassy and begged—literally begged—to become a spy. Kulikov's hatred for the Foreign Minister had blinded and engulfed him. His once promising career had turned to ashes. France had blessed him with the only happiness he'd ever known in his life. Spying gave him the means to strike back at his aged superior, while serving his beloved surrogate country.

Kulikov's Gallic friend was sympathetic, and made the necessary arrangements.

The Foreign Minister had already left for his Black Sea dacha at Vilkovo, and Kulikov was walking through the giant GUM department store on his Friday-afternoon lunch break. He took his time, pretending to window-shop here and there, then made his way outside and walked up to Karl Marx Prospekt with a copy of *Pravda* tucked underneath his arm. He pulled his gray wool coat close around him and was grateful for the fox-fur hat on his head. The snow was still falling, and the pedestrians—like all Moscow pedestrians—were walking briskly, with eyes to the front. No one took notice of Kulikov when he stopped, dropped his *Pravda* in a trash can, and put his foot up on a sidewalk bench to tie his shoelace. After the bow was redone he sauntered back down the Prospekt, leaving the newspaper behind.

A few moments later a stranger walked by, and he, too, was afflicted with the same malady of the shoelace. After retying the strings, the stranger retrieved the copy of *Pravda* from the trash can and continued his stroll.

Inside the paper was an exposed strip of Minox film.

Day 3, 1110 Hours Zulu, 6:10 A.M. Local
SPACE TELESCOPE OPERATIONS CONTROL ROOM, GODDARD SPACE FLIGHT CENTER, GREENBELT, MARYLAND

Spread over eleven hundred acres of beautiful rolling Maryland countryside was a complex of twenty-nine buildings that was, in essence, the Cheyenne Mountain of America's civilian and scientific space effort. Named after Robert H. Goddard, the founding father of rocketry science, the Goddard Space Flight Center controlled a panoply of satellites orbiting the earth. Satellites that pursued exotic scientific knowledge—such as measuring solar winds, tracing magnetospheric particles, sampling a comet's tail, calibrating crustal dynamics, and pointing an X-ray telescope at a neutron star. While Cape Canaveral and Houston Mission Control might be the arms, eyes, and ears of NASA, Goddard and its 8,600 employees—many of them leading scientists—were the brains.

218

The flagship of Goddard's scientific efforts was an instrument hailed as the greatest leap forward in astronomy since Galileo first turned his telescope on the heavens. This instrument was the Hubble orbiting space telescope, which enabled astronomers to see distant galaxies above the veil of earth's polluted atmosphere. It was controlled by a special team at Goddard, twenty-four hours a day, and it was the personal pet project of Dr. Percival Leeds, Director of the National Aeronautics and Space Administration. The very *idea* of SPACECOM's tampering with Leeds's sacred ikon had the feel of rape about it. He was pacing up and down the Hubble control room like a wounded rhino.

"This is an outrage! This telescope, *my* telescope, is being perverted by those space *goons*, those soldier boys. Wait until Senator McGilla-cudy hears about this!"

The telescope controller—who was also a graduate student at Johns Hopkins University—had the phone to one ear and his finger in the other trying to block out Leeds's bellowing. Sir Isaac from Cheyenne Mountain was on the other end of the line.

"Now do you understand what we're trying to do?" asked Sir Isaac.

"Well, yes, I think so," said the controller cautiously. "But we've never done anything like this before. We can give it a try, but I'm afraid it will use up the fuel pretty fast."

"I understand," comforted Sir Isaac. "We'll get you some more fuel later, courtesy of SPACECOM. I'll be transmitting the orbital path, reference points, and timing data to your terminal in about thirty seconds."

"Okay, sir. I'm ready. After I get the data it will take me a couple of hours to reprogram the scope alignment."

"Right. And when you get that done, I want you to patch the video over to us in Cheyenne Mountain."

"No problem," said the controller. "Just tell me which satellite and the freq."

"We'll want it to come through on RealTime," said Sir Isaac. "I'll get you the specs when it's time to transmit."

The controller whistled. "The RealTime satellite? Wow, I guess you guys must rate. You know, you're gonna have a lynch mob on your doorstep when our clients find out their time on the scope has been bumped. Some of them have been waiting for two years to do their turn."

"I can empathize. Suffice it to say, we're not doing this because we want to. Okay, we're ready to transmit."

"Go," said the controller.

Day 3, 1200 Hours Zulu, 7:00 A.M. Local
ORLANDO, FLORIDA

The proprietor looked like any middle-aged man who ran his own small business. His dark hair was thinning, his middle had developed a bit of a pot, he wore wire-framed glasses, and he was attired in a khaki uniform with the name Fred embroidered above the left breast pocket. Promptly at 7:00 A.M. he unlocked the pumps and cash drawer in preparation for another day of work at his Gas Saver discount service station. He turned on the coffee machine and had begun taking an inventory of parts and accessories when his first customer of the day rolled up in a station wagon. After filling his tank with super unleaded, the customer—who wore a Hawaiian shirt and wraparound sunglasses—surveyed the area carefully, then approached the proprietor.

"Excuse me," asked the customer. "But could you take a check?"

"We are a discount station," replied the proprietor. "We only take cash."

"But I am from Milwaukee," said the customer politely.

The proprietor's face did not betray so much as a glimmer of recognition. "A check from Milwaukee is always welcome," he replied.

"That is most kind, but on second thought, I will pay cash." The customer handed over two five-dollar bills and quickly left. The proprietor extracted the small piece of paper sandwiched between the bills and tucked the money in the cash drawer.

A few minutes later, Ernie, the proprietor's unreliable, alcoholic assistant, stumbled in. The proprietor was well aware of Ernie's weakness—indeed, it was the main reason Ernie had been selected for employment. Ernie would die before betraying his boss, because the boss accepted him in spite of his affliction—and turned a blind eye to his frequent unannounced absences.

"Ernie," confided the proprietor, "I've had a family emergency come up and I may be gone most of today and possibly tomorrow. Could you handle things while I'm gone?"

Ernie's mottled face tried to express eagerness. "Sure thing, Mr. Tompkins. I done it for you before real good, you know that. You can count on me."

The proprietor patted Ernie on the shoulder and gave him a paternal smile. "I know I can, my friend. I'll be back as soon as I can."

"Hope it's nothin' serious," said Ernie.

The proprietor shook his head sadly. "Just an aunt who lives down in the Keys. Old age, I'm afraid."

"Gosh, I'm sorry."

"That's very kind of you, Ernie. As I said, I shouldn't be gone more than a day or so."

"Mr. Tompkins" left and drove to his apartment, somewhat grateful he would not be seeing Ernie for a while. Upon arriving he locked the door and pulled the drapes, then went to the bookshelf and withdrew a hardbound copy of *Don Quixote* by Miguel de Cervantes. He sat down at the kitchen table with a pad and pencil and took out the slip of paper the man from Milwaukee had given him. Typed on the paper was a series of numbers. The first two digits indicated a page number of *Don Quixote*, and each subsequent number indicated which letter in sequence should be taken from the page. Unless you knew exactly what edition of what book the man known as Mr. Tompkins was working from, the cipher would be unbreakable. It took him several minutes to finish, and when he did it took some moments for the impact of the message from Moscow Centre to sink in, for it read:

STOP SPACE SHUTTLE CONSTELLATION AT ALL COSTS

So this was it. The end of eight years of spying on the Kennedy Space Center. "Mr. Tompkins" allowed himself a few minutes of quiet reflection on his life in America, but only a few, for he had never cared much for sentimentality. Rising from the kitchen table, he methodically began his preparations to execute a contingency plan—a plan he'd literally worked years to perfect. He did not shrink from the task, for instructions from Moscow Centre were to be followed to the letter. The mere use of the Milwaukee code indicated it was vital. What the shuttle's mission was about did not concern him. He had his orders, and that was all that mattered.

"Mr. Tompkins" went to his bedroom bureau and pulled out the top drawer, then emptied the contents on the bed. With a pocket knife he pried out the false bottom of the drawer and extracted a U.S. Postal Service uniform. Then from another false-bottomed drawer he retrieved a Heckler-Koch 9mm P7 automatic pistol, a silencer, and a clip of hollow-point ammunition. He'd selected the HK P7 because of its small size and the stopping power of the 9mm slug. Lastly, from the secret compartment of a third drawer, he pulled out an object about the size and shape of a dinner plate, as well as a small cardboard box with a false bottom, and two photo identification cards—one identifying him as a Kennedy Space Center employee, and the other as an inspector with the Occupational Safety and Health Administration.

He changed into the postal uniform, checked the action of the pistol, loaded it and chambered a round, then screwed on the silencer. He put the platelike object, the gun, the false-bottomed box, and the ID cards into a valise and tossed all of his "Mr. Tompkins" identification onto the bureau. Before leaving his apartment he put on a windbreaker to cover the postal uniform shirt, then grabbed the valise and walked out to his car.

"Why, good morning, Mr. Tompkins," called his elderly neighbor.

"Ah, good morning, Mrs. Davis," he called back.

"Why are you wearing a jacket for on such a nice warm morning?" asked the nosy old woman.

"You're quite right. It's only a windbreaker, but I'll take it off when I get to work. Must go. I'm already late."

Driving off, he gave his neighbor a smile as she waved from the sidewalk. Goodbye forever, Mrs. Davis, he thought.

He made his way through Orlando to the Tanglewood Apartments on the east side of the city, and cruised through the apartment parking lot until he found the Toyota sedan he was seeking—one with the Kennedy Space Center parking sticker on the bumper. That meant his subject was in the apartment. But was he alone?

"Mr. Tompkins" parked his car and got out. He took his time peeling off the windbreaker in order to survey the scene around him. Once satisfied that most of the residents of the singles complex had gone to work, he retrieved the cardboard box and inserted the P7 automatic through the false bottom. He walked upstairs to apartment 14B, looked around once more, and knocked lightly on the door. There was no answer, so he tried again, a bit more forcefully.

"Okay, okay, hang on a minute," came a sleepy voice from inside the apartment. The door opened, revealing a young man wearing a bathrobe and a handlebar mustache.

"Mr. Leland?" asked the postman.

"Yeah, that's me," replied the occupant.

"So sorry to disturb you, Mr. Leland, but I have an Express Mail package for you."

"For me?" Leland asked groggily.

"Yes, sir. I need you to sign for it, but I'm afraid I'm all out of pens. If I may, could I borrow one of yours?"

"Yeah, sure. Just a second." Leland turned and walked toward a pencil holder by his telephone. As he bent over to retrieve the pencil, Leland heard the door slam. He spun around to see the postman pointing a pistol at his chest. "Hey, what the hell is this?" he demanded.

The "postman" kept the gun rock steady. "I must know, Mr. Leland, are we alone?"

"Huh?" Leland's mouth was wide open.

"Please do not make me repeat myself, Mr. Leland. Now tell me. Are we alone?"

"What? Uh, well, yeah, we're alone, but I don't—"

A muffled *thunt!* spat from the barrel of the P7. The 9mm hollow-point slug caught Leland square in the sternum, lifting him off his feet and pinning him against the wall. He stayed there for a moment, looking back at the postman with an empty gaze. Then his eyes rolled up and he fell over in a clump, leaving a red stain on the wall.

The postman locked the door and quickly inspected the one-bedroom apartment. Leland had told the truth. They were indeed alone. He felt for his victim's pulse, and there was none. Then he went into the bedroom, where he searched through the cluttered dresser top and found what appeared to be a work schedule. The postman looked at it carefully, and ascertained that Leland—a power systems technician—had just returned from a night shift of working on the *Constellation*. He went to the closet and extracted Leland's hard hat and a pair of the white coveralls that all technicians wore in the gantry area. The postman pulled on the coveralls, put the hard hat under his arm, and replaced the P7 in the box. He grabbed Leland's keys from the dresser and locked the door on his way out. After scanning the parking lot, he quickly made his way to the dead man's Toyota and drove off toward the Beeline Expressway and Cape Canaveral.

Day 3, 1300 Hours Zulu
ALTITUDE: 368 MILES
ORBITAL INCLINATION: 28.5 DEGREES

Orbiting above the Earth's polluted atmospheric veil was one of the most precise scientific instruments ever assembled by man. Over a decade of design, engineering, fabrication, grinding, and polishing had gone into its construction, at a cost of over $1.2 billion. But the payoff for the money, and the four million plus man-hours that went into it, was nothing less than cosmic.

The Hubble Space Telescope looked like a 43-foot-long "tall boy" beer can with blinders attached. With this goofy-looking instrument, astronomers were able to see celestial objects fifty times fainter, obtain images ten times sharper, and peer seven times deeper into the universe than with conventional earthbound telescopes.

At one end of the beer can was the heart of the Hubble—its 94-inch reflective mirror. Although smaller than Mount Palomar's 200-inch reflector, it was a great deal more precise. To illustrate its precision: if the Hubble's 94-inch mirror were enlarged to a disk three thousand miles in diameter, its largest imperfection would be four inches high.

The revolutionary mirror was made of an extraordinary material called ultra low expansion (ULE) glass, manufactured by Corning Glass Company. The ULE glass could endure the large temperature swings of outer space without expanding and contracting like conventional glass.

The Perkin-Elmer Corporation fabricated the ULE glass into a concave structure with a honeycomb base, then ground and polished the surface with a computer-controlled robotic arm for twenty-five weeks. In a heat-and-vacuum process, the mirror was then coated with a film of aluminum 2.5 millionths of an inch thick to provide it with a reflective surface.

When the telescope was pointed at a target, the image came in the open end of the beer can, struck the 94-inch primary mirror, bounced to the 12.5-inch secondary mirror, then was reflected into the telescope's instrument array, which dissected the image for analysis. The on-board electronic instruments, powered by the solar panel "blinders," transmitted the data to Goddard. It was then passed to the Space Telescope Science Institute at Johns Hopkins University in Baltimore for subsequent analysis and dissemination.

How sensitive was the Hubble? From its low earth orbit it could detect a candle burning on the moon. It expanded the observable universe by 350 times, allowing scientists to observe celestial objects fourteen billion light-years away—almost to the beginnings of time as man comprehended it.

The incredible instrument was named for famed American astronomer Edwin Hubble. When Hubble began his career, conventional astronomical theory postulated that the known universe terminated at the end of our Milky Way galaxy. Hubble demonstrated that the universe went beyond our own tiny Milky Way. Indeed, the universe contained billions of galaxies, all hurtling and expanding through space at cosmic speeds. His contribution to astronomy was perhaps greater than Galileo's.

But now, the telescope bearing Hubble's name was repositioning itself for a different purpose. The unknown Russian satellite launched from the Plesetsk Cosmodrome was traveling in a polar orbit, while the Hubble was circling the globe in a quasi-equatorial path. The orbital trajectories of the two spacecraft would roughly intersect on opposite sides of the globe once every forty-five minutes. The Soviet satellite was in the lower orbit, while the telescope was traveling above it. The technician at Goddard issued instructions for the Hubble to track the Soviet satellite as it passed underneath the telescope on the sunny side of the earth. This was like driving your car over an overpass while keeping your eyes on a car traveling underneath you from left to right.

On command from the ground controller, the telescope's maneuvering thrusters were engaged and the entire mechanism pivoted into position. When the Russian satellite passed from darkness to sunlight the scope's protective aperture door flipped open, allowing the primary mirror to capture the tiny image.

Day 3, 1345 Hours Zulu, 8:45 A.M. Local
CAPE CANAVERAL, FLORIDA

"Mr. Tompkins," who had first become the "postman," was now Leland the power technician driving his Toyota sedan across the Indian River on NASA Causeway West, approaching the Kennedy Space Center (KSC).

The reason why the genuine Leland had had to be "taken out"—KGB jargon for "murdered"—was the security system at KSC, and in particular, Pads 39A and 39B, which handled shuttle traffic. First, to obtain access to the employee parking area, an intruder would have to have the proper sticker on his bumper. If he did, then he would be waved past the security guard's hut at the main entry gate. Obtaining a forged bumper sticker from Moscow Centre was not a problem—Mr. Tompkins had done that often enough. Taking Leland's Toyota had been more of a convenience than a necessity.

But beyond the parking lot, access to the pad area became a bit more sticky. Technicians working on Pad 39A had to pass through an access/locker room building, which was the only passage through the ten-foot-high, sensor-laden cyclone fence that ringed the entire pad

225

complex. It was in this building that technicians could change clothes and shower if they wished, and that access through the security fence was controlled. An employee had to pass through a "cattle chute" where a guard checked the worker's photo ID, matched his name against an access list, and signed him in or out. Work schedules on the pad were erratic prior to launches—a technician might work ten hours, leave for six, then return to the pad for another twelve hours. That was why Leland had to be taken out. It simply wouldn't do for Mr. Tompkins to show up posing as Leland when Leland was already signed in, or have Leland show up after Mr. Tompkins had entered the complex. That would be a screaming red flag to the guard.

For two years, Mr. Tompkins had studied photographs of KSC, followed individual employees home and tracked their work patterns, and used scuba gear to take pictures from offshore. Additionally, he'd pasted a forged bumper sticker on a Chevy van and parked it in the employee parking lot to study movements, procedures, and guard changes at the access building. He'd chosen Leland only after a careful appraisal indicated the technician was unmarried and apparently had little social life. The body probably wouldn't be discovered for days.

Mr. Tompkins was waved past the KSC security guard hut at entry gate 3T, then turned left onto Kennedy Parkway North. He drove over Banana Creek and past the shuttle recovery runway on his left before turning right on Beach Road. Then he pulled into the employee lot outside the Pad 39A security access building at Gate 5C and parked the Toyota.

Mr. Tompkins was now approaching the most vulnerable point in the whole scenario. He possessed a realistic KSC Pad 39A employee ID with his own photograph laminated on it, but with Leland's name. The procedure at the security post called for the guard to look at both the ID photo and the employee to make sure the two matched. The guard would then check the name on the access list as IN, along with the time. If this particular guard happened to know Leland by sight, then the game was busted. But there were so many workers in the pad area that this shouldn't be a problem—or so he hoped.

Mr. Tompkins waited until there was no employee traffic through the access building, for he didn't want to stumble into any workers who might know Leland by name. Seeing that the coast was clear, he walked into the "cattle chute" and up to the guard booth, where he thrust out his forged ID with authority. The man in uniform perfunctorily glanced at the card, then at the face, and made a notation on the clipboard. "Leland. Nine oh seven. In," he said while scribbling.

"Right," said Mr. Tompkins, now Leland, as he walked past the locker room and out to the shuttle bus waiting area. For safety considerations, the parking lots and buildings at KSC were kept well away from the launch pads, and gantry workers were ferried back and forth between the access building and Pad 39A on small shuttle buses.

Leland didn't have to wait long for a bus, and he was alone as he boarded the vehicle. During the quick drive to the pad he switched ID cards. The second card looked much like the first, except now Leland had turned into Donald Loomis, site inspector for the Occupational Safety and Health Administration.

As the bus approached the shuttle pad, Loomis noticed something off in the distance that looked like a Roman candle shooting up in the air. He had no idea what it was, but didn't have time to worry about it.

The Northrop KD2R-5 target drone banked away from the beach near Titan Complex 40 at KSC and traveled about a quarter mile over the Atlantic Ocean. The Army specialist played with his remote-control joysticks and the aluminum monoplane turned again, coming to a course parallel with the beach at about five hundred feet altitude.

"Okay, Major," coached Warrant Officer Hogan, "put it in the circle and wait for the 'engage' light."

Mission Specialist Sandford Watkins peered through the viewfinder of the Stinger surface-to-air missile and easily lined up the propeller-driven drone, which was traveling at 80 knots. When the morning sun glinted off the drone's dark aluminum skin, the red "engage" light lit up in the viewfinder and Watkins squeezed the trigger, causing the missile to pop out of the tube muzzle. After the Stinger "jumped" about forty feet from the launcher, its solid-fuel propellant ignited and the small missile took off, leaving a corkscrew tail of smoke in its wake. Watkins watched the high-powered dart as it vectored off in the wrong direction. He would've sworn it was going to miss the drone, but then it made a sharp climbing left turn and quickly gained on the lumbering target. When the small aircraft disappeared in a ball of flame, Watkins couldn't help yelling, "Awwwright! Man, this is more fun than shooting pop-bottle rockets."

Hogan grinned. "Yes, sir. I know the feeling. I think you've got the hang of it. Now, let's try it with this contraption on."

Watkins shrugged. "Okay. I'm not sure whose idea this was, but I'll give it a try."

"As I understand it, Major," said Hogan, "some air crapper came up with this brainstorm."

Watkins laughed. "Figures. I can't tell you how nice it is to see another Army face around here, Mr. Hogan. I feel a little lonely at times."

"I understand, Major Watkins. Say, how did a ground pounder like you ever become an astronaut, anyway?"

"Beats me. Somebody in the Pentagroin must have dropped my file into the wrong in-basket. Ready? Heave."

The two men lifted up the top half of the extravehicular spacesuit, sans oxygen pack and maneuvering unit, and draped it over Watkins's torso. The major raised the clear visor so he could breath easily, and took another Stinger from the Army warrant officer. Hogan spun his finger in the air, indicating he wanted another drone launched, and almost immediately a monoplane was catapulted off its small ramp.

The first Stinger Watkins fired with the suit on went wild. Fortunately, all the nearby airspace had been closed to air traffic and there was no danger of downing an innocent Cessna. On the second shot, Watkins contorted himself so he could peer through the eyepiece with the helmet on, and the missile got close. The third Stinger was dead on.

"One more drone, Major?" asked Hogan.

"Let's do it."

And the last aluminum monoplane was scattered over the ocean.

"Help me get outta this thing," pleaded Watkins. "It's kinda hot without the cool suit on."

Hogan assisted him, then began a critique. "For your purposes, I think you can handle the Stinger with no problem, sir. Your target will be stationary, and that will make things a lot easier than tracking a moving drone. Plus, as I understand it, the *Intrepid* is quite a bit larger than our drone."

Watkins nodded. "To say the least."

"However, I must point out that what we're doing here may not really apply to an outer-space environment. The guidance fins on the Stinger will be useless in a vacuum, and this missile isn't spin stabilized. So all I can recommend is that you essentially bore sight the weapon and let 'er rip. Just stay at least four hundred meters away to allow enough distance for the warhead to arm before it impacts. Okay?"

Watkins nodded. "I hear ya. Actually, I seriously doubt if we'll need these. If we have to disable the *Intrepid*, I plan to do a little number on her OMS rocket fuel lines, and for that all I need is a big set of pliers. But if the Russkies show up, just shootin' one of these things off should scare hell out of 'em and keep 'em at bay.''

Hogan took off his soft fatigue hat and wiped his brow. "Major, just between us ground pounders, is this thing for real? I mean, are the Russians really trying to heist one of our shuttles?''

Watkins shrugged again. "All we can do is go on the evidence, and the evidence tells us that a hijack can be the only explanation. By the way, until this thing is resolved, you and your crew are quarantined here at KSC. There's a tight security lid on this.''

Hogan nodded. "I understand, sir, and so do my crew. I told 'em if they so much as opened their mouths about being here I'd turn 'em into sopranos real quick.''

The bus halted and Mr. Tompkins turned postman turned Leland turned Loomis stepped out with his valise, saying "Thank you" to the driver. He now confronted the gantry and had to make a quick decision. In order to execute his mission with the platelike device, he needed access to a vulnerable part of the launch vehicle for a few moments—unobserved and alone. That was going to be difficult, because a gantry before launch was busy as an ant hill, with white figures scurrying around, reading gauges and making system checks. Loomis gave the scene a quick once-over—he would have to attempt something at the base of the orbiter around the engine nozzles, or ride the elevator up and take his chances on one of the upper levels of the gantry. Above all, he couldn't hesitate, for that would draw attention to himself.

The decision was really made for him. There were simply too many technicians around the rocket nozzles.

So in a forthright manner he strode over to the gantry elevator and waited behind two other men clad in white coveralls and hard hats. The cagelike elevator descended and opened, and all three men got on board. One of the technicians turned the hand control knob and the cage began to rise. Loomis had studied the available literature on the shuttle many times, so when the elevator stopped he knew the level on which they'd halted. The wire doors opened and his two companions stepped out. Loomis followed.

When they were out on the gantry catwalk, one of the technicians— who had a set of barn-door ears sticking out from beneath his hard hat—turned around and inspected Loomis quizzically. "You sure you got off on the right level?" he asked. His partner turned around, too.

"This *is* the hydrogen vent access arm, isn't it?" queried Loomis politely.

"Yeah." It was a cautious response.

Loomis smiled. "Then I'm in the right place." He touched his ID card. "Don Loomis, Occupational Safety and Health Administration. We've had some complaints filed and I was sent here to verify a few measurements. Wonder if you might lend me a hand for just a minute?" As Loomis well knew, nothing squelched curiosity better than an imposition on someone's time.

The other technician, who had a pair of goldfish bug eyes, shrugged. "What do you need?" he queried.

Loomis extracted a wind-up metal tape measure and a clipboard from his valise. He handed one end of the tape measure to the goldfish-eyed technician and pointed. "Now just hold the end of this tape measure against the girder right there." Loomis pulled the tape across the catwalk and jotted down the measurement. "Very good. Now then, if you would, hold it right up here," he said, indicating the top of the elevator opening. The technician sighed and did as he was told while Loomis extended the tape to the bottom of the opening and jotted down another number.

"Say, what's this for, anyway?" asked goldfish eyes.

In a tut-tut voice Loomis said, "Safety, my friend, safety. Your safety in particular. Would you believe I once had to investigate a catwalk accident—a catwalk very much like this one, I might add—at a chemical plant. The restraining door on the elevator was left wide open and a night watchman literally walked right through the hole and fell a hundred and seventy-five feet. It was ghastly, I don't mind telling you. Absolutely ghastly. The insurance company paid a handsome settlement on that one, and quite rightly so. Now we certainly don't want anything like that happening here, do we? Certainly not. Your government has an obligation to ensure you have a safe work-place."

Goldfish eyes nodded while his flap-eared companion shifted his weight from one foot to the other and said, "Come on, Tony. We can't wait around here all day."

Goldfish eyes nodded. "You need me anymore?" he asked.

"No, no," said Loomis. "You've been most helpful. I must say, this is quite a big bird you have here." He gazed up to the top of the external tank. "When is she taking off?" he asked casually.

Tony with the goldfish eyes shrugged. "Early tomorrow morning was the last I heard. Never really know, though. Things can always go wrong."

"I'm sure." Loomis smiled. "Well, thank you so much. I can manage from here."

The two techs nodded and walked down the catwalk of the gantry arm. They were making a check on the coupling that linked the hydrogen gas vent pipe to the big orange external tank.

Loomis started making random measurements of the girders along the catwalk cage while his mind raced through the timing arithmetic. Early tomorrow morning, goldfish eyes had said. Sunrise was about 6:30 A.M., so that would probably mean the launch would be about 6:30 to 7:30 A.M. Maybe. Maybe earlier. Loomis knew that the shuttle's external tank took five hours to fuel. If lift-off was to be at sunrise, then fueling would probably begin around 1:00 A.M. If he placed the platelike device—which was a small limpet mine—on the side of the external tank, and it detonated while the tank was empty, then that would delay the mission until the tank could be replaced. But Loomis took his orders to stop space shuttle *Constellation* at all costs to mean *stop*. Not *delay*. And that meant obliteration of the shuttle. Besides, after eight years of spying in America, Loomis wanted the capstone of his efforts to be greater than a little hole in an empty disposable tank. No. He wanted it all. And that meant detonation during fueling. All he needed was a few thousand liters of the liquid hydrogen loaded on board, and the small limpet mine would turn Pad 39A into a pyrotechnic display unlike anything since the *Challenger* went down. So he guessed somewhere between 1:00 A.M. and 7:30 A.M. would be the optimum time for detonation—say, 4:30 A.M. The tank should have plenty of fuel by then.

The two technicians walked past him, heading for the elevator. Goldfish eyes asked, "You finished yet?"

"No, not quite." Loomis smiled while adjusting his wire-framed glasses. "I have a little more to do still."

"Can you operate the elevator?" asked flap ears.

"Oh, my, yes. I work on construction catwalks all the time."

They both nodded. "Okay. See you," said goldfish eyes, and they disappeared into the elevator.

Loomis kept up his measuring routine while working his way toward the hydrogen gas vent coupling. He was keenly sensitive to discovery now, but no one paid him any attention. He was just another set of white coveralls on a catwalk.

Upon reaching the coupling he knelt down and extracted the limpet mine from his valise. He set the timer for 4:30 A.M., then with some effort he peeled off the waxed-paper-like film that covered its adhesive base. On many parts of the shuttle a magnetic attachment device wouldn't work, so adhesive was used.

He laid down and carefully sandwiched the mine—which was painted a neutral cream color—between the base of the catwalk superstructure and the external tank. He had to reach out and around the bottom girder of the catwalk and push the mine against the orange aluminum surface. Since he was a devout atheist, he hoped, rather than prayed, that no one would notice his arm sticking out of the catwalk.

No one did.

Loomis backed off and inspected his handiwork. Unless you placed your eye against the side of the external tank and looked straight down, you couldn't notice the mine from the catwalk. You could probably see it from the ground, but it was in the shadows of the catwalk and wouldn't be very visible until the gantry was pulled back a short time before launch. Then it would be predawn twilight.

Satisfied, Loomis picked up his valise and walked back down the catwalk. He rang for the elevator as if he were in a hotel. The empty cage appeared and he rode it down to the ground. Without hesitation he strode to the shuttle bus, and while keeping his head low he took his place as the last of a dozen techs climbing aboard. He sat alone in a seat by the driver and gazed out the window to avoid making eye contact with the other passengers.

After the short ride the bus doors clapped open at the security building, and Loomis filed out first. He pulled the clipboard out of his valise and pretended to study it while slowly sauntering toward the security "cattle chute." He had to allow the other employees to go past so he could switch ID cards again and stay out of earshot when the guard mentioned the name Leland.

The Russian was thinking about how incredibly easy the whole thing had been when a voice from behind asked, "Do you OSHA guys do much work out here on the Cape?"

Loomis turned around. It was Tony with the goldfish eyes. He'd been on the bus. The Russian put down the clipboard and gave his companion from the catwalk a charming smile. "Oh, not too often, no. We OSHA inspectors are spread rather thin, I'm afraid."

"*OSHA*? What's this about OSHA?" demanded a baritone voice. Goldfish eyes looked over Loomis's shoulder, and immediately started backpeddling. "Nothing, Mr. Garvey. I just ran into this OSHA inspector up on the gantry and I was just askin' him a question, that's all."

"Nobody told *me* anything about any OSHA inspector," bellowed the baritone voice.

Loomis turned around again, this time to see a slender man of medium height whose green eyes possessed a singular intensity. The Russian smiled and extended a hand. "Well then, I guess I should introduce myself. I'm Don Loomis, site inspector, Occupational Safety and Health Administration."

A firm hand clasped his, and a giant's voice boomed from the man with the slender build. "I'm Ed Garvey, deputy pad manager here. Nobody told me about your coming out here today."

Loomis feigned surprise. "Indeed? It was my understanding everything had been arranged by Mr. Burke's office." Edmund Burke was director of the entire Kennedy Space Center. "I would certainly think someone in your position would have been informed."

Goldfish eyes slunk off. Garvey had a reputation as a badass manager, and the technician avoided him whenever possible. He joined the remaining employees on their exodus to the parking lot, leaving the deputy pad manager and the OSHA inspector to themselves.

Garvey's intense eyes surveyed Loomis's KSC ID with OSHA embossed on it. He'd never seen one like that before. "I'm sure you're just doing your job, Mr. Loomis, but I don't like anything happening on my pad that I'm not aware of."

The last tech filed by the guard.

"I quite understand, Mr. Garvey. Uh, may I call you Ed? Please call me Don. I have some papers in my case here"—Loomis touched his valise—"that I must confess I find rather disturbing." Loomis looked around like a conspirator, then leaned closer and whispered. "I could get in trouble for telling you this before I file my report, Ed, but I think it's only fair for you to know. There have been some serious allegations made concerning safety on this pad. My yes, serious allegations. Perhaps if you could take a look at these papers—right here and now—we could possibly nip this problem in the bud. I so dislike getting the U.S. Attorney involved in these matters. I've been in this business for more years than I care to count, and believe me, I'll bend over backward to clear something up before turning it over to those damn lawyers."

Garvey gulped. "Well, yeah, I would appreciate it. Although I must say this is all news to me."

Loomis shook his head sadly. "I'm afraid you're not the first one to tell me that, Ed. Oh, the stories I could tell you. It would curl your hair. But never mind about that. Uh, could we possibly go in here"—Loomis jerked his head toward the locker room—"to look over the papers. Besides, I could use the 'facilities'."

Garvey said, "Yeah, me, too," and followed Loomis through the heavy swinging door.

Inside was a room ringed with tall lockers that contained a few scattered benches and a shower/lavatory area. No one else was there.

"This is a terrible time for something like this to happen," lamented Garvey. "We have a critical launch underway. Even so, I just can't believe anybody's raising a ruckus about safety violations. We run a pretty tight ship here, especially where safety's concerned."

"Oh, yes, yes, I'm sure you do," soothed Loomis as he pulled out the Heckler-Koch P7 automatic from his valise.

Garvey blinked. "Hey! What are you doing?" roared the baritone voice.

"Please be quiet, Mr. Garvey, and do exactly as I say."

Garvey blinked again, then snarled, "You aren't any damn OSHA inspector."

Loomis nodded. "I applaud your deductive skills. Now, if you please, step into one of those lockers."

"What?"

"Please do exactly as I say, Mr. Garvey, and you will not be harmed. Otherwise, I shall be forced to shoot you here and now."

What disturbed Garvey the most about this man Loomis was the detached, unemotional way in which he said "shoot you here and now." The deputy pad manager gulped, then backed up and opened a locker door. Slowly he scrunched up and inserted himself into the cramped rectangular space. "What are you going to do now?" he asked defiantly. "Lock me in here?"

"No," replied Loomis, and a *thunt! thunt! thunt!* poured from the silenced automatic. Loomis slammed the locker door, pinning the corpse inside.

The P7 went back into the valise and the ID tags on the Russian's chest were switched. He walked outside and up to the security window. The guard looked at the forged ID and the man in white coveralls.

"Leland. Nine fifty-two. Out," said the guard while making a notation on his clipboard.

Leland nodded and smiled, then walked casually toward the employee parking lot.

Driving back over the NASA Causeway West, "Mr. Tompkins" turned postman turned Leland turned Loomis turned Leland took a left turn onto U.S. Highway 1 and headed toward Miami. He wished he could stay and see the result of his many years' labor, but by nightfall he would be on board a thirty-foot cabin cruiser en route to Havana.

Day 3, 1430 Hours Zulu, 7:30 A.M. Local
CHEYENNE MOUNTAIN

"So what do you make of it?" asked the CinC.

Fairchild, Dowd, and Whittenberg were huddled around a television monitor in SPADOC, inspecting the image of the unknown Russian satellite taken by the Hubble telescope.

Sir Isaac scratched his lightbulb-shaped head and examined the telescope picture intently, then he sighed an exasperated sigh. "I'm afraid these pix don't do us much good. It could still be anything."

"Bull?" queried the CinC.

Dowd shook his head in frustration. He said, "I agree, sir," and moved his finger along the torpedo-shaped object. "This could be an aerodynamic launch shroud that simply hasn't been jettisoned yet. Underneath it could be a reconnaissance bird, electronic ferret, you name it. If this picture wasn't so clear I would've even guessed a Soyuz, but as you can see, it doesn't have the escape rockets on the nose."

The Bull was referring to the small pointed mushroom on the nose of all Soyuz spacecraft that held a small cluster of solid-fuel rockets. It acted like an ejector seat in the event of an emergency on the pad, allowing the Soyuz capsule to propel itself clear of the booster. On September 27, 1983, Cosmonauts Vladimir Titov and Gennadi Strekalov were atop an SL-4 liquid booster awaiting lift-off when, at T minus ninety seconds, a fuel valve apparently failed to close at the base of the rocket and a fire started. The flames consumed the booster so quickly that the automatic launch abort circuitry was melted before it could react to the emergency. The controllers in the launch bunker had to trigger the escape rockets, and the Soyuz was blasted to an altitude of 950 meters, where its rapid-deploy parachute opened. The cosmonauts came down four kilometers from the pad. Shaken, but alive.

Whittenberg's clouded mind agreed with the assessment of his other two generals. As frustrating as it was, he recognized there was virtually nothing further he could do about the *Intrepid* until the *Constellation* got aloft. His body was screaming for sleep, and Fairchild looked worse than he did. "Sir Isaac," he ordered, "go get some sack time. Bull, you keep somebody riveted on this satellite picture during the Hubble's observation window. I'm going to hit the sack myself for a while. There's nothing we can do at the moment, anyway. Wake me if you need me.''

"Yes, General," said Dowd, but Whittenberg's mind had already shut down and the chief of staff's response didn't even register. The CinC had to rely on his body's autopilot to get him back to the couch in his office.

Day 3, 1500 Hours Zulu, 10:00 A.M. Local
THE WHITE HOUSE

Ambassador Yevgeny Yakolev was escorted through the executive mansion to the Treaty Room. The French President was in the Oval Office, and it simply wouldn't do to have the ambassador run into the Gallic chief of state.

As Yakolev entered, he found the President and the Secretary of State waiting to receive him. The Defense Secretary was absent, indicating the American saber had been put back in its sheath—for the moment.

"Mr. President," said the portly Yakolev.

The President nodded in reply and said, "Mr. Ambassador, please sit down." The old professor did so.

"Now then, Mr. Ambassador, do you have a response to my query of yesterday evening?"

"Indeed I do, Mr. President. The Foreign Ministry submitted your supposition to the Defense Ministry, and I am happy to report that the matter was investigated thoroughly and found to have no substance whatsoever. In fact, my colleagues arrived at the same conclusion I did—that you are most likely experiencing some malfunction with your spacecraft and wish to, if you will forgive me, fabricate a rumor that the Soviet Union is somehow responsible for these problems. As I mentioned, such a rumor was attempted after your *Challenger* disaster. It is painful for me to bear such a distasteful message as this, Mr. President, but there you have it."

The Secretary of State saw the President's jaw muscles start flexing.

"Mr. Ambassador," said the chief executive through his teeth. "I told you last night that there is no malfunction or mistake. Someone inside the Soviet Union is talking to our space shuttle, and I want to know what it's about." Toward the end of his rejoinder, the President's voice started to rise.

Yakolev gave an exasperated sigh, thinking this American reminded him of an obstinate graduate student. "Mr. President, please try to understand. In my message to the Foreign Minister I conveyed your very real concern about this matter. The Foreign Minister personally called the Defense Minister, who personally investigated the matter himself. I have known these men for many years and I have the assurance of the Foreign Minister that there is absolutely no substance to your allegations, and we consider the matter closed."

The pugnacious President was about to explode when the Secretary of State lifted a hand to cut him off. "Very well, Mr. Ambassador," said the diplomat. "The President and I appreciate your timely response to our inquiry. We emphasize that our position remains unchanged and we can only wait to see how the situation with our spacecraft develops. Please convey our regards to the Foreign Minister and Defense Minister, and thank them for their attention to this matter."

The President gave his Cabinet officer a funny look, but decided to keep his mouth shut.

Yakolev nodded, and rose. "Very well, Mr. Secretary. I shall leave it at that. I would like to convey my personal wishes that no harm has come to any of your crewmen aboard your spacecraft. I have always admired the courage of the space explorers—of all nations. Mr. President, I bid you good morning."

The President only nodded and the ambassador withdrew. After the door closed he turned to his Secretary of State. "And just what was that all about?"

The Secretary rose and began pacing the room. Finally he muttered, "Something's screwy here, Mr. President."

The chief executive gawked. "Well, no screamin' shit, Winston. Even *I* knew that. I was fixing to read Yakolev the riot act when you cut me off. Why?"

The diplomat leaned over the table. "Consider this, Mr. President. First of all, as we've already noted, Yakolev is a lousy liar. Plus he's an independent cuss. We know he's personally very close to the Foreign Minister and the Defense Minister, and those two are heavyweights on the Politburo. It's highly unlikely that those two would try to pull Yakolev's chain and sent a false message through him. If they did, Yakolev probably wouldn't carry the message himself. He'd push it off on a subordinate. And even if he did bring in a phony story himself, he'd have been squirming in that chair."

The President shrugged. "Okay. Keep going. I'm listening."

The Cabinet officer started pacing again. In his well-tailored pinstripe suit he really did look as if he'd stepped off the cover of *Gentlemen's Quarterly*. "Mr. President, the single hardest thing for any American diplomat to do is to get inside the Russian mind. I know. I was posted in Moscow for four years. That's because Americans are brought up in a culture of strict laws, protected rights, venerated institutions. By comparison, the Soviet government is such a Byzantine enterprise that I doubt Machiavelli himself could survive in it today—especially within the Politburo. It's nothing like an elected senate or parliament with predetermined terms of office. No. It's more like a confederation of Mafia bosses, all of them constantly jockeying for position."

The President's hackles went up over the reference to the Mafia. Less than one percent of Italian-Americans were a part of organized crime, yet it was a stereotype with which all of them—including himself—had to contend. "So, what are you saying?"

"What I'm saying, sir," continued the Secretary, "is that it's not unprecedented for conflicting, yet genuine, messages to come out of the Kremlin. During the Cuban missile crisis, President Kennedy received conflicting letters from Khrushchev almost simultaneously."

The President scratched his head. "You mean the ministers of Foreign Relations and Defense in the Politburo don't know what's going on in their own government? That's a pretty big pill to swallow, Winston."

The Secretary had to be careful now. There was a very fine line between reasonable conclusions and pure speculation. "I'm simply saying it's . . . possible."

The President's nostrils flared. "Jesus Christ, Winston. Anything is possible. I've got the deadliest weapon ever produced by man floating around in space, and some Foggy Bottom supposition isn't going to get it down for me. I think we should've given it to Yakolev with both barrels to warn the damn Russians off. Mafia bosses understand muscle, you know."

Now it was the Secretary who got his hackles up. "Mr. President, have you ever been fired?"

The former auto executive gawked again. "Huh?"

"I asked you if you'd ever been fired."

A scowl crossed the President's face. He'd once been canned in the messiest, ugliest, most publicly humiliating corporate termination in American industrial history. Although he had landed on his feet with an ailing car company and achieved a spectacular turnaround, and then gone on to capture the Presidency, the episode was still a sore subject with him. "You know damn good and well I've been fired before, Winston. Every mother's son on planet earth knows that. What's it got to do with anything?"

The Secretary was pacing again. "Well, I've been fired, too," he said in recollection. "After graduating from Dartmouth I joined the foreign service. My first embassy posting in Saigon got cut short. You see, after a long day's work at the embassy I'd hang out with some of the reporters in town. But back then I was so damn naive I didn't even know what a 'leaker' was—until I turned out to be one. The ambassador found out and didn't care for it much. He personally administered the ax." The Secretary sniffed, allowing himself a moment of reflection. "Having self-destructed my foreign service career, it was at that point I decided to enter law school at Columbia. If Dr. Kissinger hadn't rehabilitated me several years later, I'd probably be probating wills in Buffalo right now."

The President shrugged again. "So? I don't understand what point you're trying to make."

The Cabinet officer leaned over the table again. "The point is, Mr. President, that out of that whole episode, the one thing that I vividly remember is those final days before I was summoned into the ambassador's office and given the ax. Think back to your own experience, Mr. President. Remember? Your company had just gone through a friendly takeover. It looked like you would be made chairman of the surviving company. You thought everything was rosy until you walked into that board of directors' meeting—then the people you thought were your friends pulled the rug right out from under you and threw you out on the street. You didn't see it coming, did you?"

The former auto executive emitted a grudging "Correct."

"Neither did I when the ax fell on me. But think back. After you were tossed out on your ear, you probably told yourself, 'How could I have been so stupid?' In the days prior to that fateful board meeting, I'll bet your phone calls weren't returned. When you walked into staff meetings, people would clam up. Nobody wanted to go to lunch with you. You were kept out of the loop on important memoranda. You'd call up a colleague to arrange a golf game, but he would beg off and say he was busy. You were *persona non grata* in your own company and you didn't even know it. When the board finally axed you, you were *the last one to know*. Am I right?"

A nod. "Yeah," he admitted. "But I still don't see where you're going with this line of thinking. What's the bottom line?"

The Secretary pulled on his sharp chin as he walked to the end of the table, then turned around. What the hell, he thought. Go for it. "Mr. President, I believe the 'pre-termination fool's paradise syndrome,' if you want to call it that, is not a distinctly American phenomenon. In fact, I believe it to be a universal phenomenon, to which the Soviet Union is not immune. The bottom line is that if Sam's people are wrong about the *Intrepid* and there is, in fact, no real communication between our spacecraft and the Russians, then we've just made a stupid error and have some egg on our face. But if Sam's people are indeed correct, and Yakolev is telling the truth about the Soviet ministers knowing nothing about the *Intrepid* . . ."

The Secretary's voice trailed off, but the President prodded him gently: "Go on."

The Secretary sighed. "Then a leadership change may be under way in the Kremlin."

The President walked back into the Oval Office to find his Gallic counterpart reviewing a staff briefing paper. The Frenchman's long, lanky frame dwarfed the easy chair.

"I apologize for the interruption, Mr. President," said the American. "I hope we can continue our discussions undisturbed for a while."

The Frenchman removed the tortoiseshell glasses from his huge round face and bit gently on an earpiece while contemplating his American host. The two men had gotten on famously, and their personal rapport had uplifted Franco-American relations to its highest plateau in many years—perhaps decades. But the man from the Elysée Palace had discerned a peculiar change in his host's behavior from the previous day.

"If you will forgive me, *Monsieur le Président*," he said, "I could not help but notice that since yesterday afternoon you have been popping in and out of our meetings like a—how you say—cuckoo in a clock. Late yesterday afternoon. The dinner last night. This morning. Your behavior puzzles me, my friend. This protocol is, well, *à tort et à travers* for a state visit. Is there anything you wish to . . . tell me? I must confess, you do not look well this morning. You appear the victim of *une nuit blanche*."

The American sagged back in his chair. Although Whittenberg suffered from "peer scarcity," it was nothing like the loneliness experienced by the President of the United States. There was truly no person he could talk to on a peer level. Not even the Vice President. And after a while this dearth of peers took a toll. He bit his lip and eyeballed his guest. He liked the Frenchman, and felt the man could be trusted. What the hell, thought the American. If I can't let my hair down with this guy, then who? He's putting his nuts on the line to bring France back into NATO, and this *Intrepid* business is too big for one man to handle alone. I need some solace.

"Mr. President," said the American, "sit back and strap yourself in, because I'm going to tell you the goddamnedest story you ever heard."

Day 3, 1500 Hours Zulu, 9:00 A.M. Local
CHICAGO

The amount of paper accumulated in a military man's personnel file during the course of his career can be physically heavy. There are educational background forms, proficiency test forms, commendation forms, disciplinary forms, medical forms, dental forms, efficiency report forms, and security clearance forms.

Of all the forms produced by the Department of Defense, however, security clearance forms are, by far, the most unwieldy, as Lydia Strand well remembered. It had taken her a man-day just to fill out the Top Secret clearance form and its section on historical residences.

Iceberg's residence history, however, was brief. From birth to age seven he had lived at 1819 MacKenzie Street in southwest Chicago. His family—which consisted of his mother, Victoria, his father, Carl, and himself—then moved to 419 Hampton Avenue in Wheaton, a Chicago suburb, where Iceberg had lived until he entered the Air Force Academy and where his mother had remained until her death.

Strand was en route to the Hampton Avenue address in Wheaton after flying into O'Hare on a T-39 Sabreliner earlier that morning. She felt a lot better after catching six hours of sleep.

In the back of the taxi she pulled out Iceberg's personnel file and reread the FBI background investigation. The FBI agent who conducted the background check had talked to the Kapuscinskis' neighbors on Hampton Avenue in Wheaton, but hadn't bothered to follow up on the MacKenzie Street address. Apparently the agent thought the MacKenzie address was too long ago to bother with.

Strand read the agent's report on his interview with the neighbors from Hampton Avenue. Yes, the Kapuscinskis were nice people. Very quiet. The father was a plumber—we think. He died when the boy was quite young. The mother didn't talk much. Well, hardly at all, really. Only said hello. Rarely saw the child. He stayed inside and didn't play with the other children. The yard was always maintained well. They were good neighbors.

Big help, thought Strand.

"Did you say four nineteen Hampton Avenue, lady?"

She looked up. "Yes, that's right."

The taxi driver pointed. "Well, that's it."

Strand gazed out the window and saw a Wal-Mart store, surrounded by a big parking lot.

"But there must be some mistake," said Strand in a puzzled voice. "The address I want is a residence."

The bearded driver, who wore a tam o'shanter cap, shook his head. "Not anymore, lady. I remember. This thing went in about two years ago. I drove past the construction a few times. These Wal-Mart stores spring up faster than mushrooms."

"Dammit!"

The driver was taken aback by the vehemence of her remark, but he quickly forgave her. This lady was a looker. "So, you want out here?" he asked.

Strand sighed. "No."

"So where to?"

"I wish I knew."

They should pay me extra for psychoanalysis, mused the cabbie.

"Hold on a second." Strand looked through the file once more. Iceberg's father had been a plumber and his work address was listed, but he'd died when little Julian was ten years old. She had the U-Stow-It warehouse receipts and a search warrant in her purse, but decided to try the MacKenzie address first, just to be thorough—unlike the FBI agent of long ago. "Take me back to Chicago—MacKenzie Street."

"You got it, lady," said the cabbie, and he hit the gas.

Day 3, 1630 Hours Zulu, 11:30 A.M. Local
THE WHITE HOUSE

For the first time in a very long time, the liquor cabinet in the Oval Office was opened before noon. The American President poured his guest a Jack Daniel's, while the Frenchman filled his host's glass with

Courvoisier. Then they raised their glasses in a toast to each other's native drink.

The Frenchman swished his bourbon over the ice. "You are most correct, my friend. This is an incredible story. As you say, it *is* the most goddamnedest thing I have ever heard."

The American took a swig and felt the cognac burn down to his stomach. "I'm pretty much at my wit's end. There's really nothing we can do until the *Constellation* is launched. I still have a hard time believing this is really happening, but my military people insist the *Intrepid* is talking to the Russians."

The Gallic President turned somber and pulled on his Jack Daniel's. "*Entre nous*, is this, this Graser device, I believe you called it, truly as powerful as you say?"

The American nodded. "Yeah. We've had oppressive security around the whole project, but even so, everybody knows we've had a technological breakthrough. Still, we thought the specifications on the Graser and the status of our SDI platform remained secure. We've given eyes-and-ears-only briefings to the NATO heads of state, and even then we couched a lot of the technical information in careful terms. You've only been in office for six months, and we were going to wait and see how this visit went before deciding whether or not to bring you in on the loop. I made the decision not to tell your predecessor."

The Frenchman chuckled. "*Oui*. I quite understand. In the Elysée bedroom he would always wake up facing east, while I tend to face west. But even with your excessive security measures, there appears to have been a serious penetration of your project."

The President downed the remainder of the Courvoisier. "No argument there. I don't know how the hell they did it, but the Russians caught us with our pants down."

"Pardon? Pants down?"

"That means they penetrated our security when they shouldn't have been able to," explained the American.

The tortoiseshell glasses once again came off and the earpiece went between the teeth. After some thoughtful moments the Frenchman said, "We are not without our own information sources inside the Soviet Union. This matter has ramifications for all of Western Europe . . . for NATO. If you will permit me, I shall see if my DGSE can shed some light on what mischief the Russians are making."

The American perked up. "Thanks. I would appreciate it. My CIA hasn't been able to come up with squat on this whole affair."

The Frenchman drained the last of his drink and smiled. "You know, this bourbon is truly a wondrous elixir. What do you call this? *Jacques* Daniel's?"

Day 3, 1630 Hours Zulu, 10:30 A.M. Local
CHICAGO

MacKenzie Street had probably been a nice neighborhood—once upon a time. Big oak trees still lined the roadway, but now almost everywhere Strand looked she saw peeling paint, overgrown or dead shrubs, and grime. A few houses had broken-down cars parked in the front yard with parts strewn about. Two ragamuffin children, whom she guessed were Vietnamese, were bundled up against the chilly March air. When the cab pulled up to the curb they scurried away, leaving their broken scooter behind.

The old Kapuscinski house looked worse than the others. A fading FOR RENT sign on the front door dangled by a lone thumbtack, and there wasn't a single unbroken window in the entire house.

Strand got out, looking pert and attractive in her off-blue Air Force trench coat and beret. In the yard across the street, two leathered-up bikers leaned on their "hogs" and eyed her hungrily. They were obese and filthy.

"You want me to wait around, lady?" asked the cabbie tentatively.

Strand swallowed. "Yes, if you please."

"Okay. Just don't be too long."

"Roger," she replied.

"What?"

"I mean, I'll be back as fast as I can."

"Good." He locked the doors of his cab.

Strand didn't see any point in trying the Kapuscinski home, since it was obviously deserted, so she went to a neighboring house and marched up the cracked sidewalk. She took a deep breath, threw her shoulders back, and knocked purposefully on the door. She waited and knocked again. The door opened slowly to a narrow slit, and Strand could barely make out a tiny, brown-skinned woman standing in the shadows on the inside.

"*Sí?*"

Strand tried to smile. "Good day, ma'am. My name is Lydia Strand and I'm with the Air Force. I'm trying to track down some information and I wondered if I could ask you a few questions."

The woman's eyes had a wildness about them. "*Inmigración?*" she asked apprehensively with a heavy accent.

Strand felt a dead end coming on. "Oh, you mean Immigration and Naturalization Service? INS? No, no. I am not *Inmigración*. I'm with the Air Force."

"*Por favor?*"

"I guess you don't speak English, do you?" asked Strand lamely.

"*No hablo inglés.*"

"I see, well, I'm afraid I don't speak Spanish, so I won't be taking up any more of your time. Thank"—the door slammed—"you."

Strand sighed, then beat a hasty retreat. At least she'd tried.

She walked back around the old Kapuscinski home toward the second neighbor's house, ignoring the bikers' stare. On rounding the corner of a large hedge she was greeted by a rather queer scene. A little white-haired man, wrapped in a worn black overcoat, was sitting on the concrete stoop with a steaming cup in his hand. Strand guessed it was coffee. Maybe tea. She couldn't understand why he was sitting outside on the cold, hard steps. There were still a few clumps of snow on the ground and winter wasn't over yet. She shrugged to herself, then approached him. "Excuse me, sir, I'm sorry to bother you, but—"

He put his finger to his lips, indicating he wanted silence. Then he pointed to the hedge and whispered, "He in there. . . . They no leave during winter, you know."

The accent was heavy. Strand guessed Eastern European.

The elderly man reached into his pocket, pulled out some sunflower seeds, and held them in his open palm.

Strand didn't understand what he was doing until a brilliant red cardinal appeared and perched on his thumb. The bird pecked through the offerings with his beak, then seized one seed and flew off. The white-haired man then pocketed the leavings and said, "He a good friend."

Strand nodded. "I'm sure he is. And so are you, to come out and feed him in the cold."

He sipped from his cup. It was tea.

"Marta use to feed birds . . . she die . . . now I feed."

"Marta . . . was she your wife?"

He nodded and sipped again.

"I'm sorry," she said.

"Thank you," he replied softly, then looked at her carefully. "Who you?"

"Sir, my name is Major Lydia Strand and I'm with the Air Force. I'm trying to track down some information and I would appreciate it if you could help me. Can you tell me how long you've lived here?"

He returned her gaze with vacant eyes. Strand felt another dead end was in the making, for it appeared the old fella was somewhere out in the ozone.

"Long time," he said finally.

"I see. The reason I'm here is that I'm trying to find out about the family that once lived in the house next door." Strand pointed. "I can't tell you what it's about, but I would appreciate it greatly if you could answer just a few questions for me."

A shrug of the shoulders. "Okay."

"Thank you. Now, sir, over thirty years ago a family lived in the house next door. A mother, father, and small boy. The child was seven years old when they moved away. Their name was Kapuscinski and they were an immigrant family from Poland—although the boy was born in Chicago. What I'm trying to find out is—"

"No," said the old man.

Strand blinked. "You mean you never knew them?" she asked.

The little man shook his head. "No Polski," he said simply.

Strand was puzzled. "What do you mean by 'No Pole . . . skee'?"

He sipped. "They not Polski . . . no Polish."

Strand cocked her head. "You remember them then?" she asked hopefully.

He nodded.

"Then how could they not be Polish? Their name was Kapuscinski. I've seen their immigration papers. They came from Krakow, in Poland."

A shrug. "I see no papers. But I know . . . they no Polski."

Now she was irritated. "How do you know?"

He pulled out some sunflower seeds from his pocket and scattered them on the ground. Two cardinals appeared and began to forage.

"I born Warszawa . . . that Warsaw. Leave when Hitler come. Fight Germans in Free Polski paratroop with General Sosabowski. Wounded near Arnhem . . . before you born. Marta and me come to America after war. New York first. No like. Then come here." He looked up. "Marta pretty like you."

Strand blushed. "I'm sure she was. Please, go on."

"I remember. We move this house. It nice then. Not like now. I want to meet neighbor. See name on mailbox. 'Kapuscinski.' I remember. I talk to him over fence. I say, '*Dzaen dobry, aesten Jersey Woyda. Przechalem tutay z Warszawa.*' That mean, 'Hello, I Jersey Woyda. I move here from Warsaw.' That man''—he pointed next door—''he speak Polish, but he not Polski. I remember . . . they leave soon after Marta and me move here.''

Strand felt a tingling sensation. ''Are you certain? The man named Kapuscinski had been in this country seven years. He probably hadn't spoken Polish much in that time.''

''No.'' He shook his head. ''If they Polski they speak Polski in house. . . . Marta and me speak Polski when alone.'' He smiled sheepishly. ''That why my English never so good.''

''No, no,'' she reassured him. ''Your English is fine. And you made a good point. They probably would continue to speak Polish when they were alone.'' Strand rubbed her gloved hands together. ''But if he did speak Polish, how can you say for certain he wasn't from Poland?''

His eyes were mocking. ''You American. Everybody who speak English sound like American?''

She shook her head. ''I see what you mean,'' she conceded, then contemplated what he'd said. ''So if they spoke the language but were not Polish, then where were they from?''

He shrugged again. ''Don't know . . . too long time . . . Ungarn . . . Czechsi maybe. Don't know where. Just know they not Polski.''

She patted her cheeks. It was getting colder. ''What about the little boy?'' she asked. ''Did you ever see him? As I said, he was only seven years old when they were here.''

He took one last sip, then tossed the remnants in his cup on the ground. ''I remember. Marta give him piece of cake one day. He quiet. Not say much. Unhappy boy . . . Marta and me not have children.''

Strand pulled out her billfold and held open the picture section for him to see. ''That's my little boy. Noah. He's eight months old.''

The white-haired man peeked at the photo and smiled. ''He pretty baby . . . like Mama.''

Strand blushed a little once more, and said, ''Thank you.''

''You want tea?'' he asked.

She was about to beg off when the taxi's horn honked. Maybe the bikers were getting restless. ''No. No thank you. That's my cab. I have to be going. It was nice talking with you. I wish I could've met Marta.''

He smiled wistfully. ''She would have liked you.''

Strand nodded, said, ''Thank you for your time,'' then instinctively leaned over and kissed him on the cheek. Now it was the old Pole who blushed.

She turned and began walking down the sidewalk.

"Air Force lady?" he called after her.

She stopped and looked back. "Yes?"

He had an ethereal look in his eyes now, as if trying to peer through a distant fog. "When I tell neighbor I from Warszawa . . ." He paused for a moment.

"Yes?" prompted Strand.

"He scared."

Day 3, 1700 Hours Zulu
THE *INTREPID*

The image slowly crept into focus, the white dot growing larger and larger until it became vividly clear. He was in a tunnel, which turned into a hallway. The walls were white—completely white—their sterility amplified by the pungent smell of antiseptic and formaldehyde.

Like a robot, the young Julian walked down the hall, wearing his blue academy uniform. Beside him the butterball police lieutenant kept pace, looking drawn and weary from having done this sort of thing too many times before.

"I understand your father passed away when you were only ten years old. . . . You must have been very close to your mother." The lieutenant tried to make his voice sound consoling, but it came out flat, without emotion—just like a written police report.

Julian only nodded.

"Sorry," offered the lieutenant as they approached a swinging door marked:

COOK COUNTY MEDICAL EXAMINER

MORGUE

They entered and the lieutenant handed some paperwork to the white-uniformed attendant, who was sickeningly obese and was eating a Twinkie at his desk. The human white elephant thumbed through the paperwork and looked up at the plainclothes lieutenant. "Kapuscinski?" he asked absently.

"That's right," replied the cop.

The white elephant heaved himself up. "This way," he ordered. They walked through another set of swinging doors into a large room. One wall was filled with a bank of small stainless steel refrigerator doors.

The white elephant opened one of the doors and roughly yanked out a tray.

The lieutenant spoke softly. "From the crime scene it looked like she returned home from shopping and stumbled onto some burglars that were in the house. Apparently the thieves panicked and . . ." The cop didn't finish the sentence. He only nodded to the attendant.

The white elephant folded back the sheet covering the face.

Clinically, the lieutenant asked, "Do you, Julian Kapuscinski, positively identify this woman as Victoria Kapuscinski, your mother?"

Her brown hair had turned gray many years ago, and it fell raggedly on the tray. Her eyes were closed and her skin a flour white. She did not look peaceful—even in death.

"Is this your mother?" prompted the lieutenant again.

Julian emitted a barely audible "Yes."

The lieutenant nodded to the white elephant, who started to roll the tray back into the refrigerator. But Julian placed a restraining hand on the tray. He couldn't bring himself to let her go. "How did my mother die?" he asked, almost choking.

The lieutenant pretended not to hear.

"I asked you how my mother died." This time it was a demand.

The middle-aged cop sighed, then quietly said, "Stab wound."

The white elephant wanted to get back to the other Twinkie at his desk and tried moving the tray again, but Julian's strong hand still held it fast. "C'mon, kid," he said roughly. "Your momma's dead. She ain't gettin' up, I can tell you that."

Inside Julian's mind a dike broke, and a sea of blind, searing rage engulfed him. "You pig!" he shouted, and lunged over the tray to seize the white elephant by the throat. The scuffle knocked Victoria Kapuscinski's corpse off the tray, and the naked body hit the tile floor with a dull *smack*.

Julian released his grip on the white elephant's throat and collapsed against the wall of refrigerator doors, aghast at what he'd done. His mother's naked torso showed that she had not died from *a* stab wound, but from about thirty savage punctures that horribly maimed her delicate body.

*   *   *

249

Julian ran from the hellish morgue. Ran far and fast until his legs could take him no farther and he collapsed on the grounds of Chicago's Lincoln Park. It was dark, and he was alone with his panting and sobbing. How long he stayed there he couldn't remember, for his mind was consumed by the image of his violated mother.

"Julian?" It was a tender voice, imparting a sense of kindness and understanding. "Julian?"

The young Kapuscinski looked up to see a benevolent face. It seemed grandfatherly—almost cherubic. It was attached to a portly figure wrapped in a woolen overcoat. "Come with me, Julian," he said gently, but with a trace of insistence.

Numbly, Julian rose from the ground and allowed himself to be guided to a park bench.

The portly figure took a small bag of candies from his pocket and put one in his mouth. "You are a fine athlete," he said finally. "I had difficulty following you, even in my automobile."

Still numb, Julian mumbled, "Who . . . who are you?"

The grandfather figure took another candy. "In America I have had many names. The one I presently use is Philip Johnson. Very common, wouldn't you say? But my birth name is Pyotr . . . the same name as your mother's cousin who died in Byelorussia many years ago."

Julian, though in shock, showed his surprise.

"I knew your mother," whispered the grandfather, "and I have watched you grow from a small boy—but you never knew I was there, did you, Julian?"

Julian shook his head.

"Your mother. Such a remarkable woman. You saw what the Americans did to your mother?" It was more than a question. Almost a challenge.

Julian nodded.

The grandfather sighed. "A country that would allow such hooligans to run loose and commit such an atrocity on your mother—well, it is evil, is it not?"

Slowly, Julian nodded again.

The old man took another candy. "I know your secret, Julian. I was sent to look after you. You have done well to be admitted to the Americans' Air Force university." He chewed the candy slowly, savoring it as it dissolved. "The road ahead of you will be long and difficult, but if your resolve does not weaken you will be able to avenge your mother's death. You will be able to strike back at this evil country. Do you want to strike back, Julian?"

250

Firmly, Julian nodded.

"Will your resolve waver, Julian?"

"My resolve will not waver," he replied without hesitation.

"Good. I expected no less. Your mother's resolve never wavered. Such an extraordinary woman." The old man pocketed the bag of candies. "Come along. We have much to talk about." And he reached out and took Julian's arm.

But Julian recoiled from the old man's grasp and hissed with an undercurrent of rage, "My resolve will not waver, but never, ever, touch me again!"

But, in fact, there was a time when Julian's resolve did begin to waver. Although the cherubic grandfather figure named Philip Johnson kept a close watch on Julian as he progressed through the Air Force Academy, an imponderable factor entered the picture during his senior year. A girl named Felicia. Tall, lissome Felicia with the flowing red hair. Older than he, she stirred emotions in Julian that had long been dormant. But before a bond could crystallize between them, Julian graduated and was shipped off to flight training school—and then to Vietnam.

During his third week in Vietnam Julian received a letter from Felicia. She was engaged to an older man—the executive vice president of a defense contractor.

It was the final nail in the coffin, and Julian became a true psychotic. His burning rage at Felicia's betrayal was unleashed in his flying. He turned into a crazed Apache in the air, flying 223 combat sorties and shooting down six North Vietnamese MiGs. His fearlessness and cold-blooded manner earned him the Distinguished Flying Cross—and the call sign of Iceberg.

In a bizarre fashion, Vietnam further honed his resolve. For although he was in the middle of it and participated in the killing, he felt the use of such massive aerial bombing by a giant power on a primitive people was evil. An evil propagated by the ruling American elite—as personified by war profiteers like Felicia's husband. Iceberg turned a blind eye to atrocities committed by the North Vietnamese and decided that his mother had been right. Yes, as always, his mother had been right, and he would not betray her as Felicia had betrayed him.

Julian Kapuscinski—the Iceberg—awakened from the nightmare and looked out the windshield. At that moment the *Intrepid* was passing over the North American continent.

251

"No, Mother," he whispered to himself. "My resolve will not waver."

It was both tragic and ironic that Julian never learned the true identity of his mentor, Philip Johnson. In fact, Johnson was a clinical psychologist trained at the Subinskiy Institute of Psychiatry in Leningrad. He'd learned much while experimenting on American prisoners of war held in North Korea. And he used his horrifying skills to twist Julian's mind into a sickened psychotic mass.

It was Johnson who orchestrated the brutal murder of Victoria Kapuscinski.

And arranged for Julian to meet Felicia—one of Moscow Centre's more seductive agents.

Day 3, 1730 Hours Zulu, 3:30 P.M. Local
MIDAIR REFUELING OVER THE NORTH ATLANTIC, SOUTH OF THE AZORES

The air turbulence made refueling a bitch. Three times the boom operator was compelled to yank out the aluminum tube from Ghost Leader's plane, then restart the process of realigning and reinserting the probe. On the fourth break-off, he'd had enough. "Say, Skipper, it's really the pits back here," he lamented from the boom pod, located in the arse of the KC-10 tanker. "Is there something a little smoother downstairs?"

"Maybe so. Stand by." The pilot of the tanker eavesdropped a little longer on the civilian air traffic frequencies before making his decision. The Ghostflight mission of four aircraft was south of the Azores on an easterly heading. Since it was daylight they had to remain far enough away from civilian air traffic routes to avoid visual detection, but they stayed close enough to monitor the radio chatter of commercial pilots as they discussed weather conditions.

"Okay, Boomer," said the pilot over the intercom. "We're gonna take it all the way down to two-three thousand. A KLM seven-four-seven says it's silk city down there."

"Great," replied the boom operator.

"Ghost Leader, this is Ghost Four. We're taking it down to two-three thousand to finish up."

"Roger, Ghost Four," replied the Leader. "Ghost Two and Three, you go ahead and vector to one-eight-zero at four hundred knots. We'll catch up after we're full."

252

"Roger, Ghost Leader."

"Okay, Ghost Four, let's do it."

"Roger," replied the tanker. The two aircraft started descending from their bumpy refueling altitude of 33,000 feet, while the C-141 Starlifter and the other coal-black batwing turned to a heading of due south.

Ghostflight had come a long way, and still had a long way to go. From their refueling point near the Azores, they would travel south over the Atlantic to about the midpoint of the bulge of the West African coastline. When they were out of range of civilian air traffic radars, they would turn due east and fly over the desolate terrain of Mauritania, Mali, Niger, Chad, the Sudan, Ethiopia, and Somalia. No request had been filed for transit over the airspace of these countries, because this was an illegal flight. Radar detection of the batwings was not a real concern, but the tanker and cargo aircraft could be discovered; therefore, Ghostflight had to follow a carefully plotted route through the African airspace that was "unpainted" by civilian or military radars.

When the four aircraft finally crossed the East African coastline over the Arabian Sea, they would follow the southern coast of the Saudi Arabian peninsula until they reached their destination along the Gulf of Oman. There they would land on friendly territory—before the sun came up again.

At 23,000 feet the tanker and its thirsty companion once again lined up for insertion of the fuel boom. This time, the air was smooth and both aircraft remained stationary throughout the fuel flow. Midair refueling was always problematic, and the nature of Ghost Leader's machine made it particularly nettlesome. The batwing aircraft handled like a cumbersome eighteen-wheeler. That's because it wasn't designed for responsiveness. It was built with a wholly different purpose in mind.

When the tanker and the topped-off Ghost Leader started climbing back up to their cruising altitude, the boom operator's eyes remained transfixed on the jet-black aircraft. Finally, he shook his head. He still couldn't believe something that weird-looking could fly.

Day 3, 1800 Hours Zulu, Noon Local
CHICAGO

The cabbie pulled up to the U-Stow-It warehouse complex and parked. "You want me to wait this time?"

She looked around. "No. This doesn't seem too threatening. I appreciated your staying at the other place, though. Those bikers gave me the shivers.''

"Me, too," he agreed.

Strand counted out some bills for the fare, including a generous tip, then parted company with the taxi.

The U-Stow-It establishment looked like any self-storage warehouse that you could find across the country. When the household closets, attic, and garage overflowed, the mini-warehouses took up the slack—for a fee. This one had several rows of low corrugated-steel buildings with overhead doors and was surrounded by a ten-foot-high cyclone fence.

She walked over to the building with MANAGER painted over the door and entered. The office had a counter, and a doorway that led into an unkempt living room. Obviously, the management lived on the premises.

The proprietor walked through the doorway. He had a beard and wore his shirt unbuttoned, revealing a generous and hairy beer belly. He was carrying a Coors in one hand, indicating he'd gotten an early start on the first of his three daily six-packs. Although surly-looking, he brightened up when he laid eyes on the major. "Morning, er, afternoon I guess it is, now. What can I do for you today, honey?" He was trying to be charming.

Inwardly Strand winced at the primitive come-on and quickly slipped into her sergeant-major mode, as she had with Tedesco, the FBI man. In a flintlike voice she said, "My name is Major Lydia Strand, United States Air Force." She opened her purse and laid out some documents on the counter. "I have a federal search warrant to inspect the contents of warehouse number P-thirteen, leased to Julian Kapuscinski of Colorado Springs."

Upon hearing the words *search warrant,* the manager took a step backward, thinking of the hashish he had hidden in the medicine cabinet. He'd done time in Cook County jail once and didn't like it. He also didn't like that tone of voice in a woman. "Search warrant? Where does the Air Force get off handin' out search warrants? You ain't no cop."

Strand kept her posture erect. "I have special authorization from the Director of the Federal Bureau of Investigation in Washington to execute this warrant. If you wish, you may call the local FBI office. Ask for Agent Wilkerson. He will confirm what I've told you. He will also deploy additional agents if necessary. Now if you don't mind, I'm in a hurry."

Director of the FBI? Shit. He didn't want any part of this. "Okay, okay. Don't get excited." He picked up the warrant and looked at it. "P-thirteen?" he asked.

"Correct."

He went to a lockbox full of keys and extracted one. Then he put on an overcoat and picked up a crowbar. "Come on," he said.

They walked outside and down row P of the buildings, finally stopping at number 13. The manager fumbled with the keys and unfastened one of two padlocks. Picking up the crowbar, he said, "The customer gets to put his own lock on the door, too. Security, you know. I don't have no key for this one here, so I gotta break it—seein' how you got a warrant and all. . . . Stand back a little."

The major complied, and the manager inserted the crowbar through the padlock loop. He jerked a few times before it gave way. Then he lifted the overhead door and exposed the room, which held a single large wooden crate—nothing else.

"Can I borrow your crowbar?" she asked.

He looked at her skeptically. "Sure you don't need no help?"

"I'll manage," she said evenly.

Having been a student of physics, Strand knew the principles of the fulcrum. She put her purse on the floor and began working on the crate with the crowbar. Using it on just the right pressure points, she dismantled it quickly—with leverage, not brute strength.

"You need me for anything else?" he asked.

"I'll let you know if I do. I'd like to hang on to the crowbar for a little while if you don't mind."

"Right. Just be sure and bring it back. I gotta pay for it iffin you don't bring it back," he said in a self-righteous tone.

"Rest assured it will be returned."

He retreated toward the icebox of Coors.

The crate contained a two-drawer filing cabinet and an assortment of cardboard moving boxes. Strand started at one end and methodically went through them.

An hour later the contents of the wooden crate were neatly spread over the warehouse floor. Apparently they were all that remained of Iceberg's mother's estate. The two-drawer filing cabinet contained the probated will of Victoria Kapuscinski. Julian was named his mother's executor, and other documents in the filing cabinet showed Iceberg had liquidated virtually all the assets of the estate at auction. He'd also filed the appropriate estate tax returns.

255

The remaining contents were apparently the unsold items from the estate sale and family keepsakes, and they didn't amount to a hill of beans. Some old clothes, a few cheap oil paintings with ornate frames, some kitchenware, Iceberg's Air Force Academy yearbooks and memorabilia, an RCA television set, and a stack of old mystery books.

Strand was starting to get tired, and her stomach was growling. She hadn't eaten all day, and this was beginning to look like another dry hole. She had one last box to open, then she could grab something to eat and head back to Colorado.

The remaining cardboard box was sealed with tape. She split it open with the pocketknife from her purse. Inside was an ornate wooden chest with a padlock. Strand cut away the rest of the cardboard to reveal the entire chest, which was bigger than a jewelry box but smaller than a hope chest. She picked up the crowbar again and easily forced the small padlock open. Then she lifted the chest and put it on top of the two-drawer file cabinet so she could sort through it.

On top of the open chest was an inset compartment that held some costume jewelry. Strand pawed through the necklaces and bracelets but found nothing out of the ordinary. Same sort of stuff you could get at J. C. Penney. She figured it had belonged to Iceberg's mother.

She lifted the compartment out, and underneath she found an album of pictures showing Julian Kapuscinski growing up—as an infant, on his tricycle, his first day of school, high school graduation, and his first year as a "Dooley" at the academy. Strand remembered Iceberg's mother had been murdered when he was a sophomore at Colorado Springs. She had never lived to see her son graduate or get his wings and become an astronaut. A damn shame, she thought. Digging deeper, Strand found Julian's certificate to the high school National Honor Society, as well as his diploma from Pembrook High School and his acceptance letter to the academy. Typical stuff you'd find in a proud mother's heirloom chest.

Finally, on the bottom, was an item bundled in soft black velvet. Strand picked it up and took off the velvet wrapping. It was a small leather notebook. She gently leafed through the old, fragile pages, and was a little perplexed. Although it was a bound volume, the text on the pages was not printed. It was handwritten. The handwriting was definitely masculine, as well as jerky and unintelligible—and obviously not in English. In fact, the writing looked like a bunch of hieroglyphics to Strand. The elder Kapuscinski's diary, perhaps? She shrugged wistfully to herself and decided to take it back to Cheyenne Mountain.

Grabbing her purse and the crowbar, she pulled down the overhead door and left.

Day 3, 2100 Hours Zulu, 4:00 P.M. Local
THE WHITE HOUSE

The President of the United States looked out the French doors and gazed upon the White House Rose Garden. The small panes of glass that framed his view were extraordinarily thick for such elegant doors, but that was a necessary precaution. Each square was constructed of six sheets of glass laminated to interlayers of polyvinyl butyral. This created a see-through bulletproof shield that could withstand anything up to and including a .460 Weatherby Magnum fired at point-blank range.

The President's mood was one of befuddlement. He wasn't sure what to believe about this *Intrepid* business anymore. Turning to his guest, he asked, "How much confidence do you have in this Kremlin source of yours?"

The Frenchman tapped the ashes from one of his host's Don Diego cigars. "As you can understand, my friend, I cannot tell you his precise position. We have to protect our intelligence sources, just as you must. But I can tell you that he is highly placed within the Soviet Foreign Ministry, and we have found him to be extremely accurate in the past. Indeed, we have seen staff position papers even before they have crossed the Foreign Minister's desk."

The President frowned. "And he verifies everything that Ambassador Yakolev says?"

The Frenchman nodded. "*Oui.* Our source confirms that the Foreign Minister personally investigated the allegations concerning Soviet communications with your space shuttle and dismissed it as American propaganda. My intelligence people tell me we, ah, even obtained a copy of the cable message the Foreign Minister sent Ambassador Yakolev. . . . Perhaps I should not have told you that."

The American's eyebrow went up. "I must confess I am impressed. And rest assured I've already forgotten about the cable. Although it certainly validates your source. I wish my spooks could come up with something like that."

"Spooks?"

The host smiled. "American slang for 'spies.' But even with your Foreign Ministry source, I don't know how to read the situation. I told you about my Secretary of State's speculation that a leadership change may be under way in the Kremlin?''

"*Oui*. And I agree with you. It is most difficult to interpret. But it is even more difficult to believe the Foreign Minister and Defense Minister are not exercising genuine control over their portfolios, as they have for years.''

"Yeah. That's what I told Winston. And I sure hope you're right. I wouldn't want to contemplate the alternative.''

The Frenchman took a drag on the Don Diego. "What are your plans now?''

The American's gaze returned to the Rose Garden, and he took a long sigh. "There's nothing we can do, really, except get the *Constellation* up there as fast as possible.'' The President checked his watch. "Lift-off is supposed to be at four-thirty A.M. About twelve hours from now. If you're so inclined, we can watch the lift-off and part of the rendezvous from here.'' He motioned to the television cabinet.

Now it was the Frenchman who was impressed. "Indeed?''

Like a neighbor showing off a new lawnmower, the American said, "Yeah. My SPACECOM general has got a telescope in a high-flying jetliner. He calls it Spyglass, and it's up near the polar ice cap now. That way it can catch the *Intrepid* for a few minutes on each orbit.''

His guest nodded. "I would very much like to see this.''

"Fine.'' The President looked at his watch again. "I guess we can make it an early dinner, then turn in early so we can get up early. Or we can make it a long night.''

The Frenchman chuckled. "I have never been an early riser, my friend.''

Day 3, 2200 Hours Zulu, 2:00 P.M. Local
VANDENBERG AIR FORCE BASE

Col. Peter Nordstrum Lamborghini threw his T-38 Talon fighter into a savage double roll. He was nearing his approach to the Vandenberg runway, and the double roll was the only aerobatic maneuver he could execute in the tightly controlled southern California airspace. En route from Colorado Springs he'd taken a little time over the wide-open spaces of Utah to do a couple of loops and Immelmanns. He found it was a good way to relieve the stress of the last few days, and only wished there had been time for more fun.

Lamborghini knew the Talon probably as well as any man alive, because he'd flown it as a member of the Thunderbirds, the aerobatic demonstration team. One of the disappointments of his Air Force career was that he'd flown with the Thunderbirds before they made the transition to his beloved F-16. Despite its problems, Peter still thought the Falcon was one hummer of an aircraft.

The son of a road construction foreman, the SPACECOM intelligence officer had graduated from the University of Wisconsin in aeronautical engineering. Although proud of his Italian and Norwegian heritage, he always felt like a half-breed in the land of the transplanted Scandinavians, so he joined the Air Force to see other parts of the world. The first part of the world he saw after completing flight school was North Vietnam, from the front seat of an F-4 Phantom. He saw a lot of it while racking up two tours of duty, 318 combat missions, and a chestful of medals. He saw lots of flak, thousands of tracer rounds, and dozens of SAM missiles—real up close and personal. More times than he cared to count, he saw a mean-looking fighter plane and a dashing, brave American pilot disappear in a fireball in the time it takes to blink an eye. He had the opportunity to see an SA-2 SAM missile explode directly above his cockpit, and through the blur of a 400 mph ejection, he watched the parachute of his bombardier disappear into the triple-canopy jungle. He experienced the total blackness and utter terror of a night spent alone in the jungle, as well as the horror of finding his bombardier swinging from a tree in a parachute harness—perfectly fine, except that he was headless. He experienced the exhaustion and fear of running from Laotian widows and orphans as they came after him with sticks, rocks, and crossbows, seeking revenge for the errant American bombs that had snuffed out their husbands and fathers. Instead of seeing the world, Peter Lamborghini's face had been rubbed savagely in the slime pit called ''war''—and he didn't care for it much.

By the time his second Vietnam tour ground to a halt, Lamborghini had soured on the whole sordid Indochina mess, and he came very, very close to leaving the Air Force. His wife, Juliet, had soured on it long before he had; but she knew her husband. And she loved him. She wanted to see him happy, and knew the only place he would be happy was in the cockpit. She patiently explained to Peter that there was a difference between defending your country and pursuing a foreign policy gone haywire. So at her urging he kept his uniform. And in the years that followed, she went uncomplaining, rearing their two daughters, as they hopped from one Permanent Change of Station to another. It was a royal pain in the kazoo for a spouse, but necessary if her husband was to climb the career ladder in the Tactical Air Command.

Lamborghini grew and matured. He was a gifted pilot and a natural leader. And he knew his wife was right. Flying had become a fundamental part of his life. Putting Vietnam behind him, he auditioned for, and was accepted into, the Thunderbirds. The aerobatic flying became a salve that rehabilitated his wounded spirit. It also made up for a lot of the shortcomings of Air Force life—such as low pay, frequent moves, family separations, and crazy hours.

If you ever reviewed Lamborghini's personnel file, you would find plenty of commendations, medals, and outstanding efficiency reports. But you would also find that although he completed 318 combat missions, and had even flown as wingman to the Air Force's legendary Brig. Gen. Robin "Old Man" Olds, Lamborghini could not claim the title of "fighter ace." That is to say, he'd shot down four North Vietnamese MiGs, but was one plane shy of the five kills needed to possess the coveted "ace" designation—officially, that is. The circumstances surrounding the additional two MiGs he nailed, to this day, remain locked in a Pentagon basement vault under an Omega classification.

In May 1982, Peter Lamborghini had been assigned as technical adviser to the Israeli Air Force (IAF) when it took delivery on eight new F-16 Falcons, fresh out of the Fort Worth General Dynamics plant. As part of his duties, he flew with the Israeli pilots as they debugged and ironed out the kinks of their new aircraft (in the automobile business, this is called "dealer prep").

Peter chose an inopportune time to arrive in the Middle East—just two weeks before the Israelis mounted their incursion into southern Lebanon, when tensions in the region were white hot. The day before the Israeli Army went into full mobilization, he was upstairs checking out weapon systems on a newly delivered Falcon, along with an IAF captain as his wingman. The two F-16s were flying low and slow, just heading out over the Mediterranean, when four Russian-built MiG-21 Fishbed fighters screamed out of Syria and crossed over the Golan Heights. Peter didn't speak Hebrew, so he paid little attention when his companion exchanged some excited gibberish over the IAF air warning frequency. Then with a start, the Israeli streaked northeast on an intercept vector, while transmitting a terse "Come with me!" in

English. Operating purely on instinct, Peter shoved his own throttles to the stops and followed. He was smack in the middle of a dogfight with the MiG-21s before he realized what he'd been drawn into.

The Syrian MiG dove on the American from a high angle of attack, with its single 30mm cannon blazing. Peter saw the tracer rounds whiz by his cockpit; but instead of jinking away to evade and then reengage his adversary, he put the Falcon on its tail and pointed the nose directly at the oncoming Fishbed.

Besides a complement of missiles, the F-16 is armed with a General Electric M61 A-1 Vulcan 20mm cannon that looks like a latter-day Gatling gun. When activated, the Vulcan's six barrels rotate and fire simultaneously, and they can run though six thousand rounds of ammunition in a mere sixty seconds. It is an awesome weapon. However, the 20mm shells are quite heavy, so the F-16 carries only 515 rounds in its magazine when it goes aloft. That means the Falcon can spit out its entire load of ammunition in just five seconds—which is exactly what Peter did. He waggled the F-16's hand controller and mashed the red firing button at the same time. This put the muzzle of the Vulcan in a spiral pattern that sprayed the air with a wall of 20mm slugs—a wall through which the MiG-21 had to pass. As the Syrian Fishbed shot past him, Peter caught a glimpse of its shattered canopy.

The American didn't waste a millisecond trying to confirm his kill, but immediately started looking for other MiGs. He spied one coming across his beam at a distance of about four miles and began to close the gap. But before he could line up his targeting circle (called a "pipper") on the Syrian plane, the Fishbed erupted in flames before him. His Israeli wingman had gotten there first.

The two remaining MiGs did a 180-degree turn and scooted back for the Syrian border; and at that point, in a technical diplomatic sense, Peter should have broken off the engagement and returned to base. But he didn't. Instinct and training—and anger—had taken over.

The American scanned the sky. "How many were there?" he demanded.

"Four," responded the Israeli. "Two left."

Peter illuminated his Falcon's Westinghouse AN/APG-66 digital pulse Doppler radar and scanned the airspace for the retreating Fishbeds. The radar connected, flashing the range, position, and speed of the bandits onto his head-up display. He kicked in the Falcon's Pratt & Whitney F100 turbofan afterburner to pursue, and his Israeli wingman followed.

Peter closed the gap and spied one of the MiGs as it headed for cover in a cloud bank of giant thunderheads. The Syrian pilot was no fool. His own equipment had detected the radar surveillance, and he wanted to at least get out of visual range and into some protective concealment. Conversely, Peter had to close within visual range because his Falcon was armed with infrared, not radar-guided, missiles. The American peered through the head-up display and started to line up his shot, but it was a struggle to put the targeting "pipper" on the Fishbed's jinking Tumansky engine tailpipe. Then finally, just as his Falcon crossed into Syrian airspace, Peter heard the familiar *grrrrrrrr* of the AIM-9L Sidewinder in his headphones, and he let the missile fly. A split second before the MiG plunged into the cloud bank, it disappeared in a puffball of yellow and orange flame. There was no chute.

Peter yanked his F-16 quickly back toward Israel. He knew the Syrians possessed the deadly effective SA-6 Gainful surface-to-air missile, and he wanted to hightail it out of there before any Syrian battery commanders could lock on to him. He'd seen all the SAMs he ever wanted to see over North Vietnam, and they'd scared him shitless.

In his after-action report to the Department of the Air Force, Lamborghini took pains to explain that he did not understand the Hebrew language, and honestly didn't know what was afoot until he saw the Fishbed MiG diving on him. Then it was a matter of self-defense. Up to a point. Perhaps he should have reined himself in before crossing the Syrian border; but after all, he'd been trained as a fighter pilot for the better part of fifteen years. What did the Air Force expect?

The Air Force accepted the report without comment and buried it deep. Way deep. The slaughter and mutilation of innocent women and children in the Sabra and Shatilla Palestinian refugee camps by Israeli-sponsored Phalangists had evoked a great revulsion in the United States toward the incursion into Lebanon. The last thing the Air Force needed was an AP story about how an American pilot had shot down some Syrian planes—one of them over Syrian airspace—while in the cockpit of an Israeli fighter. No. That just would not do. And if the Air Force disciplined Lamborghini for violating Syrian airspace, there was always the danger he might get miffed and go public about the incident. That wouldn't do either. So the report went into the bottom of the Omega vault. Never to see the light of day, ever again. And in the world's eyes, Peter Lamborghini never made it to "ace."

*　　*　　*

The wheels of the Talon squealed as they touched down on the Vandenberg runway.

Day 3, 2200 Hours Zulu, 5:00 P.M. Local
KENNEDY SPACE CENTER

The space shuttle possessed a mind-numbing array of exotic systems that all had to work properly if the spacecraft was to leave the ground, and the responsibility for checking all of those systems and sub-systems—from the fuel cell heat exchanger to the on-board comput-ers—fell on the shoulders of the pad manager. That is why Jacob Classen (white-haired and antsy even in the best of times) bought and consumed aspirin and Rolaids by the six-pack. He was constantly haunted by the image of that one switch left off when it was supposed to be on, by the loose wrench dropped inside the external tank, or by the valve that didn't close when it was supposed to. The strain was enough to make a religious man turn to drink, or make a drinking man turn to religion.

Classen was as careful as they came. He never, ever, had gotten over the *Challenger*. If another shuttle ever went down, he swore it wasn't going to be because somebody on his pad screwed the pooch. That's why he insisted on employing the best technicians, and rotated them during prelaunch to ensure they got enough rest. Bleary-eyed technicians were bound to make mistakes. He also employed a first-class deputy pad manager by the name of Ed Garvey to be his resident son of a bitch. On the pad, Classen was the "good guy," while Garvey was the "bad guy" who kicked ass, jumped up and down, and screamed to make sure all the ducks were in the proper rows before launch.

And now Garvey had disappeared. Classen had sent his deputy home to get some sleep prior to the final, frenetic prelaunch hours, when things really started hopping. Garvey had left and had never come back. Classen had called his home. Not there. Local hospitals were called. Not there either. KSC Security was notified. "We'll keep an eye out," they promised. In desperation, Classen called the police and highway patrol. "We have to wait seventy-two hours until someone can be classified as a missing person," they said, "but we'll put out a bulletin anyway and let you know if we hear something."

Despite Classen's frantic search, the dependable, always reliable

Garvey couldn't be found. It was as if he'd vanished into thin air. Classen was bone-tired, and unless his deputy showed up, the pad manager was afraid he might collapse before the *Constellation* lifted off.

Neither Classen, nor KSC Security, nor the police or highway patrol thought to check the employee parking lot outside Pad 39A. Had they done so, they would've found Garvey's Ford Bronco, waiting patiently for its owner's return.

Day 3, 2215 Hours Zulu, 3:15 P.M. Local
CHEYENNE MOUNTAIN

Whittenberg, Dowd, and Fairchild were alone in the conference room. Whittenberg was talking on the phone from the roll-out commo panel beside his chair at the head of the table. Sir Isaac was pouring coffee for the group when the CinC hung up.

"Chet is wrapping things up at the Cape," said Whittenberg. "He'll be flying back to CSOC and will be there in time for the *Constellation*'s lift-off. I ordered him to get some sleep before he left."

Dowd nodded. "Good idea. That guy doesn't know when to quit."

The CinC and Sir Isaac had gotten some sleep and were reasonably coherent. Dowd was starting to fade again and was keeping alert by pumping a constant stream of coffee and Maalox into his stomach. The three of them were dealing with a collage of frustration, exasperation, and feelings of impotence. All they could do now was monitor preparations at the Cape and at Vandenberg, and keep an eye on the mysterious satellite.

The conference-room door opened and CM/Sgt. Timothy Kelly walked in, looking incredibly weary. He tossed his cap on the table and plopped into a chair. Not standing on protocol, Sir Isaac poured him some coffee.

"So how was Boston?" queried Dowd.

Kelly scowled. "Complete waste of time," he said after a gulp of coffee. "Major Mulcahey is the quintessential all-American. I talked with his parents and brother. He was an altar boy, an Eagle Scout, March of Dimes supporter—you name it. I can't believe he could turn; but if it is him, he never left any tracks we'll ever find. Has Major Strand or Agent Tedesco gotten back yet?"

In answer to his question, the door opened and an Air Police security guard appeared, along with the FBI man. Kelly nodded to the AP guard, and he withdrew. Then he introduced Tedesco to the three generals. Whittenberg was amazed at the G-man's resemblance to Mike Ditka.

"Any luck?" asked Kelly.

Tedesco shook his head. "I can tell you that I don't see any possible way it could be Rodriquez," he declared. "I talked with his mother. She said he wanted to join the Marine Corps after graduating from Cal Tech, but she persuaded him to stay in school. No. This isn't the guy. My instincts tell me the same thing, too."

Whittenberg made a sound like a low growl. "Sounds like you and Tim had the same results. Guess that leaves us with Kapuscinski, and I find that equally hard to believe."

"I agree, General," said Kelly ruefully. "The man holds the DFC and flew over two hundred combat missions in Vietnam. The major said he despised the Russians . . ." His voice trailed off.

Sir Isaac shrugged. "Looks like we may never know who it is unless the *Constellation* gets a peek inside the cockpit." He puffed on his pipe and thought about the Stinger missiles being loaded onto the *Constellation* and wondered if they'd be used. And if they were used, whether they would work. . . . Maybe it had been a bad idea to begin with. He allowed himself a sigh, and reflected that desperate men do desperate things.

The door opened for the third time, and in walked Lydia Strand. She, too, plopped into a chair and was offered coffee.

"So, how'd it go with you?" prompted Kelly.

Strand didn't know what to think. Or report. All she had, really, was the hazy recollection of an old man who might be sinking into senility—a recollection that was over thirty years old. The more she thought about it, the less sense it made.

"I don't know what to make of it." She sighed. "It looks like a total blank to me. I ran into an old man who said he'd been a neighbor of the Kapuscinski family for a brief period over thirty years ago. Nice old guy, but he seemed a little daft. He claimed that Iceberg's father spoke Polish, but wasn't a native of Poland, as stated on the immigration records."

Dowd's brow went into a furrow. "Not from Poland? Then where did he come from?"

Strand reached behind her head and unclipped her hair. Damn the regulations, she thought. She shook her head, causing her luxuriant brunette locks to tumble down over her shoulders. None of the generals present voiced an objection. "That's just it," she said in response to Dowd's query. "I asked him that very same question and he said he didn't know where the Kapuscinskis came from. That it was too long ago. It's been over three decades, after all."

"Yeah," agreed Kelly. "Maybe Iceberg's father was just speaking a different dialect of Polish."

"Possibly," mused Strand as she rummaged through her purse. "I went through some old papers and stuff Iceberg had stored in a warehouse in Chicago. The only curious thing I found was this." She passed the leather notebook to Tedesco. "I had no idea what it was. Everything else in the warehouse was junk."

Tedesco carefully thumbed through the delicate pages. Then he shrugged and passed the notebook to the Bull, who thumbed, shrugged, and passed it to Whittenberg, who thumbed, shrugged, and passed it to Sir Isaac, who thumbed, shrugged, and passed it to Kelly, who thumbed but didn't shrug.

"Well, I guess there's nothing more that we can do about it now," lamented Whittenberg. "I'd hoped we could shed some light on who our turncoat was, and maybe why he turned. It might have helped us retrieve the *Intrepid* somehow. Looks like we've got nothing but dry holes."

There was a depressed silence until Kelly held up the leather notebook and said, "Sir, if you don't mind, I'd like to take this back to my office for a few minutes."

The CinC shrugged once more and said, "Sure."

Twenty minutes later Kelly returned with the leather notebook and a thick tome tucked under his arm. During Kelly's absence, curiosity had started to build as to why he'd left.

"So what've you got, Tim?" asked Sir Isaac.

"Well, sir, I'm not exactly sure." He opened the notebook.

"This handwriting looks like a bunch of mishmash, I know. It's a very heavy-handed style and the paper has faded badly. But what intrigued me was that the handwriting didn't appear to be in any alphabet or language with which I was familiar."

"How do you mean?" asked Whittenberg.

"Well, sir, whatever these pages are, they certainly weren't written in the Roman alphabet."

Dowd chuckled. "I wouldn't be too sure about that, Sarge. You can't tell my handwriting is in English, either."

Kelly nodded. "I understand what you're saying, sir. But if this is not the Roman alphabet, then that means it wasn't written in any of the Romance or Germanic languages—like French, Spanish, German, or Italian. It also eliminates the Western Slavic languages like Czech, Slovak . . . and Polish." Kelly scratched his head. "Also, this writing is in neither the Greek nor the Cyrillic alphabet, which would preclude its coming from Greece, Bulgaria, Byelorussia, Macedonia, the Ukraine, or Serbia. In fact, this handwriting looks more like Arabic or Armenian than anything else, but I know a little about those two languages and it doesn't appear to be either of them."

"What about Hungarian?" asked Sir Isaac.

Kelly shook his head. "No, sir. Hungarian is Finno-Ugric. That's in the Roman alphabet, too."

Sir Isaac fired up his pipe. "So as a process of elimination, you ascertained this handwriting wasn't Eastern or Western European, Armenian, or Arabic writing?"

"Yes, sir."

Dowd's bull-like face betrayed the trace of a scowl. "So what is it? Chinese?"

"No, sir," replied Kelly. "I don't believe it is." He opened his large book to a specific page. "I could be wrong, but I think this may be written in an alphabet known as Mxedruli." Kelly spun his book around so everyone could see a chart of letters representing the foreign alphabet he'd referred to:

MXEDRULI
(Transliteration to Roman Alphabet)

a	b	g	d	e	v	z	t	i	ḱ	l
m	n	o	ṕ	ž	r	s	t́	u	p	k
y	q́	š	č	c	ʒ	ć	č'	x	ǯ	h

Dowd was starting to show his irritation. "Well, just what the hell is this, this Mix-a-drool-eee?"

Kelly cleared his throat. "Mxedruli is the alphabet used in the language spoken by approximately three to four million people in a region north of Armenia—specifically, in the Georgian Republic of the Soviet Union."

There was a period of silence as a host of eyebrows went up. Sir Isaac lifted Kelly's book so he could see the cover. The title was *The Languages, Peoples and History of the U.S.S.R.*

"In short, sir," concluded Kelly, "I think this may be written in the Georgian language."

It was another queer twist, in an affair laden with queer twists, and Whittenberg was stunned.

"Well, let's not jump to conclusions," cautioned Sir Isaac, while pulling on his hawklike nose. "If these pages are, in fact, written in Georgian, there could be a reasonable explanation for it. The paper is obviously very old. Maybe it belonged to a grandparent of Kapuscinski's who emigrated from Soviet Georgia to Poland. A family heirloom, of sorts." Sir Isaac didn't think he sounded very convincing.

Whittenberg picked up the notebook again. "Are you sure about this, Tim?" he asked gently.

Kelly sighed. "No, sir. I'm not. I'm only going on a comparison of these pages against this reference book here. As you can see for yourself, the handwriting is nothing more than a chicken scrawl, and the Mxedruli alphabet is very cursive. As this book points out, there are some hundred thirty languages spoken in the Soviet Union, from Yakut to Kurdish—and about half of those have been reduced to written form. I'm just making an educated guess."

Sir Isaac had taken the notebook from the CinC and was carefully comparing the pages against the reference book. "Well, Tim, you're the resident expert here. If we wanted to obtain a clarification on your thesis, who should we go to?"

Kelly didn't hesitate with his answer. "There are some fine people at the Agency who could take a pass at it. But if it was up to me, I'd run it by the guy who wrote that book," he said, while pointing at the tome. "Professor George Brennan. He's with the Averell Harriman Institute for Soviet Studies at Columbia University. There's not a man alive who knows more about Russian history and language than he does. I worked with him during the Belenko debriefing."

"Do it," ordered Whittenberg.

Day 3, 2300 Hours Zulu, 6:00 P.M. Local
COLUMBIA UNIVERSITY, NEW YORK CITY

Professor George Kirtwell Brennan had held the Donald Kendall Chair of Russian Language and History at Columbia University ever since it was endowed by the PepsiCo executive seventeen years before (Pepsi-Cola was still the only American soft drink you could buy in Moscow). The seventy-four-year-old scholar—known for his ever-present bow tie and domelike bald head—had written fourteen books on the Soviet Union, and his personal library in his Long Island home rivaled that of many midsized colleges. Although he was first and foremost a teacher, he'd been retained on many occasions as a consultant to the CIA, State Department, Defense Department, and National Security Agency (or their predecessors). As a newly minted Oxford graduate and "whiz kid" linguist during World War II, Brennan had landed in a place called Bletchley Park, where he'd helped decipher German dispatches with the Enigma cipher machine. In short, he'd been one of the Founding Fathers of the Ultrasecret while still in his early twenties. It was a heady experience for one so young; but now he was an old man, and he could no longer keep up the feverish pace he'd maintained for some fifty years.

It was Friday evening and Brennan was leaving his office at the Harriman Institute on the Columbia campus. The professor and his wife were departing in the morning for a four-day holiday at their vacation home in Maine, where they would get together with their children and grandchildren. The old professor was just closing the door of his office when the phone rang. He guessed it was his wife, calling to make sure he was on his way home. She'd been looking forward to the Maine trip for months. He picked up the phone and muttered, "Brennan."

"Professor Brennan?"

"Yes, that's correct. Who is this, please?"

"Professor, this is Chief Master Sergeant Tim Kelly calling from U.S. Space Command headquarters in Colorado Springs."

There was a pause as Brennan reached back into his memory bank for the name. It rang a bell, but he couldn't immediately place it.

"You remember, Professor," prompted Kelly. "I was with the Defense Intelligence Agency then. We worked together on the Belenko debriefing."

A light bulb went on. "Oh, yes! Of course! Tim, I'm sorry. My memory lapsed there for a moment. How are you? My goodness, it's been years.''

Kelly laughed. "Yes, sir, it has. And I'm afraid I haven't been a very good correspondent.''

The professor chuckled, too. "I'm often guilty of that myself. Well, to what do I owe the honor of this call? You know, I was always disappointed you didn't enroll in our doctoral program here. I was very impressed with your work on the Belenko affair. Not having any second thoughts about joining us, are you?''

Kelly laughed again. "No, sir, I'm afraid I'm a little old for that nowadays.''

"Rubbish!'' spat the professor in a good-humored voice. "You're never dead until you stop learning. But be that as it may, if you're not interested in enrolling, what can I do for you?''

Kelly cleared his throat. "Professor, I have something of a bizarre situation here. I can't tell you what it's about, but I can emphasize that it's very important . . . make that critically important. I have come into possession of a handwritten document that appears to be written in the Georgian Mxedruli alphabet. At least, I think that's what it is. I would greatly appreciate it if you would examine this document and give me a rough translation of its contents. I need to know if it is, in fact, written in Mxedruli. If it's not in the Georgian language, I'd like to know what you can make of it, in any case.''

"Certainly, Tim,'' comforted the professor. "Anything for an old friend. Just drop it in the mail and I'll have a look at it as soon as I get back from my place in Maine. I was just leaving to go there on a holiday.''

Kelly took a deep breath. "Professor, timing is a bit of a problem on this. I would appreciate it if you could look at these documents now.''

A pause.

"Now?'' asked Brennan.

"Yes, sir.''

"Well, Tim, don't misunderstand me. I'd be happy to help you out. But as I said, I was just walking out the door to go on a holiday. My wife's been planning this for some time and I've strained her patience already, I don't mind telling you. But you pop it in the mail and I promise to look at it the minute I get back.''

There was another pause.

"Professor,'' Kelly said imploringly. "This stuff is hot.''

The tone of his old friend's voice got the professor's attention. "Exactly what do you mean by 'hot,' Tim?''

"I mean hotter than Belenko, Professor. Maybe a hundred times hotter. My boss says he'll get the White House to call you and verify the seriousness of the situation if need be. We need your help, Professor, and we need it now."

That knocked down the old scholar's objections. "My, well, if that's the case then I would, of course, be happy to assist you, Tim. But I really don't know how. I mean, in order to do what you ask, I would need to inspect this document you speak of, and I believe you said you are residing in Colorado."

"Hmmm," pondered Kelly. "You wouldn't happen to have a facsimile machine there, would you?"

The professor never had been one to embrace technology. "Is that one of those contraptions that will send a picture of a document through the phone?" There was a trace of irritation in his voice.

"Yes, sir. That's it."

"Well, I believe there's one in the department chairman's office, but everyone's left for the weekend and I don't know how to operate it."

Kelly thought fast. He wasn't about to let Brennan off the hook. "Well, Professor, tell you what. Just get on the phone by that facsimile machine and tell me what brand it is. I'll have one of our technical people explain to you how to operate it."

The old professor sighed. He was very tired and just wanted to go home. "You're sure this won't keep?"

"I'm sure, Professor. On the level."

A fatigued voice said, "Very well."

Twenty minutes later, replicas of the first fifteen pages of a notebook found in a Chicago warehouse began rolling out of a Minolta facsimile machine on the Columbia campus.

Day 3, 2300 Hours Zulu, 3:00 p.m. Local
VANDENBERG AIR FORCE BASE

Monaghan craned his neck to look up at the Kestrel. It was poised in a sling over the Titan 34-D rocket, and the technicians in the payload assembly hangar were preparing to attach the tail end of the spaceplane to the booster. The vehicle had never been fitted to a booster before, so things were progressing slowly, as was the case with any prototype. Monaghan decided it was about time to leave and go over to the launch control bunker, where he could start reviewing the flight plan.

"So how's it going, Mad Dog?" asked a voice from behind.

Monaghan turned around, and his face immediately brightened. There stood Lamborghini in his green flight suit. "Hey! Hot Rod! Long time no see! How the hell are you doin'?" He clapped the colonel on the back and pumped his hand.

Lamborghini smiled. "Not too bad, Mad Dog. And yourself?"

Monaghan grimaced. "Could be better. There's some pretty heavy shit going down around here. I guess you know about it?" He jerked a thumb up toward the Kestrel.

Lamborghini nodded.

"Yeah. And if that wasn't enough, my backseater is in the hospital, and that lawnmower McCormack has been crawlin' all over my ass. I tell ya, that's one two-star who must have been abused by a sailor when he was a child. He has a stroke every time he sees my anchor."

Lamborghini laughed. "Don't take it so hard," he comforted.

Monaghan sighed. "Oh, well, no sense in my pissin' on your leg. What brings you out here anyway, Hot Rod?" (There had never been any doubt what Lamborghini's call sign would be.)

"Well, actually, I'm here about your backseater."

"Oh, you got one lined up?" asked Monaghan.

"Yep."

"No shit? Who is it? Anybody I know?"

"Yeah, I think so. You're looking at him."

Monaghan was stunned. "You?"

"Me."

"How come?"

"Process of elimination," Lamborghini explained. "The Kestrel has always had super-tight security. Only one prototype crew has been trained. I was the only one familiar with the weapons systems who was flight-qualified. Either I came on board or the mission was scrubbed. Simple."

Monaghan shook his head. "Well, just between us girls, I hope that the *Constellation* can take care of this *Intrepid* crap without our lifting off. I didn't plan on goin' up in this thing for almost another year. The whole operation feels jerry-rigged to me. And after my last run-in with McCormack, retirement is looking mighty good."

Lamborghini laughed again and looked at his watch. "Listen, I'm starved. What do you say we run out and grab a steak, then we can shag ass over to Edwards for some simulator time. You can bring me up to speed on the systems over dinner."

"You got a deal, Hot Rod. You're the first friendly face I've seen in I don't know how long." He looked back up at the Kestrel and grinned. "Hot damn. Mad Dog and Hot Rod. That sounds like somethin', don't it? Anybody gets in our way, we'll kick his ass."

Day 3, 2345 Hours Zulu, 6:45 P.M. Local
COLUMBIA UNIVERSITY

Professor George Kirtwell Brennan slammed down the magnifying glass. "Good God!" he exclaimed. "It *can't* be!" The elderly scholar's fatigue vanished as he leapt from his chair and bounded to one of the bulging file cabinets in his office. He rummaged through the papers until he found a certain document in a special envelope. He returned to his desk and placed the file-cabinet document alongside the facsimile copies which had been transmitted from Cheyenne Mountain. He picked up the magnifying glass and carefully examined both documents several times.

Finally, he slammed the magnifying glass down once more, this time almost breaking it. "Good God!" He gulped. "It *is!*"

He reached for the phone.

Day 3, 2400 Hours Zulu, 5:00 P.M. Local
CHEYENNE MOUNTAIN

In the conference room, Whittenberg's commo panel buzzed and he picked up the receiver. After a few murmurs he turned to Kelly. "It's for you, Tim. Professor Brennan in New York."

"Oh, good. That was quick." Kelly motioned to the box on the table. "Why don't you put it on the speakerphone, sir? That way we can all hear it."

"Good idea," said the CinC, and he punched a button on his console.

"Tim?" asked a voice from the box.

"Yes, Professor. I'm here. We've got you on a speakerphone. Besides myself there is Rodger Whittenberg, Commanding General of the Space Command, our chief of staff, the deputy chief of staff for operations, and my boss, Major Lydia Strand.'' Kelly thought it better not to mention that an FBI agent was also in the room, and he exchanged an understanding nod with Tedesco.

"Gentlemen, and lady,'' greeted Brennan in a nervous voice. "Tim, I must ask you. Where on earth did you get these documents?''

Kelly flashed a glance at Whittenberg, who shook his head.

"Well, Professor, I'm afraid I'm not at liberty to say at the moment. Besides, it's a situation that would be very difficult to explain over the phone.''

Brennan emitted a "harrumphf,'' then added, "I'm not surprised. Do you have any idea what you have here?''

"No, Professor, we don't. Only that it appeared to me it was written in the Mxedruli alphabet.''

"I see. Well, my dear fellow, I've got something to tell you. I've only made a cursory examination, you understand, but I'm almost certain of my findings. You were quite right. They are written in the Georgian language. These documents appear to be an excerpt from the original handwritten text of a series of articles entitled, *Anarkhizm ili Sotsializm*, which, as you know, translates to *Anarchism or Socialism*. These articles were published serially in some Georgian political periodicals after the turn of the century, and were written by a young Georgian revolutionary named Iosif Vissarionovich Dzhugashvili.''

Kelly's jaw dropped to the table.

"And who is this Eye-Owe-Siff, whatever you said his name was?'' asked Dowd in a laconic voice.

"Iosif Dzhugashvili is the original birth name of Generalissimo Joseph Stalin.''

"*Stalin?*'' cried a chorus of voices. Everyone's voice except Kelly's. He had recognized the name Dzhugashvili.

"But—but—'' stammered Dowd. "I don't understand. I thought Stalin was Russian. Wouldn't he have written in Russian Cyrillic writing?''

"That's a misconception a lot of people have,'' said the voice through the speakerphone. "Stalin was born in the small Georgian town of Gori. He was brought up in the Georgian language and didn't start to learn Russian until he was about ten years old. Georgian is a distinctly different language from Russian, and, in fact, Stalin spoke Russian all of his life with a thick Georgian accent.'' Brennan let his words sink in, then continued, "After ill health forced Stalin from the seminary in 1899, he became politically active. His early writings were in the Georgian language—like the documents you sent me. I compared them to a personal letter written by Stalin—in the Georgian language—that I have in my files. I'm not a handwriting expert, but that rough style is most distinctive. It's my opinion that your documents, and my sample, came from the same hand. And the content of the documents you sent me should eliminate any question. It's definitely from *Anarkhizm ili Sotsializm.*"

"Professor, this is Rodger Whittenberg. I doubt if you remember me, but you were a guest lecturer when I was getting a master's degree at Georgetown. Are you saying that in your professional opinion, these documents were written by the hand of Joseph Stalin himself?"

"Precisely."

Whittenberg's head was throbbing. "Professor, I must ask you. Are papers of this type something that is available on the open market? You know—historical documents that specialty dealers handle. I've purchased a few letters from a dealer myself that were correspondence between Napoleon and Murat at Austerlitz. Could this document be obtained that way?"

The box barked a sarcastic laugh. "Hardly. This isn't something you pick up at a Sotheby's auction. Stalin's writings are exceedingly rare. Particularly his earlier writings. You were lucky to have contacted me. I doubt if there are three or four people in the country who have a sample of his early Georgian handwriting. I obtained the few samples I have from an academic friend of mine in the Soviet Union. As you're probably aware, Stalin has been an extremely sensitive subject with every Russian leader since Khrushchev. Essentially, he became a nonperson. It's been difficult to come by anything relating to him for the last thirty years. The mere possession of these documents, particularly outside the Soviet Union, is, well, nothing less than extraordinary. That's why I was so curious how you obtained them."

All eyes were on the CinC for a response. "Professor Brennan, if I told you how these documents were obtained, you wouldn't believe it. Just as I'm not sure I believe it. If it's all right with you, I would like to send the original documents to you by special messenger so you can examine them and verify your preliminary findings. Rest assured you'll be compensated for your time."

"The opportunity to examine the original will be compensation enough, General. I'm sure our Bakhmeteff Archive here at the university would appreciate the opportunity to obtain these documents—if that ever becomes a possibility."

"Very well, Professor. I'll see what I can do. We can't thank you enough for your assistance."

"Certainly, General. I'll look forward to receiving the originals. Goodbye, Tim."

"So long, Professor Brennan," said Kelly. "I'll be in touch."

There was almost a minute of silence before anyone could recover from the shock. Finally, it was Whittenberg who spoke. "So it's Iceberg," he said softly. "It has to be."

Dowd gripped the little leather notebook so hard that the veins on his hawserlike forearm stuck out. He wished his fingers were encircling Kapuscinski's throat instead. "Goddam," he spat through his teeth. "Joseph fucking *Stalin.*"

Day 3, 2400 Hours Zulu
THE *INTREPID*

Stalin was mad—stark, raving, rabidly mad. Some historians claim he was simply a flint-hard, consummate politician of supreme ruthlessness. But that is wrong. He was mad. Mad in a most evil, calculating way—like a latter-day Ivan the Terrible, carrying Satan's blood bucket across the Eurasian continent. Mass murderers like Tamerlane, Genghis Khan, Adolf Hitler, Napoleon, and the Ayatollah Ruhollah Khomeini all pale in comparison to Josef Stalin. Indeed, so overwhelming were the "Generalissimo's" crimes that the river of blood which flowed from his hands would turn the Black Sea red.

What forces turned little Iosif Dzhugashvili into a madly evil spirit? No one can say. Quite possibly it was his father—a drunken cobbler who beat him savagely. But whatever the reason, once Stalin—a name Iosif took which roughly translates into "Man of Steel"—seized power in the wake of Lenin's death, he never relinquished it for the rest of his life. No other dictator who has ever lived has wielded such sweeping, absolute power—or spilled so much blood.

And the man who became the high executioner for Stalin's bloodthirsty purges—a Russian Himmler, if you will—was a henchman so evil and sinister that the very whisper of his name would chill the spine of the most hardened Politburo member. This was Lavrenti Pavlovich Beria, *komisar* of Stalin's dreaded secret police, the *Narodny Komisariat Vnutrennii Delo* (People's Commissariat for Internal Affairs), or NKVD.

Beria was a hulking, phlegmatic figure—at once malevolent and benign. With his stoic face, bald head, and pince-nez glasses, he looked more like a schoolteacher or the family doctor than a secret police chief. Yet the veil of his unassuming appearance concealed the blackest of hearts, and a mind that was consumed by intrigue, deception, and sexual perversity. This perversity—particularly with young children—was his eventual undoing. In the power struggle following Stalin's death, his repulsive behavior had so alienated him from the rest of the Politburo that even his diabolical scheming couldn't save him. In a poetic end, Beria was accused of spying, and after a six-day Star Chamber trial, he was executed on December 23, 1953.

But in 1945, as the Great Patriotic War began winding down, Beria's position and influence were approaching their zenith, and he was in a position to exercise his own wicked, visionary powers. Beria knew that with Germany defeated, the Generalissimo would need another great enemy to challenge—for dictators need great enemies to stay in power. Beria's calculating mind also knew that Britain, Western Europe, and Japan were finished as potential adversaries. No. They were passé. The next great confrontation would be with the United States—a naive but formidable opponent. To engage the United States in a confrontation—which might lead to war—would be a dangerous but necessary endeavor. After all, little Germany had almost defeated the Motherland, and Germany's resources were puny in comparison to America's vast treasure house. In order to deal with such a potent enemy, Beria knew, extraordinary measures would have to be taken, utilizing all of the Soviet Union's skills of guile, duplicity, propaganda, patience, and spies. Yes, a great many spies would be needed if this adversary was to be slayed. It was in this context —searching for an unconventional spear—that the wicked Beria hatched his long-range, diabolical plan to plant his "seedlings" on American soil. "Seedlings" that would one day rise up and strike the American giant from within.

February 1945.
Moscow.
Heavy snow in Red Square.
The German Army had collapsed and was in retreat toward Berlin, its spine broken by four Russian winters and the horde of Marshal Zhukov's Soviet divisions. The mood in Moscow was of impending victory and relief, for the invaders had been pushed back to the Oder River and the end was only a matter of time.

277

In the basement of the Council of Ministers Building in the Kremlin, a peasant woman who looked much older than her twenty-seven years was trying to restore some order to the paperwork files of the Public Works Ministry. In October 1941, when the German panzer units had been a mere hundred kilometers from Red Square, the files and records of the Soviet government had been hastily extracted from the Kremlin, loaded onto trucks, and moved to storage facilities east of the Urals. But now that the war was coming to an end, the boxed-up files had slowly made their return journey to Moscow, where they were being sorted and returned to their proper place. Even in war, the Soviet bureaucracy survived.

The peasant woman, Viktoria, and her friend Ludmilla worked methodically under a single naked light bulb, in temperatures cold enough to make their breath visible. But they did not complain. For every lump of coal they saved could be used to heat and light an armaments factory. Armaments that could be used to kill Germans.

The door opened and their supervisor entered—a woman, for most Russian men were at the front.

"Viktoria—I must see you," said the supervisor nervously.

Viktoria looked up, then put aside her work and followed the supervisor up to a better-heated ground-floor office. Inside the door stood a strapping NKVD guard with a Kalashnikov rifle. "You are to go with this man," said the supervisor uneasily.

Viktoria nodded and was led outside to a spectacular sight. It was an automobile. And what an automobile! Viktoria had never seen anything like it. So shiny. So clean. So large. Somewhat in shock, she was placed in the backseat of the Packard limousine with the guard and driven the short distance to the building at 2 Dzerzhinsky Square.

Upon arrival she was ushered upstairs into a spacious office which featured a large desk and couch. Viktoria noticed that the temperature in the room was comfortably warm, and the walls were covered with a quiltlike padding, which she thought odd. Little did she know that the padding was soundproofing material, designed to contain the screams of innocent girls who were sexually violated in this room.

Behind the desk sat a hulking figure wearing a thin necktie, a vest, and pince-nez glasses. He was smoking a pipe and had a glass of mineral water sitting beside a closed file. He leveled his eyes on the woman and drummed his fingers on the file for some seconds before ordering, "Viktoria Petrovna Kaminskaya, step forward."

The peasant woman obeyed and approached the desk.

The *komisar* inspected her up and down. She was rail thin, with scraggly brown hair that was tied back with a *babushka* scarf. Her dress was little more than a rag, but her brown eyes were intriguing. A sign of intelligence, perhaps?

"You know who I am?" he asked.

Viktoria nodded. "You are the *komisar*. I have seen your picture."

Lavrenti Beria took a drink of his mineral water. "You are correct, Comrade Kaminskaya . . . quite correct." He took another sip and opened the file in front of him. "Where were you born, Comrade Kaminskaya?" he asked in a formal voice.

"Gantsevichi," she replied stoically.

"In Byelorussia," stated the *komisar*.

"In Byelorussia," she affirmed.

"And when were you born?"

"October 28, 1917."

Another sip. "A child of our glorious revolution," he said in a voice tinged with drama, then returned his gaze to the file. "Your parents were White Russian sympathizers who declared their allegiance to the Czar. Regrettably, they were executed on . . ." He checked the particulars. "On April 22, 1918, for their misplaced loyalties. Yet you, their daughter, joined the Party on June 19, 1943. Tell me, Viktoria Kaminskaya, why did you join the Party of our glorious revolution?"

The peasant woman shrugged and said, "The Germans," as if that curt reply explained it all. And for a White Russian like Viktoria, it did. Byelorussia—White Russia—felt the full brunt of Hitler's Operation *Barbarossa* as German panzers stormed across the Soviet border in June 1941. By the time the Great Patriotic War had ended, one fourth of the White Russian population had died.

"Yes . . . the Germans," repeated the *komisar* softly as he turned a page of the file. "Your uncle Oleg, who raised you? What was his fate at the hands of the invaders?"

"Dead," said Viktoria.

"And your aunt Ekaterina?"

"Dead."

"And your cousin Pyotr?"

"Dead."

Another sip. "And you survived." It was a statement, not a question.

Viktoria nodded.

"How did you survive, Viktoria Kaminskaya?"

The *komisar* had not invited her to sit, so she remained standing in front of the desk and recited her story. "The Germans came," she recalled with a glassy look in her eyes. "My village, Gantsevichi, was near the Polish border. They came very fast. My family was trapped before we could move east. Still, we tried to escape. We were caught by a German patrol. My aunt, uncle, and cousin were shot. I was to be next, but the Germans raped me first," she continued clinically. "Seven of them. While they raped me a partisan group found us and killed the Germans. The partisan leader was our village *komisar*—a brave man. They took me. We moved east by night and slept by day. Finally we slipped through the lines and reached Moscow before the Germans."

The *komisar* regarded her thoughtfully, then refocused his eyes on the file for some seconds. "Your story is incomplete, Comrade Kaminskaya," he said finally. "You failed to mention that there were originally thirteen partisans in your band, but only three of your number completed the journey to Moscow. You neglected to mention that you killed eight Germans yourself—with a knife. You failed to mention that you reached Moscow near starvation, yet shortly thereafter worked on the construction of the city's defenses. You failed to mention that you were awarded the Order of Lenin. You failed to mention"—his voice rose—"that you are a heroine. I know this, Comrade Kaminskaya. I know everything about you. The report by the village *komisar* who survived the journey with you was quite complete. Your Party file is quite complete. The state security file on you is quite complete. There is nothing that I, the *komisar*, do not know about Viktoria Petrovna Kaminskaya."

Beria slapped the file shut and rose to gaze out the window—a calculated move to intensify the artificial drama of the moment. "You joined the Party, Comrade, because the Party saved you, sheltered you, fed you, decorated you, and found you work. That is why you joined the Party. Am I correct?"

Viktoria sensed it would not be wise to disagree with this man, even though he'd touched on her true feelings. "Yes, *komisar*. You are correct."

Beria lowered his voice. "And there is nothing you would not do for the Party. Is that correct?"

"Correct," she said reflexively.

The *komisar* turned and leaned over the desk. "That is what I expected to hear, Comrade. Sit down."

Viktoria did as she was told, and Beria continued. "The Generalissimo has given me a mission. A vital mission that will require the dedication and sacrifice of comrades with unquestioned loyalty. Comrades like yourself.''

''The Generalissimo,'' whispered Viktoria reverently. Beria might as well have said the mission had been handed down directly from God. Upon arrival in Moscow, Viktoria had been weak, sick, and half starved. Yet she immediately joined a horde of weary Muscovites in digging a tank trap that encircled the city—a colossal trench designed to stop Guderian's panzers at the city's gates. One day her work party had looked up, and there he was. The Generalissimo himself. He raised a clenched fist, then disappeared into his car as quickly as he'd come. The inspiration was overwhelming. Viktoria's work party, one of thousands digging the huge excavation, grabbed their picks and shovels and attacked the trench like a pack of wolves.

''You would do anything for the Generalissimo, would you not, Comrade?'' asked the *komisar* harshly.

''Anything,'' replied Viktoria without hesitation.

Beria continued staring at her with his cold, foreboding eyes, until finally saying, ''Good.'' Then his voice took on a challenging tone. ''There is a special mission that must be undertaken for the sake of the Motherland, Viktoria Petrovna. A vital mission that is lifelong. Do you understand? Lifelong. The element of danger will be small, and you will live well, but the requirement for secrecy is all-important. Yes, secrecy. It is crucial. So secret is this mission that I cannot tell you the nature of it until you have accepted the task.'' Beria smiled his phelgmatic smile. ''A dilemma, is it not, Viktoria Petrovna? You cannot learn the secret until you accept the mission. Only the most devoted of the Party have been selected for this task. The Generalissimo himself approved of your selection. Tell me, Viktoria Petrovna —tell me the absolute truth—do you accept this mission without hesitation? Are you truly worthy of being the Generalissimo's chosen one?''

Any other Russian would have been frightened half to death over this confrontation, but the war had dulled Viktoria's sense of fear, and steeled her devotion to the Generalissimo and the Party. Her village *komisar* had saved her. She regretted her parents' death, but she had never really known them. All she knew was that Viktoria Kaminskaya had survived the war, when twenty million Russians had not, and she had actually laid eyes on the Generalissimo. And now he summoned her.

''I accept,'' she said flatly.

Beria nodded. ''Good,'' he said, then added another ''Good'' for emphasis. "The Generalissimo knew you would not refuse him." Beria did not tell Viktoria that had she refused, she would not have left Dzerzhinsky Square alive.

Beria rang for tea, and for the next two hours he explained in patient detail to Viktoria how she would soon be wed to another loyal Soviet, also handpicked by the Generalissimo. The couple would receive intensive language training, and after the war's end would be packed onto a train for Poland. From Warsaw they would emigrate to America, along with thousands of displaced persons pouring into the promised land after the war. They would enjoy a hidden source of money and raise one child and one child only, who would be taught from the cradle to be a loyal Soviet and to obey the instructions of his parents.

"Go to your home and collect your possessions, Viktoria Petrovna, then return here. Your training will commence at once. Never forget, you are the Generalissimo's chosen one."

Viktoria nodded and left.

The Packard transported her back to the apartment in Moscow that she shared with eight other women. The hovel was empty because the other occupants were working. Viktoria had no reservations about leaving the miserable apartment behind. Perhaps this "mission" she had accepted would lead to something better. But there was one thing she was not about to leave behind. From beneath her cot she withdrew a small wooden chest that was padlocked shut. On a string around her neck she kept a key, which she now used to unlock it. Inside were two baubles of cheap jewelry—and a leather notebook. Carefully she placed the notebook in the dirty cloth sack that served her as a handbag.

Initially, she thought her summons to Dzerzhinsky Square might concern the notebook. And although Viktoria no longer frightened easily, she was relieved to learn the *komisar* knew nothing of it.

Two months previously, Viktoria had reported for work at the Council of Ministers Building, only to find two Red Army soldiers posted at the door. These were not the old, toothless men or young boys found in Moscow these days, but real soldiers with rifles. Like the ones at the German front. They stopped Viktoria at the door until her supervisor appeared. With an urgent manner, the supervisor ushered her downstairs to an area of the basement where she'd never been allowed before. Her superior pointed to a door. "Go inside and help Ludmilla. We must finish and lock this door quickly."

Viktoria did as she was told, and when she entered the room, Ludmilla nearly jumped out of her skin.

"Oh, Viktoria!" cried Ludmilla. "Thank heaven it is you. I was so afraid it was one of the guards."

Viktoria confronted a bizarre scene. Her friend was surrounded by file boxes. But these were not the boxes made of pine or rough cardboard to which they were accustomed. No. These file boxes were made of finished rosewood. Beautiful, smooth, polished rosewood. They were finer than anything Viktoria had ever seen. One of the fine boxes had fallen from its stack, and the paper contents had spilled at Ludmilla's feet.

"Ludmilla," asked Viktoria with a sense of wonder, while touching one of the boxes, "what are these?"

Ludmilla gulped. "They were delivered only minutes ago."

Viktoria nodded. "Yes . . . but what are they?"

Ludmilla gulped again and drew Viktoria close. "These boxes," she whispered, "are the papers of the Generalissimo himself."

Viktoria gasped. "The Generalissimo?"

Ludmilla nodded vigorously. "*Da*, Viktoria. We are to stack these boxes against that wall." She pointed. "I was moving this one when it slipped." Ludmilla started to whimper. "I am so afraid. What will they do to me when they learn I dropped the Generalissimo's papers?"

Viktoria comforted her friend. "Do not fear, Ludmilla. I will repack this box. You begin stacking the others. We will tell no one that the box slipped. We can stack it so any scratches will be hidden."

"Oh, yes, Viktoria, let us do that," said Ludmilla, and she quickly put her heavyset body to work stacking the file boxes against the wall.

Viktoria knelt down and began repacking the strewn papers back into the rosewood box, trembling at the knowledge that what she held had passed through Stalin's own hands. A small leather-bound notebook had been badly smudged by the basement room's grimy floor. If anyone opened this box later he would find the dirty volume. So Viktoria made a quick decision. She would clean the notebook off and return it to the box later, when she had the chance. She dropped it into her raggedy cloth handbag and began helping Ludmilla.

But Viktoria never had the opportunity to return the notebook. The door to that special room was locked and sealed off, and Viktoria could not enter. And besides, she'd become attached to the diminutive leather-bound volume. It was her link to the Generalissimo. And now he summoned her for this lifelong mission. She couldn't bear to part with the little book. So she kept it.

*   *   *

A year later, when Victoria Kapuscinski and her husband walked down the boat ramp at Ellis Island in New York Harbor, her belly was already swollen with their first and only offspring.

The pilot at the controls of the American space shuttle *Intrepid* was a ''seedling'' planted by Lavrenti Beria.

THE FOURTH DAY

"A deep plant," murmured Tedesco softly. "It has to be."

"What did you say?" asked Strand.

The FBI agent's brow had turned into deep furrows beneath his widow's peak. He took a slow breath and said, "Something called a deep plant. It was a rumor. Pure supposition that was bantered about in the Bureau from time to time. I always thought it was some kind of fairy tale left over from the Hoover era. A myth, like a unicorn or a mermaid. But in view of this, I guess it has to be real. Still, God, I can't believe it."

"I don't understand," said Whittenberg. "Explain what you mean by this term 'deep plant.'"

Tedesco took another breath before continuing. "The Bureau, I'm sure just like the Air Force or any big agency, gets more than its share of crackpot phone calls. Like every once in a while some psycho will call us up and claim J. Edgar Hoover is still alive and running things from the basement of the Bureau building. Well, I remember one crazy story that circulated around the Bureau, oh, ten or fifteen years ago. Some guy had walked into our Tulsa office off the street. Said his parents immigrated to the United States from Bulgaria after the war, but that they were really Russian agents. Claimed they tried to indoctrinate him when he was a kid—wanted to turn him into a lockstep Communist. He said that after his parents died he was contacted by someone who professed to be with the KGB. But this 'walk-in' said he renounced his parents, told the KGB contact to go to hell, and decided to contact the Tulsa FBI office to let them know he was a good American."

Tedesco sipped some coffee. "Well, as you might imagine, the walk-in was dismissed as just another wacko. But in view of this Russian connection with Kapuscinski, it looks like he might have been for real."

Sir Isaac was rubbing his eyes when all of a sudden he jerked bolt upright in his chair. "McKenna!" he exclaimed.

Tedesco eyeballed the brigadier and was puzzled. "Who is Mc-Kenna?"

Strand explained. "Jarrod McKenna was on the *Intrepid*'s original flight manifest as mission commander. Four days before lift-off he came down with intestinal flu—at least that was the diagnosis. Iceberg was the backup pilot and took over." Strand shook her head ruefully. "Intestinal flu. Pretty damned convenient if you ask me. I'd bet the family farm that Kapuscinski laced McKenna's shrimp salad with something that made it look like he had the flu."

Sir Isaac nodded. "I'll have the medical people test McKenna. See if there's a trace of whatever Iceberg gave him."

A wave of bitterness swept over those present as they realized that for years they had been hoodwinked and betrayed by a traitor in their own midst. The amount of damage that could have been inflicted by Iceberg—even without the *Intrepid*—was nothing less than devastating.

"I can guess what you're probably thinking, General," comforted Tedesco. "But something like Kapuscinski is, well, unprecedented. There really is no defense against a penetration like this."

Whittenberg sighed. "It's kind of you to say so, Mr. Tedesco. I only hope Admiral Bergstrom and the President will be as understanding." He picked up the phone.

Day 4, 0130 Hours Zulu, 3:30 A.M. Local
KALININGRAD FLITE CONTROL CENTRE

Lt. Gen. Likady Popov was in the cavernous Flite Control Centre, leaning over the mission commander's shoulder. The stocky general was trying to enlist the blond-haired Malyshev into his plan, but the young colonel was resisting—and sweating. Philosophically, Malyshev agreed with his general, but the omnipresent KGB henchmen floating around the room caused him to waver.

"Listen to me, Oleg," implored Popov with a whisper. "Hijacking a shuttle is one thing. Deliberately shooting one down is quite another. Do you want more blood on our hands? There is no way to predict how the Americans will react. If they do launch a rescue shuttle from their Florida cosmodrome, you will be in charge of firing the antisatellite weapon. All you have to do is hesitate for a few seconds before hitting the activation button. That will give the American rescue shuttle enough time to pass out of range. We must stop this madness."

The Slavic-looking Malyshev was about to give a slow, careful nod when the door opened and in walked the KGB Chairman, along with a tall, spidery man who wore a Vandyke beard.

"General," announced Chairman Kostiashak, "I believe you know Comrade Pirdilenko."

Ivan Pirdilenko took off his gloves and fur hat, while a KGB corporal stepped up to help the scientist with his coat. "Yes, yes, of course," said Pirdilenko. "Popov and I have known each other for many years, have we not, General?"

Popov nodded a grudging acknowledgment.

"In view of Comrade Pirdilenko's credentials as an expert with our antisatellite weapon, I thought it would be, ah, helpful, to bring him here from Plesetsk. Perhaps you could turn the antisatellite preparations over to him. That would allow you to concentrate on launching our own cosmonauts from Baikonur." The little Chairman's smile remained fixed.

Pirdilenko didn't give Popov a chance to respond. "Of course, I'm certain the General would be delighted to turn these matters over to me. Is that not correct, Popov?" Not waiting for an answer, Pirdilenko bored right in. "Now then, who is in charge of monitoring the American shuttle's flite path and activating the arming sequence?"

Slowly, Popov pointed at Malyshev, the mission commander.

"Ah, very good," said an enthusiastic Pirdilenko. "It is not often that we are allowed to put one of our weapons to a genuine test. Is that not correct, General?"

Popov said nothing. He only looked at the little KGB chieftain with the gaze of a defeated man.

Day 4, 0130 Hours Zulu, 8:30 P.M. Local
THE WHITE HOUSE

After explaining the incredible discovery of the Stalin notebook in a Chicago warehouse to Admiral Bergstrom, the Secretary of Defense, and the Vice President, Whittenberg was now relating the story for the fourth time to the President over the phone.

The chief executive was in the living quarters of the mansion, and his mood was disbelief. "I know you have to respect the evidence, but still—Joseph *Stalin?*"

"Yes, Mr. President," replied Whittenberg, "that's what it appears to be. I am having the original text of the notebook flown out to

Professor Brennan at Columbia so he can verify his initial findings, but given the rarity of these kinds of documents, it would appear his preliminary conclusions are on the mark.''

"Jesus. Every time I think this *Intrepid* business can't get any crazier, it does. It's damn well gone over the edge. A renegade shuttle. A Russian ambassador and a couple of Politburo members who haven't a clue what's going on. A mysterious satellite. And now a link to Joseph Stalin? This is insane.''

"I quite agree, Mr. President. But we have to face facts, and the facts indicate Kapuscinski is the traitor. How or why he came into possession of Stalin's own notes is beyond me, but it establishes an irrefutable link with the Soviet Union. A link that cuts through everything else and gives credence to Agent Tedesco's thesis.''

The chief executive shook his head. "Well, if the turncoat is Kapuscinski, then what do you suppose has happened to the other two crew members? Mulcahey and Rodriquez?''

There was a pause on the other end while Whittenberg took a deep breath. "Dead . . . most probably.''

The President shuddered. "Has there been any change in the *Intrepid*'s behavior?''

"No, sir. Orbit unchanged.''

"So, if the *Intrepid* is, in fact, damaged as you suspect, that means the Russians still have to go up and get it. Right?''

"Yes, sir,'' replied Whittenberg.

"Any activity on their launch pads?'' asked the President.

"We've been keeping an active surveillance on all Soviet cosmodromes. Except for the mystery satellite that was launched twenty-one hours ago from Plesetsk, we've seen no activity. But I should point out that the Soviets are able to roll out and launch their boosters in very short order—as they did with that mystery satellite out of Plesetsk.''

"Do you have any idea what that thing is?'' The chief executive's face betrayed his concern.

"As we discussed previously, sir,'' recapped Whittenberg, "there's no way of telling. The configuration of the satellite indicates it could be virtually any kind of vehicle that simply hasn't jettisoned its launch shroud yet—anything from a photo reconnaissance bird to an ASAT.''

The word *ASAT* gave the President pause. "What if it is an antisatellite weapon?''

An exasperated sigh came through the line. "My crystal ball is no better than the next person's, Mr. President; but if it is, in fact, an ASAT, then it could very well destroy the *Constellation*, its crew, and the *Intrepid* right along with it. And as I said, we would be powerless to stop it."

"Hmmmm. What about that spaceplane?"

"The Kestrel?"

"Yeah. Could that thing handle an ASAT?"

Whittenberg's voice contained the equivalent of a shrug. "An ASAT going against the Kestrel in a reciprocal—that is to say, opposite—orbit would be something of a Mexican standoff, sir. It would just depend on which spacecraft could lock on and fire the fastest."

"You mean . . . a quick-draw contest?"

"In a manner of speaking, yes, sir."

"Well, if that spaceplane can at least defend itself, should we forget the *Constellation* and launch the Kestrel instead?"

"We could, sir, but it would mean trading capability for time. The *Constellation* is completing preparations now. Fueling will commence" —Whittenberg checked the giant watch on his wrist that all aviators wore—"about three hours from now. Preparations on the Kestrel are under way now, but the earliest we could make it ready for lift-off would be twenty-seven hours *after* the *Constellation*'s first launch window. During that time the Russians might get something aloft."

"You're not giving me very attractive options, General," grumbled the President.

"That's correct, sir. And make no mistake—that mystery satellite up there could very well be an ASAT. We simply don't know. If it is, the *Constellation* could be destroyed and the crew killed. General McCormack has already informed the *Constellation*'s crew of the potential risks. However, if we wait and send up the Kestrel, we're giving the Russians another twenty-seven hours to try to bring down the *Intrepid* for themselves. I won't make this easy for you, sir. The *Constellation* or the Kestrel. You've got the facts, and it's your decision. Which one do we send up?"

The President felt excruciatingly alone. It was a clear choice now. No more staff papers. No more study. No more counseling or recommendations. Decision time. His and his alone. He could be dead right or dead wrong. He felt like waffling, but then he remembered Dr. Sharp's comment about the rubidium isotope and the twenty trillion watts of power released in a single Graser pulse.

"Launch the *Constellation*," ordered the President.

"Yes, sir."

Day 4, 0230 Hours Zulu, 5:30 A.M. Local
ROYAL OMANI AIR FORCE BASE, MUSCAT, OMAN

The sky was a purple twilight, indicating that dawn was almost upon them. To be seen in the daylight would be unforgivable; therefore, Ghost Leader was grateful when he finally heard the squeal of his tires on the runway. As his speed decreased, he turned the aircraft onto a high-speed taxiway and headed for a darkened hangar.

Waiting inside the hangar were the Omani air base commander, the senior military attaché from the U.S. Embassy (an Army colonel), and two U.S. Air Force advisers who were on loan to the Royal Omani Air Force.

The barrel-chested American colonel, complete with desert fatigues and sidearm, didn't like having the Omani air base commander present—but that was the price you paid for using the Sultan's real estate. Although he grumbled, the American knew he had no real cause for a gripe. The Sultan's rich but sparsely populated little country was within spitting distance of Iran, across the Gulf of Oman. His Highness had to go eyeball to eyeball with the Ayatollah on a daily basis, and the fewer Americans on his soil, the better he liked it. Yet when the chips were down he'd play ball, just as the Secretary of State said. When the U.S. Army's Delta Force had embarked on its abortive mission to rescue hostages in the U.S. embassy in Teheran, the Sultan had allowed the Americans to use his Masirah Island as a staging area. He was a gutsy little guy.

As Ghost Leader's plane approached, one of the American Air Force advisers guided the aircraft into the darkened hangar with a bright flashlight wand, then gave the signal for the pilot to kill his engines. The process was then repeated with Ghost Two, while the C-141 Starlifter and the KC-10 tanker were directed to a different hangar.

The air base commander flipped a switch and the hangar doors rolled forward on their tracks until they closed, which plunged the hangar into total darkness. He then turned on the interior klieg lights to illuminate the black batwings, and the sight that greeted him almost caused his knees to buckle. He stood there some moments with his mouth agape, then warily approached Ghost Leader's plane.

"You understand you are to speak to no one about this?" said the American colonel sternly. "Absolutely no one."

The air base commander nodded absently. "Yes, yes, I understand. I was not told what type of aircraft we would be receiving." He gulped. "Tell me. What *is* it?"

Before the colonel could answer, a hatch on the underside of the batwing flipped open, and a flight-suited figure wearing a crash helmet nimbly dropped onto the tarmac. "Where's the bathroom?" he demanded.

Day 4, 0430 Hours Zulu, 11:30 p.m. Local
PAD 39A, KENNEDY SPACE CENTER

On the northeast corner of Pad 39A, a valve was turned and the liquid contents of a giant spherical vessel began flowing into an underground fuel line. The fluid draining from the 850,000-gallon storage tank was liquid hydrogen, chilled to minus 423 degrees Fahrenheit. In liquid form, the hydrogen was incredibly light—a full gallon weighed only half a pound. And because it weighed so little, no pumps were required to transmit the fuel down the vacuum-jacketed transfer line. Instead, a small amount of the liquid H-two was allowed to "boil off," or vaporize at the top of the storage vessel, and the resulting pressure was sufficient to push the fuel down the pipeline toward the launch pad.

At the pad, the fuel traveled into a tail-mast umbilical at the bottom of the *Constellation*, where it gushed backward through the orbiter's own pipeline system and into the orange external tank. Like a bubbling caldron, the tank's H-two fuel compartment began filling from the bottom up, and shortly before lift-off at 4:30 A.M., the vessel would be topped off.

At launch time, the only thing that would stand between the limpet mine and 383,000 gallons of the volatile liquid hydrogen was a thin layer of the external tank's aluminum skin.

Day 4, 0430 Hours Zulu, 8:30 p.m. Local
EDWARDS AIR FORCE BASE

"I got a bandit at two o'clock low, moving laterally from starboard to port. Range three-eight-seven miles and increasing slightly."

"Want an attitude adjustment?" queried Monaghan.

"Negative," responded Lamborghini. "At least not yet. He's coming across our beam. I'll track him with the cone for now." He twisted the handle on the radar focusing controller, which caused the small radar dish in the Kestrel's nose cone to align with the bandit. The adjustable radar dish allowed him to sweep the airspace without having to pivot the spaceplane.

"You want to move in on this one?" asked Monaghan. The Kestrel could maneuver closer to a target if they were traveling in roughly the same direction.

"Negative," replied Lamborghini. "The cross angle might be too severe. It may not do us much good. I think we should go for this one now with the Phoenix."

"Take the shot," ordered Monaghan.

Lamborghini punched some buttons on the armament panel and set the missile for dependent guidance, which meant the Phoenix would follow the Kestrel's own radar beam to the target unless otherwise instructed. He pressed the red FIRE button and there was a flash of bright light, but no sound, and the two pilots watched as the white dot of flame disappeared into the night sky.

"He's following the beam," observed Lamborghini. He tried twisting the radar dish farther to the left to keep the bandit onscreen, but the controller couldn't go any farther. "Bring us to port twenty degrees and drop the nose ten. The bandit is getting to the edge of my scanner."

"Roger," replied Monaghan, and he joggled the Kestrel's hand controller, causing the spacecraft to pivot.

"Okay, he's closing, but it looks like it's going to be close. Range is four-five-seven miles. Switching to independent lock-on." Lamborghini flipped a switch that illuminated the missile's own Doppler-pulse radar. When he heard a tone in his earphones, indicating the missile had acquired the target, he flipped the guidance switch from DEPENDENT to INDEPENDENT.

The two blips had almost converged when they disappeared off the edge of his screen, out of range of the Kestrel's radar. "I lost 'em," grumbled Lamborghini. "Looked like it was close, though."

"The one that got away is always the sweetest, Hot Rod," comforted Mad Dog. "We've been at this for a while. What say we take a break?"

"You got it . . . maybe the Phoenix was able to close on its own?"

Monaghan said, "Don't count on it," and pulled a lever to engage an electric motor. There was a whirring sound as the canopy of the Kestrel simulator raised itself up.

The two aviators were in the hypersecret Kestrel simulation facility at Edwards Air Force Base. It was a room crammed with computer consoles, as well as the simulator module which looked like some sort of carnival ride on stilts. The stilts were actually hydraulic jacks that could pitch the simulator cockpit up, down, and sideways to give the occupants the feeling of maneuver.

Having once been deputy director of the Kestrel project, Lamborghini was intimately familiar with the simulator and the Air Force Flight Test Center at Edwards, where virtually every fighter aircraft in the Air Force inventory had undergone development testing.

The two pilots climbed out of the simulator and pulled off their helmets as a tech sergeant walked over from the simulator control panel. "Close, but no cigar on that last one, sir," he told Lamborghini. "That problem has a deceptive degree of difficulty. You should have listened to Commander Monaghan and closed a little bit before engaging. That way you might have just tagged the bandit before he dropped off your screen."

Lamborghini scowled. "Closing the gap takes fuel. I figured we might need it for later."

"You were correct to put the missile on independent guidance, though. Unfortunately, our simulation model says your Phoenix ran out of propellant before it could connect." Lamborghini continued to scowl.

"Just wait till next year," offered Monaghan. "Come on, Hot Rod. I'll buy you a drink."

The two men went down the hall to a small vending area. Lamborghini was gratified to discover the soft-drink machine carried Dr Pepper. He'd developed a taste for it while stationed in Texas. After dropping in Mad Dog's coins, they sat down in a pair of plastic chairs at a plastic table.

In appearance, sitting across from each other, each man seemed to be the antithesis of the other. The abstemious, raven-haired Lamborghini was lean, angular; his movements were precise and analytical. Monaghan, on the other hand, was sort of, well, round. The extra poundage on his stocky frame indicated he hadn't missed too many meals, and his Irishman's crop of red hair was perennially unkempt. As he lit up a Marlboro, a cloud of smoke enveloped a set of craggy features that demonstrated he'd obviously enjoyed "the good life." Yet despite the differences, the two pilots liked each other, and Monaghan could tell that his friend was starting to have reservations.

"Relax, Hot Rod," he comforted. "In the first place we ain't going up. And if we do, you'll do fine. Trust me."

Lamborghini swished his Dr Pepper over the ice in the paper cup. "I hope you're right. This will teach me to have more respect for backseaters. There's a lot more finesse to handling that hardware than meets the eye. I feel comfortable with my grasp of the equipment, but using the systems and computing target solutions is a lot tougher than I figured. It takes a lot of practice.''

"No sweat, Hot Rod. If we do go up, the *Intrepid* will be sittin' pretty. I'll bring us in so close you can shove a Sidewinder right up Iceberg's ass.''

Lamborghini swished his drink again and thought about the phone call he'd received earlier from his deputy, Lydia Strand. "Yeah. Iceberg. Brother. I still can't believe it. The guy has the DFC. Who would've thought?''

Monaghan tossed down his Seven-Up. "I would've thought. In fact, I had a pretty strong inkling it was him.''

Lamborghini was surprised. "You? I didn't know you knew him.''

Mad Dog nodded. "Yeah. I came to know him in an intimate way, you might say.'' Monaghan described the Red Flag competition for Lamborghini, and how Iceberg had tried to lead him into a death trap.

Lamborghini's jaw dropped. "You should've told somebody. I've flown in Red Flag, too. They're pretty tight about safety at Nellis.''

Monaghan shrugged. "My gun camera ran out of tape just before it happened. I was on air-crap turf—no offense—and nobody would have believed a crybaby swabbie.''

Lamborghini whistled softly. "I dunno about that. . . . Guess it wouldn't bother you to get Iceberg in your sights, would it?''

Mad Dog nodded, and his friend was chilled by the look in the man's eyes. It made Lamborghini wonder how much of Monaghan's life-of-the-party demeanor was a veneer.

Lamborghini checked his watch. "My deputy talked to the chief of staff at SPACECOM. He's going to have the *Constellation* launch and rendezvous patched into the Edwards commo center from SPADOC. We can watch it if you want.''

Monaghan nodded. "I want, Hod Rod.'' Then he scratched his mop of red hair. "Say, I always meant to ask you—you any kin to that sports car outfit over in Italy?''

Lamborghini laughed and shook his head. "No. No, I'm not. Just happen to have the same name. Funny thing, though. The guy who founded that sports car company was a man named Ferruccio Lamborghini. He made his fortune in the tractor business, and then started the sports car operation. Maybe it was sort of like a hobby for him. Anyway, there's hardly a week that goes by that somebody doesn't ask me if I'm related to the sports car family. Yet in my whole life, not one single person has ever asked me if I was related to the tractor manufacturer.''

Day 4, 0630 Hours Zulu, 1:30 A.M. Local
KENNEDY SPACE CENTER

Marine Lt. Col. Phillip Heitmann, Air Force Maj. Jack Townsend, and Army Maj. Sandford Watkins walked through the insulated crew access arm of the gantry tower toward the entry hatch of the *Constellation*. To the graying Heitmann—a onetime linebacker for Michigan State—walking down that ramp was like walking out of a locker room before a big game. The ground crew's eyes were upon them, and the sense of excitement never failed to make his pulse start thumping.

At the hatch of the orbiter, they slipped off their felt boot covers and dropped them into a plastic bag held open by a white-suited technician. The crew access gantry arm was a ''clean'' room, designed to prevent foreign substances from polluting the orbiter's delicate electronics and environmental control system when the hatch was open.

Now came the tricky part. Because the orbiter was pointed nose up, the astronauts had to twist like gymnasts to maneuver themselves up into the upper deck and into their flight chairs. After a few grunts and strains they made it, while trying to ignore the four crates of Stinger missiles lashed down in the crew deck.

Once in their seats, Heitmann and Townsend pulled out the first of several three-ring binders which contained the voluminous preflight checklist. Although computers handled the bulk of the checklist chores, there was still a lot with which the crew had to contend. To begin his *de rigueur* preflight checks, Heitmann propped the binder into its special holder on the console panel, being careful not to let it slip. Since the *Constellation* was facing nose up, a dropped notebook would fall all the way to the back wall, possibly catching Watkins right between the eyes on the way down.

Mission Specialist Sandford Watkins didn't have a whole lot to do during the preflight checks, so he studied a manual on the operation of the Stinger missile to make sure he hadn't forgotten anything about the arming and firing sequence.

Outside in the gantry arm, two technicians closed the hatch door, then engaged the electronic actuator which caused the twenty-eight latches on the hatch ring to pop into place. With his hand-held radio, a technician told the systems engineer inside Firing Room Two that the hatch was closed.

"I copy," said the engineer, who, in turn, notified the Cap Com—the person who handled all communication with the spacecraft crew.

"*Constellation*, this is Launch Control," said the Cap Com. "Your hatch is closed."

Heitmann looked at the green light on his console under SDE HCH—one of the 2,040 dials, switches, gauges, and instruments on the orbiter's control panels. He radioed back, "Roger, Control, I copy side hatch closed."

Day 4, 0830 Hours Zulu, 1:30 A.M. Local
FALCON AIR FORCE STATION, COLORADO

Maj. Gen. Chester McCormack strode into Mission Control at the Combined Space Operations Center (CSOC) looking tired and unshaven and wearing his green flight suit. He'd just parked his Talon at nearby Peterson Air Force Base. Despite Whittenberg's order to get some rest, he'd slept very little before leaving Cape Canaveral.

When Senators and Congressmen visited the Mission Control room at CSOC, or its civilian counterpart at NASA in Houston, they were always surprised at the smallness of the enclosure. "It always looks so big on TV," was the usual remark, and that was true. During the Mercury, Gemini, Apollo, and shuttle programs, the Mission Control room in Houston was always photographed by the networks with a wide-angle lens, making it appear giant size. Perhaps that made things more dramatic. But in fact, it was a small room. The Kaliningrad Flite Control Centre was much larger, because it did not rely as much on computers and required more people to perform many of the tasks.

McCormack went straight to the mission director. "What's the status at thirty-nine?" he asked, meaning Pad 39A.

The chubby and balding director—an Army lieutenant colonel—had his checklist ready. "Fueling is about complete. No problems there. Manipulator arm circuit breaker is having some glitches again, but since we're not doing anything with a payload that shouldn't matter. Primary heat exchanger in crew deck environmental system has a clogged tube, but backup is working all right. Hydraulic line on speed brake isn't testing right. Could be a malfunction on the test circuit, but can't say at this point. And the Ku-band transponder is kaput. Have no idea why. In short, nothing abortable.''

With a machine as complex as the shuttle, it was rare when everything worked without a glitch. In fact, having a flawless space vehicle prior to launch never happened. But small glitches were permissible. A big glitch—like a bad valve on the liquid oxygen feed—was not permissible and could abort a launch.

"What about the flight plan?" asked McCormack.

"Navigation has it all computed and it will be loaded into the BFS computer fifteen minutes before lift-off," said the director. "If we get off on schedule, the rendezvous shouldn't be any problem at all.''

McCormack sighed, "Good," then collapsed into the mission director's chair.

The mission director looked his boss over carefully. McCormack's "rakish" appearance was undercut by his ashen face, and for the first time there appeared to be some gray in that perfect head of blond hair. "General," said the mission director charitably, "if you don't mind my saying so, you look like hammered shit.''

Day 4, 0900 Hours Zulu, 4:00 A.M. Local
CENTRAL INTELLIGENCE AGENCY HEADQUARTERS, LANGLEY, VIRGINIA

The Director of Central Intelligence, or DCI, looked out the picture window of his seventh-floor office into a void of pitch-black darkness. Had it been daylight, he would have seen a beautiful Virginia forest, and perhaps a deer striding across a distant meadow. But now it was dark. Impenetrable. Much like this whole damned *Intrepid* affair, he mused.

After attending the White House briefing on the rogue spacecraft, he'd sent out an ALL CHIEFS OF STATION URGENT cable for something—anything—on this *Intrepid* business and had come up with absolutely zero. Nothing. About every hour the Vice President had called him, fishing for something. The gangly framed DCI with a toothy grin had nothing to give. Zip. It was frustrating. He'd been in the intelligence business most of his professional life, coming up the signals intelligence route through the Army. He'd run into stone walls before, but never like this. Frustration—and no sleep. But sleep was a nasty habit he'd shaken years ago.

The door burst open without the prelude of a knock. It was the professorial-looking deputy director, waving a cable in his hand. "I'm not sure, but we may have something," he said, trying to contain his excitement. "How it figures into the *Intrepid* business I can't say, but this just came in on a one-time disk from Canberra." The DCI grabbed the cable, put on his reading glasses, and scanned the message. Twice.

"Hmmm," he murmured. "A phony shuttle?"

"Yeah," concurred the deputy. "The source is on the scene at Baikonur, too, and Australian SIS says he's solid gold."

The DCI scratched his head. "Well, at least it's something. I'll get this to Bergstrom. Send a copy on a one-time disk to Whittenberg at SPACECOM. Maybe he can make something out of it."

"Gotcha."

The deputy exited and the DCI picked up his secure phone to inform the White House about the message. But then he stopped. Although the DCI felt confident about using the secure Oracle system, the fact remained that electronic "ferrets" operating in the Soviet Embassy could monitor *70 percent* of all telephone microwave traffic in Washington, D.C. With something as important as this Baikonur source, the DCI wasn't willing to take so much as a minuscule chance of its being compromised. He put down the phone and grabbed his coat. He'd hand-carry it to the White House himself. Slow, but secure.

Day 4, 0900 Hours Zulu
SPYGLASS, ALTITUDE: 62,000 FEET ABOVE THE ARCTIC ICE CAP

"Rabbit's Nest, this is Spyglass. We're in position, just waiting to take a picture of the *Constellation-Intrepid* rendezvous. Let us know pronto if any of the *Constellation*'s specs change after lift-off. In the meantime, we'll just hang around up here and keep the coffee warm."

"Roger, Spyglass. . . . Say, I'm curious. What's your exterior temperature?"

The chief master sergeant leaned over his console to check the readout on the outside air temperature. The high altitude-767 observation platform was accustomed to temperature extremes. "Looks like a minus seven-three degrees, Rabbit's Nest. Fahrenheit-type."

"Whooooweee," replied Rabbit's Nest from inside Cheyenne Mountain. "That's Cream of Wheat weather, isn't it? Stay up there, Spyglass. We'll keep you posted on the *Constellation*."

Day 4, 0902 Hours Zulu, 4:02 A.M. Local
PAD 39A

Jacob Classen felt, and looked, as if he'd run back-to-back marathons. His white coveralls were smudged, there was stubble on his chin, and under the orange hard hat his snow-white hair was even whiter. That was because his deputy pad manager, Ed Garvey, had never returned, and Classen didn't know whether to feel angry or worried. But in any case, he was exhausted and it was less than thirty minutes until launch—way past time to clear the pad area. Fueling was almost topped off now, and the final on-site check of the gantry by the section chiefs was under way. Classen held up his radio and mashed the transmit button. "Alpha Chief, report."

"Alpha Chief here," squawked the transceiver. "Decks one, two, three, and four, all clear."

"Acknowledged. Bravo Chief, report," ordered Classen.

"Bravo Chief reporting. Decks five, six, seven, and eight, all clear."

"Acknowledged," said Classen. "Charlie Chief, report."

"Decks nine, ten, eleven, and twelve, all clear, Jacob."

"Good," replied Classen. "Everybody bust ass down here so we can clear out. We're miles behind schedule."

"Roger," said Alpha.

"Roger," said Bravo.

"Roger," said Charlie.

With half a million gallons of volatile liquids close by, the section chiefs needed no prodding to climb down from the superstructure. They'd just made a final check to ensure that there were no injured technicians or loose equipment lying about on the gantry decks, and were now descending to ground level in the elevator cage. If Classen had had the energy, he would have impatiently tapped his foot as he waited by the shuttle bus. But he'd depleted his energy reserves long ago. The vehicle was filled with technicians who were waiting to call it a day—or, rather, a night.

After some minutes, the elevator finally disgorged the three section chiefs. They walked briskly under the gantry lights and onto the shuttle bus. Classen was the last one on board. "Move it," he ordered the driver, while looking at his watch. They had twenty-two minutes until the 0430 launch. That was cutting it close. Too close.

Mike Rossen, a hydraulics technician on the pad, was a fastidious person. He didn't like to go home dirty and was one of the few techs

301

on Pad 39A who made use of the shower and locker room at the security access building. He'd hustled through his shower so he would have enough time to change and get a good vantage point to watch the launch. That was half his pay—watching those giants lift off. Especially at night. Unless you have personally witnessed a night launch of a space shuttle, there is no earthly way to comprehend the staggering power that is unleashed. The tiny image you see on television in no way imparts the violence of the conflagration, the fearsome thunder of the engine noise, or the brightness of the exhaust plume. Rossen couldn't wait to experience it again.

Drying off, Rossen walked over to the locker which contained his clean clothes. He was reaching for the door handle when he spied some rivulets of a dark, almost black substance at the base of a locker near his. Puzzled, he looked closer, but still couldn't figure out what it was. If he didn't know better, he'd have guessed it was dirty hydraulic fluid, but it couldn't be that. Curious, he opened the locker door.

And out tumbled the bloodstained corpse of Edward Garvey.

The doors of the shuttle bus clapped open, allowing Classen and his crew to disembark and make their way toward the security "cattle chute." Although the security building was a safe distance from the shuttle, they still wanted to get in their cars and put a little more real estate between themselves and the volatile behemoth they'd left on the pad. The group was approaching the security window when a buck-naked man ran out of the locker room screaming, "Help! Help! Dead man! Dead man!"

Initially, the group was stunned by the scene. But then Classen recognized the man and led his group forward in a surge, just as a burly security guard appeared from around the corner.

Classen grabbed the naked man by the shoulders and shook him. "Mike! Get hold of yourself! What is it?"

He pointed at the door. "In there! Dead man!"

Everyone froze, not knowing what to do, until the rough-looking security guard drew his .357 magnum and plunged through the door. There were a few moments of tense silence, then Classen and his troops heard the security guard yell, "Somebody get in here!" En masse the group piled into the locker room, where they found the guard kneeling over Ed Garvey's body.

For a few moments Classen stood there in total shock. Then slowly he knelt down beside his friend and carefully touched Garvey's hair. "Oh, no," he moaned.

The security guard holstered his pistol and scanned the faces in the room. "Anybody know anything about this?" he demanded.

There was a stunned silence until one throat cleared. It was a technician with goldfish eyes named Tony. "Uh, well," goldfish eyes offered carefully, "when I was leaving off my last shift I saw Mr. Garvey here talkin' to that OSHA inspector."

Classen whirled around. "OSHA inspector? What OSHA inspector?"

Goldfish eyes gulped. "I dunno, Mr. Classen. Billy and me was up on the H-two access arm—you know, checking the coupling. Some guy I never saw before rode up with us and started making some measurements on the catwalk. We asked him what he was doin' and he said he was from OSHA, making a safety inspection. He had an ID. I saw it."

Classen felt his stomach knotting up. "No visitors are supposed to be on the pad during prelaunch. Didn't you know that?" His eyes were starting to well up with tears.

Goldfish eyes blinked and he cleared his throat again. "Well, uh, yessir. I thought about reportin' it, but when Mr. Garvey started talkin' to him right outside here, I figured, well . . ." The voice faded.

Classen felt his throat choking up. Tony had seen the "OSHA inspector" talking to Garvey, and now Garvey's dead. Dammit. Jesus God in heaven, Ed. Forgive me. When you didn't show I should've known something like this had happened. Goddammit, I should have *known*. "Where did you say you saw this OSHA inspector?" he demanded.

"Uh, the H-two access arm," replied goldfish eyes.

"Were you with this 'inspector' the entire time?"

Tony stammered, "Well, gosh no, Mr. Classen. Billy and me had some other things to get done before we finished our shift. And that inspector said he had to take some more measurements. So we left him."

"So he was *alone* on the H-two arm?" Classen's voice was little more than a squeak.

"Yessir."

Raw panic seized Classen. He looked at his watch, then leapt to his feet and grabbed the bus driver. "Come with me!" he ordered. "The rest of you clear out!"

Day 4, 0915 Hours Zulu, 4:15 A.M. Local
THE CONSTELLATION

"*Constellation*, this is Launch Control, commence loading OPS-One flight plan into BFS computer."

"Roger, Launch Control," replied Heitmann, then without pausing he asked Townsend through the intercom, "Error log switch?"

"Error log switch, negative," said Townsend. (A light on the error log would have indicated a fault in the guidance and control system.)

"Enter SPEC nine nine PRO," ordered Heitmann.

"Roger," said Townsend as he punched in the proper strokes on the computer keyboard. "SPEC nine nine PRO entered."

"I copy launch trajectory on CRT two," said Heitmann.

Townsend looked over to make sure—two sets of eyes were always better than one. "I confirm launch trajectory on CRT two," he said.

"Initialize GPC Mode Five—Run," ordered Heitmann.

Townsend hit the correct button. "GPC Mode Five is running."

"Enter OPS one zero one PRO."

Townsend put in the keystrokes. "OPS one zero one PRO entered."

"Control, this is *Constellation*," said Heitmann. "OPS-One flight plan is entered."

"Roger, *Constellation*. We copy OPS-One loaded."

The launch was in the computers' hands now.

Day 4, 0919 Hours Zulu, 4:19 A.M. Local
PAD 39A

The shuttle bus screeched to a halt. Classen jumped out and yelled, "Get out of here!" to the driver. The bus jockey needed no prodding; he nearly put the vehicle into a wheelie as he sped away.

Classen looked at his watch and his heart jumped into his throat. It was 4:19 A.M.—eleven minutes until they lit the candle. Frantically, he scanned the exterior of the orange external tank near the hydrogen vent coupling. The catwalk, which provided access to the coupling, had been retracted an hour earlier and only the umbilical pipeline remained.

When the liquid hydrogen boiled off in the external tank and expanded into a gas, it had to be vented from the vessel—just like the liquid oxygen. However, gaseous hydrogen is many times more volatile than gaseous oxygen. Therefore, the vapors were vented from the external tank through the "closed system" of the umbilical pipe until the H-two valve was closed. At the moment of lift-off, the umbilical vent cord would automatically disconnect from the tank and fall away against the gantry.

Several precious moments elapsed before Classen finally saw it. There. Just below the coupling. It was hard to see, and from the ground it appeared no larger than a muted, cream-colored dot. But it wasn't orange, like the tank. It didn't belong there. He reached to his belt for his hand-held transceiver to inform Launch Control that the lift-off might have to be aborted, but he came up empty-handed. In the confusion of the locker room, he'd left it by Garvey's body. He would have cursed his own stupidity, but couldn't take the time.

Like a gazelle, Classen bounded across the concrete tarmac and into the gantry elevator. He shoved the hand controller to the UP position and the steel cage started skyward. No matter how hard he pressed the controller, the lift rose at a maddeningly slow rate. In frustration, he kicked the side of the cage and yelled, "Move!" But it continued up at its leisurely pace. Classen alternated between praying and cursing —now that he had the time.

When level nine was finally reached, he jumped out and lunged for the instrument panel which controlled the hydrogen vent access arm. He shoved the lever forward, and the catwalk arm started rotating toward the external tank.

Day 4, 0924 Hours Zulu, 4:24 A.M. Local
FIRING ROOM TWO, LAUNCH CONTROL BUNKER, KENNEDY SPACE CENTER

A red light twinkled on the pad systems engineering console in Firing Room Two. The engineer who monitored the board blinked his eyes several times in surprise and muttered, "What the . . . ?" The red light indicated the hydrogen vent access arm was not retracted into its proper lift-off position. The engineer looked up at one of the four large television screens which pictured the *Constellation* on Pad 39A—and gasped. Eschewing his headset, he jumped up from his console and yelled at the launch director: "Chief! Look at the center left screen! The H-two arm is moving!"

Every head in the room bobbed up to look at the screen, and the launch director's eyes nearly popped out of their sockets. "What the hell?" he said in a soft voice. Then he barked at his deputy, "I thought Jacob cleared the pad fifteen minutes ago!"

The bald, squat-looking deputy looked like a ghost. "He did," came the croaky reply.

"Well, somebody's got to be up there!" barked the tall, skinny launch director who had two days' growth of beard on his face. "Get Classen on the radio! Photo, give me a zoom on the H-two arm! Pad systems, get that arm retracted and back into place!"

The deputy started talking nervously into his microphone, but Classen was not on the air. The pad manager's little hand-held transceiver was still in the locker room. "I can't raise him," whined the deputy.

The engineer in charge of photography systems fiddled with some control knobs, and the television image of the access arm enlarged until it filled the screen.

The pad systems engineer punched a bunch of buttons, but the H-two catwalk kept moving toward the external tank. "I can't retract the arm. Somebody's controlling the manual override from the gantry."

"There's somebody up there!" yelled the flight surgeon while pointing at the screen. And sure enough, the image of someone in white coveralls appeared, running down the catwalk. It halted at the coupling.

"Give me max zoom!" ordered the skinny launch director.

The image on the screen grew some more, but because of the magnification and the limited illumination of the klieg lights, the shadowy figure was terribly grainy. All that could be discerned was that he wore white coveralls and had an orange hard hat on his head . . . and only one person on Pad 39A wore an orange hard hat.

"It's Jacob!" exclaimed the deputy.

"What in God's name is he doing up there?" thundered the launch director. He poised his trembling hand over the big red console button marked ABORT.

Day 4, 0925 Hours Zulu, 4:25 A.M. Local
PAD 39A

When the arm had extended all the way to the tank wall, Classen flew down the catwalk. Upon reaching the coupling, he knelt down and inserted his arm between the edge of the catwalk and the tank. Everything felt cold from the liquid hydrogen as he fingered the platelike device. It was a bomb, of course. It had to be a bomb. That was why Ed Garvey had had to die. He'd found out. Was it rigged to go off if tampered with? Classen didn't know shit from Shinola about bombs, and the tampering question hadn't occurred to him until now.

But never mind about that. He still had to try, even though he was afraid. Deathly afraid.

Getting a proper grip from his kneeling position was impossible, so he lay down flat on the catwalk and reached around the superstructure to get a handhold on the rim of the limpet mine. He caught the edge. There. That was it. He pulled. It didn't budge. He pulled again, harder. Rock solid. *Oh, Lord, give me strength. Now.* He took a deep breath and with every last ounce of grit and muscle he heaved once more, while groaning, "Damn you, damn you, damn you."

Day 4, 0926 Hours Zulu, 4:26 A.M. Local
FIRING ROOM TWO

"He . . . he's pulling something off the tank," stammered the deputy.

The launch director was almost dancing now, his lanky frame hopping from one foot to the other. He didn't know what to do. He was the one person at KSC who'd been told the score—the *whole* score—on the *Intrepid*. If his launch crew didn't light the candle now, it would be another twenty-four hours before they'd have another chance at a rendezvous with the *Intrepid*. That would give the Russians another full day and night to intervene. He looked at the digital clock. Less than four minutes to ignition. Everything was controlled by computers now, but he could shut the launch down by punching the ABORT button. However, the launch time window was so small on this mission that once the ABORT button was pushed, they couldn't recover in time and still catch the *Intrepid* rendezvous on this pass. It was up to him. Go or no-go.

"He's got it!" yelped the squatty deputy. "Whatever it is, he's got it!"

Day 4, 0927 Hours Zulu, 4:27 A.M. Local
PAD 39A

Like a giant scab, the plate finally peeled away from the orange skin of the external tank—slowly at first, then as the leverage increased, the adhesive yielded so quickly that Classen nearly dropped the limpet device as it fell into his hand. Carefully, he brought it around the edge of the superstructure and clutched it to his chest, then scrambled to his feet and flew back down the catwalk, where he smashed the control lever into the RETRACT position.

Day 4, 0928 Hours Zulu, 4:28 A.M. Local
FIRING ROOM TWO

The firing room crew watched the catwalk superstructure start moving away from the external tank.

"Pad systems!" screamed the launch director, forgetting his headset. "Tell me when we've got enough clearance from the H-two catwalk for lift-off!"

The pad systems engineer checked his board. "We've got it now!" Then added, "Oxygen vent hood is starting to retract!"

The launch director pulled his thumb away from the ABORT button. His body was shaking. "Okay," he announced. "Okay, we're go for launch!" Then he gulped and almost cried. "Get out of there, Jacob," he implored. "Get the hell *out* of there."

Day 4, 0928:30 Hours Zulu, 4:28:30 A.M. Local
PAD 39A

The H-two catwalk had moved back several meters when Classen heard a creaking sound. He looked above him and his blood went cold. The metallic hood that covered the liquid oxygen vent was retracting, too. That meant he had maybe a minute to ignition. He looked back down the catwalk to the hydrogen vent coupling, and when he figured the catwalk had enough clearance, he released the lever. Ignoring the elevator, he sprinted to the far side of the gantry.

Classen knew there was only one way out now. He fled to the hanging baskets of the emergency exit system, and like an Olympic diver he dove headfirst into one of the steel mesh baskets, clutching the bomb in one hand and slapping the release bar with the other. Immediately the basket began hurtling toward the arresting crash net.

The emergency exit system was a simple device, designed to put a lot of distance between the astronauts and a shuttle accident (say, a fuel spill) in a *hurry*. It consisted of several wire mesh baskets, which hung from steel cables on sets of rollers. The cables sloped at a severe angle from the eighth level of the gantry structure to a landing zone on the ground alongside a blast bunker. The harrowing slide down the cable took less than thirty seconds, and during that time the basket traveled 1,200 horizontal feet and dropped 147 vertical feet. This rate of descent meant the astronaut went from zero to a top speed of nearly 50 miles per hour during the slide—but that was the easy part. The hard part was going from 50 mph to a complete stop in 1.2 seconds when the basket crashed into the arresting net at the bottom of the cable.

However, Classen didn't have time to ponder the exact physics of the situation. All that registered in his brain at the moment was that he was upside down in a steel basket, plummeting down at a high rate of speed, with a powerful explosive beside his head. With great difficulty he righted himself, and in the process he lost his hard hat and started the basket swinging from side to side. He fumbled with the plate. He'd never thrown a discus before. What a time to try! Clumsily he grabbed the disk and curled his fingers around the edge, then, holding on to the side of the swinging basket, he summoned up all of his strength and heaved the plate into the darkness.

For Classen, the basket's crash into the nylon arresting net was nothing but a blur, but he seemed to remember hearing a distinct *whump!* and catching the image of a starburst flash, just before his bare head bashed against the basket's forewall. For a few moments he remained on the floor of the still-vibrating vessel, too stunned to move. Finally, like a weak kitten, the pad manager climbed up and over the rim of the steel basket, only to have the wind knocked out of him as he fell to the ground with a dull thud. With his last ounce of strength he forced himself to stand, and like a zombie he limped the final few steps to the sheltering bunker.

What was left of Jacob Classen pushed through the door and fell into the concrete dugout, just as the earth began shaking violently beneath him and a deafening roar rumbled over his spent body. He covered his ears with his hands, then curled up into a ball and pressed his knees on top of his hands.

"*Stop that noise!*" he pleaded. "*Stop it!*"

Day 4, 0930 Hours Zulu, 4:30 A.M. Local
THE *CONSTELLATION*

The *twang!* reverberated through the flight deck as the orbiter lurched forward on its brackets.

"Three greens on main engines!" shouted Townsend over the thundering roar.

The solid boosters fired.

"SRBs are green, too!"

The three astronauts felt the vibrations from the 6.5 million pounds of thrust erupting below them, then watched as the klieg lights slowly passed by the cockpit windows.

The *Constellation* had started her ascent.

Heitmann, Townsend, and Watkins had been totally unaware of the drama unfolding so near them. The H-two catwalk was on the opposite side of the external tank, and after the Cap Com had recovered from the shock of the episode, he saw no point in alarming the flight crew. There wasn't a blessed thing they could've done about it anyway.

"You are go for roll, *Constellation*," radioed the Cap Com. "Roger," replied Heitmann. "Starting roll maneuver now." Although his hand rested on the hand controller, it was the shuttle's computers that ordered the engines to "gimbal" and roll the spacecraft into its standard heads-down position. But instead of arcing over the Atlantic, the *Constellation* thundered on a trajectory into the southern night sky.

Day 4, 0932 Hours Zulu, 4:32 A.M. Local
YEEHAW JUNCTION, FLORIDA

Seymour Woltman was the night wire editor for the Miami bureau of the Associated Press. He was pudgy, dark-haired, middle-aged, divorced, and his career had pretty much plateaued—or, rather, regressed.

Woltman had been a good reporter for the *Herald* once. A helluva reporter. Then a helluva editor. Then a hard-drinking editor. Then it was just hard drinking. Before his career started on a downward slide, he'd been an assistant managing editor at the *Herald*. Now he was a night wire editor.

But Woltman was determined to bounce back. He'd finally gotten a handle on his drinking, and through an old friend he'd lined up an interview for the metro editor's job at the *Atlanta Constitution*. After he'd gotten off work from the bureau at 2:00 A.M. that morning he'd gone home and packed, then headed out north on the Florida Turnpike toward Atlanta. He figured he'd visit with his old buddy over the weekend, then face the job interview on Monday.

But Woltman had neglected to gas up his car before leaving Miami, so as the fuel gauge neared empty he left the turnpike to hunt for a gas station in the tiny town of Yeehaw Junction. Luckily, the small community—which was about sixty miles south of Cape Canaveral—had an all-night self-service station.

He'd just gotten out of his car to plug the gas nozzle into the tank when he saw—no, he perceived its presence. The darkness around him seemed to take on a slightly yellowish tint, as if someone had turned on a row of distant streetlights. But in Yeehaw Junction there were no distant streetlights. He looked up, and the sight he beheld caused him to stagger. It was an orange torch, traveling across the heavens. He stood there—mesmerized and stupefied by the image—until a thunderclap *boom!* made him jump two feet in the air. The *Constellation* had just cracked the sound barrier.

He was tired and worn out, but Seymour Woltman's brain cells came alive—really alive—for the first time in years. He'd covered a dozen space shots out of Cape Canaveral. He knew that NASA never launched its rockets south over populated areas. Never.

Until now.

Woltman didn't have to be a genius to figure out that something was wrong. Terribly wrong. Horribly wrong. Catastrophically wrong. Maybe a damned rocket was out of control!

The orange torch could still be seen in the distance, but Woltman didn't wait. He jumped into his station wagon and tore out for Miami and the bureau office. He'd never put a flash message on the wire before. Now was his chance. This could be his ticket back to somewhere. Hot damn! For the first time in a long, long time he was on a story.

Day 4, 0932 Hours Zulu
THE *INTREPID*

As his spacecraft passed over the western edge of Greenland, Julian Kapuscinski tried to sleep, but sleep would not come. He'd been riding a roller coaster of exasperation, nightmares, boredom, and tension for almost seventy-two hours. All of the emotional firepower that had been bottled up inside of him for over forty years was clawing to break out now. He'd envisioned the *Intrepid*'s touchdown in Russia as an emotional catharsis for his soul, expunging all of the hurts and slights he'd endured for so many years. Endured at the hands of people inferior to himself. Iceberg, they called him. They all thought the call sign was so amusing. Kapuscinski didn't, and hijacking the *Intrepid* was his opportunity to even the score. For the hurt. For the death of his mother. For the betrayal of Felicia. But instead of exhilaration in completing the mission of a lifetime—literally, a lifetime—he was trapped inside a crippled vessel like a caged animal, and all he could do was wait . . . wait . . . and wait some more. Iceberg's emotional bottle remained corked.

So he floated there in the left seat of the cockpit, simply staring into space. The multitude of stars in the heavens failed to excite or inspire him. He only gazed morosely ahead.

From his upside-down vantage point above Greenland he could see the sun starting to creep over the horizon to his right, while the path in front of him and to the left remained cloaked in darkness. Without the polluted veil of the atmosphere to impair his vision, it was amazing how far he could see from his perch above the earth.

It was barely perceptible, but with his exceptional eyesight he saw it. There. Just above the curve of the black horizon, perhaps a couple of thousand miles away. It looked like nothing more than a tiny, tiny firefly in the far distance—but nonetheless, it was unmistakable.

The realization was like a cold slap that snapped Iceberg out of his semisleep. He emitted a little cry as he fearfully punched up the *Intrepid*'s ground track on the NavComputer. It showed that his spacecraft was above Greenland, on a course that would take him directly over Florida.

"No!" he shrieked. "No! No! No! They would not do it!"

But "they" did.

In the distant void, Iceberg saw the *Constellation* rising to meet him.

Day 4, 0933 Hours Zulu
THE *CONSTELLATION*

The flash from the explosive bolts filled the windshield for a split second. The solid boosters had separated from the external tank and were now beginning their long tumble down to a parachute landing in the Caribbean Sea.

"CSOC, we have SRB separation," radioed Heitmann. "Throttling main engines up to a hundred percent of rated power."

"Roger, *Constellation*. We copy SRB separation. You're looking good from here."

The solid booster separation had been delayed for forty-five seconds to ensure that the descending projectiles would clear the southern coast of Florida and touch down in the Caribbean.

Day 4, 0933 Hours Zulu, 11:33 A.M. Local
KALININGRAD FLITE CONTROL CENTRE

"Launch detection, Comrade General!" barked Mission Commander Malyshev, holding the headphone to his right ear. "It is coming out of the Kennedy cosmodrome, bearing one-eight-seven degrees. I am punching up the ground track from the Aerospace Defense Warning Centre."

A stubby luminescent line appeared over eastern Florida on the giant Mercator map projection.

The General Secretary's swarthy face turned a pale white. He was stunned. "You were correct to take precautions, Vitali," he whispered softly. "The Americans are attempting a rescue."

Kostiashak's response was nothing but a nod, while his dark features remained somber. His KGB agent in Florida had failed to stop the *Constellation*. Now it was up to Pirdilenko to shoot it down. General Secretary Vorontsky, Kostiashak, and Popov were standing behind Mission Commander Malyshev, and seated beside him at a computer station was the spidery Pirdilenko, who was furiously tapping at a keyboard. All of a sudden he quit tapping and looked at the screen with a blank expression on his face. With a raspy voice, he said, "It appears we have a problem."

Day 4, 0937 Hours Zulu
THE *CONSTELLATION*

. They were entering the final minute of main engine burn. The *Constellation*'s computers had just throttled the three giant infernos back to 85 percent power in preparation for engine shutdown, when a red annunciator light started blinking and a *bzzzzz! bzzzzz! bzzzzz!* filled the cabin.

Townsend scanned the instruments. "Low pressure turbopump failure on number two oxidizer!"

"Feather two!" ordered Heitmann.

One of the pumps feeding liquid oxygen into the orbiter's center main engine had failed. For what reason, Townsend had no idea, but

313

he quickly flipped the switches to shut down the liquid oxygen and hydrogen feed to the combustion chambers in engine number two. At the same time, Heitmann's muscular hands shoved the throttles forward on engines one and three, increasing their power output from 85 percent to 100 percent. This would help compensate for the loss of power on the center engine.

There was no danger that the *Constellation* would fail to reach orbit. The vehicle was already in the shallow dive maneuver to point the external tank back to the sea. The loss of the engine would affect their orbit insertion OMS burn, but that was all.

"CSOC, this is *Constellation*. We had to feather number two. Some kinda O-two turbopump problem. I've switched from auto to manual and have increased rated power to a hundred percent on one and three."

A few moments passed before Heitmann heard: "Roger, *Constellation*. We copy the shutdown. Any other problems? Over."

"Negative. Coming up to tank separation now. Pulling power back down to sixty-five percent." Heitmann pulled back on the throttles and watched the readout on the console fall to "65."

"Roger, *Constellation*," said the CSOC Cap Com. "You are go for main-engine shutdown."

Heitmann pulled the throttles down to zero and fired the explosive bolts for tank separation. Then with the hand controller he maneuvered the spacecraft clear of the empty orange vessel.

"CSOC, this is *Constellation*. Please advise on initial OMS burn. Quickly."

"Wait one, *Constellation*," came the reply, and a few more seconds ticked by before the Cap Com returned. "Navigation officer says do a manual OMS burn now with the same specifications as your programmed burn. Then do a manual insertion burn at forty-three minutes, fifty-eight seconds elapsed time. You'll have to make a third correction burn to reach your rendezvous, but it shouldn't be too much of a problem. We'll run the numbers on it and advise you shortly. You're in the ball park as it is. By the way, Eagle One says nice move on the shutdown, guys. Over."

"Roger," replied Heitmann. He and Townsend had practiced emergency engine shutdowns in the simulator until they had become second nature to them. But now they were preparing to conduct their initial OMS burn manually, and this required some concentration.

Townsend watched the readout from the NavComputer while Heitmann operated the hand controller. "Pitch up three degrees," ordered the copilot. "Yaw left six degrees. . . . I'll fire the OMS on my mark. . . . Three . . . two . . . one . . . mark!" Townsend hit the red switch and the engines fired silently.

Because they had not completed the shallow dive maneuver, the *Constellation* was actually a little ahead of where it was supposed to be.

Day 4, 0937 Hours Zulu, 11:37 A.M. Local
KALININGRAD FLITE CONTROL CENTRE

"*Problem*?" bellowed the General Secretary. "What do you mean by 'problem'?"

Pirdilenko's aloofness had been replaced by distilled fear. There had always been a small chance that this could happen. Quite small. Incredibly small. But there it was. He should have warned them of this contingency, but . . . "Well, ah, General Secretary," stammered Pirdilenko, "it appears the launch of the American rescue shuttle was, ah, ill-timed for our antisatellite weapon."

"What do you mean by 'ill-timed'? Speak simple Russian, you fool!"

Beads of sweat appeared on Pirdilenko's brow as he took a deep breath. "When a shuttle is initially launched," he explained, "it goes into an elliptical orbit, which is shaped much like an egg. When the spacecraft reaches the apex of this ellipse, it fires the maneuvering rockets to push it into a circular orbit. I intended to fire the antisatellite device as the rescue shuttle was climbing to the apex of the ellipse—that is, when the *Intrepid* would still be a safe distance away from the *Constellation*. You will recall our discussions at Plesetsk." Pirdilenko cleared his throat. "However, I, ah, failed to mention that if the rescue shuttle lifted off from the Florida cosmodrome during a certain three-minute 'blind spot' of the antisatellite weapon's orbit, then our device would be unable to hit the rescue shuttle during this ascent phase. The weapon would not be within range until *after* the rendezvous with the *Intrepid* spacecraft was completed. . . . Much to my surprise, the Americans happened to launch during this, ah, 'blind spot' period."

The General Secretary—a former hammer thrower—seized the spidery scientist by the throat and shook him with such violence that his spectacles were knocked to the floor. "Blind spot? I will show you a blind spot, Comrade! Get back on that machine and shoot down that goddam rescue vessel! Do you understand me? Shoot it down! Or I will

315

strap you to one of your own goddam rockets! How would you like that?'' With a final shake, the General Secretary slammed Pirdilenko back into his chair.

With studied casualness, the KGB Chairman reached down and retrieved the eyeglasses from the floor, then handed them to Pirdilenko. ''You may need these, Comrade.''

Day 4, 0950 Hours Zulu, 2:50 A.M. Local
CHEYENNE MOUNTAIN

Whittenberg, Michael Dowd, and John Fairchild were all in the SPADOC Crow's Nest, monitoring the flight of the *Constellation*. Dowd was on the phone to McCormack at CSOC. He hung up and turned to Whittenberg. ''Chet says they're going to manually fire the orbit insertion burn, then they'll compute a corrected flight plan for a rendezvous. It may take another orbit or two, but the rendezvous is not in jeopardy. Could've been a lot worse.''

Sir Isaac nodded. ''Maybe our luck is beginning to change.''

''Let's hope,'' added Whittenberg, and he picked up the green phone to inform Admiral Bergstrom.

Day 4, 1014 Hours Zulu
THE *CONSTELLATION*

''Ignition!'' ordered Heitmann. Townsend mashed the red firing button, and for sixty-eight seconds the orbital maneuvering system engines fired, propelling the *Constellation* out of its elliptical path and inserting it into a circular orbit—a little bit ahead of the *Intrepid*.

Townsend gazed out the window. The *Intrepid* was out there— somewhere—and like the *Constellation*, it was above the southern Indian Ocean, hurtling north at 17,000 miles per hour.

Day 4, 1015 Hours Zulu, 3:15 P.M. Local
KOUNRADSKIY RADAR STATION, DZHEZKAZGAN REGION, KAZAKHSTAN, CCCP

On the northern shore of the giant Lake Balkhash in southern Kazakhstan stood a structure not unlike an Egyptian pyramid. This was the long-range phased-array radar (LPAR) complex at Kounradskiy.

The pyramidlike structure was, in reality, a giant transmitter and receiver that blanketed the sky with its electronic waves. With its powerful signal, the LPAR pyramid easily detected the two American shuttles approaching from the south. Their radar signatures were identical, and they were approximately two hundred kilometers apart.

The electronic detection was routed to the Aerospace Defense Warning Centre in Magnitogorsk, where the tracking data were processed and stored in computer banks. These data files were routinely accessed by the computers in the Kaliningrad Flite Control Centre.

Day 4, 1030 Hours Zulu, 12:30 P.M. Local
KALININGRAD FLITE CONTROL CENTRE

Pirdilenko was tapping furiously at his keyboard now. His concentration was so intense that he ignored the drops of perspiration falling from his forehead and onto the backs of his hands. There was a chance now. A very real chance, and he was not about to bungle it. The Americans had muffed their flight plan somehow, and the radar data showed some separation between the *Constellation* and the *Intrepid*. Only a scant two hundred kilometers, but that was enough for Pirdilenko to take a shot now. He feared for his life if he didn't.

The antisatellite device was currently over the eastern United States, while the two shuttles had just crossed the southern border of Russia. All three spacecraft were approaching the polar ice cap on a northerly heading, at a mutual closing velocity of 34,000 miles per hour. Pirdilenko's margin for error was absolute zero.

"When are you going to take action, Comrade?" huffed Vorontsky, who was leaning over the scientist.

"Quiet!" barked Pirdilenko. So severe was his rebuke that even the General Secretary retreated a few steps. The tension in the room was taut as a violin string.

Pirdilenko allowed himself a quick glance at the Mercator map projection. The two American shuttles were on identical ground tracks—both heading north. The *Constellation* was about two hundred kilometers ahead of, and a little below, the *Intrepid*. That tallied with the data on his computer screen.

In the time it took him to recheck his computations, the two American orbiters had already passed over the Soviet Union and crossed the northern coast of Siberia. The ASAT missile was over

Greenland, also hurtling north toward the Arctic ice cap. All three spacecraft were now being tracked by the phased-array radar complex at Pechora.

Everything was ready, and although his spectacles were smeared with perspiration drops, Pirdilenko could see the computer screen well enough. The digital time readout was moving rapidly in reverse. Thirty seconds now . . . twenty . . . ten . . . five, four, three, two, one.

Pirdilenko's heart thumped as his trembling finger came down on the button marked ACTIVATE.

Day 4, 1042 Hours Zulu
THE ASAT

The ASAT warhead was little more than a spaceborne blunderbuss, consisting of a large ceramic cone filled with stainless-steel pellets. The cone was secured to a base made of plastique explosive, but the golf-ball-sized pellets contained within the vessel were not explosive themselves—they didn't have to be.

Upon receipt of Pirdilenko's "activate" command, the ASAT missile deployed its two small Doppler-pulse radar dishes, and like a couple of electronic bird dogs, they began sniffing the ether for their quarry. When a signal bounced back, the microchip in the ASAT's brain rapidly computed distance, speed, time, and intercept vector to the *Constellation*. Then, at the precisely correct millisecond, the liquid-fuel engines ignited, and the missile roared off for its target in the lower orbital plane.

Day 4, 1041 Hours Zulu, 3:41 A.M. Local
CHEYENNE MOUNTAIN

Lt. Keith Brunswick was bored. Bored to tears. The former collegiate football guard liked action, and there was certainly no action on this shift in SPADOC—where all he had to do was monitor the Hubble space telescope television transmission every forty-five minutes or so. The image of the torpedo-shaped "mystery satellite" on the TV monitor was the same time after time, and Brunswick didn't even know what he was supposed to look for. "Just keep an eye on it and holler if it does anything suspicious" was what he'd been told.

Brother, how do you know if a satellite looks suspicious? What a bunch of crap, he thought.

Impatiently, Brunswick drummed his fingers on the console, then once again looked at the empty television monitor and the digital chronometer. It was about time for another pass but the mystery satellite hadn't appeared on the screen yet. Because he didn't have anything else to do, Brunswick started eavesdropping on the major in the monitor slot on his left. The major's call sign was Rabbit's Nest—and he was the officer who controlled the Spyglass observation aircraft cruising over the Arctic ice cap. Brunswick knew that Spyglass was supposed to photograph the *Intrepid-Constellation* rendezvous, but there had been a glitch on the *Constellation*'s launch, so the rendezvous wouldn't take place for another couple of orbits. Nevertheless, Rabbit's Nest was lining Spyglass up to take a practice shot on the *Constellation* now, just to test out the systems.

A test pattern picture from the high-flying 767 Spyglass was relayed to SPADOC via the RealTime communications satellite, and it was being projected on the big center screen. The *Constellation* hadn't appeared yet, but it was due any second now. From Brunswick's vantage point, he couldn't see the big center projection screen in SPADOC very well. It was like sitting in the front row of a movie theater. But he was curious. So he started leaning over to look at the major's television screen to get a better view of the Spyglass picture—and in the process he began to ignore his own monitor. He watched the major's TV for some seconds, waiting for something to appear. Then all of a sudden, bingo! There it was, the *Constellation*, making a nice picture on the small monitor. Gee, that was neat, thought Brunswick. The major punched some buttons, and the test pattern on the large center projection screen was replaced with the image of the winged orbiter.

Brunswick felt a tap on his shoulder. "Say, Keith?"

He turned to face the lieutenant who sat at the neighboring monitor station on his right. "Yeah?" he replied.

"Did you see that?" asked the lieutenant.

"See what?" replied Brunswick.

"That flash," said the lieutenant, pointing at Brunswick's monitor.

Brunswick trembled. "What flash?" he asked nervously.

"That satellite you've been watching. I happened to see it just as it came up on your screen. There was a flash and it disappeared."

Brunswick's heart skipped a beat. His monitor screen was completely blank now. Oh Lord! he thought. I missed it! "You say there was a flash?"

"Yeah. A bright flash and then it was gone. I think the engines must have fired."

Engines! Oh, dear God, *no.*

Up in the Crow's Nest the CinC's phone buzzed. He picked it up and said, "Whittenberg."

"General!" cried Brunswick. "Station Nine here! It looks like that satellite we've been tracking with the Hubble telescope just fired its engines!"

Whittenberg's entire body gave an involuntary jerk. "When?"

"Just now, sir. There was a flash and it disappeared."

Whittenberg looked at the ground tracks of the two American shuttles and the Russian mystery satellite that were projected on the left screen. They were all converging over the polar ice cap. He grabbed the phone that was a direct line to CSOC.

Day 4, 1043 Hours Zulu, 3:43 A.M. Local
COMBINED SPACE OPERATIONS CENTER

Chester McCormack was standing over the Cap Com when the console phone from SPADOC buzzed. He picked it up and said, "CSOC."

"Chet!" yelled Whittenberg. "We just had a visual on that unknown satellite! It just fired its engines . . . I think it's an ASAT!"

McCormack's spine vibrated. He shoved the Cap Com out of the way, grabbed the console microphone, and slammed down the transmit button. "Phil! Jack! Get outta there! An ASAT is coming at you!"

Day 4, 1043 Hours Zulu
THE CONSTELLATION

Heitmann and Townsend looked at each other. Each man's face betrayed his own stark terror. "Say again, CSOC!" demanded Heitmann.

320

"I said an ASAT's coming at you! Boost your orbit, lower your orbit, I don't give a damn, but get the hell out of there! *Now!*"

Heitmann needed no more coaxing. He grabbed the hand controller and pivoted the *Constellation* into position for an orbit boost.

"Hit the OMS!" he ordered, and Townsend mashed the red firing button.

The engines responded, but it was already too late.

Day 4, 1043 Hours Zulu
THE ASAT

An impulse from the ASAT's microchip brain ran through the satellite's circuitry, triggering the explosive bolts that held the protective launch shroud in place. As the aerodynamic cover peeled off, the missile's ceramic warhead became exposed and glistened in the sunlight. A moment later another impulse was transmitted, and the warhead's plastique explosive base was detonated—blasting the ceramic container apart, and spitting out the pellets in a scatter pattern three kilometers wide.

The *Constellation* and the spaceborne buckshot approached each other at a mutual closing velocity of nine miles per second, so it didn't take long for their paths to cross—they met almost at the very moment Townsend engaged the OMS engines.

The first steel pellet slammed into the *Constellation*'s nose with the kinetic energy of a three-inch artillery shell, cleaving the spacecraft's snout in two and venting the flight deck to the hostile vacuum of space. The destruction of their spaceborne chariot was so violent and quick that the three astronauts never truly comprehended what hit them. The initial shock wave mercifully whiplashed them into unconsciousness before their bodies were ripped apart by the pressure imbalance.

The second ASAT projectile passed cleanly through the left wing, doing little more than punching a hole through its delicate skin. But the third steel ball smashed into the midsection of the shuttle's soft underbelly, rupturing the liquid hydrogen and oxygen tanks that supplied the on-board fuel cells. The resulting secondary explosion immolated the *Constellation*, blasting the fragile spacecraft into a billion shards of aluminum, silica, and plastic—and scattering its remains across the black sky, like funereal ashes on the sea.

321

Day 4, 1043 Hours Zulu, 5:43 A.M. Local
THE WHITE HOUSE

"*Jesus!*"
"*Mon Dieu!*"
"*God in heaven!*"
The small group of men standing before the television in the Oval Office collectively leapt back from the Spyglass picture on the screen, shocked by the utter devastation they'd just witnessed.

It was the President who recovered first. "Sam," he ordered in a gravelly voice, "find out what . . . what happened."

The Secretary of Defense picked up the phone on the coffee table and punched in the connection to the National Military Command Center in the Pentagon. He spoke rapidly, then waited for the reply. After a few more hushed words were exchanged he looked up with a red face. "Admiral Bergstrom says it was the Russians, sir. That mysterious object of theirs was apparently an antisatellite warhead. The admiral says SPACECOM caught a photograph of the missile just as it was firing to intercept the *Constellation*."

"All right! That does it!" The President's face turned purple with rage. "Tell Bergstrom to push the Strategic Air Command up to DEFCON Two! I want the Russians to see a goddam hornets' nest on their radar screens!"

"Yes, sir!"

His fury still building, the President turned to the Secretary of State. "Winston, go get Yakolev over here! Hog-tie him if you have to, or take some Marines and break down his goddam embassy door! But get him over here now! We're going to find out what the hell is going on!"

"Yes, Mr. President."

"I'll go with you to the embassy, Mr. Secretary," offered the Vice President, "and help you with the collection of the ambassador."

"I appreciate that, Mr. Vice President," said the diplomat grimly. "Your assistance may be required."

"Sam!"

The Defense Secretary looked up from the phone. "Yes, Mr. President?"

"Tell Bergstrom to launch that spaceplane and send in the stealth bombers if he has to, but the Russians are *not* getting their goddam hands on the *Intrepid*!"

"Yes, sir!"

322

The President felt a large but gentle hand on his shoulder. "Steady, *mon ami*," whispered the voice. "Steady."

Day 4, 1044 Hours Zulu, 3:44 A.M. Local
CHEYENNE MOUNTAIN

Everyone in the giant room stood as if riveted to the floor. No one could move. No one could speak. No one had been trained for something like this. Instant death on a giant screen a few feet away. It couldn't be real. Someone on one of the front consoles began sobbing.

In the Crow's Nest the green phone buzzed and the CinC picked it up with a shaky hand. "Whittenberg," he said in a whisper.

A few moments passed before Bergstrom said, "We were watching it here. It was an ASAT, wasn't it?" Even the old salt sounded subdued.

Whittenberg's throat was dry and he had a hard time forming the words. "Yes, Admiral. It was. The Hubble had it on camera just as it fired its engines."

There was another pause, and Whittenberg heard a buzz in the background. "Hold on a minute," said Bergstrom. There were some murmurs before the admiral returned. "That was the Secretary of Defense. They saw the whole thing at the White House. The President says get that spaceplane up there and shoot the son of a bitch down if you have to."

"I understand, sir," replied Whittenberg solemnly.

"I'll call you back in a few minutes," said Bergstrom. "I've got to talk to General Dooley right now. The President is pushing SAC up to DEFCON Two." The line went dead.

As Whittenberg hung up his receiver, the glass door to the Crow's Nest opened. The major who was in charge of handling the Spyglass aircraft walked in, holding a sobbing lieutenant named Keith Brunswick by the arm.

"General," said the major, "I thought I'd better bring the boy up here. He wanted to tell you something."

The CinC looked at the sobbing young officer and said, "Sir Isaac, get him a chair." Fairchild quickly provided one and the lieutenant sat down with his face in his hands.

"What is it, son?" asked Whittenberg.

In a stammering voice, the stocky lieutenant sobbed, "General . . . I . . . I killed them."

"What?" asked Dowd numbly.

In a staccato voice punctuated with more sobs, Brunswick said, "I was on station nine. I was supposed to watch that Hubble telescope picture of that unknown satellite. I got . . . distracted by what the major was doing and started looking at his Spyglass monitor instead. I didn't see the satellite fire its engines. The guy in the next station saw it and asked if I'd seen it. If I'd been watching it . . . like I should have, they might've had enough warning. . . . Oh, God, I'm sorry." The sobs continued.

Whittenberg felt like unloading on someone, but he knew this wasn't the person or the time. He extended his hand and squeezed the young officer's arm. "There's nothing you could've done, son. They were probably as good as dead when they lifted off. It's not your fault. It's mine." He looked at the major. "Take him down to the dispensary. Have the medics give him something to quiet him down."

"Yes, sir," replied the major, and he guided the lieutenant out the door.

"Bull?" asked Whittenberg.

"Yes, sir," replied Dowd softly.

"In just a second I'm going to call Chet. He pushed himself so damn hard getting the *Constellation* aloft, I'm afraid this may put him over the edge. I want you to go out to CSOC and . . . stay close to him. You two are friends, I know. Make him get some sleep. We'll need him fit for the Kestrel launch. If he gives you any trouble, call me and I'll send a medic over there."

"Right away, sir." And Dowd left.

"Sir Isaac," continued the CinC, "I want you to stay on top of things at Vandenberg. Let me know if there's so much as a whiff of a foul-up with the Kestrel."

Fairchild responded with a gentle, "Yes, sir," and left for his operations office.

Whittenberg stared at the CSOC phone for a full thirty seconds, then closed his eyes and slowly picked it up.

Day 4, 1044 Hours Zulu, 2:44 A.M. Local
EDWARDS AIR FORCE BASE

They were both stunned beyond words, and could only gape at the debris filling the screen.

Finally, Monaghan recovered enough to ask in a croaky voice, "Who . . . did you say was . . . on board?"

324

Lamborghini couldn't reply at once. His mind was groping for some equilibrium. The same dizziness had struck him when he witnessed the *Challenger* disaster. The shuttle was such a magnificent machine, yet so vulnerable. To see one atomized in the blink of an eye was more than the mind could absorb.

"Pete . . . you okay?" asked Monaghan gently.

Lamborghini's eyes were still glazed, and all he could manage was a feeble half-nod.

"We're going up, Pete. You understand that, don't you? We have to go up and nail the fucker. I need you, man. Don't crap out on me now."

Lamborghini nodded again. More firmly this time.

Monaghan turned to the tech sergeant in charge of the commo room, who was also shell-shocked. "If anybody wants us, tell 'em they can find us in the simulator hangar."

Monaghan didn't wait for a response. He took his friend by the arm and led him out of the building.

Day 4, 1045 Hours Zulu, 12:45 P.M. Local
KALININGRAD FLITE CONTROL CENTRE

Every eye in the Flite Centre was focused on the map projection showing the ground tracks of the *Intrepid*, the *Constellation*, and the ASAT missile converging over the Arctic ice cap. The ground tracks were unchanged, even though Pirdilenko knew the ASAT missile had fired its engines and detonated its warhead. When a space vehicle altered its orbit, it took some seconds for the Aerospace Defense Warning Centre's computers to "digest" the new data and adjust the projection screen accordingly.

General Secretary Vorontsky saw the unchanged orbits and was snorting and pawing like a fighting bull. "Your antisatellite weapon has failed, Comrade. What do you have to say for yourself now? You may not have thought I meant what I said about—"

Pirdilenko stuck up his hand, indicating he wanted silence. His gaze remained on the map projection, and after a few seconds elapsed, the white lines denoting the *Constellation* and the ASAT missile disappeared from the screen.

There were no cheers from the room. Just a collective wince. Albeit American, three brother space pioneers had just been vaporized, and almost everyone squirmed a little. The General Secretary, however, did not squirm. Instead, with wide eyes, he asked, "Is it done?"

Pirdilenko stood up from his chair. The aloofness had returned. "Of course, General Secretary. There was an unexpected gap between the two spacecraft. Narrow, but a definite gap. I was able to trigger the device at such an angle as to destroy the rescue vessel without damaging the *Intrepid*." Pirdilenko's attack strategy had been quite clever. He'd placed the ASAT in a higher orbit than the target, so the downward plane of attack would destroy the *Constellation* and take the pellets out of the *Intrepid*'s orbital path. It was a "pop-down" rather than a "pop-up" maneuver.

"Excellent work, Comrade!" Vorontsky was exultant again. "I knew all along you could do it."

Pirdilenko cleaned his sweat-stained glasses with the tail of his white laboratory coat, and in an acerbic voice he replied, "I am honored to have had your confidence. Now, if you do not object, I will be going." And he strode from the room.

"Comrade Popov?" asked the diminutive KGB Chairman.

The mournful general had placed a comforting hand on Malyshev's shoulder. He withdrew it and turned. "Yes, Comrade Chairman?" he replied in a weary voice.

"Is there any danger of the Aerospace Defense Warning Centre investigating the, ah, 'disappearance' of the two spacecraft?"

Popov sighed. "Probably. But it will take them at least a week to process the data. They track fifteen thousand objects in orbit, after all. The fact that the American rescue shuttle traveled south out of the Florida cosmodrome may raise some questions. But it will take some time to look into the matter, and any investigation would not commence until after the weekend has passed."

"Very good," said Kostiashak. "When will we launch our Soyuz spacecraft?"

Popov looked at his watch. "Baikonur will be in position in approximately fourteen hours. Vostov should have loaded the docking collar into the launch shroud by now, and our cosmonauts are completing the review of their flite plans."

Kostiashak nodded. "My compliments, General." He then turned to his companion, and while stroking the lapel of his English-tailored suit, he said, "You see, General Secretary, as long as we anticipate events we can deal with any problems that arise."

Vorontsky thumped Kostiashak on the back. "As usual, you are correct, Vitali. But I must confess, the tension has left me exhausted."

"I quite understand, General Secretary," comforted Kostiashak. "It has been an ordeal for you, I know. Since it will be some hours before our spacecraft is launched from Baikonur, please allow me to escort you back to your apartment in Moscow. You can bathe and get a few hours' sleep in your own bed. I will monitor the situation and make sure the preparations are in order."

The bleary-eyed Vorontsky did not argue. "That is an excellent suggestion, Vitali. Let us go." He started to leave the Flite Centre, but then his hulking body stopped abruptly. "The Americans," he said rhetorically. "We have shot down one of their spacecraft. They may react." He sounded apprehensive again.

Kostiashak was soothing. "Rest assured, General Secretary. My people in Washington are watching the American situation very carefully. We will be notified the moment anything suspicious arises. Besides, we will have their spacecraft in a matter of hours."

The former hammer thrower shrugged. "Very well, Vitali. I leave it in your hands. Let us go."

The KGB Chairman stubbed out his cigarette and smiled at Popov. "I will not be long, General."

Popov did not reply.

Day 4, 1047 Hours Zulu, 4:47 A.M. Local
WURTSMITH AIR FORCE BASE, MICHIGAN

Maj. Rusty Tipton was settled in for the rest of the night on a bunk in the ready room—as settled in as he could get while sleeping in his flight suit. At least he didn't have to wear those infernal steel-toed flight boots when trying to sleep on alert status. The red-haired aviator had obtained a pair with Velcro wraparound tops so he could jump out of the bunk and slip on the boots in under ten seconds. Sometimes five.

B-52 crews, like Tipton's, were not like normal people who worked during the day and slept at night. Their regular routine might be twenty-four hours aloft in one of the big black monsters, down for forty-eight, airborne for twenty-four, then down for seventy-two (which would include time for classes, training, simulator, briefings, and preflight checks), then on standby status for forty-eight, which could mean one takeoff and landing after another in the black monster. The *old* black monster. The Stratofortresses that Tipton and his fellow pilots flew had been built before he was born.

Tipton's crew had already been up once since midnight for a practice alert, and he hoped that was all the action for this go-around. He was due to go on leave at the end of this alert shift—to Hawaii, where it was warm for a change. Tipton wanted everything to remain quiet until he signed out at headquarters. But with CinCSAC Bernie Dooley, you never knew—that four-star son of a bitch kept everybody on a very short leash.

The sandman was just letting Tipton drift off to slumberland when a *whaaa! whaaa! whaaa!* blared through the loudspeaker. Reflexively, the former Northwestern basketball forward pivoted out of the bunk, then shoved his feet into his boots and secured the Velcro flaps. He grabbed his parka and joined the mob running pell-mell down the ramp for the transport trucks, which were lined up in herringbone fashion along the tarmac. When each vehicle had its full crew complement loaded, the skipper would knock on the cab and the driver would tear out. Tipton had great confidence in his ability to survive in the air; however, surviving the ride to the aircraft was something else again. In a nuclear war, getting off the ground in one piece was half the battle. In fact, most of the Pentagon's simulated nuclear war scenarios called for half the U.S. bomber force to get nailed on the ground before takeoff. That's why speed, speed, speed was always the byword in getting the lumbering bombers airborne. Tipton was convinced the Air Force recruited frustrated drag racers for runway transport drivers.

The weather was frosty as the truck screeched to a halt in front of aircraft number 41/652 of the 379th Bombardment Wing. The ground crewmen, wrapped up in their snowsuits, were already there as Tipton and his flight crew scurried up the hatch ladders. After the electronic warfare officer was on board, the ladder was removed and the hatch buttoned up.

Tipton and his copilot gave a thumbs-up sign to the ground crew chief, indicating they were ready. The two aviators had developed a knack for starting the B-52's eight engines and putting on their helmets simultaneously. All eight engines fired in sequence, the wheel chocks were pulled, and Tipton began to taxi while his copilot lowered the windshield flash protectors.

In a nuclear war environment, the fusion fireball of a hydrogen bomb—even at a distance—could easily blind a pilot. Therefore, during takeoff, flash protectors covered the windshield of the B-52, and the pilot navigated through dual, electro-optic periscopes mounted in "chin turrets" underneath the B-52's nose. The filtered infrared and low-light TV periscope system enabled the pilot to see the runway at night, or through the flashes of nearby nuclear detonations (at least, that's how it was supposed to work).

Tipton was rolling into his place as number four in the takeoff line when the commo officer got the alert status through his VHF radio. It was SAC policy to let bomber crews know early on what sort of alert they were carrying out. The commo officer listened sleepily until he heard a certain code word, causing him to wake up real fast. "Skipper!" he yelped through the intercom.

"Yeah?" Tipton responded. He was next in the takeoff roll.

"Base commo transmits 'Brushfire.' "

Tipton and his copilot looked at each other in disbelief.

"Brushfire? Are you sure?"

"Dead sure, Skipper," replied the commo officer.

Brushfire meant it was the probable Real Thing and the bombers were to proceed to their "Cocked Pistol" points to wait for a "go—no go" authentication signal from SAC headquarters in Omaha. Brushfire was one level below a Wildfire alert, which meant it already was the Real Thing.

Although the aircraft in front of him hadn't lifted off yet, Tipton shoved the throttles forward and started his takeoff roll. Water was injected into the Pratt & Whitney TF33-P-3 turbofan engines, goosing the thrust of the Stratofortress so it could get off the ground. Inside the monster's weapons bay were twenty nuclear-tipped cruise missiles.

Day 4, 1120 Hours Zulu, 6:20 A.M. Local
THE WHITE HOUSE

Ambassador Yevgeny Yakolev had the distinction of being the only diplomat on record to have been personally manhandled by a Vice President of the United States and a Cabinet officer. Wearing only an overcoat, a pair of hastily thrown-on trousers, and a shirt, the diplomat was literally shoved through the door of the Oval Office by the two Americans.

Stunned and groggy, Yakolev confronted a bizarre scene. Seated behind the desk was the President of the United States, and standing to his left—as was often the case—was the Secretary of Defense. But then there was something unexpected. Seated at the right side of the desk was the tall, lanky-framed President of France. The ambassador didn't like the looks of the situation as he gave a perfunctory nod to the Gallic chief of state. *"Monsieur le Président,"* he mumbled, then turned to the American. "What is the meaning of this, Mr. President? Why have I been abducted by your Vice President and Foreign Minister? This is an outrage!"

"Shut up, Mr. Ambassador," snapped the President, "and don't talk to me about outrage. I told you earlier that any tampering with our spacecraft would be considered a hostile act. I tried to warn you off then, but you wouldn't listen—"

"Is that what you have kidnapped me for? Are you still pursuing your hijacking fantasies? I told you earlier, Mr. President. The Foreign Minister and Defense Minister investigated this matter themselves at my behest. Your story of a spacecraft hijacking is nothing but a fabrication."

The door opened and an Army major stepped inside. "Mr. Secretary? Here it is, sir," said the officer as he held out a videotape.

"Thank you, Major. That will be all." The Secretary of Defense took the videotape and opened a hidden cabinet in the wall of the Oval Office, revealing the television and a videotape player. He turned on the set and dropped in the tape. "Mr. Ambassador, if you please," he said, while motioning the Russian to approach the set. "This videotape was just prepared by the White House press office from imagery supplied by United States Space Command."

He punched a button and the picture appeared. The Secretary adjusted his horn-rimmed glasses and began his narration: "This is a picture of a Soviet satellite taken by the Hubble space telescope orbiting three hundred sixty-eight statute miles above the earth. The satellite you see here was launched from the Plesetsk Cosmodrome at zero-four-three-six hours Greenwich Mean Time yesterday in an orbital inclination of eighty-three degrees at an altitude of two hundred twenty miles."

The picture switched to a brilliant nighttime lift-off. "This is the space shuttle *Constellation* lifting off two hours ago from Kennedy Space Center in Florida. Three American astronauts were on board." The image changed again. "This is a picture of the *Constellation* just after it reached orbit. This was taken from one of our high-altitude observation aircraft." The picture changed once more. "This is the Russian Plesetsk satellite again. As you can see, it is firing its engines on an intercept course for the *Constellation*. And this is . . ."

The final image of the *Constellation* erupting in a white ball spoke for itself, and a jolt passed through the ambassador's body.

It took some seconds for the shock to subside, and when it did, Yakolev knew something was very, very wrong. His mind raced. Had the Foreign Minister and Defense Minister misled him? Inconceivable. It would be political suicide for the two Politburo members. It could not happen. Yakolev was certain of that. But what had happened? This was no American propaganda ploy now. The destruction of their shuttle had to be genuine. The ambassador had to sort things out. But he needed time. Time to find out what was happening. "This is a fabrication," stated Yakolev flatly. "Nothing more than American technical trickery—"

"I can assure you this is no trickery, *Monsieur l'Ambassadeur*," said the Frenchman in an icy tone. "I have been a witness to this entire affair, and I can attest to its genuineness. Three American space pilots have been killed. Do you understand? Murdered. I came to the United States to explore the possibility of France rejoining NATO, and this unspeakable act will undoubtedly thrust my country back into that alliance as a full partner. You may even see a joint European-American space defense pact as a result of this treachery. It has set Franco-Russian relations back thirty years. And when the other leaders of the Western Alliance learn of this murder they will react as I have." He turned to his host and nodded. "Mr. President."

The American returned the nod, then refocused on the Russian. "Now you listen to me, Mr. Ambassador. I have placed the Strategic Air Command on its highest peacetime alert status, Defense Condition Two—better known as DEFCON Two. It hasn't been that high since the Cuban missile crisis. The bombers are in the air. In short, you're looking down a gun barrel, Mr. Ambassador. If you tamper with our space shuttle *Intrepid*, you will get a military response in return. Do you understand that? A military response. Now you have been warned. Get out of here and convey this information to General Secretary Vorontsky immediately. Along with our demand that we expect full reparations for the loss of our spacecraft, and compensation to the families of the astronauts who were murdered."

For Yakolev, this had turned into a nightmare, and words failed him. He could only stumble out the door and retreat to the limousine for refuge. In the safety of the backseat, the scene continued swimming in his mind. A spacecraft destroyed. France back into NATO. A Euro-American space defense program. DEFCON Two. Military response. This was madness! He had to stop it. A cable must be dispatched at once.

"Thank you," said the American softly.

"It was the simple truth," replied the Frenchman. "But I must say, in view of the information provided by my intelligence source, it appears there may be some substance to your Secretary of State's theory."

"What do you think, Winston?" asked the President.

The Secretary with the male-model looks shrugged. "I wish I was wrong, but I'm afraid I may not be. This was a hostile act of which the Russian leadership apparently was not aware. We have no choice but to put our forces on alert. However, I feel we must be extremely careful until we find out what's happening and who's truly in charge on the other side."

"I would agree," said the Vice President.

"And I," added the Frenchman.

The President turned to his Director of Central Intelligence. "Bobby, is there any further light you can shed on this thing, other than the fact the Russians have a fake shuttle?"

The DCI was a frustrated man, and his trademark toothy grin was absent. "I can only say that the unusual thing is what hasn't happened. Radio traffic analysis from NSA indicates nothing abnormal. Military forces are at their standard level of readiness. Higher-level telephonic intercepts indicate nothing out of the ordinary. As far as I can tell, it's as if no one in Russia knew about the *Intrepid*. Business as usual, you might say."

The President didn't like that and started to get himself worked up again. His drill-sergeant face began twitching. "This is insane. A country that has five million men under arms and twenty-five thousand nuclear weapons, and we don't know who's really in charge? It's crazy." He rubbed his temples in disbelief.

"Try to understand, my friend," comforted the Frenchman. "We are dealing with *Russia*."

Day 4, 1120 Hours Zulu, 4:20 A.M. Local
CHEYENNE MOUNTAIN

In the SPADOC Crow's Nest, Whittenberg slowly read the cable Lydia Strand had given him. He was still in a daze from the horrific destruction of the *Constellation*, and had just received a report on the murder of Ed Garvey at the Cape and the attempted sabotage of the *Constellation*. Now this. He reread the message from the Central Intelligence Agency one more time, then passed it to Fairchild.

"A fake shuttle?" asked Whittenberg absently.

"Yes, sir," replied Strand.

The CinC's giant black hand pulled on his chin. "This is new information. Why would the Russians have a replica? We know their shuttle works. We even have photos of it in retrofire." He kept pulling on his chin. "Maybe they wanted us to think they have more shuttles than they really have?"

Sir Isaac puffed on his pipe. "I'm afraid a theory like that doesn't dovetail with their behavior," he countered. "Whenever the Russians conducted shuttle landing tests, they always tried to time their tests so our recon satellites wouldn't be overhead. We were lucky whenever we caught one out in the open. Why have a replica when you're trying to hide the real one?"

There was silence while they all tried to make some sense of it. And nothing seemed to make sense anymore. The shock of the *Constellation* had numbed their minds.

"What you say may be true, sir," said Strand, "but I think you have to come back to the fundamental question. Why have a replica in the first place?"

A moment or two drifted by until Whittenberg said, "To make us think something is there when it's not."

"Exactly. And what was the location of the plastic replica?" she asked, using the Socratic method.

Sir Isaac scratched his aquiline nose. "At Baikonur," he said finally.

"Yes, sir," she continued. "So if we followed that logic pattern, that would mean they wanted us to think they had a shuttle at Baikonur when they really didn't."

Sir Isaac chewed the stem of his pipe. "But as the general said, we have a Spyglass photo of their shuttle in retrofire, and we took satellite pix of it on the ground at Baikonur minutes after it landed. We haven't seen it since."

Whittenberg had turned and was looking blankly at one of the big SPADOC screens, which still had the ground track of the *Intrepid* projected on it. The flight paths of the *Constellation* and the ASAT were no longer there. His mind drifted, until somewhere in his subconscious a door opened, causing him to quickly spin around. "But what if those pix on the Baikonur runway were of the replica shuttle?"

Sir Isaac furrowed his brow. "Well, I don't see how that would be possible. That would mean the shuttle landed somewhere else, and I don't know where that could be, or . . ." He gasped. "*Or . . .*"

"Or it didn't land at all," said Strand excitedly.

"Son of a bitch!" exclaimed the CinC. "Major, I want you to pull out all of the historical pix we have on the Russian shuttle. Especially those pix we got back in November after the shuttle's last flight. Sir Isaac, check the historical orbital patterns on that reentry. Maybe we missed something.''

Day 4, 1130 Hours Zulu
THE *INTREPID*

"You need not worry,'' came the subdued voice over the radio. "The American spacecraft has been destroyed.''

"Destroyed?'' exclaimed Iceberg.

"That is correct, *Intrepid*. As I told you before, we were watching the American situation carefully.''

Iceberg took a deep breath. "I am impressed, Flite Centre. That took some balls.''

"Say again, *Intrepid*. Balls?''

"Never mind. When are you launching your people?''

"In approximately fourteen hours, *Intrepid*. Will you be ready?''

"I was ready when I left Vandenberg, Flite Centre. Keep me informed. *Intrepid*, out.''

Iceberg killed the mike and leaned back. So the *Constellation* got its ass blown out of the sky, he thought. Goddammit, that's great. Shove it to those holier-than-thou bastards. The Iceberg allowed himself a smile. He figured he was going to like Russia.

Day 4, 1300 Hours Zulu, 3:00 P.M. Local
THE KREMLIN

Aleksandr Kulikov, aide-de-camp to the Foreign Minister, read the cablegram intently. This was serious. Deadly serious. The Americans claimed the Soviet Union had shot down one of their space shuttles. France would rejoin NATO. A military alert. Saint Kirill, help me, Kulikov thought. The aide-de-camp knew he must notify the Foreign Minister immediately, so he picked up the phone; but before he could start dialing, the door opened—and Kulikov froze.

"Good afternoon, Comrade Kulikov,'' said the KGB Chairman in a warm voice. "It is a cold day, is it not?''

Kulikov sat there in shock, staring at the little man with the slicked-back hair and double-breasted suit. It was as if a viper had just slithered into his office.

334

Kostiashak looked around for an ashtray, but the abstemious Kulikov was a nonsmoker, so he flicked the ashes onto the Persian rug. "Correct me if I am wrong, Comrade Kulikov, but you were in the process of telephoning the Foreign Minister in Vilkovo—is that not so?"

Kulikov's head slowly nodded.

Kostiashak smiled again. "You are an intelligent man, Comrade. I could make it most attractive for you to refrain from making that telephone call."

Kulikov was stunned. "*Not* make the call?" he asked.

"Precisely," replied the Chairman.

"But why should I not make the call? We have a serious situation with the Americans. The Foreign Minister must be informed immediately."

Kostiashak flicked another ash and studied his manicured fingernails. "Let us say, I am in a position to know that the situation is not what it appears to be. And it would be unwise to inform the Foreign Minister at this time."

Like ninety-nine percent of all Russians, Kulikov loathed the secret police, and his closeness to the Foreign Minister gave him some insulation from their tentacles. "I regret I cannot comply with your request, Comrade Chairman," he said testily. "I must make the call."

Kostiashak pulled on his Pall Mall and slowly exhaled before saying, "Very well, Comrade Kulikov, but if you insist on communicating with your superior, you will force me to arrest you on charges of espionage."

Kulikov's androgynous face turned white. "Espionage?" he repeated softly.

The KGB chieftain nodded. "Yes, my dear Comrade. You may recall—oh, approximately three years ago—visiting the apartment of a friend of yours. A French diplomat, I believe. You really should have gone to the park when you pleaded with him to make you a spy. A listening device had been installed in the gentleman's flat long before your visit. It was such an infantile mistake for you to make. And you are a Russian. Did your parents teach you nothing?"

Kulikov's throat was dry. "You have known? . . . From the beginning you have known?"

Kostiashak smiled again. "But of course, my dear Aleksandr. You know"—he allowed himself a chuckle—"your French controllers should have given you some instruction in the tradecraft of espionage.

Your attempts at avoiding detection were so clumsy that my surveillance teams had a most difficult time containing their laughter.'' Now Kostiashak laughed himself. ''It was truly most amusing.''

Obviously, Kulikov did not find it amusing. ''But why? Why did you wait until now to confront me? Did you not know I was passing documents to the French?''

Kostiashak stroked his silk tie. ''A fair question. I did not arrest you for two reasons. One, it has been my experience that the Foreign Ministry deals with matters that are of little consequence; therefore, the materials you were passing to the French were of little consequence. Two, I felt you could possibly be useful to me in the future. And I was correct.''

Kulikov's gaze remained wary. ''What is it you wish me to do?''

''Simply hang up the phone and send a reply cable, over the Foreign Minister's name, to Yakolev in Washington. Instruct the ambassador not to contact the Americans, and to wait at the embassy until further orders are received.''

Kulikov wavered. ''Issue a cable under the Foreign Minister's name without his authorization? I . . . I do not believe I could do that.''

The KGB Chairman folded his arms and assumed a studious pose. ''My dear Aleksandr, the choice is yours. You can refuse to send the cable, and spend the night in Lefortovo Prison awaiting your trial on espionage charges, or you can do as I ask and be on an Air France flight for Paris tomorrow night.''

Kulikov felt faint. He couldn't believe his ears. In a voice that was little more than a whimper, he said, ''Paris?''

Kostiashak nodded. ''With, perhaps, a little something extra waiting for you at the branch office of the Credit Suisse Bank when you arrive.''

Kulikov blinked . . . then hung up the phone and picked up his cablegram pad.

Day 4, 1300 Hours Zulu, 8:00 A.M. Local
MIAMI

Seymour Woltman couldn't believe his own stupidity. He'd torn out of the gas station in Yeehaw Junction without filling up with gas, and was on the Florida Turnpike when his station wagon went *chug . . . chug . . . chug* and died—the victim of an empty tank. It took him a couple of hours to get refueled and back on the road. He was sure someone had beaten him to the story, but when he returned to the bureau office he checked the wire, and there was no mention of a torch sailing across the southern Florida sky. Maybe everybody had been asleep. Maybe there was cloud cover and witnesses were few. But whatever the reason, he was going to be ahead of the pack. He dashed off his story, entered it in the computer, punched in the codes to put it out on a flash circuit, and hit the transmit button.

FLASH . . . FLASH . . . FLASH
Z2552DQNTG
FL-ROCKET 0179
   (MIAMI) — AN UNIDENTIFIED SPACECRAFT WAS LAUNCHED AT 4:35 A.M. SATURDAY FROM KENNEDY SPACE CENTER ON A TRAJECTORY THAT PASSED OVER SOUTHERN FLORIDA. FLIGHT TRAJECTORIES OVER POPULATED AREAS ARE SPECIFICALLY PROHIBITED BY THE NATIONAL AERONAUTICS AND SPACE AD-MINISTRATION, AND MAY INDICATE A MALFUNCTION IN THE SPACE VEHICLE. A LAUNCH VEHICLE MALFUNCTION OVER POP-ULATED AREAS COULD ENDANGER HUNDREDS, IF NOT THOU-SANDS, OF LIVES.
AP 08:03 EST

In newspapers and broadcast stations across the country a *ding, ding, ding, ding, ding* would be sounding on teletype printers, telling the news editors there was some heavy-duty shit going down at Cape Canaveral. But Woltman had the jump on the story, and he wasn't about to relinquish it to anyone. He pulled out the three-ring binder that held the office and home telephone number of everybody he knew that was worth knowing. In some cases he also had the numbers of their girlfriends or boyfriends. He turned to the page marked ''NASA'' and picked up the phone.

Day 4, 1330 Hours Zulu, 6:30 A.M. Local
CHEYENNE MOUNTAIN

Whittenberg took the stereoscopic magnifying glasses and went back and forth between the photos, then looked up. ''I see what you mean,'' he said to Strand. ''When were these taken?''
Strand pointed. ''The one on the left was a nighttime shot taken almost immediately after the second flight of the Soviet shuttle over

three years ago. It had just landed on the recovery runway at Baikonur. As you can see, the infrared image is irregular. It shows up bright on the extremely hot leading edges of the orbiter, and becomes less so as you move in toward the top of the fuselage.''

"Uh-huh,'' agreed Whittenberg as he peered through the glasses again.

"The second photo,'' continued Strand, "was taken after the most recent Soviet shuttle flight back in November, shortly after we got a Spyglass picture of it during retrofire. Unlike the other photo, it shows no irregularity in the orbiter's skin temperature. It's essentially uniform across the entire wing and fuselage surface.''

Whittenberg went back and forth a few more times, then shoved the pictures and glasses across the conference room table to Dowd, his chief of staff. "You're right, Major,'' the CinC said absently. "What's your assessment?''

"I would say, sir, that the earlier image was taken after a genuine shuttle landing, because of the bright image generated by the leading edge of the wing. That's where the hottest temperatures occur during reentry. The uniform temperature on the second photograph would indicate to me that it's artificially induced—perhaps electrically, or even chemically. In short, I'd bet the second image is of the replica.'' Strand turned and focused her gray eyes on Fairchild. "Sir, did you come up with anything on the orbit path?''

Sir Isaac shook his head. "I'm afraid not. It would've passed right over our GEODSS tracking station at Diego Garcia, but it was down for maintenance at the time. Looks like all we have to go on is what you have here.''

"There's a definite difference,'' observed Dowd through the glasses. "The photo boys maybe shoulda caught this before.'' He shoved the pictures to Sir Isaac.

"So if that shuttle with the uniform heat dispersion is the dummy, and we caught the real shuttle during retrofire, then . . .'' the CinC's voice drifted off.

"Then the real thing didn't make it through reentry,'' said Dowd with finality. "Damn grisly way to die.''

"So what does it mean?'' queried Whittenberg.

Sir Isaac looked up from the photos. "Remember—prior to their shuttle launch last November, the Russians hadn't launched a shuttle in over a year. Maybe the same thing happened then.''

"You mean, maybe they've burned up *two* shuttles on reentry?'' asked Dowd.

Sir Isaac nodded.

"Jesus," muttered Dowd. "That would mean they had a problem. A severe problem. A problem that was . . ."

"Fundamental," said Strand. "A fundamental engineering glitch they couldn't solve. And they burned up two shuttles trying to fix it, but couldn't." She held the thought for a few moments. "That would mean the Russians were . . ."

"Behind," said Sir Isaac.

"Way behind," added Dowd.

Sir Isaac fired up his pipe again. A sure sign the wheels were turning inside his light bulb-shaped head. "So if they haven't got a viable shuttle, and don't have a PRISM battle management system, or a Graser, that would mean they were really behind on an SDI program . . . so far behind they'd never catch up. So far behind . . ."

"They'd do something desperate," said Whittenberg. "Something desperate like stealing the *Intrepid*. So desperate they'd even try to sabotage the *Constellation*—and failing that, they'd go so far as to shoot it down."

Everyone took a moment to absorb their deductions. Then Whittenberg picked up his green Pentagon phone.

Day 4, 1400 Hours Zulu, 5:00 p.m. Local
BAIKONUR COSMODROME

Chief Designer Grigory Vostov breathed a sigh of relief as the final fastener finally closed on the launch shroud. The mating collar with the Progress engine was now firmly ensconced within the aerodynamic shell and could now be attached to the SL-14 booster. Getting the mating collar fitted with a launch shroud had taken more time than he'd expected. Too late he'd discovered there wasn't one of the proper size in the Baikonur inventory. He had to have one flown in from the Plesetsk Cosmodrome and that took time. But now it was ready and he felt relieved.

The launch commander—an elfin lieutenant colonel in a heavy overcoat—walked up and announced, "We are prepared except for the baseplate attachment, Comrade Vostov, and that will not take long to complete."

"Very good. Make haste, Colonel. How are the cosmonauts, Lubinin and Yemitov?"

The launch commander looked at his watch and said, "They will be awakened in approximately one half hour. They will undergo their final flight briefing, meal, and preflight dress, then load onto the Soyuz.''

Vostov nodded. "Not a minute to waste now.''

Day 4, 1530 Hours Zulu
STRATEGIC DEFENSE PLATFORM
ALTITUDE: 430 MILES;
ORBITAL INCLINATION: 83 DEGREES

"Would somebody be kind enough to tell me just what the hell is going on down there?'' demanded Col. David Colquist. "First the *Intrepid* doesn't show up, and now the *Constellation* has gone off the air. . . . You'd tell us if our spacecraft were being abducted by UFOs, wouldn't you?'' Colquist, commander of the SDI prototype platform, was in the communications room of the hexagonal structure, floating upright in front of the transmitter microphone.

The speaker box replied, "I can tell you it doesn't have anything to do with UFOs, sir. But that's all. Eagle One says stay off the air except for routine reporting.''

In a mocking voice, Colquist said, "Well, please be sure and tell Eagle One not to forget us, and that we're still waiting for our delivery. There's not much to do up here until we receive the final package, you know.''

"I will do that, sir,'' squawked the speaker. "CSOC, out.''

Colquist slapped the mike switch off, then in frustration the former gymnast stomped on the "floor" and did a backward somersault up to the "ceiling" of the commo room. "Damn,'' he cursed. "I don't like being in the dark.''

"Yessir,'' replied the commo officer. "Not much we can do about it, though. I just hope everything's okay.''

"Yeah,'' said Colquist, while putting himself in a slow cartwheel to relieve some of the tension from his body. One thing the former gymnast didn't like about long-term spaceflight was that the weight-lessness caused his well-developed muscles to atrophy. "Something tells me things are not right.'' He sniffed. "This whole prototype assembly has gone way too smooth. It's like we've been leading a charmed life up here. We were due for some bad luck, and now I think we've got it. In spades. If they'd just tell us what the problem was, I could handle it a lot better.''

340

"Yessir," comforted the commo officer.

"Well, no sense wasting time here. If anyone should call, I'll be in Reactor Control."

"Yessir."

Colquist executed a beautiful jackknife and propelled himself into the passageway.

Day 4, 2000 Hours Zulu, 11:00 P.M. Local
BAIKONUR COSMODROME

Usually, cosmonauts boarded their Soyuz capsule from a gantry tower after the SL-4 booster was hoisted into a vertical position. However, rolling the crew access gantry into place and then retracting it took time. So to expedite matters, Lubinin and Yemitov were climbing into the crew compartment of their spacecraft while the SL-4 booster was still lying sideways on its flatcar transporter.

The Soyuz-T spacecraft into which the two cosmonauts were gingerly crawling looked like an hourglass mounted on a stubby tin can.

The stubby tin can section was the instrument compartment of the spacecraft. It was about nine feet in diameter and contained the life-support and power-supply systems, the long-range voice and telemetry radio transmitters, the on-board computers, and the liquid-fuel retro rockets. After the Soyuz reached orbit, a pair of blinder-like solar panels would deploy from the compartment into a thirty-foot span and provide the spacecraft with its electricity.

Sandwiched between the stubby tin can of the instrument compartment and the top sphere of the hourglass was the descent module. It was here that Lubinin and Yemitov would sit in conformational seats during lift-off and reentry. The module contained little more than the seats, an instrument panel, and a television camera that allowed ground controllers to keep an eye on the cosmonauts. After retrofire, the descent module would detach itself from the rest of the Soyuz and position itself for reentry. It would then descend to earth like the old Mercury-Gemini-Apollo capsules, except for one aspect—the descent module had a deceptive aerodynamic shape that reduced reentry g-forces for the cosmonauts to a maximum of three to four g's. (The American capsules, and the early Vostok and Voshkod capsules, inflicted eight to eleven g's on their passengers during reentry.) At 25,000 feet the Soyuz descent module deployed a drogue chute, followed by a main chute. Then a scant meter-and-a-half above the ground, a cushioning rocket was fired to absorb much of the landing impact.

The second half of the hourglass was the orbital module, which was a spherical vessel about eight feet in diameter. It contained storage compartments, as well as instruments, along its interior walls. Food, scientific equipment, and excess gear were stowed here, and it was in this sphere that the cosmonauts worked, ate, and sometimes took their sleep breaks. The sphere possessed three hatches—one on top that provided ingress and egress through a docking collar, one on the bottom that provided access to the descent module, and one on the side that allowed the cosmonauts to enter the spacecraft from the outside.

Climbing into the orbital module, and then into the descent module, was slow work for Lubinin and Yemitov, because they were already wearing their extravehicular activity (EVA) suits, which were bulkier than the regular Soyuz cabin suits. Wearing the EVA suits as they went aloft would save them considerable changing time when they reached orbit.

All in all, the Soyuz was very much a Russian vessel. It was simple, functional, utilitarian; it got the job done. Comparing the Soyuz to an American space shuttle was like comparing a Chevy Nova to a Mercedes. One vehicle was cheap, the other expensive and elegant, but both could transport you across town.

Once inside, Lubinin and Yemitov were "buttoned up" as the hatches and launch shroud were secured. The launch commander monitored the preparations, and when everything appeared to be in order he instructed the locomotive to fire up its engines and roll the SL-4 booster out to the pad.

Like the Soyuz, the Baikonur Cosmodrome reflected another facet of Russian nature. In most ventures they undertook, Russians did not exhibit a proclivity for being the best in a qualitative sense; but they certainly had a passion for being the biggest, as exemplified by their cosmodromes. The Baikonur complex possessed eighty launch pads and was seven times larger than the Kennedy Space Center—and KSC was not a small launch facility. Huge hangars dotted the landscape, along with office buildings and living quarters, while a latticework of rails connected the pads and hangars.

Lubinin and Yemitov felt the vibration of the locomotive as the booster was rolled out to its pad.

"So, Sergeivich, we begin our journey," said Lubinin, trying to sound cheerful.

Yemitov was morose. He initially had been inspired at the prospect of capturing an American shuttle, but that feeling evaporated when Vostov told him about the destruction of the *Constellation*. He had always admired his fellow American space travelers, and didn't like the feeling of being an accomplice, of sorts, to their murder.

Lubinin seemed to read his comrade's thoughts, and his false cheerfulness disappeared. "I understand how you feel, Sergeivich," lamented the elder cosmonaut, "but what could we have done?"

Yemitov's pale blue eyes stared back at his friend. "Nothing," he replied simply.

Day 4, 2100 Hours Zulu, 4:00 P.M. Local
MIAMI

Finally, thought Woltman. Finally, we're getting somewhere. The AP bureau office was abuzz about the launch. The bureau chief had notified the Washington office and they were tracking the story from that end, while Woltman and two reporters from the local bureau were tracking it from the Florida end. Woltman was now on a conference call with the Kennedy Space Center press office. He'd been badgering everyone he knew in NASA all day long and had come up with a big zero. The lid was down tight on this one. Nobody would say anything. Not in Florida or Washington. They'd run into such a stone wall that his bureau chief had even started to question if there had actually been a launch. Now Woltman was glad he'd put it on the flash circuit, even though that was supposed to take the bureau chief's approval. The flash had finally triggered enough pressure to make the KSC press office squeal. Woltman had the phone in his hand, waiting for the NASA public relations guy to speak on a conference call.

"UPI, are you there?" asked the disembodied press officer.

"Yeah, I'm here," said the UPI reporter.

"AP?"

"Present and accounted for," replied Woltman in an acid tone.

"ABC, NBC, CBS, are you there?"

"Yeah."

"Yes."

"Yeah."

"I'm here, too," said the man from the *Herald*.

The voice on the phone cleared his throat. "This statement is from the Kennedy Space Center press office and is for discretionary release.

No questions will be entertained after the statement is read. . . . 'At four-thirty A.M., Eastern Standard Time, a space vehicle was launched from KSC on a trajectory that took the spacecraft over southwest Florida. The launch was executed flawlessly without injury to the civilian population. The nature and purpose of this mission is related to the Strategic Defense Initiative and, therefore, must remain classified. While launches over southern Florida are without precedent, the particular trajectory of this vehicle traveled over sparsely populated areas and did not present an excessive danger to the civilian population. It was specifically authorized by National Command Authorities.' End of statement.''

"What kind of vehicle was it?" asked the UPI reporter.

"As I said initially, I'm not going beyond the statement," said the press officer firmly.

"Listen, buster!" barked Woltman. "I got a press release in front of me that was put out by your office a week ago. It says a shuttle—the *Constellation*—is slated to launch five days from now to carry a COSMAX telescope and a communications satellite into orbit. That wasn't, by any chance, the 'vehicle' you spoke of, was it?"

A few moments passed before the public relations man responded tersely: "I'm not going beyond the statement."

Woltman knew when he'd hit a nerve. "Listen, babyface, if I hire a helicopter and fly past your shuttle pads and *don't* see a *Constellation* sitting there, you're gonna look like an asswipe in every paper from Boston to Honolulu, so you'd better come across now. I'm asking you again, was it the *Constellation*?"

The disembodied voice cleared his throat once again, then finally emitted a barely audible "Yes."

Woltman jumped out of his chair. "What! You launched a *shuttle* over south Florida! Are you guys nuts? Didn't you ever hear of the *Challenger*? What if that thing took a wrong turn and wiped out downtown Miami? Better yet, Palm Beach? Is something screwed up on this Star Wars business? Is that what it's about? You got a meltdown on that platform reactor of yours? What's happening, sweetheart? C'mon, what gives?"

"Yeah, what gives, turkey?" echoed the man from ABC.

"A shuttle. You'd better come up with something better than a cardboard press release," demanded the *Herald* reporter. "This is industrial-strength shit."

"I'm not going beyond the statement," said the press officer defiantly, and the connection was terminated.

Woltman stared at the receiver in his hand. Gad. A shuttle. This was bigger than he'd ever dreamed. It had to be. Woltman had been without sleep for almost thirty-six hours now, but the vestiges of fatigue evaporated as his mind raced forward. The launch meant there was trouble. Trouble on the SDI platform. The SDI program was controlled by the Pentagon and the White House, and they were in Washington. He knew it would be impossible to get into the vortex of the story from where he sat in Miami. He'd spent two years with the *Herald*'s Washington bureau, and still had some friends up there. He made a quick decision. He was going to D.C., with or without his stingy bureau chief's sponsorship. This was *his* story, and he was going to stay on top of it. He strode into the chief's office, trying to keep the words "Pulitzer, Pulitzer, Pulitzer" from intruding on his thoughts.

THE FIFTH DAY

Day 5, 0130 Hours Zulu, 4:30 A.M. Local
BAIKONUR COSMODROME

Like dual pyrotechnic projectiles rising into the night, the SL-4 and SL-14 boosters painted two orange streaks across the black sky with their blazing tail cones.

Chief Designer Grigory Vostov should have monitored the lift-off from the launch bunker—but he didn't. Instead, Vostov stood alone in the freezing night, watching the two tongues of flame grow smaller in the distance. When they finally disappeared, he shrugged to himself and trudged off to the sleeping quarters. He'd done everything he could possibly do.

Day 5, 0132 Hours Zulu
ALTITUDE: 22,300 MILES
ORBITAL INCLINATION: 28 DEGREES

The eyes of the Teal Sapphire launch detection satellite were its high-resolution lenses, but its heart was the on-board mosaic of electro-optic sensors called charged coupler devices, or CCDs. These CCD mosaics were stimulated by radiant energy passed on to them by the satellite's infrared scanner—which is to say, temperature changes within Teal Sapphire's field of vision were rapidly detected.

Against the cold nighttime backdrop of the Kazakhstan steppes, the twin infernos shooting out of the Baikonur Cosmodrome caused the satellite's CCD mosaics to go crazy.

Day 5, 0132 Hours Zulu, 6:32 P.M. Local
CHEYENNE MOUNTAIN

Brig. Gen. John Fairchild was minding the store in the Crow's Nest again when one of the phones buzzed. He picked it up. On the other end was a captain who was monitoring the Teal Sapphire satellite. The young officer said, "Launch detection, sir. Headed

349

south out of Baikonur . . . no, wait—check that. I've got some separation in the signatures. Make that a dual launch. Two separate boosters. I'll get you a configuration analysis and a bearing in a minute."

Sir Isaac looked at the ground track and position of the *Intrepid* on the center projection screen. There was no question in his mind what was happening. He picked up another phone and buzzed Whittenberg in his office. "General," he reported, "the Russians are headed upstairs. In two vehicles."

Day 5, 0135 Hours Zulu
THE *INTREPID*

Iceberg heard the transmission crackle in his headphones: "A Soyuz and a cargo vessel have lifted off successfully, *Intrepid*, and are en route to their rendezvous with you."

A wave of exhilaration washed over him. There was a chance to succeed now. A real chance. "Outstanding, Flite Centre," he radioed. "I'll be looking for them."

The *Intrepid* was now communicating with the Kaliningrad Flite Control Centre via the Kosmos 1700 satellite system, which allowed him to stay in constant contact. It was less secure than communicating with earth stations, but that didn't seem to matter much anymore. Besides, his transmissions were still scrambled.

"How do I communicate with your people who are coming up in the Soyuz?" asked Iceberg.

"You may transmit and receive on this same S-band frequency, *Intrepid*; but be aware, our Soyuz crew does not possess an encryption device that is compatible with yours, so you will have to transmit in the clear. Keep your communications to essentials."

"Roger, Flite Centre." Another thought occurred to him. "Are your people going to require my assistance outside the orbiter? If so, I need to start some oxygen prebreathing for EVA."

"Negative, *Intrepid*. You remain inside the spacecraft."

"Roger, Flite Centre."

Iceberg scanned the horizon, looking for some sign of the Russians, but the tail plumes of the SL-4 and SL-14 boosters were much smaller than the *Constellation*'s, and Iceberg couldn't detect them against the inky horizon.

Day 5, 0138:50 Hours Zulu
THE SOYUZ

Cosmonauts Vasili Lubinin and Sergei Yemitov felt their spacecraft separate from the last stage of the SL-4 booster. They were in orbit now, and Lubinin threw the switch to deploy the spacecraft's solar panels. He went through a systems check to make sure the on-board electronics were working properly for the upcoming correction burn that would enable them to close in on the *Intrepid*.

Day 5, 0147 Hours Zulu, 3:47 A.M. Local
KALININGRAD FLITE CONTROL CENTRE

Mission Commander Oleg Malyshev tried to ignore the troika that had become a permanent fixture in the Flite Centre. Popov, the KGB Chairman, and the General Secretary kept hovering around him like husbands whose wives were in labor.

"I have the correction burn computed, Commander," said the navigation officer through the intercom.

Thank God, thought the exhausted Malyshev. "Very well, transmit the data to the Soyuz. We will fire the cargo vessel's correction burn first, then the Soyuz. Are you ready?"

"Ready on the cargo vessel, Commander," replied the navigation officer. "It will be a short burn. There is only seventy kilometers separation from the American spacecraft."

Malyshev wiped his sleeve across his sweaty forehead. "Very well. Fire at your discretion, Navigation Officer."

Day 5, 0203 Hours Zulu
THE *INTREPID*

The ground track of the orbiter passed from darkness to daylight as the spacecraft looped under the bottom of the earth—high above the white frozen wastes of Antarctica. Inside the *Intrepid*, the psychotic Iceberg in human form scanned the space around him for the arrival of his rescuers. Flite Centre had told him the correction burns had been fired smoothly, and they should be coming close any second. He saw the torpedo-shaped cargo vessel first. The *Intrepid* was traveling in a heads-down position, and Iceberg tracked the Russian craft visually as it traveled underneath the orbiter and disappeared from view. He grabbed the hand controller and rolled the spacecraft so he could keep it in sight. Tiny maneuvering thrusters at the base of the cargo vessel flared, causing it to halt some three hundred yards from, and a little above, the American orbiter's position and attitude. Whatever heart Iceberg possessed leapt into his throat when he saw the Soyuz. There it was! He was going to make it!

The Soyuz pivoted and fired its braking thruster, and it came to rest not a hundred yards from the *Intrepid*. Iceberg moved his hand controller a little more so the orbiter's directional S-band nose antenna would be pointed directly at the Russian spacecraft. "Soyuz, this is *Intrepid*, do you read me? Over."

Day 5, 0207 Hours Zulu
THE SOYUZ

Lubinin switched radios, disengaged his voice scrambler, and began speaking in English. "We read you, *Intrepid*. Our ground control will jettison the launch shroud of the cargo ship in a moment. Stay off this channel until we have exited our capsule and gone into EVA. The radios on our EVA suits are much less powerful than the transmitters aboard our Soyuz, and we will be able to talk more freely. Do you understand?"

"Roger, Soyuz. Will comply. *Intrepid*, out."

Lubinin switched radios and engaged his on-board voice scrambler—a Soviet-made device that was much less sophisticated than, and incompatible with, the American Oracle scrambler—then began speaking in Russian again. "Flite Centre, this is Soyuz. We are in position. You may jettison the launch shroud on the cargo ship at your discretion."

"Roger, Soyuz. Stand by."

Yemitov watched the cargo vessel through the porthole in the descent module. He saw sparks pepper the seam of the shroud as the explosive bolts fired. He lifted his thumb to Lubinin and said, "Good."

"Flite Centre," radioed Lubinin, "we have separation of the shroud. We are prepared to go EVA at your command."

"We read you, Soyuz," came the reply. "You are cleared for EVA. Good luck."

Lubinin nodded to Yemitov, and the younger man unfastened his restraining seat straps. He kept his helmet visor closed so he would stay on pure oxygen and not breathe the nitrogen/oxygen atmosphere of the cabin.

Before astronauts went EVA they had to prebreathe pure oxygen for two hours to "wash" the nitrogen from their systems. Otherwise, the lower-pressure spacesuits would cause nitrogen bubbles to form in their bloodstreams, inflicting them with a deadly case of the bends.

Yemitov pointed at the hatch, and Lubinin checked the gauge. "Pressurized," said the pilot.

Yemitov spun the wheel and pulled down the lid. He then took a deep breath and disconnected his oxygen and intercom umbilicals that extended from underneath his seat. He pulled himself through the hatch and into the spherical orbital module, where he attached his oxygen line to the environmental portion of the EVA backpack. When the tiny gauge showed oxygen was flowing into his suit, he began breathing again. Yemitov flipped himself around and pulled the hatch closed, then struggled into his environmental gear. He wouldn't put on the maneuvering component of the backpack until he was outside the spacecraft. He pulled the depressurization handle, and the module's atmosphere began venting into space. When the indicator light turned from red to green, he began turning the hatch wheel on the top of the sphere and carefully opened it. Then, with a gentle hand, he pushed the maneuvering portion of the backpack outside, being careful not to bump it or lose its tether line. If he lost the backpack he wouldn't be able to maneuver in the void of space.

Once outside, Yemitov closed the hatch and began wrestling into the maneuvering component. It was difficult to get the thing on by himself, but it could be done. Lubinin was inside, repressurizing the orbital module. After some struggling, the component finally snapped into place. Yemitov flipped the appropriate switches and began testing his thrusters. He floated slowly away from the Soyuz for a short distance before stopping himself. He felt comfortable now—back in his own element. He propelled himself to the porthole of the descent module and gave Lubinin an "okay" sign. "Everything is fine, Vasilivich," he radioed.

"Good, Sergeivich," replied Lubinin. "I will be out shortly."

"Roger. I will check on the American." Yemitov toggled his joystick and the backpack thruster released its jet of compressed nitrogen gas, pushing him toward the *Intrepid*. What a magnificent spacecraft! thought Yemitov. It looked very much like the Soviet shuttle, except the Russian model did not have the big, reusable main engines on the tail—all of the Soviet shuttle's lift-off engines were on the Energia booster vehicle. The Russian orbiter only had small retro rockets on its tail section.

Lubinin and Yemitov had not been in the Soviet shuttle training program, but the cosmonaut figured their status would change if they could capture this American orbiter.

Yemitov slowed as he approached the windshield of the winged spacecraft. The cabin lights were on. He didn't quite know what to expect, and his curiosity heightened. What would the American be like? Then he spied the astronaut, sitting in the left seat.

The pilot inside the orbiter did not raise a hand in salutation. He only stared at the Russian with a pair of coal-black eyes that were recessed in a gaunt, almost cadaverous face. Yemitov started to wave, but didn't. This astronaut had killed two of his own crewmates, and the thought caused the Russian to shudder. Instead, the cosmonaut backed off and hovered directly above the S-band nose antenna.

"*Intrepid,* can you hear me?" asked Yemitov.

"I hear you fine," replied Iceberg brusquely. "What's the plan from here?"

This American did not care for small talk, Yemitov concluded, so the Russian quickly outlined how they would attach the Progress engine and execute retrofire. Upon completing his explanation, Yemitov asked, "Do you understand everything I have said, *Intrepid?*"

"Yes, I understand," came the curt reply. "Is everything ready at Baikonur?"

"Affirmative, *Intrepid.* Your reentry window will open in approximately nine hours."

"Okay. Let's get on with it. I'm tired of being marooned up here. . . . Looks like your friend is coming out to join you."

Yemitov executed a pirouette and saw Lubinin exiting the Soyuz. Then he gazed back at Iceberg. "Very well, *Intrepid,* we will proceed to attach the collar and engine. Communicate with us if you must."

"Roger. *Intrepid* out."

Yemitov propelled himself back to the Soyuz and helped his comrade with the maneuvering component of his backpack. In Russian, Lubinin asked, "Did you speak with the American?"

" *Da,*" replied Yemitov quietly.

"And?" prompted Lubinin.

Yemitov's delicate features looked at his friend through the visor. "I do not care for him," he said finally.

Lubinin's heavy eyes stared back and seemed to convey his understanding. "Come along. We must not waste time."

The two cosmonauts propelled themselves toward the cargo ship. In his wake, Lubinin pulled an auxiliary hand thruster and a webbed canvas tether line.

When they reached the cargo vessel, the cosmonauts found the launch shroud still hanging on at the base. A small nudge from Yemitov caused it to break completely free. Lubinin then pulled on a lever and the collar/engine was released from the engine, along with the small container that held the clamps.

Lubinin handed Yemitov the small auxiliary thruster—which was nothing more than an Aqua-lung-sized tank of compressed nitrogen gas with handgrips attached. He also gave Yemitov one end of the canvas strap and said, "Hold this." Then, with the other end in his hand, Lubinin circumnavigated the mating collar. Upon completing his circle, he took the other end back from Yemitov and threaded it through a buckle, pulling the canvas belt tight around the girth of the mating collar like a saddle cinch strap.

"You get the clamps. I will take care of this," ordered Lubinin. Yemitov retrieved the container, while his comrade attached the loose strap end to the auxiliary thruster and pulled taut the four meters of slack. "Here we go!" radioed Lubinin, and with that, he triggered the aux thruster, which yanked him and the mating collar toward the *Intrepid*.

The two cosmonauts were cautious as they moved toward the shuttle. This was no training exercise. It was the real thing, and they had to take each movement slowly and carefully, for a tiny mishap could scuttle the entire mission. As they closed on the orbiter, Lubinin deftly brought the aux thruster to the opposite side of the mating collar and started applying little braking squirts of gas to halt their advance. Finally, he brought the collar to a complete standstill just a few meters from the *Intrepid*'s tail.

"Excellent work, Vasilivich," complimented Yemitov.

"Thank you, Sergeivich. Now, let us move this contraption into place—with caution, my friend." Lubinin removed the canvas strap, then moved to the rear of the collar with Yemitov. Each with one hand on his joystick and the other on the exit nozzle of the Progress engine, they gently guided the anterior male end of the mating collar into the center main engine nozzle of the orbiter. There was no sound as metal began scraping against metal, but the cosmonauts could feel the vibrations through their gloves. When the male end struck home, there was a slight whiplash that pushed the two Russians away. "It is in place!" exclaimed Yemitov.

"And it fits perfectly!" shouted Lubinin as he began circling the collar to make sure the lip of the anterior end rested flush against the flange of the shuttle's exit nozzle. It did. "Comrade Vostov did as he promised," observed Lubinin. "Now, let us get the clamps in place."

Day 5, 0327 Hours Zulu, 8:27 P.M. Local
CHEYENNE MOUNTAIN

Chief of Staff Michael Dowd scratched his large bald head. "What the hell are they doing?"

The picture from the Spyglass observation aircraft was displayed on the center projection screen in SPADOC.

Sir Isaac absently rubbed the single star insignia on his epaulet. "Obviously they're attaching something to the tail of the *Intrepid*. What it is and why, I can't say."

Strand's gray eyes peered at the screen carefully. "It looks like some kind of engine . . . but that doesn't make sense. The shuttle has backup systems to ensure the OMS thrusters work."

"Well, whatever's happening," mused Whittenberg, "they've got to be close to bringing the *Intrepid* down. Sir Isaac, what's the status on the Kestrel?"

"The launch vehicle looks in good shape, sir," replied Sir Isaac, "and the weapons systems are getting their final tech out. We'll be ready for a rendezvous launch in about nine hours." The skinny brigadier pulled on his hawklike beak before saying, "It could be close."

"Yeah." The CinC was grim as he picked up his red phone to the White House.

Day 5, 0414 Hours Zulu, 6:14 A.M. Local
KALININGRAD FLITE CONTROL CENTRE

Popov, General Secretary Vorontsky, and KGB Chairman Kostiashak leaned over Mission Commander Malyshev's shoulder to listen to the speaker box.

"We are back in the Soyuz," radioed Lubinin. "The mating collar is in place and it fits perfectly. The Chief Designer is to be commended."

Popov exhaled a sigh of relief.

"The spring clamps have also been installed, and the American pilot has been informed of the retrofire procedures. All is in readiness. We must only wait for the reentry window."

"Very well, Soyuz. Well done," replied Malyshev. "Keep in contact and try to rest. You have approximately seven hours until retrofire."

"Acknowledged, Flite Centre. Soyuz out."

The General Secretary was rested, refreshed, and ebullient as he thumped Popov on the back. "Well, Comrade, the American shuttle will soon be ours. We have done it."

The stocky general looked up at the former hammer thrower with irritation. "Yes, General Secretary," he replied with a tinge of sarcasm, "*we* have done it."

Vorontsky then turned to his diminutive partner in the double-breasted suit. "This is marvelous, Vitali. It is hard to believe we will soon possess an American shuttle. In one brilliant stroke we will be on our way to parity with the United States. Their spacecraft, their weaponry payload—it will all be ours. It was your plan, my friend. An audacious plan, a fantastic plan, a brilliant plan. You are truly a grandmaster."

Kostiashak gave a modest shrug.

"With this shuttle and its payload," Vorontsky boasted, "my position as General Secretary will be unassailable."

"Unassailable," echoed the little Chairman softly.

"And the Americans can do nothing to stop us now."

Kostiashak's smile was disarming. "Absolutely nothing," he agreed.

Day 5, 0617 Hours Zulu, 9:17 A.M. Local
MIDAIR REFUELING OVER THE ARABIAN SEA, OFF THE COAST OF IRAN

The aluminum pipe was retracted from the batwing's fuel vent.

"You're topped off, Ghost Leader," radioed the boom operator. "We'll be here when you get back. Go nail that son of a bitch."

"Roger, Boomer," came the reply, "and thanks. We'll put your name on one of the Paveways. Ghost Leader out."

The KC-10 tanker banked westward, back toward Oman. The stealth bombers would be gone for at least ten hours, so the tanker crew might as well cool it on the ground for a while.

The two batwings came together in a loose formation and turned due north toward the coast of Iran. Beyond the Shiite nation lay the Soviet Republic of Kazakhstan.

Day 5, 0630 Hours Zulu, 1:30 A.M. Local
THE WHITE HOUSE

The National Security Council's EXECCOM had convened in the Cabinet Room. Their mood was fatigued, tense, and grim, with an undercurrent of smoldering anger. Admiral Bergstrom was muttering into a red phone. He finally finished and hung up. "That was General Dooley from SAC in Omaha. The stealth bombers have just crossed the Iranian coast, Mr. President. After they receive their verification go-ahead signal at the Soviet border, they will proceed to a holding station near the Baikonur Cosmodrome. If the *Intrepid* comes down before we launch the Kestrel, the bombers will be able to hit it after it lands on the Russians' shuttle recovery runway."

"I'm not sure I understand, Admiral," queried the Secretary of State. "Are you saying there's a chance the *Intrepid* could come down before the space fighter launches?"

"Yes, sir, there is," replied the old salt. "You see, the Baikonur Cosmodrome is on almost the exact opposite side of the earth from Vandenberg Air Force Base. Just a few longitudinal degrees off the identical meridian. That means our launch window from Vandenberg is the same as the *Intrepid*'s reentry window to Baikonur—except for one difference."

"And what would that be?" asked the Treasury Secretary while stroking his walruslike mustache.

Bergstrom crushed out his foul-smelling cigar and explained. "The *Intrepid* has considerable flexibility when it returns from space. As long as the spacecraft's orbital ground track falls within a reentry zone that is twelve hundred miles wide, it can still reach its recovery runway. That means the reentry window is two orbits wide. Conversely, the Kestrel's lift-off is ballistic in nature, with trajectory parameters that are extremely narrow in relation to the *Intrepid*'s reentry. In short, the *Intrepid* could be executing its reentry shortly before the Kestrel could lift off on an intercept flight plan. That's why we have to have the stealth bombers as backup.''

The man from Foggy Bottom grimaced. ''And if both the Kestrel and the stealth bombers fail?''

The admiral's gold braid seemed to weigh heavily upon him as he took a deep breath. ''The USS *Tennessee* has moved in close to the Iranian coast. If the President gives the order, it will launch a Tomahawk cruise missile carrying a one-and-a-half-kiloton nuclear warhead. That's enough to knock out anything on the recovery runway, as well as their shuttle hangar complex and a chunk of the cosmodrome.''

''Hmmm,'' mumbled the Treasury Secretary. ''How can we be sure that cruise missile would be accurate enough to hit the runway?''

Bergstrom's response was flat. ''This is an upgraded version of the Tomahawk cruise missile. It has a hybrid inertial/terrain-following navigation system that is highly accurate. If you wanted me to put a Tomahawk in the Rose Bowl, I could send it through the uprights. Additionally, the missile can operate dependently with the NavStar Global Positioning satellites, and with the accuracy of that system I could hit the crossbar of the uprights if you wanted.''

''Well, if this gizmo is so accurate,'' countered the Secretary of State, ''why not use a conventional warhead with it?''

''We considered that, Mr. Secretary,'' said the admiral, ''but there are too many unknowns. The recovery runway is three miles long and runs east to west. We don't know from which end the *Intrepid* will approach it. Nor do we know how long it will stay on the runway before being removed to their hangar complex—presumably they would want to get it under cover as quickly as possible. Also, we don't know on which orbit the *Intrepid* will come down, and it will take five hours for the Tomahawk to travel the distance from the *Tennessee*. In short, sir, if we are going to use conventional weapons we must have the flexibility of putting the ordnance down immediately after the *Intrepid* lands, and we need a pair of eyeballs on the scene in order to hit the target. The cruise missile does not give us that flexibility, but the stealth bombers do. In order to have any chance of success with the Tomahawk cruise missile, we have to use a nuclear warhead.''

No one spoke for several seconds.

''*Monsieur le Président*,'' said the Frenchman carefully, ''I must protest any action involving a nuclear device.'' The Gallic chief of state had now become a *de facto* member of the NSC EXECCOM, and everyone was attentive to his words. His long, lanky frame leaned forward as he said, "You have every right to try to prevent your spacecraft from falling into Soviet hands. You have my full support in combating this act of piracy. But to send a nuclear missile into Russia—well, that is something else again. No Soviet leader could stand by and not respond in kind, even though the Soviets have blood on their hands from the destruction of your *Constellation*. Indeed, we are not even certain who is in control in the Kremlin at the moment. I endorse your use of conventional weapons. But a nuclear missile? No, my friend. I implore you not to take that step. It could push the civilized world into an abyss."

"I must agree with our guest, Mr. President," said the Secretary of State. "There are too many imponderables on the Soviet side. If we cross that nuclear threshold—no matter how vital the *Intrepid* and its payload—there may be no return."

The President scratched his upper lip. "Sam—what do you think?"

The Secretary of Defense, his bony features looking troubled, said, "Sir, if you give the order, the *Tennessee* will launch. But my advice is that we stick with conventional weapons. The risk is just too great otherwise. The whole purpose of the *Intrepid*'s payload was to prevent a nuclear exchange in the first place."

The chief executive turned to the Vice President and raised an eyebrow.

The Veep ran a hand through his bristly crew cut and nodded. "I agree. Hold off on the nukes. Everything else is open season, though."

The President sighed. He was relieved, in a way. "All right, Admiral. Tell the *Tennessee* to return to its regular station. But keep SAC at DEFCON Two. Since Yakolev has disappeared into his embassy, we're not going to lower our guard an inch until we nail the *Intrepid* one way or another."

"Yes, sir," replied Bergstrom as he picked up the red phone.

While igniting a cigar, the Treasury Secretary looked across the table at Bergstrom and said, in a conversational tone, "Well, I suppose this is a bit of a disappointment for you, isn't it, Admiral?"

Bergstrom looked up and furrowed his brow. "I beg your pardon, Mr. Secretary?"

The President's money man kept puffing. "Well, I'm sure you military types must be disappointed you can't unload one of those nuke missiles of yours. What did you call it? A Tomahawk? I bet you've been waiting to shoot off one of those for years. I mean, that's sort of your thing, isn't it?''

Bergstrom came out of his chair like a bullet, and if an ebony table had not separated the two men, he would have ripped the Cabinet officer's face off. The admiral's own countenance turned beet red as he hissed in a gravelly voice, "You listen to me, Mr. *Secretary*. In Korea I got my ass shot out of the sky while tangling with MiGs in my Corsair, and I got to spend six fun-filled months in a North Korean prison camp. I've scraped the burned entrails of kids, and I mean *kids*, off a carrier deck after a crash. I've written more letters to widows and orphans than you've ever thought about—all the while bastards like you stayed home and made a potful of money—''

"That will be *enough*, Admiral!'' barked the President. Bergstrom's scrambled-egg chest was still heaving, but he obeyed his commander in chief and lowered himself, inch by inch, back into his chair—like a saber sliding slowly back into its sheath.

The President scowled at his money man. "Milton, you will apologize to the admiral.''

The former investment banker sat there in wide-eyed shock, twitching his walruslike mustache and puffing smoke like a locomotive.

"*Now*, Milton.''

The Treasury Secretary cleared his throat. "Well, I, ahem, I didn't mean to give offense, Admiral. I, uh, that is to say, I apologize.''

Bergstrom's face was still red. "Your apology is accepted, Mr. Secretary. And had I been asked, I would have said I agree with our guest about the use of nuclear weapons. But I recognize the military shouldn't make policy. They should be an instrument of policy. It's my job to point out options, no matter how distasteful they may be to me personally. I don't get my jollies popping nukes at the Russians.''

Now it was the President's turn to clear his throat. "Your point is well taken, Admiral. Now then, if you please, just shoot the *Intrepid* down . . . with conventional weapons.''

Day 5, 0638 Hours Zulu, 10:38 P.M. Local
VANDENBERG AIR FORCE BASE

The dream was surreal, and frightening as it was bizarre. The *Constellation* was floating in a water-filled placenta, suspended in a black void. It floated there. Helpless. Vulnerable. Then out of the void a shooting star smashed into the placenta, causing the *Constellation* to erupt in a burst of white light. Lamborghini came violently awake with a cry, his breathing rapid, his face in a sweat. He felt another presence in the room.

"You okay, Pete? . . . Time for us to suit up." The voice was gentle.

"Mad Dog . . . is that you?"

"Yeah, Hot Rod, 'tis I. Guess I came in at a bad time." Monaghan flipped on the light in the BOQ room and tossed his friend a towel. "C'mon. Let's saddle up. I just got word Ivan is already upstairs. Time's a-wastin'."

Day 5, 0730 Hours Zulu, 9:30 A.M. Local
KALININGRAD FLITE CONTROL CENTRE

Nothing could contain Vorontsky's ebullience. The General Secretary was wandering up and down the aisles of the Flite Centre, slapping backs and joking with the officers and engineers like an old Boston pol. Although they were still saddened by the fate of the *Constellation*, the men within the giant room welcomed some relief from the constant strain they'd endured for the last several days. If the General Secretary was happy, they were happy.

Popov was out of the room, grabbing some sleep, as Kostiashak leaned over Mission Commander Malyshev's shoulder. "At what time will the American shuttle land at Baikonur?" he asked softly.

With great fatigue, Malyshev checked his chronometer. "Assuming the *Intrepid* comes down on its first reentry window, it should touch down approximately six hours from now."

Kostiashak nodded, then inhaled a deep lungful of smoke before approaching the former hammer thrower, who was swaggering down the aisle. "General Secretary," he said, "this is a momentous capstone to an incredible adventure, is it not?"

"Absolutely, Vitali," replied a grinning Vorontsky. "I have never known such exhilaration. The American shuttle will soon be ours. The Politburo will be in the palm of my hand, and the world will see the invincibility of the Soviet Union. Indeed, the world will be mesmerized at how we outwitted the Americans with our brilliance and guile. Harrumph. So much for their impregnable space defense. We outsmarted them, did we not, my friend?"

"Most certainly, General Secretary," agreed Kostiashak, "and our triumph has caused me to think. Would it not make a spectacular picture if you were at Baikonur to greet the American when he landed?"

Vorontsky was a bit surprised by the suggestion, but after a few moments the thought took root and Kostiashak could see his superior's mind racing. "Of course, Vitali. What a vision! It would show the Politburo—no, it would show the entire world—that I am the indisputable leader of the Russian people. That it was *I* who captured the American spacecraft which was a threat to our country."

"I agree, General Secretary. I have spoken with the mission commander. If you were to leave now, you could arrive in Baikonur shortly after the *Intrepid* lands. Think of it. A photograph of you embracing the American pilot with the spacecraft pictured behind you. It would be stupendous." The General Secretary was entranced by the thought, and Kostiashak gave him a final prod. "My helicopter is just outside. It can transport you to your Ilyushin, and in a matter of minutes you can be on your way to Baikonur."

The former hammer thrower smacked his fist into his palm. "Excellent idea, Vitali. I shall leave at once."

Kostiashak beckoned to his aide. "I will have Colonel Borisov escort you to your plane."

The General Secretary looked surprised. "You are not coming, Vitali?"

Kostiashak shook his head. "I think it best I remain here, General Secretary. I feel it would be imprudent for both of us to leave the Flite Centre at this particular time."

Vorontsky agreed. "Of course. You are always the wise one, Vitali. Very well, Colonel Borisov, let us be off. I will see you when I return, my friend, and we shall celebrate this triumph together." And he clapped his partner on the shoulder.

"Yes, General Secretary." Kostiashak smiled. "We will make it a glorious celebration."

Vorontsky returned the smile and strode off through the door held open by the KGB colonel. After the large man lumbered past him, Colonel Borisov turned and looked back at Kostiashak with a questioning gaze.

The grandmaster allowed himself a moment's hesitation, then gave a quick, almost imperceptible nod.

Borisov nodded in reply, and let the door swing slowly shut.

363

Day 5, 0730 Hours Zulu, 12:30 A.M. Local
CHEYENNE MOUNTAIN

Back in his office, Rodger Whittenberg leaned back in his big leather chair and closed his eyes. He'd just about reached the end of his rope. What else could happen? A rogue spacecraft. Joseph Stalin. A Russian deep-plant agent in control of the *Intrepid*. An immolated *Constellation*. It was more than any one person could absorb. If he could just go back to the simple world of, say, flying combat, things would be so much easier.

His red SAC phone buzzed. He quickly grabbed it and said, "Whittenberg."

"Yeah, Rodg," came the reply, "it's Bernie."

Whittenberg was never so glad to take a phone call. "Hello, Omaha. I can't tell you how good it feels to hear a friendly voice."

"I read you," said CinCSAC Bernard Dooley. "I've been talking with Bergstrom about this *Intrepid* deal—he's got us at DEFCON Two, so I can't gab for long. Haven't talked to you since our SR-71 flyby. Just wondered how you were holding up."

Whittenberg chuckled for the first time in a long time. "I feel as if I were in the twenty-seventh mile of a twenty-six-mile race."

Dooley allowed himself a little laugh, too. "I hear ya . . . Bergstrom said you had a little 'surprise' going up to hit the Russkies."

"Yeah," replied Whittenberg, his grimness returning. "They sure surprised us on the *Constellation*. I don't know if you saw it, Bernie. It was horrible—maybe worse than the *Challenger*. Dammit, I should have known something was screwy with that satellite."

The CinCSAC lent a sympathetic ear to his friend. "C'mon, Rodg. Lighten up. Your guys knew the score. So did my SR-71 crew. That's what we get paid for. Sometimes you get lucky, sometimes you don't. You did the best that you could with an impossible situation."

Whittenberg sighed. "Yeah. My best."

"*C'mon.*" Dooley's voice became harder. "We've got these fucking Bolsheviks in a box now, only they don't know it yet. It's our turn to spring a surprise. If your space fighter doesn't nail the *Intrepid*, my stealth boys will."

There was a pause, until Whittenberg said quizzically, "Stealth?"

The moment Whittenberg popped the one-word question, Dooley knew he'd just violated security. Apparently his friend had been kept out of the loop on the decision to use the stealth bombers. "I guess Bergstrom didn't tell you," he said finally.

"Tell me what?" queried Whittenberg, not masking his curiosity.

Dooley felt chagrined, but figured his friend had a right to know what was happening. He proceeded to explain how the stealth bomber prototypes were currently flying through Iranian airspace—on a bearing of true north toward the Baikonur Cosmodrome.

Barbara Kelso, Whittenberg's secretary of four years, kept herself busy in the outer office by working on the CinC's backlog of correspondence. Although a civilian and not privy to all the details on the *Intrepid* affair, her perceptive antennae told her something very big was afoot. So she'd packed a bag from home and made up her mind to stay at her post until this business was settled.

Her phone buzzed. "General Whittenberg's office," she said in her soft Missouri accent.

"Barbara?"

"Yes."

"This is Peter," said Lamborghini in a surprised voice. "What on earth are you doing there at this time of night?"

"The same reason you're at Vandenberg, Colonel," replied Kelso. "Or is it Edwards this time?"

"It's Vandenberg. I guess nobody can keep a secret from the CinC's secretary. Is the general free?"

Kelso looked at her phone board. The red light was on, indicating that Whittenberg was talking to Dooley. "I'm sorry, Colonel, he's on the phone with General Dooley at SAC right now. You know how it is when those two get together. Should I break in?"

"No," Lamborghini said quickly. "No, don't do that. Just take a message, please."

"Certainly."

Lamborghini took a few moments to phrase what he was going to say in precise language. "I'm afraid I have to leave now. Just tell the general that I've left an envelope with the base commander here. . . . If for any reason it becomes necessary, tell him I would appreciate it if he gave the envelope to Juliet personally."

Kelso shuddered and a lump formed in her throat. "I'll tell him, Peter."

"Thank you, Barbara."

Day 5, 0805 Hours Zulu, 12:05 A.M. Local
VANDENBERG AIR FORCE BASE

Lamborghini hung up the phone, then walked out of the small anteroom and into the preflight suit-up area. Monaghan was already wearing his helmet. Lamborghini nodded to the airman, who stepped forward and carefully lowered the pressure helmet over the colonel's head, then sealed it with a quarter turn. Lamborghini raised the visor and plugged a tube into his suit from the portable briefcase-sized air conditioner. Lastly, he pulled on his flight gloves and screwed the aluminum wrist seals shut. He and Monaghan were wearing the full "closed" orange space suits—the kind worn by the flight crews of the SR-71.

The two aviators walked out of the crew area and into a van that would transport them to the Titan 34-D gantry. They were escorted by two white-suited technicians, and the journey was made in silence. One Air Police car with armed guards traveled in front of the van, another behind. The convoy pulled up to the gantry, and the party of four disembarked to walk to the elevator.

The service gantry for the Titan 34-D was like any at Cape Canaveral, except it possessed an aluminum-leafed canopy that prevented the launch vehicle from being observed by Russian spy satellites. When the rotating portion of the gantry rolled away, the leaves of the canopy folded back like a lady's fan.

The elevator stopped and the party exited to walk down the gantry access arm—just as the *Constellation*'s crew had done less than twenty-four hours before. The ground crew at Vandenberg, however, was somber.

Monaghan and Lamborghini doffed their boot slippers and stepped into the clean area, where they disconnected their air-conditioning hoses and allowed the ground crew to help them squiggle into the Kestrel's tandem seats. Mad Dog went first, followed by his friend. They connected the air-conditioning and oxygen tubes to their suits and closed the visors, then Monaghan lowered the canopy. After the CLOSED light lit up on his panel, Mad Dog said through the voice-activated intercom, "Commo check."

"I read you five by five," responded Lamborghini evenly.

Monaghan began his instrument check. "You've been awful quiet, Hot Rod."

From a zippered pocket Lamborghini extracted a small photograph of Juliet and their two daughters. He wedged it between a couple of toggle switches on his control panel. "Yeah," he said finally. "I was just wondering."

"Wondering what?" asked Monaghan.

"Wondering if the Russians have any more ASAT surprises up there we don't know about."

Day 5, 1007 Hours Zulu, 12:07 P.M. Local
THE STEALTH BOMBERS OVER NORTHERN IRAN

They looked as if sorcery had taken wing—like two giant black batwings cruising menacingly through the clouds. If an aviation historian had been granted a close-up peek at the unearthly objects, he'd probably say they resembled the old YB-49 Flying Wing, and indeed, the Flying Wing was part of their heritage and pedigree. But whereas the Flying Wing was designed with the intent of reducing aerodynamic drag, the stealth bomber was designed with a much different purpose in mind—it was conceived, designed, and built to be invisible to radar.

After World War II, the marriage of aviation, radar, missiles, and electronics caused a new, intriguing axiom to emerge, and that was: If the enemy could see you, he could kill you. So compelling was this axiom that it ultimately triggered a quest for the perfect warplane—an invisible warplane. One that could not be detected by the omnipresent tentacles of enemy radar. However, in designing an invisible airplane, there was a fundamental "Catch-22."

To understand this Catch-22, assume for a moment that your household flashlight is a radar beam. Now then, sit in a darkened room and hold up an ace of spades playing card and shine the light on it. The light hits the card and is reflected back into your eyeball. Held face toward you, the card is easy to see.

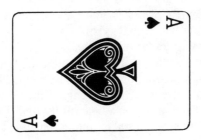

A radar beam works on much the same principle. When its electronic signal hits a reflective surface, it bounces back to the receiver and shows up on an operator's green screen. In electronic parlance, this reflective surface is called Radar Cross Section, or RCS. The ace of spades turned broadside toward the path of the light beam presents a highly reflective surface, or high RCS.

Now then, take the ace of spades and turn it sideways, then shine the flashlight on it.

It now has a low RCS and is much harder to see, and the same dynamic applies to radar. To be invisible, simply present an extremely low RCS to the enemy radar transmitter.

Simple in theory. Difficult in practice. Particularly for a bomber, because by their very nature bombers tend to be a tad bulky. Items like the tail section, the fuselage, the jet engine intake nacelles, and the spinning turbine blades produce a beautifully high RCS. To design a bomber that was invisible to radar, the aeronautical engineer had to eliminate, or reshape, these fundamental parts—and that was a sticky problem.

It took fifteen years, $5 billion, and several crashes before Northrop produced a reliable production prototype, but it was, at long last, achieved.

The stealth bomber was shaped like a boomerang with a jagged trailing edge that truly did give it the appearance of a batwing. The body of the winglike structure was smooth and no bulkier than six feet at its thickest point—except for the crew compartment and air intake nacelles which rested on the top side of the aircraft in pods that tapered smoothly into the skin. The single-wing design and tapered pods reduced the aircraft's cross section and allowed radar beams to "roll over" the aircraft. And to further enhance its low RCS, the bomber's skin was not made of metal, but of intricately patterned anechoic carbon fiber composites which absorbed—rather than reflected—radar energy. Additionally, the entire exterior of the plane was painted with a substance called retinyl Schiff base salts, which further enhanced the absorption of radar waves.

To conceal the spinning turbine blades from radar, the air flow traveled from the topside air intake nacelles into a set of S-shaped ducts that funneled the air into the four General Electric engines. The GE power plants did not hang from exterior wing pylons as on a commercial airliner, but were implanted along the underside trailing edge of the body, further reducing the cross section.

Although it possessed ailerons and elevators along its trailing edge for banking, climbing, and diving, the stealth bomber had no vertical tail stabilizer with a rudder for turning. Instead, the aircraft's engine thrust was vectored, or directed, by exit nozzles that pushed the aircraft in the direction the pilot wanted to go. These vectoring nozzles on the tail exhaust provided an additional benefit, in that they helped conceal the bomber's hot engine thrust and made it less vulnerable to infrared sensors or heat-seeking missiles.

Although stealthy, the flying batwing was not small. Its wingspan was only slightly less than a B-52's, and it could carry an ordnance load of up to forty thousand pounds. However, unlike the B-52 or the FB-111, the stealth bomber did not have a single large weapons bay or carry its ordnance on exterior pylons. Instead, four mini-bays were arrayed along the belly. This eliminated the need for stacking the bombs in one large bomb bay.

The aircraft was not invisible to radar in the absolute sense of the word. Rather, its RCS was reduced to the point that it was no bigger on an enemy radar screen than a ringtail hawk. Unless the search radar had been tweaked to a high degree of sensitivity and the radar operator was experienced with stealth radar "signatures," then for all practical purposes, the bomber could not be detected.

The cockpit of the aircraft was set back slightly from the leading edge of the wing, where the crew members sat in chairs that were severely reclined. This was comfortable, but often tempted them to fall asleep. The wraparound windshield was almost like a skylight, in that it provided a grand view of the airspace above and slightly forward of the aircraft, but the pilot's field of vision directly in front of and below the bomber was poor to nonexistent. To compensate for this drawback, the aircraft had three television cameras mounted in the nose that provided views of the blind airspace.

The crew was configured much like that of an FB-111 or an A-6 Intruder—just two people. The commander of the aircraft was the pilot in the left seat, while the person on his right was the electronic systems officer. The ESO was a navigator, bombardier, and communications/electronic warfare officer all rolled into one; and he was invariably referred to as "Whizzo."

"Authentication signal coming through now, Skipper," said the ESO.

The message, which had originated in the Pentagon, traveled to SAC headquarters in Omaha via fiber-optic cable, then was relayed to Ghost Leader's aircraft by a Milstar communications satellite. The encrypted message came through the Oracle scrambling system and was automatically stored in the commo panel's microchip brain. The ESO could call up the encrypted message on the commo panel's small digital display, but he preferred to work from the paper tape. He punched a button and the thermal printer quickly rolled out the hard copy of the five-digit code groups. Working from a notebook on a tummy-level desk board, he quickly decoded the message from a one-time pad. It read: THOR'S HAMMER. He ripped the message from the pad and handed it to his pilot. Ghost Leader and the ESO each withdrew a sealed envelope from his own flight suit, ripped it open, and extracted a plastic 3-by-5-inch card with printing on it. The message—and the two plastic cards—all read THOR'S HAMMER.

Ghost Leader was a pro. A full colonel who'd been in SAC for twenty-three years and was the chief test pilot on the stealth bomber development program. His hair was gunmetal gray and his face deeply lined. Yet despite all his experience and the years and years of training, nothing quite prepared him for such a moment as this. His throat felt dry and he gulped. Hoping his voice sounded reasonably confident, he said to the ESO, "I authenticate Thor's Hammer."

"Confirm," echoed the ESO—a major who was somewhat in awe of the veteran pilot and didn't detect any nervousness in the older man's voice. "I authenticate Thor's Hammer."

Ghost Leader gulped again and said, "All right, Whizzo, let's proceed to the holding station. We'll wait there for a go or abort signal. How far to the Soviet border?"

Whizzo took a glance at his Global Positioning System. The bombers were still in Iranian airspace. "A hundred twenty-three nautical miles to the Russian border, Skipper."

"Okay," said Leader evenly. "Is the laser channel open to Ghost Two?"

"Hold on," said Whizzo, while twisting a hand controller.

A problem often encountered by aviators on combat missions was the nettlesome requirement that they maintain radio silence. Ships at sea could sometimes get around this nuisance by using blinker signal lights, but aircraft could rarely resort to such a time-consuming technique. So to remedy that shortcoming, Ghost Leader's bomber possessed a communications laser beam on its belly. The beam could be aimed at a receiver grid on the dorsal side of his wingman's aircraft. Secure voice communications could travel back and forth between the two bombers as long as the laser beam could stay aligned with the receiver grid—and that was the tricky part. Keeping the beam on a three-square-foot grid while the two aircraft lumbered along at 500 mph was a bitch. Ghost Leader and Ghost Two were about three hundred feet apart—Leader on top and Ghost Two below in a "stacked" formation. The two aircraft maintained enough distance to prevent them from forming a discernable radar signature, but were close enough to allow the ESO to aim the laser beam with his hand controller.

"Okay, Skipper, we're connected," said Whizzo, "but talk fast. There's some turbulence out there and we could lose the connection at any time."

The pilot keyed his mike switch. "Ghost Two, this is Ghost Leader. I authenticate Thor's Hammer."

"Roger, Lead," came the response, "I confirm Thor's Hammer."

"Okay," said the veteran pilot. "Stay below me within laser-beam range. We may need to talk again."

"Roger, Lead. Ghost Two, out."

"All right, Whizzo, here we go. If you know any prayers, say 'em now.'' Ghost Leader turned the wheel on his control stick gently to the right. He didn't push the rudder pedal, because the bomber had no conventional rudder. Instead, on-board computers guided the vectored thrust nozzles into the correct position, pushing the giant black batwing into a slow, banking turn toward the southern border of the Soviet Union.

Day 5, 1103 Hours Zulu
THE SOYUZ-*INTREPID* RENDEZVOUS

Vasili Lubinin carefully pushed the maneuvering unit of his space backpack through the hatch of the Soyuz orbital module. Yemitov was already outside, and he grabbed the contraption as it drifted out of the portal. Before leaving the capsule, Lubinin switched on the spacecraft's radio repeater, which would relay the voice transmissions of the cosmonauts to the Kaliningrad Flite Control Centre. He then retrieved the remote-control triggering transmitter—which looked like a hand-held walkie-talkie—and exited the Soyuz. Once outside, the two cosmonauts helped each other clip their maneuvering units into place.

Lubinin spoke into his voice-activated microphone. ''Flite Centre, this is Soyuz. Do you read? Over.''

''Roger, Soyuz, we read you. Inspect your chronometer. It should read thirty-three minutes to retrofire . . .'' There was a pause. ''. . . now.''

''Roger, Flite Centre. I copy thirty-three minutes to retrofire. The chronometer is operating properly. We are departing now for the American spacecraft to make final preparations.''

''Roger, Soyuz. We will monitor you. Good luck.''

''Thank you, Flite Centre.'' Lubinin turned to Yemitov. ''Come along, Sergei. Let us send the American on his way.''

The two spacesuited figures engaged their thrusters, and like two bumblebees floating from flower to flower, they transversed the void to the *Intrepid*, coming to a halt over the orbiter's nose. Iceberg's black eyes stared back at them through the windshield.

Lubinin transmitted in English. ''*Intrepid*, we are approaching the time for your retro fire. You are to put your spacecraft into the same reentry attitude as you would normally. The thrust and timed burn of our replacement engine should provide you with the same retrofire characteristics as your own reentry engines. We will read off the countdown and fire the engine from outside with this remote-control triggering device.'' Lubinin held up the small transmitter. ''We will

372

set the timers on the explosive bolt clamps so they will automatically release after you are positioned in your final reentry attitude. As I understand it, your navigational computer is self-contained and can guide you to the recovery runway without external assistance."

"Yeah," replied Iceberg. "The NavComputer can do that. Better move out of the way. I'm going to close the doors and put it into reentry position now."

"Very well," replied Lubinin. The two Russians backed away from the shuttle and watched in admiration as the *Intrepid*'s cargo bay doors closed and the orbiter executed a lazy pirouette into its retrofire position. The spacecraft was now traveling "heads down" and backward, with its nose inclined slightly toward earth. From this position, the thrust from the Progress engine would brake the *Intrepid* and propel it toward the ground at the same time.

After the orbiter had frozen its position, Lubinin and Yemitov traveled to the tail section, which held the mating collar and Progress engine. Yemitov wished they had had time to go on board and explore the *Intrepid*, but there would be time enough for that after the American was finally on the ground.

Lubinin checked his chronometer and did some mental arithmetic. There were now seventeen minutes to ignition. Allow three minutes for the retro burn. Another five minutes for the spacecraft to reposition itself for atmospheric reentry. Another three minutes for a safety margin. That meant a total of twenty-eight minutes before firing the explosive bolts. "Set your timers for twenty-eight minutes on my mark, Sergei."

"Roger."

"Three . . . two . . . one . . . mark." The cosmonauts each set two timers that were equally spaced around the flange of the rocket nozzle. This would fire all four explosive spring bolts at roughly the same instant.

Inside the *Intrepid*, Iceberg was punching the reentry data into his navigational computer. The ultrasophisticated NavComputer was really a nifty device. All the pilot had to do was enter the latitude and longitude of the target landing zone and engage the digital autopilot. The autopilot would read the data from the NavComputer and guide the spacecraft down through reentry, through the braking S-turns, and into the final approach. The *Intrepid* also possessed an Autoland system, but that wouldn't work without the TACAN microwave landing system on the ground. No matter. Iceberg figured he could handle the landing manually. No sweat. He knew how good he was.

Day 5, 1120 Hours Zulu, 3:20 A.M. Local
VANDENBERG AIR FORCE BASE

"Kestrel, this is Launch Control."

"We read you, Launch Control," replied Monaghan.

"CSOC in Colorado says we'll have a go–no go decision on your launch in a few minutes. The *Intrepid* is coming up on its first reentry window. If it doesn't go through retrofire on this pass you'll be able to get within range on the next go-around."

"We can hardly wait," radioed Monaghan. "No sense getting all dressed up with nowhere to go."

Day 5, 1131 Hours Zulu, 2:31 P.M. Local
KALININGRAD FLITE CONTROL CENTRE

Mission Commander Malyshev watched intently as the digital chronometer raced backward. Once again his blond hair was pasted to his forehead in sweaty streaks. "Four minutes to ignition," he radioed.

"Roger, Flite Centre," squawked Lubinin's voice through the speaker box. "Everything is in readiness."

Kostiashak turned to Popov, whose rumpled uniform looked like a potato sack. "Not long now, General. This is a glorious moment, is it not?"

Popov shot the little man a sideways glance. "That still remains to be seen, Comrade Chairman."

Day 5, 1135 Hours Zulu
THE SOYUZ-*INTREPID* RENDEZVOUS

"Thirty seconds!" crackled in Lubinin's earphones.

"Thirty seconds, *Intrepid*," relayed Lubinin. "Are you ready?"

"Yeah," said Iceberg irritably. "I've been ready for days. The NavComputer is locked in. You just light the candle."

Lubinin watched his wrist chronometer and read off the final countdown, while Yemitov poised his thumb over the red firing button of the remote-control triggering device.

"Seven . . . six . . ." Lubinin's voice grew more strained as he ticked off the final seconds.

"Five . . . four . . . three . . . two . . . one . . . fire!"

374

Yemitov mashed the red button.
And nothing happened.

Day 5, 1134 Hours Zulu, 4:34 A.M. Local
CHEYENNE MOUNTAIN

The Crow's Nest in SPADOC was crowded, with Whittenberg, Fairchild, Dowd, and Lydia Strand watching the advancing ground track of the Soyuz-*Intrepid* rendezvous. The blinking light on the projection map indicated the two spacecraft were above the South Pacific—out of range of SPACECOM's Spacetrack radar stations in Hawaii and the Marshall islands. To fill in the blind spot, a NASA tracking ship had been dispatched to that corner of the South Seas to ensure the reentry window was covered.

Chief of Staff Dowd was on the phone to the Spacetrack monitors on the floor below, while Whittenberg was holding the receiver on a direct line to Admiral Bergstrom. Sir Isaac and Strand were monitoring a green CRT screen.

"I calculate they're entering the first retrofire window . . . now," announced Sir Isaac. "They can initiate reentry within the next two minutes."

Whittenberg relayed Sir Isaac's information to Bergstrom, and seconds crawled by one at a time, until two minutes elapsed. Dowd muttered into his receiver to the Spacetrack monitor one last time, then looked up and announced, "No change in orbit, General."

"Give it one more minute to be sure," ordered the CinC, and another sixty seconds dragged by.

Dowd spoke into the phone again, waited for a response, then said, "It's definite, General. No retrofire on this pass."

"Good. Call CSOC and tell McCormack it's a definite go on the Kestrel." The CinC then spoke into his own phone. "There was no retrofire on this pass, Admiral, and we're sending the Kestrel up."

Day 5, 1136 Hours Zulu
THE SOYUZ-*INTREPID* RENDEZVOUS

"Fire it, Sergei! Fire it!" pleaded Lubinin.
"I am trying!" yelled Yemitov, as he repeatedly mashed the red button.

"What's the problem out there?" barked Iceberg.

Lubinin cursed. "We do not know, *Intrepid*. We have some type of malfunction. . . . Sergei, what is wrong?"

Yemitov gave up trying. "I do not know, Vasili," he said in an angry voice. "It could be something on this unit, or there could be a problem with the receiver and igniter on the Progress engine."

Lubinin swore again. "You return to the Soyuz and retrieve the backup remote device. I will disengage the timers on the explosive bolts. Then we must try again."

Day 5, 1137 Hours Zulu, 1:37 P.M. Local
KALININGRAD FLITE CONTROL CENTRE

"What do you mean, a *malfunction*?" demanded Kostiashak.

Popov had had it. "How the hell am I supposed to know?" he fired back. "The damned thing did not fire! You know as much about it as I do!"

The Chairman's cool veneer had finally cracked. Without the *Intrepid* on Russian soil, his plan was on the rocks. "What can we do?" he asked ruefully.

Popov sighed. "Not a great deal. I will contact the Chief Designer at Baikonur and have him patched into the communications link. Maybe there is something he can do, but I doubt it. It is all up to the cosmonauts now. Perhaps they can diagnose the problem, but they must do it quickly. There are only eighty-seven minutes to the next reentry window."

Kostiashak got a grip on himself. He must, he told himself, "play out the play." He summoned Colonel Borisov and rapidly scratched out a message. "See to it that this message is transmitted to the General Secretary's aircraft."

"At once, Comrade Chairman."

Day 5, 1144 Hours Zulu, 2:44 P.M. Local
THE STEALTH BOMBERS

"Message coming in now, Skipper," said Whizzo. "Gimme a sec." He rapidly decoded the four-letter epistle and handed it to the pilot.

"Damn!" Ghost Leader grimaced as he glanced at the message. It read: HOLD.

The two black batwings were flying a rectangular holding pattern in Soviet airspace near the Initial Point (IP) for their bomb run. The Baikonur runway was some 250 miles distant. They had remained undetected by radar, and visual detection was highly unlikely because a quilt of giant cumulonimbus clouds blanketed the Kazakhstan steppes. The two bombers were still flying in a loose "stacked" formation—one on top of the other—about three hundred feet apart at an altitude of thirty-three thousand feet. They were ducking in and out of the fluffy towers, and although flying inside the clouds made for a bumpy ride, the extra concealment was welcome.

"Is the laser channel open?" asked Ghost Leader.

"Roger, Skipper," replied Whizzo.

The pilot keyed his mike switch. "Ghost Two, this is Lead. Did you copy the message?"

"Roger, Lead."

"Okay, then. It looks like we gotta kill another ninety minutes up here. We'll stay in the clouds as much as possible until we get a go–no go from Omaha. Apparently that shuttle hasn't started to come down yet."

"I copy, Lead," said Ghost Two. "We're with you."

Day 5, 1210 Hours Zulu
THE SOYUZ-*INTREPID* RENDEZVOUS

The antenna which fed into the triggering device for the Progress engine was sticking out of a tiny hole at the base of the engine.

"The base is sealed shut," said Chief Designer Vostov in a tired voice, "and it is inaccessible from your position. All you can do is feel the antenna itself to determine if it is firmly attached to its anchor point on the igniter inside the engine."

Lubinin reached out and gently probed the thin wire. "It appears to be securely fastened, Comrade Chief Designer."

There was a pause on the other end. "Very well," said Vostov finally. "All you can do is use the backup remote-control trigger. Perhaps there was a flaw in the first one. Try to position yourself as close to the antenna as you dare when you engage the trigger. Remember, the signal is line-of-sight."

Lubinin sighed. "Yes, Comrade Chief Designer."

* * *

Inside the *Intrepid*, Iceberg had almost blown a fuse. All he knew was that the jerry-rigged engine hadn't fired, and that was followed by a lot of radio chatter in Russian—which he couldn't understand.

Yemitov floated into view and hovered over the nose.

"So what's the holdup?" demanded Iceberg.

"There was some type of malfunction of our triggering device. We are going to try again"—Yemitov checked his wrist chronometer—"in forty-three minutes. We will use a backup transmitter."

Iceberg was not pleased. "What's your name, anyway?" he asked the Russian.

Yemitov hesitated a moment. He was repelled by Iceberg's black eyes. They seemed to bore right through him. Carefully he replied, "Sergei."

"Yeah, well, I have something to tell you, Sergei."

Yemitov felt a chill. "And what is it that you wish to say to me?"

Iceberg's eyes were flint hard. "Don't fuck it up this time."

Day 5, 1210 Hours Zulu, 2:10 P.M. Local
THE GENERAL SECRETARY'S ILYUSHIN JETLINER

General Secretary Vorontsky's private Ilyushin was a sumptuous vehicle that was divided into three compartments. The forward section was a lounge area with a small bar. The middle compartment was a study, possessing a custom-made desk and chair, while the rear cabin was a bedroom.

One of Vorontsky's greatest pleasures was taking the jetliner to Western capitals for state visits. He enjoyed the pomp and circumstance of an airport arrival, while his wife enjoyed shopping sprees at Harrods or Saks Fifth Avenue with her American Express card.

On other occasions he would take the jetliner into Siberia for a fishing trip at Lake Baikal—often in the company of someone other than his wife.

The aircraft's bartender had just handed the General Secretary his third vodka when the captain came out of the cockpit with a message. The General Secretary quickly scanned the note and looked up at the pilot. "This message is from Comrade Kostiashak. He says General Popov thought it best to bring down the American spacecraft after one more orbit, and that it will land at Baikonur at approximately six P.M. When are we scheduled to arrive there?''

"At approximately the same time, depending on the headwinds," replied the pilot.

The General Secretary smiled and sipped his vodka. "Marvelous. Perhaps we will be able to watch it land after all.''

Day 5, 1237 Hours Zulu, 4:37 A.M. Local
VANDENBERG AIR FORCE BASE

Like the sands of an hourglass, the remaining time on Peter Lamborghini's digital chronometer quickly evaporated. When it hit 00:00:00, he heard, "Ignition!" and felt the vibration of the Titan 34-D's rumbling engines.

The Titan's propulsion system was similar to the shuttle's in that it possessed two solid-fuel boosters mounted as outriggers to a center liquid-fuel engine. When all three elements worked together they produced 3.5 million pounds of thrust.

As the vibrations increased, Lamborghini remembered the lift-off of his orientation flight aboard the shuttle *Antares.* That launch was daunting, to be sure, but riding aloft in the Kestrel gave him a more intimate feeling with the booster—as if the Titan rocket were strapped right to his ass. He watched the gantry disappear from view and heard, "Lift-off, Kestrel! We have lift-off! Everything's looking fine. Transferring you to CSOC. Good hunting.''

"Roger, Launch Control," replied Monaghan, "and thanks."

Lamborghini felt the cabin pressurize while the mounting g forces pushed him back into his seat. The Titan 34-D was ascending rapidly, punching a hole in the night sky and pushing up the needle on the machometer. As the speed increased, Lamborghini's confidence —which had been shattered by the destruction of the *Constellation* —seemed to return, and he found he liked the idea of springing this surprise on the Russians. It was time to even up the ledger. He looked out the side window, and even though it was night, he could begin to make out the curvature of the earth.

"How're you doin', Hot Rod?" queried Monaghan.

"Doin' okay, Mad Dog. Let's nail these bastards."

Monaghan liked the firmness in his partner's voice. "Awright, that's my guy.''

Day 5, 1240 Hours Zulu, 2:40 P.M. Local
KALININGRAD FLITE CONTROL CENTRE

The liaison officer, who kept tabs on activity at the Aerospace Defense Warning Centre, was rocked out of his lethargy by the *beep* coming from his computer terminal. He'd been focusing on the upcoming reentry procedure of the *Intrepid*, like everyone else, and the last thing he'd expected was an alarm. He immediately began tapping on his keyboard, and when the data appeared on his screen, he yelped, "Launch detection, Commander!"

Popov, Kostiashak, and the mission commander looked up.

"Where?" demanded Malyshev.

The liaison officer kept tapping rapidly. "Coming out of the Vandenberg cosmodrome . . . wait one moment . . . vector one-eight-seven degrees. I am putting it on the plot board." He hit the proper keys and a short ground-track line appeared out of California, far south of the Soyuz-*Intrepid* rendezvous position. The Soyuz and the *Intrepid* had just crossed the Arctic Circle and were on a southerly heading toward their next retrofire attempt over the South Pacific.

"What is it?" demanded Kostiashak.

"I have no idea," replied Popov. "But if you thought the Americans were going to sit on their hands while we destroyed one of their shuttles and tried to steal another, then you are a fool."

The Chairman's eyes flashed, but he contained himself. "How long until the next reentry attempt?"

Popov looked at the time display. "Twenty-three minutes. It would appear the American rocket will approach our vessels approximately the same time as we retrofire."

Day 5, 1240 Hours Zulu, 5:40 A.M. Local
CHEYENNE MOUNTAIN

Strand watched her green CRT screen, which was receiving a data readout on the Kestrel launch from CSOC. "Solid boosters have separated on the Titan," she announced. "So far, so good."

The ground tracks on the giant center projection screen showed the spacecraft were heading south and approaching the equator. The Kestrel would cross it first, but the Soyuz and the *Intrepid* were rapidly gaining because of their greater velocity.

Day 5, 1243 Hours Zulu
THE KESTREL

Mad Dog felt a vibration as he checked the control panel. "Liquid booster has separated," he radioed. "We're clear. Lining up orbit insertion burn now." The Kestrel was completely free of its Titan booster and would now rely on its own orbital maneuvering system (OMS) engines.

"Roger, Kestrel," said the Cap Com from CSOC. "You are go for insertion burn."

Monaghan checked his attitude direction indicator to confirm it was in the inertial mode and that the digital autopilot was engaged. The NavComputer was wired into the autopilot and would execute the firing of the OMS engine to insert them into orbit. Mad Dog kept his hand off the pitch and yaw controller and let the computers take over. "Here we go, Hot Rod."

"I'm with you," replied Lamborghini.

The flight plan called for the Kestrel to be inserted into the same orbital vector as the Soyuz and *Intrepid*, but the space fighter's initial position would be two hundred miles behind and fifteen miles below its target. The strategy was to initially keep some distance, in order to guard against any ASAT weapons the Soyuz might have brought along. From two hundred miles away, Lamborghini would scan the *Intrepid* with the long-range radar and engage it with the Phoenix missiles. Then the space fighter would close the gap to inspect the damaged shuttle, or finish it off with the Sidewinders.

Because the Kestrel was traveling in a lower orbital plane, it could catch up to the *Intrepid* like a sprinter who had the inside track around a curve.

No attempt would be made to disable or board the *Intrepid*. Monaghan and Lamborghini were to simply blast it out of the sky.

Day 5, 1253 Hours Zulu
THE SOYUZ-*INTREPID* RENDEZVOUS

"They what?" cried Iceberg.

"Just as I told you, *Intrepid*," explained Lubinin patiently. "We have received word from our Flite Centre that the Americans have launched a vehicle from your Vandenberg cosmodrome. It is approaching our position on this same axis of advance. Flite Centre wants to know if you have any idea what it could be."

Iceberg began sweating as his mind raced. What could it be? Not an ASAT missile. Those had been destroyed under the treaty. Besides, they were launched from an airborne F-15 fighter, not from a launch facility like Vandenberg. Another shuttle? No way. They couldn't possibly have prepped another shuttle in just a few days. And it couldn't be a manned vehicle. The shuttle was the only manned launch vehicle in the U.S. inventory. What could it be, then? Some ASAT improvisation? Or a photorecon bird? Yeah. Recon. Now that made more sense.

"Tell your Flite Centre I don't know for sure, but it's my guess it's some kind of reconnaissance satellite coming up to take close-up pictures of what's going on."

Lubinin wasn't convinced, but said, "Very well," and informed Kaliningrad.

Iceberg was impatient. "How much time until we try your retro engine again?"

"Eleven minutes," replied Yemitov.

"Good," said Iceberg. "I'll be out of here before they can do anything with that Vandenberg vehicle, whatever it might be."

"Yes," observed Lubinin. "*You* will be."

Day 5, 1258 Hours Zulu
THE KESTREL

After the OMS engines shut down, Monaghan jettisoned the launch shrouds covering the Phoenix missiles on the topside wing pylons. Then he activated the reaction control thrusters so he could maneuver the space fighter.

The three spacecraft were now orbiting on a roughly common ground track in single file, heading south above the South Pacific. The *Intrepid* was in the lead, followed closely by the Soyuz. The Kestrel was 217 miles behind.

"Take a look, Hot Rod. See what you can find."

"Roger," said Lamborghini, and he turned on the powerful AWG-14 Doppler-pulse radar. Using the hand controller, he rotated the slotted planar antenna in the nose cone to search for the rogue spacecraft. Around and around he went, peppering the target space with electromagnetic pulses from the LTV radar, but his tactical

382

information display (TID) screen remained blank. "I'm not getting anything, Mad Dog."

Monaghan's earphones crackled. "Kestrel, this is CSOC. Please advise on your status."

"Nothing yet," replied Monaghan. "We're still scanning with the radar. Anything you can tell us?"

"Wait one," ordered the Cap Com. "The *Intrepid* is already being scanned by the NASA tracking ship. We're waiting for you to come into range. Yeah. Okay they've got you! We mark you two-one-seven miles behind the *Intrepid* and one-seven miles below. Also, your ground track is slightly west of the target. You copy that?"

"Roger, CSOC," said Monaghan, and he yawed the space fighter a bit to the right. "Try it now, Hot Rod."

Again, Lamborghini swept the ether with his planar antenna. "I've got something!"

Mad Dog whooped. "That's gotta be them. CSOC, we got 'em in our sights."

"We copy, Kestrel," replied the Cap Com in Colorado. "Eagle One says take the shot as soon as you can."

"Roger," said Lamborghini as he began powering up the electronics in the Phoenixes. "It's hard to say for sure at this range, Mad Dog, but the TID screen says we're picking up two signatures."

"You probably are," said Monaghan. "A big one and a smaller one, I bet."

"Yeah. Very little separation between them, though."

"I figure the big one is Iceberg," speculated Monaghan, "and the small blip is that Russian Soyuz. Better take 'em both out to be sure."

"Roger," said Lamborghini. "Seems a shame to blast the Soyuz, too. Those Russian cosmonauts are probably just following orders."

"Yeah. That's a shame," agreed Monaghan. "Now nail the fuckers."

Lamborghini flipped on the Phoenix AWG-14 fire-control system, then punched in some keystrokes on the armament panel, which assigned a target, and a target priority, to each missile. He set both Phoenixes for dependent guidance, so they would be guided by the Kestrel's radar for most of their death journey. Lastly, he popped open the safety cover on the red arming switch and flipped it to ENGAGE. The two blips on his TID screen started blinking, indicating the missiles were locked onto their targets in the priority sequence he had assigned. All Lamborghini had to do now was press the red button on the hand controller. "We've got lock-on, Mad Dog."

"Take 'em!" ordered Monaghan.

There was a white flash as the first Phoenix leapt off the left pylon. Monaghan instinctively blinked, and the Kestrel wobbled slightly from the missile's release. But the fire-control computer quickly readjusted the spaceplane's attitude so it would regain its stability for the next shot. A few moments elapsed, and with a second flash, the final Phoenix raced into the night sky.

As Monaghan watched the two white dots streak off in the distance, he said, "God, Hot Rod, that was weird. I didn't hear a thing."

Lamborghini watched his screen. "The TID's readout says five minutes, thirty seconds to impact."

Day 5, 1300 Hours Zulu
THE SOYUZ-*INTREPID* RENDEZVOUS

"Five minutes to retrofire," radioed Lubinin. He and Yemitov were a mere sixty feet from the tail of the *Intrepid*, and as close to the Progress retro engine as they dared be. They could only hope their backup trigger transmitter would function properly. "If the device works this time, *Intrepid*, the American spacecraft will be too late to prevent your escape."

"Just make sure it does work this time," replied Iceberg. "I don't want to have to ride down with you guys in that Soyuz capsule."

Lubinin didn't tell the American that if they failed, they'd all be better off just staying in orbit.

As the seconds dragged by inside the *Intrepid*, Iceberg found himself perspiring again, and the little droplets of sweat remained suspended around his face. It had to work this time. The success of his lifetime mission now rested on a silicon chip inside a hand-held device. Would it work or wouldn't it? He cursed, but whispered no prayer. If an atheist could be devout, then Iceberg was devout. His god had become the mission—the final, complete obedience to his mother.

Day 5, 1305 Hours Zulu
THE KESTREL

Lamborghini was glued to his TID screen now. The range to target was rapidly shrinking as the Phoenix missiles homed in on their targets at 2,500 miles per hour. "Sixty seconds to impact," he said in a tight voice. "Switching to independent guidance now." He punched the appropriate button on the armament panel, and the missiles' on-board planar antennae became active. From this point, the Phoenixes would guide themselves in for the terminal kill phase.

"Forty seconds," announced Lamborghini.

Day 5, 1305 Hours Zulu
THE SOYUZ-*INTREPID* RENDEZVOUS

"Seven . . . six . . . five . . ." Lubinin read off the countdown one last time. ". . . Four . . . three . . . two . . . one . . . fire!"

Yemitov mashed the red button, and the Progress engine erupted before them, silently belching out a tower of yellow flame.

"We have ignition!" shouted Lubinin as the *Intrepid* started moving away.

For Iceberg, the vibration from the jerry-rigged engine imparted an almost sexual feeling of release. At last—at long last—he was on his way. Yet instinctively, he peered out the window—as if he might be able to see the American bogie that had been sent up from Vandenberg.

Day 5, 1306 Hours Zulu
THE KESTREL

Lamborghini had become mesmerized by the TID screen.

"How's it lookin'?" asked Mad Dog.

"Thirty seconds," came the clipped response, then, "Hold on a minute—what is this?"

"What is what?" demanded Monaghan.

Lamborghini blinked a few times to make sure he was seeing it correctly. "Mad Dog, I'm picking up a third radar signature."

"What? A *third* signature?"

"Yeah, a third image," replied Lamborghini. "It's moving away from the other two and becoming more distinct. Its range is increasing . . . and it's *descending*."

"What about the other two?" asked Monaghan.

Lamborghini was flustered now. "Still stationary. The first Phoenix will impact in five seconds."

385

Day 5, 1306 Hours Zulu
THE SOYUZ-*INTREPID* RENDEZVOUS

Yemitov's blue eyes watched the *Intrepid* grow smaller and smaller in the distance. "We did it, Vasili! We did it!" cried the cosmonaut in exultation.

Lubinin was about to echo his compatriot's excitement when, over Yemitov's shoulder, he noticed a white flash in the distance. Puzzled, he pointed with his gloved hand. "Sergei . . . I saw something over there."

Yemitov was turning to look behind him when the nearby Soyuz silently exploded in a burst of light, sending fragments spinning in all directions.

Day 5, 1306 Hours Zulu
THE KESTREL

"We have impact on one!" shouted Lamborghini. "And two!"

"What about the third one?" demanded Monaghan.

Lamborghini watched the screen. "It's still there . . . range still increasing . . . and descending. I don't understand. Where could it have come from?"

The answer was painfully simple. One of Lamborghini's targets—which the $128 million Phoenix-VII prototype had destroyed—was the spent launch shroud that had covered the Progress engine and mating collar while they were transported on the Russian cargo booster. After being jettisoned, the launch shroud had drifted a mile from the other two spacecraft—reflecting a lovely radar signature.

At the same time, the Soyuz was poised directly between the Kestrel and the *Intrepid*, where the butterfly solar panels of the Soviet spacecraft blocked Lamborghini's radar sweeps before they could strike the American shuttle. When the *Intrepid* retrofired and moved out from behind the "mask" of the Soyuz, the Kestrel's AWG-14 radar picked it up—too late to assign it as a target for the Phoenix missiles.

"Range still increasing." Lamborghini was reluctant to admit what was coming into focus as the bitter truth. "Mad Dog . . . I think that's Iceberg getting away."

Monaghan didn't even take time to think. With his four thousand

386

hours in jet fighter aircraft and his Irish chromosomes, nothing but distilled instinct governed him now. He spat, "My ass!" then disengaged the autopilot from the fire-control computer and quickly flipped the Kestrel so it was traveling upside down and backward. He checked the attitude direction indicator to make sure his alignment was correct, then without hesitation he mashed the trigger button to fire the OMS engines.

As the spacecraft vibrated, Lamborghini shouted, "Mad Dog! What the hell are you doing?"

Monaghan felt himself sink into his seat as the braking action of the OMS engine took effect. "I'm going after that son of a bitch!"

Day 5, 1300 Hours Zulu, 5:00 P.M. Local
A MIG-29 FULCRUM OVER THE KAZAKHSTAN STEPPES

Oh, joy! *This* was flying!

Lt. Fyodor Tupelov put his MiG-29 into a double snap roll and howled in absolute delight.

The young aviator had been a top graduate from the Frunze military academy, as well as the number-one graduate in his flite school class. His proficiency, his Party activism, and the fact that his father was a high-level Party *apparatchik* had enabled Tupelov to land a plum assignment—flying the highly sophisticated MiG-29 Fulcrum fighter with the 77th Interceptor Regiment at Tbilisi. It was a rare honor for such a young man, and he was one of only two lieutenant pilots in the entire regiment. Such expensive and sophisticated aircraft were usually entrusted to older, more experienced aviators.

And what an aircraft this Fulcrum was! The athletic, blond Tupelov often boasted that with a Fulcrum he'd gladly go to the newly reoccupied Afghanistan for a chance to tangle with one of those vaunted Pakistani F-16s. Yet because he was a young officer, Tupelov rarely got the opportunity to push his sophisticated MiG-29 to the edge of its performance "envelope." The Fulcrum was an expensive plane, and despite his flite school credentials, Tupelov was young. Therefore, tight controls were consistently imposed on his flying. Always, from the moment he took off until he landed, his every movement was monitored by senior commanders and ground controllers. On any given training mission, Tupelov was told when to take off, when to join the formation, when to peel off from the formation, what training maneuver to execute, when to execute it, when to stop, and when to rejoin the formation. Everything was done within strict parameters. He never had a chance to truly let loose and bore holes in the sky—no opportunity to become one with the aircraft.

Until now.

Tupelov had just picked up a brand-spanking-new Fulcrum from the air-maintenance depot at Tselinograd and was en route to join his regiment at Tbilisi near the Black Sea. His new Fulcrum had been outfitted with its complement of AA-10 and Aphid missiles, along with external tanks to carry the aircraft through the 3,000-kilometer journey. Tupelov was alone with his aircraft, flying over the Kazakhstan steppes, which were covered with a patchwork quilt of giant cumulonimbus clouds. The young pilot was having the time of his life, snaking through the canyons created by the giant white thunderheads —rolling, climbing, and playing tag with the airborne pillows to his heart's content. He'd always dreamed flying could be like this, and now his dreams were fulfilled.

But Tupelov wasn't one to let his headiness carry him too far. In zipping over and around the clouds, the last thing he needed was a midair collision. He checked his map and saw that he was crossing into another air traffic control division—Sector 23-R. He set his radio for the proper frequency and keyed his mike. "Air control division, two-three-Romeo, this is MiG seven-seven-echo, do you read? Over."

"Roger, seven-seven-echo," came a detached voice over the radio, "we read you, over."

Tupelov said, "I am flying on air defense flite plan number niner-seven-whiskey-foxtrot, from Tselinograd to Tbilisi, on vector two-three-two at eight thousand meters altitude. I am on visual flite rules. Is there any traffic in my area? Over."

"Stand by," came the robotic voice. A few seconds elapsed, then, "Negative, seven-seven-echo. You have no traffic in your sector except for an Aeroflot jetliner. It is seventy kilometers east of you at eleven thousand meters altitude en route to New Delhi on vector one-five-seven."

Seventy kilometers east, and Tupelov was traveling west. The path ahead of him was clear as could be. "Roger, air control two-three-Romeo. Thank you. MiG seven-seven-echo, out."

But the ground controller wasn't finished yet. "We have noticed your course has been somewhat erratic, MiG seven-seven-echo. Are you having any difficulty with your aircraft?" The question was asked in a quasi-threatening tone, and this caused Tupelov to be wary. Ground controllers were always snoopy—and arrogant. They acted as if they owned the airspace. Tupelov wanted to give a response that was plausible, yet not offensive. Something that would not stir up any trouble, but allow him to keep having a good time. He keyed his mike and tried to sound authoritative. "There is no problem, air control. I am checking out the performance on a new aircraft." Which was true. "Request clearance for discretionary climb and descent between seven thousand and twelve thousand meters on my present vector."

"Very well, seven-seven-echo. Proceed at your discretion, but you are advised not to deviate from your flite plan."

That meant no loops or backtracking, but as long as he kept heading for Tbilisi, he could play as much as he wanted to—until he came within range of his regimental radar control centre. Then he would have to play it by the book. "Thank you, air control two-three-Romeo. MiG seven-seven-echo will comply with your instructions. Out." The young pilot smiled. Evidently he'd sounded authoritative enough. Now he could have some more fun.

Tupelov was cruising along the top of a puffy field of clouds at eight thousand meters altitude, but ahead of him the clouds billowed up into two Goliath thunderheads, extending to fifteen thousand meters in height and creating a giant canyon between them. Tupelov hooted, then shoved his throttles in and climbed up the middle of the canyon. At eleven thousand meters he leveled off and wove back and forth between the canyon walls—brushing up against one fluffy side, then the other. Ahhhhhh! Complete delight! He was deep into the canyon gorge now, and he brought his aircraft midway between the white towers to put the Fulcrum into a slow, lazy barrel roll. Tupelov was halfway through his aerobatic maneuver—poised in the heads-down inverted position—when two giant black batwings roared out of the cloud bank, sandwiched his Fulcrum between them, and then plunged into the far canyon wall—vanishing as quickly as they had appeared.

Day 5, 1305 Hours Zulu, 5:05 P.M. Local
THE STEALTH BOMBERS

Had Ghost Leader not been held firm by his shoulder harness, he would have leapt out of his seat as he screamed, "*Shit!*"—and yelped at his companion, "Did you see that!?"

Whizzo's bug eyes were transfixed on the nose-camera video screen. "Yeah!" he replied in a quaking voice. "And I think I saw some missiles under the wing!"

389

Ghost Leader uttered another high-pitched "Shit!" Then he gulped and asked, "Is the laser channel open?"

Whizzo nervously fiddled with his hand controller before saying, "Open, Skipper."

The pilot keyed his mike. "Ghost Two, this is Lead. Did you see that?"

"*See* it?" came the excited reply. "I nearly took his fucking tail section off!"

Lead's stomach started knotting up. "Oh, great, just what we need. Did you catch what it was?"

"I dunno," said Ghost Two anxiously. "It was too fast. A Fulcrum? Maybe a Flanker? Can't say. Whatever it was, it had a double tail—I can tell you *that* for sure. It didn't clear my windshield by more than ten feet. You think they got us spotted?"

"I don't know. Hold on." Leader was sweating as he turned to the major and asked, "You picking up anything?"

The Whizzo scanned his instruments. "Nothing, Skipper. Threat board shows only normal search radars working. Nothing in the X-ray or India bands."

"My Whizzo says we're not picking up any SAM search, air-to-air search, or lock-on," said Leader to Ghost Two. "Only normal navigational search."

"My Whizzo says the same thing," replied Two. "But how did they know where to look for us?"

"Damned if I know," said Leader through his teeth. "Listen, we better split up and take evasive action. If Omaha transmits the go signal, you take the alternate southern approach to the target and I'll come in from the north. Stay in the clouds as much as you can. They may be looking for us, but I bet we're still blind on their radar."

"Roger, Lead. We'll see you back in Muskrat"—slang for Muscat. "If we get the go, put your load where it counts."

"You got it, Ghost Two. Good luck. Lead out." After cutting the transmission, Leader said through the intercom, "All right, Whizzo, I don't know how they found us, but it looks like we've been spotted. Even so, we're sticking with the game plan. I think we'll be okay as long as we stay in the clouds. If we get the go, Ghost Two will approach from the south and we'll come in from the north. Keep an eye on that threat board."

"Roger, Skipper."

Leader pushed his control stick forward and turned the wheel. The batwing responded and began a lumbering, diving turn to the northeast.

Day 5, 1306 Hours Zulu, 5:06 P.M. Local
THE FULCRUM

Fyodor Tupelov tried to hold the Fulcrum steady in level flight, but he was shaking so violently from fright that it was difficult. And when his shaking turned into sobs, it became almost impossible. God in heaven! What had he seen? Those big, black, sinister creatures had come out of nowhere and almost swallowed his Fulcrum. They did not look of this world. Tupelov clutched the control stick with two hands. He'd never known such panic. He forced himself to take long, even breaths. Good. That helped . . . deeper breaths now. Better. He kept the oxygen going in and out, and slowly the terror subsided. Tupelov was regaining control of himself and his aircraft. As the clouds whipped by his cockpit, he told himself to go back to flite school basics. Identify the problem, then correct it.

First, what *were* they? They were unlike anything Tupelov had ever seen. The concept of a UFO was foreign to him, so it didn't even enter his mind. He knew that however bizarre, those flying black batwings were of this earth. And if they were in Russian airspace, that meant the ground air traffic controllers *had* to know about them; for in the Soviet Union, no one *ever* left the ground without filing a laborious flite plan. And if that was the case, the air controller in Sector 23-Romeo had been grossly negligent, incredibly stupid, or had deliberately lied to him. When this thought took hold in Tupelov's mind, his fear was quickly supplanted by anger—a deep, searing, blinding fury—and he keyed his mike. "Air control division, Sector two-three-Romeo, this is MiG seven-seven-echo. Do you read? Over."

There was a pause until a bored voice came on the air. "Roger, seven-seven-echo, we read you, over."

Tupelov recognized the voice as the one that had given him his original clearance. "Air control, on our last transmission I thought you said there was no air traffic in my area!"

There were some moments of silence before the controller came back: "Affirmative, seven-seven-echo. I have you on my screen at one-one-zero-seven-eight meters altitude, bearing two-two-niner-degrees. There is no traffic in your area except for the Aeroflot flite you were advised of earlier."

Tupelov's face turned scarlet. "You listen to me, you stupid ass! I just avoided a midair collision by no more than three meters with two unidentified aircraft! Why did you not advise me of them?"

The controller responded in a puzzled voice, "You say you almost had a midair collision?"

"Yes, you ass! How many times do I have to repeat myself? Your negligence could have gotten me killed!"

There was a pause before the controller said, "You are mistaken, seven-seven-echo. I see nothing on my screen in your area but your aircraft."

"*Mistaken*! I could have touched those bogies if I had wanted to! Are you asleep down there? Or just stupid? Or both?"

There was another pause, longer this time, and a different voice came on the radio. "MiG seven-seven-echo, this is the commander of Sector two-three-Romeo air traffic division. You claim you had a near miss?"

The fact that the ground control commander was on the radio stole some of Tupelov's thunder, but nevertheless, he pressed his case. "Yes, Commander, that is correct."

"Describe the aircraft to me," ordered the commander.

"There were two aircraft," said Tupelov precisely. "Delta shaped. Black in color. No markings that I could see. Very large. Bigger than a Backfire bomber. Perhaps as big as a Blackjack."

A moment of silence. "Big as a Blackjack bomber?"

"Yes, Commander," replied Tupelov.

It was a biting voice that came over the radio now. "You listen to me, MiG seven-seven-echo. If we can see your tiny aircraft on our screen, do you not think we would be able to see two huge Blackjack-sized airplanes?"

Tupelov was careful. "Yes, Commander, I would think so. Are you saying you are not tracking them?"

"That is exactly what I am saying, seven-seven-echo," replied the commander. "We are tracking no aircraft of any kind near your location, except for the Aeroflot jetliner that is far from you. How do you explain that?"

Puzzled, Tupelov said, "I cannot explain it, Commander. I only know what I saw. The two aircraft were very large, and I almost collided with one."

A grunt came over the air. "Would you be suffering from hypoxia, seven-seven-echo?"

Tupelov was startled at this suggestion. "Absolutely not, Commander. My oxygen is working fine."

Another grunt. "Your flite plan shows you are assigned to the 77th Interceptor Regiment at Tbilisi. Is that correct?"

"That is correct, Commander."

The ground control commander's voice was hard now. "You are hereby ordered to continue on your flite plan. I am preparing a report about your hallucinations that will be on your commanding officer's desk when you arrive. In the future, I suggest you stay away from the vodka before piloting one of the Motherland's aircraft."

"But Comrade Commander," protested Tupelov, "I saw—"

"Our radar can *see* better than your vodka-filled, bloodshot eyes, MiG seven-seven-echo. In fact, I can *see* you now on my screen, but I do not *see* these two Blackjack-sized aircraft you claim to have nearly collided with. Now quit hallucinating, get off this channel, and report to your commanding officer in Tbilisi at once! Preferably sober. Sector two-three-Romeo, out."

Now another kind of fear gripped Tupelov. If such a report made it to his commanding officer's desk, his military career would be finished before it even began. Now he wished he'd kept his mouth shut. . . . But no. He'd seen those two—whatever they were—with his own eyes. That meant they were still out there somewhere. Why in the world couldn't the damn fool controllers see them? Tupelov was a bright young man, and he made a quick decision, for he knew it was his only chance. In order to avoid being hauled up on the carpet, branded a drunkard, and busted out of the service, he had to find those mystery aircraft and report their location. He scanned his instruments, and rapidly computed time and distance back to where the near collision had taken place. His external fuel tanks were almost empty now, but the fighter's organic tanks were full. To do what he was about to do was a violation of a ground control order. A court-martial offense. But what did he have to lose? Could jail be any worse than a humiliating dismissal from the Air Defense Force? Tupelov figured one fate was just as distasteful as the other. He gulped, jettisoned his external tanks, and whipped the Fulcrum around in a 180-degree turn to begin his hunt for the flying black batwings.

Day 5, 1308 Hours Zulu
THE *INTREPID*

Iceberg felt the vibrations of the Progress engine cease, causing him to experience relief like nothing before in his life. Whatever the Americans had sent up from Vandenberg, it was too little, too late, to stop the *Intrepid* now. In about fifty-five minutes he would be touching down on the Baikonur runway, and he was home free. He engaged the

393

reaction control thrusters and rotated the spacecraft into the correct attitude for atmospheric reentry. The explosive bolts holding the Progress engine in place would fire shortly.

Day 5, 1308 Hours Zulu
THE KESTREL

"Monaghan!" Maj. Gen. Chester McCormack's voice reverberated in Mad Dog's earphones. "What kind of crazy stunt are you trying to pull now?"

"We missed the *Intrepid*, Eagle One," said Mad Dog in a flat voice, "and now we're going after it. Give me the coordinates for the Baikonur Cosmodrome."

"You weren't authorized for—"

Monaghan's voice turned mean. "Save it, Eagle! I don't have time for your bureaucratic bullshit. You want to put me in jail after we get back home, then that's just Jake by me. But if we're going to catch that son of a bitch Iceberg, I need those coordinates—now!"

"Now you listen to me, *Commander*—"

"Beg pardon, sir," cut in Lamborghini, "but Mad Dog is right. We've already gone through de-orbit burn, and there's no way to reverse it. If we're going to have a chance at catching the *Intrepid* we need the coordinates at once."

There was a pause. "All right, hang on." Another few moments passed before McCormack returned. "Okay . . . the coordinates for the Baikonur Cosmodrome are forty-seven degrees forty-one minutes north, sixty-six degrees eleven minutes east."

Monaghan rapidly punched the numbers into the NavComputer and engaged the digital autopilot. The two astronauts immediately felt a change in the Kestrel's attitude and a quick eight-second burn of the OMS engine. Monaghan had executed a "seat of the pants" retro burn, and now the autopilot was correcting the spacecraft's course alignment for its descent to Baikonur.

"So what's your game plan?" asked Eagle One.

"We'll try and reacquire *Intrepid* by radar," replied Monaghan, "then see if we can close it up enough to fire the Sidewinders before we start heating up on reentry. If not, then we'll try to pick him up after we exit the blackout."

Another few moments passed, until McCormack asked in a resigned voice, "Do you go along with this, Pete?"

Lamborghini sighed. "Call me a late convert, but yes, sir. I think we have no choice but to try to nail the *Intrepid*. Whatever the risks." Now it was McCormack's turn to sigh. "Since you'll be coming down in Russia, make sure you find some way to destroy the Kestrel when you land. I would say the odds of our extracting you out of there are just about zero."

"Aye, aye, sir," replied Monaghan. "Now if you don't mind, we've got some hunting to do. Okay, Hot Rod, fire up your radar."

Day 5, 1310 Hours Zulu, 6:10 A.M. Local
CHEYENNE MOUNTAIN

Whittenberg, Fairchild, Dowd, and Lydia Strand stood in open-mouthed shock as they monitored the transmission between McCormack and the Kestrel. It was inconceivable that Lamborghini and that loco Navy pilot were going straight into Soviet airspace to chase down the *Intrepid*. It was insane. But there wasn't a blessed thing any of them could do about it.

If Whittenberg had had thirty seconds' warning that Monaghan was going to try something so stupid, he could have warned the lunatic off and told him about the stealth bombers. But it was too late now. And Whittenberg wasn't going to put out word about the stealth bombers over the radio without good reason. Maybe the Russians could descramble their transmissions, too. It seemed there was nothing they couldn't do these days—and now the Kestrel was flying into their midst. The CinC felt a load of depression sink into him. He figured Lamborghini was as good as dead.

"Mad Dog," muttered Strand softly.

Whittenberg turned. "What was that, Major?"

Strand shrugged. "I understand Commander Monaghan's call sign is Mad Dog . . . I guess that says it all."

Whittenberg nodded. "I guess it does." He was silent for a few moments before saying, "I shouldn't have let Pete go."

Day 5, 1311 Hours Zulu, 5:11 P.M. Local
THE FULCRUM

Fyodor Tupelov was back in the vicinity of his encounter with the flying black batwings. The ground radar station had detected his course reversal, and the controller was now issuing shrill orders and vile threats over the radio. But Tupelov had made his decision, and he turned off his radio receiver to keep the ground chatter from distracting him.

Now then, what to do? He could chase off in the same direction he'd last seen the mystery aircraft, but that didn't feel like the right move. He remembered a holiday trip he and his father had once taken into Siberia to hunt for caribou. They'd found some tracks of a small caribou herd in the snow, and the impetuous young Tupelov had started off after them. But their Yakut guide had quickly admonished the boy. "You do not want to be where they have *been*," he explained. "You want to be where they are *going*." The old trapper had taken Tupelov and his father off on a course that was at a right angle to the path of the animal tracks, and sure enough, they'd caught the caribou as they circled around on a feeding circuit.

Tupelov figured that was as good a strategy as any, and banked his aircraft sharply to the right. He'd travel due south for a hundred kilometers, then make a search pattern to the southeast until his fuel ran low and he had to put down somewhere. He was scared. But there was no turning back now.

He cut in the Fulcrum's afterburners.

Day 5, 1317 Hours Zulu, 3:17 P.M. Local
KALININGRAD FLITE CONTROL CENTRE

"The explosive bolts on the engine clamps have fired," squawked the speaker box, "and I maneuvered the orbiter around so I could see if the docking collar pulled free. It did. So there should be no problem on reentry."

In a relieved voice, Mission Commander Malyshev said, "Excellent, *Intrepid*. Stay in contact until you reach the transmission blackout."

"Roger, Flite Centre," replied Iceberg.

The Mission Commander looked at Popov, who nodded. Malyshev keyed his mike, and asked, " *Intrepid*, can you tell us anything about our Soyuz crew? They went off the air shortly after your retrofire."

"I have no idea, Flite Centre," said the flat voice. "Maybe that American spacecraft out of Vandenberg had something to do with it."

"Yes . . . perhaps so, *Intrepid*," said Malyshev bitterly.

Popov covered his eyes with his hands. "Vasili . . . Sergei," he whispered mournfully. Somehow he knew they were dead. More blood on his hands.

Day 5, 1320 Hours Zulu
THE KESTREL

The OMS engine died as the fuel ran out.

"Dammit!" Mad Dog was pissed. Without more fuel, the Kestrel couldn't close the gap to the *Intrepid*. "Can you take him now, Hot Rod?"

Lamborghini scanned his TID screen. "He's right on the edge of Sidewinder range at one hundred twenty-five miles. I'd hate to waste another shot. How close can we get to him on the backside of the blackout?"

"Probably pretty close," replied Monaghan. "I can put the Kestrel into a little bit steeper descent gradient than the shuttle. The NavComputer says we can make it to Baikonur as is. So we may have a chance."

"Then I vote we hold off and pick him up on the backside. I think we're just wasting a missile if we try it now."

"Okay, you got it," said Mad Dog.

There was a period of silence, but Lamborghini could hear his own heart thumping. He still couldn't believe they were going down into the Soviet Union. The typical emotions of air combat—which combined the gut-wrenching fear of dying with the exhilaration of being alive—washed over him. "Say, Leroy?" he said, in a jabbing use of Monaghan's Christian name.

"Yes, Peter?" replied Monaghan in an equally mocking voice.

"You really are mad as a hatter, aren't you?"

Monaghan chuckled nervously. "You betcha. A regular U.S. Government certified Section Eight." Then in a more somber tone he added, "Guess I should've asked you if you were game for this action before I hit the retro switch."

Lamborghini emitted a high-strung laugh. "Guess it's a bit late now, but no sense in having second thoughts. I pull on the blue suit every morning, and I know what that means."

"Yeah," agreed Monaghan. "But still, if you'd like to get out now, it's all right with me."

Lamborghini emitted another high-pitched laugh. "Thanks, but I think I'll tag along, if you don't mind."

397

Day 5, 1320 Hours Zulu
THE *INTREPID*

Iceberg was over Antarctica now, making preparations for atmospheric reentry. Like the machine he was, he ran through the procedures from memory.

First, he dumped the unused fuel from the orbital maneuvering engines, which Rodriquez had crippled. Since the engines had not been used much, there was a considerable amount to jettison, and it was necessary to get rid of the excess liquid so the orbiter would be properly balanced for reentry. Luckily, Rodriquez had not damaged the purge, vent, and drain circuitry.

He then flipped a series of switches into their proper position: Antiskid to ON. Nose Wheel Steering to OFF. Air Data to NAV. ADI Error to MED. ADI Rate to MED. Hydrazine Main Pump to NORM.

Finally, he corrected the orbiter's attitude until its nose was pitched up 32 degrees. This ensured that the silica tiles on the underbelly were properly positioned to absorb the horrendous atmospheric friction during the black hole of reentry.

Day 5, 1323 Hours Zulu, 5:23 P.M. Local
THE FULCRUM

Desperation was starting to cloud Lt. Fyodor Tupelov's thoughts, which were already punctuated by images of a dismal prison cell. He'd traveled a hundred kilometers south after a quick spurt from his afterburners, and was now flying a slow, sawtooth search pattern on a southeasterly course. There was no sign of the mystery planes as his Fulcrum flew in and out of the clouds. He wished he'd held his temper with the radar controller, but it was too late to worry about that now. Besides, the near miss had frightened him to his core, and there was no way he could have capped his anger.

He kept searching. Whenever the Fulcrum flew into a gap between the clouds, his eyes would dart back and forth, looking for some sign of the black batwings. But there was none. He activated his on-board radar and swept the airspace in front of him, but his screen showed no return. The image of the jail cell was becoming all too intrusive on his thoughts. . . . Then suddenly—there it was! At ten o'clock low! Over two thousand meters beneath him!

Tupelov's Fulcrum flew into the clouds again for a few moments, and when the fighter broke into the clear, the mystery aircraft was gone. He threw the fighter into a diving left turn and headed for the spot where he thought he'd seen the black batwing. Was his mind really playing tricks on him? Maybe he was suffering from hypoxia? No. He rejected both scenarios. His eyesight was excellent, and his oxygen system was working perfectly. He'd seen the . . . whatever it was.

Again he illuminated his on-board radar, and again there were no returns. Dammit. Where had the infernal thing gone? The young pilot's lip was starting to quiver when the black batwing popped out of a small thunderhead above him at two o'clock high, traveling on the same vector. Tupelov howled in relief and brought his fighter up to about three hundred meters behind and a hundred meters above the mystery machine.

Inside his oxygen mask, Tupleov's jaw dropped as he studied the bizarre vision before him. What on earth *was* it? The aircraft was unlike anything he'd ever seen. It had no vertical tail stabilizer, and no engine pods, as far as he could see. He squinted to look for markings, but he was too far back to discern the subdued black-on-black USAF lettering on the wings. And where was the second batwing? No matter. He had this one in his sights, and that was enough. He turned his radio back on. "Air control division, Sector two-three-Romeo, this is MiG seven-seven-echo. Do you read? Over."

The response was not long in coming. "Seven-seven-echo! This is the commander of Sector two-three-Romeo. You are to consider yourself under arrest! I order you to put down at the nearest airfield immediately! Is that clear?"

"I must disregard that order, Comrade Commander," replied Tupelov. "I have located one of the mystery aircraft that I almost collided with. I am on its tail at this very moment."

"I have had enough of your hallucinations, seven-seven-echo! I have you on my screen and there are *no* other aircraft in your vicinity! Do you understand me?"

Tupelov was incredulous. How could it not be on radar? It was right there, in front of him. And this was no hallucination. "I do not understand, Comrade Commander. I have the 'bogie' in sight not three hundred meters ahead of me. As I said before, it is approximately the size of a Blackjack bomber."

"Enough of this lunacy!" screamed the radar commander. "You listen to me, seven-seven-echo—"

"No!" shot back Tupelov. *"You* listen, Commander! I think you are

the one who is drinking the vodka. I have in my sights, at this moment, a large unidentified aircraft. I demand you connect me with your superior so I may report this sighting. You are obviously incompetent and unfit to execute your duties.''

"You are a dead man, seven-seven-echo! I will personally see to it that you are court-martialed and shot! There is *no* unidentified aircraft!''

Tupelov heard desperation in the commander's voice, so he played his trump card. "Very well, Comrade Commander. You give me no choice. If you do not patch me through to your superior, I am going to shoot this nonexistent aircraft down. Do you understand me? Shoot it down—that is my mission as an interceptor pilot, after all. Then when an investigation team finds the debris of this nonexistent aircraft, you will have to explain why you could not locate such a large airborne object on your radar. Then we will see which one of us hangs. . . . Now patch me through to your superior. At once!''

There was a long pause before a chastened voice responded: ''Wait one . . . I am patching you through to the Aerospace Defense Warning Centre.''

Day 5, 1330 Hours Zulu
THE *INTREPID*

Iceberg watched the external temperature gauge start to inch up. His altitude was 400,000 feet above the earth, traveling at 16,500 mph, and the external tiles were beginning to warm up. He jettisoned the remaining fuel in the forward reaction control tanks to further improve the spacecraft's balance, then inflated his anti-g pressure suit and switched the pitch, yaw, and roll controls to AUTO. In five minutes he would be in the grip of the blackout, and until he took back manual control, the guidance of the spacecraft rested in the hands of the NavComputer and digital autopilot.

Day 5, 1330 Hours Zulu
THE KESTREL

Monaghan hit the switch, and the pylons which had held the Phoenix missiles in place on top of the wings were released. Lamborghini watched them drift up and away from the spacecraft, and felt the pressure inside his spacesuit increase.

"The outside is heating up," said Monaghan. "On the way down I'm gonna make the S-turns a little tighter than programmed so we can reel in Iceberg on the flip side of the blackout. We're not gonna have that much time to find him before we have to put down somewhere, so let's keep the radar warmed up."

"I'm with you, Mad Dog."

Day 5, 1328 Hours Zulu, 4:28 P.M. Local
SOVIET AEROSPACE DEFENSE WARNING CENTRE

In the Crow's Nest of the Warning Centre, Col. Valery Leonov felt harried, frustrated, and tired. His uniform was rumpled and his wavy gray hair disheveled. He was still way behind on the stacks of paperwork left over from the fiasco caused by that contemptible American Blackbird spy plane a few days ago. He was having to explain to every general in the Soviet Air Defense Forces why he'd missed shooting the damned thing down. And if that wasn't enough, the Americans had gone crazy and increased their military posture to an incredibly high degree. On the large screen depicting the Northern Hemisphere, there were no fewer than a hundred American bogies—undoubtedly bombers and tankers—prowling above the Arctic ice cap. For what reason he couldn't fathom. There had been no notification of the exercise through normal channels, and the Russian-language BBC broadcasts—which he secretly monitored at home—had said nothing about international tensions. He could not understand what prompted such a massive unannounced exercise. In any event, increased American bomber activity required a heightened Soviet alert posture, which consumed more of his time, and that meant he would fall further behind on his paperwork.

His phone buzzed. He grabbed it and irritably said, "Yes, what is it?"

"Yes, Comrade Colonel," replied one of the controllers. "I have the commander of radar Sector two-three-Romeo in Kazakhstan on the line. He says he has an unusual situation in his area that requires consultation with you."

Leonov sighed. "Very well. Put him through."

There were some clicks and buzzes before another voice came on the line. "Comrade Colonel?"

"Yes, yes. What is it you want?"

"Ahem, yes, Comrade Colonel. This is Major Kubasov of Sector two-three-Romeo in Kazakhstan. I have a, ah, bizarre situation here that, I am afraid, must have your attention."

Just what I need, thought Leonov. More craziness. "Very well. Speak up. What is it?"

Major Kubasov of Sector 23-R quickly recounted his problem with the Fulcrum pilot, but, of course, couched it in such terms to make Tupelov sound like a lunatic. ". . . and he insists on talking to you, Colonel," concluded Kubasov.

In a resigned voice, Leonov said, "This entire week has been madness. Why stop now? Put him through."

"Yes, Comrade Colonel." A few more squeaks came through the line. "Go ahead, Colonel."

Leonov keyed his mike. "MiG seven-seven-echo, this is Colonel Leonov, duty officer commander of the Aerospace Defense Warning Centre. I understand you wish to speak with me."

There was static on the line until a young voice came through. "Yes, sir. This is Lieutenant Fyodor Tupelov, second battalion, 77th Interceptor Regiment, stationed at Tbilisi. I was flying a routine transport mission from Tselinograd to Tbilisi when I had a near midair collision with two unidentified aircraft in the clouds. I informed radar control division, Sector two-three-Romeo of the sighting, but was told there were no aircraft in my area except my Fulcrum, and I was ordered to land at my base. Sir, I felt the situation was serious, therefore I disobeyed those orders and commenced an air search for those unidentified aircraft. I located one and now have him in visual contact."

Hmmm, thought Leonov. This pilot did not sound deranged. "Wait one, MiG seven-seven-echo," he said, while rotating a dial to zoom in on Sector 23-R of his large projection screen. "I see you on my screen, MiG seven-seven-echo. Southwest of the Baikonur Cosmodrome. Is that correct?"

"Yes, sir."

"I see no other aircraft in your vicinity," said Leonov. "But you say you have this bogie in sight?"

"Yes, Comrade," replied Tupelov.

The colonel scratched his wavy gray hair. He found this intriguing. "Describe it to me," he ordered.

"Yes, sir. It is unlike anything I have ever seen. It is somewhat delta-shaped, but elongated. Black in color. Approximately the size of a Blackjack bomber. It is not propeller-driven, yet I see no engine pods for jet engines."

"Hmmm. How odd. Any markings on the wings or tail?" asked Leonov.

There was a delay in Tupelov's response. "No, sir. There are no markings on the wing or tail. In fact, sir, there is no tail stabilizer on this aircraft."

Leonov had only been curious about what the young lieutenant was saying, but when the words "no tail stabilizer" were mentioned, everything suddenly came into focus with horrifying clarity. All at once the American bombers over the Arctic ice cap made sense. The "invisible" mystery aircraft over Kazakhstan made sense. Even that Blackbird penetration made sense now. It was unthinkable. The Motherland was under a surprise attack!

Leonov looked at the screen once more. It showed only the Fulcrum. His heart leapt into his throat. "Lieutenant! That is an American stealth bomber!"

Tupelov was bewildered. He'd never heard the term "stealth bomber" before. That was because only senior officers received briefings on such advanced American technology. "I am sorry, Comrade Colonel. I do not know what a . . . 'stealth' bomber is."

"It is an American warplane designed to avoid radar detection!" shouted Leonov. "And it apparently works! Shoot it down! Shoot it down now!"

Day 5, 1332 Hours Zulu, 5:32 P.M. Local
THE FULCRUM

"Shoot it down! Shoot it down now!" screamed through Tupelov's headphones.

"At once, Comrade Colonel!" responded Tupelov. The young man's hands began trembling. Dear God, he thought. I am actually going to shoot down an American bomber. He tried to control his nervousness and remember his training. Missiles! Use the missiles! Tupelov eased back on his throttle and let the distance between him and the black batwing increase. His AA-10 radar-guided missiles had to travel at least two kilometers before the warhead would arm. He hung back four kilometers, losing sight of the target in the clouds ahead. The loss of visual contact bothered him as he illuminated his monopulse radar in the fighter's nose, which was directly in line with the bomber's tail.

Day 5, 1332 Hours Zulu, 5:32 P.M. Local
THE GHOST TWO STEALTH BOMBER

The electronic systems officer heard the warble in his earphones even before the visual warning appeared on the threat board. "We've been illuminated, Skipper! In the India-band. No missile lock yet."

"Dammit!" cursed the pilot as sweat spurted from his brow. "Maybe they don't have us on visual."

"Let's hope," said Whizzo in a tremulous voice.

"Yeah, let's see if we can shake 'em." Then the pilot heaved the stick forward and turned the wheel as sharply as he dared.

Day 5, 1333 Hours Zulu, 5:33 A.M. Local
THE FULCRUM

Tupelov's mouth was agape. He knew his nose radar was dead on, but he was not getting a return.

The lieutenant had never been briefed on the stealth bomber and had no idea of its true capabilities, but he knew the aircraft was very large. He'd seen it, and had it at virtual point-blank radar range. Yet it still would not generate a return. That was impossible, he thought.

Actually, it was possible. If Tupelov had dived straight down on the flat dorsal side of the aircraft, he would have gotten a radar return. But aimed directly from the side the radar signals were deflected or absorbed.

"Well, speak up, man," demanded the colonel over the radio. "Have you shot it down yet?"

Tupelov gulped. "I do not understand, Comrade Colonel. I am directly on the aircraft's tail, but my missiles will not lock on."

"What is your armament?"

"AA-10s, sir."

"I told you," huffed Leonov, "the American bomber is designed to avoid radar. Have you other missiles?"

"Yes, Colonel. Aphid heat-seekers."

"Then use them, you fool!"

"Yes, sir." Tupelov was still whipping in and out of cloud patches.

He looked ahead and the mystery aircraft was gone. His heart sank until he spied it below him, banking to the right. He wasn't about to lose it again, so he cut in his afterburners to close within two kilometers. He lined up the lumbering craft once more and activated his Aphid infrared missiles. But again, the projectiles refused to lock on—this time defeated by the bomber's rectored exhaust, which covered the heat signature of the engine.

By now, Tupelov was a basket case. "My Aphid missiles will not lock on either, Comrade Colonel."

A groan came back through the radio. "Then use your cannon, man! Your cannon!"

The young pilot was now mimicking the wide, serpentine turns of his target to stay on its tail. He hadn't thought about his single 23mm cannon, and didn't even know if the magazine was loaded. He turned on the arming switch, and felt a wave of relief when the green light indicated that some conscientious technician had filled the magazine with cannon shells before his Fulcrum left Tselinograd. He pressed his thumb against the red button on his control stick to clear the gun, and a washboard of vibrations ran through his seat—inducing a strange calm into Tupelov. He looked at the clumsy bomber, trying desperately to hide. It was pitiful, really. He knew it was no match for his nimble Fulcrum.

He pulled back on the stick and brought the Fulcrum up until it was four kilometers above the batwing. Remembering his training, he pushed the stick forward in an assault dive, and placed the target —God, it was big—in the fixed aiming circle of his head-up display. The Fulcrum continued to close on the batwing, but Tupelov waited until it almost filled the entire circle before pressing the red button.

Day 5, 1334 Hours Zulu, 5:34 P.M. Local
THE GHOST TWO STEALTH BOMBER

The pilot was beginning to hope the radar illumination had been a random sweep, but then he felt the vibration and heard the rapid *thump-thump-thump* of the 23mm cannon shells ripping into his fragile aircraft.

The stealth bomber's greatest strength was also its greatest weakness, in that all of the aircraft's defensive eggs had been placed into one basket—its maneuverability and speed had been traded off for the cloak of radar invisibility. But once that veil of invisibility was penetrated, all that was left for the bomber was a funeral dance. As the first slugs tore into the composite fiber body, the pilot knew it was all over. The cannon shells ripped through fuel tanks, hydraulic lines, electronic components, and on-board computers. The pilot and the Whizzo watched the control panel go haywire just before they were pitched forward into it by centrifugal force. The big bird was spinning out of control.

"Whizzo!" pleaded the Ghost Two pilot over the intercom. "Send the burst! Then eject! Eject! Eject!"

His companion hit the button which sent a high-speed, prerecorded "burst" message to the Milstar communications satellite, then reached under his chair and yanked on the eject handle. The section of ceiling above him disappeared with a *BANG!*, followed by the *KA-POW!* of his ejector seat exploding. With a swift kick in the butt, the rocket-propelled chair shot him through the opening in a blur.

Day 5, 1334 Hours Zulu, 5:34 P.M. Local
THE FULCRUM

Tupelov watched in fascination as little black puffs erupted on the dorsal side of the giant batwing. He then pulled his Fulcrum up in a tight loop so he could make ready for another pass, if need be—but he quickly saw that it wasn't necessary. The plodding aircraft seemed to sag to one side before cartwheeling down in a slow death spiral.

"I hit it!" cried Tupelov. "Comrade Colonel, I hit it! It is going down!"

There was a howl of exultation over the radio. "Outstanding, Lieutenant! Outstanding! I have your location plotted and I am dispatching a search party immediately."

"Roger, Colonel. I see a parachute deploying now . . . and another."

"Excellent," replied the colonel. "The search party will pick up the prisoners. Now, Lieutenant—I daresay it will soon be Captain—did you say you observed two stealth aircraft during your near miss?"

"That is correct, Colonel."

"Where is the other one?"

Tupelov was taken aback. "I do not know, Colonel. I was lucky to find this one with a visual search. I have not seen the other one. They must have taken separate vectors after the near collision."

Some seconds elapsed before the colonel returned. "Lieutenant, listen carefully. We do not know for sure, but these stealth aircraft may be carrying nuclear weapons. I have scrambled the 61st Interceptor Regiment at Balkhash to assist you, but it will take them at least forty-five minutes to reach your location. We must find that second bomber quickly.''

"Yes, Colonel. But I am starting to run low on fuel.''

"Damn the fuel!'' bellowed Leonov. "Find that other plane! Find it!''

"Roger, Comrade Colonel.''

Tupelov didn't know what else to do, so he started his sawtooth search pattern anew, in the direction his Fulcrum was pointing—which was northeast.

Day 5, 1335 Hours Zulu, 5:35 p.m. Local
GHOST LEADER

Ghost Leader was still flying an evasive pattern northwest of the Baikonur Cosmodrome when the ESO handed him a terse decoded message. The pilot read the paper, which said, simply, GO. He looked at his companion. "Okay, Whizzo, it's confirmed. We're going in. How long until the shuttle puts down on the target runway?''

The electronic systems officer checked his notes and the digital display on the NavComputer. He then rechecked it with his own navigation program on his personal Hewlett-Packard 41C calculator. "Looks like twenty-four minutes until the shuttle touches down. We've got eleven minutes to the IP from here, plus seventeen minutes on the bomb run. That's a total of twenty-eight minutes to target, which means the shuttle will be on the runway for four minutes before we drop—assuming our data on the shuttle landing time is accurate. . . . Also, all this chasing around up here has sucked up a lot of our fuel. I'm not sure if we can make it back to our refuel rendezvous as is.''

"Let's handle one thing at a time,'' countered Leader. "Just give me a bearing to the IP.''

Whizzo checked his instruments. "Come to one-five-four, Skipper.''

"Roger,'' replied Leader, and he began his turn. They were flying in an area where the cloud cover had thickened, and he felt confident that his aircraft was once again invisible. Ghost Leader had been on the inside track of the stealth prototype's development for years. He knew his warplane's capabilities as well as he knew the capabilities of the Russian radar system. He still couldn't explain how that fighter had spotted them visually, yet he was certain they were undetected by radar—because if the Russians had somehow acquired them on their radar screens, his bomber would've been blown out of the sky long ago. As long as they stayed in the clouds, he felt they were safe.

"I like this soup," said Whizzo, referring to the cloud cover. "It's a shame we have to drop under it for the bomb run. What do we do if there's a flock of fighters circling the target runway?"

Leader shrugged. "If that happens, we'll see if we can get a visual on the shuttle, then go back into the clouds and drop the load with the Norden Computer. That would be a long shot for such a pinpoint job, but that's the best we can do. No sense losing the bomber and our respective asses if we can't make it through to the target."

Whizzo nodded. Both men had guts, but they were also aware of their aircraft's painful limitations when it was exposed. Even a B-1 bomber with its Mach 2 speed, swing-wing maneuverability, and defensive systems wouldn't stand much of a chance against a pack of fighters out in the open.

"I wonder how Ghost Two is doing?" muttered the electronic systems officer, thinking about his buddy Whizzo on the other bomber.

In a reassuring voice, Leader said, "He's probably coming up to the alternate IP now."

Day 5, 1340 Hours Zulu, 8:40 A.M. Local
THE WHITE HOUSE CABINET ROOM

"Goddammit!" yelled Bergstrom as he slammed down the phone.

"Now what?" demanded the President.

The admiral's face had turned purple. "That was General Dooley at SAC in Omaha. They just received a burst radio transmission from one of the stealth bombers. It looks like one of them has been shot down."

The chief executive sagged in his chair, and in a voice that was numb from too many surprises, he asked, "What else can happen now?"

"Not much, I would say," said the Vice President.

"General Dooley says the burst message indicated the bombers were spotted visually by a Russian fighter aircraft," added Bergstrom. "The two stealth bombers split up and tried to evade detection by staying in some cloud cover. As far as General Dooley can tell, the other bomber is still in the air."

"They were spotted visually?" queried the Vice President.

"Yes, sir."

"Hmmm. How did the Russians know where to look?" asked the Secretary of State.

"Beats the hell outta me . . . sir," grumbled the admiral. "I've seen what that stealth bomber can do, and I don't think there's any way in hell it could've been picked up on radar. Our one consolation is that it assuredly broke into smithereens when it impacted on the ground."

Day 5, 1337 Hours Zulu
THE *INTREPID*

Iceberg watched his instruments carefully as the *Intrepid* plunged through the inferno of the reentry communications blackout. His eye was fixed on the Pascal air pressure indicator. When the readout clicked up to 480 Pascals—roughly equivalent to ten pounds of pressure per square foot—it meant there was enough airflow over the ailerons to generate a roll response from the orbiter.

The indicator kept moving up, and when it passed 960 Pascals, Iceberg knew the orbiter would now respond to the elevator control surfaces as well.

The *Intrepid*'s altitude was now 230,000 feet above the Indian Ocean. At that height the atmosphere was almost nonexistent, and it was the orbiter's 15,000-mph speed that generated enough air pressure over the wings to transform the vessel from spacecraft to aircraft.

Iceberg turned his attitude direction indicator rate switch to HI, then disengaged the digital autopilot and manually took over the steering of the vessel with his hand controller. The autopilot could have continued to handle the descent, but Iceberg liked to be in control. He watched the altitude and chronometer readouts on the NavComputer display screen, which showed that the *Intrepid* had already plummeted to 200,000 feet and was sixteen minutes to touchdown.

Iceberg carefully moved the hand controller to put the *Intrepid* into its first of four braking S-turns.

Day 5, 1337 Hours Zulu
THE KESTREL

Monaghan's heart was thumping now. All his instruments told him everything was fine with the spacecraft, but his windshield was covered with a glowing orange hue. The external thermometer said the Kestrel's skin temperature was approaching 1,800 degrees Fahrenheit, and he felt his spacesuit's cooling system working overtime.

"Damn," muttered Mad Dog. "This is a lot different from the shuttle. The flames weren't so . . . close."

"That's for sure," agreed Lamborghini, who felt himself growing warm, but didn't know if it was for real or just his imagination. "Mad Dog, I just thought of something."

"Yeah. . . . Like what?" asked Monaghan.

Lamborghini could feel sweat on his upper lip. "The infrared sensor in the nose. I'm not sure how this reentry heat will affect it. Maybe it could foul things up."

In a voice that was devoid of his usual confidence, Monaghan said, "Okay."

Changing the subject, Lamborghini said, "Dammit. I wish I knew what that second radar signature was that we hit with the Phoenix."

"No sense pissin' and moanin' about it now," mused Mad Dog. "Maybe you got some kinda false echo, maybe there was some space junk out there. Maybe the damned system was busted. Who the hell knows?"

"Yeah," came Lamborghini's rueful reply.

Mad Dog checked his NavComputer. "Okay, Hot Rod. Hang on. We're going into the S-turns now. I'm going to have to cut this very nicely if we're gonna surprise Mr. Iceberg."

Monaghan began playing the hand controller like a virtuoso, slicing the thin air with just the right edge to give the Kestrel a little faster braking than the *Intrepid*.

Lamborghini looked down and saw they were just crossing over the coast of Pakistan.

Day 5, 1347 Hours Zulu, 5:47 P.M. Local
GHOST LEADER

Whizzo double-checked the Global Positioning readout on the NavComputer display screen. "We're almost to the IP, Skipper.

410

Come to one-nine-seven . . . now. We're at IP. Seventeen minutes to target."

"Roger," replied Leader, and he turned the wheel to line up his aircraft for the final bomb run. "Whizzo, I'm going to stay up in the clouds at one-seven thousand, then thirteen minutes out from the drop point I'm going to begin a descent to two thousand feet for your final run."

"No sweat, Skipper," replied Whizzo. "Just get me in the ballpark and I'll lay in the Paveways nice and pretty." He checked his NavComputer again. "Sixteen minutes to target . . . speed four-four-two knots."

Day 5, 1348 Hours Zulu, 3:48 P.M. Local
KALININGRAD FLITE CONTROL CENTRE

"The spacecraft is responding well," said Iceberg's voice through the speaker box. "Approximately twelve minutes to touchdown. Altitude one-seven-seven thousand feet, speed eight-one-two-zero miles per hour."

"Excellent, *Intrepid*," replied Mission Commander Malyshev. "Be advised, conditions at the landing zone are heavy cumulonimbus clouds, ceiling at four thousand meters—that is, approximately twelve thousand feet. Wind from the northeast at seventeen kilometers per hour."

A moment of silence passed, betraying a crack in Iceberg's confidence. "I don't like the cloud cover, but there isn't much I can do about it. Since you don't have the microwave landing system, I won't have much time to line up the runway visually. That means I'll have to rely on the NavComputer almost exclusively. Are the coordinates you gave me for the runway precise?"

"Absolutely precise, *Intrepid*."

"They'd better be. Since the wind is coming from the northeast, I'll make my approach from the west."

"Because of the weather we did not make arrangements for a chase plane, *Intrepid*. You could collide with each other in the clouds. Are you sure you will be able to make it down?" asked Malyshev.

Another moment passed before the speaker box said, unevenly, "I'm sure."

Day 5, 1348 Hours Zulu, 4:48 P.M.
SOVIET AEROSPACE DEFENSE WARNING CENTRE

On Col. Leonov's projection screen there was still only Tupelov's Fulcrum to be seen. The 61st Interceptors from Balkhash were thirty minutes away, and the other American stealth bomber was still out there somewhere. Who knew—maybe there were more than just the two of them. The thought caused the colonel to swear. How could they defend against something they couldn't *see*? In frustration he keyed his mike. "Anything yet, Tupelov?"

"Negative, Comrade Colonel," replied the young pilot mournfully. "The area is totally socked in with thunderheads, and I am finding no gaps at all. I climbed to fifteen thousand meters to search for some holes in the cloud cover, but it is useless. I do not even know if the American bomber is in this vicinity . . . and I only have twenty minutes of fuel left."

"Never mind that. Stay up there as long as you can. You are authorized to eject if you have to."

"Roger, Colonel."

Another phone on Leonov's console buzzed, and he grabbed it. "Yes?" he snapped.

"Comrade Colonel," said one of the radar controllers, "I have Caspian Station on the line. They are picking up two, uh, unusual objects that have just crossed into Soviet airspace from Afghanistan."

"Marvelous," spat the colonel. "Just what I need at a time like this. What are the unidentified aircraft?"

"Two objects, Comrade Colonel. One is leading the other by approximately three hundred kilometers. Their course is almost due north, altitude fifty-two thousand meters, and their speed is—" The controller cleared his throat. "Their speed is approximately Mach thirteen."

Leonov didn't think he'd heard correctly. "What was that speed and altitude again?"

"Fifty-two thousand meters at Mach thirteen, Comrade Colonel."

"Mach thirteen? That is thirteen thousand kilometers per hour! Has everyone around here gone insane?"

"Look at the board, Colonel," offered the controller. Leonov spun the console dial and the projection screen zoomed out to reveal most of the Kazakhstan Republik. To the northwest there was a government aircraft—beeping its identification transponder and heading southeast at about 1,000 kilometers per hour—but the colonel didn't pay any

412

attention to that. Instead he looked to the south, and sure enough, there were two bogies moving north at an incredible speed and altitude. They were traveling twice as high and four times as fast as the American Blackbird spy plane. They did not have the ballistic characteristics of an ICBM, but they were unlike any aircraft he'd ever seen or been briefed about. For Leonov, this was the last straw, and he was convinced the intent of these bogies—whatever they were—had to be hostile. He guessed that the American stealth bombers, and now these bogies, were undoubtedly some kind of spearhead for the horde of enemy bombers hovering over the Arctic ice cap. Who knew? The Americans might launch their ICBMs at any moment. Leonov reached for the phone that was a direct line to the duty commander of the Soviet Strategic Rocket Forces. As he raised the receiver, his hand trembled. He felt he had no choice but to recommend a first strike against the Americans.

Day 5, 1349 Hours Zulu, 5:49 P.M. *Local*
BATTLE CENTRE, SOVIET STRATEGIC ROCKET FORCES, CHELYABINSK, CCCP

The command and control structure of the Soviet Strategic Rocket Forces was typically Russian, which was another way of saying it was typically Byzantine. There was one hierarchy that controlled the rockets themselves, and this structure was populated by professional officers in the Soviet military. However, a separate and distinct hierarchy existed for control of the nuclear warheads, and this was staffed by a special department within the Committee for State Security.

The control station within each missile silo was partitioned into separate compartments. In one compartment were two officers responsible for fueling and firing the missile if the launch order and verification code came through the communications link with the Chelyabinsk Battle Centre. In the second compartment of the silo were two KGB officers who exercised control over arming the warheads. Technically, the military officers could launch the rocket with an unarmed warhead, but that didn't make a whole lot of sense. Unless the two KGB officers worked in unison with each other to activate the warhead, the missile would remain a dud.

Similarly, this dual control structure existed at the apex of the Strategic Rocket Forces command pyramid. In the Battle Centre, which was much like the American SAC headquarters in Omaha, there

413

resided a general officer duty commander in the Rocket Forces, as well as a general officer duty commander of the KGB. They sat side by side in yet another Crow's Nest, overlooking yet another gigantic room with a large map projection screen.

The phone on the Crow's Nest console, which was a direct line to the Aerospace Defense Warning Centre, buzzed. The general put down his *Pravda* and picked up the receiver. "Battle Centre," he said casually.

"Yes, Comrade General, this is Aerospace Defense Warning Centre. We have detected two unidentified objects which have just crossed into Soviet airspace from Afghanistan. . . . It appears they may be space reentry vehicles of some kind. Also, one of our interceptors has just shot down an American stealth bomber in Kazakhstan province, and there are a hundred American bombers over the Arctic, poised to strike. Comrade, it appears the Rodina may be under attack! A nuclear attack! I am recommending a first strike against the Americans before it is too late!"

"A stealth bomber, you say?" asked the general.

"Yes, Comrade. A Triple Red-Omicron alert must be issued to the War Council of the Central Committee immediately," pleaded Leonov.

"Certainly. You have done well to notify us, Comrade. I will implement the alert at once."

Leonov was somewhat befuddled by the general's conversational tone. "Yes, Comrade General. I urge you not to delay."

The general's voice became sharp. "You need not tell the Strategic Rocket Forces how to fulfill their duties, Comrade!"

Chastened, Leonov retreated, "Of course, General, I only meant—"

"Very well, get off this line. I will see to this matter from here."

In a somewhat puzzled voice, Leonov said, "As you wish, Comrade General."

The KGB general hung up the phone and returned to his *Pravda*, just before his counterpart in the Strategic Rocket Forces walked back into the Crow's Nest. "So how are you feeling now, Vladimir?" asked the portly KGB general with an air of concern.

The wiry Rocket Forces general groaned. His face was green and he was holding his stomach. "Worse, I am afraid. And I simply do not understand what is the matter. I felt fine this morning, then all of a sudden it is as if I had contracted dysentery. I have not enjoyed spending most of the day in the toilet."

"Perhaps it was something you ate," suggested the KGB general in a sympathetic tone.

The Rocket Forces officer groaned again. "Do not speak of food, Arkady, please. All I have consumed today was our morning tea. It certainly could not have been that. We drank from the same samovar. You poured the cups yourself, and you are fine."

"Yes," agreed the KGB man, "absolutely fine. Perhaps you should go to the dispensary."

The Rocket Forces general emitted a grunt. "And let those incompetents go to work on me with their leeches? No thank you. I shall wait until our duty shift is over, then I will go to the Party clinic in town to see a real doctor."

"Yes, perhaps that is best, Vladimir," concurred the general in the green serge uniform.

Vladimir sat down gingerly and looked over at his KGB counterpart. Usually the heavyset KGB general was somewhat arrogant and aloof. But today he had been all kindness and understanding. Perhaps he had misjudged this man. "Arkady . . . I would just like to say, I appreciate your covering for me while I have been . . . indisposed."

The KGB general shrugged. "Think nothing of it, Vladimir."

Vladimir was turning a darker hue of green. "Has everything been quiet today?"

"Extremely so. In fact, I just had a routine communications check from the Aerospace Defense Warning Centre. Everything is quiet there as well."

Vladimir nodded, then groaned again and ran back through the door toward the toilet.

After watching Vladimir run off, the KGB general patted his breast pocket, which held a vial of pills given to him by the KGB Chairman himself.

One of the pills had gone into Vladimir's tea earlier that morning.

Day 5, 1352 Hours Zulu
THE KESTREL

During combat, or other moments of high stress, Mad Dog Monaghan would relieve some of the tension by repeating the same curse over and over, putting emphasis on the last word. As he surveyed the blanket of giant cumulonimbus clouds before him, the old habit returned.

415

"Dirty *bastard*! Dirty *bastard*! Dirty *bastard*!"

"So what's the deal, Mad Dog?"

"Dirty *bastard*! Listen, Hot Rod, we're in a pickle, and I think this is our only shot. The Baikonur area is totally socked in by those clouds ahead and below us. They're thirty thousand feet thick if they're an inch. I think Iceberg is probably somewhere in front of us, but there's no way we're gonna be able to search for him visually in that soup. And since we have to keep the Kestrel trimmed up for gliding, we can't move your radar around much."

Lamborghini's frontal view from the backseat wasn't very good, so he had to rely on the pilot's assessment. "So what do we do?"

"I'm killing the air brake," said Monaghan, and Lamborghini felt the spacecraft-turned-glider lurch forward a bit. "I'm going to eliminate the last braking S-turn and take the Kestrel in a wide semicircle. That will eat up time, but still let us retain some speed and kinetic energy."

"Speed and kinetic energy for what?" queried Lamborghini.

"To keep us airborne long enough so Iceberg can get on the ground. As we execute the semicircle we'll still be descending while coming around one-eighty degrees. I'll try and time it so that when we finish the maneuver we'll be under the cloud cover and have enough steam left for one pass over the cosmodrome. Maybe we can find him on the ground and nail him there. The *Intrepid* will be nice and hot from reentry, so you should be able to get a lock-on with the Sidewinders."

Lamborghini could have faulted a lot of Monaghan's ideas, but he had to admire the man's rapid-fire diagnosis of their situation—and they obviously didn't have time for thoughtful debate. "Sounds good to me, Mad Dog. Go for it."

"Roger," replied Monaghan, and he put the Kestrel in a slight bank to the left. They were traveling at Mach 3.3 and had just dropped through ninety thousand feet.

Day 5, 1351 Hours Zulu, 5:51 P.M. Local
GHOST LEADER

"Thirteen minutes to drop point," chanted Whizzo. "Altitude one-seven thousand, ground speed four-three-nine knots."

"Roger," said Leader, while pushing the stick forward. "Starting descent now. Get ready."

"I'm ready, Skip," replied Whizzo, as he checked his fire control systems for the umpteenth time.

Day 5, 1352 Hours Zulu, 5:52 P.M. Local
CONTROL TOWER, SHUTTLE RECOVERY RUNWAY, BAIKONUR COSMODROME

By the time he reached the glassed-in observation platform, Grigory Vostov was huffing, puffing, and swearing at the climb up the stairs. He wondered why they had not installed an elevator in the damned tower.

"Good afternoon, Comrade Chief Designer," greeted the tower controller. "I was told you would be arriving."

It took some time before the overweight Vostov could regain his breath to ask, "Binoculars?"

The controller was helpful. "Of course, Comrade. You are welcome to use mine," he said, while lifting off the neck strap.

Vostov took them without thanks. "The communications link to Kaliningrad?" he puffed.

The controller pointed to the phone. "That receiver there."

Vostov nodded, then lifted the Carl Zeiss lenses to his eyes.

Day 5, 1355 Hours Zulu
THE *INTREPID*

The top fringes of the towering cumulus clouds were still below the *Intrepid* as it came out of its fourth and final braking S-turn. Iceberg was transfixed on the NavComputer now. There was only one chance to hit the runway, and all he had to rely on was the NavComputer, the altitude/vertical velocity indicator, and the other instruments on his craft.

The *Intrepid* was now entering the terminal area energy management phase of its landing approach—five minutes and fifty-five miles from the runway, traveling at 1,700 mph, and rapidly descending through 75,000 feet. Iceberg was carefully husbanding the kinetic energy of the vessel now, trading speed and altitude for lift and distance. The remaining energy had to be managed precisely so the huge spacecraft would be able to execute its critical flare maneuver just prior to touchdown.

Iceberg pitched the hand controller to the right and gently applied

417

pressure to the right rudder pedal. He was putting the orbiter into proper alignment with where the runway was supposed to be. His flight suit was becoming sweat-soaked as the digital altimeter ran backward through 60,000 feet and the *Intrepid* plunged into a giant thunderhead.

Day 5, 1355 Hours Zulu, 5:55 P.M. Local
THE FULCRUM

Fyodor Tupelov was about to throw in the towel. His computations showed his remaining fuel would keep him aloft for twelve or thirteen minutes at the most, and he wasn't about to punch out at sixteen thousand meters altitude. At this height, he figured his blood would freeze in an instant. The colonel be damned. He would give it five more minutes, then he was going to dive through the clouds and hunt for an airfield.

Day 5, 1355 Hours Zulu, 5:55 P.M. Local
GHOST LEADER

The black batwing broke through the clouds at twelve thousand feet. Leader and Whizzo scanned the screens of the nose cameras to look for the recovery runway, but the scene was somewhat hazy from the overcast and they couldn't locate it. "Hit the zoom," ordered Leader. His companion turned a dial and the images of all three screens enlarged.

"Still don't see it," muttered Whizzo.

"We'll stay on this heading," grumbled Leader. "What's your readout?"

Whizzo checked his instruments. "Altitude eleven-two hundred and descending. Speed four-four-two knots. Nine minutes to drop. The computer says we're in the groove."

Day 5, 1358 Hours Zulu, 5:58 P.M. Local
THE *INTREPID*

Iceberg cursed. He was still in the clouds, but his altimeter showed he'd just gone through fourteen thousand feet and was eight miles from the runway. He would have to enter the last phase of the runway approach blind, and that meant there would be very, very little margin for lateral adjustment if his position was wrong, because from this point the *Intrepid* would be dropping almost like a stone and its maneuverability would be severely hamstrung. He pushed the hand controller forward to put the orbiter into a 22-degree glide slope—a descent gradient seven times steeper than a commercial airliner. The orbiter would cover the last seven miles and drop the final thirteen thousand feet to the runway in just eighty seconds. If the runway wasn't where it was supposed to be, he was in deep shit. Even with a name like Iceberg, Kapuscinski had a dry throat now.

The airspeed indicator showed 411 mph as the *Intrepid* broke into the clear.

"There it is!" Iceberg shouted to himself. Right in front of him, but just a shade to port. No problem. Iceberg, the master pilot, eased the hand controller a little to the left and applied left rudder. He also decreased his air brake a bit to maintain the 22-degree glide slope. Perfect.

Once aligned, Iceberg retrimmed the orbiter and watched the altitude/vertical velocity indicator on the head-up display as the runway rushed up to meet him.

Day 5, 1359 Hours Zulu, 5:59 P.M. Local
THE BAIKONUR CONTROL TOWER

"There he is!" shouted Vostov. He discarded the binoculars and grabbed the phone. "Popov! I have him in sight! He will touch down in a matter of seconds!"

The tower controller said nothing as he snapped pictures at five frames a second with his 35mm Nikon motordrive camera.

Day 5, 1401 Hours Zulu, 6:01 P.M. Local
THE *INTREPID*

5,000 . . . 4,000 . . . 3,000 . . . . It almost seemed like the digital altimeter couldn't run backward fast enough. At two thousand feet, Iceberg pulled back heavily on the hand controller and increased the air brake to put the *Intrepid* into its final flare maneuver. The nose pitched

419

up from 22 degrees to a 1.5-degree glide slope, and the last remnants of altitude and kinetic energy clicked off. Iceberg armed the landing gear. Everything came down to this moment. Fourteen seconds to touchdown, speed 268 mph, altitude ninety feet. Iceberg hit the LANDING GEAR DN switch and the tricycle gear exploded out of the nose and wheel wells.

The tarmac came up to meet the *Intrepid*, and at 216 knots, Iceberg felt a rumble as the rear wheels met the 5,000-meter runway at the Baikonur Cosmodrome. He put the air brake to 100 percent and gently eased the hand controller forward. The nosewheel squealed as it touched down and Iceberg immediately popped the braking parachute. The drogue quickly deployed, then the main chute, and the braking action caused Iceberg to pitch forward a little. But the *Intrepid* still continued to roll. It had landed with a full load in its cargo bay, and the additional mass required more braking power to stop it. When the speed slowed to 100 mph, Iceberg pushed on the pedals to apply the wheel brakes. Slower . . . slower . . . slower . . . until finally, a mere eighty meters from the end of the runway, the *Intrepid* came to rest and the braking chute collapsed like a deflated balloon.

"*Yeeeaaah!*" shouted Iceberg, in an exultation unlike anything he'd experienced in his life. The landing was like a catharsis, uncorking his emotions from some inner psychological dungeon. "I have done it! Mother, I have done it!"

Day 5, 1402 Hours Zulu, 6:02 P.M. Local
KALININGRAD FLITE CONTROL CENTRE

"His roll speed is decreasing," came Vostov's voice through the speaker box. "Still rolling . . . rolling . . . rolling. Dear Lord! He's running out of runway! . . . Wait . . . no. He is slowing rapidly. Now. Yes. It has stopped. He has done it! Yes, he has landed!"

A cheer rose up from the entire room. Popov looked up at the ceiling in supplication before plopping into a chair—exhausted.

The relief in the Flite Centre was palpable as Kostiashak patted Popov on the shoulder. "You have done well, General. You are to be congratulated, as is everyone here."

Popov could not have cared less what the little bastard thought. "You are too kind, Comrade Chairman," he said bitingly.

Day 5, 1402 Hours Zulu, 6:02 P.M. *Local*
GHOST LEADER

"I think that's it," said Ghost Leader coldly while pointing at a small white line on the screen.

Whizzo nodded. "I think you're right."

Leader looked closer. "Can't tell if the target is there or not, but I'm starting the bomb run now. Leveling off at two thousand." And he pulled back on the stick. "Any bad guys?"

Whizzo looked at the threat board. "Negative, Skipper."

"Guess our luck is holding," said Leader in a hopeful voice.

"Four minutes to drop," chirped Whizzo. "Speed four-six-four knots."

Day 5, 1401 Hours Zulu, 6:01 P.M. *Local*
THE KESTREL

Monaghan's digital altimeter read 11,877 feet as the space fighter popped out of the clouds.

"Son of a *bitch*! Son of a *bitch*! Son of a *bitch*!" yelled Monaghan in frustration. "Hot Rod, I'm afraid we aren't gonna make it. Our airspeed is down below six hundred knots. . . . We can't glide much farther. You see the runway anywhere?"

Lamborghini's hawk eyes scanned the horizon. It was still hazy from the overcast and sunset was approaching, but there was no rain. "Dog, I think that's it over to port. Way in the distance."

Monaghan looked over to port but couldn't see anything. Hot Rod must have some kind of zoom lenses in his eyeballs, he thought. "I don't see it," Mad Dog said in defeat. "No way we could make it anyway. We'd better look for a place to set her down." He focused his eyes on the ground to search for a landing zone, and saw a bizarre object cross his beam at an obtuse angle—something that looked like a giant black manta ray skimming over the sandy bottom of the ocean. Mad Dog immediately threw the Kestrel into a slight banking left turn to give Lamborghini a better view, and to come to a parallel course with the strange craft. "Hot Rod! Do you see what I see?"

Lamborghini looked down, and although it was a shock, he knew immediately what it was. He'd seen it in a hangar at Nellis Air Force Base during a supersecret briefing with General Whittenberg. It took

421

him a moment to digest it all, but then everything fell into place. What had Whittenberg's secretary said? "He's on the phone with General Dooley. You know how it is when those two get together." Dooley meant SAC. And SAC meant bombers. "Mad Dog! That's a . . ."

"A stealth bomber?"

"Yeah. I saw it once at Nellis. I bet SAC sent it in to nail the *Intrepid* if we missed."

"Shit," cursed Monaghan. "Why didn't that son of a bitch McCormack tell us about it?"

Lamborghini's mind raced. "Because there was no reason for McCormack to know about it. We weren't supposed to be here. Remember?"

"Oh, yeah," came the sheepish reply. Monaghan took a moment to absorb the situation, then said, "Well, you think we should tail him?" He checked the altimeter, which showed they were passing through ten thousand feet. He figured the stealth bomber was six to seven thousand feet below them.

Lamborghini quickly said, "No. If we're being picked up on ground radar we could draw attention to the bomber. We'd better break off. Maybe our radar signature will decoy the Russians away."

Mad Dog had a hard time taking his eyes off the black manta ray, which was a couple of miles ahead of them now. God, what a freaky-looking contraption. "Yeah. Okay. You're right. Let's get outta here and find someplace flat to set down." He was about to put the Kestrel into a banking turn to the right when something roared out of the clouds—not four hundred yards in front of them.

Day 5, 1402 Hours Zulu, 6:02 P.M. Local
THE FULCRUM

Tupelov shot out of the clouds in a powered dive, then began pulling up to look for an airstrip. Ground radar would have to help him, no matter what that colonel said. His eyes started scanning the ground when—Saint Kirill! There it was! Right below him! Excitedly he keyed his mike. "Colonel! I have found the second American bomber!"

"Excellent, Tupelov!" hooted the Colonel. "Shoot it down at once! It may be carrying nuclear weapons!"

Having learned that his missiles were worthless against it, Tupelov again put his Fulcrum into an assault dive and began lining up the black

422

monster in his aiming circle. All he could think about was another American flag painted on the side of his MiG-29.

He pushed the throttle forward slightly, and the batwing started growing in his sights.

Day 5, 1402 Hours Zulu, 6:02 P.M. Local
THE KESTREL

"*What is it?*" yelled Lamborghini, while trying to peer over Monaghan's shoulder.

"Shit! I think it's a Flanker. No. Wait a minute. No. Not a Flanker. It's a Fulcrum . . . and he's taking a bead on that stealth bomber! Hot Rod, see if you can take him with the Sidewinders!"

Lamborghini began swearing. He'd already tested the spacecraft's infrared sensor during their descent, and he'd been right about the Kestrel's heated exterior screwing up the instrument. The TID display was nothing but garbage. Sweat poured off Lamborghini's forehead like raindrops. "Dammit! The IR sensor is still fucked up!" There was desperation in his voice now. "Mad Dog, drop the nose! Point it right at the Russian's ass!"

"Roger!" replied Monaghan, and he shoved the hand controller forward.

Lamborghini set the Sidewinders for independent guidance and retracted the silica plates that covered the wing nacelles. All he could think to do was bore-sight the missiles and fire them, hoping their own sensors could lock on to the Fulcrum's tailpipe. He punched the red button on his hand controller, and a Sidewinder jumped out of the left wing and ignited, followed by its partner two seconds later.

The space versions of the Sidewinder were unlike the conventional kind in that they possessed no aerodynamic fins to stabilize them as they traveled through the atmosphere. The effect was much like shooting an arrow with no feathers on the tail of the shaft—the projectile wobbled in flight.

However, the space Sidewinders did have the vectored thrust that helped keep them on track. But as the wobble action of the missiles became greater and greater, the on-board microprocessor had more and more difficulty compensating for the increased jerky motion of the weapons—until finally the vectored-thrust tail nozzle of the first Sidewinder couldn't compensate fast enough and the first missile started to pinwheel as it closed on the Fulcrum.

"Shit!" yelled Mad Dog. "One of the Sidewinders went wild! And I see tracer rounds!"

Day 5, 1402 Hours Zulu, 6:02 P.M. Local
THE FULCRUM

Tupelov was just pressing the cannon trigger on his control stick when a swirling pyrotechnic torch flashed by his cockpit. He instinctively flinched, and before he could fix his eyeballs on the object, his Fulcrum bucked violently and began tumbling end over end. He wrestled with the control stick and the rudder pedals, but all he kept seeing was a rapid-fire sequence of earth-clouds-earth-clouds-earth-clouds. Tupelov groped for the eject handles, but the tumbling was so fast now that the centrifugal force kept him pinned against his shoulder harness. "Mayday! Mayday! Mayday!" he cried into his radio. "Seven-seven-echo is going down!" His fingers were finally able to curl around the handle, and he yanked with every fiber of his strength.

Day 5, 1403 Hours Zulu, 6:03 P.M. Local
THE KESTREL

"*We got him!*" screamed Monaghan. "We got him! Just barely, but we nailed him. The second Sidewinder sliced his tail fins clean off. He's tumbling down."

Lamborghini heaved a sigh of relief. "Any more bandits?" Not that we could do anything about it, he thought.

Monaghan did a quick sweep. "Nothing that I can see. That Fulcrum just popped a chute, though." His gaze turned back to the stealth bomber, which was pulling away. "Go get that motherfucker Iceberg!" Mad Dog yelled after the batwing. "Nail him!"

Day 5, 1404 Hours Zulu, 6:04 P.M. Local
GHOST LEADER

On the belly of the stealth bomber a panel rotated, revealing a washtub-sized pod with a faceplate of zinc sulfide glass. Inside the pod resided an AAQ-9 forward-looking infrared (FLIR) camera, and a

424

yttrium-aluminum-garnet (YAG) laser, which were aligned together in precise calibration.

Inside the bomber, the crew was blissfully unaware of the air battle that had taken place in their wake—the Fulcrum's initial rounds had gone wide.

Whizzo shoved his face against the hood covering the FLIR video screen and flipped the camera to 2x power magnification. "I think I've got it," he intoned through the intercom. "Come to port four degrees." He felt the aircraft move, and adjusted the controls to keep the camera aimed on the same spot. "Yeah, that's gotta be it. Jesus, that shuttle is hotter than a pistol," he said, while inspecting the brilliant infrared image.

Looking at his center video screen, Leader said, "I've got it, too," and asked, "What's the range?"

Whizzo put the cross-hair cursor on the bright object and hit the YAG laser rangefinder. A digital readout flashed on the screen just above the cross-hairs. "Range two-three kilometers. Maintain this speed and altitude. Opening weapons bays and activating fire control now." The major's voice was growing strained. He always wondered what the Real Thing would be like.

The doors on the four weapons bays slapped open while the fire control computer ordered the laser to lock its invisible light onto the *Intrepid*. Once the beam was locked on, the stealth bomber could jink, climb, or bank to a fare-thee-well, but the belly pod would rotate and keep the laser fixed on the orbiter.

"Range one-five kilometers. Come starboard two degrees," ordered Whizzo. "Speed down to three-five-zero."

"Starboard two degrees," echoed Leader. "Speed three-five-zero. Let me know when you've got control."

Whizzo locked the fire control computer into the digital autopilot. "I've got it," he said tersely, with his face still married to the screen hood.

The fire control computer digested the time, distance, and speed to the target and rapidly calculated the precise point of bomb release. The device then transmitted this information to the autopilot, which flew the aircraft in exact conformance to the fire control instructions. The crew was no longer in the loop. They were now passengers on a flying weapons system.

"Six kilometers to drop . . . five . . . four . . ." The *Intrepid* grew bigger on the FLIR screen. "Three kilometers . . . two . . . one . . . bombs away!"

Eight Mk 83 Paveway bombs dropped cleanly from their racks, causing the aircraft to lurch upward as it became lighter by four tons. Each of the Mk 83 projectiles deployed their tail fins as the Texas Instruments Paveway guidance system came alive. On the nose of each Mk 83 was a mushroom-shaped snout, which held a silicon detector array that was tuned to the 1.064-micron wavelength of the YAG laser. As the Mk 83s arced through the air, the detector array sensed the laser light reflecting off the *Intrepid* and transmitted the information to the bomb's on-board guidance computer. The tail fins were rapidly adjusted so that the trajectory of the projectiles would intersect with the laser reflection on the side of the orbiter.

Like a school of airborne sharks, the Paveway bombs sensed the laser blood splashed on the *Intrepid*, and were plummeting down to savage their victim.

Day 5, 1406 Hours Zulu, 6:06 P.M. Local
THE INTREPID

Iceberg had unhooked his shoulder harness and was quickly tending to the post-landing checklist. He paused to look up, and saw how close he'd come to the end of the runway. Earlier models of the shuttle did not have the braking parachute. Without one, the *Intrepid* would've undoubtedly sailed off the end of the tarmac. He looked out to the side and saw a covey of ground vehicles rushing up the runway access road with their strobe lights flashing. Coming to greet their new hero, he figured—and that started him thinking about what kind of deal the Russians were going to set him up with. Hell, he could probably move into the Kremlin if he wanted to. In fact, he figured he could have anything he wanted now. Because he—Julian Kapuscinski—had just pulled off the grandest hijacking in the history of piracy.

The first thing he'd do was hold one of those press conferences. Now *that* would be something. Finally, he could shove it to those American bastards in spades. For what they'd done to his mother. And for what Felicia had done to him. All those years he'd played by their rules just so he could keep his secret. He'd even up the score now. Think of it. The Iceberg who was decorated by the President would host a press conference out of the Kremlin to tell those Americans he'd played them for fools. Yes, this was going to be sweet.

*   *   *

426

As Kapuscinski was contemplating his future, the first Paveway sailed over the top of the *Intrepid*—clearing it by a hair—and went on to impact on the far side of the runway. The force of the blast rocked the spacecraft so violently that Iceberg's face was thrown into the control panel, shattering the glass CRT screen of the NavComputer and crushing some of the indicator lights. Iceberg was dazed and barely able to lift his bloodied countenance from the broken instruments. The last thing that registered in his brain before he left this life was the sight of broken shards of bloodstained glass sticking out of the NavComputer display.

In rapid succession the second, third, and fourth Paveways plowed broadside into the soft aluminum skin of the orbiter's cargo bay, detonating simultaneously and blasting the innards of the *Intrepid* apart like a harpooned whale. The remaining four Paveways joined the conflagration, turning what was left of the spacecraft into a funeral pyre of flame and dust for Frank Mulcahey, Geraldo Rodriquez, and Col. Julian Kapuscinski.

Day 5, 1406 Hours Zulu, 6:06 P.M. Local
THE BAIKONUR CONTROL TOWER

Caught in a wave of sheer ecstacy, Vostov watched the army of ground vehicles rush toward the *Intrepid*, while the tower controller continued to snap pictures with his Nikon camera. What a coup! thought Vostov. What a victory! He could almost smell his seat on the Politburo now.

He was savoring the triumph when, out of nowhere, a bizarre, unearthly black batwing rose up into the air and soared over the runway, just as the *Intrepid* erupted before him.

The blast shook the tower, shattering one of the large panes of glass and throwing Vostov to the floor, along with the controller. "Alert the air defense battery, you fool!" yelled the Chief Designer. "We are under attack!"

Day 5, 1406 Hours Zulu, 6:06 P.M. Local
GHOST LEADER

"*Bull's-eye! Bull's-eye! Bull's-eye!*" howled Whizzo. "We got him, Skipper! We blew it away! Good Christ, there's nothing left but smoke now!"

427

"Great shooting, Whizzo! Great shooting! Okay, let's bust outta here and send the message! Yahoo!" Ghost Leader pulled back on the stick and the black batwing climbed toward the protective concealment of the puffy clouds.

Day 5, 1407 Hours Zulu, 6:07 P.M. Local
THE KESTREL

After the Fulcrum was shot down, Monaghan spied a flat plateau—a mesa—and turned the Kestrel toward it to make a landing. His speed was less than 400 mph now, and they had just passed through 2,500 feet.

"Mad Dog, I see some smoke over to port," said Lamborghini with excitement. "Maybe they got him."

"Jeez, I hope so. Can't worry about that now. I'm gonna try to put down on that plateau up ahead."

"*Beeeeeeeeeeeeppp!!*"

Lamborghini's threat warning receiver emitted its distinctive warble. "Mad Dog! We've been locked on!"

"Oh, shit!"

Lamborghini scanned the sky above him but saw no bandits. Then he looked down, and his blood froze. There it was. A jinking little pinpoint of light with a smoky tail. The last time he'd seen something like that was over Thai Binh, North Vietnam. "Mad Dog! SAM coming up from nine o'clock low!"

Monaghan looked down, and felt absolutely helpless. His aircraft had no power, they couldn't climb, they couldn't maneuver. They were dead in the water. "Hold on, Hot Rod!" he said in a squeaky voice. What he was about to try was crazy, but he couldn't think of anything else to do. He watched the pinpoint grow bigger and bigger, until at the last possible moment he yanked on a lever beside his leg.

The braking parachute billowed out from the Kestrel's tail, cutting its speed just as Mad Dog shoved the space fighter into a dive.

The SAM couldn't compensate quickly enough and whizzed by the Kestrel, exploding moments later. But neither Monaghan nor Lamborghini saw the blast, because now the Kestrel was headed straight down.

The flat-top plateau was rushing up at them. Monaghan jettisoned the braking chute and the Kestrel started falling even more rapidly. "Here we go, Hot Rod!" yelled Mad Dog as he deployed the landing gear. When the plateau filled the spacecraft's entire windshield, he pulled the hand controller all the way back, putting the Kestrel into an extremely sharp landing flare.

Lamborghini felt a washboard rumble as the landing gear touched down on rough terrain. He was violently shaken in the backseat, but after a few seconds he could feel the spacecraft's speed slowing. Lord! Evading a SAM and making a dead-stick landing on a Kazakhstan mesa. What a piece of flying!

Monaghan felt like he was in a bronc's saddle, but it looked like he'd pulled it off. The Kestrel had slowed to seventy-five mph and Mad Dog had a grin on his face.

But then the Kestrel sailed into a gently sloping trough in the center of the plateau. Monaghan gasped as the spacecraft's wheels momentarily left the ground, then came down hard. The tricycle gear snapped off like so many pretzels, and the Kestrel skidded along the bottom of the trough until it was pitched up into a cartwheel by the upsloping side.

Instinctively, Monaghan wrestled with the hand controller and refused to give up, cursing, "Come on, you son of a bitch!" But it was useless. In the windshield the sky was swirling, swirling—until, in a heartbeat, it was replaced by a rock formation that seemed to reach out for them. "Oh, Christ, Pete," he cried, "I'm sorry . . ."

And the Kestrel impacted on the Kazakhstan plateau.

Day 5, 1408 Hours Zulu, 4:08 P.M. Local
KALININGRAD FLITE CONTROL CENTRE

"It is utterly destroyed!" wailed the speaker box. "There was some type of giant plane. It came out of nowhere and dropped dozens of bombs, then disappeared. Some of the ground vehicles were destroyed and their crewmen killed. It is a disaster! An absolute disaster!"

Vostov's wailing hit poor Popov like a sledgehammer, and he collapsed back into his chair, totally crestfallen. "I cannot believe it," he mumbled. "All of that work . . . the danger we faced . . . our cosmonauts dead . . . all for nothing. Nothing."

The little KGB Chairman patted Popov on the back. "You need not be upset, General," he comforted. "Having the *Intrepid* intact no longer matters."

Popov looked up in disbelief. "No longer matters? What the hell do you mean, it no longer matters? Two of our men have been killed! The

American astronauts have been killed! And you say it no longer matters?''

The diminutive Chairman extended his gold cigarette case with a charming smile. "The deaths were a pity, to be sure, but I assure you, the *Intrepid* is no longer important. . . . Cigarette, General?''

Dumbfounded, Popov extracted one of the Pall Malls.

Day 5, 1415 Hours Zulu, 6:15 P.M. Local
THE GENERAL SECRETARY'S ILYUSHIN JETLINER

As he approached the Baikonur Cosmodrome, the pilot of the General Secretary's Ilyushin saw a dark plume rising in the distance. The sky was at dusk, but there was no mistaking the nature of that dark tower. It was smoke. Puzzled, the pilot set his radio to the cosmodrome's air tower frequency and keyed his microphone.

"Baikonur Tower, Baikonur Tower, this is Alpha Gold One. Do you read? Over.''

"Roger, Alpha Gold One. We read you, over.''

"Baikonur, I am approaching your location from the northwest, speed five-eight-three kilometers per hour, elevation two-three hundred meters. I see a tower of smoke in your direction. Please advise us of the origin of this smoke, over.''

There was a pause. "Negative, Alpha Gold One. We cannot advise you. This is restricted airspace and you are not authorized for that information.''

"Not authorized?'' The pilot almost laughed. "Listen, you swine. This is Alpha Gold One. Do you have any idea who I have on board?''

"That does not concern me, Alpha Gold One. You are not authorized for any information on your sighting.''

Bureaucrats, cursed the pilot. "Very well, Baikonur Tower. I will let you speak to my passenger personally. That will change your mind—and quickly.''

The pilot turned the aircraft over to the copilot and left the cockpit. He found the General Secretary reading White TASS dispatches and presiding over still another vodka.

"Are we there yet?'' The General Secretary's speech was a bit slurred. "Almost. General Secretary, could I ask you to step into the cockpit for a moment? There is something I think you should see.''

The American shuttle is probably on the ground, thought the

430

Russian leader. Too bad we missed the landing, but it would be interesting to see it from the air. "Certainly," he said, putting down his vodka.

The General Secretary never made it to the cockpit. As he rose from the divan, the kilogram of plastique explosive—which Colonel Borisov had secretly placed in the wheel well—detonated, transforming the shiny airliner into an orange ball that lit up the dusky sky.

Day 5, 1415 Hours Zulu, 9:15 A.M. Local
THE WHITE HOUSE

Bergstrom's phone buzzed, and he grabbed it. After listening for a few moments, he leaned back and looked at the ceiling through the heavy cigar smoke in the room. "They got him," he said finally. "The second stealth bomber got him. They transmitted 'Touchdown.' That means complete success."

The NSC EXECCOM exhaled in mass relief.

"What about the space fighter? And the crew?" asked the Vice President.

Bergstrom shook his head mournfully. "Who the hell knows? Dead probably."

Day 5, 1507 Hours Zulu
ALTITUDE: 129 MILES
ORBITAL INCLINATION: 83 DEGREES

They were passing over Antarctica again, approaching the Indian Ocean. Lubinin looked at his wrist chronometer once more—not that it made any difference now. He examined the debris scattered around them, which was all that remained of their Soyuz. Initially, he'd been amazed and grateful they were unharmed by the spaceborne shrapnel —but now he was wondering if a quick death might not have been preferable.

Lubinin turned to his friend. Yemitov's face was red and his breathing rapid. Soon his countenance would turn purple and the breathing would cease, for his tanks were empty and he was relying only on the residual oxygen left in the suit.

431

"My indicator . . . has been red . . . for some minutes, Vasilivich.
. . . How long . . . for you?"

Lubinin looked at his oxygen gauge. "Perhaps three minutes,
Sergeivich."

Yemitov was struggling to form the words now, for asphyxiation
was a painful death. "If . . . I have to die . . . what better way . . .
for a cosmonaut . . . than to die in space . . . with a friend."

Lubinin reached out and took his comrade's gloved hand.

"Vasilivich . . ." Yemitov was purple now, and could barely whisper through his grimace. ". . . I am glad I . . . am going first . . .
I was always afraid of . . . dying alone."

Yemitov's tight grip on Lubinin's hand suddenly weakened, but the
surviving cosmonaut did not let go. From a zippered pocket in the
sleeve of his suit, Lubinin extracted a tiny gold ikon on a chain. It was
a gift from his grandmother which he always secretly carried with him
when he flew. "Fear not, my friend," he said softly to his dead
companion. "We will be together again soon."

Day 5, 1600 Hours Zulu, 5:00 P.M. Local
VILKOVO, ON THE BLACK SEA, CCCP

The Defense Minister drank heartily from the crystal goblet. The
day had been delightfully warm, and while lying by the pool, he and
the Foreign Minister had consumed two bottles of potent wine.

"Ahhhh," sighed the Foreign Minister as he drained his own
goblet. "There is nothing quite like fine Moldavian wine. Is that not
so, Konstantin?"

"You are absolutely correct, my dear Comrade," replied the
Defense Minister. "It has been a most enjoyable afternoon, and I
implore you to stay and be my guest for dinner."

"I would be delighted, Konstantin," purred the old diplomat
gratefully.

"I have ordered pheasant for our meal, and I have obtained some
American films for us to watch on my videotape device after dinner."

"Excellent, Konstantin. You are a gracious host." The Foreign
Minister took another sip, then chuckled. "Can you imagine how
cold it must be in Moscow? We were wise to come south for the
weekend."

"Most wise," agreed the military chieftain.

At that moment, the host and his guest heard a heavy-handed knock on the door, but they thought nothing of it, for it was soon followed by the echo of a servant's footsteps going to answer the summons. But then some disturbing noises were heard. Sounds of raised voices and heavy boots tramping on the marble foyer. The two ministers turned to see a KGB general and eight KGB troops, armed with Kalashnikov AK-47 submachine guns, exit the house. The troops quickly formed a phalanx at one end of the pool.

The two Politburo members, trying to look defiant in their swimming trunks, rose up. "What is the meaning of this?" roared the Defense Minister. "Who the hell are you?"

"I am of the Committee for State Security, Defense Minister," said the general evenly. "You and the Foreign Minister are hereby placed under arrest."

"Arrest?" barked the aging diplomat. "On what preposterous grounds do you think you are going to arrest *us*?"

The general was quick to reply. "You are charged with crimes against the state. Specifically, warmongering and placing the Motherland in jeopardy of a nuclear attack, as well as failing to defend the Rodina from an attack by American bombers."

"This is madness!" bellowed the old soldier, and he screamed, "Igor!" to summon his Cossack bodyguard.

From behind a hedge, an apelike man appeared, wearing the uniform of a sergeant in the Soviet Army and brandishing a sidearm. No one could fault the bodyguard's loyalty or bravery as he charged forward with his pistol blazing. Nor could anyone fault his marksmanship, for he was able to drop two of the KGB troops with his well-placed shots. But the frontal assault demonstrated that Igor was more than a little stupid, for the six remaining AK-47s opened up and split him apart like a ripe watermelon. He was blasted back into the pool, and his blood quickly turned the crystalline water to red.

The two ministers stood in shock, and offered no resistance as they were handcuffed and led away to the waiting armored van.

Day 5, 2237 Hours Zulu, 12:37 A.M. Local
THE KREMLIN

As the snowflakes drifted down onto the onion domes of the Kremlin, they caught the reflections of the incandescent lights that illuminated the grounds. It made the late-night scene look like something out of the *Nutcracker*.

But the eleven disgruntled men gathered around the large conference table ignored the beautiful scene. They were all irritated at having their Sunday evening disturbed with a summons to an emergency Politburo meeting—a meeting convened well after midnight for reasons that still remained unknown.

As they sat there, grumbling amongst themselves, the adjoining door to the General Secretary's office opened and in strode KGB Chairman Vitali Kostiashak, carrying three bulky files under his arm. He took his seat at the head of the table—the chair usually reserved for the General Secretary. A flurry of eyebrows went up over this breach of protocol.

"Comrades," began Kostiashak with a mournful voice, "I apologize for summoning you here so abruptly. But while I was resting at my dacha this weekend, certain events were brought to my attention that demonstrated—with the most conclusive evidence—that the very security of our Motherland was placed in jeopardy these past few days. Yes! The very security of our nation was endangered by the most monstrous scheme ever conceived in our history. Absolutely monstrous!"

The eleven men were taken aback by the forcefulness and vehemence of the little man's speech. They looked at each other in bewilderment.

"And what is this monstrous plot you speak of, Comrade Chairman?" inquired the burly Agriculture Minister.

Kostiashak tapped down a Pall Mall, then slowly went through the motions of lighting it up, allowing the drama to build. "Early this morning I was contacted by a patriot. A Soviet patriot who—despite the danger to himself—possessed the courage to come forward and expose this treacherous crime against our Motherland. Against our Party. . . . The substance of this incredible crime is that General Secretary Vorontsky, the leader of our Party, the leader of the Rodina, executed a plan on his own authority"—Kostiashak looked up and down the table—"to hijack an American space shuttle and bring it down to the Baikonur Cosmodrome!"

The group uttered a stunned gasp, then mumbled among themselves until the portly Mining Minister said, "Steal an American space shuttle? I do not understand. Why? How?"

Kostiashak leaned forward. "Concerning the why, the motivation is obvious. As we all know, Vorontsky's position as General Secretary has been precarious ever since the loss of our own two space shuttles—the *Buran* and the *Suslov*. I have spoken with each of you individually concerning this matter. In any case, he embarked on this desperate act of piracy—apparently thinking that capturing an American spacecraft would solidify his position as General Secretary. Without the knowledge or consent of the Politburo or the Central Committee, he took it upon himself to exercise his authority over the Space Ministry to put this treacherous plot into action. . . . That explains the why, Comrade. To answer your question of how, I give you the patriot who courageously came forward to expose this despicable crime." Kostiashak nodded to Colonel Borisov, and the door was opened to allow the stocky-looking patriot to enter.

"Lieutenant General Likady Popov," said the KGB Chairman stonily, "I have brought you before my fellow members of the Politburo so that you could bear witness that General Secretary Vorontsky, acting illegally and without authorization, somehow inserted his own agent aboard the American space shuttle *Intrepid* and forced you to use your position as Director of Spaceflite Operations to receive the spacecraft at the Baikonur Cosmodrome."

Kostiashak fondled an ivory button on his double-breasted suit and continued. "You are here to bear witness that General Secretary Vorontsky conspired, and acted in concert with, Ivan Pirdilenko of the Plesetsk Cosmodrome to shoot down a second American shuttle which was launched by the Americans to prevent the loss of their stolen spacecraft. This was done in violation of our antisatellite treaty with the United States.

"And you are here to bear witness that the American shuttle *Intrepid* did, in fact, land at the Baikonur Cosmodrome." Kostiashak reached into a file and pulled out a stack of photographs which depicted the *Intrepid*'s landing. He shoved them down the table, and each Politburo member grabbed one.

"Finally, General Popov, you are here to bear witness that for the last month General Secretary Vorontsky and his dastardly accomplices have kept a gun to your head, and forced you to cooperate with them. And it was only at great personal peril to yourself that you were able to contact me at my dacha this morning and expose this crime. Will you bear witness, General Popov, that all I have said here is the absolute truth?"

Popov was no fool. If he replied, "No, Comrade Chairman, that is incorrect," the general would face a torturous interrogation, followed by a one-way trip to the cellars of Lefortovo Prison. But on the other hand, if he said, "Yes, Comrade Chairman, that is true," a kinder fate might await him.

Popov said, "Yes, Comrade Chairman, that is true." Kostiashak released a puff of smoke that clouded his dark features. With a humble voice, he said, "You are to be commended, General. The Rodina is in your debt."

The burly Agriculture Minister picked up the photograph of the *Intrepid* touching down at the Baikonur runway and muttered, "This is unbelievable. Absolutely unbelievable. We have hijacked an American space shuttle? It is too much to accept, and I profoundly resent that this was done without our knowledge. But still . . . as I think about it, I fail to see the harm in stealing an American spacecraft. In fact, this idea appeals to me."

Kostiashak was on the man like a wolf. "You stupid oaf! What do you think this is? Some kind of schoolboy prank?" He motioned to Borisov. "Bring in the Colonel."

The door opened again, and a middle-aged, overweight colonel with wavy gray hair entered—his knees quaking. He wore the uniform of the Soviet Air Defense Forces.

"Colonel Leonov," said Kostiashak gently, "you were the duty officer at the Aerospace Defense Warning Centre in Magnitogorsk earlier today, is that correct?"

The colonel cleared his throat and said, "Yes, Comrade Chairman."

"Would you be so kind as to describe the events of this afternoon?"

Leonov gulped. Never had he been so scared. "Very well, Comrade," he began cautiously. "When I came on duty today at Magnitogorsk, I found the American Strategic Air Command at an unusually high level of readiness. More than a hundred bombers and tankers were over the Arctic ice cap, holding their positions—almost within range of a cruise missile launch." Leonov gulped again. "I have never seen such a high level of readiness," he continued, "and it surprised me because we received no notification of this military exercise through the normal channels. As you know, we have an agreement with the Americans for mutual notification of major military exercises. Because of this lack of notification, our interceptor forces in the northern defense districts were placed on a high level of alert. . . . Then this afternoon, one of our interceptor planes spotted two American stealth bombers in Soviet airspace near the Baikonur Cosmodrome."

"*Stealth* bombers?" asked the aging Party ideologue.

"Yes, Comrade Minister," replied the colonel. "They are American warplanes designed to avoid radar detection, and I am sorry to say they are most effective. Had our pilot not stumbled upon them and made a visual sighting, we would never have known they were there.''

"That is most disturbing," said the portly Mining Minister in a low voice.

"Continue, Colonel," instructed Kostiashak.

"Yes, Comrade. After our pilot made a visual sighting he was able to shoot down one of the bombers—"

"Marvelous!" shouted the Agriculture Minister while raising a big fist in the air. "A triumph of our Soviet defenses."

"Yes, Comrade," agreed Leonov. "But the pilot lost sight of the second bomber because of cloud cover. . . . At this same time our phased-array radar station on the Caspian Sea picked up two unusual objects entering Soviet airspace from Afghanistan. They were traveling at an incredibly high altitude and speed. It was only later that I learned the objects were an American space shuttle and a smaller space vehicle of some kind, but at the time I did not know this. In any case, because of these reentry vehicles and the stealth aircraft, I became convinced that the unannounced American bomber exercise over the Arctic ice cap was no exercise at all. I felt it could only mean that the Soviet Union was under a surprise attack. I then notified the Strategic Rocket Forces Battle Centre and recommended a Triple Red-Omicron alert.''

"Triple Red-Omicron?" barked the willowy, bespectacled Science Minister. "That is a recommendation for a first strike against the Americans."

"That is correct, Comrade Minister," agreed Leonov, "but with the presence of the stealth bombers and the unusual space vehicles, I felt I had no other choice but to recommend such an action."

The Science Minister was enraged. "I am a member of the National War Council. Why was I not informed?"

"An excellent question, Comrade," said Kostiashak. "I am a member of the War Council myself, and I was not informed either. Why do you think that is so, Colonel?"

Leonov was almost stammering now. "I have no idea, Comrade. I can only tell you that the Strategic Rocket Forces duty commander was notified in accordance with prescribed procedures, and the duty commander—a general—said he would implement the Triple Red-Omicron alert.''

"Well, if that is the case, I should have been informed via my special communications device," said the Science Minister bitterly.

"As you should have, Comrade Chairman."

"Most certainly," concurred Kostiashak. "That will be all, Colonel. You have performed your duties well. You may go." Leonov almost sprinted from the room.

"So there you have it," said Kostiashak with venom. "The American shuttle was hijacked, American bombers were poised to strike with their cruise missiles, and an American invisible bomber had penetrated Soviet airspace." The KGB Chairman turned on the Agriculture Minister. "Now do you think stealing an American shuttle is a schoolboy prank?"

The burly minister hunkered down in his chair. "Well, nothing happened, after all."

"Nothing happened?" barked Kostiashak. He pulled out another stack of photographs and shoved them down the table. The Politburo members picked them up and saw the blackened craters on the Baikonur runway, with part of the *Intrepid*'s tail section and a landing gear sticking out of the ground. "The second American invisible bomber blasted the spacecraft to pieces. And the Americans were obviously prepared to do more than that to prevent their precious shuttle from falling into our hands. Does a hijacking still appeal to you now, Comrade Minister?"

The Agriculture Minister hunkered down in his chair even further and remained silent, his eyes glowering from under his heavy eyebrows.

"But still," commented the Mining Minister. "These measures seem extreme for the loss of one shuttle. One would expect protests. Even threats. We did that when the traitor Belenko defected with his MiG-25 to Japan. But to send warplanes into Soviet territory? And their nuclear bombers so close? All for one shuttle? That puzzles me as much as it disturbs me."

"Exactly," agreed Kostiashak. "But my intelligence sources informed me that the payload aboard this particular shuttle contained some components for their space defense platform. Critical components relating to their technological breakthrough. The cargo included some highly sophisticated computer parts and an isotope for something called"—Kostiashak studiously checked his notes—"a gamma-ray laser."

"Ah," said the willowy Science Minister. "That explains it. No wonder they went to extraordinary lengths to destroy it." The scientist pondered the ceiling, then took off his glasses. "Had the situation been reversed, we might have been forced to do something desperate ourselves."

"Absolutely," agreed Kostiashak. "And the Americans are a very excitable and unpredictable people. Worse than the Afghans. That is why the General Secretary's crime was so heinous. He almost plunged us into a nuclear exchange with the Americans in an attempt to solidify his own position. It was folly, my Comrades. Criminal folly!"

The Agriculture Minister wasn't giving up so easily. He leaned forward and put his muscular forearms on the table. "You expect us to believe that General Secretary Vorontsky, acting completely alone on his own authority, conspired to steal an American shuttle without our knowing it? I find that impossible to believe. If that had truly happened, the Americans would have been screaming for blood. Where are the protests? The threats? The howls of defiance about this hijacking?"

"You are quite right, my dear Comrade," said the little Chairman. "The General Secretary did not act alone. He had accomplices. And, as you say, the Americans did, indeed, scream." Kostiashak adjusted his silk tie before turning to Borisov. "Bring in the prisoners."

Once more the door opened, and this time two manacled figures were thrust inside. The portly Defense Minister was not wearing his usual resplendent uniform with its acre of ribbons and medals, and the Foreign Minister was sans his Italian tailored suit and Borsolino hat. Instead, they were wearing the rough gray woolen garments worn by guests registered at Lefortovo Prison.

"What is the meaning of this?" shrieked the Defense Minister.

"I demand to be released from these chains at once!" bellowed the Foreign Minister.

Kostiashak was unmoved as he slapped open the file. "Defense Minister Konstantin Zholobov, you stand accused of crimes against the state. You stand accused of deliberately cutting off the Triple Red-Omicron notification warning from the Strategic Rocket Forces to prevent the War Council from learning of your treachery. You stand accused of failing to defend the Rodina's borders against American bombers who dropped their bombs on Soviet soil. You stand accused of thrusting your country perilously close to a nuclear exchange. How do you answer these charges?"

The Defense Minister strained so hard against his chains it looked as if they might break. "What is happening here? What alert? What bombing attack? This is madness! It is a conspiracy!"

"And I would wager you know nothing of a shuttle hijacking?" challenged Kostiashak in a mocking tone.

"What?" screamed the Defense Minister in an incredulous voice.

Kostiashak nodded to Popov. "General?"

Oh, what the hell, thought Popov. In for a penny, in for a pound. Sorry, old friend, he thought, it is either you or I. The stocky general gave a reluctant shrug, and said, "It was the Defense Minister who held the gun on me much of the time. I was truly frightened."

"Incredible," wheezed the Science Minister.

"Take him away," ordered Kostiashak.

"Likady! What are you saying?" screamed the Defense Minister as he lunged against his chains, but one of the KGB guards whacked his solar plexus with a truncheon and the old soldier went down like a sack of potatoes. He was dragged from the room.

"And as for you, Foreign Minister," seethed Kostiashak. "I would like you to explain these cables, which were obtained from the ministry's message centre." Borisov distributed copies. "The first cable is from Ambassador Yakolev. He relays the Americans' allegation that the Soviet Union is in communication with their space shuttle. Your cable in reply states that you and the Defense Minister investigated the matter, and that there was no communication—a bald-faced lie if I ever heard one. The next cable from Ambassador Yakolev expresses the Americans' outrage over the destruction of their shuttle—the *Constellation*—which they sent to intercept the *Intrepid*. He warns that the Americans are threatening a military response. And what do you do? You send this reply"—Kostiashak shook the pages in his hand—"instructing our honored ambassador to do nothing and to remain silent. Silent!"

"The first two cables are genuine," said the old diplomat. "The Defense Minister and I *did* investigate, and we found nothing suspicious. I know nothing of the other two cables."

"So you admit to misleading our ambassador. And as for knowing nothing of the other two cables, Foreign Minister, these documents came from your own ministry's message centre. The instructions to Yakolev went out under your name. And you claim to have no knowledge of them?"

"That is correct," said the old diplomat defiantly. "My aide handles all of the cable traffic in and out of my office. You have only to ask him, and he can tell you the other two cables are fabrications."

Kostiashak barked a laugh. "You mean your aide, Aleksandr Kulikov—the lackey who always kept your tea cup filled during our Politburo meetings?"

"Yes!" responded the Foreign Minister angrily. "Bring him here and he will tell you this is all some kind of fantasy!"

"I would hardly use him as a character reference, Comrade Minister. Your aide-de-camp is a French spy."

The entire room gasped again as Kostiashak pulled out yet another file and shoved it down the table. "It is all there. Transcripts of clandestine meetings with French 'diplomats,' wire taps, photographs of message drops. Yes, it is all there. Your aide-de-camp was working hand-in-glove with the French."

The Foreign Minister was not to be put off. "I demand Kulikov be brought here for questioning!"

"Unfortunately," said the KGB Chairman softly, "Kulikov is not available. Prior to my learning of this plot only this morning, Kulikov escaped on an Air France flite to Paris. My passport control officers said his special diplomatic exit visa was personally signed by you."

The old diplomat visibly sagged. He knew his survivor's luck had finally run out.

"Take him away," ordered Kostiashak.

Not wanting a truncheon in his old gut, the Foreign Minister went without complaint, looking incredibly feeble.

"There you have it, my Comrades. The Rodina has been the victim of a power-mad dog in our midst. General Secretary Vorontsky has brought us to the edge of a nuclear war through an evil conspiracy. Had it not been for the courageous actions of General Popov, I shudder to think of what might have happened."

The Science Minister shook his head and turned to Popov. "You are to be praised, General. I must confess this is all difficult to accept. We must bring General Secretary Vorontsky before us at once for interrogation."

Kostiashak looked down, and in a subdued voice he said, "I am afraid that is not possible."

The Science Minister's eyebrows went up. "Not possible?"

"That is correct, Comrade," replied Kostiashak mournfully. "I have been informed that the General Secretary's airplane crashed while on approach to the airfield at the Baikonur Cosmodrome. All on board were lost. Apparently he was en route to take personal charge of the scene at Baikonur. Alas, he will never be able to face Soviet justice."

There was a shocked pause, until the portly Mining Minister said in a daze, "Well, I am at a loss as to what we should do."

In a somber tone, Kostiashak said, "I, too, share your feelings of profound betrayal, Comrade. This has been a shameful chapter in our history. But the situation with the Americans is still tenuous. I recommend that we send a message to the American President at once. We inform him that the Soviet Union is under new leadership, and that we totally refute the hostile actions taken by the late General Secretary Vorontsky. We ask them to recall their bombers, and call for a summit meeting to demonstrate our sincerity. Speed is of the essence."

The Mining Minister nodded. "I would agree," he said, "but we must now choose a new General Secretary."

"True," agreed Kostiashak, "and I must confess that in view of the severity of this crisis, and my position as guardian of the Party, I see no alternative nomination for the post of General Secretary than"—he paused for effect—"myself."

Fifteen minutes later, Vitali Kostiashak walked out of the Politburo conference room as the new General Secretary of the Communist Party Central Committee of the Soviet Union.

After the KGB Chairman had placed his name in nomination, the remaining Politburo members took one look at the empty chairs of the Defense and Foreign Ministers, and another look at Vitali Kostiashak sitting at the head of the table—the place reserved for the General Secretary.

They got the message.

The gauntlet had been thrown down.

If the Politburo members wanted to try to dislodge Kostiashak from the General Secretary's chair, it would mean going toe to toe with the man who controlled the gargantuan KGB apparatus. And the loser of such a confrontation would, indeed, lose *everything*. The idea of putting their country dachas, Western tailored suits, Zil limousines, lavishly appointed apartments, special medical clinics, and girlfriends (or boyfriends) in jeopardy had little appeal, so the remaining cabal of men inside the conference room decided that this young Kostiashak fellow would do just fine as General Secretary. The vote was unanimous.

After a quick champagne toast, Kostiashak dispatched Colonel Borisov to the Kremlin's communication centre with a message for the American President, then he brought Likady Popov into the adjoining baronial office of the General Secretary for a private word. "You should have been an actor, General," Kostiashak said with genuine admiration.

"I saw little choice," replied Popov in a straightforward manner. Kostiashak nodded. "You have labored hard, General, and we still have much to discuss. But you must be weary. My driver will return you to your wife. Tell her the new General Secretary is in her debt for enduring your absence for so long."

Popov nodded, but did not leave. "I cannot help but wonder. What about Pirdilenko? You mentioned him. And Vostov? Both men have friends—and influence. They could talk. Make trouble."

Wistfully, the new General Secretary sighed and looked out the window. "I am afraid I did not tell you the tragic news, General. Comrade Pirdilenko's helicopter went down while en route back to Plesetsk . . . and Comrade Vostov, alas, he was killed during the attack by the American bomber at Baikonur."

Popov was stunned. "Killed during the attack? But we talked to him *after . . .*"

"The Comrade Chief Designer was killed in the attack," repeated Kostiashak. Then he returned his gaze to Popov. "I know you find this distasteful, General, but in the intelligence world we refer to this as 'tying up loose ends.' "

Popov was still stunned, but nodded his understanding. Warily he eyeballed the little man. "And what about me? Am I one of your 'loose ends,' as you put it?"

The new General Secretary was gentle in his response as he touched the general's stocky shoulder. "No, my Comrade, you are not a 'loose end.' You see, Vostov and Pirdilenko were ambitious men, and as you mentioned, they could have made trouble. You, on the other hand, are not overly ambitious. Therefore you are not a threat to my plans."

Popov appeared relieved. But his conscience could not blot out the lives that had been lost. "It appears you have achieved what you wanted to achieve—General Secretary. I must now take my leave and inform the families of cosmonauts Lubinin and Yemitov of their deaths."

Kostiashak took Popov's arm and guided him toward the door. "General, throughout this adventure I have admired your concern for your men. We will talk more later, but before we part, I must leave you with two thoughts. First, do not take all that has occurred during the last few days at face value—things are not always what they seem. And second, never, ever, embrace the notion that I have done what I have done in the pursuit of selfish ambition. You will find that I—like you—am a patriot. . . . Good night, General.'' And Kostiashak closed the door on a befuddled Popov.

Finally alone, the new General Secretary walked to the large bay window and sat down on the bench-style windowsill. He took out the last Pall Mall from his gold cigarette case and fired it up with the Dunhill lighter, then gazed out on Cathedral Square and saw that the snow had stopped falling. The incandescent lights had been extinguished for the night, and the clouds had parted to reveal an inky sky full of shimmering stars.

Kostiashak leaned back to contemplate the scene and allow the tension to ebb from his body. His mind wandered back over the tumultuous events of the last five days, and as he began to relax, his thoughts reached farther back in time—once again returning to his studies at Princeton. As a student, Kostiashak had not only studied the American President Franklin Roosevelt, but had also scrutinized the life and writings of a Florentine nobleman and diplomat named Niccolò Machiavelli.

Kostiashak had always felt history had treated Machiavelli unfairly, because—for some unfathomable reason—the sixteenth-century diplomat's name had become synonymous with deceit and treachery. But in fact, Machiavelli was an extremely capable public servant with high ideals whose actions were governed by a bare-knuckled pragmatism. In reviewing the previous week's events, the new General Secretary recalled one particular passage from Machiavelli's masterpiece, *The Prince*, which he had read while studying at the Firestone Library and had put to use this very day: "A prince being thus obliged to know well how to act as a beast must imitate the fox and the lion, for the lion cannot protect himself from traps, and the fox cannot defend himself from wolves. One must therefore be a fox to recognize traps, and a lion to frighten wolves."

Day 5, 2353 Hours Zulu, 6:53 P.M. Local
THE PENTAGON

T/Sgt. Jack Donley, United States Army Signal Corps, was leaning back in his chair, sipping a cup of coffee and thumbing through his copy of *Sports Illustrated*. The sandy-haired former semipro second baseman was just getting settled into his shift, looking forward to reading an article on his hometown Chicago Cubs, when the teletype suddenly clattered to life. The surprise *brrraaap! . . . brrraaap! . . . brrraaap!* of the high-speed printer almost caused him to spill his coffee. He looked at the clock and was even more surprised. What the hell was the matter? There were still thirty-seven minutes until the hourly circuit test. But the printer continued with its litany of *brrraaap! . . . brrraaap! . . . brrraaap!*

Donley got up and went over to the printer, which was spitting out a stream of Cyrillic letters. Then it dawned on him. Jesus! This wasn't a test. This message was for real! He rang for the interpreter.

Donley was a shift operator for the Washington-Moscow "Hotline" teletype. Established in the wake of the Cuban missile crisis, the Hotline (officially known as the Direct Communications Link) was established to allow rapid, direct communications between the American President and the top Soviet leadership. Initially, the device utilized a landline cable system, but was later upgraded to a satellite link that hooked into the Russian Molniya and American Intelsat communication birds. Although Hollywood reinforced the false perception that the Hotline was a telephone, it was, in fact, a teletype system which was tested on an hourly basis. The Russians would transmit in Russian, and the Americans in English.

The Hotline was first used extensively in June 1967 during the Arab-Israeli Six-Day War, when President Lyndon Johnson and Premier Aleksei Kosygin fired messages back and forth. It allowed the two leaders to probe for each other's trigger points during the fast-moving crisis without the nettlesome delay of diplomatic communications or the danger of garbled messages.

The interpreter walked into the communications center. He was a bookish, bespectacled Navy lieutenant who was a doctoral candidate in Georgetown University's modern language department. "What have you got?" he asked casually.

"Beats the shit outta me, sir," replied Donley. "Why don't you get to work on the translation? I'll notify the general staff duty officer and the commo center chief."

"You got it," said the interpreter, and he quickly set to work on the translation.

After the officers were notified, the interpreter finished the English translation, which Donley rapidly typed into a computer terminal. He then hit a TRANSMIT button to send the English version of the Russian epistle across the Potomac to a printer in the White House Situation Room. It read:

MOLNIYA II
CIRCUIT4/2353 GMT
MESSAGE 1/1
TO: PRESIDENT OF THE UNITED STATES OF AMERICA
FROM: CENTRAL COMMITTEE OF THE COMMUNIST PARTY OF THE
SOVIET UNION
MR. PRESIDENT:

DURING THE LAST HOUR IT HAS COME TO THE ATTENTION OF THE CENTRAL COMMITTEE THAT GENERAL SECRETARY VORONTSKY, ACTING CRIMINALLY, AND WITHOUT AUTHORIZATION FROM THIS COMMITTEE, ENGAGED IN AN ACT OF AIR PIRACY AGAINST THE UNITED STATES.

SPECIFICALLY, WE HAVE LEARNED THAT GENERAL SECRETARY VORONTSKY ARRANGED FOR THE HIJACKING OF AN AMERICAN SPACE SHUTTLE AND THE DESTRUCTION OF ANOTHER.

WHILE THE CENTRAL COMMITTEE HAS EXPRESSED ITS VOCIFEROUS OBJECTIONS TO YOUR SO-CALLED STRATEGIC DEFENSE PLATFORM, WHICH IS IN VIOLATION OF EXISTING ANTIBALLISTIC MISSILE TREATIES, THE CENTRAL COMMITTEE IN NO WAY CONDONES THE PIRATE ACTIONS OF GENERAL SECRETARY VORONTSKY. THIS MESSAGE IS TO EXPRESS OUR REPUDIATION OF THIS ILLEGAL, UNAUTHORIZED ACT.

IN VIEW OF THIS UNPRECEDENTED SITUATION, AND OUR DESIRE TO REDUCE THE CURRENT TENSION, WE HAVE TAKEN THE FOLLOWING ACTIONS:

ALL SOVIET MILITARY AIRCRAFT ARE GROUNDED UNTIL FURTHER NOTICE. THIS HAS BEEN DONE TO DEMONSTRATE OUR PEACEFUL INTENTIONS.

THE BODY AND EFFECTS OF THE AMERICAN KILLED DURING THE ATTACK WILL BE RETURNED WITH ALL DELIBERATE SPEED.

AMERICAN SURVIVORS OF THE ATTACK WILL RECEIVE APPROPRIATE MEDICAL CARE, AND WILL ALSO BE RETURNED WITH DISPATCH.

AN AMERICAN INSPECTION TEAM WILL BE ALLOWED TO SALVAGE THE REMAINS OF YOUR EQUIPMENT WHICH WAS DE-

STROYED BY THE SOVIET AIR DEFENSE FORCES DURING YOUR BOMBING STRIKE ON THE BAIKONUR COSMODROME.

THE SOVIET UNION AGREES TO PAY REPARATIONS TO THE UNITED STATES FOR THE LOSS OF YOUR SPACECRAFT, AND TO THE FAMILY OF THE DECEASED AIRMAN.

GENERAL SECRETARY VORONTSKY WAS KILLED IN A PLANE CRASH BEFORE HE COULD BE BROUGHT TO JUSTICE. THE SOVIET FOREIGN MINISTER AND DEFENSE MINISTER HAVE BEEN RE-LIEVED OF THEIR DUTIES FOR THEIR DUPLICITY AS CO-CONSPIRATORS IN THIS CRIMINAL ENTERPRISE.

THIS MESSAGE HAS BEEN SIMULTANEOUSLY TRANSMITTED TO AMBASSADOR YAKOLEV, WHO HAD NO KNOWLEDGE OF THIS ILLEGAL PLOT.

THE CENTRAL COMMITTEE HAS SELECTED VITALI KOSTIASHAK, CHAIRMAN OF THE COMMITTEE FOR STATE SECURITY, AS THE NEW GENERAL SECRETARY OF THE COMMUNIST PARTY. WE CALL FOR A SUMMIT MEETING BETWEEN YOU AND HIM IN ORDER TO FURTHER REDUCE TENSIONS BETWEEN OUR TWO COUNTRIES.

TO REPEAT, THE CENTRAL COMMITTEE WAS TOTALLY UN-AWARE OF THIS CRIMINAL ACT BY GENERAL SECRETARY VORONTSKY. WE HAVE ACTED SWIFTLY AND OPENLY TO COR-RECT THIS TRAGEDY. WE OFFER OUR APOLOGIES TO THE UNITED STATES AND OUR CONDOLENCES TO THE FAMILY OF THE SLAIN CREWMAN.

CENTRAL COMMITTEE OF THE COMMUNIST PARTY
OF THE SOVIET UNION
-END MESSAGE-

After typing in the translation, the sandy-haired Donley turned to the general staff duty officer—a Marine brigadier. In a voice that was three octaves higher than his normal tone, he asked, "Just what on earth is going down, sir?"

THE SIXTH DAY

The President looked at his reflection in the mirror and straightened his tie. "Are you sure this is the way we should handle it, Harry?" he asked laconically.

Harry Funkweiler, the garishly dressed White House press secretary (and former vice president of marketing at the chief executive's old car company), said, "Oh, absolutely, Mr. President. First of all, nobody would believe the truth about this whole disaster, and in the second place we just don't have all the facts yet. We'd look like horse butts if we let it all hang out and then the Russkies did a change-up on us. Just go out and say we had some serious problems with a shuttle mission to the SDI platform, and we had to launch a rescue shuttle over southern Florida. Unfortunately, complications arose with that launch as well, and life has been lost. Say it's all national security, and only take three questions . . . make that two questions."

The President didn't know what to think. But he always relied on Funkweiler's judgment. He was the best media flack in the business and could play the press like a pipe organ. He'd been instrumental in engineering the President's election landslides. Yet the President was always uneasy when throwing a "slider" to the press. He always figured it could backfire. He turned to his Secretary of State, who was the only other adviser in the room. "What do you think, Winston?"

Having studied under Henry Kissinger, the diplomat had fewer qualms about using a little sleight of hand in dealing with the press. "I agree with Harry, Mr. President, but for different reasons. I think we have to withhold the whole story until the Russian leadership has had a chance to solidify. Then we can reassess the situation."

The President sighed. "Hmmm. Well, okay. Let's get on with it. How long till I go on the air, Harry?"

Funkweiler looked at his Spiro Agnew wristwatch—a collector's item—and said, "Seven minutes, Mr. President."

The three men filed out of the Oval Office and headed for the East Room of the White House.

* * *

Seymour Woltman sat among the press corps, unshaven and giving off a foul odor. He was unable to recall when he had last shaved and showered. Although the East Room was crammed with reporters and photographers for the Presidential press conference, Woltman's stench enabled him to enjoy an empty seat on his left and right.

Woltman was exhausted, but pleased. His trip to Washington had been a success. He believed his constant hammering of everyone he knew at NASA, the Pentagon, and the White House had built enough momentum to compel this press conference. They'd been told the President would make a brief statement concerning the shuttle launch, then take a few questions.

Woltman noticed everybody was standing up. He got to his feet and saw the President marching down the red carpeted hallway toward the podium.

As the President strode down the long hallway, he passed a series of portraits that were hung along the wall. The images of Washington, Jefferson, and Lincoln seemed to scowl down at him as he walked past with the prepared press release in his hand. The prepared release was less than the whole truth. Which meant it was a lie.

He mounted the podium and faced the lights and television cameras. Through these electronic windows he would be talking to a hundred million Americans—"the Boss," as he called them.

He looked down at his statement, and was silent for some moments as his thoughts returned to the images of Washington, Jefferson, and Lincoln. Lincoln's scowl had been particularly haunting, causing the President to pause. He figured his predecessors deserved better than an "inoperative" press release. "The Boss" deserved better, too. So with great ceremony the President ripped the prepared statement in two and walked around in front of the podium.

The boom operator was caught off guard by this unexpected move, and jumped to reposition the reedlike microphone above the chief executive's head. The assembled gaggle of reporters was intriqued by the deliberate paper shredding, and collectively leaned forward.

"Ladies and gentlemen," said the President tiredly, "I have an incredible story to tell you."

For the next forty-five minutes an open-mouthed press corps, as well as an entire nation, remained silent in rapt attention as their national leader explained in precise detail how an American-born Russian agent had hijacked the *Intrepid,* how the Soviets had destroyed the *Constellation,* how SAC had gone to DEFCON Two, how a pair of stealth bombers had been sent into Russia and how one of them had blown the *Intrepid* apart, how there had been a palace coup within the Kremlin, and how he'd ordered SAC's bombers recalled.

At the end of his monologue he returned to the podium, took a sip of water, and said, "Are there any . . . questions?"

A full ten seconds of shocked silence elapsed—then the East Room exploded in pandemonium.

THREE WEEKS LATER

The Army colonel—who could have doubled for Arnold Schwarzenegger—hung up the phone and walked out of the guard booth. "Okay, sir," he told Whittenberg, "we can go across now. Just remember to stay on our side of the line."

"Right," responded the SPACECOMCinC.

The colonel nodded to the gate guard, and the barrier was raised. Whittenberg turned to Maj. Lydia Strand and CM/Sgt. Tim Kelly. "Let's go collect our man," he said, and the three of them strode past the barrier into no-man's-land—a patch of earth in the heart of Berlin where the geography and ideology of East and West met in an uneasy truce. Behind Whittenberg, Strand, and Kelly came the colonel and an Army medical team.

Across the way, Whittenberg saw the barrier go up, allowing a lone Soviet officer to approach. The CinC thought this odd, for he knew that Russians liked to move in packs—particularly in touchy situations like this. But be that as it may, the rather short, stocky-looking Russian came forward by himself, extended his hand, and asked in a heavy accent, "General Whittenberg?"

The big black man took the Russian's hand and shook it. "That is correct, sir. And you are?"

"I am Marshal Likady Popov, Minister of Defense of the Soviet Union. I have been sent as a personal emissary of General Secretary Kostiashak to ensure that you are satisfied with the repatriation of your people."

"Popov?" asked Whittenberg quizzically. "The same Likady Popov who is Director of Soviet Spaceflite Operations?"

The stocky Russian shrugged and looked at his feet, trying to conceal his pleasure at learning he was important enough for the Americans to maintain a dossier on him. "My former position, General. I have recently taken on new responsibilities."

Whittenberg nodded. "Apparently so. . . . May we proceed with our transfer?"

"By all means," replied Popov, who motioned to a guard by the

457

East Berlin barrier. A man who was wearing gray coveralls and had his arm in a sling walked forward. "First, I am presenting you with one of the crewmen from your bomber that was shot down. You will find that all of your men have been treated well and have not been interrogated."

"I am glad to hear that," replied the CinC.

As the pilot of Ghost Two crossed the white line, the Army colonel took him under his wing.

"Next," said Popov, "your two injured aviators. One from the bomber, and one from your small spaceplane. I must admit you caught us by surprise with your space fighter. We had no idea you were working on such a device."

Whittenberg nodded. "I daresay, Marshal Popov, our surprise has been far greater than yours."

Popov did not reply at once, but instead motioned again to the guard. Two stretchers were brought forward, each carried by a pair of Russian Army medics. "You will be pleased to know they have received the finest medical care."

Whittenberg peered at the stretchers as they approached. "Would you have them brought over here first?" he asked.

"As you wish," replied Popov, who turned and uttered a command. Then he said to Whittenberg, "The injured will be followed by the fatality from your spaceplane."

Again, Whittenberg nodded, and stepped back as the first stretcher crossed the line and was passed to U.S. Army medics. He didn't recognize the face. "What's your name, son?" he asked.

"McKinley, sir," the patient replied weakly. "Captain Jack McKinley. I was the Whizzo on Ghost Two."

Whittenberg patted his shoulder. "You did good. We received the burst message you sent."

The Whizzo smiled. "That's good to know, sir."

"You take it easy. We'll visit more later." The CinC stepped back and the medics carried the stretcher toward an ambulance parked behind the American barrier.

The second stretcher was transferred and brought forward, and Peter Lamborghini's bandaged face looked up at the big black man, the brunette major, and the sergeant with the bullet-shaped head. A weak smile came across his face. "Sir . . . Lydia . . . Tim . . . sure good to see you."

Whittenberg took his hand. "Good to see you, too, Pete. Juliet and your girls are waiting for you at Rhein-Main in Frankfurt. We're flying you out to the Army hospital there."

Lamborghini had a faraway look in his eyes. "That's good," he said meekly.

Strand couldn't hold back. "That was a crazy thing Commander Monaghan did."

Lamborghini looked at her, and then at Whittenberg. "Tell me . . . that was a stealth bomber we saw, wasn't it?"

Whittenberg was surprised. "I guess the Russians kept you separated from the other guys after you were captured, but, yes, it was a stealth bomber. Did you see it?"

Lamborghini's response was slow and pained. "We lost the *Intrepid* in the clouds on the way down. Thick soup. We tried to pick it up on the ground, but couldn't find it. Saw the stealth bomber just as a MiG was lining up for a shot. We nailed the MiG. . . . Tell me, did the bomber make it through?"

"It got through and blasted the *Intrepid* into spare parts," replied Whittenberg. "And I guess we have you two guys to thank for that."

Lamborghini turned his head slightly so he could watch the covered body bag being transferred into American hands. "After we nailed the MiG, we would've both been killed by a SAM, but Mad Dog saved me. . . . He didn't survive the impact."

Whittenberg, Strand, and Kelly all looked at each other. None of them quite understood exactly how Monaghan had saved the Kestrel from the SAM. "You rest easy, Pete," ordered the CinC. "You guys did a great job. After you get better you can tell the President and me all about it. In the meantime we'd better get you to Rhein-Main. Lydia and Tim will go with you."

The stretcher headed toward the ambulance, with Strand and Kelly acting as escorts.

Finally, Whittenberg and Popov were alone.

"I trust you found the transfer satisfactory?" inquired the Russian.

"Yes, Marshal Popov. It looks like Colonel Lamborghini is lucky to be alive."

Popov agreed. "Most fortunate. I was told he suffered a concussion, several broken ribs, an injured hip, a broken cheekbone, and internal bleeding. Some surgery was required to reduce pressure on one of his lungs." Then the perceptive Russian observed, "It would appear the two of you are close."

Whittenberg checked to make sure Lamborghini was safely inside

American territory before saying, "That's true. He's my intelligence staff officer."

Popov showed his surprise, while Whittenberg took some satisfaction in knowing the Russians would be galled to learn the SPACECOM intelligence chief had slipped through their fingers. Popov couldn't ignore the zinger. "I must say, General," he remarked, "you live up to your dossier."

Whittenberg raised an eyebrow. "Why, thank you. I think."

Popov extended his hand. "This should conclude our business, General. It has been an honor to meet you. I hope you will convey to your President that the transfer was conducted satisfactorily."

Whittenberg took the stocky man's hand. "I shall, Marshal Popov. And the President asked that his regards be passed along to the new General Secretary."

"It will be done." Popov gave a curt bow, turned and walked away.

"Marshal Popov?" called Whittenberg.

The Russian stopped and turned. "*Da?*"

"It was Kapuscinski, wasn't it?"

Popov was caught off guard and hestitated, but then softly said, "*Da.*"

Whittenberg nodded, then gave the Russian a salute. Popov brought himself to attention and returned the gesture.

THE FOLLOWING DECEMBER

The Vice President, who was now the President-elect, absently stoked the logs in the fireplace with an ornate bronze poker, sending up a small plume of swirling sparks that were reflected in his energetic eyes. However, his mind was far from the glowing embers—he was still trying to absorb what the General Secretary had just told him.

The President, the Vice President, and the General Secretary were in the oak-paneled den of the Chateau Fleur d'Eau in the wooded outskirts of Geneva. It was here, in this very room, that the first Reagan-Gorbachev summit had been held. But this meeting had a much different dynamic. Billed as the "Transition Summit," it included both the incoming and outgoing American chiefs of state, as well as the new General Secretary. And because the General Secretary spoke fluent English, the meetings could be held without those nettlesome interpreters. Although interpreters were considered trustworthy, national leaders always felt the presence of another set of eyes and ears in the room, and were inhibited from speaking with unvarnished candor. But English was not a problem for Vitali Kostiashak, and he spoke to the two Americans with absolute candor.

The Vice President, still somewhat numbed by the General Secretary's remarks, put the poker aside and turned. "You mean to tell us, General Secretary, that the hijacking of our space shuttle *Intrepid* was nothing more than an engineered *plot* to topple your predecessor?"

Kostiashak exhaled a lungful of smoke. "That is correct, Mr. Vice President."

The Vice President shook his head, causing the firelight to glint off his steel-gray crew cut. "That's incredible. Unbelievable. I've always figured you Russians as a conspiratorial lot, but this *Intrepid* business. Well, it's hard to accept. Good God, didn't you know we were at DEFCON Two? We even considered launching a nuclear cruise missile to destroy the *Intrepid*."

"You must have been clean out of your mind," said the President bitterly. "To bring our two countries so close to a nuclear exchange is unthinkable. Yet you did so just to satisfy your own personal ambitions. That is contemptible, General Secretary. Contemptible and insane. You must be off your rocker.''

Kostiashak exhaled again. ''Gentlemen—if you will permit me to finish. I want you to know that I have shared this information with no one—absolutely no one—inside or outside the Soviet Union, except yourselves and my Defense Minister. And I trust I can rely on your discretion, for you will see that confidentiality will be in your best interest.''

Kostiashak leaned forward and helped himself to a Swiss chocolate from a tray on the coffee table. ''I ask that you judge my conduct not as an act of simple ambition, but as a calculated move in a broader context.''

The President's drill-sergeant face gave him a sour look. ''What broader context?''

''Your country and mine, Mr. President, have been prisoners on an inexorable treadmill from which we have been unable to escape. Like a dog chasing its tail, the faster we chase, the more frustrating it becomes.''

''I take it you mean the arms race?'' said the Vice President.

''Correct,'' replied the Ukrainian.

''If you want to know who is responsible for the arms race, General Secretary,'' said the President with irony in his voice, ''you have only to look in the mirror.''

Kostiashak shrugged. ''Mr. President, you and I can waste a great deal of time pointing fingers at each other. While it is true that the Soviet Union has spent vast sums on the military, you should be mindful that we have been invaded twice in this century by aggressors—and we lost twenty million souls in the Great Patriotic War. Had that happened in America, your perspective might be different.''

The President harrumphed. ''Be that as it may, what are you getting at?''

Kostiashak unwrapped the chocolate. ''Mr. President, I am a devoted Communist. Although I was educated in your country, I totally reject your weak and decadent system of commercial exploitation. However, I am also a pragmatist, and my education demonstrated to me that your country has certain strengths and attributes that the Soviet Union cannot match.''

''No shit,'' observed the President.

The Ukrainian ignored the comment. ''When you achieved your

technological breakthrough in space defenses, I knew that the Soviet Union could not compete in that arena. My years at Princeton taught me this. The race to the moon taught me this. Trying to compete with the United States head to head in advanced technology was folly. No matter how many of our resources we applied to the effort, I knew we would always be a few steps behind. The playing field, as your expression goes, was not level." Kostiashak looked into the fire.

"Unfortunately, the Soviet leadership which had been entrenched for some time—particularly the military—did not have the benefit of my Princeton experience, and my understanding of American culture. They reacted to your technological breakthrough in typical Russian fashion, born out of two invasions on our soil in this century—as I have pointed out. The Politburo and the military reacted with enormous additional space research expenditures, as well as enormous expenditures for space vehicles. General Secretary Gorbachev was unable to quell these conservative forces, which rallied around an unholy alliance of GOSPLAN Minister Vorontsky, Defense Minister Zholobov, and the Foreign Minister. Even if he had lived and remained in power, Gorbachev would have found himself a prisoner of that troika of conservative forces. But Gorbachev was killed, Vorontsky seized power, and the military spending binge continued unabated. The Politburo fell into the firm grip of the militarists.

"In any case," he continued, "these increased space defense costs, on top of our expenditures to reinvade Afghanistan, were particularly onerous. Our defense budget as a percent of gross national product climbed to *twenty-seven percent*. I believe yours remains at six percent."

"Six and a half," corrected the President.

"Six and a half," echoed the Ukrainian softly as he continued to gaze into the fire. "My country was caught in an impossible situation. We could not match you technologically, and we could not afford the combination of space defense research, the war in Afghanistan, and the maintenance of our large conventional forces. The fabric of our society was starting to crumble. Mothers could not feed their children." The Ukrainian turned to face the American. "Yet in spite of all this, you did the most stupid thing."

The President sat up straight. "And what was that?"

"You refused to negotiate any limits on space weapons."

The President almost laughed. "General Secretary, if you think I'm going to buy some type of bleeding-heart story—from you, of all people—intended to get me to negotiate away our space defense shield, you've got it all wrong. The United States will never negotiate from a position of weakness. My country has had a consistent policy that it will develop and deploy our Strategic Defense System. It has been developed, and we are deploying. So much for your Princeton education. You have totally misread us.''

Kostiashak took a very long drag on his Pall Mall and exhaled ever so slowly. He then looked at the American for some moments before saying, in his viper's voice, "It is you, Mr. President, who have misread your adversary.''

The Ukrainian's tone was unsettling, causing the President's drill-sergeant face to start twitching. "How so?'' he asked cautiously.

"You are wise to negotiate from a strong position, Mr. President. We Soviets admire strength. For us, it is a virtue, and to deal with someone who is strong evokes our respect. Unfortunately, your technological breakthrough has done more than evoke feelings of respect. It has brought out feelings of genuine terror—of deep vulnerability. I can tell you categorically that unless you and I reach an accord that will limit your space defense deployment, you will thrust the Soviet Union into an act of desperation.''

The President scowled. "The Soviet Union has nothing to fear from a defensive weapon system,'' he said flatly.

"That is entirely wrong,'' said the Ukrainian in an analytical voice. "It is our perception that a protective space shield over your ballistic missiles creates an imbalance. It destroys the balance of power—what you refer to as MAD, or Mutual Assured Destruction. If you launched your missiles in a first strike, we would be unable to retaliate effectively. And Russia will not allow itself to become vulnerable again—*ever* . If you continue to prosecute your deployment of a space defense platform, I would be unable to halt our defense spending, yet I still could not match you technologically. You would leave me with no choice but to embark upon an . . . unprecedented act.'' The Ukrainian fell silent.

"And what is this 'unprecedented act' you refer to?'' queried the Vice President.

The General Secretary reached into his Gucci leather attaché case and withdrew a file. From the manila folder he extracted a color photograph and placed it on the coffee table. It was a picture of Red Square, with the Kremlin's onion domes in the background. In the foreground was a KGB major standing next to a simple 55-gallon oil drum, which was painted a bright red, white, and blue.

The two Americans looked at the picture. "So?" asked the President.

Kostiashak pulled out a second photograph. The same KGB major was now in civilian clothes, standing in front of a Ford van with the panel door open. Inside the van was the same red-white-and-blue 55-gallon drum. But the onion domes of the Kremlin were no longer present. Instead, the background of the photograph clearly showed the White House.

The President's neck hairs rose up. "What are you trying to prove?" he asked sharply.

The Ukrainian adjusted his silk tie. "It is amazing how small nuclear weapons can be made these days. Even thermonuclear deuterium-tritium weapons in the fifty-kiloton range. They can be reduced to the size of an ordinary oil drum." The General Secretary sighed. "You Americans pride yourselves on having such 'open' borders and unrestricted travel within your territories. So be it. That is your choice. But I can tell you that your borders are pitifully porous. South American drug merchants smuggle in illicit cargo by the *ton*, do they not? And you are powerless to stop them. The oil drum you see pictured here was unloaded from a commercial vessel in the Mexican harbor of Veracruz, then flown by private plane to a desert landing strip in your state of Utah. It was then transported by this van to the tourist parking area near your residence, Mr. President. . . . No one lifted a finger to stop my agent. In fact, a courteous highway patrolman in your state of Nebraska assisted him when his vehicle suffered a tire puncture."

The two Americans were speechless.

The diminutive Ukrainian's charm evaporated now, and his eyes turned hard. "If you continue with your SDI deployment, Mr. President, you give me no alternative but to find other means to deliver nuclear weapons. That would mean prepositioning weapons on your soil to circumvent your spaceborne defensive shield. It would be a simple matter to park a genuine nuclear weapon by the White House, by the Pentagon, near major military bases, or in New York's Central Park."

"You wouldn't dare," said the President cautiously.

Kostiashak studiously toyed with the gold band of his Piaget watch. "Who is to say I have not done so already?"

The President shot out of his chair. "You couldn't have!"

The Ukrainian softened his tone, and the charm returned. "Of course not, Mr. President. I am only trying to demonstrate what could happen if you continue to push me into an impossible corner. I understand you are quite knowledgeable concerning automobiles, but have you learned nothing from history? Gunpowder defeated the bow and arrow. The machine gun defeated the cavalry. The tank defeated the machine gun. Air power defeated the tank. What made you think your Star Wars system could not be countered as well?''

The two Americans eyed each other. ''So what's the bottom line?'' asked the Vice President.

''Ah, a businessman,'' said Kostiashak as he crushed out his cigarette. ''How fortunate. The 'bottom line,' as you say, is that if you are willing to halt the deployment of your Star Wars platform, I am in a position to make you a very attractive offer. Very attractive, indeed.''

Both men cocked their heads forward. ''Go ahead,'' said the President. ''We're listening.''

The Ukrainian spoke quickly. ''I propose a moratorium on the space testing and deployment of any and all space weapons by both nations, but terrestrial research may continue to your heart's content. We will agree to cut strategic arms by fifty percent. Further, I am willing to reduce Warsaw Pact conventional forces to a one-to-one ratio with NATO forces in soldiers, armored vehicles, aircraft, and artillery pieces. Any Soviet forces in excess of this one-to-one ratio will either be demobilized or withdrawn to positions east of the Ural Mountains. Soviet forces in Afghanistan will be withdrawn immediately under UN supervision, and Soviet support for liberation forces in Central America, Cuba, and Africa will be greatly reduced. Additionally, attractive joint-venture terms will be offered to American firms for development of natural resources in Siberia, and they will be permitted to repatriate their profits. Finally, all of these treaty elements will be offered with stringent, on-site verification terms.''

The Vice President looked at him with disbelief. Warsaw Pact forces vastly outnumbered those of NATO. ''A one-to-one ratio with NATO and a fifty percent strategic arms cut? You just told us that Gorbachev couldn't get a handle on your conservatives. Why should we believe you can make your military buy a deal like that?''

Kostiashak contemplated the fire once more before saying, ''The conservative unholy alliance I spoke of is no longer operative, and I currently have some exceptional influence with the military. But unless we rapidly reach an accord, that influence will evaporate and new conservative forces will emerge.''

The President looked at his Veep—the man who would soon be his successor—and said, ''You know my feelings on SDI, but you're the

President-elect. This is going to have to be your call. He could be deposed tomorrow," said the President, while pointing to the Ukrainian. "Then we'd be back to square one. And I don't like the feeling that we're being blackmailed."

Kostiashak unwrapped another chocolate. "I can assure you both that if we walk out of this room without striking a bargain, I will either be overthrown or forced to embark on a prepositioning strategy." He pointed at the photographs on the coffee table, then popped the chocolate in his mouth and rose from his chair. He approached the President-elect, who was standing by the fire. "I delayed this summit meeting until your election was past, Mr. Vice President, because I wanted to deal with someone who would be in office for a considerable time. You have my proposal, and I have outlined in crystal-clear terms the alternatives. I must halt my country's insane arms expenditures and redirect our resources to the civilian sector, but I am powerless to do so without an agreement limiting deployment of your space weapons. Believe me when I say I find the alternatives just as distasteful as you, if we do not reach an accord."

The Vice President picked up the poker and started stoking the fire again. Like the President, he was a businessman. But he was more of a historian than the former auto executive. While a student at West Point, the Vice President had carefully studied Operation *Barbarossa* —Hitler's ill-fated invasion of the Soviet Union—and he knew that when the Russians had their backs to the wall they'd fight harder than a band of Comanches. When the Wehrmacht panzers were rolling toward the Kremlin, the Russians had been willing to trade ten of their own lives to kill one German. A Russian respected strength, to be sure, but when cornered, a desperate Russian was a dangerous thing. Maybe too dangerous. Castrating the Soviets' nuclear arsenal with a space defense shield might push them past a deadly trigger point.

The President-elect gave the coals one last jab before placing the poker aside. He turned to the dark-skinned Ukrainian and asked, "No restriction on earthbound research?"

"No restriction on terrestrial research or testing," replied Kostiashak. "Only on deployment."

"A one-to-one ratio in Europe on conventional arms, a pullout from Afghanistan, and a fifty percent cut in strategic arms?"

"A one-to-one ratio, a pullout, and a fifty percent cut," echoed the General Secretary.

"Stringent on-site verification?"

"Stringent on-site verification."

The American thought for a moment, then added, "Draconian verification?"

Kostiashak nodded, and said, "Draconian verification."

The President-elect brushed the soot from his fingers, then stuck out his hand and said, "Deal."

Epilogue

Comdr. Leroy Monaghan, United States Navy, was awarded the Congressional Medal of Honor posthumously. He was buried at Arlington National Cemetery with full military honors, along with Maj. Frank Mulcahey and Geraldo "Jerry" Rodriquez.

Posthumously, Col. Julian Kapuscinski was stripped of all military rank and decorations.

Of the twenty-three "seedling" couples that were planted on American soil by the *Komisar* Lavrenti Beria, three did not bear children. Of the remaining twenty couples: two of the offspring died young; twelve were simply assimilated into American society; three wound up in mental institutions, being unable to resolve the conflict between their environment and their parents' instructions; and three "took root." Of the three seedling offspring that took, one was Iceberg; one is currently a sergeant in a cable platoon at the U.S. Army Signal School at Fort Gordon, Georgia; and the last is an import/export official in the Department of Commerce in Washington. The two remaining seedling offspring show no particular promise, nor do they have access to highly classified material. Far and away, Iceberg was the star.

The new President was sworn in, and because of his conservative credentials, was able to get the new arms treaty through Congress. The NATO alliance, including its new member, France, embraced the treaty like a long-lost grandchild, and it was with a sense of awe that Europeans watched Soviet troops withdraw from their long-held positions along the border and head east toward the Urals or demobilization. Mostly demobilization. Hundreds upon hundreds of ICBMs in the Soviet Union and the United States were yanked out of their silos and sent to the shredder. There were so many inspection teams crawling over the Russian landscape that one American sergeant quipped, "If a soldier in the Red Army farts, we can tell you what flavor borscht he had for dinner."

Gen. Rodger Whittenberg, having anticipated a somewhat inglori-ous retirement, was surprised when he was tapped by the new President to replace Admiral Bergstrom as the new Chief of the General Staff of the United States Armed Forces. From time to time he exchanged personal letters with the Russian Defense Minister.

Memorial services were held in Red Square for cosmonauts Vasili Lubinin and Sergei Yemitov. Their families were granted special dispensation to continue living at Star City. Yemitov's widow bore her dead husband a daughter, whom she named Nadja.

Lt. Fyodor Tupelov was awarded the Hero of the Soviet Union medal and promoted to captain.

The flight crews of the stealth bombers were awarded the Silver Star, en masse.

Slowly at first, then with a bit more frequency, refrigerators and television sets became easier to obtain in Moscow, and food availabil-ity seemed to increase a bit. Instead of spending her average two hours a day in shopping lines, the typical Moscow housewife had cut it down to an hour and twenty minutes.

Senior managers with McKinsey & Co. and other American consulting firms started flying to Moscow with greater frequency.

Lydia Strand stayed at SPACECOM, even though the command's space mission had been curtailed to a great extent. She was on the promotion list for lieutenant colonel.

Peter Lamborghini healed. Slowly, but he healed. He was offered the Congressional Medal of Honor, but turned it down. Having survived the wild ride, Lamborghini didn't feel he was Monaghan's equal. He was then offered the Distinguished Flying Cross, and at Whittenberg's urging, he accepted it.

By special order of the Chief of the General Staff, Lamborghini was appointed Commander of the 388th Tactical Fighter Wing (F-16s) at Hill Air Force Base in Utah. And by special appointment of the President, Juliet Lamborghini was named as Assistant United States Attorney in Salt Lake City.

But perhaps the greatest and most tragic irony of the entire *Intrepid* affair was the fact that there was never anything wrong with the two Russian shuttles that were incinerated during their reentry. The *Buran* and the *Mikhail Suslov* were perfectly sound spacecraft.

Prior to the respective final lift-offs of the *Buran* and the *Suslov*, a KGB agent—dressed in the white coveralls of a technician—gained access to the gantry tower and threw a beaker of sulfuric acid onto the fragile silica tiles of the orbiters' underbellies. Although only a few tiles were affected by the corrosive acid, their loss allowed the air friction to gain a foothold and tear a seam of tiles from the bellies in a "zipper effect." This exposed the orbiters' soft aluminum skin to some 1,800 degrees Fahrenheit, which quickly turned the delicate metal into liquid, causing the spacecraft to break apart.

Four innocent cosmonauts died and two magnificent spacecraft were vaporized because of the acid. But Vitali Kostiashak was a ruthless man, and if his audacious plan to topple the "unholy alliance" of the Politburo and steer Russia onto a new course was to succeed, then the *Buran*, the *Suslov*, and their crews were expendable. Indeed, he considered their demise as a necessary strategic move to push General Secretary Vorontsky into an act of desperation—to lure him into bringing the *Intrepid* down onto Russian soil. And once the American spacecraft had touched down at the Baikonur Cosmodrome, the final trap could be sprung.

It was an intricate chess game, of sorts, and the diminutive grandmaster often wondered if Roosevelt and Machiavelli would have approved.